June Flaum Singer lives in Bel Air, California, with her husband, painter Joe Singer. They have three daughters, Sharon, Brett and Valerie, and one son, Ian – all writers. Born and raised in New Jersey, she attended Ohio State University before experiencing a brief stint as a starlet in Hollywood. After the success of her first novel, the bestselling *The Debutantes*, she believed she enjoyed the best of all worlds. She has also written *Star Dreams*, *The Movie Set*, *The Markoff Women*, *The President's Women* and *Sex in the Afternoon*, all published by Corgi Books.

BRILLIANT DIVORCES

June Flaum Singer

CORGI BOOKS

BRILLIANT DIVORCES
A CORGI BOOK : 0 552 13504 6

Originally published in Great Britain by Bantam Press,
a division of Transworld Publishers Ltd

PRINTING HISTORY
Bantam Press edition published 1992
Corgi edition published 1993

Set in 10/11pt. Linotype Bembo by
Falcon Graphic Art Ltd
Wallington, Surrey

Corgi Books are published by Transworld Publishers Ltd,
61-63 Uxbridge Road, London W5 5SA,
in Australia by Transworld Publishers (Australia) Pty Ltd,
15-25 Helles Avenue, Moorebank, NSW 2170,
and in New Zealand by Transworld Publishers (NZ) Ltd,
3 William Pickering Drive, Albany, Auckland.

Made and printed in Great Britain by
Cox & Wyman Ltd, Reading, Berks.

ACKNOWLEDGEMENTS

Many thanks to Mark Barty-King and Diane Pearson, not only for their professional expertise, but also for the generosity of their good friendship.

I would also like to thank Miriam Hope Bass, Ben Haller and Kathleen Hughes for their delightful *Lifelog* which proved to be a wonderful source of reference.

And as always, my thanks to Joe for the best of everything.

'The clever and very rich Mrs Vanderbilt always said that every woman should marry twice – the first time for money, the second for love. But I always say that the first time should be for love and then after you've got all that lovely romantic nonsense out of your system, the second time should be for convenience. Then the third time round should be just once – for the fun of it. And after that, one should certainly marry for money because that's what really lasts. But when you have all four in one package – the love, the convenience, the sex and the money, why then you've got it all – a brilliant marriage!'

NORA GRANT

BEFORE THE PARTY

Los Angeles
June 1990

Nora opened her bedroom window wide to breathe in the clear morning air drifting in on a gentle, balmy breeze. It was a golden day, a wondrous day for a garden party, a June day so rare a bride could dance barefoot in the sunlight at her own wedding and Grantwood Manor – situated on nine acres of prime Bel-Air real estate with its bright green lawns, tropical plantings, lush gardens, sparkling pool and multicoloured hills forming a magnificent backdrop – was the picture-perfect setting for a wedding.

She thought back to that first time she saw Grantwood Manor when she came to live there as the newly wedded wife of Hollywood's legendary moviemaker, T.S. Grant. She hadn't been *really* young even then by Hollywood standards and certainly no longer virginal. Still, in many ways she'd been as starry-eyed as any young bride with a head full of dreams. TS's Grantwood had been quite shabby then, its grounds neglected, the house badly in disrepair and she had renovated and transformed it, furbished, refurnished, polished and burnished until the manor glowed like a jewel. She had intended it to be a restorative haven for those who dwelled there as well as a showcase for glorious parties, a truly magical kingdom where all dreams could come true . . .

It was time for her to get dressed for the party; still,

9

she tarried at the window looking out over Grantwood's splendid vistas. To the left of the mosaic-tiled pool was the guest house, and just beyond it, the three-hole golf course with its reproduction of the tiny pro shop at St Andrews, Scotland's quintessential golf course, which was easily as legendary as Hollywood's Grantwood Studio.

To the right lay the tennis court and if she squinted she could almost make out the figures of a long-legged girl and a golden-haired boy-man – TS's fiery-haired daughter, Sam, and her beautiful son, Hubie. They were moving with such youthful grace in their tennis whites it was as if they were dancing a ballet rather than merely hitting a ball back and forth. But when she opened her eyes wide, the figures vanished.

Behind the court, enclosed in its own grove of stately palms, was the three-room doll's house where a fourteen-year-old queen of France might have amused herself before she lost her head. She concentrated hard now so that she could *almost* hear three fourteen-year-old Hollywood princesses – Sam and her two very best friends, Honey and Babe – playing at being adults, fantasizing about a time when they'd be all grown-up and life would be perfection, as perfect as it could only be in one of TS's studio's star-studded extravaganzas.

But that was twenty years ago, and today only Grantwood Manor remained the same, as if freeze-framed, a timeless great English estate, but conforming to Hollywood tastes – a British transplant intertwined with the dazzling flora of luxe LA accoutrements, much like she herself seemed to be. Everything else was changed. TS was dead, the three Hollywood princesses were all grown up, her sweet prince of a son, Hubie, was long gone, and Grantwood Manor was *her* queenly domain even if her stepdaughter, Sam, thought it should be hers – along with Grantwood Studio – by right of birth and all the laws of basic morality and royal ascension. And today, she, who was almost as famous for the parties she gave as she was for her four-and-a-half marriages, was throwing not a wedding party, but a celebration of a divorce.

And before the day was over, one way or another, she intended to celebrate another kind of divorce. Like there were all kinds of marriages, there were also all kinds of brilliant divorces . . .

PART ONE

THE CLUB

Los Angeles
June 1990

1

The stunning blonde in the white Corniche convertible, wearing oversized sunglasses, a white silk suit and a wide-brimmed white hat, cruised west on Sunset Boulevard. She braked for red lights and accelerated again, switched lanes when the traffic demanded it, then made the right turn at Bel-Air's East Gate, all by rote, her concentration elsewhere.

All morning she hadn't been able to get a certain picture out of her mind – second graders jumping rope in the schoolyard. One girl jumped as two girls turned rope while the rest of the girls clapped hands and chanted a rhyme, waiting breathlessly for the current jumper to miss so they could get *their* chance, though sometimes a girl was so good and so lucky, she didn't miss for what seemed like hours.

But at last it was *her* chance and her heart was beating so fast while the other girls recited:

> *'First comes love,*
> *Then comes marriage,*
> *Then comes Honey with the baby carriage . . .'*

And then on the last line one foot got entangled in the rope and she fell.

Oh yes, first had come the love . . . From the first moment she saw him, from the first words they'd exchanged, she'd believed that true love was what they shared. She had loved him so much she had vowed to be anything he wanted her to be.

Then came the marriage . . . Everyone called it the

15

marriage made in television heaven. Nora Grant, the one person she respected above all others (except for her father Teddy), had even pronounced it a *brilliant* marriage.

But there had never been a Honey with a baby carriage!
First comes love,
Then comes marriage,
Then comes Honey with love's miscarriage.
Love's miscarriage . . . After all, wasn't that what a divorce was all about?

She pulled up close to the stanchion guarding the iron, gilt-touched gates of Grantwood Manor so that she could push its buzzer and talk into its receiver without stretching. There was a bit of static and then an anonymous voice: 'Yes?'

She gave her name and at the same time removed the sunglasses and the big hat to reveal a mass of golden-blond hair, then flashed her wide, ultra-white smile so that she would be easily recognized on the manor's closed-circuit television, its recording camera nestled in a royal palm overhead. These were automatic reflexes based on an inherent modesty – there probably wasn't a person over the age of five in all of the civilized world who wouldn't recognize the image of the Honey Rose. Especially here where once she'd visited so frequently she'd been referred to as an adopted daughter by the members of the household, both family and staff.

Now the iron gates slowly swung open admitting her to Grantwood and its enchanted castle. At least, that was how she had envisioned the great English country house when she first saw it. She'd been so excited that afternoon as she sat in the Grants' limousine between her two new schoolfriends, Babe and Sam. The fanciful Sam had told her and an awed Babe that the three of them would be the enchanted castle's reigning princesses. But of course it was only Sam who was the *true*, to-the-manor-born aristocrat who called Grantwood her ancestral home.

16

But it had taken her only a few visits even back then to realize that it wasn't the manor itself that was truly enchanted but its inhabitants – they who proved not who and what they appeared to be at first sight. Not the indomitable, redoubtable Nora whom everyone, with the exception of Sam, adored. And not Sam's father, T.S. Grant, either. Not even Sam, and not Hubie, gone from Grantwood before she herself ever set foot there. Still his spirit had hovered, perhaps more intensely felt *in absentia* than it had ever been with his actual presence.

And today she knew something that at fourteen she would have been incapable of understanding – that in spite of Grantwood Manor's lovely pedigree, it was, like TS's movies, only a Hollywood fabrication, its look of the grand English manor being more a matter of cinematic wizardry than anything else, and as such – like its inhabitants – never *quite* as presented. Still, it had taken some time before she realized that behind its idyllic façade and tropical plantings lurked a few dark secrets that one would ordinarily only associate with gloomy, mysterious Gothic castles . . .

But today she wasn't visiting. She was only picking Sam up so that they could go on to lunch with Babe who was flying in from Washington. It was Babe who had chosen the setting for their luncheon – Beverly Hills's Bistro Garden, where the ex-first lady, Nancy R., and her friends were the bunch who regularly lunched, all in matching Adolfos, the Chanel pump and the Judith Leiber pocketbook. These days, it seemed, though it *was* hard to believe, Babe admired Nancy Reagan as much as her mother Catherine always had. And these days, since Babe called Washington, DC home more than LA, she and Sam didn't get to see that much of her, so today was a special luncheon – a chance for them to catch up with Babe as well as a celebration of her very own divorce.

She drove up the sun-dappled driveway lined with king palms to the bricked courtyard with its huge terracotta pots spilling over with masses of multicoloured impatiens to find that there were at least twenty cars of all colours and denominations already parked there – Jag, Honda, Land-Rover, all making congenial enough neighbours, and she wondered to whom all these cars belonged.

But just then, Sam, tall and slender in emerald-green silk and matching, dangerously high-heeled, strapped sandals – her long red hair swirling around her shoulders as if of one piece – threw the manor's massive oak doors open and cried, 'Welcome to the club, Honey Rose!' And Honey's heart quickened and there were little goosebumps of remembered recognition running up her spine. The day she'd met Sam – the very same day Sam had brought her home to Grantwood Manor for the first time – that fourteen-year-old sophisticate had invited her to join a club and it would prove to be the most *fateful* moment of her entire life. After that, it was as if she had passed through a strange door to enter a whole new world and left innocence behind for ever . . .

Honey stepped into the Great Hall. 'OK, Sam, what club is it this time?'

Ever since that first club, it had been one club or another with Sam, some new group or cause. People claimed Sam changed affiliations as often as some women changed their good leather handbags or even their husbands. But it wasn't true in either case. There'd been many more handbags in Sam's life than clubs, and far fewer husbands.

'Come on, I'll show you.'

Sam took her by the hand to pull her down the long hall to the rear of the house and into the galleria that overlooked the terrace surrounding the pool. Ordinarily with its expanse of windows that allowed the sun to filter softly in through multiprisms of age-faded stained glass and its huge Oriental pots filled with exotic palms and blooming orchids, the room was an oasis of cool serenity. But today, drifting in from the terrace came an unceasing buzz of female voices with an accompanying swell of laughter.

'What club *is* meeting out there today?' Honey asked again, thinking that most likely it wasn't one of Sam's after all but her stepmother's since Nora was known for her philanthropies and fund-raisers as much as for her 'just for fun' parties. When Sam's father was alive, all the old Hollywood institutions like Cary Grant (no relation), Henry Fonda and John Huston, had gathered at the manor to sit at the great moviemaker's feet, to talk Industry talk, to wine and dine and make merry. And now that he was gone, the institutions of a later day like Nicholson, Beatty and Streisand, and all the new major moviemakers and the more recently arrived studio heads – the rich and the famous and the powerful – came to pay homage to the perennially ageless and effervescent Nora.

'What club the girl asks!' Sam hooted and drew Honey over to the windows to look out so that she could see the bevy of round pink-draped tables shaded by pink-and-white umbrellas, waiters carrying silver trays of tall champagne flutes and squat cocktail glasses, a maid in a pink uniform passing hors d'œuvres, and the thirty or so women who, dressed in everything from Valentinos and major jewellery to sweats and outrageous Melrose Avenue funk, milled and trilled.

'Take a look around, fool! What club would this be but the Hollywood Exes, or – the *Hexes*? Get it? A hex's a curse and all these women would love nothing better than to put the foulest kind of curse on their less-than-beloved exes.'

'I didn't know there was a club called the Hollywood Exes,' Honey said mournfully.

'Come on!' Sam's green eyes gleamed with sly amusement. 'I was only kidding. There *isn't* any such club. But from this gang gathered here it sure looks like we could get the club chartered today. Now, if we *were* to form this club who do you think should be president?'

'All right, I'll play along. Who?'

'I'll tell you *who* – the gal who scores the highest at

19

marriage and divorce roulette, the clever little exée who lands with both feet on Mr Ex digging her Ferragamo spikes into his bleeding, gory guts.'

'Sam! Must you be so graphic?'

'Don't you start getting fastidious on me, Honey Funny, or I'll flay *you* bloody.' She pushed Honey down into an overstuffed sofa abloom in chintz roses and sat down next to her. 'Let's dish a few secs before we go out to do battle with those cats at which time it will be next to impossible to get a word in. Now, getting back to that body dripping bloody guts,' she exhaled with relish, 'all I meant was to convey an image of the ex-wife as a winner, the rare female who comes out of the marriage holding not only *all* the loot but the bastard's gonads too. *That's* the woman who has to be the president of our club.'

Honey was uncomfortable with the turn of conversation but she knew from experience that the only thing to do when Sam was doing one of her numbers, was humour her. 'As I recall, Samantha, *you* were the president of every club I ever belonged to so I can't imagine electing anybody but you to the presidency of *anything*.'

'Ah, but that was when we were in our gloriously innocent pubescence. Now that we're grown up I hardly qualify to be president of the Hexes. I told you, the president has to be a real winner at the game and I, even with my three big Bs – beauty, brains, and breeding – can hardly qualify.'

Honey couldn't keep from laughing. 'Well, of course there is that *other* big B – your big mouth.'

'I will ignore that. Actually the gal I had in mind for the president of the Hexes is *you*, Honey Bunny. After all, what's the worst hex you can put on an ex? Stripping him down to his Speedos. And *you're* the clever exée who's going to end up with the very last pair of his jockeys.'

Honey's smile faded. 'Look, Sam, I'm really not in

the mood for this. And since that gathering out there is *not* a meeting of the Hollywood Exes, what *is* going on out there?'

'All right, spoilsport, I'll tell you. It's a party in your honour. You know, like Nora gave you a bridal shower before your wedding? Well, since tomorrow's the big day when your award is being announced, this time Nora's throwing you a divorce shower in anticipation of the fantastic award.'

'Settlement, not award,' Honey corrected her.

Sam shrugged. 'Same thing. Settlement, award, half of the community property. Does it matter what you call it?'

'It matters to me. As far as I'm concerned, award signifies something one is *given*, or a prize, maybe, that one has won. I want only what I've *earned*, that which is *due* me.'

'But how many of us get what's due us? And how many cocksuckers get what's *not* due them like my old steppie Nora? Didn't she get everything that was *my* due? Anyway, settlement or award, everyone's talking about *it*, waiting to see if you actually get it – every last cent you're asking for as well as that mausoleum you call home, Crown House.'

Honey grimaced. She was very much aware of the speculation the question of her settlement had sparked in the Hollywood community . . . in all its chic watering holes, across the tables of its power breakfasts, as well as in its bedrooms from the Hollywood Hills clear out to Malibu. It would have been bad enough if all the speculation had only been local, but like it or not, she was like Liz Taylor or Madonna or Princess Di – a spectacularly public figure and for months her divorce had been the stuff of national conjecture. One headline in a publication with a huge supermarket circulation had read: THE BIG AWARD: HOW MUCH HONEY WILL TV'S QUEEN BEE SUCK FROM THE PRINCE OF PRIME TIME'S GARDEN OF GOODIES? The speculation had even superseded the discussion about how big a slice Ivana was going to cut out of Donald's crumbling pie.

'I know only too well how interested the public is in my settlement,' Honey sighed. 'It's almost as if it were their God-given right to know every article of Crown House's inventory down to the last solid gold toilet seat everyone insists we have though we never had anything vaguely resembling that description.'

Sam arched an eyebrow. 'Are you sure? Have you counted lately?' Then, 'Well, you can hardly blame people, Honey Bunch. Even I when I think of how much you're asking for – Well!' She went into a mock faint.

Honey laughed but the laughter was forced. 'Asking doesn't mean getting.'

One thing she knew: no matter how large her settlement might turn out to be, it could never compensate for all the pain, the long months of acrimonious in-fighting, for the notoriety and exposure of the last intimate detail of her marriage. And the truth was, she didn't think anyone – not her sweet father or even Sam and Babe – really understood that the settlement she was seeking was not about money or revenge, but only validation of herself as a flesh-and-blood woman, not just some revenue-producing Barbie doll complete to the last appropriate accessory – furs, jewels, leather minis and purple workout suits, dreamhouse and dreamy white Rolls convertible. And she didn't think that even Nora, who always seemed to know everything, knew that going after all that money was about vindication rather than vindictiveness, and that no matter how much money she ultimately ended up with, she was still going to feel incredibly devastated that the marriage that had started out with *how much* as in Elizabeth Barrett Browning's 'How much do I love thee?' was going to end up with *how much* money she was going to squeeze out of the man she had once loved so desperately.

She remembered how just before she walked down the

aisle on her father's arm, he had softly recited Browning's sonnet to her about the depth and breadth of love. '*Freely, purely, passionately, with breath, smiles and tears . . . I shall but love thee better after death . . .*'

But that line was definitely *passé*. The updated version would read, 'I shall but love thee better until we split up the assets . . .'

> First comes love
> Then comes marriage
> Then comes splitting up the assets . . .

But she didn't want to think about that now. To change the subject, she teased, 'I don't know, Sam. You said this divorce shower was Nora's idea but it sounds more like something *you'd* dream up.'

Sam grinned a bit sheepishly. 'Well, I must admit that when Nora said she wanted to throw you a party, I did kind of suggest a divorce shower would be fun. But what's the diff? I mean, think how happy Nora is making this party for you. She's always been so fond of you. Remember how she always called you that "darling little girl" ever since the first day I brought you home? She used to chirp to Daddy, "Isn't that Honey the sweetest thing? It's really too bad that—" She never finished, but Daddy and I both got the point. *You* were the sweet little thing and I was the little shit even though I was nearly six feet tall even then. But as they say, it's all *herstory*. I just want you to understand that while I did suggest making this party a divorce shower, I was only trying to help Nora out.'

'Help Nora out?' Honey hooted. 'How come? *Opposing* Nora usually makes your day. And just a second ago you—'

'Isn't it possible I had a change of heart?' Sam chuckled and touched a long, red nail to Honey's nose. 'I can see from the look on that beautiful, but suspicious, face that you don't buy it – that I've had a change of heart about Nora.'

'You're right. I don't buy it.'

23

'OK. I confess that I have an ulterior motive in trying to get along with her these days. That's why I moved back into the house again. You see, I'm getting these vibes, these feelings deep down in my gut that Nora is about to make a decision about the studio, that she's finally having an attack of conscience and is thinking about giving me back that which she stole from me. And I'm not just talking about the studio or this house. I mean my trust fund, too.'

Honey started to object but Sam held up her hand. 'Please, no lectures about what a grand old gal Nora really is and how totally wrong I've been about her all these many years. Give me a break. Anyway, all I'm saying is that I'm getting these vibes that she's about to make her move with the studio and I'm on my best behaviour, just in case. I'm doing everything possible to get along with her outside of calling her Mummy, even though just the thought of making nice with her is enough to make me barf. Oh, let's not talk about it any more now or I'll just get depressed, OK?'

'OK,' Honey agreed, but if she herself hadn't been depressed before, she certainly was now. She, too, had a feeling Nora was about to make a move with the studio, only her own feeling was backed up by a rumour going around town, and if the rumour were true, Sam would not only despise Nora more than she already did, her heart would be broken . . . this time, perhaps, beyond repair.

But, of course, the rumour wasn't true, Honey reassured herself. Nora would never undercut Sam like that. No matter what, she herself was convinced that deep down Nora really *cared* about Sam, and she couldn't be *that* far off the mark.

Honey gave Sam's hand a squeeze. 'I'm sure everything's going to work out if you give it half a chance.'

'Really? I just wish you sounded a bit more sincere. But enough of me and my travails. Today is *your* day, Honey Buns, and you're going to enjoy it even if it kills you and I can only pray that when you walk into that courtroom tomorrow you get the full, record-breaking amount you're suing for. *One quarter of a bil!* Oh my, what a lovely sum! How enterprising of you to demand such a nice, round figure.'

'I don't want to think about that now. What I need right now is a good dose of our little Babe. But I didn't see her out there on the terrace. She *is* coming to my incredible divorce shower, isn't she?'

'Yes. At least, we're expecting her. She was supposed to fly in from Washington this morning. But either her flight was delayed or darling hubby decided he couldn't make a speech or whatever without her adoring eyes fixed upon him.'

'Oh, I hope not. I haven't seen Babe in ages and I'm dying for a sight of her.' Actually, she'd been eager to see Babe who was still ecstatically happy after her many years of marriage because Babe would understand, if no one else did, how destroyed she was feeling about the end of her own.

'So, tell me, Sam,' she said with determined cheeriness, 'before I go out there, what exactly happens at a divorce shower so that I'll be prepared. Naked body builders jumping out of the double-fudge chocolate cake?'

Sam snapped her fingers. 'Oh shit, I knew I'd forgotten something! And personally, I would have adored seeing your private parts violated by a bunch of muscular studs. I mean, men have to be good for *something!* Oh well, we'll do that one at your *next* divorce shower. In the meantime, you know how everyone brought gifts to your bridal shower? Well, at a divorce shower instead of gifts, the ladies – rad fems, wives, live-ins, divorcées, pals, etc. – all bring stories about marriages, both legal and not, and divorces, their own or maybe their best friend's, or just plain gossip – hopefully hot about some celebrated but sordid relationship.'

Honey had to laugh. When Sam got going, there was no stopping her. There just was no one else in the whole wide world quite like her. If nothing else, Sam was an original.

'Hold the laughter, please, until I'm through,' Sam held up her hand. 'Actually, any story that includes *any* ex – real or significant other – will do, or any weepy tale of a romance gone sour with a man who was bad news from the start, specially a blood-curdling story of unusual marital abuse. And any frank report on a *really* kinky marriage is acceptable, but only if none of the details are left out. And now, if you're ready – But wait, before we go out there, I want to make sure you look the part of a quarter-of-a-billion dollar baby!'

Honey smiled thinly. 'I thought I always did—'

'Of course you always *looked* the part,' Sam cooed, 'but you didn't always *have* it and now you're going to!'

'I didn't actually *have* it and I still might not get it, but I did *earn* it, didn't I? All of it, every penny?'

'Of course you did, Honey Money, but we've been through all that. What is it with you? Are you feeling guilty about going for the big one? Didn't you learn anything from that woman you admire so much, Ms Nora etc., etc., etc., Grant? How do you think she got where she is without grabbing every damn thing she could lay her greedy, oft-married little claws on?'

'Sam!'

'OK, I'll stop and we'll focus our attention on you. I just want to make sure that those hyenas out there don't think that just because you've cut the first notch on the old divorce pistol, the dew is off the Rose. We have to show them that the Honey Rose still lives to bloom another day.'

She crouched down into a photographer's stance pretending to look through a camera viewer. 'Now, let's see the famous Honey Rose smile, if you please.'

Honey obliged with as big a smile as she could muster but Sam wasn't satisfied. 'Oh no, that won't do at all!'

Honey tried again showing more teeth, but Sam shook her head. 'If you can't do better than that, you know what I'll have to do. I'll have to *tickle* you into a big grin and you know how you always hated to be tickled in the good old days.'

The good old days . . . before we grew up to get married so that we could get divorced . . .

'No, no tickling, please!' Honey begged more to please Sam than anything. 'I'll be good! How's this?' And she flashed an even wider smile, a smile as big as the Ritz.

'*Give it to me,*' he urged. '*A smile as big as the Ritz.*'

She had had no idea how big the Ritz actually was, but he had said, 'Give it to me,' and whatever he asked for, he got. That was the way it had been with them whether it was a big smile or a kiss or anything else she had to offer. He took and always demanded just a little bit more.

'Beautiful! Gorgeous!' Sam cried, leaping forward to whip at Honey's hair with her long fingers as vigorously as if she were enthusiastically hand-tossing a Caesar salad. Then she stepped back to view her handiwork. 'That's better! *That's* the famous Honey Rose Tousle!'

'*More hair! Bigger hair!*' he ordered the hair stylists. '*It has to be a definitive statement.*'

He'd stood over the hair stylists for hours, suggesting, instructing, correcting and harassing in turn, while she sat mute with her heart in her throat, frightened that he might never be satisfied and then *what*? But finally . . . magically . . . he *was* pleased and she was able to breathe again.

'Now give us that notorious Honey Rose come-hither with the ol' topazes. You know, the "Look!"' Sam cajoled.

The Look! Think sex, he had instructed her.

That hadn't been difficult. Every time she looked at him she had thought sex. Thought of him poised above her as she looked into those deceptively soft eyes,

27

felt him inside her, so fully and beautifully inside her. Thought of how it felt when *she* was positioned above *him*, easing him into her. But, of course, that had never been *his* favourite sexual position.

She obliged Sam now by thinking sex just as she had always obliged him and Sam breathed, 'Oh *yeah*! That's the "Look"! Now, do you think we might hike the hemline up an inch or two? We need a little more leg here.' Even as she spoke Sam tugged at Honey's waist to raise her skirt, then went back into her crouch. 'This is good! *Really* good! You look almost as delectable as you did in that wet T-shirt poster that set world records for whacking-off from Jackson Hole, Wyoming to Peking, China.'

Thinking about the poster, Honey sighed. All by itself it had generated millions of dollars, selling two hundred thousand copies in Tokyo alone. As a birthday present, he'd had the poster blown up to five times its size and framed in gold leaf to hang incongruously along-side the Picassos, the Renoirs and the Warhol silk-screen rendering of a pistol packing Honey in short shorts and thigh-high cowboy boots.

Who would get the art collection? Would it be a trade-off for Crown House? He loved the collection almost as much as he loved the house. And he loved the house almost as much as he loved Royal Productions.

Then she heard Sam groan in mock gratification. 'OK, Honey Rose, I think we're ready. Let's go out there and kill 'em!'

2

When the women cheered as she and Sam stepped out onto the terrace, Honey felt ridiculous. It was as if she'd saved the world from nuclear destruction instead of merely demanding a shocking amount of money and an outrageously extravagant home as her fair share of the community property. Then, when Nora, looking incredibly attractive in a red silk caftan and chandelier earrings of diamonds and rubies, her pale blond hair swept back into a chignon, rushed up to hug her, murmuring, 'Congratulations, love, on a brilliant divorce!' her eyes filled up.

Nora, seeing the tears now, whispered, 'Oh, my dear, you mustn't. It only hurts for a little while and that's where the money helps. It makes the pain go away. And you look much too beautiful to ruin the effect with tears. I always say it's much more important to look beautiful when one is getting a divorce than when one is getting married.'

Despite her vow to be nice to Nora, Sam couldn't hold back completely and, voice tinged with irony, she drawled, '*Why* do you always say that, Nora?'

Choosing to ignore any possible taunt, Nora smiled. 'I say it because it's the truth. A wedding, if you think about it, is actually an ending – a culmination of two people meeting, courting, breaking up and getting back together again finally to unite their souls into one. So loverly, but still an ending, and endings are sad. On the other hand, the divorce! That's saying goodbye to the past and hallo to the future and I always say we must begin anew looking beautiful and feeling positive because it's good karma. It attracts the best of everything. Especially new and exciting men!'

'And *rich*! That's important, isn't it?' Sam persisted.

'To be sure, my dear,' Nora said, refusing to be goaded.

'There you go, Honey!' Sam cried. 'Another brilliant observation from the lady who has a brilliant saying to cover every subject, be it men, marriage or divorce. And as *I* always say, no one is better qualified to do this than our Nora.'

Nora's laugh tinkled out and she patted Sam on the cheek before she turned away to instruct the butler to bring out a few more bottles of the Cristal while Honey hissed, 'I thought you said you were going to try to get along with her—'

'I know I did.' Sam lowered her lashes in mock remorse.

'Then why were you being so snide and sarcastic?'

'You know the story of the frog and the scorpion? They come to a stream they have to cross and the scorpion says, "I can't swim. Let me ride on your back," and the frog says, "But if I let you ride on my back you'll sting me and I'll drown," and the scorpion says, "Don't be ridic! Of course I won't sting you! If you drown, so will I." So the frog lets the scorpion get on his back and sure enough, midstream the scorpion stings him and as they're both drowning the frog croaks, "But you knew this would happen. Why did you sting me?" and the scorpion says, "Because I'm a scorpion."'

'Did it ever occur to you *not* to be a scorpion?'

Sam laughed. 'Of course it's occurred to me, but that's the very point – I *am* a scorpion.'

'Honey, you're really *doing* it!' Lakey Owens, the star of a prime-time soap, pounded Honey on the back. 'You're even putting Francie Lear to shame. *She* only got one hundred and fifteen mil!'

'*Only?*' Chris Campbell, who'd been a divorcée for five years after having been married to a rock star for six months, was indignant. 'I'll take that *only* any day of the week! I barely got enough to pay the rent on my one bedroom.'

'And you were lucky to get that,' Lakey retorted, snatching a glass of champagne from the passing waiter's tray. 'Poor Francie was in her sixties and had given Norman her best years. How can you compare six months with Wild Bill Boynton to the kind of time Frances put in with Norman?'

'And you never understood the value of public relations,' Pammi Petrie of Petrie Public Relations, decked out in rhinestone-studded leather, added. 'Look at Alana Stewart. *She* really dug the dynamics of publicity. She married Rod with everybody looking and parted from him in the public eye with shots of her and Rod's kids hitting you in the eye every time you opened a rag. Now she's living it up with fantastic support and fancy digs. Why? Because who, even a rocker, wants to look like a SOB who doesn't give a shit about his kids? Now if *you'd* been smart, you would have stuck it out with Wild Bill for a couple of years, had a kid or two, and had it all documented with lots of togetherness photos.'

'Had a couple of kids? Stuck it out for a couple of years?' Chris fumed. 'How the hell was I supposed to manage that? Once he married me, he stopped pronging me. And then when I was out shopping at Saks one afternoon he moved one of his groupies into my bed and all my stuff out into the garage. And I didn't even have the garage remote with me!'

'Pathetic!' WeeGee Gosset, columnist for the *Beverly Hills Recorder*, observed, slurping a Cajun oyster. 'Don't you know that when you marry a rocker you need a special clause written into the marriage contract? No balling groupies.'

'Or, at least, you should have always carried your garage opener with you,' Bambi Winters snickered, getting a big laugh, since everyone knew the story of how the petite Bambi had won the family manse (which had only her husband's name on the grant deed) by simply refusing to move out even after her ex called the cops on her, contending she was trespassing.

But Mary Lou Walters, the beauty queen from El Paso recently divorced from the CEO of a major studio, moaned, 'That's not funny,' and there was a few seconds of silence out of respect for Mary Lou's depression. Her ex had just announced his engagement to young and hot Mavis Madding, who'd been spotted only a month before

31

holding hands with Warren Beatty at the China Club for a dazzling nine nights running, the same Marvellous Mavis her husband had first strayed with.

'The truth is that sooner or later, they *all* stray,' the middle-aged gravel-voiced sitcom writer, Rae Peters, in an orange running suit and lime Reeboks, lamented. 'When you're hot, *they're* hot. But as soon as you give up what made you hot so you can baby *them*: rub their backs, run their baths, fix their drinks, arrange their social schedules and listen to their bullshit about how hard they have it out there, they chill out so fast it makes the blood run cold. Then, instead of *banging* you, they're letting you *take* their temperature while they find someone else to *raise* it, the moral of which is if you sublimate your own career to his, you're really up shit creek without a paddle.'

'*She* should talk,' someone snorted in an undertone. 'Whose temperature did she ever raise?'

'Some women are really smart. They hold on to their careers, give up zilch and still come out on top. Look at Amy. She didn't give up her career for Steven and now she not only has lots of fancy real estate, nearly a hundred mil in cash, Steve's kid as well as her current boy-friend's, she's managed to keep the big man's friendship, too. She and Steve are still having dinner together.'

'Yeah, it's nice that the Spielbergs stayed friends.'

'It's even nicer that Amy has enough cash now to call the shots on her career. She can afford to pick and choose.'

'Never mind Amy, look at our Honey. She's still going to have her career *and* Crown House and two hundred and fifty million dollars!'

But not the things I *really* want, Honey thought, and certainly not Joshua's friendship.

She looked at Sam, eyes begging: *Save me!* and Sam took her by the hand. 'Excuse us, we have to get Honey here a little nourishment. Just thinking about that

32

two hundred and fifty million dollars, you know. A *huge* expenditure of calories.'

Before they moved on the raspy-voiced Rae advised, 'Take your money, Honey, and do something really *big* with it.'

'Yeah,' Lakey Owens agreed. 'Francie started *Lear's* with her millions which really told Norm off in spades.'

'What does she mean?' Honey asked Sam as they made their way toward the buffet table. 'How did Frances Lear starting up her own magazine tell Norman off?'

Sam laughed. '*Lear's*, the magazine for the *older* woman, if you'll pardon the expression, is also known in certain circles as the "Fuck you, Norman" publication.'

'But why?'

'Because it's a feminist magazine and Francie used Norm's millions to launch it. She didn't just sit on her money. She used it to start a new life for herself and at the same time, to thumb her nose at Norman. And that's what *you* should do.'

Honey laughed. '*What* should I do? Start a magazine or thumb my nose at Norman?'

'I'm serious. You should start a new career with your settlement money and at the same time stick it to Josh – show him you can make it on your own in terms he understands.'

'*New* career? And what do you mean by terms he understands?'

'What did you always want? A career as a *serious* actress. That *would* be a new career for you, all things considered. And what means the most to the hotshot?'

'I guess his company, Royal Productions.'

'There you have it! He loves Royal Productions beyond anything and if you took your settlement money and bought a studio – a *real* studio that produces real movies and not just grist for the TV mills, then did the serious stuff he claimed you were incapable of doing, wouldn't that be thumbing your nose at him, showing him that you were *never* just a T and A bimbo? And if you really

33

made a success of it, wouldn't that be the ultimate in the fuck-you department?'

'But—'

'Not now. Here come some more of the gals. Smile and have some *rotelle*. You *know* it has to be yummy because the steppie hired the Yum-Yums to do the food. Trust Nora to always have the best and the latest in edibles. That's what they call keeping *au courant*.' She took some *rotelle* on her own plate and tasted. 'Yep, it's entirely yummy-yummy.'

But Honey, mulling over what Sam had just said, barely tasted the *rotelle*. She wondered if there was a particular company Sam had in mind as her 'fuck-you' studio.

Actually it was a fascinating concept. In all the years they'd been married she couldn't honestly say that she had ever fucked Josh in the non-literal sense. And she hadn't fucked him too many times in the literal sense, either. It was he who had almost always *fucked her*, though sometimes she had attempted to assume the more aggressive position on top rather than the supplicant one under, enabling her to choose when to ease him gently into her, or savagely to impale herself upon him . . . to set the tone, to ride him as furiously as she desired or at a tantalizingly deliberate rhythm . . . to make *him* cry out in unbearable desire and plead with her to quicken her pace or to slacken it . . . No, he hadn't permitted that too often. Josh was a man who could relish life, love and sex, only if he called the shots.

Maybe if she wanted to be honest, that was what her divorce and her demands were *truly* all about – fucking him – and not vindication and validation of self, or even the money she had justly earned. Maybe it had been simply the 'fuck you' divorce right from the start.

She looked up to see Nora watching her. And startled, she realized that Nora's expression was *sorrowful*. But then as their eyes met, Nora shifted her mournful gaze. What had she been thinking that made her look so sad? Honey wondered.

Nora had just a while ago congratulated her on making a brilliant divorce. Brilliant because of the money. Still, on her wedding day, Nora had congratulated her on making a brilliant marriage which by Nora's definition included love, convenience, fun (which translated into sex) and money. But married or divorced, the money part was still viable, so she wasn't feeling sorry for her about the money. Was Nora feeling sad then that she was going to miss out on great sex?

He was on top, his full lips moving sensuously against hers, then moving down tortuously slowly to her throat, her shoulders, her breasts. Then they mouthed her nipples – those twin erections as hard in their desire as his own erection which she invariably pleaded for. 'Now! Oh yes, please! I love you so much! Please . . . I love you!'

She had always ended up begging for that final thrust, the final fulfilment, as if he were holding back on the best part of himself though she always promised herself she *wouldn't* beg – not for his body nor his love, not for all the best things in life he had promised her. But she strongly doubted Nora was feeling sorry for her because she was going to lose great sex. After all, this *was* Hollywood and sex was Hollywood's cheapest commodity. Besides, Nora had no idea of whether the sex had been good, bad or indifferent.

Convenience, then? But Nora would hardly think she'd lost a marriage of great convenience. Everyone knew that if her marriage had been a marriage of convenience, it had always been more Joshua's than hers, and that left only the love.

But love was the *tricky* part, the part that could fool you. Oh, she had loved him, but had he ever truly loved her? As she'd just told Sam, he had loved Royal Productions above all else, and probably he loved Crown House next, which was the reason she'd insisted on getting it as part of her settlement. Then if she did walk away with the house, she would at least have one of the two things he loved best. Even now she didn't know if she had ever come close to being third on the list of the things he called the best things in life.

But what did Nora know about that love that she herself didn't? And for at least the hundredth time she wondered: of all Nora Grant's marriages, which was *her* most brilliant and which had been only for love? She thought that if she had the answer to those questions then maybe she'd understand why Nora was looking at her with so melancholy an expression . . .

'When the legal beagle gave me the four alternatives he said he always offered his clients: negotiation, litigation, capitulation or assassination, I didn't hesitate. I told him I was out to murder Jack!' As she spat out the words, Dawn Harris twisted the huge emerald encircling her engagement finger as viciously as if it were her husband's neck. 'I knew that Jack was cheating on me all over town and that he had to pay through his teeth for the humiliation he'd caused me. I not only wanted half of every last thing he owned including his sapphire cuff-links, I wanted his blood.'

'And did you get it? Did you cut Jack's balls off?'

'We're *still* slugging it out. Murder isn't as easy as it sounds. We're not all as lucky as Honey.'

Honey vaguely thought about straightening out the record – *she'd* never opted for murder. She'd never wanted blood.

Or did I? But if anyone had done any killing, it had been *he*, not she. He was the one who had killed their love and their marriage with his disregard of her needs . . . his false promises . . . his lying kisses.

But she didn't want to be filled with bitterness. She wanted to walk away clean. Maybe someday, when he realized that she was a real person and not a Barbie doll, she and he could even be friends.

'What about it, Honey?' Sallee Foster demanded.

'Did your lawyer talk you into going for the jugular?'

Honey shrugged. That was like the question – *when* did you stop beating your wife? Why did everyone assume she had gone for the jugular instead of just wanting what was rightfully hers? Besides, most probably, not one woman here was really interested in hearing her say that her attorney, Press Rudman, had, on the whole, urged her to be fair rather than venal. These women only wanted to hear the worst.

'I don't know,' Jill Halpern sighed. 'It seems some women have it so easy. Look at Brigitte Neilsen. She was scarcely married to Rambo when she walked off with six mil.'

'Yeah, but there was more to that than meets the eye. I read there was a kitchen drawer full of kinky pictures – you know, *ménage à trois* stuff.'

'You're not serious? But who was the third party?'

'I don't know the details, but the story goes that Mom accused the Rambette of playing cosy with her lady secretary.'

'I'm glad it was only the secretary. I had this feeling you were going to say it was Mom she was cosying with. But let's go back a way and consider the case of Joanna Carson.'

'But Johnny and Joanna's brawl no longer has any relevance considering what's going down these days.'

'Still, there was no scandal there, at least none that I heard and Joanna didn't do bad for the time she put in.'

'They, at least, were married something like ten years.'

'Yes, but she was so *incredibly* greedy she gave the necessities of life a crappy name. She had the gall to ask for two hundred and twenty thousand dollars a month in temporary alimony saying it was the least she could live on and then she listed a six thousand dollar payment on Johnny's life insurance which was made out to her as one of *her* monthly expenses. *That's* what you call *chutzpah*.'

'Well, what about that Swede and Joan Collins?

He tried to take her to the cleaners although he had a sweetie on the side – the one they called the Passion Flower. Now, *that's* what I call *chutzpah*. Lucky for Joanie she had a prenup.'

'Oh, I don't know. I think prenuptial agreements show a lack of trust which doesn't bode well for a marriage. I mean, look at Donald and Ivana. He had that prenup updated about a half-dozen times. He had to have something in the back of his mind all along, you know? Did you have a prenup, Honey?'

Honey started to say, 'Hardly. I—'

'Did *he* have a passion flower on the side?'

Honey pretended she didn't hear the question while a pale blonde groaned: 'They *all* have a passion flower on the side, but it doesn't matter. What people can't get through their heads is that a California divorce is *not* affected by adultery – that that big A is for Assets, not Adultery.'

Nora joined the group clustered around Honey. 'Well, everyone looks like they're having a good time. Whose reputation are we destroying now?' she asked cheerfully.

'We were just talking about prenups and the big A – whether it stands for assets or adultery,' Sam grinned slyly. 'Considering your vast store of experience, Nora dear, is there anything you'd care to add to the discussion?'

Nora chuckled. 'Oh my, I think not. By now I've already forgotten more about prenups, assets and adultery than any of you would ever really want to know.'

Honey turned to Sam who was nibbling away at a crabcake dripping black bean sauce, using her fingers instead of cutlery, but still managing to carry it off with *élan*. 'Have I done my duty?' she asked, *sotto voce*. 'Don't you think I've earned a little time-out? And Babe's still not here. Don't you think we should check and find out what happened to her?'

Oh, she *needed* to see Babe now – Babe with her wonderful, successful marriage.

38

'OK. We'll go make a couple of calls and see if we can find her.' Sam licked the sauce from her fingers. 'We'll just kind of sneak off to the library to make the calls.'

'You know what's funny?' Honey whispered as they tiptoed down the hall. 'Out of that whole group and all that talk, I didn't hear one good word said about *any* man.'

'Well, did you think that you would?' Sam chortled. 'These women *are* the Hollywood Exes.'

'Still you'd think that there'd be *one* woman willing to say, "OK, we didn't make it, but he's a terrific guy and I wish him the very best."'

'Yeah, you'd think, but I guess it's the nature of the beasties that it doesn't work that way. And what about you, Honey? Are you willing to make that statement?'

'Well, let's say I'm not entirely *unwilling* to say it. And I *do* wish him the best.'

The very, very best. And who knows? It's quite possible that I will always wish him love . . .

3

'I'll call Washington, but if we don't get any satisfaction on that end, *you'll* have to call Babe's mother,' Sam said, closing the library door. 'Frankly, I'm not up to Catherine today. You know how she answers the phone with that Queen Mother irritation in her voice? As if you interrupted her just as she was having an orgasm on the crapper?'

'Oh, God!' Honey giggled, shaking her head.

'I always greet *her* nicely enough, enquiring after her health politely,' Sam said, going to the massive oak bar, the focal point of the panelled room, to take down a bottle of Courvoisier. 'But it's always the same old shit with her.'

She poured a little brandy into two snifters, then judiciously measuring with an eye, poured a little more into each glass before handing one to Honey. 'It's always, "Oh, it's *you*, Sa-*man*-tha. I suppose you want Babette?" and I always feel like answering, "No, actually I want Babette's daddy, your husband, the Judge. It's been awfully long since we've been between the sheets and I wanted to ask him over for a quickie." But being a nice person, I never have.

'Anyway, if Babe *isn't* there, Catherine loves to say that she hasn't heard from her in *weeks* just so I'll be sure to worry that something's wrong. Then she asks, "Is there anything *else* I can do for you?" as if she'd already moved a mountain and then I'm tempted to say, "Yeah, you can bend over and touch your toes while I stick a hot poker up your ass!"'

'All right,' Honey conceded after she finished laughing, 'you call Washington and if you have no luck, I'll call Catherine even though I really don't know why this great privilege should be mine. What did I ever do to deserve it?'

'You deserve it because everyone knows how famously you get along with Catherine Tracy, *almost* as well as you get on with old Nora. That's your style, Honey Buns. You're the girl every mother loves to mother.'

Not quite, Honey thought. I can think of one notable exception – my own.

'That was Babe's social secretary,' Sam said, hanging up. 'I didn't even know she had one. She really *needs* one of those? Anyway, Ms Prissy said Babe left Washington at eight-thirty their time, was supposed to land eleven-thirty our time and was coming straight here, which means she should have been here by twelve-thirty, one at the latest.' She checked her watch. 'It's almost three

40

now so something or somebody is off-schedule.'

'She said Babe definitely took the eight-thirty flight?'

'Yes. She said Senator Ryan's chauffeur took Babe to the airport. Hmm . . . A social secretary for her, a chauffeur for him, that big house and all that fancy entertaining. They're living pretty high on Catherine and the Judge's money which leads to an interesting question – if *they* get a divorce, how will they split up all that Tracy community property?'

'Don't trouble your little head, Sammy dear. Babe's marriage is as solid as a brick wall.'

'Maybe so, but even brick walls disintegrate and you know how it happens? One brick at a time when the mortar starts to crumble. That brick wall is only as good as the mortar's formula which has to take into consideration weather conditions, wear and tear, and compatibility of materials. And the mortar that binds Babe's bricks? I'd say there's too much Tracy mixed in with the sand and water.'

'But what about that thing called love? Doesn't that count for anything in that formula?'

'It all depends on what kind of love you're talking about and who's in love with whom. Personally, I think Greg is in love with Babe's parents and they're in love with him which is all fine and good – I'm all for swell in-law relationships. Still, where does that leave Babe? Who's left to love *her*?'

'Why do you have to think the worst about everyone and everything, Sam? Why can't you accept the fact that Babe has a good marriage? Sometimes, you know, you just have to take certain things and people simply on faith.'

'Was that what you did when you waltzed down the aisle with the blinders on?'

'Oh, Sam!' Honey's stricken voice reproached. 'That's attacking me where I'm most vulnerable!'

'I'm sorry, Honey, I guess that *was* hitting below the belt. But you know I love you and between *us* we have

41

some pretty great mortar, don't we? Do you forgive me?'

Honey waved a hand in exasperation. 'I guess I have no choice. You're forgiven. Now, I think we should call the airline and find out if Babe's plane arrived on time. Did her secretary say which airline?'

'Yes, TWA. She also asked that since Mr Wonderful always likes to know where Babe is in case he has to be in touch, would I be so good as to call her back when Babe shows up.' Sam smirked. 'Fat chance, lady, fat chance.'

She flipped through a Rolodex and dialled. It took only a couple of minutes to establish that Babe's plane had landed on time. 'It touched down at eleven-thirty.'

'I guess there's nothing to be done then but for me to call Catherine,' Honey sighed and started to dial while Sam went back to the bar to refill her glass.

After volleying with Catherine Tracy for at least five minutes, Honey, laughing, reported: 'It appears that Catherine hasn't seen or heard from Babe in *weeks*. Maybe *months*. Would you believe *years*?'

'You see? What did I tell you? She always says that no matter what, just so you'll have an anxiety attack. You didn't tell her that we expected Babe almost three hours ago?'

'I didn't.'

'Good. Not that Catherine doesn't deserve a little anxiety attack herself.'

'But what do we do now?'

'*Nada*. Maybe Babe decided she didn't like what she was wearing and went shopping instead of coming straight here.'

'Shopping for three hours after she got off a plane?'

'Why not? You know Babe was always a Rodeo Drive freak.'

'Don't you think we should call Babe's secretary back and tell her we can't locate her? Maybe they'll want to start checking from their end.'

'For God's sake, Honey, give Babe a break! We're talking about three hours here, not a missing person.

Maybe between her mother and her husband and that secretary, the poor girl desperately needed a few hours to herself. And did you ever stop to think that maybe she took this opportunity discreetly to check into a motel for a little off-the-record dicking? And the least we can do for her is not turn her in to the cops.'

'Very funny. So, what *shall* we do?'

'We shall sit tight and *get* tight while we wait for Babe to show up in her own good time.' Sam went to the door to lock it. 'If anyone comes a-knockin', don't you make a sound. We'll just wait right here until that menagerie out there is gone and Babe gets here. In the meantime, how about a refill?'

Honey held up her glass to show that it still had liquid in it and while Sam went to replenish her own drink, she thought about all the times they'd done this very same thing in this very same room – locked themselves in to hide from the world. Sometimes they'd sat for hours no matter who pounded on the door while Sam, refusing to open up, calmly read aloud to them from a book she'd pulled at random from one of the floor-to-ceiling bookshelves.

Still, no matter how frequently they'd done this, she herself had always been shocked anew by Sam's cool indifference to the order: 'Open up!', while Babe, her black-cherry eyes sparkling with excitement, was enraptured by the show of open disobedience. But, at the same time, it was always a nervous kind of excitement because while Babe found Sam's audacity awesome, she herself would have been terrified to pull a stunt like that in her own house which was something Honey always completely understood. While the Tracys hadn't believed in corporal punishment, their silent treatment and 'confinement to quarters' discipline *was* inhibiting, which explained why Babe had always begged, 'Let's go to your house, Sam, or yours, Honey, any place but mine!'

'But what if it's Nora who comes to the door, Sam?

You're going to *have* to open up. You're not a rebellious kid any longer. Well, not a kid, anyway. And this *is* her house.'

'Tell me about it!'

'In all fairness, Nora has given you a home here any time you want, regardless of how—'

'Sure she has. As long as I remember that it's *her* house, just as Grantwood Studio is *her* studio. Besides, she wants me here so she can remind me of what a fuck-up I am, not to mention that she wants to control me just like she did when I was a kid . . . just like she always controlled Daddy.'

They were going over old material. It seemed to Honey that no matter where the conversation began it always ended up with Nora. With Sam it was *always* Nora . . .

'The truth, Sam, is that Nora controlled your father as much as he *let* her control him.'

Sam made a hissing sound. 'He was putty in that little calculating, manipulative hand of hers. Why else would he have left her *my* studio and *my* house, damn it?'

'Oh, Sam!' Honey remonstrated softly. 'It was never *your* studio. It was *his* and he chose to leave it to the woman who made him happy. Sooner or later you'll just *have* to come to terms with that, and stop tearing yourself apart.'

'But I can't bear it!' Sam cried out, throwing herself down on the sofa next to Honey, rubbing her hot face again and again against the comfortingly cool leather. 'It's mine! I'm his daughter! It's his blood that runs in my veins just like making movies ran in his. That studio belongs to *me*! You know she doesn't give a damn about it. She's let strangers run it ever since Daddy died. It's never meant anything to her except for the money it made.'

'But she's always been willing for you to work there. In fact, she urged you to—'

44

'Oh sure. She wanted me to work at the studio as a gofer. But what she really wanted was to humiliate me.'

'Come off it, Sam. The problem was that you wanted to start at the top producing fifty-million-dollar pictures and Nora wanted you to start at the bottom so that you could learn the business thoroughly. She thought that—'

Sam sat up straight. 'How the hell do you know *what* she thought? You really don't know anything about it! Just like you don't know *why* she tried to make my father hate me or *why* she sent Hubie away just because he loved me.'

Honey didn't know what to say to that. It had been years since Sam had mentioned Hubie.

'And you don't know for sure why she got me out of the way when my father was dying. Or the number one question – why my father left everything to her – even my trust fund, *to be disbursed at her discretion*!' Sam snorted. '*Disbursed*! That doesn't even sound like TS . . .!'

'If you weren't still so blinded by all that faky charm you'd see that it all adds up to just one thing – that she's an out-and-out bitch who completely snowed a trusting man and the fact that she could do that to *him* – fool him – just shows what a good and pure heart *he* had. Only the good and the pure can be manipulated like my father was by Nora. Oh, what's the use of talking to *you*? But, one of these days, you're going to have to take a stand, you know. Decide whose side you're really on. Hers or mine.'

But I've already done that, Sam, Honey ached to cry out. *I took sides a long time ago when I betrayed Nora by not telling her the truth about TS and I did it only to keep the truth from you.*

'Oh God, why did my father ever marry her? Why? She's such a terrible bitch and he was *so* wonderful, wasn't he?'

Honey hesitated a moment or two before nodding and Sam, who was usually so acute at catching these small

45

nuances, was so worked up she didn't notice the slight pause. Instead, she burst into tears and Honey rocked her back and forth, trying to comfort her. Never had she seen Sam like this – her spirit so broken. Sam who, no matter what, always appeared so strong and self-sufficient.

'Everything will be all right, Sam. You'll see.'

'You'll help me, then? You'll be on my side?'

'Oh, Sam, I've always been on your side and of course I'll help you. That's what friendship means. The good times, the fun – that's the *easy* part. But you're not going to need my help. You said that you had this feeling that Nora might be ready to turn the studio over to you. Well, if it turns out that she *isn't* ready to do that, maybe she'll at least be ready to give you a chance at running it, and then if you prove yourself, you could work together to hammer out some kind of a deal – a partnership, maybe, or a trade – your trust fund money for at least a share of the studio. . .'

Sam sat up, pushed the heavy hair back away from her face, wiped at her cheeks. 'I don't know. You make it sound so easy. And it never is, is it? Easy? It never has been.'

Honey tried to smile. 'Maybe this time it will be.'

Still, Sam sank into one of her funks and then Honey thought about the conversation she and Sam had had over the *rotelle* about what she should do with her settlement money.

If you took your money and bought a studio – any studio or production company – you'd be starting a new creative life for yourself and at the same time sticking it to Josh . . . showing him that you were never just a T and A bimbo.

Had Sam been implying that the studio she should buy was Grantwood? Buy it for *both* their sakes? Or had she just been talking idly as she often did, enjoying her own conversation?

But just now Sam had asked her if she'd be on her side – if she would help her. Was that the help Sam was really referring to? Suggesting that she take her blood money –

46

that's what it amounted to when all was said and done – her money and Josh's blood – and invest it in Grantwood Studio? But that was something she wouldn't dream of doing in a million years. Owning a studio was the last thing she wanted. And did she really *want* to stick it to Josh?

Honey said a little silent prayer that Nora, who was so much wiser than they, would do the right thing and soon. *And please, dear God, don't let that rumour I heard be true!*

Lost in thought, she was startled to hear Sam's harsh, abrupt laugh. 'From the first day I met Nora all I prayed for was that Daddy would divorce her. But I see now that it's *I* who really needs a divorce from her and if I finally get my hands on Grantwood Studio, at last I'll be getting it and I'll never have to look at her again.'

'But all this time, Sam, ever since your father died – ever since you've been old enough to be on your own – you didn't *have* to see her. You didn't have to live here or even talk to her. No one forced you to keep coming back here. To tell the truth, Sam, I've always wondered why you *did* keep coming back to Grantwood Manor.'

'It's my home,' Sam said defensively.

'Not any more. And if you didn't want to see Nora—?'

'There *was* the matter of my trust fund, as you well know. I had to keep after her for that, didn't I?'

'Not in person you didn't.'

'Look at it this way, Honey. You wanted to be divorced from your husband, right?'

Honey shrugged.

'But you didn't just walk *out* of Crown House, did you? And you didn't just walk *away* from Royal Productions even though, legally, you never owned any part of it, did you? You stayed to fight for what was yours. What makes you think that I would walk away from my marriage to Nora without getting my share of the goodies, without getting *my* brilliant divorce any more than you did, any more than Nora herself would have?'

Honey had no ready answer. Perhaps Sam was right. There were all kinds of marriages so there had to be all kinds of divorces, too . . .

'I guess someone's finally come to look for us,' Honey whispered when there was a hard rapping on the locked door.

Sam put a finger to her lips. 'Sh!'

But Honey felt foolish hiding from the guests at a party given in *her* honour. She and Sam were no longer schoolgirls to be playing these silly games. And what if it were Nora? She, if not Sam, could hardly refuse to respond.

She half-rose from the sofa to go to the door, but Sam pushed her back down. They tussled as Sam tried to put a hand over her mouth to muzzle her, both of them laughing soundlessly until the rapping at the door turned into a thunderous pounding and they heard a voice, harsh and ragged: 'Open up! Sam! Honey! I know you two are in there! Open up! Let me in!'

Sam raced to the door, unlocking it quickly and Babe, shiny black hair a smooth cap with bangs cut squarely across, and exquisitely turned out in a pale yellow suit – unmistakably Chanel – came tumbling into the room, high heels clattering noisily on the polished floor. But despite the fastidious grooming, an air of hysteria shimmered about her, and the very dark, hip sunglasses she was wearing were an incongruous note, clashing with the discreetly elegant fashion statement she otherwise presented.

'What's with the shades?' Sam asked, amused. Babe hadn't worn the Wayfarers she'd been addicted to as a teen in years.

Babe seemed surprised by the question as if she'd forgotten she was wearing the glasses and pulled them off to reveal eyes wild and ringed with inky, smudged

48

mascara, which struck a discordant, almost macabre note in the otherwise perfectly made-up face.

'Babe! What's wrong?' Honey rushed to her. 'Where were you? We were worried about you!'

'I had to hitch-hike here from Hollywood and Vine . . .'

'You hitched from Hollywood Boulevard in your Maude Frizons?' Sam hooted, then stopped abruptly. 'Honey, get her a drink. Now, sit down, Babe, and tell us what happened.'

'I finally took a ride from some guy in a Brooklyn College sweatshirt in a red Ferrari. It was the first offer I received from someone who looked at least halfway normal.'

'Then what happened?'

'Nothing happened. He wasn't a pervert if that's what you mean. He didn't do anything except drive me here.'

'I mean, what were you doing on Hollywood Boulevard with all the weirdos in the first place? Why didn't you come right here from the airport like you were supposed to?'

'I needed some time to think.'

'About what?'

'About what I wanted to do. So, I got into a cab and told the driver to drive around and that's where he drove. From LAX to Hollywood. Then I got out. I thought I'd walk for a while. That's when I bought these sunglasses from a kid on the street because I had lost mine. I guess he needed the money for drugs or something.'

'I don't believe this!' Sam was incredulous. 'You bought sunglasses from a street kid who needed a fix? Catherine Tracy's daughter?'

'Just let her talk,' Honey said, handing Babe her drink.

Babe took a fast swallow before handing the glass back. 'May I have some ice, please? You know I like my drinks on the rocks,' she said, sweetly reproachful.

'Oh Lordy, I think you've lost *your* rocks,' Sam moaned. 'Will you please get on with the story?'

49

'Then I discovered I'd left my purse in the cab.'

'You couldn't have left it in the taxi because you took money out of it to pay for the sunglasses, didn't you?' Honey asked, bringing back Babe's drink now clinking with ice.

This time, Babe grabbed for the glass and took several quick gulps. 'I guess you're right. But anyway, my yellow crocodile purse that matched this suit perfectly since it was dyed to match was gone, and it was from Paris, a birthday present from my mother. She'll be furious. She'll—'

'She'll what?' Sam raised her eyebrows. 'Ground you like she used to do when you were a naughty little teenybopper?'

'Never mind that, Sam. And never mind your purse, Babe. Why didn't you call for a ride?' Honey asked.

'There was *no way* I was going to call my mother for a ride. Think what she'd have to say about me parading down Hollywood Boulevard. And my father would probably send me to jail for hustling.'

'I see what you mean,' Sam acknowledged drily, 'but you didn't have to call your mother. You could have . . . *should have* . . . called *us* here. Why didn't you call us?'

'I didn't have any money. I told you, I lost my purse.' She finished off the drink.

'You don't need any money to make a call from a public phone. All you have to do is dial the operator and tell her you want to call collect. Or you could have taken a cab and we would have paid for it when you got here.'

'I didn't think of it. Why are you grilling me like this?'

'Oh, Babe darling, we're not grilling you!' Honey soothed her. 'We only want to help. What did you have to think about that you couldn't come here and think about?'

But before Babe could answer, Nora flew into the room. 'What's going on? Clara told me Babe was here

50

and—' Then she saw Babe and focused in on the glazed eyes and the smeared mascara. 'Oh, love, is something wrong?'

'She just hitched here from Hollywood Boulevard,' Sam answered, 'and don't bother asking why. We've already established that she was driving around in a cab because she had something to think about, that she got out to walk and lost her bag so she didn't have any money to phone or take another cab and now, hopefully, we're proceeding from there.'

'I'm not going back no matter what anyone says! And I'd like another drink, please.'

'Of course. Honey, will you get her a drink?' Nora directed, then turned back to Babe. 'Of course you're not going back, darling,' she reassured her. 'Why would we send you back to Hollywood Boulevard, of all places?'

'I'm not talking about Hollywood Boulevard!'

'What *are* you talking about?' Sam asked.

'If I tell you, do you promise not to tell my mother?'

'Of course we won't! Will we, Nora?' Sam demanded.

'Not until we talk about it, certainly,' Nora said. After all, Babe was no longer a child when she would have felt honour bound to tell Catherine and Judge Tracy *certain* things.

'I'm not going back to Washington . . . not to my life there, and not to my husband. Definitely not to Greg.'

Sam's eyes immediately darted to Honey, transmitting an unmistakable message: *see what I mean about brick walls?*

'You don't think I *have* to go back, do you, Nora?'

'Of course you don't have to go back!' Sam said, before Nora had a chance to say, 'You don't have to do anything you don't want to, love.' She was sure of that, no matter what.

'You most definitely don't have to go back,' Honey made it unanimous. 'But can you tell us *why* you don't want to?'

Babe considered the question for several seconds, then said quietly, 'I'll show you, if you lock the door.'

Nora told Sam to lock it and then they watched Babe stand up to kick off her shoes as if she were ready to go into a dance as she had frequently done for no reason at all when she was a teenager. But somehow they knew that if this was to be a dance, it wasn't going to be one of Babe's usual offerings.

She took off her jacket to throw it aside, unzipped her skirt and let it slip to the floor as she hummed a tune to herself, one which Nora recognized as a tune from the forties that the boys in uniform had been particularly fond of. But Sam and Honey were puzzled until they remembered that it was a song Babe had always loved in the seventies, though it had already been, even then, as obsolete as dinosaurs.

'*Take it off, take it off, cried the boys in the rear . . .*' she crooned, while Nora realized that for some bizarre reason Babe was doing a striptease. She wondered if she should stop her or let her get whatever was disturbing her out of her system. *Yes, that will be best.* She had a feeling that soon, one way or another, they'd discover what it was that had made Babe suddenly decide she wanted to leave Greg.

Babe smiled at them coyly, sitting down to remove pale pantihose, standing up again to sensuously wriggle out of a yellow half-slip heavily trimmed with lace, after which she leisurely unbuttoned a collarless silk blouse and shrugged it from her shoulders, allowing it heedlessly to slither down. Finally she was down to a yellow bra and matching bikini briefs. When she removed the bra, first pulling down each strap partially to disclose a voluptuous breast, she coquettishly threw it at her audience. Then when she removed the panties with a brazen flourish, she flung them up in the air.

Honey and Sam were so transfixed by Babe's performance – now, completely nude, she was whirling about – they didn't notice that Babe's ordinarily satin-smooth body was criss-crossed with a bevy of pink-and-red welts and marked with yellow-and-purple bruises, until Nora, determined not to show how horrified she was, went silently to Babe to still the dancing and to encompass her in her arms protectively. Then Honey gasped, Sam muttered, 'Jesus!' and Nora asked quietly, 'When did this happen, Babe?'

Babe twisted her mouth into a sickening smile. 'Last night. I was perfectly groomed when I left Washington this morning, but underneath this is what I looked like . . .'

'You don't mean—?' Honey hoarsely whispered.

'Not Mr Wonderful?' Even Sam, who had never believed Greg was wonderful at all, found it hard to believe.

'Yes, Mr Wonderful himself.' Then Babe began to laugh crazily and Honey thought the laugh was the most hideous thing she had ever heard, while Sam cursed bitterly.

'Oh, my dear love,' Nora kissed Babe, more sad for her than angry with Greg. *So much for brilliantly happy marriages. Sometimes all that's left to any of us are our brilliant divorces.*

Then, under her breath, Honey whispered, 'Welcome to the club, little Babe.'

PART TWO

THE MEMBERS OF THE CLUB

Los Angeles
June 1990

4

Taking off her red silk coat, Nora handed it to Sam, ordering her to get Babe into it. 'Then take her upstairs to bed. I'll be up as soon as I get rid of that crew out there.'

'What are you going to tell them?' Honey asked.

Nora smiled at her kindly. 'That the party's over.' Then, giving Babe a hug, she rushed out.

Yes, Honey thought, the party's over and we're all members of the club now – me, Sam, Babe, as well as Nora. But Sam was wrong when she'd said earlier that the presidency of the Hollywood Exes belonged to her. She was practically an amateur at the game, her experience limited, her qualifications nil. The right person for the position was obviously Nora. She was the oldest and the wisest, certainly the one with the executive skills and the most experience. As Sam loved to point out, Nora had been married almost as many times as that Hollywood champ, Liz Taylor, another English transplant.

They practically carried Babe upstairs and put her to bed in Sam's room in the California king with its mound of pillows, covering her cosily with a pretty floral duvet. Then, when Nora came up, having seen the last guest off, Babe asked in a wavering voice if she could stay the night.

'Of course, love. Didn't I always tell you and Honey that you were to think of Grantwood Manor as a second home?'

'Such a comforting thought to nurse on a cold and stormy night,' Sam drawled. 'Would that some kind person had ever said it to me.'

Nora, ignoring the comment, invited Honey to sleep over, too. 'Babe needs her friends with her this evening,' and Honey quickly agreed. She wanted to be with Babe and *she* herself wanted her friends around her tonight. This night more than any other night she would have felt so alone in Crown House with only her ghosts to keep her company.

Though the manor had many guest rooms there was no question that both Honey and Babe would share Sam's old room with her. This was the way it had always been when they'd slept over at the manor, laughing and talking late into the night. The room was unchanged, still decorated as it had been then, in a pink-and-white rosy chintz highlighted with bright green accents, the latter still Sam's favourite colour. It was almost as if time had stood still, Honey reflected. Only it *hadn't*, and tonight was going to be an odd kind of party with the three schoolgirls all grown up and hurting.

Sam cornered Nora at the windows where she was adjusting the floral draperies against the late afternoon sun. 'I think we're doing the wrong thing simply putting Babe to bed. We've seen only the external bruises. How do we know she's not hurt inside? I think the responsible thing to do is get her to a hospital to be examined . . . X-rayed.'

'I was planning on calling Len Silver to take a look at Babe and let him decide if she needs to go to hospital.'

'But suppose she's bleeding internally? By the time Dr Silver sends her to the hospital it could be too late!'

Nora smiled thinly. 'You're being melodramatic, Sam. I daresay that those bruises aside, the worst of it is inside Babe's mind. And what she needs is exactly what we're prepared to give her – reassurance. And Dr Silver will give her a sedative or whatever it takes to calm her and provide her a night's rest.'

'But why should we take a chance when it's just as easy to take her to the hospital now?'

'Look, Sam, I know what *you're* after,' Nora's eyes narrowed. 'You'd love nothing better than if we took Babe to hospital and called in a battalion of reporters to take pictures and all the rest of it so that the whole beastly mess would be on the evening news and in the morning papers, making sure everyone and his sister Kate takes full note that Babe Tracy Ryan was beaten up. But would it be in anyone's best interest to have this thing blown up? Would it help Babe?'

'It certainly would. After publicity like that just think how she could sail through a successful divorce. The big shot could have the hottest hotshot divorce lawyer – even Jeffrey Cohen or Raoul Felder – it wouldn't help the charm boy one tiny bit. He'd still collapse like a tired balloon.'

'I don't doubt that for a minute. At the same time all the publicity would only make it that much more difficult for Babe and Greg to iron out their differences *if* that's what Babe ultimately decides she wants.'

'Are you *crazy*? Why would she want to make up with him? It's not as if she has a bunch of kids or that she's some poor wretch with no education and no means of support. We're talking about a very attractive, talented woman with a great personality, with wealthy parents to fall back on *if* she had to, though who in her right mind would fall back on the Tracys unless she was going under for the third time? But I don't even know why we're discussing this. You heard Babe. She never wants to see the slime-bag again. She's *terrified* someone's going to force her to go back to him.'

'Really, Sam, your naïvety amazes me. I'd think that by this time, considering your considerable sophisticated maturity,' Nora sucked in her cheeks, 'you'd know more about the female psyche. How many marriages, do you think, which have lasted for several years break up over a single, isolated incident when one partner loses control for a few bad moments? Chances are that by tomorrow morning Babe will be ready to listen to her husband's apologies and to make up with him because that's what she really *wants* to do.'

'Then she'd be the worst kind of fool and Babe was never a fool except for the one time she slipped her gears and married the prick in the first place.'

'Oh Sam, haven't you learned yet we're *all* fools at one time or other? But the biggest fool is one who interferes in the relationship between two adults. There might well be extenuating circumstances here that we know nothing about.' She finished with the curtains and gave one a last tug, then turned to Sam as if she were about to give her one final tug, too. 'The best thing we can do is find out what happened – what precipitated this quarrel and why, suddenly, Greg behaved in such an uncharacteristic manner.'

'You're blowing my mind. Babe's bruised, battered and bloody and you call it a quarrel? He beat the shit out of her and you say there might be extenuating circumstances? What kind of extenuating circumstances? That getting slammed around is what Babe really craves and the bastard was just being obliging? Wait, I know what the trouble was! He had a fit of terrible but temporary insanity. Babe broke out into one of her tap dances and suddenly he saw red! All he knew was that he had to stop her from doing her "Shuffle Off to Buffalo" at any cost!'

'Really, Sam, you're not nearly as funny or clever as you think. Most likely he was drunk when he abused Babe and whether Babe would consider intoxication as an extenuating circumstance after she's had a chance to think about it would have to be *her* decision, much as you'd like it to be yours.'

For a second Sam struggled to hold her tongue, reminding herself that she was trying to get along with Nora, but she lost the battle and snapped, 'You always have all the answers. No matter what the story is we can count on you to make a reasonable analysis of the situation, giving every cocksucker the benefit of the doubt.

Everyone except me, of course. Oh, how well I remember how when I came home from school complaining that some teacher was picking on me, you always said to Daddy, "There may be extenuating circumstances." Then you made out a case for the shit no matter what. I wouldn't be surprised if when the bombs were falling on your precious London you had something to say in defence of Hitler.'

Nora laughed. 'Hardly. When the war first broke out I was barely into my teens and my mind was on boys and clothes just like any other silly girl and Hitler was just a cartoon character with a funny moustache. But yes, I believe that it's best to try and find equable solutions, no matter how beastly the situation. That's just good common sense.'

Smiling falsely, Sam went through the pantomime of holding up a microphone to Nora's face. 'Would you mind telling our audience, Mrs Grant, if this *teddibly* sweet philosophy of yours is the secret of your phenomenal success in the marriage market-place?'

'Gladly,' Nora went along with the gag. 'It's my belief that if one keeps a level head and one's sense of humour, it's the rare relationship that must end in bitterness and strife.'

Sam's fake grin disappeared. 'I'm sure you're right if you're Nora Grant who consistently ends up with everything you can squeeze out of a relationship. Like you ended up with Grantwood Manor and the studio and I ended up with a fat—'

Nora cut her off. 'Let's not get into that again. It's tedious and hardly the time. Right now we have to help Babe.'

'Yeah, sure,' Sam said bitterly. 'There's always *someone* who's getting the benefit of your loving ministrations . . . *anyone* . . . *everyone* . . . but me. Not that you didn't *play* the role of the doting stepmother convincingly. God knows you had Daddy convinced. As for Babe and Honey, it was no contest convincing them –

with their mothers they were push-overs for the likes of you.'

Sam could almost taste the sour tang of bile on her lips, but she couldn't stop the flow of words. 'The truth is that it was never, ever *my* turn with you. Just like it was never my turn at the studio that—'

'Enough!' Nora's tone was, finally, sharp and clipped. 'All that will be settled once and for all, I promise you, and sooner than you think. But right now we must concern ourselves with Babe who's in immediate need.'

'I'll say she's in need! She might even die on us because you wanted to spare her the publicity of being an abused wife,' Sam spat out, needing to have, if nothing else, the last word.

'I was thinking, Babe darling, that I'd call Len Silver to check you over just to be on the safe side,' Nora said softly.

'No! No doctors!'

'But why not, love? He's a dear friend and we can count on his discretion.'

'Yes, Babe,' Honey urged. 'I've seen Dr Silver and he's terrific. Easy to talk to . . . very sympathetic.'

'No!'

'I don't want to hear this *no* shit,' Sam said severely. 'It's either the doctor or the hospital. Take your choice.'

'But nothing really hurts me and I know nothing's broken. I'm just sore all over. And I can't have a doctor or go to a hospital! Once I went to the hospital – I thought my arm was broken – and Greg started in on me again before I explained that I *didn't* tell them at the hospital what really happened. I told them I'd fallen down the stairs.'

Stunned anew by this revelation that the beating hadn't been an isolated incident, Honey and Sam stared at one another while Nora, shocked, sank down on to the bed.

'Well, Nora,' Sam sang out in triumph, 'what bright and cheerful insight do you have to offer us now? Would you still care to call Babe's beating at her husband's hands a few bad moments in the life of a happy marriage? And what of *your* marriages? How many bad moments did *you* entertain before *you* blew the whistle? Not too many, I dare say, considering how many times you've hit the old wedding trail.'

'You *do* mean it has happened before, Babe?' Nora asked, not even looking at Sam, but it was a rhetorical question and Babe only moaned in reply.

'How many times?' Honey asked in an agonized whisper.

'Many . . .' Babe mumbled, burying her face in a pillow.

'How many?' Sam demanded harshly, forcibly turning Babe's face around with her hands.

'I don't know. Twenty, thirty . . . But after the first time, when one eye was almost closed and my lips were so swollen I couldn't talk and I couldn't leave the house for days, he never touched my face again.'

He never touched my face again . . .

It took a few seconds before the full implication of Babe's words sank in. Then Honey had a mental image of Greg, tall and tanned, his golden muscles smoothly rippling as he beat a tiny, cowering Babe while retaining so much control he remembered to spare her face . . . any part of her visible to the public eye. And that seemed more grotesque somehow, than even the beatings themselves. By comparison, her own marital grievances shrunk to a molehill and all the horror stories the guests had brought to her divorce party paled to funny tales with ironic undertones.

'Wait a minute,' Sam demanded. 'I want to get this absolutely straight. You mean to say he actually beat you while he kept his cool to the extent that he remembered not to hit you where it would show?'

'And only when he was sure there was no one in the house,' Babe whimpered. 'No servants.'

'That scumbag!' Sam's voice cracked. 'That fucking

63

slimy prick! I'll kill him myself! I swear I will!'

Nora put her arms around the sniffling Babe and gestured at Sam to desist, but Sam was too outraged to be silenced. 'And what did you do, Babe, while he was beating you up?'

'I tried to get away from him, to lock myself in a room. Sometimes I managed to do it but it was always worse when I came out. Or, he broke the door down. Sometimes I tried to fend him off – his punches – with my hands and begged him to stop. What else *could* I do? He's over a foot taller than I am and almost a hundred pounds heavier.'

'Didn't you ever think to call the police?' Honey asked, bewildered by what appeared to be a maddeningly stoical acceptance – a stultifying impotence – on Babe's part. Babe who was . . . *who used to be* . . . so spunky and full of life, who had a quick and funny quip for every occasion.

'Oh, I called the police once, but they wanted me to swear out a complaint. And how could I do that? Have my own husband arrested? It would have been in all the papers. The story would have been all over Washington. It would have ruined him! His career. So I never called the police again.'

'Ruined *him*? *His* career?' Sam sputtered. 'What about *you*? He was ruining you and by doing nothing you were guilty of complicity – a co-defendant is what they call it!'

At that Babe broke out into wrenching sobs and Nora stood up. 'Now that really is enough, Sam! And that goes for you too, Honey. I'm calling Len Silver to come over immediately and in the meantime, I'm declaring a moratorium on all discussion. Babe's going to rest and that means there will be no more questions and answers. Do I make myself clear?'

Honey mutely nodded and Sam, watching Babe's narrow shoulders heaving under the duvet, didn't answer at all. A last unasked question still hung heavy in the air: *but why didn't you leave him before this, little Babe?*

* * *

Once Dr Silver left after having verified that Babe's injuries were only external and prescribing sedatives, Sam felt free to inundate a now-calmer Babe with more questions. 'There's still one thing I don't fully understand. How could the prick, bombed out of his skull – drunk enough at least to beat the hell out of you – still be so much in control as to remember not to hit you in the face?'

Babe sat up in surprise. 'Drunk? I never said he was drunk. Greg doesn't drink! The most he ever does is take a couple of glasses of wine with dinner. He's afraid to drink. His father was an alcoholic. I thought everyone knew that.'

'So, what you're saying is that he beat you while he was completely sober. But why? There has to be an explanation. What horrendous crimes did you commit?'

Babe looked from Sam to Honey to Nora. 'But that's *it*. I don't *know* why. Or, at least, I'm not sure . . .' her voice trailed off. Then she began again but it was as if she were talking to herself as much as to them: 'I used to think about it all the time . . . trying to figure out what I did to get him so mad, thinking if I *knew*, I'd just be sure not to do whatever it was, ever again. But there was always something *new* that would get him mad and there was no way of knowing beforehand what exactly would set him off.'

She smiled at them, as if pleading for their understanding. 'Sometimes it seemed like such a *little* mistake, really. Like the time I forgot to order a special wine he wanted to serve at a dinner party. Well, actually I *do* understand why he was upset *that* time. It *was* Secretary of State Winter who was our guest of honour and it *was* a coup to get him to come to our party in the first place, so it was only natural that Greg wanted to impress him by serving this special wine. It was a—' she faltered. 'Oh, God, I'm such a fool I can't remember!'

She looked anxiously from face to face as if her friends

might be able to help her remember the name of the wine, or at least tell her that she wasn't *really* such a terrible fool for not remembering.

Nora assured her that it didn't matter, and Honey said, 'No one cares what dumb old wine it was, Babe.'

'Still, when he first found out that we didn't have the right wine he didn't make a fuss. So I thought it was all right, but after the guests went home and the caterer's people left, he threw me against the wall and—' Her voice broke off and she licked at her dry lips with a nervous tongue.

It was so perfectly still in the room then – all of them scarcely breathing – that when Sam finally broke the silence, her voice sounded like shattering glass magnified many times over. 'So, which was it *that* time, Babe? Was that one of your *little* mistakes, or was it one of the big ones?'

'I guess it was kind of in the middle,' Babe said flatly. 'Not like the time with the tie . . . Once I said I didn't like a tie and it really ticked him off. He looked as if he wanted to kill me. He took the tie off and wrapped it around my neck and – Well, I guess I *was* being critical that time and he does have this thing about criticism . . .'

'You know, Babe, you actually sound like you're *defending* him – this monster – this sadist! What's wrong with *you*?'

'Sam!' Honey and Nora protested simultaneously but Babe said, 'It's OK. I guess I do sound as if I am defending him. But it's so hard to know. I'm not sure if my thinking is straight. But I am not really defending him. All I am doing is pointing out that I *did* criticize him. That in some way I did bring the beatings on myself . . .'

'My goodness, I would say!' Sam said, sucking in her breath. She was so furious with Babe for accepting that she was to blame in some way, that she felt like beating Babe herself. She turned to Nora: 'So, what do you say about that? Is it the duty of the perfect wife never to criticize? In all of your many marriages, did *you* criticize your man or were you always the little wife seeing only to his comfort and keeping your mouth shut?'

'I always *tried* to be the ideal wife if that's what you're getting at,' Nora said evenly. 'Which also means giving as good as one gets and that, I believe, is only reasonable behaviour. But we've talked about this enough for now. As Scarlett O'Hara once said, "Tomorrow is another day", and I think what we all need now is a bit of supper and a sip of the old vino. What do you say to that, Babe love?'

'Vino . . .' Babe repeated, then broke out into a grin. 'Oh, I remember – the name of the wine we were supposed to have that night Secretary Winter came to dinner! It was a Beaujolais! But not just *any* Beaujolais. It was Beaujolais Nouveau and the day we had the party was supposed to be the first day that the new wine was ready to drink.'

Now that Babe remembered she was more relaxed, settling back against the pillows as if to reminisce pleasantly. 'It happens every fall. All over the world, wine lovers celebrate the Beaujolais Nouveau on the same day. They ship it from France so that it arrives in time for all the celebrants to take the first sweet taste of the season in tandem. As a matter of fact once we went to a Beaujolais Nouveau festival at the Hotel Bel-Air right here in LA and they had all kinds of cheeses and pâtés. It was wonderful! The very first sweet taste of the season . . .'

Honey and Sam exchanged looks of bewilderment. Babe was talking as if her mind had really been affected.

'I'm sure it was wonderful, Babe,' Nora patted her hand. 'But right now I want you to rest. The sedative won't work if you don't help it along by leaning into it.'

'But I want to tell you all about it, Nora, so that you fully understand how *important* Beaujolais Nouveau Day is . . . how it's a celebrated tradition. And Greg *knew* that Secretary Winter was a wine lover, you see. A connoisseur, really.'

'Well, then, that explains it all,' Sam said flatly. 'Undoubtedly you *deserved* to be slammed against a wall. Good heavens, for forgetting to order that Beaujolais I'd gladly slam you against a wall myself.'

But Babe acted as if she hadn't heard Sam. She had a secret little bemused smile on her face and repeated to herself, 'The very first sweet taste of the season . . .'

Nora had dinner sent up on trays, but no one ate more than a few bites and Babe, not even that. Depressed once again, she kept repeating, 'This time I'm not going back no matter what. Not even if he gets down on his knees.'

'Of course you're not going back,' Honey placated her and Sam said, 'I just hope he shows up here! It will be the last time he shows up anywhere, I promise you.'

'But there *is* one thing, Babe—' Nora's voice was deliberately casual. 'Before I said I wouldn't call your parents until we talked about it. But under the circumstances I think I should call them now so that they can see you, hear how all this has been going on for so long. After all, your father is a judge – he'll know what steps must be taken.'

'No, you *can't* call them! You don't understand! They *have* seen. They've seen and they've heard and they know and they've always made me go back. Each and every time . . .'

Sam and Honey – faces mirrored images of one another's horror – and even Nora, stared at Babe in disbelief. While none of them had any good feelings about the Tracys, this was too much. They *knew* and had sent cute, fun-loving, little Babe back for more? Babe had to be exaggerating.

'But that can't be true, Babe dear,' Nora said. 'Your parents love you. They'd never send you back to a man who beat you. You're upset, love, and—'

'No! Yes! I am upset but I'm telling the truth. I cried and I begged but they always made me go back. You have to believe me!' She was so distraught they quickly assured her that, of course, they believed her.

'So you see, you *can't* call them. They'll only make me go back again and I can't any more. Not any more,' she said as if it were a matter of just being too worn out to do it again. 'I can't go back even if I do bring the beatings on myself. And if they make me go back again, I think I might do something really terrible. I might even set Greg on fire like that woman who spilled kerosene all around the bed while her husband slept and put a match to it. Or maybe I'll just kill *myself*. It would probably be easier that way . . .'

'Babe!' Honey cried. 'How can you say such a thing?'

'She doesn't mean it,' Sam said, but her tone lacked conviction. 'She's not about to kill anybody, not even those who so richly deserve it. She's just being dramatic so we'll all feel sorry for her instead of being mad at her for being such an incredible wimp. Now, you cut it out, you wimp!'

'Of course she doesn't mean it,' Nora soothed, holding a cup of tea to Babe's lips. 'You mustn't say such things, love, not even in jest. It's so silly. Killing is such a messy business and so unnecessary. In this day and age of the easy divorce no one has to kill anyone, least of all one's self. That's all it takes – one little divorce and it's all over. Then you'll be a free woman, free to start all over.'

'Then you *won't* call them? And you won't let them in no matter what?'

'Not tonight, at any rate. Tonight, you're going to get a good night's sleep. You'll take another of Dr Silver's little pills and tomorrow, when you're all rested, we'll talk some more and decide when to call your parents. All right?'

'I don't see why they have to be told anything!' Sam raged. 'After what they've done? It's criminal! The Judge is the one who should be sent to jail! That shit-heel!'

'But why did they want you to stay in spite of the beatings?' Honey implored. 'Why *did* they send you back?'

69

Babe opened her eyes wide, surprised that Honey . . . all of them . . . *still* didn't understand. 'Because they think that one of these days he's going to be president and they want me in the White House with him! The First Lady of the land . . .'

She closed her eyes. 'You all know how Catherine always said that the most important thing in the world was to be a lady. And who could be more of a lady than *the* First Lady? Now I'll be a divorcée and you know what *that* means?' She giggled before she began to cry. 'I'll be a little nobody again . . . the silly little fool Catherine always said I was.'

Then they thought they understood why Babe hadn't left the seemingly affable, good-looking, ambitious Greg who had got along so well with the Tracys before. But now there was another question hanging brooding and oppressive on the otherwise pleasant breeze blowing in from the west. Would the woman Babe was today be strong enough to stand up not only to the rigours of a divorce battle, but to the united front Greg and the Tracys would undoubtedly present? If she hadn't been able to resist them before when there had still been remnants of the old spunky Babe, how was she to resist them now?

Nora wished she had the answer to that one.

5

'I know you don't think so right now, but you're going to feel much better about things in the morning, love.' Nora kissed Babe on the top of her head. 'Let's see a smile on that sweet face.'

Babe managed to comply, but the smile was a weak

little thing, her mind more on what the morning would bring. She was sure that she wasn't going to feel better about things at all. Her parents were certain to show up even if Greg didn't and they'd not only be furious that she was leaving him – or at least making the attempt again – but that she had fled to Grantwood Manor and Nora, instead of going back to them.

Catherine, even more than the Judge, would resent that. Nora had never been one of Catherine's favourite people. She considered Nora's style too flamboyant, her exterior too flashy – all that ostentatious jewellery (diamonds with lunch which flouted even the most extreme limits of good taste), her friends (all those movie people and so many Jews among them) slightly *déclassé*. But not the least of Nora's crimes was that she was a major Democrat. The Tracys did not suffer Democrats lightly, especially those who were so prominent, who had their pictures in the newspapers so often.

'If my parents do show up tomorrow, do you *have* to let them in, Nora? Can't you say I'm too sick to see them?'

'If I said that, it would sound as if I was trying to keep them from you. I *could* say that you *refuse* to see them. I'm quite willing to do that but that wouldn't be a real resolution of the problem, either. They'd only keep pestering you until they saw you. The best thing would be for you to see them and tell them very firmly what you plan to do, leaving no room for argument. That way you'd get it over with once and for all. But you don't have to decide now. You can decide tomorrow after you've slept on it. Now, I have to see about a few things. I'll be back in a while to say good night.'

Sam, already in an emerald-green satin night-gown, frenetically pacing back and forth while attacking her hair with a hairbrush, held the door open for Nora with a flourish and a bow. 'We'll be here waiting for you with bated breath.'

'And well you should, my dear,' Nora smiled, leaving.

Sam closed the door softly after her though she felt like slamming it shut.

'"*And well you should, my dear*,"' she aped. 'What do you think she meant by *that*? Oh well, she's probably just trying to get under my skin, but I won't let her. But she's right, Babe. You *should* see your parents and get it over with. And I know exactly what you should do and say – the very best thing you *can* do and say.' She laughed even before she spoke. 'You confront them coldly with your nose in the air as if you just *barely* know them. Then you look them in the eye and say with great hauteur, "I really don't care to discuss it. My attorney will be in touch." Can't you just picture the look on Catherine's face? I *love* it! Don't you love it, Babe? Honey?'

'I love it,' Honey laughed, 'but isn't Babe supposed to say that to Greg? About the attorney being in touch?'

'Oh, for God's sake. *That's* what's funny – saying it to *them*! Catherine will be so infuriated she'll go out of her fucking mind! As for Greg, Babe can say it to him, too.'

If it were only that simple, Babe reflected morosely. If only she could do it, just tell them to fuck off.

'Is it *so* much worse for you to tell your parents than Greg?' Honey asked, though, she *knew* it was. Telling Catherine anything at all had always been hard for Babe.

'In the beginning it will be. They'll be so mad . . . and *he* won't be. Mad, that is, not at first. Each time, afterwards, he's sorry. And then he always tries to make up, swearing it will never happen again. He's very sweet then and he always makes love to me . . .'

Sam's hairbrush stopped in mid-air. 'Makes love to you? You *do* mean sex?'

'Yes, of course, sex.'

'And you *let* him screw you right after he's beaten you up?'

'Well, not *right* after.'

'But as soon as he says he's sorry?'

72

'Yes . . . I suppose.'

'You either do or you don't? Which is it?'

'I don't know,' Babe moaned. 'Does it matter?'

'Yes, it *matters*! How do you think it's going to sound in court that you want a divorce because your husband repeatedly abused you, but each time, practically immediately after, you let him prong you? That doesn't sound like a woman who's been degraded and abused. It sounds more like a woman who's turned on by the beatings. *Hurt me! I love it!*'

'But it wasn't like that! It was more like I was – I don't know – like a woman who's about to be raped, but it's hopeless to resist so she decides to lean back and enjoy it.'

'Oh my God! That's *revolting*! That's insulting to every woman who's ever been raped or abused. How *dare* you say such a thing? And tell us, *did* you enjoy it? Did you enjoy getting screwed by the man who had just beaten you?' Sam demanded furiously.

'Of course not! That's just an expression people use. Accepting the inevitable. I was only trying to explain a certain attitude a helpless woman can assume. Why are you being so mean to me, Sam?'

'Yes, Sam,' Honey said angrily. 'Why *are* you being such a bitch? What was the point of Dr Silver giving Babe sedatives if you're only going to upset her all over again?'

'I am *not* being mean. Not deliberately, anyway. I'm just trying to get things straight. Everything has to be clear in *your* head, Babe, so you can go out there fighting.'

'But I told you, it's just an expression. Why would you assume that I meant it? That I enjoyed it?'

'Oh, Babe! We all know how you are when it comes to sex.'

'Now what does that mean?' Babe's voice was ragged. 'How *am* I when it comes to sex? Go on, I want you to say it!'

Honey's heart beat faster. They were treading on dangerous ground here. Sam pushing, Babe on the defensive . . . Too much might be said, too much revealed and the secret that she and Babe had kept so long from Sam and Nora would be out in the open and then what? Then there would be no going back. She yearned to intervene, to say something . . . anything that would halt the flow of words but it was as if her brain was immobilized, her throat constricted.

'Oh, Babe, you were always so *greedy* for sex!' Sam's voice was soft now despite the harsh reality of her words. 'The three of us always made a joke of it but the truth is that you *always* wanted to get laid and you didn't care who laid you, where or even how. The only thing on your mind besides the fucking was that Catherine and the Judge didn't find out.'

Honey held her breath waiting for Babe's answer. But Babe didn't respond, she only gave an abrupt sob and Honey almost collapsed with relief and gratitude. But then seeing the misery on Babe's face she again felt the urge to say something – to take Babe's part against Sam, to help Babe deny what was essentially only the truth. While Sam had always *talked* a good game of sex, it was Babe who *had* embraced it greedily.

But she said nothing. It was better now to keep quiet, she thought. Not confirm but not deny, either. She was sick to death of denial. And how guilty the three of them were when it came to that, pushing away the reality for the fantasy. And what had it got them but membership in the club – the Hollywood Exes?

She looked at Babe – miserable and whipped, with her face again buried in a pillow. Then she looked at Sam, almost as miserable as Babe, remorseful now that she had driven Babe further into her depression. What had Nora said? That she had always tried to maintain her sense of humour. Maybe that was the answer. You kept your sense of humour while you tried to regroup. She sat down on the bed and deliberately laughed.

'Oh?' Sam glanced at her hopefully. 'Have I overlooked something highly humorous here? Or even something *slightly* amusing? If so, I'd love to be filled in.'

'I was just thinking about the time Babe and I slept over when we were fourteen and there was a big party going on. Cary Grant was here that night, and Henry Fonda, and we decided to smuggle some bottles of wine upstairs. Remember?'

Sam's face lit up and she sat down on the opposite side of the bed. 'How could I forget? What about you, Babe? Do you remember?'

When Babe didn't respond Sam kept tapping her on the shoulder with her hairbrush insistently until Babe finally sat up and tried to shove the hairbrush back in her face. 'Remember?' she cried indignantly before the corners of her mouth began to curl up suspiciously. 'How could I forget, you wiseass? If you recall, it was *you* who made me carry one of those damn bottles between my thighs, for God's sake, and I couldn't move my legs to take a step, much less go up a flight of stairs. And then all of your folks' company very politely came out into the hall to wish us good night as we went up to bed. It was a nightmare!'

Now she struggled to choke back the laughter. 'Nora thought something was wrong with me – that I'd been suddenly struck with paralysis of the legs. She kept asking me if I was all right and I kept saying I was fine, but there I was – unable to move. Then your father came from behind to give me a boost up the stairs, half-pushing, half-picking me up, practically throwing me into the air, and then it was all over. I don't think I'll ever forget that bottle slithering down my thighs and me trying to catch it at the knees, but missing, and then it dropping to the step below where it stopped for a second before it began to roll down the stairs while everyone's eyes were glued to it, until it landed right side up, miraculously unbroken! Then everyone clapped their hands like it was a feat of magic I'd performed! Even Cary!'

'Still, I was positive your father was going to send for the car to take me home right then and there and that Nora would write a note to my parents denouncing me as a teenage alcoholic and then the Judge, for sure, would send me to that home for disturbed girls he was always threatening me with. But then your father broke out laughing and said he was going to stick that bit into one of his comedies and Nora said, "Well, it's just as well, Babe. You really wouldn't have enjoyed that wine anyway. I sampled some of the same bottling the other day and it was bloody sour."' She shook her head. 'I'll never forget that night but I still can't imagine how you ever thought that I'd make it up the stairs with that thing between my thighs, Sam.'

'Well, you really can't blame me for thinking you could,' Sam said ingenuously. 'You always were the champ at managing big things between your thighs. I guess it's just a knack some girls are born with. But seriously speaking, I thought you could do it because you were such a whiz-kid at gymnastics and you were always doing all those splits and things. I thought you had complete control of all those wonderful muscles in your legs. How was I to know that they'd fail us when we needed them most? But fortunately, I already had a couple of bottles of wine stashed away in my panties' drawer.'

'Speaking of panties, what about the bottle of wine you made me stash away in *my* panties?' Honey demanded. 'And I had to walk up the stairs in front of everyone looking like I was seven months pregnant. And I wasn't worried so much about the darn bottle falling out as I was that it would leak and the wine would start trickling down my legs and Cary Grant wouldn't only think I was peeing in my pants, but peeing *red*!'

'Damn!' Sam howled. 'If only it had happened! A memory like that would be worth a mil!'

'Oh yeah?' Honey grinned. 'What about me getting sick from the wine and throwing up in your closet all

76

over your shoes? How's *that* for a memory? You really didn't think it was so funny at the time, if I recall.'

'No, I guess I didn't, Honey Bunch,' Sam admitted. 'But how was I to know that you'd get so polluted you'd mistake my closet for the bathroom and my beautiful riding boots for the toilet bowl? Now, Babe was a much nicer behaved drunk. All she did was take off her jammies and dance for us in the buff.'

'Oh, but she wasn't *completely* naked. She was wearing a long, chiffony scarf wrapped around her neck and trailing it as she did her bumps and grinds against the hat stand.'

'Of course I was wearing a scarf around my neck! I was doing my imitation of Isadora Duncan.'

'Only I seriously doubt old Isadora had a pair of bazooms like yours to wave around in the breeze,' Sam snorted.

'Well, it wasn't my fault I was well-developed for my age. As a matter of fact, Sam, you were always insanely jealous of my tits. Admit it!'

'If you must know, I feared for you, considering how short you were. I was always afraid you were so top-heavy you were going to topple over and fall flat on your face.'

'Huh, I just bet you were! At least I didn't have to wear padded bras like some indecently tall but under-developed individuals,' Babe retorted.

'Of course you didn't wear a padded bra – how could you when what you wore resembled a harness more than a bra?'

But then, instead of retaliating with a well-turned phrase, Babe turned morose again, her face and body visibly drooping. 'I know . . .' she said mournfully. 'Catherine was always *so* embarrassed by my breasts. She said it was *déclassé* to have so large a bosom . . . that only Jewish women, country singers and TV actresses flaunted their obscene chests—' She caught herself and cast an apologetic glance at Honey. But Honey was just

77

sorry that Babe, who had been enjoying herself, had been brought down to earth again.

'Don't worry that you hurt my feelings, Babe. Your mother wasn't talking about *me*, after all. Honey Rose didn't even exist then. And even if Catherine *had* been referring to me, I still wouldn't be insulted. I'm not ashamed of my body or that I flaunted it playing Honey Rose. And despite everything, I'm very fond of that incarnation of Honey Rosen and she'll always be part of me. So no long faces, please!'

Still, Babe shook her head despondently. 'She was so ashamed of my tits she'd never even go with me to buy the bras. You remember how she always sent the housekeeper and told her to make sure to get the kind that minimized.'

'Oh, forget it, Babe!' Sam said, sorry now that she had ever brought up the subject of Babe's breasts. 'Let's face it – your mother always was a shit, she's still a shit, and it's likely she'll always be one, and if you can just get past that awful truth and accept it, *finally*, you'll be OK. The truth is that Catherine the Great was always jealous of your magnificent titties because she herself was flat as a board. You certainly didn't get those fancy hooters from her. She's just a bazoomless old bag.'

'But how come if *she's* the shit, everything *I* touch turns to shit?'

'Oh, Babe, that's not true,' Honey said quickly. 'We all have our ups and downs – experiences that turn sour on us.'

'Like my marriage, for instance? Whose marriage was *quite* as sour or shitty as mine? *Yours* wasn't, Honey.'

'No, it wasn't,' Honey conceded. 'Still, *any* marriage that fails is a soured marriage and can break your heart, and really, who's to measure to what degree?'

'And just consider the statistics that at least one marriage out of three, and probably more, will eventually end up in the divorce courts,' Sam added. 'How do you know how shitty exactly all those marriages are? So you'd just

78

better stop thinking you're the only one who continually steps into the stuff.'

'But I'm not just talking about my marriage. I'm talking about *everything* I touch. Even the little things. Like with those bottles of wine. I had a bottle of wine between my thighs and it fell down in full sight of everyone. Honey had a bottle of wine stuck into her panties, but did it fall out to humiliate her? And you were the instigator, Sam. But were you embarrassed in any way? Of course not! Only I was caught out.'

'OK, enough of that,' Honey commanded. 'We're not going to listen to you bad-mouth yourself any more. The truth is we've all had our ups and downs. But we're not going to dwell on the downs and we *are* going to rise like the phoenix from the ashes. Remember our old pledge?'

'Yes, I remember. That we'd always stick together and that come hell or high water we'd emerge victorious because our hearts were strong, pure and innocent.'

'Right! And are we going to lose the faith just because there've been a few stumbling blocks in our path?'

'Hell, no, we still go!' the three of them shouted in unison, another bit of their teenage ritual.

'OK, put it there!'

Honey stuck out her hand palm up, Babe put her hand on hers palm down, then Sam put her hand over both of theirs and it was a pledge renewed. But then as she went into the dressing room to put on the lime-green night-gown Sam had lent her for the night, Honey realized that the pledge no longer applied. Their hearts might still be strong – that was yet to be proven – even pure (and that was open to debate), but they were hardly innocent . . . hadn't been for a long time . . . not since they were fourteen and experiencing that first sweet taste of their season.

6

Finally, they were all in bed and hopefully, ready for sleep – Sam and Babe in the big bed, Honey on the sofa bed lying between the familiar peppermint striped sheets and under the same peony-pink duvet that had always been hers when she'd slept over at Grantwood. But they didn't turn off the lights. They waited for Nora to do that when she came back to make her good nights – part of the bedtime ritual they had always followed at the manor.

Nora would make sure that at least one window was open to admit the evening air. 'It's the fresh air that puts the roses in the cheeks, m'dears,' she'd always said before tucking them in, kissing Honey and Babe, but never Sam, since Sam always made a big thing of shrinking back from her touch. But even Sam pulling back as Nora smoothed her duvet in place had become one of the manor's bedtime rites, though Honey always suspected that this bit of business was at least, half-pretence, as far as Sam was concerned. No matter how she felt about Nora, how could Sam *not* crave a motherly touch as she went to sleep, as much as she herself and Babe craved it?

Then Nora would turn off the lights and croon the magic words: 'Sweet dreams . . .' Honey had always believed the words were a lucky charm, more solemn promise than mere wish.

Occasionally, in a more playful spirit, Nora would say, 'Nighty night, now don't let the bedbugs bite.' And then she and Babe always chortled at the childish foolishness and responded in one voice that they'd be sure not to let the bad old bedbugs get them. But not Sam. Instead, she would mutter something desultory under her breath or recite one of the rhymes about Nora she was always making up:

> *'The only thing that's bound to bite*
> *in the middle of the night –*
> *with great pleasure and delight –*
> *is Nora, the dirty, rotten blight.*
> *That, you see, is my plight*
> *because, no matter how I fight,*
> *in the end she'll surely bite.*
> *Alack and alas, I know I'm right!'*

But tonight – even if Nora left them with her admonition about the bedbugs – Honey doubted that Sam would recite a rhyme. It wasn't that kind of night. Tonight, though the three of them were sleeping over at Grantwood once again, they *were* thirty-something, all grown up and chastened by life, and if they were to list all the spectres that might haunt their dreams, bedbugs would certainly be at the bottom of the list.

'Well, are my little chickadees ready for the sandman?' Nora, her burnt-orange taffeta *peignoir* rustling as she moved, her face illuminated by a brilliant and ironic smile, came rushing into the room as if she were late for an important date.

'All your chickadees are ready and waiting, Mommy Hen, for you to give them their beddy-bye pecks,' Sam answered in a chirpy voice. 'And don't you look purty? How about a peek at the nightie you're wearing under that swellegant robe?'

Nora agreeably parted the *peignoir* to reveal an apricot satin and lace confection underneath.

'Oh my yes, right purty. Isn't that so, chickadees?'

Honey and Babe murmured their agreement but Sam, as usual, wasn't satisfied to end the by-play there. 'But all that lushy pulchritude, those tantalizing peek-a-boo glimpses of creamy-skinned, rosy-tipped titties can't be

81

all just for us chicks. Is Mommy Hen planning to party tonight? Is there, perchance, a new candidate for the Nora Grant matrimonial sweepstakes panting in her bed even as we talk?'

'Forsooth, no,' Nora affected regret. 'All this pulchritude, as you so nicely put it, Sam, is just being prepared for any eventuality. Suppose I was taken ill in the middle of the night and had to go to hospital?' Then when Sam raised a quizzical eyebrow, she added, 'And you'd be surprised at all the attractive men I keep meeting in my dreams.'

Then, laughing at her own nonsense, Nora went about the familiar routine – checking out the windows, making the remark about the fresh air bringing the roses to their cheeks. It occurred to Honey then, that the air coming into the room was hardly as fresh as it had been twenty years before when Nora had first made that observation.

Then again, neither are we . . .

Nora moved to the beds now, tucking, patting and smoothing, bending to kiss Honey's brow and then Babe's, but not Sam's, all according to prescribed ritual. But this time Sam broke with tradition. 'What?' she demanded archly. 'No bedtime kiss for Sammy-girl?'

'Oh, I have something even *better* for you, Sam.'

'You do?' Sam asked, and sat up straight. It *had* occurred to her that Nora was acting strangely tonight. Still, she was caught off-guard.

'Oh yes, an announcement about the studio,' Nora drawled.

Now, Honey sat up, too, and even Babe – forgetting her own problem for the moment – came to full attention, propping herself up on an elbow as Honey and Sam exchanged a swift, taut glance. This was what they'd been waiting for! As in a divorce, Honey thought, this was the final step. The announcement of the financial settlement . . .

'Yes—?' Sam could scarcely believe the moment had

82

actually come, that Nora was finally going to give her her rightful due. 'Yes?' she said again.

'Yes, Sam. As you've probably sensed the studio has been much on my mind lately. But I wasn't sure what I wanted to—'

'Oh, for God's sake, Nora,' Sam's voice was ragged with tension, 'will you get on with it?'

'Be patient, my dear, and hear me out. You've waited so long for the resolution of this business, surely you can bear with me for a few minutes more,' Nora said, her tone not unkind. 'As I was saying, I was rather dragging my feet about making a definite decision. I was considering all the possibilities since it wasn't only I who would be affected by my decision. There was my son to be considered, of course—'

'Hubie!' Sam was more astonished than anything. She'd been so centred on the studio being the bone of contention only between Nora and herself, she had never even thought about Hubie's possible involvement.

'And then, of course, I thought of you, Sam, and that bloody conviction of yours – how making moving pictures was in your blood as it was in your father's.' She laughed. 'Oh dear, have I made a pun? I didn't intend to, you know.'

Sam grew unbearably impatient, her nerve-ends screaming. She had never wanted to strangle Nora more than at this moment. Then it was on the tip of her tongue to remind Nora that there was also the matter of her trust fund to be taken into account if she was considering the possibilities. But she forced herself to hold back. Nora did seem unusually amiable now and her smile was as sweet as any Sam could remember. Everything was looking good . . . even hopeful. Why introduce a negative note into the proceedings?

Again Sam glanced at Honey for reassurance and Honey nodded at her encouragingly as if to say: *victory is at hand!* Then Sam thought she could actually smell victory's presence in the room, its aroma more intoxicating than the scent of the night-blooming jasmine coming in through the open window.

'And while I was considering all the options – perplexed as to what to do, something quite extraordinary happened! Out of the blue I received an offer from an unexpected quarter!'

Honey's pulse quickened. Then the rumour she'd heard about an offer being made for the studio was true!

'What quarter?' Sam demanded, inner antennae quivering.

'I'm afraid that will have to remain my little secret.'

'But did you tell them what they could do with their offer?' Sam's voice was a hoarse whisper. 'That they could stick it where—'

'Oh, my dear, of course I didn't! It was an excellent offer and – Well, I'm already talking to my lawyers.'

'But how can you? The studio is mine . . . it's all I've ever thought about. It's my sweet dream,' Sam croaked, her voice so desperate it practically broke Honey's heart.

Nora's smile disappeared as swiftly as her manner abruptly changed. '*Your* sweet dream!' she scoffed. 'You know that we orchestrate our own dreams, Sam, and the dreams are only as sweet as our imaginations. In your case, I'd say your imagination did you a disservice. It led to your deluding yourself, always a foolish thing to do. The dream was so sweet you assumed that you were automatically entitled to it without doing a thing to make it come true. All you ever did was whine and complain and demand.' There was a growing anger in Nora's voice as its volume mounted. 'And whatever made you think that when it came down to it – to choosing between *giving* the studio to you and getting a pile of money for it – I'd choose you? Because you're a charity case and I'm one hell of a philanthropist? Or because you've been such a loving, sweet stepdaughter? Was that part of the dream too? Or was it only some more of your incredible arrogance?'

Then her voice was diamond-hard rather than angry. 'Don't you know, Sam, that there are *no* sweet dreams? There's only reality. Just like in a marriage. We all dream of how it will be – a sugar-coated fairy-tale. Then comes the real thing and all it boils down to is how we deal with what *is* instead of how we dreamed it would be.' Now her gaze fixed on Babe. 'Isn't that right, Babe?'

Not expecting to be drawn into the dialogue, Babe gasped in pain, but Nora went on. 'But in both cases – the dreams and the marriages – there's always a bottom line and sometimes the bottom line is only a row of dollar signs as there might be in a divorce. Don't *you* agree, Honey?'

Honey stared at Nora. She was not only shocked that Nora was actually selling Sam's studio out from under her – something she had never believed Nora would actually do – she was confused. *How had they moved from selling Grantwood Studio to Babe's marriage and then her own divorce?*

There was only the sound of Babe's faint sniffling until Sam's furious voice rang out: '*Your* bottom line might be a line of dollar bills, but I think there's another bottom line here. That the much-married Nora is very much the greedy whore I always thought she was. And there are a couple of questions I might ask you – how greedy *exactly* is a greedy whore and where, damn you, is my money that my father entrusted you with?'

But Nora only laughed. 'Keep on dreaming, Sam. Perhaps one of these days you, and your friends, too, for that matter, might wake up with the right answers.'

'Go fuck yourself!'

'Naughty, naughty,' Nora chided. 'Surely, if nothing else, I taught you better manners than that. Besides, it's much more fun and eminently more profitable to find another husband to perform that act for me.' With that she gracefully circled the room, turning out the lights. When the room was dark except for the glow of the slice of moon coming in through the open window, she went to the door and Honey held her breath. Would Nora *dare* wish them 'sweet dreams' now?

But Nora didn't. Still, as if the thrall of ritual was too strong to break and she couldn't leave them without *some* word, she bid them her other admonition of old: 'Nighty night, girls. Now don't let the bedbugs bite.'

'But *you're* the fucking bloodsucker and you've already done your biting,' Sam said tiredly now, without heat or passion. At this point she was beyond heat and passion.

Then there was the sound of the door closing softly and after that an awesome silence, disturbed only by Babe's kitten-like whimpers, while Honey bitterly mulled over what Nora had just said about there being no sweet dreams – no wish, no good-luck charm, no promise.

She felt so incredibly cheated. She had *believed* in Nora's sweet dreams. Yet the truth was that life's rich and early promise *had* eluded all three of them. Was it because Nora herself had never truly believed? *But what did we do that was so terrible that everything went sour for us?* What was the answer and what about the ultimate question? Could they still reclaim the promise of their youth or had they, only in their thirties, already run out of time?

Once Nora closed her own bedroom door, she leaned back against it heavily, exhausted. While she hadn't expected that the day would go easily, she hadn't anticipated Babe's posing yet another dilemma to be coped with. But, for better or worse, the bomb had been dropped, and all that remained was to observe the fallout in the morning, begin the sweeping up and then, perhaps, the rebuilding.

Well, nobody ever said war wasn't hell. She only hoped she had said the right things, taken the right course of action. Then, feeling suddenly cold and alone, she went to the phone to call the one person she knew she could count on for warmth and reassurance.

86

7

Listening to the little noises of distress Babe was making in her drug-induced sleep, Honey wondered if Babe could still come back to play another day. Her spirit was so broken and she had behaved and spoken so oddly tonight, as if she had already cracked under her stress. All that nonsense about the Beaujolais Nouveau . . .

Babe's situation was disastrous. She could only make it *if* she could reclaim some of her spunk . . . *if* she could make it through the divorce given the pressures that would be exerted . . . *if* she was able to turn her parents around and get them to support her or *if*, best of all, she could declare her independence from them.

It was certainly her parents more than Greg who had betrayed Babe. He had been no more than a stranger really – a stranger who had come into her life and promised her a glorious future. And, of course, he had promised her love.

Don't they always promise you love?

That was a fact. But then, instead, he had provided her with a unique kind of sex – sex after pain.

But the Tracys were her parents, and wasn't it the obligation of parents to love and protect their child, to guard her against those strangers from whose lips false promises flowed like wine?

And what about Sam?

She herself had always insisted on believing that no matter what, Nora would be there for Sam, but what was there to say about that now?

She found herself wishing that her father was there so that she could ask him what he thought about what had happened between Sam and Nora tonight. Surely no one believed in Nora more than Teddy did, but at the same time, she knew she could count on his being fair.

Then hearing Sam's painful tossing again, she called out softly, 'Sam?'

'Go to sleep, Honey. I don't want to talk. There's nothing to say anyway. It's all been said a thousand times.'

It was the first time Honey could remember Sam actually refusing to talk. Talking was practically an addiction with her. But she sounded so defeated . . . so worn out. Was it possible that Sam, who had always been so gutsy, had finally, like Babe, run out of steam and wouldn't be able to snap back?

She thought of Sam's real mother who had run out of steam early in the game. Was it possible that a propensity for that sort of thing – being too tired to fight back – was transmitted in the DNA and carried in the bloodstream, just like Sam claimed the genius for making movies was? Was it remotely possible that Sam would follow in her mother's footsteps? Like mother, like daughter . . .

Isn't that what they said about me when I became Honey Rose, TV's sex symbol? Like mother, like daughter . . .

Though God knew it hadn't ever been what she had intended for herself, the last thing she had wanted was to follow in her mother's footsteps. Her friends knew that. Her father knew that. Why hadn't the man she married known it? Believed it? How many times had she told him that over the years? A hundred? A thousand? Two hundred and fifty million times?

Her thoughts, like mice scurrying around mindlessly in her head, switched back to Sam. She wished that there was some way she could help her get through this. Wasn't that what sisters were for? And Sam was more than a sister. Sisters, like other members of a family – mothers and fathers, stepmothers obviously and husbands for sure – could fail you. But Sam had never failed her. Sam's love had always been constant.

And wasn't that what life's sweet promise was really all about? *Love*?

Then, as they invariably did, her thoughts bounced back to Joshua, out of habit if nothing else. For so many years he'd been the first person she thought of when she awoke each morning, even before she turned to him in bed; the last person she thought of as she drifted off to sleep only to dream of him, even after she had just kissed him good night.

Oh, *he* had promised her love along with a glorious future and stardom, along with a fortune of money – money that she had never cared about. Not then, anyway. And he had promised her love and babies and a castle to live in. But then he had delivered his own version of love which had never equated with hers. And he had delivered the castle, but it turned out to be only an enormous empty house no matter how magnificent, with no babies to fill it. And he had delivered the glorious future, only it wasn't the same future she had envisioned for herself.

And now there was *no* future for them . . . not together.

Then she wondered if he too, less than a mile away, was lying awake tonight, staring into the darkness, contemplating the future. Or was he, too, mourning the past?

Was he tossing and turning, sleepless with worry that she might actually walk out of that courtroom with that quarter of a billion dollars? Was he was quaking in terror that she was going to snatch his beloved Crown House away?

If asleep, was he dreaming? And if he were dreaming, was it a sweet dream? Was he dreaming of the woman who had been his wife or the woman that had been his star?

Was he holding her in his arms in the dream, whispering his false promises in her ear? Was he burying his lips in her throat, caressing her breasts, kissing her moist thighs, tonguing her most receptive parts, sipping of her nectar?

89

Was he piercing her with his thrusting phallus, pounding at her, lost in a wild lust? Or was he calling out her name in ecstatic rapture? And if so, which name was it? Honey, my sweet love? *Or was it Honey Rose, my sweet golden goose?*

Of course there was always the possibility that he was very much awake neither worrying nor mourning but making passionate love to another woman, her replacement. But this woman – whoever she might be – would have to be her replacement both in his bed and on his set. Otherwise, it would never work for him – not the sex, not the marriage.

Oh God, how he had cheated her! Much more than Nora had cheated the three of them with her false promise of sweet dreams! Well, at least there would be the money – the money she hadn't valued before. At least he was going to have to deliver on that!

What had Nora said that afternoon – the money helped the pain go away? And what was money anyway? It wasn't love. Not even Nora had ever said it was love. But if you used it to make the pain go away, why then it was *almost* as good as love. Was that what Nora had been telling her? And even if Nora had lied about the sweet dreams, that only made her a liar, it didn't make her any the less wise.

If the money couldn't make her own pain go away, it could still help Sam's to disappear . . .

'Sam—?' Honey tentatively whispered again, not wanting to wake Babe.

'Why aren't you sleeping?' Sam grouched. 'Besides, I thought I told you I didn't want to talk.'

'It's not over, Sam. The business with the studio.'

'Forget it. It's over. *Finis.*'

'Oh, Sam! That's not like you. To give up so easily.'

'Well, you heard her. It's over. My studio is gone.'

'What she said was that she was talking to her lawyers. And a deal is only a deal *after* the names are on the dotted line. Your father always said that. And if you offer Nora as much money as those other people have, why wouldn't she sell to you instead of them?'

'Oh, Honey! You still don't understand. Or is it that you're hopelessly naïve? Maybe it's just that you're as foolish as I was when I thought it was remotely possible that the cat would change her spots and give me back what was mine. But this whole business of her selling the studio – it's as much about *hurting me* as it is about money.'

'But—'

'There are no buts. Everything else being equal, she would *prefer* to sell to them. She's aching for it like some women ache for a man! Besides, where would I get the money?'

There was a pause. 'From me.'

'You?'

'Yes, me.'

'You mean your award money?'

'My *due*, but yes, that's what I mean.'

'I couldn't ask you to do that – to give me that money.'

'But you're not asking me – I'm offering. Besides, I'm not *giving* you the money. I expect to be an equal partner with you making the pictures and me getting the choice roles. Just don't get any big ideas about giving me less than my share, kid.'

'Oh Honey, I appreciate what you're trying to do. But owning a studio wasn't part of your dream for a new life.'

'Well, sometimes dreams just need updating. Besides, I *liked* what you said this afternoon. How if I owned my own studio I could do whatever projects appealed to me, the serious roles I've always wanted to do and at the same time I could thumb my nose at the man who said I couldn't do them . . . who wouldn't even let me try.'

'Oh, what do I know?' Sam laughed sadly. 'You can't go by anything I say. I just talk because I love the sound of my own voice. Besides, suppose I took your money

– the money that represents fifteen years of your life and lost it? Suppose Nora is right – that I'm just an arrogant bitch who *thinks* she can run a major studio, but who actually has a pretty lousy track record when it comes to success?'

'But I trust you even if you *are* an arrogant bitch. You're still the smartest girl I ever knew.'

'In spite of all my fuck-ups?'

'In spite of every last one.'

'Hey, there haven't been *that* many.' Sam was perking up.

'Oh Sam, I *know* it's a risk. But isn't everything? Living is a risk. Trusting someone enough to be your best friend is a risk. Loving someone. Getting married. But that doesn't mean we can stop living or loving, trusting friends or even getting married. If we did the world would come to an end and then where would we be?

'Besides, I don't really care about the money as *money*. I tried to explain that to you. What would I do with it anyway except put it in a bank? Several banks, I suppose, and live off the interest like they tell you to do. But that doesn't sound like much fun and this way, we both get a new chance. And it's exciting to have a new, *really big* venture!'

'Oh, Honey, you almost have me convinced,' Sam said wistfully, 'but it won't work. For one thing Nora won't sell it to me . . . to us, for the same price she's getting from that unexpected quarter.'

'Why wouldn't she?'

'I told you. Because she wants to break it off in me. You saw, you heard what she did to me tonight. She played with me. She dicked me around. She – Anyway, we'd have to offer her a hell of a lot more money than *they* are.'

'What kind of money are we talking about?'

'I'm not sure, but at least a half.'

'Half a billion dollars? Why, that's a fortune!'

Sam laughed at the amazement in Honey's voice. 'It

sure is and if anyone should know, it's you. What did you think?'

'I don't know. I guess I didn't think about it. But I suppose that figure sounds about right. Grantwood Studio has to be worth *at least* as much as Royal Productions is, if not more. And that's what the accountants say Royal Productions is worth. That's why we're asking for half of that.

'But look, no matter how much money I end up with, won't the banks lend us the rest? At least that's what my clever ex always says. That when you *already* have plenty of money, everyone bends over backwards to lend you more.'

'I'm sure that's true but the thing is if we have to better the other offer – Well, Nora could name a figure that's completely out of the ballpark. One that might be a lot more than the studio is actually worth. One that may mean committing financial suicide before we even made our first movie. No, Honey, I can't let you do it.'

'Look, Sam. You're tired now and understandably depressed and therefore, negative. But in the morning you're going to feel differently. You're going to be my old Sam again, putting on the gloves, ready to come out fighting. Isn't that what you told Babe? We're *both* going to come out fighting and we're going to make Nora an offer. I'm counting on you, Sam. You can't let me down. You won't, will you?'

'Well, if you put it that way – OK, it's a deal! We won't let each other down. At least, we'll give it the old GAM try. We'll pitch the bitch.'

'Oh, Sam!' Honey leaped out of bed and ran to the big bed to give Sam a hug. Sam laughed and hugged her back. 'Here, get in,' she said, moving over to the middle of the bed. 'There's room enough in this bed for all of us tonight.'

Disoriented, Babe slowly came awake as Honey snuggled under the covers. 'What's happening? Did something happen?'

'Not yet,' Sam told her. 'But it's going to – *tomorrow*. Tomorrow's Independence Day for the GAMs and it might very well be the day we're finally going to triumph over all.'

Babe moaned, remembering that tomorrow was the day her parents were going to come pounding on the manor's front door. 'I wish I could believe that, but tomorrow might be the day Catherine and the Judge force me to go back to Greg again.'

'No! Wrong! Tomorrow is the day you're going to tell them to go fuck themselves and Greg, too! And tomorrow is the day Honey's going to court and sticking it to the Prince of TV. And tomorrow is also the day we're going to pitch that bitch Nora and just maybe – before night falls – I might well end up being the President of Grantwood Studio and then I can tell *her* where to stick it! Right, Honey?'

'Wrong! Before night falls *I* might end up the President of the studio and you might end up being the VP.'

'Oh, all right, spoilsport,' Sam said goodnaturedly. 'I can see the power's already gone to your head. Soon you're going to insist that we stop calling you Honey and start calling you Madam President.'

'Wrong. *Ms* President, if you please.' And Honey knew that she had made the right decision – to give Sam the money that was *almost* as good as love to make her pain go away. 'And with that said, I propose to get some sleep so I'll be bright-eyed and bushy-tailed in the morning, and I suggest that both of you, dear Sam and sweet Babe, do the same.'

Still, Honey found it impossible to sleep. She couldn't stop thinking about what Sam had always said about Nora . . . that she was a cunningly clever witch-bitch who always, in some mysterious fashion, knew everything and manipulated everyone around her for her own ends.

'*She wants us all to fail so that she can play the saviour*

94

. . . wants everyone to love her to the exclusion of everyone else while she loves only herself. She's as avaricious for love as she is for money . . . a modern-day vampire who lives only by sucking everyone else's blood dry . . .'

Of course she and Babe had never taken any of Sam's silly charges seriously. But tonight, somehow, Nora herself had changed all the rules. Was it possible Sam really had a righteous case and that all these years she and Babe had been incapable of seeing the truth because they'd been, as Sam insisted, under Nora's spell?

Had Nora really wanted all of them to fail? Had she *programmed* them for failure? Had *all* of them been manipulated – she herself, Sam, Babe, as well as all those husbands?

And what about those husbands . . . that quote she was known for? *Once for love and once for convenience, once for the fun of it and once for the money . . . all four in one package – a brilliant marriage.*

Nora *had* stamped her marriage to Joshua as brilliant. But today, as smooth as silk and as glib as ever, she'd declared the end of the brilliant marriage, brilliant, too.

Was her quote just a witty, cynical saying said with tongue in cheek then, or was it the code she had actually lived by? Even if those marriages weren't all conceived in greed as Sam claimed, they couldn't *all* have been only for love, sweet love, either. How many of them had been approached with cold calculation? And the fact was that – at least, in her last marriage to TS – she *had* ended up with all the goodies.

And the hard fact was that she *had* sent Hubie away. What truly loving mother could have done that? Not even her father, Teddy, trusting soul that he was, had ever come up with a reasonable explanation for that, saying only that if Nora had done it, then there must have been a good reason.

Who was Nora really? The warm and loving woman she and Babe had always believed her to be or the manipulator complete? Surrogate mother or avaricious whore? Or was she only a charming fraud – just another stranger from whose lips flowed lies sweeter than truth?

Will I ever know for sure?

Suddenly, she heard a sound in the stillness and sat up. 'Did you hear that, Sam? I think it came from the courtyard.'

'I didn't hear anything. Besides, what could it be? The security alarm would have gone off if someone was out there. It probably was a squirrel or maybe even a coyote down from the hills. There've been a lot of them around lately.'

'No, it wasn't an animal. It wasn't that kind of a sound. Listen, there it is again!'

Now, Sam sat up. 'That's the garage door closing! It makes that whooshing sound going up and down.'

Then they heard the screech of tyres and Sam leaped from the bed to run to the window, Honey and Babe at her heels. They were just in time to see Nora's silver Jaguar rounding the curve before disappearing down the driveway towards the entrance gates.

'Where can she be going at this time of night?' Honey wondered. 'She was already in her night-gown and négligé.'

'Maybe she's going to see my parents,' Babe speculated. 'To tell them about—'

Sam hissed. 'At midnight? I hardly think so, Babe. More likely she's off to see the people who want to buy the studio. She probably wants to tie up the deal real fast just to make sure that in case she dies in her sleep tonight, I *still* wouldn't end up with the studio.'

Then Sam laughed unpleasantly. 'I bet I know where she's really going. Remember what I said before when she came into the room all jazzy in her night-gown and négligé and made up to the teeth? I asked her if she had a lover or a potential husband waiting in her bed and she said no. Well, I guess he *wasn't* in her bed or she wouldn't have needed her car.'

'And that's where you think she went? To her lover?' Babe sounded wistful.

'Actually, I lean more to the potential husband theory,' Sam said thoughtfully.

'But you're only speculating,' Honey said.

'Well, where *would* she be headed at this time of night in full make-up and a peek-a-boo nightie with her tits spilling out all over the place?' Sam demanded.

'I suppose it *is* a possibility,' Honey granted.

'I wonder who he is,' Babe mused longingly.

'It doesn't matter. The only one who matters right now is *you*.' Honey put her arm around Babe to lead her back to bed. 'You're supposed to be resting and you've hardly closed your eyes all night.'

They weren't back in bed more than a few minutes before Sam sat up again. 'I'm *sure* it's not her lover. It's her next husband! I'd swear my life on it.'

Honey sat up. 'How can you be so sure?'

'Because it's her *pattern*. Don't you see? Any woman who marries so many times has to have a pattern. And what's been hers? Not that bullshit she spouts about the first time for love, the second time for – you know how it goes. That's *all* bullshit, still Madam Grant's pattern *is* to do it by the numbers. First, she marries a rich and important man, second, she sheds him by one means or another, third, she picks up all the marbles before moving on to the next sucker.

'So what's she doing now? *Repeating the pattern*. After marrying my father and eventually getting rid of him – I'm still not convinced she didn't murder him – she's picking up all the marbles by selling off the studio and probably this house as well. I mean, I wouldn't be a bit surprised to learn that she already has Grantwood Manor listed with the brokers. And why now? Because she's ready to move on to a new man and her *next* marriage. Don't you see? *It's her pattern!*'

Sam's theory was crazy, Honey told herself. As usual, she was letting her imagination run away with itself. But

97

crazier still, in some crazy way, it all, somehow, made sense.

If only there was some way they could know for sure. If they knew for sure they might find the answers as to why their own lives were such a tangled mess. They might even find a way to go. A way to make the dreams come true . . .

'Well, I guess, as they say, only time will tell. And in the meantime, sweet dreams, Sam, sweet dreams, Babe.'

It wasn't a lucky charm. It certainly wasn't a promise. It probably wasn't even a wish. Maybe it was nothing more than a wistful hope. But Sam returned the hope. 'Sweet dreams, sweet Honey. Sweet dreams, little Babe.'

Then Babe took up the call. 'Sweet dreams, Sam. Sweet dreams, Honey.' Then she said something which at first struck Honey as odd. 'You know what sweet dreams remind me of? Beaujolais Nouveau. You know, that first sweet taste of the season . . .'

Then, thinking about it, Honey realized that she knew exactly what Babe meant . . .

PART THREE

THE FIRST TIME AROUND

London
1943–51

8

Pretty, blonde, blue-eyed and curvaceous, with a good nature and an eye for the lads (and they for her), Natalie Hall changed her name to Nora (thinking it much more sophisticated), when she left the beautiful Cotswolds to go to a London at war. She wasn't so much seeking work but a lively time of it since there were no young men left at home.

Part of the baggage Nora carried with her to London was her virginity, which probably would have stunned her old neighbours who would have wagered that the high-spirited, eighteen-year-old crumpet was a bit of a tart. But the truth was that Nora had always coupled her love of a good time and her admiration of men in general with a healthy self-respect, holding neither her person nor her virtue cheaply and, at heart, was the complete romantic. She wasn't waiting for marriage to yield up her virginity, but true love.

Untrained for most work, but with a repertoire of bawdy songs (her sole legacy from her mother the barmaid), Nora quickly found a job in a cabaret. Boasting only a fair voice but great enthusiasm, she was a big favourite with the boys in uniform, including the handsome Captain Hubert Hartiscor, with whom she fell in love at first sight. She swore that at that moment – as in the song – her heart really stood still.

She was grateful that Hubert's wartime assignment precluded his leaving London – he wasn't about to kiss her hallo to only kiss her goodbye a fortnight later. Not to mention that he wouldn't be getting himself killed off either, unless he fell prey to the nightly bombings, which wasn't all that likely. At least the odds were with him . . . *with them.*

It was Hubert's assignment to organize entertainments for the men who went off to do the actual fighting. He did little that was really crucial to the effort. Still he did his job well enough since he was of an artistic bent with an ear for music and an eye for the look of the thing, plus an intuitive sense of what was in good taste and what was truly deplorable.

But all Nora really knew about Hubert was that she had never known anyone as charming or quite so beautiful, and if she had but known how, she would have written an ode to his manly beauty – the mane of yellow hair that waved back from the unfurrowed brow; the lofty cheek-bones; the chiselled nose; the square jaw; the clefted chin; the dimples which appeared like a marvellous surprise when he smiled, but which in no way took away from his masculine image. The odd thing about her finding him so excruciatingly beautiful was that anyone seeing them together unfailingly remarked how much alike they looked down to their exact colouring, so much so they might have been brother and sister. Then Nora always said: 'Oh, but there's nothing sisterly about how I'm feeling.'

Nora also knew that Hubert talked as sweetly as he appeared with the kind of manners and style she'd never before encountered, that he enjoyed a good time and seemed to find her as attractive as she found him, which was enormously so.

What she didn't know about him would have filled a book. While she recognized that he was upper class, she had no idea that he had the distinction of being called Lord since his father was the twelfth Earl of Hartiscor and one of the richest men in the country – the family's landed estate exceeding 100,000 acres of fertile English countryside, and a few hundred acres of even more fertile London brick and cement. And even if she had known this – not reading anything more serious than the tabloids or the occasional fashion magazine – she would scarcely have been aware that in addition to being a member of the House of Lords, Hubert's father, Lord Jeffrey, was a prestigious member of high-placed society on many different levels – a world renowned financier, an expert on the economy, a respected political analyst and the intimate of every person of consequence in his radius, even the Prime Minister himself.

But it didn't take long before more knowing friends filled her in, giving her fair warning. She was wasting her time, whether she was just mucking around or silly enough to fall in love with the likes of Hubert Hartiscor.

'If you believe there's a chance in hell he'll marry you, then you'd believe that *I'm* the queen,' her friend Pat told her. 'And what's more, laddie doesn't have a shilling. Without an allowance from the old boy he can't set *himself* up in style, much less a girl-friend. And what do you think would happen to that allowance if Da got wind that he's smooching around with the likes of you – a singer in a third-rate club?'

Furthermore, what kind of presents was he offering? Flowers. The occasional bottle of bubbly. Maybe a packet of sweets. Not like some of the Yanks who could magically produce a pair of stockings or a carton of American cigarettes by way of saying thanks for a good time. The consensus of opinion among her friends was that she should sleep with Hubert if she couldn't resist, but that she shouldn't expect anything but a few nights of rolling around in the sack, after which he'd most likely give *her* the sack, which was what men like Hubert Hartiscor always did with girls like her.

But Nora was too young to listen to any cautionary advice and too much in love by this time. While a woman of more experience might have recognized certain flaws when she came up against them, Nora had never even heard of a flawed diamond, much less a flawed character. But at the same time she had too much basic common sense to have expectations of marriage. Besides, what she felt for Hubert was wildly beyond the consideration of whether he would marry her or not, and at this point, hardly her dilemma. Her problem with Hubert was that while she ached with the need to surrender herself to him, yearned with desire for the feel of him, the smell of him, for the swell of him pressing against and finally into her, he himself made no move in that direction.

Not that they weren't friends. Sometimes she thought she would never again have such a wonderful friend. And not that there weren't intimate moments – murmured conversations, heads close together; laughter, lips inches away; long walks, fingers interlaced; dancing, cheek to cheek, thigh to thigh, even belly to belly; friendly hugs and sweet kisses, occasionally even hungry kisses, and lingering good nights, as if the nights themselves were too good to let go of.

Yet, that was as far as it had gone. There had been no foreplay, no entrance, no final thrust, no cries of joy and release, and Nora – craving sexual fulfilment until she was almost ill with it – came to the conclusion that Hubert was just too much the gentleman to make the first move.

Then, beyond caring about ladylike delicacy, she decided she herself would make that first move and invited him to her flat for dinner which she'd often done before, but in a casual way. This time it would be a very special dinner.

By trading away her meat rations for months, she was able to dig up a decent roast, and then on the big night she set the table with a lace tablecloth and pink candles in Bristol-blue candlesticks. As for herself, her blond hair was freshly washed and set – a wave dipping over one eye like a film star – her blond eyebrows darkened with brown pencil, her lashes twice coated with cake mascara, her mouth painted a dark red with a lipstick called Raven Red, and she was wearing a pink gossamer négligé. Underneath the négligé she wore the kind of intimate apparel no decent shop carried – lingerie that left nothing to the imagination – just black lace scraps and a shocking pink garter belt that held up the last pair of black net stockings she owned.

When the buzzer sounded, she rushed to the door, at the last second thinking that their dinner would, after all, wait, and she didn't give a bloody damn if the bloody roast dried up like a bone. She herself had already waited far too long.

She flung open the door and without even giving Hubert a chance to take a good look at her in all her seductive glory, threw herself at him, causing him almost to drop the bottle of wine he was carrying in one hand. (He *did* drop the bunch of flowers that he held in the other.) But when he drew back in surprise, she laughed in delight, thinking that she had really knocked him for a loop.

She swooped to pick up her posies, pulled him into the room and slammed the door shut after him. But then he stood there motionless, his mouth slightly open, his eyes hooded so she couldn't read them, taking all of her in. Naturally, he wanted to savour the look of her, she thought. That *was* the idea. And any second he would say something, breathe her name, move to touch her, embrace her, crush her in his arms.

She laughed again, removing the wine from his inert hand to place the bottle and the flowers on the table. Then she shrugged off the négligé and went to him, standing just inches away and placed her hands on her hips the better for him to take in the full image of her in her high-heeled, pink, marabou-trimmed slippers, breasts spilling from the inadequate bra, thighs emerging from the lacy scanties, garters meeting stockings with a creamy expanse of flesh in between.

But instead of saying anything – even breathing in ragged gasps – Hubert remained mute, transfixed, until not able to bear his silence another moment, she cried, 'Don't you have anything to say? Have you been struck deaf and dumb? Oh, say something, Hubert! Say something wonderful!'

Still, rather than coming towards her to take her in his arms, to mash his lips against hers, to force her mouth open with a demanding tongue or run his hands down her body, he remained motionless as if he had turned into a pillar of salt.

Was he petrified with desire or simply terrified by her brazenness? Nora agonized. Then when she saw a look of intense pain cross his beautiful face, she herself grew terrified. 'What is it, love? What—?' In a frenzy she slid her arms around his neck and, placing her hands on the back of his neck, rubbed her body against his. Then she drew his head down to hers so that she could press her lips to his, attempt to force them open with her tongue. When that still didn't make him move, she ran her fingers over his groin feverishly, groping to find an erection . . . *which simply wasn't there.*

'Oh, my sweet Nora,' he finally spoke. 'I'm so sorry.'

'What are you sorry about, love?' she asked quickly, misunderstanding, smiling, trying to hide her disappointment.

Her friend Rose, who had been around the block more than a few times, had told her that this sort of thing happened frequently – blokes could be so excited that instead of a hard-on they had a limp-on.

'These things happen, Hubert love . . . but we'll take care of that in no time.'

She reached for his testicles again, to stroke them, mould them, squeeze them. And then she felt for his penis, to fondle it, rub it persuasively with the heel of her palm. When she still didn't feel it respond to her touch, she took his hand and placed it between her breasts so he could feel their heat, and then between her thighs so that he could feel their wetness. And when he only threw his head back not in exultation but in a gesture of defeat, she placed his hand under her panties and forced it to rub against her there.

'Don't,' he muttered as if in profound distress.

'Sh!' she whispered, still not understanding, unzipping

his fly to find the opening in his shorts to free his penis so that it could emerge in all its fiery tumescence . . . but then she found it wasn't tumescent at all, but *flaccid*.

She fell to her knees to wet it with her kisses, to caress it with her lips, to make love to it with her tongue, finally to take it in her mouth, to suck on it, lick at it, to tease it gently with her teeth, but the only thing that happened was that he put his hands to either side of her head and forced it back, and she fell back on her heels to look at him pleadingly. 'What am I doing wrong? Tell me what to do!'

He looked down at her, his eyes filled with tears. 'It won't help . . . Don't you understand? *Nothing* will help.'

'But why not?' she raged. 'Why don't you want me like I want you? Aren't I good enough for you just to *want* me? I never asked you to marry me or even to love me. I just want you to *make* love to me. Aren't I good enough for that?'

'Too good,' he whispered. 'I thought you understood.'

'Understood what?'

'Understood that I have never in my life loved a woman . . . made love to a woman . . .'

At first she was bewildered. But when she did finally understand, her face flushed with the sickening heat of this ultimate rejection and she could feel the humiliation coursing through her. She struggled clumsily to her feet from her kneeling position and stared down at herself – at the absurd underwear, the silly suspender belt, the obvious net stockings, the foolish satin mules with their silly stiletto heels and useless fluff of marabou. Never had she felt so pathetic, so ashamed and so degraded!

She kicked off the slippers, tore at the stockings until there were big rents in them, tugged at the garter belt until the fastenings gave way and she pulled it off, still grotesquely attached to the torn stockings. But her rage was unabated. She ripped off her bra as if it were searing her flesh, pulled at the panties until they were in tatters.

'I'd like to kill you!' she screamed and moved to the table to pick up dish after dish and send it crashing to the floor.

He rushed over to pull her to him, to try and put his arms about her, to comfort her somehow, but it was too late for comfort and so far from what she needed that it only enraged her further.

'What did you think you were you doing? Playing with me, amusing yourself, laughing behind my back with your fairy boys? Laughing at the barmaid's daughter who was mad about the elegant gentleman and just grateful for his attentions? How could you be so cruel to someone who loved you so? Why, in God's name, did you do it?'

'Because I love you, Nora.'

'Oh no, don't you dare say that to me!'

'I love you,' he said again. 'And I tried so hard! I wanted so much to love you like a real man. You're such a wonderful woman – a woman any man would die to make love to. And I thought that if it could happen with anyone it would happen with you,' he cried, the tears rolling down his cheeks.

She believed him. That was the worst of it – that she *believed* that he loved her and she had lost, been cheated of the greatest love story ever told . . .

She fell into his arms to sob against his strong, manly chest and he picked her up and carried her into the bedroom, laying her naked body tenderly on the bed. Then he quickly undressed and kneeled over her to lower his head to her and made love to her with his lips and tongue. It wasn't *quite* the same, but it was love just the same – a gift of love, she thought – and when she climaxed, she cried out in sweet relief before she cried salty tears as he did. Then they licked the tears from each other's face.

They spent the night in each other's arms and in the morning they swore eternal love, the love of best friends. Still, Nora wondered, would she ever love another man like she had . . . *did* . . . love Hubert Hartiscor?

*   *   *

A week later, Nora, in a knock-out satin gown, was singing, 'Roll me over, in the clover, roll me over, lay me down and do it again', when Corporal John Wayne from Butte, Montana, tall and lanky, loped into the Cock 'n' Bull with his American buddies. Johnny, whom his pals referred to as 'the Duke' because he shared his name with the movie star, encouraged by dares from his fellow Yanks, asked Nora if she'd like to do some rolling over in the clover with the best cocksman in the whole USA. 'It'll be an experience you'll never forget,' the Duke promised. But then he almost dropped in shock when she invited him to go home with her to prove it.

She lay on top of the chenille bedspread, waiting for the Duke to come out of the lavatory, more nervous than aroused. This was the big moment. Before morning came she would know what it meant to be made love to by a real man – an expert 'fuck artist', as the corporal had bragged. And at last and at least it would be over. She would be virgin territory no more and what was still a mystery would all become clear.

Thinking that the Duke would want to undress her himself, she still wore her pretty dress and party sandals. But then she remembered her stockings. She couldn't risk a ladder and Johnny in the throes of passion might remove them too roughly. She sat up to remove her shoes, stockings, and suspender belt, then lay back again with closed eyes, to try and visualize what it was going to be like, how it was going to feel and tried not to think of Hubert, with the tears rolling down his cheeks.

Finally, he emerged and she was shocked to see that his upper half was still fully clothed, his tie only loosened which made his exposed penis – as long and lanky as the Duke himself, but standing at attention – seem ridiculously out of place. And she thought that if Hubert were there, they would both probably laugh at how silly it all was. But Hubert wasn't there.

She waited for the Duke to approach her, to kiss

her and fondle her, to murmur sweet nothings in her ear before he took off her clothes. But as he loped over to her, his legs as bowed as they were long, the Duke said, 'You better pull up your dress and take off your panties.'

He wasn't going to undress her, after all.

He should know, she thought. He was a real man, a cocksman to be precise, and thoroughly experienced. Maybe it *was* sexier this way, he still in the upper pieces of his uniform, she in her dress, so she obeyed, wriggling out of the pink step-ins and throwing them to the floor, pulling her dress up to her waist. Then, quickly, he was on top of her, crushing her, each of his hands mauling a breast through the satin, and she thought that this must be what was called foreplay and how lucky it was that a man had two hands and a woman two breasts to make everything work out so evenly.

But the foreplay was over by the time she even finished thinking the thought, and his penis was masterfully attempting to find its rightful home, straining against her vaginal membrane but getting nowhere. 'Jesus!' he muttered, the sweat dripping from him and staining her dress. 'Don't you English girls even have a hole? Maybe you'd better blow me.'

Something clicked inside her head then and she wanted to tell *him* to blow it . . . right out of his barrack bag. But in for a penny, in for a pound, and he was already on top of her and she was already lying under him, and her dress was probably already ruined. She had might as well get it over with.

'Oh, we English girls have holes all right – if we get a real man with a real cock who knows how to fill it!'

'I'll show you a real cock!'

Straining with frustration and panting, he pounded away unmercifully, the thrusting growing more furious and vicious with each shove until finally she could feel herself tearing, and him entering. Then, as if the sound were far away, she heard a groan to realize that it was *hers*, one of pain.

Moments later, she heard another – the Duke's – as he erupted within her, and she groaned again as he collapsed on her chest, his weight crushing the breath from her.

She waited a few polite seconds while a line of a ditty danced in her head: *Thank you kindly, Sir, she said, As he broke her maidenhead.*

Then she said, 'Would you be so kind as to get off? You're crushing me.'

He rolled off. 'Did you—?'

She guessed at his meaning. 'Not really, cocksman.'

'I'll finger-fuck you if you want,' he offered generously as befitted a Duke, a bit of *noblesse oblige*. 'Personally, I don't go in for diving the muff, if you get my meaning.'

'I do and that's all right, I don't go in for it myself. And I'll pass on being fucked by a finger, if you don't mind, since if that's what I *had* in mind, I got ten of me own.'

When Nora discovered that she was pregnant and pondered her options with her best friend, Hubert asked her first if she really wanted the baby, and when she said yes, that she was already filled with love for it, he proposed a 'marriage of sweet convenience'.

'A marriage of sweet convenience . . .' she rolled the phrase over her tongue. 'But who am I going to marry? You don't mean Johnny the Duke? He's long gone. Besides I wouldn't marry him even if he was a real duke or even a king.'

'Marry *me*, Nora.'

She looked at him in shock, then in bemused sorrow before she asked, 'And who would it be convenient for, besides me?'

'For the baby, of course, and me . . .'

'You?' she scoffed in mournful disbelief. She didn't believe he really meant it. He was just being kind and

111

talking nonsense. 'I can just picture how convenient it would be for you to marry me, two months preggers with the bastard of a bastard of a Yank.'

God, what a nit I was! For the same results, I could have picked a nice Yank.

'What would your father say . . . *do* if you married a girl who sings at the Cock 'n' Bull, even if he didn't know she was already two months gone? He'd more than not have a stroke.'

'No, not really.' Hubert's laugh was just barely bitter. 'Perhaps if it were my brother Rupert, he who is beyond reproach, Father might be put off somewhat. After all, the woman Rupert marries will be the future Countess of Hartiscor. But his younger son, the charming but very black sheep in the family–? He probably won't turn a hair.'

'I don't believe you're serious. You're just teasing.'

'But I'm not. I am very serious. Even sincere.'

'Well, even if your father didn't perish from shock, he'd cut you off without a quid . . .'

'Look, when I proposed a marriage of convenience I meant exactly that. For the both of us. Don't you see? The old boy is quite on to me and more than fed up with my little . . . er, shall we call them peccadilloes? Actually, he's been threatening to cut off my allowance for months now. But if we were to wed and you were pregnant with my child, he'd be reassured. Who could doubt the manhood of a chap lucky enough to be married to a lusty woman like Nora Hall? Especially when the chap's already planted the noble Hartiscor seed in the rich, luscious loam of her? What I suspect will happen is that Father will be so thrilled he'll give me an allowance three can live on very well. Please, Nora, do it for us both and for the baby.' He kissed her hand as he gazed into her eyes the exact shade of blue as his own. 'And who knows – maybe you'll even make a real man of me.'

That was the clincher.

'Oh, Hubert, do you really mean it?' she screamed in delight. 'I warn you, I'm not a quitter.'

He laughed. 'That's exactly what I'm counting on.'

It was an offer and a challenge Nora couldn't refuse and she vowed to herself that she would do everything in her power to make the marriage work. A marriage of sweet convenience was already all the sweeter when you loved a man *so much* you'd be willing to die for him, much less just live for him.

Still, much as she hated the idea of lying, passing off her baby as Hubert's, it disturbed her even more to tell Lord Jeffrey that they were first getting married when she was already pregnant. 'It's embarrassing. It makes me look like a you know what.'

'All right. We'll just tell him we're getting married then and won't say a word about your being preggers. We'll wait a couple of months and then we'll announce it. You won't be the first bride who gave birth to a seven-month baby.'

'No, that will be even worse. In a couple of months I'll be sure to be showing and then I'll not only look like a liar, but an idiot as well.'

'In that case, there's only one thing to do – tell Father that we're already married, that we were married three months ago. Then we can say you're pregnant and still have a month to spare. What do you say?'

'I guess that will have to do, only I do hate all this lying.'

'You *are* an old-fashioned girl. Don't you know that a few lies keep things interesting?' Hubert laughed. 'But since we are going to tell Father that we're already married, we'll go see him right away, quick before you change your mind. Then we can get married later, secretly but leisurely.'

Nora was ready in an hour, though their appointment with Lord Jeffrey was still an hour away. Dressed in her best – a two-piece pink rayon with hat to match –

she was tottering and quaking in her four-inch heels. She couldn't have been more nervous if they'd been going to Buckingham Palace to take tea with the Queen. No matter how much Hubert reassured her that things would go smashingly, she wasn't convinced.

'You'll see. In his way, Father is a man with a very clear vision. That's why old Winnie depends on him so much; even had Father along with him when he met with Roosevelt to draw up the Atlantic Charter. Father will see clear to your heart and realizing what a treasure you are, he will love you as much as I do.'

Since Hubert didn't love her the way she yearned to be loved, what did it really matter if Lord Hartiscor loved her as much? Nora wondered. But she couldn't say this to Hubert. It would only bring that look of helpless pain to his face and since things were the way they were and neither smiles nor tears would change them, she much preferred to see him smiling. She herself felt enough pain for two.

'Why would he love me as much as you do? Is he *daft* then, like you?' she teased. 'But it must be me who's daft even going there today.'

'Don't worry so much. We have an advantage.'

'And what would that be?'

'You're the picture of my sister Anne.'

This was the first Nora heard of Anne. 'I didn't know you had a sister. Why didn't you ever mention her before?'

Hubert shrugged. 'I'm five years younger than Anne, and when I was still a boy, she up and ran off to Australia. She married a chap from the outback and we never saw her again.'

'Oh, that's awful. And your father? What did he do?'

'He tried to be in touch, but Annie said she was no longer a Hartiscor and that was the way she wanted it. We should just *consider* her dead. And after that, Father refused to talk about her. Not even after Mummy died. He adored Anne. She'd always been his favourite. And I

114

know he still thinks about her. I've seen him sitting for hours just staring at all the old snaps of her he keeps locked in his desk.'

'That's so sad. But why did Anne run off like that? Wanted the family to think of her as dead?'

'I'm not sure. But there was always bad blood between her and Miranda.'

'Miranda?'

'Mummy. Anne used to say Mummy hated her because Father loved her so much. Anne thought Miranda was jealous of her. It *did* seem as if Mummy couldn't stand the sight of Anne.'

'Still, she must have been crushed when Anne ran off.'

'To the contrary, Mummy seemed relieved,' Hubert laughed. 'But then she still had me, her little boy, and she always said I was the most smashing of the litter. Looks, you see, went a long way with Miranda.' He laughed again. 'And she always said that I was the only one who was full of fun just like her.'

'So you were her favourite?'

'Decidedly. Of course, Father always claimed she was spoiling me rotten, not that he did much to stop her. I suppose he wasn't that wrong. I *am* a bit of a rotter, you know,' he smiled at her beguilingly.

'Oh, hush. I don't want to hear you say that, not even in fun. But what about Rupert?'

Then, as always when she questioned him about the brother who was off fighting the Germans, his face closed up. 'What do you want to know about Rupert?'

'Well, you said your father was crazy about Anne and your mother favoured you over Anne. Did she favour Rupert, too?'

'Hardly. But she didn't dislike him the way she disliked Anne – it was more that Rupert wasn't exactly Mummy's cup of tea. He never laughed, never even cried. Miranda always said Rupert was born old, without a bit of charm or humour. He was always well-behaved and did the right thing but old Mummy didn't give too many good

115

marks for those qualities. Besides, Rupert was dark and brooding and not at all cheerful like her. No, it was I who dear Mummy always took into her bed to tickle and giggle with and play little bedtime games.'

'And your father? Did he treat you and Rupert alike?'

Hubert chuckled. 'I suppose he tried. All the same it was pretty clear whom he preferred. Not that I can blame him. If you were my father – a man of high purpose and accomplishment boasting one of Britain's greatest fortunes and everyone's respect – whom would you prefer? The good son or the one's that not only a black sheep but the family clown?'

Nora protested, but Hubert put a finger to her lips. 'It's true and I'm the first to own up to it. But Father plays the sport, tries to make the best of it – *me*, that is. Stiff upper lip, you know, and he keeps trying to find a niche for me, make provision so that I won't be left entirely in the cold when he chucks it and Rupert becomes the Earl of Hartiscor . . . unless, of course, I get lucky.'

'What do you mean – *lucky*?'

'Well, I'm next to inherit if Rupert buys it in the bloody war . . .' Hubert grinned.

'Oh Hubert, that's a terrible thing to say . . . even to joke about!'

'It would be if I didn't hate Rupert's guts quite so much.'

Nora dropped the subject. *Poor Hubert!* It must be terribly hard to be the black sheep of the family or even its clown, when there's another son who's thought of as the *good* son whom the father respects *and* the one who would inherit.

On the other hand, it had to be hard for Rupert, too, to have been the one second in his mum's heart – the son she never tickled, nor took into her bed, with whom she never played little bedtime games.

Lord Jeffrey, taking both her hands in his, held Nora's eyes with a sharp, shrewd gaze, and Nora's heart dropped

116

into her stomach. While she hadn't expected him to love her, she had hoped that he would accept her. But the way he was looking at her now – as if seeing through right through her – she was afraid that he knew instinctively that she was an impostor, trying to pass off another chap's child as his son's, and would order her out of his house.

But shockingly, Lord Jeffrey kissed her on both cheeks. Then he said that he was delighted that she and Hubert were married, and that soon he would be a grandfather. Then, even more shocking, he not only granted Hubert a generous increase in allowance, he also asked them to make their home with him.

'This is a very large house, my dear, and of course Hartiscor Castle is even more enormous, and both homes are very, very empty with everyone gone—'

When his voice drifted off, Nora presumed that he was thinking of his late wife, the cheerful Countess Miranda, and Anne, the daughter he had loved so much who was as if dead to him, but he went on without mentioning either.

'It seems like years since Rupert went off to war and Hubert moved out to live on his own the way children will. And with so many of my old staff – they were like old friends, really – off to do their bit for the effort, I really am at a loss. You will be doing me a wonderful favour, Nora, gracing my home with a real family again. Oh yes, I'm in great need of a woman's presence, to organize things and create a warm atmosphere. And there's always so much entertaining to do. Beyond me, really. And if you'll forgive my selfishness, what a relief it will be to have so charming a young woman as my hostess.'

Nora noted that he had said *will be* instead of *would be* . . . as if it were all settled, and she was flabbergasted.

'But you have to understand, Lord Jeffrey, that I know nothing about these things – about grand houses like this.' She gestured wildly at the opulent furnishings, at the crystal chandeliers, the walls hung with tapestries and paintings. 'Why, this place is practically a palace. And I couldn't know less about entertaining the kind of people who—' she stopped abruptly and smiled, 'Oh, you're just twitting me, Lord Hartiscor, like Hubert is always doing, aren't you?'

'Ah, but I am not. I'm quite serious. And you must call me Jeffrey.'

'But I wouldn't even know what to say to the kind of people you entertain. They would most likely laugh at me . . . at my ignorance, at the way I speak. And to tell you the truth, Lord Jeffrey, I don't even know a port glass from a sherry glass. As for my clothes, I might have some idea of what I shouldn't wear, but not what I *should*—'

Lord Jeffrey waved his hand. 'Mere trifles. I won't take no for an answer. I already consider the matter settled. My only regret is that by marrying in secret you two cheated me out of the pleasure of a grand wedding. Still, we must toast your marriage and drink to the coming event – the birth of your and Hubert's child.'

He pulled the bell cord and when an elderly man answered the summons, he introduced Nora as proudly as he might have introduced one of the royal princesses before telling the old gentleman, 'We are making *two* toasts today, Edward, so be sure to bring both a port *and* a sherry. And Edward, you sly dog, be sure to bring out those bottles I know you've been hoarding waiting for this bloody war to be over. I have a strong feeling victory is at hand. Don't you think so, Hubert?'

'Oh positively, Father,' Hubert agreed, puffing on a cigarette contentedly. But, to Nora, it seemed almost as if he were, by some invisible line, removed from the proceedings.

Then Jeffrey called after the butler, 'Oh, Edward, be sure to bring glasses for yourself. You must join in our toast to the new Lady Hartiscor.'

Lady Hartiscor! Now Nora really felt the impostor and regretted having told Jeffrey that they were married. It was bad enough to be passing off Duke Wayne's child as a Hartiscor. But it seemed that one lie always led to another. They'd have to get married in a hurry so that at least they'd have only one lie on their mutual conscience.

As Edward filled first the Waterford port glasses, and then the sherry, Nora could hardly fail to get her father-in-law's point. This was her first lesson. The port glasses were tall and long-stemmed with a small bowl on top, the sherry glass had a shorter stem and was tapered. And, of course, she would never again *not* know the difference between the two. Simple. If only all of it would be this simple.

Lord Jeffrey nodded and chuckled, as if reading her mind. 'Nearly all problems are solvable for a bright young woman. Before you know it, you'll know everything Edward knows and you'll soon discover that that in itself is no small accomplishment. As for our Hubert, don't let him deceive you. He's fond of hiding his lights under a bushel, but he knows more than he lets on about many things – art, architecture, literature, music, decoration. Miranda always said Hubert's eye was infallible. When she herself was in doubt about what gown to wear, she always consulted him, and he a mere boy then. Remarkable, really. Rupert, on the other hand, has no eye at all. Before he went off to war, his only interest was the business of money. "Money is what makes the world go round," he said even when he was a young chap. But be that as it may, you must get Hubert to advise you on your wardrobe.

'And when it comes to charities, Hubert will be able to help you out there too. He's always been a remarkable success at running things for various charities. Fund-raising efforts, you know. Once he's dragged into it, that is, fighting and screaming all the way,' he chuckled. 'Everyone assumes this success is due to Hubert's inestimable charm, but I believe he has a remarkable flair for organization even though he'd be the last to admit it. And it's a shame to let all that talent go to waste. You'll have

119

to get him to share it all with you, my dear. Left on his own, Hubert has a tendency to slack off, but you mustn't let him – you must persevere so that Hubert will. And I'm sure you're a young lady with many talents of your own. You and Hubert will each teach the other. That's only as it should be in a good marriage.'

Suddenly, Hubert – silent the whole time his father had discussed him as if he weren't in the room – drawled, 'Was that how it was with you and Mother, Father? Each teaching the other, as it should be in a good marriage?'

Jeffrey acknowledged this question with a dark look before he remembered to smile. 'Oh, I think Nora and I are in agreement as to what constitutes a good marriage, my boy.'

While Nora took note that Lord Jeffrey hadn't really answered Hubert's question, she realized that one way or another, she and the Earl of Hartiscor had already made some kind of a pact. Then she remembered her mother advising her, 'Be careful who you be making your bargains with, me girl . . . that it isn't the devil himself.' But Jeffrey was no devil – he was not only younger than Hubert had led her to believe, he was much warmer and friendlier and she reflected how really fortunate she was to have not only Hubert, but Lord Jeffrey as her friend. Really, more than she had bargained for . . . much, much more . . .

9

Nora and Hubert moved into Hartiscor House bag and baggage and immediately Nora's lessons in being a proper lady began. And almost immediately, Lord Jeffrey insisted on giving a reception to introduce his new daughter-in-law to his friends and associates. What with one thing or another, by the time they had a chance to slip away to tie the knot in secret, Nora's pregnancy was already obvious for all to see. Then she was too embarrassed to show up at her own wedding with an extended belly, and they decided to wait until after the baby was born.

Bright if uneducated, Nora was a quick learner and in only a few months, she was (with Hubert's assistance) involved in various war charities, and – attired in tasteful maternity dresses (Hubert's fine hand again) – playing the hostess at Lord Jeffrey's dinner parties (with him at her side to guide her) when he entertained some of London's most powerful, men like Sir Winston and Hugh Cantington, the American ambassador.

She performed surprisingly well, utilizing her natural wit, charm and good humour. By the time she was about to give birth – having learned a little about politics, the arts and philanthropy, and quite a bit about how to walk, talk, dress, give a party (all under Hubert's guidance) and run a great household (this last with Edward's devoted assistance) – it was as if she'd been born to be Lady Hartiscor.

While thrilled with her success Nora insisted that she couldn't take the credit. 'It's one part your doing,' she told Hubert, 'and two parts your father's.'

'There you go,' Hubert pretended to pout, 'giving me just a little credit while giving the other side most of it.'

'Oh, Hubert, your father's not on the *other* side. You and he and I are all on the same team, like the Allies. Besides, I can't give you as much credit as your father because you already knew and believed in me while your father took me on faith alone. That's probably the best thing anyone can do for another person. It makes you strong because then you feel you *must* live up to their expectations.'

Hubert was thoughtful. 'Yes, I suppose.' Then he

laughed abruptly. 'I can't say anyone ever had that kind of faith in me. Certainly not Father.'

'But your mother? You said that—'

'That I was her favourite, her adorable pet, even her playmate. I never said she *believed* in me.'

'But she loved you so much.'

'But it's not the same thing, is it? Loving someone and believing in them?' He was mournful.

'I can't imagine loving anyone and *not* believing in them. For instance, I can't imagine not believing in you.' She cradled his head against her breasts.

'You're not just saying that?'

'Of course not. I love you so much, Hubert, and I *do* believe in you.'

'And I believe that you believe because while it takes a liar to know a liar, by the same token it takes a liar to recognize the truth. Oh, Nora, I'll try to live up to your belief in me, I swear it!'

'Oh, Hubert, I believe in that, too!'

Little Hubie was born just days before the war was over. Hubert took one look at the baby and told Nora, 'Our son's the most beautiful thing I've ever seen besides you,' and Lord Jeffrey, dubbing Hubie the Victory Baby, said, 'Remarkable. He looks exactly like Hubert did when he was born!'

Then he produced several photograph albums to illustrate his point and Nora saw that there *was* a marked similarity between the two Huberts. But it was more luck than remarkable – everyone always said that she and Hubert bore a strong resemblance to one another. The luck was that Hubie resembled her, rather than his father, the Duke of Butte, Montana.

With the war over and Hubert a civilian again, Nora believed things were falling into place. One of these days they'd manage to find the time to go out of town to be married quietly, and in the meantime, all she had to do was to be patient, put her faith in God and Hubert and then, if her luck held, she and Hubert would be living and making love as they were meant to, and all of them would live happily ever after.

Everything she had bargained for and more . . .

But the one thing she hadn't bargained for was that Rupert, home from the wars, would take up residence again in his ancestral homes, Hartiscor House and Hartiscor Castle, and that changed the family portrait quite a bit. Where before there'd been a doting grandfather, a proud daddy, a loving mummy and a bouncing baby boy, there was now also a brother and an uncle who, by his mere presence, cast the dark shadow of old hostilities, spoiling the cheery picture.

Of the two brothers it was Hubert who was openly hostile, his usual good humour deserting him whenever Rupert was about, whereas Rupert adopted a proper, if less than warm, manner. On the one hand, Nora couldn't blame Rupert for his reserve in the face of Hubert's open animosity. On the other, *did* she detect a certain snideness in Rupert's every chance remark, each glance?

Was Rupert subtly condescending toward Hubert, or was she imagining it? *Was* his attitude toward *her* patronizing, or was she imagining that, too? She wasn't sure. Still, sometimes she could almost *feel* Rupert's eyes burning into her, boring into her back, fixed on her face. Was he taking her measure? But wasn't that a natural enough curiosity about the woman of common background who had married his brother? Did he picture her as a trespasser, an opportunistic poacher? Or was it but a manifestation of his resentment against Hubert?

Then, she wondered about his feelings toward Hubie. Did Rupert see him as an encroachment on his ancestral terrain, resenting Jeffrey's affection for the baby, thinking of how Hubert had once displaced him in his mother's affections? Still, Rupert *did* say the right things – that Hubie certainly looked a healthy specimen, that he had a good nature, always gurgling and cooing, just as he remembered Hubert as a baby.

Sometimes his comments were even accompanied by a rare smile. But then Nora had to ask herself: was it a forced smile or not a smile at all but a smirk? A sneer, as if he *knew* that Hubie wasn't Hubert's son? Or was it that she herself was projecting, sensing an attitude that wasn't there – her *own* sympathetic reaction to Hubert's hostility?

Actually, from everything Hubert had said, she had formed a mental image of Rupert which was completely different from the reality. She had imagined him as darkly brooding – a kind of aristocratic Heathcliff, the churlish gypsy boy out of *Wuthering Heights*, the movie she'd seen at least five times as a young girl, entranced by its romantic, if tragic, qualities. (She had even visualized Rupert looking like the handsome Olivier.) But while Rupert *was* seemingly humourless, it was more that he was distant than brooding. And while he wasn't nearly as good-looking as Olivier, if one wanted to stretch a point, there *was* a slight resemblance – the elegant nose, the smouldering eyes, an almost palpable pent-up intensity.

This intensity was Rupert's most disturbing quality, Nora thought. Yet at the same time, she had to admit to herself, it was his most compelling, even attractive, feature.

But all this notwithstanding, Nora wondered how they were all going to continue living under the same roof under the circumstances. How could she raise Hubie in such an oppressive atmosphere and expect him to grow from a contentedly cooing baby into a happy boy? Something had to be done to effect a reconciliation between the two brothers, and while she wished Jeffrey would take the initiative, he obviously had no such intention. It was as if he were either oblivious to the situation or deliberately choosing to ignore it. If this was how it had been when the three Hartiscor children were growing up, with Lord Jeffrey seeing no disharmony and Countess Miranda showing such poor judgement as to make a pet of Hubert

at the expense of the other two, no wonder Anne had fled
. . . had run for her very life.

Then it occurred to Nora that maybe Jeffrey was
simply waiting for *her* to effect a reconciliation. Perhaps
that was part of the tacit bargain they had made that day
when Jeffrey first met her. If this was so, she could hardly
let him down.

Since she could scarcely approach Rupert and it *was*
Hubert who was the openly hostile brother, she begged
him to take a more conciliatory attitude towards Rupert.
But Hubert smiled at her tightly, going to the drinks table
in the library to pour himself a whisky, and said, '*Et tu,
Brute?*'

'Don't make a bad joke out of this, Hubert, and at
the same time imply that I'm being disloyal to you. I am
not taking Rupert's side and I'm not asking you to love
him. All I'm asking you to do is act a little bit nicer, a
little bit friendlier, and I'm sure Rupert will respond to
that and in turn, he'll act nicer and friendlier, too.'

Hubert tossed off his whisky and poured another.
'So little Nora Sunshine thinks that's all it takes, does
she?'

'Please, Hubert. I'm not trying to make *little* of
how you feel about Rupert. I'm sure whatever your
resentments are, they're well-founded. But they *are* a
hangover from your childhood and probably neither
you nor Rupert is responsible. The responsibility lies
with your parents and the British system of entail and
primogeniture that—'

Hubert's eyes slitted. 'Look at little Natalie Hall
from the country now. She's using words like "entail"
and "primogeniture", words she probably never heard
of before she came to London and got herself an education by marrying into the brilliant Hartiscor family.
Oh, we've schooled you well, little Nora, haven't we?
Now you can bounce phrases off Hubert's little pointed
head with the best of them.'

It was the first time Hubert had been even a tiny bit

sarcastic, but she forgave him. In his pain, he was just lashing out blindly. 'Oh, Hubert, it's not Rupert's fault that he's the older son . . . that he's going to inherit. How can you blame him?'

'You don't know anything about it, Nora, so the best thing you can do is keep out of it. Don't ask me to kiss his bloody ass and don't talk about things you don't understand!'

'But, Hubert, I *want* to understand.'

'Then understand *this*. Remember when I told you that if I got lucky, Rupert would get himself killed off in the war? With your innocent little heart you thought I was simply making a joke, one not in the best of taste but still, a joke. But it wasn't. It was my fondest dream, my most fervent wish. And then I cursed *God* the day Rupert returned from war. You see, I had prayed to Him at least a thousand times that Rupert wouldn't live to walk through the door again.'

Nora was shocked into silence. She could understand a childhood hostility generated by jealousy and small resentments lingering on into adult life. At best, their situation didn't lend itself to strong feelings of brotherly love even if Rupert had been a more lovable person to begin with, and Hubert less vulnerable. But a hostility of this magnitude! To *call* upon God to strike his brother dead? And Hubert, of all people, to whom almost everything had a humorous side . . . who could always manage to find something in any situation or subject to laugh at . . . even himself.

Then, having failed with Hubert, Nora felt she had to try with Rupert. But not wanting Hubert or Jeffrey to know that she was appealing to Rupert for his co-operation, she chose a time when she knew Rupert would be at home, and *they* wouldn't be – at six, since this was the time Jeffrey could usually be found having a whisky and soda at his favourite gentleman's club, the time Hubert was most often making the rounds of *his* favourite hangouts ('just keeping my ear to the ground for an interesting project . . .'), and the time Rupert invariably returned home from his office where he administered to the various Hartiscor enterprises.

Accordingly, dispensing with the footman's service so that she and he would be entirely alone, she was lying in wait for Rupert with the fire lit and radiating a cheery glow, and the tea table set in the Venetian sitting room (so designated because it was dominated by several Turner paintings from the artist's Italian period). She had chosen this room as her setting because Rupert had once idly mentioned that it was his favourite room – that he found its pale yellow and eggshell-blue colour scheme pleasing to his eye. She wanted Rupert in the best possible frame of mind when she prevailed upon him to extend his hand in friendship to his younger brother.

Rupert permitted himself a tiny smile as he sipped from the delicate Spode teacup. 'Forgive me, Nora, but aren't you being a bit presumptuous?'

'Perhaps I am, but you'll have to forgive me. When so much is at stake – a pleasant home for my child to grow up in – I can't afford to stand on ceremony or worry if I'm so rude as to violate the boundary lines of what you consider proper.'

'Well yes, I can see that you have a problem. And yes, I can understand that you're too upset to – as you put it – stand on ceremony. But this is a complicated matter between my brother and me, one of long standing. Did it ever occur to you that the easiest solution would be for you, your son and your husband simply to clear out? Oh, I know it will be difficult for Hubert to provide for his little family and that certainly must appear to you as a major problem . . . as if there weren't already *enough* problems for you to face, being married to our Hubert. But we don't have to talk of them since we're both well acquainted with *all* of them, aren't we?

'Still, the necessities of life – or should I say the more opulent luxuries of life since I'm sure that's what you feel

127

are at stake here – are really not something you have to be concerned about if the three of you were to strike out on your own. I'm sure Father would make provision for Hubert as he always has, and of course that would include you and Hubie.' Then he sighed pointedly before saying, 'As I suppose *I'll* have to as well when it's my turn.'

Despite her declaration about not standing on ceremony or caring if she were so rude as to be presumptuous, Nora felt ill. She'd made a humiliating mistake in approaching Rupert. He was being more than snide – he was being insulting, every bit as hateful as Hubert thought him, with those remarks about Hubert's inadequacies and the implications that she had married Hubert for his name and his father's fortune . . . for the opulent luxuries of life.

'You're right, Rupert,' she said, fighting for control so as not to give him the satisfaction of seeing her lose what remained of her dignity. 'I *was* presumptuous in coming to you, but not in the way you mean. I was presumptuous in thinking that you, as the older brother, would feel a responsibility to extend yourself, that you'd be big enough to overlook childhood grudges. I was presumptuous in thinking that you – the brother who will eventually inherit everything – might find in his heart a generosity of spirit for a younger brother who's less fortunate than you.'

'Less fortunate?' Rupert sneered. 'You make Hubert sound like a character out of *Oliver Twist*. Does Hubert have you reading Dickens now as part of your on-going education?'

She could feel herself losing control now and didn't care. No wonder Hubert hated him so much.

'Don't you patronize me, you arrogant son of a bitch! I might be an uneducated barmaid's daughter and you *want to think* that I married your brother for the name and the money, and the privilege of living in this house and wearing dresses like this' – she tugged at her dress, a Lanvin, – 'but it just isn't so. Yes, I have a wardrobe fit for a queen and yes, it's pleasant to take tea in a lovely room like this, but believe me, this is not the essence of a good or rewarding life. Your father told me that as a child you used to say that money was what made the world go round. I guess that was a clever thing for a little boy to say, but as an overbearing, nasty adult, I can see you haven't learned a bloody thing!

'It's *love*, Rupert, that makes the world go round, something you know nothing about. And while I can appreciate that you might wish us gone so that you wouldn't have to look at us so happy in our love for one another, I promise you you're never going to see that happen in your father's lifetime. He's still in charge and he wants us here and I made a promise to him that I would stay and do my best to live up to his expectations of me, and I don't intend to fail him.

'But you believe what you want. Because *you're* such a loveless bastard, I guess it makes you feel better *not* to believe that I married your brother because I loved him! And another thing. You don't have to concern yourself with my problems with Hubert. If you want to know the truth, I pity *you* because while you'll have the prestige and the fortune and the title, you'll never be the sweet and loving man your brother is or experience the kind of love Hubert and I share.'

With that said, her anger spent, she stared into her teacup. Despite her fierce words she was on the verge of tears. How could she have shamed Hubert like this, gone behind his back to beg this unfeeling bastard whom he rightfully despised to be *nice* to him, as though Hubert himself was nothing but a petulant child that had to be indulged. But then she looked up to see that the cold, hateful Rupert actually had tears streaming down his cheeks. *What in God's name?*

He leaned forward to grasp her hand, to hold on to it tightly. 'Forgive me, Nora, I beg you. Everything you said about me is true. I *have* been an impossible, insufferable, bloody bastard! But I beg you to understand.

129

The truth is I've always been jealous of Hubert. You see, I *do* know that love is what makes the world go round, at least it's what makes life worth living. And no matter what he did or didn't do, Hubert was the one everyone always loved. Oh, how Mother loved Hubert! And even Father after Anne left. It's me he respects, but it's Hubert he really cares about, whom he worries about. Even Anne – it was Hubert she always confided in. And now there's *you*. Who wouldn't be jealous of a brother who's lucky enough to be loved and so well by a woman like you? Can you understand, Nora?'

She nodded. How could she not? Rupert was still the little boy who had been 'tolerated' by his mother, not taken into her bed to be cuddled, coddled and loved.

'So will you forgive me?' he begged.

Her first tendency was to cry out, 'Of course!' But *was* it her place to forgive him or was it Hubert's? And if she herself forgave Rupert, would Hubert ever forgive *her*? Or would he forever see it as an act of betrayal?

Still, there was Jeffrey to consider. She had made a pact with him and he had made a place in his heart for *her* son. How could she not find a place in her heart for his older son who seemed to be as much in need as the younger?

Then she was startled to hear, 'Ah! What do we have here? And who's holding whose hand?'

It was Hubert standing in the doorway with a funny smile, and she realized that Rupert was still holding on to her hand. She disengaged the hand now to run to Hubert. 'Darling, Rupert and I have been having the most wonderful talk. He's been telling me how sorry he is that you and he haven't been friends all these years and how he wants it to be different. He *wants* to be your friend . . . our friend. He wants all of us to be one, happy family. What do you say to that?'

Hubert smiled and shrugged. 'Only an Englishman who's no gentlemen could refuse so generous an offer and never let it be said that Hubert Hartiscor is no gentleman.'

At first Nora suspected that Hubert was a bit swizzled.

But then she wasn't so sure about that when Rupert came over to extend his hand to Hubert, and Hubert lifted his right arm high, placing his hand out of Rupert's reach and wiggling his fingers, laughing. 'Oh, you don't want to shake this hand, big brother. I've just soiled it doing something with it that I shouldn't. You know how it is. But it's no matter since you've already shaken hands with Nora and God knows, she's a better man than either one of us.'

And then he laughed so hard that one would have thought he had just told the funniest joke on earth. He laughed so hard he had to wipe the tears from his eyes and then Nora was left to wonder how slender, really, was that thin, invisible line that separated laughing from crying. Probably no thicker than the line that separated love from hate.

Then for the second time that afternoon, she wondered if she had done the right thing . . . wondered if all this was going to end up being much more than she had bargained for . . . much, much more . . .

10

Although it was Hubie's second birthday they were celebrating that evening, it was Nora who was the recipient of a spectacular present from Jeffrey, a diamond and ruby tiara. 'I wanted you to have it to wear to the party tonight.'

'It must be the loveliest thing I've ever seen!'

'Yes, it is a beautiful piece. It was created by Cartier in 1925 here in London, and these are Burmese rubies which are considered the finest in the world.'

'But Jeffrey, it's not my birthday,' she protested. Still she ran over to the gilt-encrusted pier-mirror to try it on, holding her head this way and then that way. 'What have I done to deserve such a magnificent present?'

'You've wrought a miracle, undone all the harm that Miranda—' He broke off and began again. 'I don't know how you did it, but you've brought Rupert and Hubert together.'

Nora sighed, removed the tiara, put it down on the console table as if it were very heavy. 'Not *together*, not really, though Rupert's been wonderful. He's trying *very* hard. He's even getting down on all fours to play horsie with Hubie.'

She smiled, thinking about Rupert in his banker's grey suit, down on the floor, with Hubie yelling, 'Giddy-up!' digging his heels into Rupert's sides, whipping at him with a sofa pillow.

'And I suppose Hubert's trying too. At least he says, "Good morning" to Rupert every day at breakfast and sometimes he discusses sports with him. Yesterday he even asked Rupert what he thought of Dior's New Look and poor Rupert was quite thrown – he never heard of a New Look. But the thing is when Hubert speaks to Rupert there's a huge grin on his face and I suspect that all this friendship business is a big joke to him. That he's having us all on. I think, at best, an armed truce exists between them rather than friendship.' She smiled wistfully. 'In light of that do you think you want your tiara back? Maybe it's a little too grand for me anyway. It must be worth an enormous amount – a tiara fit for a duchess.'

'In that case, it's not grand enough. You should have a tiara that's fit for a queen.'

'Oh, Jeffrey, you *are* sweet. Much too good to me. But if you really want to give me a present, I'm willing to trade—' She held up the tiara as if ready to hand it back.

Jeffrey was alarmed. 'Nonsense! The tiara is yours. But what is it, my dear, that you want? What can I give you?'

'You can give *Hubert* something . . . something meaningful to do with himself, to give purpose to his day, rather than squandering it at the bookmaker's or Claridge's bar or—'

'I see. Do you have something specific in mind?'

'Well, Rupert has all the financial companies to run. I think it must be something on a par with that.'

'But what would that be? The mines? The farms? I hardly think that Hubert would be interested and I seriously doubt he'd contemplate leaving London for the rural life.'

'No, of course not. It has to be something that's suited to his talents.'

'But we've tried various things with Hubert, Nora,' Jeffrey said wearily. 'Nothing's ever worked out.'

'That doesn't mean we can just give up,' her voice sharpened. 'It only means we haven't hit on the right thing. And I've been thinking – a foundation might be the answer.'

'What kind of a foundation?'

'The Hartiscor Foundation to endow various endeavours for—' She groped for the right words. 'For the good of mankind. And Hubert will head it.'

'That sounds like an excellent idea but perhaps we should be more specific as to what kind of endeavours we're talking about. Medical research, endowments for the arts, what—?'

'We leave that to Hubert. He must be the one to make the decisions. He must be completely in charge. You have to stop treating him like a child. He's *not* a child. He's a man in his thirties and you must start treating him like a man.'

As she herself was trying damned hard to . . .

'Very well, it will be as you say. We'll get started on it at once. I'll speak to Rupert about it and—'

'Rupert? I'm not sure that's the best way to proceed.'

Jeffrey smiled at her now as if she were the child. 'I'm afraid you don't understand how these things work,

133

darling girl. A foundation must be funded. A great deal of money must be allocated. A trust will have to be set up and Rupert's the proper person to see to that. It's not like we can say to Hubert, "Here's the cookie jar, dear boy, help yourself to whatever you need and when the jar is empty, just let us know – we'll bake up a new batch."'

It was a kind of joke and Nora smiled politely but she wasn't convinced that was the way to proceed. Even if they were reasonable facsimiles of friends, Hubert would be put off, his back up, if Rupert held the purse strings. But she didn't see how she could argue the point with Jeffrey. As he said, she really didn't understand these things and neither did Hubert, for that matter.

'Then it's all settled,' Jeffrey said. 'And just think, with Rupert and Hubert working together, they might even get to be real friends. Now you must go upstairs to get ready for the party. Our guests will be arriving soon. I hope that you're wearing a gown that will go well with the tiara? We must show everyone what a real countess looks like.'

Nora was startled. *A real countess?* But the late Miranda had been the real countess, and she herself wasn't even a sham one. It was a funny slip of the tongue for Jeffrey to make and she chided him, 'Am I being demoted so quickly? Only minutes ago we were talking about a tiara fit for a queen, or at least a duchess. Now you're relegating me to a mere countess.'

As Hubert in his white tie and tails did up the hooks of her wine-red evening dress, Nora exulted over its colour. Even if she'd known that Jeffrey was going to give her the ruby tiara, she still couldn't have made a better choice.

'While I'm about it,' Hubert said, brushing the nape of her neck with a kiss to send goose bumps running down her spine, 'I might as well fasten your necklace in place, too. Are you going to wear your pearls? I think they'd

134

be exactly right nestling in that glorious cleavage.'

He buried his lips in the valley between her breasts and she bit her lip as the familiar tingling of desire futilely coursed through her body. But she only smiled teasingly at him. 'Oh, I know *you're* the fashion expert around here, m'Lord, but I think I won't wear any jewellery except for the ring you gave me for Christmas.' She wanted the tiara to be a surprise and she didn't plan on putting it on until after Hubert went downstairs before her. 'Between my ring and this gown I think I'll be quite fancy enough, no?'

'Quite!' He rolled his eyes appreciatively. 'And you're right. Why clutter up the effect of that exquisite view with any distracting note?' He kissed each breast in turn.

She shivered at this caress of his lips and thought that if nothing else, Hubert *was* a gentleman. Even if he didn't follow through, at least he always said the right thing and went through all the right preliminary motions.

'Are you ready then? Shall we go down?'

'No, you're to go down ahead of me. It's Jeffrey's plan. He wants to handle the reception line along with you and Rupert, and then after everyone's here, I'm to come down with Hubie. Poor baby. It's his birthday party but at least half of adult London is going to be here. Your father's invited every last lord in the House, but not another child and we're serving only refreshments unfit for two-year-old consumption. I'm sure Hubie would gag if we tried to feed him an oyster.'

'Why did you allow Father to take over the guest list? The whole party? You really must take a firmer stand with him. Miranda would never have let him get away with that.'

'Really, Hubert. First of all, I'm *not* your mother. And do you really think I'd get into a row with your father over Hubie's party? I think it's terribly sweet of him to take such an interest. He's so proud of Hubie I'm just happy he wants to show him off to his friends.

Besides, I'll throw another party for Hubie next week with little boys and girls and party hats and balloons, all the proper birthday-boy treats.'

'I'm relieved to hear that. But why don't you let Nanny bring Hubie down so that you can receive the guests too?'

'No, that would spoil the effect of the grand entrance your father wants us to make. You see, Hubie and I are going to match. Me in this dress and Hubie in his little red velvet suit. Won't that be a spectacular entrance?'

'Smashing. I'll be waiting with bated breath.'

Poised at the top of the staircase, tiara in place, and with Hubie clutching her hand, Nora was unprepared for *how* spectacular an entrance they were making. First a buzz swept through the assembled crowd, and then there was a hush, followed by a total silence, with all eyes fixed on her and Hubie as they descended the stairs slowly, each step a major accomplishment for Hubie's stubby little legs. It seemed as if *everyone*, not only Hubert, was waiting with bated breath.

There wasn't a sound until they finally took the last step on to the black-and-white marbled floor and Jeffrey broke the silence with his applause at which all his old friends came rushing up to wish the birthday boy happiness, but with all eyes focused on her breathtaking tiara. And then it hit her! When Jeffrey had said, 'We must show them what a real countess looks like,' it had been no slip of the tongue. It *was* Countess Miranda's tiara she was wearing! Then when she saw Hubert's paper-white face and Rupert's stunned look, she knew that not only was she wearing their mother's tiara, but that it was an electrifying jolt to both her sons.

As she and Hubert prepared for bed, Nora set the tiara down on the dressing table. Grimacing, Hubert nudged it with a finger. 'Shouldn't you put that thing away in the safe in Father's study? Or call Rowens to do it?'

'It's so late and Rowens must be exhausted. It can wait until tomorrow morning. Unless the sight of it upsets you?'

When Hubert didn't answer, she went on: 'Is it because it reminds you of your mother? It *was* hers, wasn't it?'

This time Hubert answered but barely. 'Yes . . .'

'Oh, I'm so sorry. It must have been a shock for you. So painful to remember your mother wearing it. Sometimes the most wonderful memories are the ones hardest to bear.'

'What are you talking about? What wonderful memories?'

'When your mother was all dressed up for a special party, wearing her tiara. She was probably so happy and looking very beautiful. That would be a wonderful memory for you – remembering her that way. But of course it would hurt at the same time because she's gone . . .'

'But it wasn't that way at all. There *was* a party here that night—'

'What night?'

'The first time Mother wore the tiara. It was her birthday and Father had just given it to her. Most of the people here tonight were there that night, too. And yes, Miranda *was* looking very beautiful, standing at the head of the stairs ready to descend. But that was the first and only time she wore the tiara. It was the *last* time . . .'

'I don't understand—'

'That was the night Miranda fell down the stairs and broke her neck.'

'Oh, my God, I didn't know! You never told me how she died!'

'You never asked.'

'But Jeffrey didn't say a word. When he gave me the tiara I didn't even know that it had been your mother's. All he said was that it came from Cartier's and – Well, if I had known I never would have worn it. You must

137

believe me! Frankly, I don't even know why he gave it to me under the circumstances. It must be a terrible memory for him, too.'

'One would think so, wouldn't one? Especially since he was standing right next to her when she fell and if he'd reacted a bit quicker perhaps he could have—'

'Oh, dear God, how awful for him! I wonder why he even *kept* the tiara. Why he didn't sell it or something? Why do you think he gave it to me?'

'Perhaps he wanted to pretend . . .'

'Pretend *what*? That I'm your mother?'

'Hardly,' Hubert laughed hollowly. 'If it came to that, he'd much rather pretend you were Anne. Maybe he just wants to pretend to himself that you're the Countess of Hartiscor.'

'What does *that* mean? You're not making any sense.'

The whole thing didn't make any sense. Hadn't Jeffrey realized that it would be a terrible shock for everyone who remembered that night to see the woman they thought was his daughter-in-law walking down the same stairs wearing the same tiara? Especially shocking for Hubert and Rupert! How could Jeffrey have been so insensitive? It was so unlike him.

She picked up the tiara as if it burned her fingers and put it away in one of the vanity drawers to get it out of sight. 'Do you know what I'm going to do? I'm going to give it back to him tomorrow. Then he can sell it, or lock it away in a vault or whatever. He could even give it to Rupert's bride when he marries, if Rupert's willing.'

'*If* Rupert ever marries which I doubt he'll ever do in *my* lifetime,' Hubert muttered, sitting down wearily on the edge of the bed to remove his shoes. 'But you won't give it back.'

'Why do you say that?'

'Because Father would be upset and you're Miss Sunshine. You wouldn't do anything to upset Father, now would you?'

'I know you think you're being smart,' Nora bristled,

138

'but you're right. I wouldn't *want* to do anything to upset your father. Not deliberately, anyway. Why would I?'

'Don't ask me. You're the one with all the answers. But don't worry, Sunny. Even if you stop being Nora Sunshine, you still have your other title to fall back on: Lady Hartiscor, the Happy Matchmaker. She who brings people – all kind of unlikely people – together again in the happiest of matches.'

She didn't have to ask him what he was getting at. It was just one more barely oblique reference to her efforts to effect a reconciliation between him and Rupert.

Then it dawned on her – the real reason Jeffrey had given her Miranda's tiara. This afternoon he'd said it was in appreciation of the miracle she had wrought undoing all the harm Miranda had precipitated between her sons. In Jeffrey's mind giving her the tiara constituted some kind of convoluted trade-off – an evening out of the score. But it had been a bad idea. Besides, no matter what Jeffrey thought, she had managed to undo very little. Hubert was hardly less bitter about Rupert than he had ever been.

And what had Hubert meant by that remark: *if Rupert ever marries which I doubt he'll ever do in my lifetime?* But now was hardly the time to open up another can of worms. One of them might bite.

'Oh, Hubert, I'm sorry about everything. I was just trying to help.'

'I know, Nora, I know,' he said tiredly, dropping a shoe as if it were too heavy to hold. 'And I'm sorry about what I just said. You're the last person that I want to hurt. But there are some things . . . some people, even *you* can't help. Sometimes, even you must throw in the towel.'

Does he mean that I have to give up on him? It was true that he never mentioned their getting married any more and she tried to remember when it was precisely that he had stopped.

'Sorry, mate, but I'm fresh out of towels.' She grinned

139

at him and kneeled to help him remove his socks.

'What are you doing now?' he asked in exasperation.

'You seem so tired. I'm just helping you out.'

She had planned to tell Hubert about what she and his father had discussed before the party and the decision they had come to – that they were going to set up this marvellous foundation to dispense largesse to deserving projects and *he* was going to be in charge. But now was clearly not the time.

No, she would let Jeffrey tell him about it, directing him to leave her out of it entirely. The idea would be much more palatable to Hubert if he thought it had originated entirely with his father, a symbol of the faith Jeffrey had in him. And she would speak to Rupert, too – ask him to keep a hands-off policy once the financial details were settled, to leave the rest of it entirely up to Hubert. Let it be *his* effort altogether.

For now she had a concern that had to take precedence and any talk of matters irrelevant to that concern was an intruder in the night. An intruder in the conjugal bedroom where she had to continue to wage her campaign to transform their would-be marriage into a very ordinary one. One in which she and Hubert made their good nights the way ordinary husbands and wives were supposed to, and not like two great chums who, out of necessity, shared a huge room with only one very small bed.

Tonight, just like nearly every other night of their marriage, she'd try again even if it often seemed she was losing ground rather than gaining it. But how could she give up? That was part of the original bargain she'd made with Hubert when she had accepted his proposal of sweet convenience – that she would never give up on him.

It was also part of the implicit bargain she had made with Jeffrey. And now there was Hubie to fight for, too, since he was part of the same bargain. Not to mention that she loved Hubert no less than she loved

Hubie, loved Hubert no less than that first time she had tried to seduce him.

Now instead of talking about the Foundation she turned on the radio so that there would be music to make love to, or at least, music for her to dance to. Then she was whirling about, a nude nymphette in a dreamlike trance, caught up in the hope that somehow, suddenly, Hubert would be entranced – at last seduced, set on fire with a burning desire. Oh yes, any moment now he'd call for her to come to him, to impale herself upon the erect and throbbing symbol of his manhood . . .

11

It had been on Nora's mind for some time that she *could* seek outside help for her and Hubert's problem – a medical solution. She was aware of hormone therapy, had even heard of a serum made from bulls' urine (or was it live cells extracted from the testicles of unborn bulls?), and had read of tonics that wrought miracles. In addition, she had listened to the gossip continuously making the rounds at parties about what was going on in those infamous Swiss clinics.

A typical story went: 'Did you hear about Ronnie Ashton? He hadn't had an erection in his entire life until he went to the Weiner Institute in Lausanne where they pumped his ass so full of monkey glands with a horse-sized needle the next thing anyone knew he was under arrest for trying to rape a woman on Kingsbridge Road in broad daylight! He was walking around so horny the damn fool couldn't even wait for the cover of dark.'

Another story related that a cousin of Fruity Marlowe, who was related to Lady Stilton on his mother's side and lived in a pink chalet just above Vevey to escape the taxes, was given a potion at some clinic which was made from the horns of rhinos ground into powder. It had such powerful results that his wife had to be 'sewn up' to repair the damage, the operation being performed by a London surgeon who was known on the q.t. to work on women who needed to present themselves as virgins.

Then again, if one had *any* flagging organ in need of revitalization, there was a spa in Zurich where they injected a mysterious formula directly into the organ itself, which was awfully convenient if one wanted to visit one's money stashed away in one of Zurich's banks at the same time.

But she could hardly ask Hubert to go to Lausanne to submit his bum (as well as his tender sensibilities) to the horse's needle on the off-chance that he wouldn't turn into a monkey, or to Zurich to have his prick pricked.

Of course, there was the analyst's couch. She knew that if she insisted, Hubert would comply with her demands to undergo psychotherapy. But the idea of *forcing* Hubert to expose his problem . . . his inadequacies . . . to a third party, was repugnant. If he were to choose that path himself she'd be delighted but what good could come of coercion? As her mother always said, 'You can lead a horse to water but you can't make him drink.' Or as Hubert put it, 'You can lead a hor-ti-culture but you can't make her like it.'

She was afraid theirs had to be a private war waged without benefit of allies and as far as she could see, seduction was her only weapon. Accordingly, she tried various costumes: barmaid, French maid, little country maid. She tried being luscious siren, shy siren, depraved siren – satin on her body, filthy words on her lips. She even tried dressing up as a little girl in white socks and Mary Janes, having read that 'doing it' with little girls was a fantasy that appealed to many men.

A nanny with a sharp voice, ruler in hand, was another

fantasy, but Hubert only burst out laughing, 'Sorry, darling, but it just isn't you.' Then she burst out laughing too, grateful that they, at least, could still laugh about it all.

Occasionally, she won one of the skirmishes and then for a couple of days, she went about her routine bubbling over with hope, singing bits and scraps of happy tunes. But mostly, nothing worked even though it was the most intense kind of effort – humiliating, frustrating and exhausting, anything but sexy. And while she knew that that wasn't the way love was supposed to be, it still didn't make her love Hubert any less. Sometimes she thought it only made her love him all the more, the struggle intensifying her own passion.

She had always heard the proverb that anything worth having was worth fighting for. She changed that to anyone worth loving was worth the struggle, and she never doubted for a moment that Hubert was worth every drop of love she had in her, except for the love that already belonged to Hubie.

Then when even the tiniest of victories became only a distant memory, she still didn't consider hoisting the white flag though Hubert – never one for the long haul – was clearly losing heart. But as he grew more and more unresponsive, his lack of interest only served to spur her on to new heights of creativity, even if in her heart of hearts she knew that these were acts of desperation.

She determined to develop more expertise then, consulting various manuals. Still, she came up with very little that she already didn't know or hadn't tried. The only dividend of any significance was that her vocabulary in this area became a bit more extensive: Indian names for sexual practices that sounded too impractical to follow, a few Latin terms and an assortment of vulgarisms for acts and objects with which she was already familiar under their more common labels.

The terms only filled her head with questions and

143

certain pictures that increased her agony all the more. Hubert refused to hold still for her, forcing her to speculate if sex was more acceptable to him when performed by a man, and *why*? Did it really make any difference who was the perpetrator? As for anal penetration, why was it that *her* anus was less acceptable, less interesting to him than a male lover's? Weren't her buttocks as lovely as any man's and could the male organ really differentiate between male cheeks and female cheeks?

Her desperation increased by the day, but she would not give up and she went back to reading whatever she could find, discovering something called urethral masturbation which she had never heard of before but which was considered highly effective in stimulating carnal passion. True, it sounded bizarre but perhaps bizarre translated into exotic which could translate into erotic which could translate ultimately into plain lovemaking, neither bizarre nor fancy but fulfilling.

In urethral masturbation, she read, the passage from the bladder to the outside was stimulated by inserting objects into the urethra and moving them about gently, a form of stimulation more effective in women since an object so small as a hairpin or even a rubber band (*A rubber band? What did one do, precisely, with a rubber band?*) could be the tool of insertion, a woman's urethra being extraordinarily sensitive situated as it was between the clitoris and the vagina with nerve connections to both. But with a man, a longer object was needed – a piece of tubing, a length of wire—

Then she could bear it no longer and flung the book against the wall. Was she going mad to even think of teasing the man she loved into performing sex by sticking a piece of wire up his willie? What would she be willing to do next? Dress up like some ruddy bloke, hook up a dildo (one of those kinky Japanese ones with two heads) to her snapper and stick it up his arse? Or sneak a few dashes of Spanish fly into his brandy and make him so crazy with

144

the itches that he would be so mad as to have the itch for the likes of her?

She buried her face in her hands and sobbed helplessly. All she wanted seemed like such a small thing, a simple thing. Nothing bizarre, hardly exotic, not extraordinary in any way. All she wanted was for him to love her like any plain and simple man might, and not like his best friend.

The possibility that she was fighting the wrong enemy became a suspicion only when the Hartiscor Family Foundation blew up, in a manner of speaking, in their collective faces. And it was not with an explosive pop but only a diminutive hiss, more like a tired balloon, its air escaping into the atmosphere without so much as a ripple.

In not quite a year the Foundation, funded with an extraordinary amount of money – two million pounds – was bankrupt, the last drop of its life's blood exhausted, and the hundred or so recipients of its scientific grants (such as a Dr Milton Crawford who was conducting a study into the sex life of the tussah in a flat in Mayfair) were left high and dry with their studies incomplete. There wasn't one finished report, nor was there a shred of evidence to be found anywhere that humankind had benefited in any way, manner or form.

Jeffrey was, of course, furious, not so much with Hubert as with Rupert whom he had charged with the administering of the trust. But all Rupert would say in his own defence was that he had tried to endow Hubert with as much responsibility, fiscal and otherwise, as possible since that was their purpose in establishing the Foundation. They'd done it not so much to aid humanity in general but Hubert in particular, to give him something worthwhile to do. He did *not* reveal that he had done this at Nora's behest, that she had implored him to employ a *laissez-faire* policy with Hubert. But when Nora herself told Jeffrey as much, he scoffed. 'Rupert had no business listening to you. His conduct was reprehensible.

145

All he did was give Hubert enough rope to hang himself. You're blind to certain facts when it comes to Hubert but Rupert knew better – *knew* he wasn't to be trusted.'

'What are you implying?' Nora demanded angrily, defensive as always when it came to Hubert. 'Why isn't he to be trusted? Because he's a fool or because he's a cheat?'

But Jeffrey said that the whole topic was too painful to talk about, begged her to desist.

When she went back to Rupert to recount her conversation with Jeffrey, Rupert smiled sadly. 'You needn't have gone to Father. I could have told you what he'd say. But what conclusion have *you* come to after talking with him? Who is to blame for this two-million-pound fiasco? You, because you're an innocent and asked me to give Hubert a free hand, or me because my conduct was irresponsible – that I gave Hubert autonomy when I knew he couldn't handle it? Or is Hubert to blame because he's a fool or a cheat, or a little of each?'

'You tell me, Rupert. What do you think?'

'I think the fault rests with a *what* rather than a *who* – something called a lack of moral fibre.'

'You're referring to *Hubert's* lack of moral fibre, I take it?' she asked resentfully, defensive again.

'I think we must start with Hubert's since his *is* outstanding, but then we must proceed to yours since you, too, display a lack of moral fibre, a weakness of character, when you refuse to admit that Hubert has this lack. And then I must confess to my *own* weakness of character.'

'Oh, I'm glad you're not letting yourself off the hook,' she said caustically. 'So tell me, Rupert, how did you display *your* weakness of character?'

'I didn't have the strength to resist giving Hubert his head when I knew very well that I shouldn't.'

'And is that what your father meant when he said your behaviour was reprehensible?'

'I suppose, but Father is not one to talk. He displays

his own lack of moral fibre when he tries to get others to do what he doesn't have the taste to do himself, or tries to lay off his guilts on others.'

'Now what does *that* mean?' Nora was losing her patience. They were getting nowhere with this philosophical discussion. 'What guilts are you talking about?'

'You know how Father always makes it sound like we'd have been one happy family if not for Miranda. As if *everything* was her fault. Well, it wasn't – not *everything*.'

The last thing she wanted to get into now was a discussion about the relationship that had existed between Jeffrey and Miranda. She had enough trouble dealing with Hubert's and her relationship. 'Well, who knows about these things? I'm sure that in any family there are always resentments. But speaking of resentments – your father said you gave Hubert enough rope to hang himself. That sounds like he was implying that you did so deliberately knowing that Hubert would make a mess of things. Is *that* true?'

Rupert laughed. 'Oh that. Father has this thing about people having enough rope to hang themselves. You might say it runs in the family. There was an Earl of Hartiscor back in the seventeenth century who hanged himself from the rafters and then in our own century, there's my sister, Anne.'

'Anne hanged herself?' Nora was stunned. 'But I thought she was alive in Australia . . . that she just considered herself dead to her family.'

'Father didn't tell you that. He wouldn't. His way is simply to refuse to talk about things, especially Anne. It must have been Hubert.'

'Hubert *did* say something about Anne being dead, but I guess I misunderstood. I thought he was talking figuratively.'

Had she misunderstood? But what did it matter? It was only Hubert who mattered and there was much she still didn't understand. 'So finally we're down to the bottom line,' she said. 'Considering your family's predilection for hanging themselves, and knowing that giving Hubert complete autonomy might well be a disaster, you still allowed him to run it, and I want to know *why*. Why, Rupert, why?'

'But I thought you understood. I went against my better judgement and my father's specific orders for one reason only – because *you* asked me to.' He gazed into her eyes. 'Don't you know, Nora, that I would do *anything* for you?'

It was time to end their talk, she thought, but wanting to make light of what he'd just said, she laughed, 'In that case I'd better be very careful about what I ask you to do for me.' Then she turned to leave.

'Yes,' he laughed too. 'Especially if what you have in mind is *murder* . . .' Then he asked: 'What about Hubert?'

Startled, she spun around. 'What *about* Hubert?'

It was foolish of her, of course, but she was relieved when all Rupert said then was, 'Have you asked *him* why he mucked up?'

Perhaps she might have if she knew where Hubert was but she didn't. She had seen him only once since the news of the Foundation's bankruptcy had broken, and that was only when he had come home to change his clothes before leaving again for ports in a storm where nothing more demanding than pushing money across a polished bar was required of him.

But she wasn't about to tell Rupert that. 'I don't have to ask him. Obviously, like you, he used poor judgement.'

'*Touché*, Nora, *touché*. Forgive me if I offended you.'

She sighed. She *was* offended . . . *and* angry, but only with herself. One shouldn't ask questions if one wasn't prepared for the answers. And wasn't she – just like Rupert accused Jeffrey of doing – trying to lay off guilts by blaming others?

'It's all right, Rupert. I appreciate your honesty and that you thought you were acting out of friendship.'

'We're still friends, then?'

'Of course, Rupert.'

'But just in case you *do* decide to ask Hubert a few questions, would you ask him one for me? The project the doctor in that fancy Mayfair flat was working on – the sex life of the tussah? Well, I'd love to know what a tussah is.'

'The tussah is a worm.'

'And you knew *that* without even asking? Astonishing!'

'Not really. You see, Hubert often talks about worms. He thinks they're fascinating.'

What she didn't care to disclose was that she believed Hubert's preoccupation with the species was because that was how he saw himself – a lowly creature wriggling about on the ground. It was only a shame that so much money that could have done a lot of good had been wasted on something Hubert already knew – that the tussah and the rest of his species not only had a wretched sex life, but were indeed the lowliest of God's creatures and besides, who really gave a damn?

Still, that didn't stop her from going to Jeffrey with a new proposal soon after. 'The problem with the Foundation as far as Hubert was concerned was that it was more a matter of administration than something really up Hubert's alley or suited to his talents. But an art gallery would put all his best talents to use. I think that's the answer and it would require a very small investment compared to the Foundation.'

Jeffrey quickly acquiesced. 'Of course. Anything you want, Nora. I'd do anything for you.'

Then she only wished that what he said hadn't been that close to what Rupert had said and that he – Hubert's father – was doing it for Hubert, rather than for the woman he believed was Hubert's wife.

12

Nora and Hubert were planning a gala, their supposed fifth anniversary only a week away and, feeling like the worst kind of fraud as well as a desperate fool, Nora planned one more seduction scene. Maybe this one would be a triumph, she prayed, the *pièce de résistance* Hubert would not be able to resist. Then maybe they'd be able to look into each other's eyes when the subject of their getting married came up, rare as those occasions had become.

She was nude except for black shiny boots and a black mask which covered half her face. In one hand she held a whip, in the other a black scarf and a white silk handkerchief. A voice, clipped and cold, whipped out Hubert's orders: he was to undress himself and kneel before her so that she could blindfold him with the scarf and gag him with the handkerchief, after which he was to lie face down on the four-poster bed with his legs spread. Hubert's eyes turned to the bed to see that ropes were already attached to all four of its posts. Then when he looked at her again, she saw the expression on his face and it wasn't one of sexual arousal – it was a look of horror and then *she* was filled with horror.

Doesn't he know that this is only one more of my silly fantasies? That even if I blindfold him, gag him, flay him with the black snake, criss-cross his body with bloody welts, I couldn't really hurt him. How could I when I love him so?

Then she saw the tears in his eyes and she tore the mask from her face. 'Oh Hubert, why are you crying? Don't you know how much I love you?'

'I do. And I see what the love of me has brought you to. This final degradation! Isn't that reason enough to cry?'

She dropped the whip as if it were burning her fingers. 'Hubert, no! Please, don't! I—'

'All these years you've played the masochist so well. No matter what I did you kept loving me while I kept breaking your heart. But you went on trying to make me into something I can't be. And now this! From masochism to sadism. Why can't you get it through your head? I'm a poof, a fag and I'm never going to love you the way you want to be loved, and your turning yourself into less of a woman with these grotesque charades isn't going to make a better man of me. All you'll succeed in doing will be to defile yourself more than I've already defiled you.'

'Stop, Hubert, stop!'

'No, *you* stop! Stop debasing yourself. How humiliated you must feel dressing up like a trick dog in the circus, trying to win my sexual favours. And for what? Why don't you know what everyone else knows? That I'm not worth it.'

'Hubert, please! I'm so sorry!'

'But do you even know what you're sorry for? For humiliating me by humiliating yourself? Or only for trying to turn me around with a whip? Oh, Nora,' he said mournfully, 'I might have allowed you to be a masochist, but I refuse to let you be a sadist. Not my sweet, warm, loving girl. If you love me, then don't let me do this to you! You think it's nothing – another trick that you're willing to try in the name of love, but you don't know how it corrupts the soul.'

'No, Hubert, no!'

'If you won't give up for your sake, then do it for mine. Don't make me a party to the corruption of your soul. Don't you understand? You make me feel like I can't sink any lower. Let me put it this way – if you're a real sadist, then you'll go on with it. But if you really love me, you'll give it up!'

151

She rushed to him to press his face to her. 'I promised you I'd never give up!' But even as she spoke she knew that she might have to break her promise. She had no choice. Still she whispered bitterly, 'But I promised . . .'

'Oh Nora, I thought I'd taught you to be a sophisticated woman and by now, God knows, you've had enough experience to know about promises. Some promises are made *only* to be broken and some promises can never be kept no matter how hard the heart cries out.' He pulled away from her. 'For once, I'm giving the orders and what we're going to do is get married finally so that Hubie has the Hartiscor name legitimately and then we're going to get a divorce.'

'No, I'll marry you, but I'll never divorce you!'

'Oh, for God's sake, Nora! Get on with it and get yourself a bloody lover!'

She looked into his eyes. 'Is that what *you've* done?'

'Not yet. Not once since the day we've been together.'

She believed him. 'But you *want* to? *Yearn* to . . . ?'

'*Need* to . . .'

'I see.' And she did. 'Well, then you must.'

There was a great silence as he fully absorbed her words. That she had, at last, released him.

'And you'll marry me, then, and divorce me?'

'No. Marry or not, I'll never leave you.'

'But if we stay together, you *will* take a lover? Tell me you'll take a lover! I want you to!'

She shook her head sorrowfully. 'I don't know if I can. Maybe someday . . . After I've learned how to love you less. No, I take that back. I will *never* love you less. Make that when I learn to love you like my best friend.' She smiled at him even as she licked at the tears salting her lips.

He put his arms around her to hug her tightly. 'You really should marry and divorce me, you know. Start all over. Hubie would have the Hartiscor name and Father loves you. He'd provide for you both. He'd probably even give you a dowry for your second time around.'

152

She covered his mouth with her fingertips. 'No, Hubert, no dowry. I'm not going anywhere where I'll need one.' Even as she spoke she yearned for him, ached for him to make love to her.

Will the ache ever stop?

She tried to smile. 'I told you long ago, I'm a clinger. The only way you're ever going to be free of me is when one of us is dead. And maybe not even then. Most probably I'll follow you into the grave trying to pull you out. Or if I'm there first, I'll drag you in after me. No, Hubert Hartiscor, you don't get rid of me so easily . . .'

He didn't laugh as she thought he might. 'You make it sound like a curse. And it's never been that. Not even with all the pain. You've been the best thing that's ever happened to me. Hubie too. I *do* love him, you know.'

'I know that, Hubert—' She tried so hard not to cry but it didn't work. 'And you've been a wonderful father, really you have. Hubie loves you very much.'

His lips twisted into a grimace of a smile. 'Some people would say what a lucky man I am with a sweet little boy for a son and a woman who loves me so much she won't even cheat on me when I beg her to.'

She wiped at the tears with the back of her hand. 'Well, even a charmer like you can't have *everything* you want, my darling. But one thing you must promise me and *mean* it. You *will* be discreet in taking a lover, won't you? For Hubie's sake, for your father's.'

'For Hubie's sake, anyway. But what about you, Nora? What do I do for *your* sake?'

She realized how tired she was then and she sat down on the edge of the chaise to look up at him. 'There are several things you can do for me. You can continue to try and get along with Rupert, for everyone's sake, even if it kills you.'

'Oh God, Nora. You may think you're being funny, but it probably will, you know. Kill me.' He came over to sit on the floor next to the chaise.

153

'I'm sure not and it will mean so much to your father.'

'I wonder. They're both so clever, Father and Rupert. God knows what they're dreaming up. I wouldn't be surprised if one of them was plotting how to kill off the black sheep.'

He was kidding, of course, a bit of black humour, and she smiled sadly: 'You *are* a fool, why would they want you dead?'

'Oh, maybe because I'm a dark blot on the precious family name or maybe because they're both in love with the fool of a black-sheep's wife and each one wants her for his very own.'

She couldn't tell now if he were clowning or dead serious, but she would have to play it as if he were just teasing. 'Oh, what an impossibly daft thing to say. Really, Hubert, you are a sweet but impossible fool!' She leaned down to kiss his brow, thinking it was such a lovely brow.

'Ah, but that's the paradox and possibly the key to the puzzle. *I'm* the fool who has you and doesn't know what to do with you and they're the ones not only clever enough to want you, but smart enough to know exactly what to do with you, and then some. Tell me, Nora, what happens when one fool comes up against two sharpers too clever by far for the fool's good?'

But now, played out emotionally, Nora couldn't bear to go on with this conversation. 'Enough of your nonsense, Hubert Hartiscor, and I'm quite serious now. I love you no matter what, and one thing I will not tolerate is you running yourself down. I won't hear another word about your being either a fool or a black sheep.'

Wearily, she leaned back in the chaise. Only then, she remembered that she was still done up for the farcical seduction scene that had been scheduled to take place and feeling ridiculous, she sat up to remove the black boots.

But Hubert pushed her back against the pillows. 'Here, let me.' He pulled off each boot, kissing each toe

154

in turn, and she bit her lips not to let a moan escape her lips. Then, after tenderly covering her nude body with the pale pink cashmere throw, he asked, 'What else can I do for you? And don't mention either Rupert's name or Father's, I warn you.'

'You can try very hard to make a go of the art gallery. Its success will please me more than you can imagine.'

'Granted. I will try very hard to make the art gallery a brilliant success. What else?'

'Set an example for our son. Be sweet and kind, good and true, strong and brave.'

'I swear I will to the best of my ability. And that's a vow. But you. I must do something specifically for *you*.'

'All right then,' she tried to make a joke of it. 'Swear you'll never love another woman as much as you love me.'

He got up from the floor to lean over her. 'Oh, Nora, *you're* the fool. Don't you know that no matter with whom I *make* love, I'll never love *anybody* the way I love you?'

She felt as if she were breaking apart inside.

'Oh, Hubert, kiss me! Kiss me quick! Kiss me and tell me you love me over and over and over again! And then just this *once*, make love to me . . . the very best way you can!'

First tearing off his clothes, then stripping away the cashmere throw that separated their bodies, he did all of these things – he kissed her quickly, he told her over and over again that he loved her, and then he made love to her the very best way that he could . . .

Later as Hubert slept in her arms, Nora thought that as pure sex the lovemaking hadn't been brilliant, but at the same time it had been an exquisite act of love. And whether or not they ever legally married, that was something to hold on to because whatever else it was, this act of lovemaking was the last time she and Hubert would

155

ever again share an intimate physical expression of their love. This part of their lives was over for ever . . .

13

For a long time Hubert was so discreet Nora had no inkling if he had a lover or several, or how often he loved, or where. They never talked about it. Part of their tacit understanding was that it was not a matter for discussion. But one day dropping by at the gallery on the off-chance Hubert would be free to take her to lunch, she discovered him in a back room making love to an assistant, Pepe, a small black man from the Indies.

Heartsick (would she ever be able to erase the study in black and white from her mind – the weird juxtaposition of the main elements of the composition against a blur of immaterial background), she spoke only of discretion. He *had* promised to be discreet. But incredibly, Hubert insisted he had been discreet. After all, he *had* used the back room.

She was infuriated. How dare he think he could laugh off his outrageous behaviour by treating it as a joke? Her hand reached out with a will of its own to crack his face. But then immediately she burst into tears, not sure why she was crying. Because she had lost control? Or because, while she had granted him permission to take a lover, the reality of it was too much to bear?

'Oh, very well,' Hubert, moved by her tears, said ruefully, 'I suppose it *was* a bit of poor timing on my part, but at the time, the timing seemed perfect.'

Another joke . . . Again rage engulfed her and when he smiled at her, showing her his dimples – as if this would assure her not being able to stay angry with him

156

– her arm ached with the urge to crack his face again, but she resisted.

'And now, what about lunch? The Savoy?'

Lunch? The Savoy? He is incredible!

Her arm swung up again but this time he caught it in mid-air. 'Oh, all right. It was *definitely* a bit of poor judgement. Now, are you satisfied?' He released her arm which dropped limply to her side, the anger gone, replaced by despair. *A bit of poor judgement? Or a lack of moral fibre? A weakness of character?* Was it possible that Hubert had never really known the difference between what was and wasn't outrageous behaviour? Was there an actual void – a blank, in some corner of his brain?

'Are you upset because of the gentleman in question's colour?'

'Oh Hubert, this has nothing to do with anyone's colour! It's this whole sordid affair – carrying on with an *employee* in a public place of business, never mind the back room or the front. It's in the worst possible taste and the Hubert that I know and love is *famous* for his exquisite taste. Oh, I don't pretend to understand the manner of your passion but surely you can confine it to what is appropriate. Or is it that you're so far gone you've lost all sense of what constitutes appropriate behaviour?'

He gave her a crooked grin. 'What makes you think I ever had one?'

She was taken aback by the question. *What, indeed?*

But what was the point of going on with this? Nothing she could possibly say would change anything. Accordingly, she pasted a smile on her lips, redid her face and they set off for the Savoy where over a salad, an excellent fillet of sole and a fine Sauterne, a subdued Hubert promised to do better, for whatever his promise was worth.

This time Hubert's promise was worth about six months until he was arrested in a public washroom in Victoria Station for behaviour best described as unbecoming to an English gentleman. Her heart was broken all over again,

157

but she was grateful that, at least, the whole business never made the tabloids, thanks to the Hartiscor influence and probably a great deal of hush money.

When a silently contemptuous Rupert (who could really blame him?) brought a shamed Hubert home from the lock-up, she took Hubert to their room, which now had two beds instead of one. There, instead of lecturing him, she took him into her arms, but only to comfort him, much as she did with little Hubie when things did not go his way. Still, she wondered: a lack of moral fibre? No sense of what constituted appropriate behaviour? *Or is it simply a deficiency of will?* An inability to make the required effort to curb one's excesses, no matter how excessive . . .

Then she realized that *all* of these flaws – *flaws of character in an otherwise perfect physical specimen* – had always been there, existing as a completely separate entity from his sexuality, plain enough for anyone with a grain of sense to see. Only *she* hadn't been in full possession of *her* senses. She had been too absorbed in her own obsession – her pitiful quest for a Hubert Hartiscor who never existed, to view anything in a realistic light. All this time she'd been fighting for a Hubert who could never be when she should have been battling to save the Hubert who *was*.

But it was too late to think about that, too late even for self-recrimination. It was only the end result that counted now and how it affected the people she loved – Jeffrey . . . Hubie . . . her poor darling Hubert himself. She had to do something to keep him from slipping down the drain, the victim of his own flawed character.

She decided that it was time for the psychotherapy that she had once rejected because she couldn't bear for Hubert to be forced to expose his inadequacies. But that had been *her* weakness, *her* flaw, *her* own inadequacy.

At first mention of undergoing analysis Hubert drawled: 'Is that your idea or Rupert's? Dada's? Little Hubie's? Or is it a consensus of opinion?'

She ignored the sarcasm. 'I haven't discussed this with Rupert or your father. You know I wouldn't do that, Hubert. It's totally my idea.'

Then he was only sad. 'So, Nora, you haven't given up? I should have known. Still think you can turn me around?'

'Oh Hubert, your sexuality is not my concern. I've made my peace with that. What I'm concerned with is how you're throwing away your life – all the wonderful things you can still be. Please, Hubert, do it for me, for Hubie, and no one else has to know. Just promise me that you'll seek help.'

But then remembering that Hubert had a problem with promises, she herself went to consult psychiatrists and feeling a certain sympathy flowing from one James Webster on Harley Street, she set up the first appointment and followed up by checking to see that Hubert kept the appointment. After that, leaving it to Hubert to make his own appointments, she always enquired about how things were coming along but only in a general way, knowing that Hubert wasn't supposed to talk about his sessions with the doctor.

Still, she was gratified when Hubert *elected* to discuss his treatment with her, recounting what he said to the doctor and what the doctor said to him in full detail. Sometimes it seemed as if he must have been recounting their fifty-minute conversations almost word for word.

'You know, I think Dr Webster and I really had a breakthrough today.'

'Oh, Hubert, really? So soon? How wonderful!'

'Yes, old Jimmy seems to think that most of my problems probably relate back to my childhood when Mother preferred me over Rupert, and Father – Rupert over me. You see, Father was the stronger influence. I respected him more than Mummy and when he rejected me in favour of Rupert—'

'But I'm sure Jeffrey never *really* rejected you, Hubert.'

159

'Dr Webster seems to think he did,' Hubert took a chiding tone. 'Now I know that you've come a long way from the girl you were, Nora – one who didn't know a port glass from a sherry or a Renoir from a Picasso – but do you presume to question the judgement of the good doctor who spent years training and accumulating experience in the field?'

'No, of course not.'

'Well, then—' He spread his hands eloquently.

When next he told of her of the recurring dream he had recently related to the doctor about Rupert sneaking into his bed at night and buggering him up the asshole as he slept, she was appalled. *What a horrid dream!* But out loud she only made objection to his choice of words: 'Surely you didn't use that language when you told the doctor about the dream?'

'But of course I did,' Hubert said reprovingly. 'I can see you don't know how analysis works. The main thing is *not* to soft pedal the facts. And it's *supposed* to hurt. You know what they say: there's no healing without pain. The important thing is to get it all out – a verbal regurgitation of all the muck. But you're focusing on the wrong thing. Don't you want to hear what Dr Webster *made* of the dream? He thinks it *really* happened!'

'You don't mean that? I can't believe that the doctor actually—'

'But it's true. Dr Webster believes that when we were young lads Rupert actually climbed into my bed at night and buggered me. And then I didn't tell Father about it either because I was afraid he'd call me a liar because he never believed *me* when it was my word against Rupert's, or I *did* tell him and he *did* call me a frigging liar. Either way, I repressed all memory of the incidents which is the reason I'm having the recurring dream.'

'But I can't believe it of Rupert! Besides, Dr Webster can't be certain this really happened – that it's a dream that has its basis in reality.'

'No, he can't know for certain,' Hubert agreed.

'He can only draw conclusions, as we all do. But of course *his* conclusions are based on objective, scientific observations that are more trustworthy than *our* subjective non-scientific ones, wouldn't you agree?' he asked reasonably. 'Besides, if we can't accept their professional judgements, why should we consult these head doctors in the first place?

'And if you recall I always *did* have that instinctive antipathy towards Rupert. I always hated his bloody guts until you told me that I was wrong – that Rupert was really my great chum. Well, if all this really happened as Dr Webster believes, and if I repressed all memory of it, that would explain those vague feelings of hatred I always felt towards Rupert. You *must see* how it all ties together.'

'I don't know, Hubert,' she agonized. 'It's so difficult to know what to believe. But what does Dr Webster think you should do? Confront Rupert?'

'No, he said that would be the worst thing I could do . . . for the present, anyway.'

'But you must do something to come to terms with this—'

'Yes,' Hubert laughed. 'And do you know what the good doctor suggests? That I get more exercise and fresh air. I haven't got much of either lately since I've been so busy with the gallery. I haven't been riding in ages. Not since the Hunt at the Athertons.'

She was bewildered. 'I must be missing something here. What does fresh air and exercise have to do with your dream? With what Rupert did? With your problems?'

'Old Jimmy believes that the better one takes care of one's body, the healthier the mind. It's quite progressive of him, really, for a psychiatrist. You know how most of these doctors are. If they're medical, they totally ignore the head, and if they treat the mind, they don't even acknowledge the body's existence. All in all, I think Webster was an excellent choice. Thank you so much, darling.'

161

'For what?'

'For everything. But especially for choosing James Webster as my shrink. I'm sure it wasn't pleasant for you interviewing all those doctors, washing our dirty linen, so to speak, so many times before you settled on him.'

No, it hadn't been pleasant. And while she *was* pleased that Hubert was pleased, she found it difficult to accept the doctor's theory that Rupert had sodomized Hubert. In fact, though she didn't want to argue the point with Hubert – he had to believe in the doctor if the therapy was to work – she rejected the doctor's theory completely.

All the same, it was difficult for her then to look at Rupert without wondering . . . without an involuntary repugnance . . . without thinking that maybe, if it hadn't been for him, she and Hubert might have—

No, she couldn't do this, she told herself. If she started thinking this way, she'd go out of her mind. Still, sometimes she couldn't bear looking at Rupert at all and at other times, she couldn't keep her eyes off him, studying him as if he were some bug under a microscope. What kind of man was he, really, and what kind of a little boy had he been?

Sometimes her eyes followed Rupert so intently that he couldn't help but notice and comment. Once, when Jeffrey was in the room, too, Rupert, smiling enigmatically, observed, 'You watch me so closely, Nora. If I didn't know better – if I didn't know how besotted you are with Hubert – I might think you were falling in love with me . . .'

She didn't honour *that* with an answer but looked away and then felt *his* eyes burning into her. But when she looked up again, it was Jeffrey's eyes that were fixed on her and she wondered what *he* was thinking – if Jeffrey had any more idea than she what Rupert was all about . . . if he knew how to distinguish truth from dreams . . .

Months later she would think that if there hadn't been so many details, so many obscure embellishments . . . if

Hubert hadn't gone on and on repeating at length each weekly dialogue between doctor and patient, she herself wouldn't have been so blind to the truth.

Hubert's birthday was coming up and she was at Blackley's trying to choose a new riding crop for his present since he had taken up riding again with a vengeance, when she spotted Hubert's psychiatrist.

'How wonderful that I've run into you Dr Webster. Since you're responsible for Hubert's renewed mad interest in riding – he hardly misses a day – you're just the person to advise me. You must help me choose the most beautiful, elegant crop ever for Hubert's birthday.'

James Webster blinked, totally at a loss.

Of course he doesn't recognize me, she thought. They had only talked in person that once. She reintroduced herself.

'Yes, of course I remember you, Lady Hartiscor. And your husband from the one time I saw him. But as for my being responsible for his renewed interest in riding, I have no idea to what you're referring.'

'You mean you *haven't* been seeing Hubert regularly?'

'No, I'm afraid not. After that one time he never returned. But that's not unusual, my dear. It happens all the time for reasons best known to the person himself. But I trust that you've both been well.' He smiled and moved away from her rather hurriedly, prohibiting further conversation.

Dear God! All this time! All those lengthy discussions about all those sessions that had never taken place . . .

And Rupert! How could she look him in the face after she had half-believed Hubert's fabricated account of his brother's incredibly perverted behaviour? If nothing else, she had certainly made a serious error in judgement. She had thought she'd taken care of Hubert's problem with promises by setting up the first appointment with the doctor herself. But after that she had not taken into account Hubert's cynical view of lying. *There's nothing*

163

like a few little white lies to keep things interesting . . .

Still, what would be gained by telling Hubert that she had run into Dr Webster and knew the truth? He would only look charmingly hang-dog for a moment or two, then he would not only make new false promises, but would probably throw in a few more lies, white or otherwise. And she couldn't bear to listen to the lies any more – it was as painful for her to hear them as it was demoralizing and degrading for Hubert to be telling them, even if he didn't know it.

She told Hubert that she thought it best if they no longer discussed his therapy since the sessions were supposed to be confidential, only between patient and doctor. Then, even when Hubert persisted, insisting it *helped* him to go over their dialogue with her, she forced herself to turn a deaf ear to him. That was a first for her, and it was hard, but she knew it was time . . .

14

It didn't come as a shock to Nora when the Hartiscor Art Gallery was finally forced to close its doors owing to what Rupert called an abysmal lack of attention to business and a questionable diversion of funds. While there'd been no intention to defraud since Hubert always intended to take care of the matter at some future date (or so he claimed), the fact was that many of the artists the gallery represented had never received the payments due them on the sale of their paintings. The money had simply vanished in that place where misappropriated funds usually did – thin air. She was only grateful that Rupert was there to take care of the details of bankruptcy and that Lord Jeffrey was there with his purse to make good the monies due the artists, some of them in dire financial straits. It was wonderful to have people one could depend on, come good times or come bad.

Still, though the proceedings resulted in much less adverse publicity than they'd anticipated, and Hubert acted properly repentant, she saw that there truly were no more avenues to be explored and that the time had come for another first in hers and Hubert's relationship – detachment. Not cold – it could never be that – but still, *firm* detachment.

This was necessary for her own survival and she had to survive for Hubie's sake. It was a matter of attention, as in a family when there were two children and one was in greedy need of more than his fair share. Hubie was almost six and he needed and was entitled to a mentally healthy mother's devoted attention more than a child-man was whose fate had been sealed long before she met him. As for her poor Hubert, he'd have to sink or swim on his own. She prayed he was a stronger swimmer than any of them assumed.

But Hubert proved a weak swimmer, as she should have known. He had so far to go and with his indifferent form, limited endurance and that deficiency of will peculiar to him, he was equipped only to swim a much shorter race.

When a stunning female impersonator – those who had seen his act swore one couldn't tell the performer from the real thing – was found dead in his flat, with his lovely torso thoroughly and methodically slashed in geometric patterns, his testicles separated from his body and his penis stuffed into his mouth, the police immediately perceived that he was the victim of a jealous lover. Then when it became part of public lore that the scion of one of England's foremost and wealthiest families had been the gorgeous entertainer's most frequent and dedicated lover, Hubert was taken into custody.

Never for a moment did Nora wonder if Hubert was

the killer. While there was that void – that lack of perception as to what constituted appropriate behaviour along with his inability to resist temptation, she knew that Hubert was essentially a gentle and loving man incapable of committing so heinous a crime. And she was sure that it was only a matter of time before everyone came to that conclusion and the dark cloud of suspicion hovering over him dissipated.

Still, she was filled with dread in the days immediately following the murder, not leaving the house at all as the family was literally under siege from the members of the media, foreign as well as British. She occupied herself mostly with trying to keep Hubie's daily schedule as near normal as possible (difficult, since she couldn't allow his governess to take him outside) and looking after Jeffrey.

Immobilized by anxiety, Jeffrey was relying on Rupert to act as the family's spokesman and liaison officer with the police, lawyers and the media. He himself barely left his study even to dine; mostly he sat and stared into space, stirring himself now and then to pour himself another whisky while Nora carried in trays, urging him to eat.

Still, while she tried not to think about anything else but keeping up a brave front for Jeffrey's sake and shielding Hubie from gossip – the servants were forbidden to discuss the case among themselves under threat of instant dismissal and all newspapers were burned in the fireplace immediately after a swift and painful scanning – she couldn't stop unbidden thoughts from entering her consciousness: why had an imitation of a woman, however gorgeous and stunningly feminine, been so irresistible to Hubert when he already had the real thing at home? Then she'd berate herself for thinking about anything so hideously incongruous, so foolishly irrelevant to the matter at hand – salvaging Hubert.

She was grateful that at least Jeffrey, when he did speak, reiterated his belief in Hubert's innocence. 'Preposterous!' he raged, only to repeat the word again seconds later, his voice muffled with despair. But she wasn't quite sure what Rupert really believed and this uncertainty caused her to agonize over whether he was doing his utmost for his brother, then minutes later to chastise herself for questioning his loyalty. He *was* devoting all his time to Hubert's predicament, meeting with the lawyers to develop strategy, pressuring the police for his release, trying to spare them all as much public humiliation as possible.

In fact, he urged her to take Hubie and leave London for their country estate, leaving him to deal with the mess. Their nearest neighbours in the country were a distance away and decent enough not to intrude on her privacy, and she'd be out of the range of the media. Too, she wouldn't have to look out of her windows to see the group of curiosity-seekers who gathered outside their gates each morning, not leaving until nightfall despite the presence of the security guards.

'Here, you and Hubie are practically prisoners. There, Hubie would at least be able to go outside to play,' Rupert urged. 'And if you could get Father to go with you, it would be even better. I'm truly concerned for his health.'

'Jeffrey will never leave London while Hubert's under suspicion and neither will I. It's out of the question at least until the police release Hubert. Then we can all get away for a while until everything quietens down. But tell me, Rupert, why haven't they released him yet? They haven't charged him. How can they continue to hold him?'

'They say it's only for questioning and the solicitors and I believe it's wiser not to lean on them too hard at this stage of the game.'

'At this stage of the game? What does that mean, Rupert? Do you expect things to get worse?'

'I wish I could say no, but I have to be honest with you. You want that, don't you?'

She stiffened. 'Yes, honesty is a quality I appreciate.'

'Well, it doesn't look good.'

'But *you* believe in Hubert's innocence?'

He smiled at her enigmatically. 'I do if you do.'

'That's no answer! You must believe in Hubert on your own!' She wanted to shake him, to *make* him believe.

'I'm doing whatever I can, Nora. What difference does it make if *I* personally believe or disbelieve?'

'Because you're the one who's out there fighting for Hubert and how can you fight for a cause you don't really believe in?'

'Mankind has been doing that for centuries.'

'And *winning*?'

Rupert shrugged. 'Sometimes . . .'

'*Sometimes* isn't good enough! This is Hubert – not some vague cause! For his sake you must fight very hard to win! Harder than you've ever fought.'

'Oh, I'm fighting to win, Nora, believe me. But as for whose sake–? Let's just say it's for *all* our sakes and leave it at that. Fair enough?'

Fair enough, she thought, but not exactly reassuring.

It was already seven days after the murder and Hubert was still being detained without being charged and her nerves were at breaking point. To make matters worse, she hadn't seen Hubert since the police had taken him into custody. If only she could see him, take him in her arms and tell him that everything was going to be all right! But while she wasn't officially prohibited from visiting him, both Rupert and Jeffrey thought it unwise. The leeches from the tabloids and the bastards with their TV cameras would have a field day, would make her attendance at the jail seem like the bereaved wife visiting the husband who had already been accused, tried and convicted, and she had no choice really but to accede to their superior wisdom.

If only she were convinced that Rupert was doing his best by Hubert – that he was telling her everything, every nuance of what was really going on . . .

She was sitting in the room adjoining Jeffrey's study and about to go in to check up on him when she realized Rupert was already in there with his father and she

168

remained hidden behind the nearly closed door. She had to know what Rupert was really thinking, what was really happening, and all the things he'd likely reveal to his father and not to her.

She heard Rupert say, 'I'm really surprised that anyone even thinks that Hubert has the guts to commit this kind of crime. Lesser ones, yes – a bit of embezzlement, as in the case of the gallery, certainly. But I really don't think Hubert has the stomach for murder, or the temperament. I'd say what he has most of all is an aptitude for shaming us so thoroughly and so disgustingly we'll never be able to raise our heads again.'

She felt herself burn with fury but she forced herself to stay where she was instead of rushing in to confront Rupert.

'Never mind that now,' she heard Jeffrey's voice tremble, 'I want to hear about the police. What do they say?'

'They're still not ready officially to charge Hubert, if that's what you mean. Perhaps in a way that's a pity. At least if he were charged, tried and convicted, we'd all be able to get on with our lives.'

Nora had to fight to control herself, then not to rush in to tear at Rupert's face with her fingernails, especially when she heard Jeffrey cry out in pain at his callous words. But Jeffrey rallied sufficiently to say, 'I won't listen to this kind of talk, Rupert! What I want to know is why they're still holding him, damn it!'

'They say they're holding him for questioning, Father.'

'But for how long? Men who have been arrested can secure release by posting bail, but *my* son, a Hartiscor, is being held without being charged and therefore has no right of bail? It's outrageous! Is he to be denied all his rights?'

'They say they're holding him for his own protection as well as for questioning.'

'Damn it! What are they protecting him from?'

'They say that *if* the killer is still at large – assuming

169

Hubert *isn't* the killer – there's a possibility Hubert might be next on the killer's agenda since Hubert was the murdered man's number one lover.'

'That's absolute rot! We must insist he be released at once! Immediately! You know how to lean on people, Rupert, how to exert influence. Do it!'

'I'm afraid they're not about to listen, Father, no matter how hard we exert or how hard we lean. It's possible that even without sufficient evidence to indict Hubert, they still want to make an example of him in some way – show the public that even the son of a very wealthy member of the House of Lords is not above question – will be held accountable—'

'How dare they pick on my son for their bloody example? The law is the law and they cannot detain a man indefinitely without charging him! And obviously they can't charge him because they don't have the evidence to back it up! And what the bloody hell are our lawyers doing? Why aren't they getting Hubert released? I won't have it – Hubert sitting in a cell when he's no more guilty than a babe in arms!'

'He could be sitting in worse places, Father.'

'Worse? What's worse than sitting in jail for a man who is innocent?'

'*If* he's innocent. But innocent or guilty, I'd say the worst place Hubert could possibly be would be that special place they reserve for those destined for the gallows.'

First, Nora heard herself gasp, then Jeffrey. Then Jeffrey must have started to pour himself a whisky because she heard Rupert say, 'Don't you think you've had enough, Father? You must keep your wits about you and listen to me. There's a decision to be made—'

'What decision? We know what we must do. Get them to release Hubert and dispel any suspicions that—'

'Perhaps we shouldn't be in such a big hurry to see Hubert released. At least this way the Press can't get at him. Once he's out, they're bound to catch up with him and then all hell will break out. Come, Father, you know

170

Hubert as well as I do. He's too much the arrogant fool to even keep his mouth shut. He'll be sure to stick his foot in it.' He gave a short laugh. 'Well, at least that would be a big improvement on some of the other things he's stuck in his mouth.'

With that, Nora could no longer restrain herself and she rushed into the study. 'How can you say these things? Isn't the situation bad enough without you adding your venom? And doesn't your father have enough to deal with without—'

'Enough to deal with, you say? *I'm* the one who's dealing with this stinking cesspool your precious Hubert has dragged us into. It's I who's trying to hold those swine from the Press at bay, off yours and Father's back. And it's I who has to make statements on behalf of the family when there's nothing I can say that doesn't leave people snickering in my face. All of London, all of Britain, is snickering in our faces! How they love to see how low the high and mighty have fallen. Or is the more appropriate word *sunk*?

'And you, Father, ask what our lawyers are doing. Who do you think it is who's crawling on his hands and knees, begging them – men who are supposed to be your friends – to take Hubert's case? And why do I have to beg? Because this mess is so filthy they don't want to befoul their hands. They're afraid the stink will never wash off. And who's playing games with the police, *trying* to throw the weight of the Hartiscor name around while they're laughing behind my back and who can blame them? They know what the name stands for! Everybody knows! Faggot! Bugger! Cocksucker!'

Jeffrey covered his ears with his hands while Nora lunged at him, but Rupert caught her arm and held it fast. 'You said you wanted honesty, Nora, and that's what I'm giving you. But don't hold me responsible for what Hubert has wrought. The other day you asked me if I believed in Hubert's innocence. Yes, I believe he's innocent of murder but he's guilty of other crimes, isn't

171

he? He's guilty of placing himself in this situation where he *can be* suspected . . . guilty of bringing this offal down on us all until we're smothered in it!'

He threw himself into a chair as if he were exhausted. 'And my concern isn't even for Father or myself. We can survive this scandal what with our money and our prestige. But when I think of what Hubert has done to *you*! How you suffer, how you bleed! And Hubie – so young, so innocent, so vulnerable. That's what makes me so bloody angry that I can't control myself. I know how society is. When I think of how all this will affect him and his future, oh, I bleed – but for Hubie, not for Hubert.'

Tears escaped his eyes and trickled down his cheeks. 'Oh my dear Nora, how can you doubt that I'll do anything for you and Hubie, and ultimately for Hubert? No matter what I feel, in the end I know there's only one truth – I know that I *am*, after all, my brother's keeper . . .'

When she saw the tears and heard the ring of sincerity in his voice when he spoke of his concern for Hubie, when she heard that phrase – *I am, after all, my brother's keeper* – Nora was deeply touched . . . ashamed that she had ever doubted him. She even forgave him his cruel words. She took her handkerchief to dab at the tears glistening on his cheeks. 'We're all so upset, none of us knows what we're saying any more. If only this nightmare would end!'

'I think I know what we must do,' Jeffrey said fervently. 'I should have thought of it sooner. We must hire our own investigators to find the real killer.'

'Yes, Father,' Rupert said evenly. 'I've thought of that. In fact, I've already arranged for it. But I have another idea – a plan that can save Hubert just in case everything else fails. That's what I meant when I said there was a decision to be made.'

Jeffrey's face brightened. 'What is the decision? What's your plan?'

'I think we have to move *now* . . . before Hubert is

172

officially accused. Have him declared incompetent – of unsound mind – unable to distinguish between right or wrong. But we have to do it immediately!'

'You mean insane?' Nora cried out. 'No, Rupert!'

'The term I used is of unsound mind. It's not quite the same thing. The lawyers will probably call it *legally insane* which isn't exactly the same thing either.'

'In effect it will be exactly the same!' She turned to Jeffrey. 'We can't do this to Hubert!'

Jeffrey mopped at his brow with his handkerchief, so agitated he was beyond making a decision. 'But we don't even know that they're going to accuse Hubert of murder, Rupert. It's precipitous, if nothing else! Why must we do it now?'

'Because if we wait until he *is* formally charged, it will be too late. No court, no judge would go along with it then. All we'll be able to do then is plead Hubert's innocence, but believe me, it will be very difficult to find twelve good men in all of London who haven't already made up their minds that he's as guilty as hell. I've been talking to people – I can smell the climate out there. Believe me, if Hubert were to stand trial tomorrow, there isn't a jury anywhere that wouldn't convict him.'

'No, I won't accept that!' Nora cried.

'I'm sorry, but you might have to—' Rupert caught her hand. 'Listen to me and listen well. Realizing that this might very well be the case – that it would be next to impossible to get a not-guilty verdict for Hubert – a barrister might think Hubert's only chance *is* to plead him not guilty due to insanity. In such instance, everyone would assume that Hubert is *so* guilty that this is the only defence we could come up with and thus give the insanity plea no credence. But if we move now to have him declared of unsound mind based on his moral turpitude and degenerate behaviour, we might find a judge willing to go along with it and then – if and when – well, we've already established a defence.'

'But if we do that now it will still look like *we* believe

Hubert is guilty before he's even been accused. And if we, his own family, believe him guilty, why shouldn't everyone else? Besides, suppose we *do* do this now? What does it mean? What would happen to Hubert?'

She asked the question of Rupert but it was Jeffrey who answered, 'It means, that aside from the question of whether or not Hubert committed murder, we who ask that he be declared of unsound mind must also ask that he be confined to a mental institution. Otherwise, there would be no reason to have him declared of unsound mind in the first place.'

'No, I won't stand for it!' Nora began to cry.

'Oh, Nora, Nora,' Rupert said in sympathetic despair, 'do we really have a choice? Don't you see, once everyone's conscience is clear and they can tell themselves that the man has been declared mentally ill, they'll be perfectly happy *not* to convict him of murder. They'll feel that justice will have been served. Who *really* gives a damn that Hubert disposed of some filthy scum society is better off without?'

'But they'll lock Hubert up! We can't do that to him!'

'Even if it means saving his life?'

But we'll be killing his dear, sweet soul . . .

'You know, having a person committed doesn't mean it's irreversible, Nora. Any time the doctors feel he at least shows considerable improvement, he can be released. *Will be* released . . . remaindered into our custody. Am I right, Father? Tell Nora I'm right.'

At first Jeffrey blinked as if he were having difficulty comprehending exactly what it was Rupert was right about but then he nodded. 'Yes, Nora, I think Rupert is quite right. We must do everything . . . *anything* that is necessary . . .'

Rupert squeezed Nora's hand. 'I know how painful this must be for you, Nora.'

She pulled her hand away. 'I'm not thinking of how painful this is for *me*.'

'Of course. But you know, this treatment – well,

it might not be anything more demanding than Hubert saying, "I'm sorry that I've been a bad boy and I'm going to be a very good one from now on." Then Hubert will not only be scot-free but forgiven all his sins as society grasps him back to its bosom. There's nothing the world loves more than a penitent.'

Nora saw that it was hopeless to argue. Hubert's father and brother, wiser than she about how the world worked, had made up their minds, and Jeffrey was already wearily giving Rupert his approval to proceed. 'Let us not talk about it any more. Just do it, Rupert. Tell the solicitors to take care of it immediately.'

The Lord who would one day be in charge had proposed and the Lord who was still in charge had disposed and who dared question the ways of the Lord?

The whole matter became academic the following day when another female impersonator, one quite butch, with a heavy body, hirsute legs and considerable expertise in wielding a knife – butchering had actually been his trade before he traded in his knives for high heels and lipstick – confessed to the crime and a broken Hubert came home to his family.

Rupert was actually very sweet to Hubert, for which Nora was grateful. There wasn't a word of recrimination, only sympathy for what Hubert had suffered. However, he still made vague noises about having Hubert declared mentally incompetent, defending that position with the logic that it would help salvage Hubert's tattered reputation. But with Hubert home and out of danger, Jeffrey no longer had the heart for it. 'The sooner Hubert's out of the news, the sooner people will begin to forget.'

Nora concurred, grateful that, at least, Hubert would be spared this final degradation.

Still, the tabloids chose to go on exploiting the case – the sheer scandal of it still having news-stand appeal. And they continued to make Hubert the main focus of their sensationalism, the Hartiscor name carrying more weight with a public avid for lurid details of life among the sordid rich than a mere female impersonator done in by one of his own.

These publications managed to keep the public interest at a feverish pitch by running a series of daily segments on the degenerate life and times of Hubert Albert Hartiscor who, while married to the former cabaret singer, Nora Hall – she 'notorious' for her voluptuous charms – sought more exotic thrills among the freaks and perverts of London's netherworld. Whatever dirt they managed to dig up was eked out by sheer creative invention and supplemented by interviews with several of Hubert's lovers who came crawling out from under the rocks to tell their own tales in excruciatingly sordid detail.

The tabloids were fortunate in that when, inevitably, public interest began to wane, the story regained instant notoriety when Hubert took his own life . . .

They would have preferred it if he'd committed the act in some grislier, more dramatic fashion, shooting himself in the mouth perhaps, or better yet, his sexual parts, and allowing himself to bleed to death. But Hubert passed on these methods. Rather, he went up to the attic and quietly hanged himself from a rafter. As Rupert had once told Nora, the Hartiscors had a predilection for death by hanging.

On the attic floor stood a nearly empty bottle of his father's finest brandy but no farewell note. But there *was* a note in a special place about which only Nora knew – she and Hubert had frequently left notes for one another in an illustrated volume of human anatomy, a kind of private joke. And while the note tore at her heart, she mused that no poet out of all the poets Hubert had familiarized her with could have said it all as eloquently as her sweet, darling Hubert.

The moment she began to read, she knew this wasn't a suicide note at all but a love letter. It asked her forgiveness while attempting to assuage the sorrowful regret with which he anticipated she'd be consumed:

> Don't ever feel that in some way *you* failed, darling girl. Only true gamblers know that sometimes the odds are too great even for the most daring of betting men. And only God knows how much I loved you and only fate knows how cruel a joke it played on us. But maybe in the grand scheme of things there *is* a place and a time for us and perhaps some day, years from now, we'll meet in another lifetime and it will be the way it should have been the first time around.
>
> But in the meantime and in this lifetime, know you that whatever true happiness I experienced was at your hands. Therefore, you are still obligated to me as is one who saves another's life, and thus I charge you: live and be happy and do not cry for me. Find a man who will love you in the way you deserve to be loved and take care of our 'sweet convenience' and provide for him the way I yearned to, but could not find the strength to make a good job of it. And no one knows better than you that I am not talking about the fripperies of life such as money or titles, but of its very heart.

I'll try my best, she silently vowed. But there was one thing that he asked that she *couldn't* do – she could not *not* cry for him. It was quite possible that in her heart she would cry for him till the end of time.

She kissed his signature and blurred it with her tears, thinking that this was not a farewell note so much as a love letter. But the following day, another written document – a legal notice, properly notarized, placed and paid for by Hubert Albert Hartiscor just before he took his life – appeared in all the newspapers, including the tabloids which featured it on their front pages. It stated that the woman, Nora Hall, commonly known as Lady

Hartiscor, the wife of Hubert Albert Hartiscor, was not and had never been his legal wife, and that her issue – the male child commonly known as Hubert Winston Hartiscor – was not of his loins.

Then Nora knew this public disavowal, which branded her as a woman who had lived a lie and Hubie as a bastard, but which separated them from his taint, was the true love letter.

PART FOUR

ONCE FOR THE NAME

England
1951–5

15

'I feel so guilty,' the seemingly disconsolate Rupert told Nora after they returned home from the private graveside service, and Jeffrey took to the seclusion of his study. 'As if I could have done more to save him—'

'I'm sure we all did what we could, Rupert, and you mustn't blame yourself,' Nora told him tiredly, making an attempt to comfort him though it was difficult for her to summon up the words – she felt too drained, too empty.

'But it was *my* responsibility as head of the family.'

She was startled. It was an odd thing for him to say. 'Your father may be shaky at the moment, Rupert, but he's always been and still is the head of your family. At least, what remains of it.'

He stared at her for a moment as if disoriented. 'Of course. What I meant was that it was my place to look after my younger brother. Besides, you know how Father is about assuming responsibility.'

'I don't think I understand, Rupert. How *is* your father about assuming responsibility?'

'He *doesn't* . . . ever.'

Then she remembered. This wasn't the first time Rupert had mentioned Jeffrey's dislike of accepting responsibility. But she was hardly in the mood for this conversation. In fact, she wasn't in the mood for any conversation at all. 'Personally, I think your father was wonderful with Hubert, always trying to help him, always forgiving him no matter—'

'But that was *after* the fact, that was *his* guilt!'

The last thing she wanted right now was to get into

181

discussion of Jeffrey's possible guilt. All she wanted to do was to go to her room and be alone with her thoughts. But she couldn't cut Rupert off when he so obviously needed to talk.

'I'm exhausted, Rupert, but tell me – what *did* your father have to feel guilty about?'

'He *knew* what was going on with dear old Mummy and little Hubert and he didn't do a damn thing about it!'

Her heart skipped a beat. 'What are you saying, Rupert? *What* went on with Mummy and Hubert?'

'Didn't Hubert ever tell you about the games Mummy played with him in her bed? How she sucked on his little tippie?'

She was appalled rather than shocked. 'Stop right there, Rupert. Hubert never told me any such thing and I refuse to listen to it now.'

She started for the stairs but Rupert ran after her. 'It's true! I swear it!'

'I don't want to hear this. I'm going upstairs and I'm going to forget you ever said—'

'But that *was* what was going on! Why won't you believe me?' Now Rupert was actually crying.

Oh, God! Will it never end?

She sat down on the bottom step of the staircase wearily. 'Frankly, I don't know *what* to believe. Maybe it happened and maybe it didn't. Maybe you only *thought* it happened because you were sick with jealousy. And that was your mother's fault because she played favourites so blatantly. But to think that Jeffrey knew and didn't do anything about it? *That's* unbelievable, Rupert, and you can't fall into the trap of not being able to separate truth from fancy.'

Rupert sank to the marble floor at her feet and buried his face in her lap. She could feel the dampness of his tears through the silk of her dress and her heart went out to him. He was still the little boy whose dutiful behaviour hadn't earned him any points with his mother.

She smoothed the dark hair back from his troubled brow. 'It doesn't matter any more, anyway. Your mother's dead and Hubert's dead and no one will ever really know the truth and probably it's for the best. As for your father, you must be very kind to him – he's lost a son and that has to be one of the worst things that can happen to a father, even—' *Forgive me, Hubert, for what I'm about to say.* 'Even if the lost son was only *second* in his heart.'

'What do you mean – second in his heart?'

'Well, Hubert always said *you* were your father's favourite . . . told me how much Jeffrey loved you and how you always came first with him.'

A half-truth. But would it help anyone if she told Rupert that what Hubert had really said was that after Anne, Rupert came first with his father?

Rupert straightened up. 'Hubert really said that? It's hard to believe. But Father – what does *he* say?'

'Oh, he's implied that he loved you best many times.'

Once you told a half-truth, what difference did it make if you embellished it a tiny bit more until it became a little white lie?

Then Rupert, so overwhelmed, forgot himself and kissed her most inappropriately, full on the lips. But Nora didn't reprove him. At best, they were all caught up in a highly inappropriate situation in the most inappropriate of times . . .

The next day, she, Hubie and Jeffrey left London for Hartiscor Castle, hoping to escape the gossip-mongers if not the bitterness of their sorrow. Rupert, acting as if the previous evening's conversation between him and her had never taken place, wished them God's speed, reassuring them that he would 'sweep up' as much as possible in their absence. Hopefully, by the time they returned, the worst of the gossip would be over and they'd be able to get on with their lives.

Nora didn't believe it. Nasty gossip had a way of

183

lingering on for years, often outliving the people it touched. But she wasn't so much concerned for herself as she was for Hubie and Jeffrey – the young and the old. Hubie had so long a time to live under its dark cloud and Jeffrey, perhaps, not time enough to get out from under . . .

Still, though she didn't find Hartiscor Castle the idyllic haven Jeffrey thought it – to her it was more gloomy than peaceful – she and he were able to share several weeks of serene, if not completely healing, respite. They spent most of the daylight hours with Hubie who was so adorable and sweet he managed to make them forget for a little while that they were in mourning, and their evenings in isolation with no visitors and without turning on the television. Rather, they took comfort in their quiet companionship, reading in the same room and occasionally looking up and smiling at each other, listening to music together, playing a game of chess or chatting about all manner of things running the gamut from gardening to Britain's political future.

They even reminisced about the unrecent past, she recalling her childhood in the Cotswolds, he his own childhood some thirty-five or so years before hers. What they scrupulously avoided was any topic that might prove painful to either one of them, which meant that there was no mention of the fact that she and Hubert hadn't been man and wife, or even that Hubie wasn't really his grandchild. By the same token, she wasn't surprised when every now and then he said, 'I can't begin to tell you how much your company means to me.'

'But you don't have to tell me, Jeffrey. I know because I feel the same way about yours.'

But the day arrived when he told her they'd have to start thinking about returning to London to 'get on with it'. The sooner they resumed the routine of daily life, the sooner they themselves would be on the road to recovery.

Nora turned away from the window where she'd been

watching Hubie play with the caretaker's little boy under the eye of the governess to face Jeffrey and see clearly now how their tragedy had aged him. It was as if in the passage of weeks he had grown small and frail, where before she had always thought of him as a vigorous figure, a tower of strength. 'You do understand, Jeffrey dear, that under the circumstances, Hubie and I won't be living with you at Hartiscor House for too long? It's time we were moving on.'

'*Moving on?*' he scoffed. 'What kind of fatuous phrase is that? It makes you and Hubie sound like a couple of vagrants, or two adventurers on the loose. Besides, where would you go? No, I won't hear of it. As far as I'm concerned, nothing has changed. Your home will always be with the Hartiscors. At least until you consider marrying which, I suppose, eventually you will but—' his voice trailed off.

'I appreciate your generosity, Jeffrey, especially after I deceived you so terribly, pretending that Hubert and I were married, that Hubie was his son. There are so many things I regret but that's probably the one thing that I regret the most – having taking advantage of your kindness.'

She went over to where he sat on a rose velvet Victorian sofa and seating herself on the floor, took his hand and pressed it to her cheek. 'I hope you've forgiven me.'

'But you didn't deceive me. Not about the boy, at any rate. Somehow I always knew, *felt*, right from the beginning that Hubert wasn't Hubie's father.'

'But why, then, did you accept me? You've always been *so* good to me. Why?'

'Because, no matter what else, Nora, *you* always gave as good as you received. Much more. And you and I have always understood each other, haven't we?' He stroked her hair as she leaned her head against his knee.

That was true, Nora thought. They *had* always understood one another. She thought back to the day when

Jeffrey had toasted her, how she had felt that she and he had made an unspoken pact.

'But even though we intended to get married, we did lie to you. And then I failed you. I didn't manage to save—'

'It wasn't up to you. And perhaps it's I who failed you by allowing you to shoulder so much responsibility. You were so young and so innocent – not able to grasp the magnitude of what you were undertaking.'

'I might have been young and innocent,' she smiled at him wanly, 'and ignorant, but I knew what I was getting into. And by accepting me you did the most wonderful thing anyone could have done for me at the time. You made it possible for me to keep my son. But now I must take it from there.'

'Let's not talk any longer about the past, Nora, except to say that in my heart you were Hubert's wife and Hubie was his son. More importantly, I can still give you and Hubie the benefit of my protection and the privileges of my position and wealth. I will not only provide for Hubie, but I will watch over him, present him with opportunities, open doors for him. For Hubie's sake, if not for your own, you must stay.'

'Oh Jeffrey, I don't think I can. Not that I don't appreciate everything you've done. And no matter how it all turned out, I still think I got the best of that bargain we made. Between you and Hubert, I learned how to be a much more accomplished person and I had the love of *two* good men and had the privilege of loving you both in return.'

'Ah, Nora, you talk of love – of my loving you and you loving me – yet in the same breath you talk of deserting me.'

'Deserting *you*?' How could Jeffrey construe her leaving as something she was doing to *him*?

'I never thought of leaving your household as desertion. First of all, there's the scandal. Much as we'd like to pretend it doesn't matter, we both know it does. You

186

know the way people talk. They'll forever refer to Hubie as 'the Hartiscor bastard who's no Hartiscor'. As for me, I'll be lucky if all they call me is 'the notorious Lady Hartiscor who was no lady, much less a wife'. But if we go abroad to live – say Paris – and start all over again, Nora and Hubie Hall will more than likely be able to melt into the crowd.'

'Nonsense. It's a small world and the scandal will follow you. And the people you'll meet in Paris won't be any different from the people you know here. They'll relish the malicious gossip just as much.'

'But don't you see? If we stay the stories about Hubert will be dredged up over and over again and you'll—'

'I'll what? I'll stand my ground, that's what, and dare any man to sneer. But you – if you run like a coward, you and Hubie will forever be sneaking around corners, ashamed of who you are. What kind of a way is that to raise your son?'

She started to protest, but he put a finger to her mouth. 'But if you stay and get some steel into your backbone, we can face the gossip together and hold ourselves proud. Then you'll not only be accepting the challenge, it will be Hubie who'll be the victor.'

Run like a coward . . . get some steel into your backbone . . . Jeffrey *was* a sly old dog. How well he knew the phrases that were guaranteed to ignite her fighting spirit.

'I wasn't going to run like a coward,' she said stiffly. 'I was just trying to face the facts and protect Hubie.'

'Protect Hubie. That's exactly my point. No matter what, *I'm* still the Earl of Hartiscor who commands more than a billion pounds. And we Hartiscors go back a long way and with a few exceptions like poor Hubert, we're a tough and hardy bunch. Dark clouds don't scare us – it can rain bloody hell and we survive while our detractors live to eat their words. And that's the kind of protection I wish to provide for you and your son and if you're the wise woman I

187

always thought you were, you'll accept, at least, on his behalf.'

'But what about Rupert?'

Jeffrey's eyes narrowed. 'What about him?'

'Well, I think he's unsure of himself and—'

'That's a refreshing thought, I must say, but I doubt it,' Jeffrey scoffed. 'But what has Rupert being unsure of himself have to do with you and Hubie?'

'If we stay he might view Hubie and me as a threat—'

'That's absurd! What kind of a threat can you and Hubie pose to Rupert? It's only money and position that concern him and he's going to have both of those, no matter what.'

'But there *are* other things of concern to him. Your love. And if Hubie and I stay, he might worry that we'll usurp him in your affections.'

'He wouldn't be far from the truth,' Jeffrey chuckled. 'But you're wrong about Rupert. For one thing, he doesn't give a bloody damn for my love. Still, while I believe him to be essentially a cold, passionless man, I think he feels a strong responsibility towards Hubie and is quite fond of you both. He would take it badly if you moved out.'

While she agreed with Jeffrey that Rupert was fond of her and Hubie, she, who had felt the wetness of his tears, couldn't agree that he was otherwise cold and passionless. As for his feeling a responsibility towards Hubie or that he would take it badly if they moved out, she wasn't sure. Whatever, she remained unconvinced that their staying on would work out.

'I don't know, Jeffrey. While Rupert doesn't appear to have any interest in any particular woman right now, there *will* come a time when he'll want to marry and have children of his own. And what then? No matter how fond he is of us, we'll be in the way. You know as well as I do that no house is large enough to accommodate two families. Hubie would be relegated to the status of what – some kind of unwanted stepchild without a legal name

188

to call his own. And what would be *my* status? Number two what? We'd both be in an untenable position.'

'Ah,' Jeffrey fingered his moustache. 'A point well taken. But no one could question your position if you were already the *Countess* Hartiscor, could they? Or Hubie's, if he were once and for all, legally a Hartiscor?'

She looked at him, puzzled. 'What does that mean?'

'It means, my dear, that I couldn't care less about whom or when Rupert marries or how he feels about you and Hubie. Do I owe it to him to give up everything for him even before I die? It means that you and I must think only about Hubie and *us*. What we want and what we owe one another. And that means that you must marry me!'

Nora's brain reeled. *Marry Jeffrey?* It was inconceivable!

Without waiting for her response, Jeffrey went on, his enthusiasm mounting with every breath: 'Yes, it's exactly what you must do! Actually, considering everything, it's fortunate that you and Hubert were never legally married. Then, according to the civil laws and the laws of the Church, it would have been impossible for me to marry you. But now I'll be able to take care of you and Hubie properly, adopt him as my own, and there's nothing Rupert could do about it even if he wanted to. And if he doesn't like it, well, he will just have to lump it . . . clear out himself.'

This was insane! Mourning had apparently addled Jeffrey's brain even as it had aged his body and his spirit!

But then she saw that even that was no longer true. She could see the vigour and vitality surging through him, his former larger-than-life presence taking over, the high colour flowing back into his face. Whereas it had taken three months to age him prematurely, it was as if she were watching him taking back the years in a matter of seconds. It was amazing! It was *all* so amazing . . .

It wasn't that during these weeks of mourning she hadn't thought about marrying . . . hadn't day-dreamed about what kind of a man he would be . . . hadn't tried to visualize him in her mind's eye. She'd have been inhuman if she hadn't – she was twenty-six with a son of six, with not a penny to her name and she had been masturbating herself to sleep for years.

And Hubert himself had charged her: *Live and be happy. Find a man who will love you in the way you deserve to be loved and take care of our 'sweet convenience' and provide for him.*

But she had thought that when and if she married, she would marry a virile man with an urgent need for her, one who would love her in the way she yearned to be loved – madly, passionately, with a burning desire.

But then looking at Jeffrey, re-energized by his proposal, she realized that he loved her in just that way – with an urgent need, madly, passionately, with a burning desire . . . had for a long, long time . . . maybe even from the beginning. And somewhere in the back of her head she had always known this.

Oh, dear God, what am I to do?

She owed Jeffrey so much. He'd been so good to her. How could she deny him? And she owed Hubie even more, and how could she deny him his own good name?

She heard Jeffrey say, 'We will wait a few months, of course, for appearance's sake, and then we'll be married.' Then he rose from the sofa to extend his hands to her and pulled her to her feet from her position on the floor.

'There's much to be done. Do you think you could be ready to leave for London tomorrow?'

She thought back to the timorous girl who had gone to meet him and had been told that she *would* live in his house, that he would not take 'no' for an answer.

'But Jeffrey! I haven't agreed! It's not settled! I—'

'Of course it's settled! It's the only decision that makes sense!' He laughed as happily as a schoolboy. 'You said you loved me before, did you not?'

'Yes . . .' she nodded tentatively. That was undeniable.

190

Caring about someone *was* loving them even if it weren't how she yearned to love.

'And I love you. Do you accept that?'

'Yes.' To say otherwise would be a lie.

'And we both love Hubie?'

She nodded.

'And our marriage will mean a secure future for Hubie, as secure a future as you could manage for him. Is *that* true?'

She nodded again. It was undeniably the truth.

'Well, there you are. It's settled then! Am I right?'

She hesitated for only a second or two before she said, 'Yes, Jeffrey, you are right.'

Maybe it had always been meant to be this way, an evening out of the score. Hubert had told her that *their* marriage would be one of sweet convenience, but being Hubert he had got it wrong. It would have *always* been for love. Love for him and love for Hubie. And then they had never married. *This* marriage, then, would be the one conceived in convenience and out of duty, but still it would be for love – Jeffrey's love for her and hers for Hubie. And she dutifully offered her cheek for his kiss.

But he took her face between his hands and kissed her hard on the lips, then kissed her again, crushing her to him, crouching to match her body to his so that all the parts of one fitted into the other. 'I have loved you *always*, Nora,' he muttered into her throat, kissing her again fervently and pressing the lower half of his body against hers convulsively.

Always . . . The word made her sad. *Always* would *always* be the way she had loved Hubert. Fiercely and for ever. But she couldn't complain. Love was love and it was a gift to the recipient as well as the giver, to be relished, savoured *and* appreciated. What had Jeffrey said when they had started this fateful conversation? *You always gave as good as you received.*

She liked that. It had a fine ring to it. And she would try to make it true again in every way.

Now she tipped her head back away from him to smile deeply into his eyes and then she pulled his head down to hers to return his kiss, hard at first, then softly as she parted her lips to draw his tongue into her mouth. Then as he groaned softly, she took his hand to insert it into the 'V' of her dress, and as she felt the heat of his fingers touch her flesh, a flash of pain pierced her breast as she remembered . . .

No, she'd never forget Hubert and she didn't want to. And though Hubie wasn't Hubert son, it didn't matter. The best part of Hubert would live on for her in Hubie, their shared sweet convenience.

Then she smiled into Jeffrey's eyes again as she lowered herself on to the sofa and pulled him down after her so that his body covered hers.

16

When they returned to London, Nora was surprised to find that as scandal, the Hartiscors were old hat. A new scandal had eclipsed them as conversation material in the town's leading salons as well as on the front pages of the tabloids – Guy Burgess and Donald Maclean had defected to Russia for whom they'd been spying. While Jeffrey took this news hard, she was only relieved that everyone had something else to gossip about.

But she was still nervous about how Rupert was going to react to the news of the impending marriage. She'd asked Jeffrey to delay telling him just as they were putting off telling Hubie since the wedding *was* several months away, but Jeffrey wouldn't hear of it. 'There's no reason to procrastinate with Rupert. *He's* not a little boy who might have reason to be upset. Besides, you're making a fuss that's not warranted. Rupert's not going to turn a hair at our news and the chances are he'll be delighted.'

They were having tea in the salon and while she was pouring, Jeffrey made the announcement. Then she had to put the teapot down, her hand trembling uncontrollably. No matter what Jeffrey chose to believe, the news was bound to be a jolt.

For a brief moment Rupert's face went blank as if frozen; then it unfroze sufficiently to permit his eyes to blink and his lips to curve into a smile before he managed to find his voice: 'Well, this *is* a surprise! May I offer you both my congratulations? No, that isn't quite right, is it? One offers the groom congratulations and wishes the bride good luck. Isn't that how it goes, Nora? I was never good at these small social graces. That was more Hubert's department, he having been trained so well by our mother the countess. But now that you're going to be the countess, we'll have to look to you for guidance, won't we? So, what do you say, Countess? Do I wish you luck or do I merely kiss the bride?'

Nora picked up the teapot to resume pouring. 'Though I'm not yet the countess, I believe I can make a ruling. I think it would be quite nice and proper if you were to offer your congratulations to us both, along with your best wishes. Don't you agree, Jeffrey?' She passed him his cup of tea.

'Whatever you say, my dear.' Having made his announcement Jeffrey was now immersed in the correspondence he had brought to the tea table – he'd been away from London so long that he had a great deal to catch up on.

Rupert took the cup Nora held out to him. 'But *do* I get to kiss the bride?'

'Hardly,' Nora smiled, 'since I'm not yet a bride. That's several months in the offing. Probably not until the beginning of next year.'

'Of course. Stupid of me, really. But very wise of

you to wait. We wouldn't want people to get the wrong notion.'

Nora glanced at Jeffrey to see if he would react to that but he was concentrating on his mail and paying no attention, so she sighed and asked, 'What wrong notion, Rupert?'

Rupert took a sip of tea. 'Oh, I say now, Nora, you added my slice of lemon cut paper thin, just the way I like it, but you forgot to put in my two lumps of sugar.' He held his cup out so that she could deposit the requested lumps.

'Two to be sure,' Nora said, dropping them in with the silver tongs. 'We wouldn't want you to have your lemon but not your sugar since that could give you a bad case of sour digestion and we can't have that.' She held up the plate of biscuits then for Rupert to choose one. 'Now that we have your sweetness quotient all taken care of, Rupert, why don't you tell us what you meant when you said that people might get the wrong notion if we married right away.'

'Well, we wouldn't want people to think that you two were so hot to trot you couldn't wait until the body was cold.'

He laughed then in the face of Nora's frigid stare. 'Just a small joke, you know.' He stirred his tea. 'Oh dear, Nora, you are scowling. I was just trying to be humorous. People are always saying I don't have a sense of humour and when I try – well, I've offended you. I guess I'm just not as good at it as Hubert was. Mummy always said Hubert could make a statue laugh.'

He tasted his tea and made a face. 'Oh my, Nora, this tea is quite tepid. You'd think the very least we could expect of the kitchen would be *hot* tea. Very, very hot.'

Nora agreed. She only wished the tea was hot enough to scald him if she did what she felt liked doing – pitching the contents of her own cup in his face.

'Don't *you* agree, Father?'

Jeffrey looked up. 'Agree? With what?'

'Don't you agree that the tea is quite cold?'

Perplexed, Jeffrey took a swallow of his tea. 'I don't know what you're talking about. My tea is sufficiently hot.'

'You're lucky, Father, because we all like it hot.' He set his cup down with a clatter. 'It just struck me – you're going to be my stepmother, Nora! Isn't that amusing?'

Nora shrugged. 'Not particularly.'

'But it does give me certain privileges. Prerogatives, you might say.' Abruptly he rose from his chair. 'Like kissing the bride *before* the wedding.' Then, before she knew what he was up to, he was standing over her and swooping down to kiss her full on the lips.

Then she was startled to hear Jeffrey chuckling. 'Good show, my boy! There, Nora, I told you he'd be delighted.'

After dinner and many glasses of wine, offering toast after toast to the upcoming nuptials, Rupert was drunk. So much so that when Jeffrey retired to his study with his paperwork, Nora decided to go to her room so as not to be alone with him.

But Rupert pleaded with her. 'Please don't go yet, Nora. I know I acted rather badly at tea today, but you must give me a chance to make amends.'

'It's not necessary, Rupert. I can understand that our news was something of a shock and that naturally you reacted.'

'Yes, I did, and not like a good sport at all.'

'I hardly think that being a good sport is at issue—'

'But it is. In any contest there are two men, sometimes even, two *good* men and—'

'But we're not talking about a contest, Rupert.'

'Oh yes, a contest, and may the best man win . . .' He laughed and shrugged. 'I guess the best man won.' He poured himself another glass of port.

195

'But it *wasn't* a contest,' she said firmly, 'and never a case of a best man.'

'You're absolutely correct. I was just trying to be sporting. Actually, I don't think the best man won at all. You should have waited, you know.'

She pushed her chair back to rise, but Rupert rose to speed round the table to put his hand on her shoulder, pressing down hard to hold her fast to her chair. Resigned then that she was going to have to listen to him but that she wasn't going to hear anything she wanted to hear, she asked wearily, 'Waited for what?'

'For me to marry you.'

She didn't look at him. 'It was never a question.'

'But I was going to, you know. As soon as a decent amount of time elapsed. I did so want to do the decent thing. That's my style and I thought you'd appreciate that quality – decency. Still, you must have known how I felt about you.'

'I don't think you should say any more, Rupert. You've had too much to drink and—'

'Yes, I *have* had quite a lot to drink but that doesn't change anything. You know what they say: *in vino veritas* . . . And there *was* a biblical tradition to be upheld, you know. When one brother in a family dies, the other brother is supposed to take up the standard to marry the merry widow and raise the orphans. Oh, I forgot. You and Hubert *weren't* married, were you? And Hubie's *not* his son. That *does* put a different face on things, doesn't it?'

She wouldn't respond. It was foolish to respond to a man as drunk as Rupert. Still, she was very upset. While she had expected that Rupert might react badly to hers and Jeffrey's news, she had never expected this. She hadn't dreamed that Rupert might be thinking of *her and him.*

But actually, Hubert had warned her. It had been that night when she had at last given up on their being lovers. What was it he'd said? *I wouldn't be surprised if both*

196

Rupert and Father were plotting how to kill off the black sheep . . . Of course it was only a sorry joke. But when she'd protested, asking why either one would want him dead, he'd answered: *maybe because they're both in love with the fool of a black sheep's wife and each one wants her for his very own.*

Oh, no fool Hubert, but very much dead just the same.

She shook off the pressure of Rupert's hand on her shoulder. 'I'm going to bed now and I suggest that you do the same. After a good night's rest I'm sure you'll feel differently about things.'

'I doubt it but I've just realized. *Of course* you wouldn't wait for me to marry you. Why would you? It wasn't so much a husband you wanted, or even a father for Hubie. It was that you couldn't wait to be the Countess Hartiscor . . .'

Lying in bed, unable to sleep, she decided that the only solution was to insist that Jeffrey ask Rupert to take up residence elsewhere even if this meant revealing to Jeffrey what Rupert had said and how much hostility simmered beneath his surface. It was not what she wanted at all – to come between father and son – but she didn't know what else she could do.

But then in the morning a roomful of flowers arrived with Rupert's profuse apologies, declaring how much her friendship meant to him and how much he wanted to play the good uncle to Hubie. And she decided that she had to forgive him his lapse. She had experienced a few of her own and she had forgiven Hubert so many. Besides, she owed it to both Jeffrey and to Hubie to give Rupert the benefit of any doubt.

A date was set for the wedding in early March. Rupert thought a very grand celebration was in order – one that would give all of London something to talk about, with a reception for a thousand guests including the aristocracy from the Continent as well as Britain's own, plus all the American friends Jeffrey had accumulated over the years, including Harry Truman and Ike. If they were going to do it at all they might as well do it right and show the world that they didn't give a damn about any still-circulating gossip.

Rupert was so enthusiastic, elaborating on every detail from the selection of the wines down to the colour of the table-cloths, that Nora was touched though she said she wanted a much smaller wedding. When he still insisted on orchestrating the proceedings, selecting the flowers, the music and planning the menu, she let him take over. She knew it was his way of making up to her.

Then, as it turned out, she had no reason to regret it – the wedding came off beautifully, there wasn't nearly the coverage by the Press that she'd anticipated and had been dreading, and the only dark shadow hovering over the celebration was the king's death a month earlier. (Jeffrey had been very fond of King George.)

In fact, every detail of the reception was so perfect, Jeffrey commented that even Hubert who had been so good at these things, couldn't have done it better. Then Rupert nodded and smiled agreeably and Nora was pleased. It looked like there was plain, if not exhilarating, sailing ahead . . .

17

Once they settled down to their daily routine, Nora discarded any lingering doubts she may have had about Rupert. His attitude was splendid in every way. He was very good with Hubie, playing games with him, teaching him to play chess, reading him bedtime stories. And he was very sweet with her, offering escort service when

Jeffrey was unavailable for some function, and whenever she needed help with some fund-raising event, he was there, generous with his time and practical business advice.

When Nora said as much to Jeffrey, he blustered: 'He *better* behave himself or I'll send him packing. I'm still the lord and master around here, not some impotent old dotard.'

Nora laughed. 'Hardly impotent and I'm willing to testify to that.'

She didn't say it only to flatter him – it was simply the truth. When it came to sex, Jeffrey was proving practically insatiable. Merely seeing her *begin* to disrobe, removing nothing more seductive than her pearls, was enough to put ideas into his head. And just the sight of her sitting at her dressing table in a négligé was enough to inspire an erection of enormous proportions, and then he'd lead her to bed where he unfailingly proved a lusty and vigorous lover.

But she couldn't say that she was thrilled by the incessant lovemaking, despite his virility and the impressive size of his organ. Rather, she quickly came to regard the arduous lovemaking as only one more of her varied duties and obligations as Lady Hartiscor – overseeing the running of the house, attending and hosting various private and public functions, or serving as chairwoman for charities that administered to the needy. Nevertheless, she threw herself into the job of satisfying her husband's every sexual demand with energy and vigorous, if simulated, enthusiasm, gratified that she could make him happy. It was the least she could do for the man who thought only of pleasing her, who was forever presenting her with some gift: a gold bracelet set with sapphires to match her eyes, or a painting she admired, even a country estate in the Cotswolds, remembering that she had told him how much she missed the place of her youth.

Calling Merrillee Manor her dowerage, he said, 'Now, when you long for a sight of your old home, all you have to do is hop in the car and before you know it you'll be home again.'

That wasn't *strictly* correct, she thought. She believed in the old adage: home is where the heart is, and the only place she could truly call home was wherever Hubie was. But it was a lovely gift and she knew that any woman who wouldn't appreciate Jeffrey and his thoughtfulness would be not only an ungrateful bitch, but a foolish one as well.

Even when it came to Hubie's education, Jeffrey was considerate of her feelings. While she knew that he would have loved nothing better than to have her every waking moment devoted to him alone, he allowed her to engage a tutor rather than sending Hubie off to boarding school since he knew that was her fervent wish – to keep her son close by her side.

No, she could not complain, and yes, everything was going smoothly, if not excitingly, and she had no right to even wish for more, she reminded herself. Certainly not for a young Prince Charming to set her pulses racing, to set her body on fire. Dreams like that were fine for eighteen year olds hungry for excitement and mad for love, but absolute rot for a mature lady of character with a child to consider, with obligations and responsibilities. And she had so much to be thankful for – Hubie, Jeffrey and maybe even Rupert.

Who knew? Perhaps if she kept trying, she could even turn Rupert around into a more well-rounded individual – even a modern-day hero as interested in feeding the poor, or in building museums and hospitals, as he was in the business of making money. She was sure Jeffrey would be pleased if she could manage that. He was forever saying that what Rupert needed was to expand his horizons.

Moreover, it would be wonderful for Hubie to have that kind of man around as a role model. While no one could have been more devoted than Jeffrey, his age and position still rendered him too remote to take the place of a father . . . to indulge in a bit of rough and tumble with Hubie, to talk over any problems a boy might have, to offer some male guidance when necessary. But Rupert was exactly the right age to play father and since he was already handy and fond of Hubie, he did seem the natural candidate. And though she hated to admit it, it was becoming evident as time went by that Hubie, who had the attention span of a gadfly, could well use some male guidance in addition to that of his tutor, whose personality was as dry as overdone toast. It was no wonder the poor man had a problem keeping Hubie's interest.

'A short attention span is a sign of the quick intelligence,' Rupert consoled her, and Nora, already convinced that no little boy was sweeter, was thrilled to hear it. But she was also convinced that quick intelligence or not, no boy was ever lazier. Hubie would go to any length to avoid doing anything for himself that others could do for him. Whenever she, determined to avoid spoiling him, insisted he remove his clothes from his bedroom floor, or pick up the army of lead soldiers scattered over the library carpet, he'd smile at her winsomely and tell her he was too tired. 'Can't Ella do it, or Mary? Mary *likes* to do it, Mummy, she told me so.'

Then when she told him that the servants were too busy and that he could rest after he had picked up the toys, his bottom lip would quiver adorably and he'd complain that his arm hurt him, or his stomach. Then when she still insisted that he get on with it, he would get down on the floor and lie there moaning as if in terrible pain. Or he'd retch all over everything making a clean-up at someone else's hands an absolute necessity. Then she'd end up marvelling at how he was able to vomit at will.

He was also determined to get around her general rule about limited amounts of sweets. He'd go into the kitchen and plague Cook for the biscuits she'd been instructed not to give him unless Nora herself gave a specific order. While this was what any child with a sweet tooth might do, it did seem to her that Hubie

201

was willing to go a bit further than the average boy to get his own way with the hapless woman. He'd plead and whine until the poor soul was out of her wits and would throw up her arms in surrender. Or he would charm her with kisses and tell her how much he loved her until the besotted woman handed over the whole jar of biscuits. And when he found it impossible to move the cook with either tears or kisses, he'd simply wait until her back was turned and *steal* the biscuits. But once confronted with his theft *after* he had already devoured them, the angel-faced biscuit thief would admit his guilt and say, 'I'm sorry, Mummy, I didn't *mean* to take them. It was just that I was so hungry and they were my favourites – the big ones with the raisins – that I forgot that I wasn't supposed to take them without permission. Don't be mad at me, Mummy. I won't do it again, I promise!'

But he did, of course, and would think up new excuses each time. Once after hearing Molly the parlourmaid telling Mary the chambermaid that the reason she had given in to temptation with a certain gentleman was that 'the devil made me do it, whispering in my ear', Hubie batted his long lashes at Nora and blamed the devil for whispering in *his* ear.

Rupert laughed heartily at that one. 'We best keep a sharp eye out for that old devil. Either that or make sure those maids make their confessionals where Hubie can't hear them relate what *else* the devil made them do.'

'Don't laugh, Rupert,' Nora protested, trying not to laugh herself. 'It's really not funny, you know.' The truth was, she was more disturbed than entertained.

Jeffrey told her she was overreacting. What scamp hadn't nicked a few sweets? Hubert, in his time, had made the pilfering of biscuits a major occupation. When he wasn't caught with his fingers in the jar, he'd deny he was the culprit, and when he was discovered in the act, he'd just promise he wouldn't do it again, but of course he did.

'Of course,' Nora smiled grimly. 'But what about Rupert? Did he steal sweets?'

'Certainly not. Rupert never misbehaved. I told you that. But sometimes when Hubert wasn't actually caught redhanded, he'd try his ruddy best to lay the blame on Rupert.'

'And Rupert was punished?'

'No, even *Miranda* didn't swallow Hubert's lies.'

'What happened then? Did she punish him for lying?'

Jeffrey laughed. 'I suppose you could call it a *kind* of punishment. Miranda's own form of justice. She'd make Hubert apologize to Rupert and then when it was time for treats, she'd give Rupert two sweets instead of one. That was to make up for his having been falsely accused. But then Hubert got two sweets, too, his reward for having apologized. I wouldn't be surprised if he got three. The truth was, Miranda just couldn't bear Hubert to do without.' He sighed. 'But I dare say, in the long run, it didn't matter.'

'While I know it's in bad taste for the second wife to be critical of the first, I think that it did matter, that it was deplorable. It was reinforcing Hubert's unacceptable behaviour pattern. If he knew that he could steal sweets, put the blame on Rupert, then be made to apologize because no one believed him, and *then* be rewarded with two treats for apologizing, he was receiving a negative message. As for Rupert, he was getting a negative message, too – being rewarded just for being falsely accused.'

'I'm sure you're right but you're making my head spin.'

She suspected that she was making Jeffrey's head spin only because he wasn't really interested. Rupert's words rang in her ears: *when it comes to family matters, Father tries never to assume responsibility.*

'So why didn't you step in?' Nora persisted. 'At least tell Miranda that you thought what she was doing was wrong?'

'Miranda and I didn't get along very well as it was and I hesitated to interfere in matters that were her domain.'

'But Hubert said there was bad blood between Anne

203

and Miranda. Didn't you feel that you *had* to step in there?'

'Anne?' His voice froze her. 'I don't discuss Anne. Her name is not to be mentioned in this house.'

He's furious with me, Nora thought. Never had he been really angry with her before. 'I'm sorry,' she said and she was. Still, she couldn't help thinking that if he had, at least, *tried* to reconcile mother and daughter, maybe Anne would never have run off to Australia, would never have succumbed to the Hartiscor disease – death by the rope.

But then Jeffrey smiled chidingly. 'Such a sad face, my dear,' he said as he kissed her. 'Do you know what I think the problem is? You've been reading too many books on child rearing. And my advice is just be glad Hubie is a high-spirited young boy and concentrate on *this* old boy's high spirits.'

He took her hand and pressed it to his erection. 'Now, isn't that much more demanding of your attention?'

She came to the conclusion that she *was* overreacting. It was just that she'd read that long before a child entered his teens, his character was shaped, and she was anxious not to make any mistakes in Hubie's formative years, like Miranda had with her children. And while she felt guilty for having the thought, she didn't think Jeffrey was that innocent either. He'd admitted that he had thought what Miranda was doing was wrong, but had shrugged off responsibility, just as Rupert said.

Finally she decided that Hubie had to go to school instead of being tutored at home, with a houseful of adults dancing attendance on him. What he needed was the company of friends his own age, the give and take of playing with other boys, learning to get along in the real world. Then, since she couldn't bear the thought of sending him away to boarding school, she enrolled him at the Treadwell Academy, only a fifteen-minute drive from home, traffic permitting.

But almost immediately there were negative reports. The outstanding charge against Hubie was that he was a disruptive force in the classroom. He was inattentive, was frequently disobedient albeit charmingly so, and seemed always to be at the centre of all the small disturbances that plagued a boys' school. Nothing monumental. A schoolyard scuffle or a small prank – a professor's note-book disappearing to be found in an unpopular boy's desk, or a paper ball fight as soon as the instructor's back was turned. According to Hubie, he was almost always innocent – the other boys made him do it, or if it were a fight, the other boy pushed first.

Nora was upset but Jeffrey usually came to Hubie's defence, especially if it were a fight. 'What would you have the lad do? Stand there and take it on the chin? Do you want to turn him into a bloody pacifist who won't defend himself?'

'Of course not. But how do I know he was only defending himself? That the other boy really shoved first? You know how Hubie always—' She broke off. She had almost said, 'You know how Hubie always lies and blames others.' She was falling into the trap of thinking that if Hubie lied once, he was lying again, finding him guilty by reputation. Then, thinking that he'd be disbelieved anyway, Hubie would not hesitate to indulge himself in any minor indiscretion.

Even when Hubert had lied about having all those sessions with Dr Webster, even when he had made up that dream about Rupert sodomizing him . . . one truth had slipped through the barrage of fabrications. *Dr Webster says I'm having this dream because it really happened. And then I didn't tell Father about it either because I was afraid he'd call me a liar because he never believed me. Or I did tell him and he did call me a frigging liar.*

Poor Hubert. Even in his fantasized dream that truth had emerged – that he'd be branded a liar automatically. Well, she wouldn't make that mistake with Hubie – call him a liar without giving him the benefit of the doubt.

And if she found out he was lying, she'd do more than accept an apology, then give him a treat. She'd try to teach him that the truth brought its own rewards and convince him that lies were the refuge of the weak and the cowardly, and brought only misery.

And one day, when he was older and she herself was stronger, she would tell him how she attempted to shroud his own birth in a lie and how it all turned out . . .

18

Since Hubie already had a tarnished reputation at Treadwell, Nora transferred him to the Wheaton School so that he wouldn't be damned before he was out of the starting gate. She tried to impress upon him the importance of starting off on the right foot. He was to follow the rules, pay strict attention to his teachers and not do any old thing that popped into his head before thinking about it twice.

'I know what you mean. Like looking before you leap.'

'Exactly!' She was delighted that he grasped the concept.

But then like a self-fulfilling prophecy, only a few days later, when confronted with a huge puddle in the schoolyard, Hubie, along with another boy, jumped right into the middle of it. Hubie and Peter Horton not only drenched themselves with filthy water, they splattered a half-dozen other boys *and* the irate assistant headmaster, who insisted that the two boys had jumped with malice aforethought, displaying a reckless disregard for the health and comfort of others. The school chose to make much of the incident and asked that Lord and

Lady Hartiscor come in to discuss the matter, along with the Hortons. But Jeffrey refused to go, calling the whole thing poppycock, and advised Nora to forget about it as well.

'But I have to go to straighten out this silly thing. To say that the boys jumped with malicious intent is ridiculous and I don't want it to be a black mark on Hubie's record.'

'What does Hubie have to say in his own defence?' Jeffrey arched an eyebrow.

'I haven't spoken to him yet. I wanted to talk it over with you first. Decide how we wanted to proceed—'

Jeffrey smiled thinly. 'Perhaps what you should do is hire Hubie a barrister and demand a trial by jury.'

Hurt, she drew back. If that was a joke it was a snide one, bordering on the caustic. Either Jeffrey really thought the matter so trivial he was making fun, or the whole business of Hubie's behaviour was growing so tedious that he wanted to drop it completely. And that led to another question. Had he ever really been that concerned about her son whom he'd adopted, or had he only pretended to be, so that she'd throw herself more wholeheartedly into the business of pleasing *him*? Disappointed, she turned to Rupert for counsel.

'Do you think the school's making a fuss about nothing?'

'Of course they are and of course the conference with the two hellions on the carpet will turn out to be a junior inquisition, but—'

'Hold on. *Hellions?* That implies guilt and—'

Rupert caught her hand affectionately. 'It's just a term, not an indictment. And I still remember Mummy saying how she couldn't *abide* a boy who didn't have a touch of the hellion in him,' he laughed. 'I don't believe she really ever forgave me for being better behaved than Hubert.'

'Oh, poor Rupert. That must have been so difficult for you. And I'm convinced that the traumas of childhood

207

are never really outgrown. That's why I want to be very careful to do the right thing now. And I especially don't want Hubie to get the reputation of being a troublemaker or a liar. Once he gets the name – well, you know how it is. He'll think if he has the name, he might as well have the game.'

'You're absolutely right. Besides, guilty or innocent, how would it look if you didn't go and defend Hubie? It would appear as if you didn't care.'

'I have no intention of defending Hubie if he's wrong.'

Rupert smiled sadly, shaking his head. 'That's what you say now, but once you get into that room with the Hortons and those prune-faced Wheatonites, you'll defend him, just like Miranda always defended Hubert. If anyone dared attack her darling, she stood ready to pluck out the offender's eyes.'

'But Rupert, I'm not Miranda and Hubie isn't Hubert.'

'Of course not. It's just that – well, Hubie *is* so much like Hubert they really *could* have been father and son.'

'Oh really?' she said frostily, though it was the same chilling thought that had occasionally flashed through her own head. 'Why? Because there's a physical resemblance? Because Hubie's so handsome, and so was Hubert? Half the people in the world probably have blue eyes and blond—'

'But even you can't deny that there's more than a *physical* resemblance. There's a similarity of personality.'

'Hubie does have the same devastating charm that Hubert did, if that's what you mean,' she said coolly, 'and the same love of a good time. Is that what you're referring to?'

'I can see you're annoyed. Let's drop it, shall we?'

'No, I want you to say what's on your mind. I insist.'

'I don't want to offend you, Nora, but – Well, it's as if Hubie *were* Hubert's son and inherited his most significant characteristic – that lack of moral fibre we once discussed, if you recall.'

Oh, she recalled all right – the lack of moral fibre he had called a weakness of character – and she felt like slapping him. *How dare he?* But she *had* insisted he say the damning words even though she knew beforehand what he was going to say. And she knew only because the same thought sometimes crept into her head to bedevil her. *A significant characteristic . . .* She herself thought of it as a condition, an affliction. *Flaws of character in an otherwise perfect physical specimen . . .*

'But I know that's foolish,' Rupert said now, repentant. 'Hubert was a grown man and Hubie's only a little boy, just full of the devil. I'm sure he'll grow out of whatever – will you forgive me for saying that? I was just—'

'Just trying to be helpful?' She tried to smile.

'Something like that. You must know by now that I only want to be yours and Hubie's friend and I want to help in any way that I can. Will you let me?'

She thought of how Jeffrey had backed away from her problem. 'Of course. I wouldn't dream of turning down a good offer, even from the devil himself.' But then she laughed at how the words sounded. 'Sorry, I didn't mean to imply—'

Rupert laughed, too. 'I know. But we do have a deal? And when you go to that beastly conference at Wheaton, why don't I go with you to lend my support?'

'Thank you, Rupert. That *will* be a help.'

She went into Hubie's room to get his side of what had now become the infamous puddle-jumping caper, but he was already asleep. She looked at him in the dim glow of the night light: his yellow hair curling on the blue pillow slip, the long lashes curling in shadow on his pink cheeks, the lips – still a baby's rosebud, curved in a smile as if he were dreaming the sweet dreams of angels. She smoothed the pure brow gently, leaned down to kiss it lightly. He didn't *look* like a boy who suffered from an affliction, a chronic condition.

How *could* Hubie's character be a carbon copy of

Hubert's? Wasn't a flawed character something that would have to be transmitted in the genes? Could it come into existence by some mysterious form of osmosis? Was it a contagious disease, the bacteria floating in the air, ready to infect the vulnerable young in close proximity? Could a little boy who looked like an angel and was as sweet as one catch the disease simply by being given a name that didn't belong to him? And if so, what other manifestations might suddenly appear? Would he grow up another sweet ne'er do-well, a charming charlatan, a foolish rogue, a man who loved well but unwisely?

As she had sometimes wondered in the past she wondered again about what kind of a man Hubie's genetic father, the Duke of Butte, Montana, had really been. Other than that he was a boorish oaf, she knew absolutely nothing else about him. It had never occurred to her, not even out of curiosity, to try and find out anything. Did he lie? Could he be sweet? Did he pilfer? Did he love his mother? Did he cheat at games? Did he betray? Did he know right from wrong? Had he made callous love because he was a callous man or was it only that he had been indifferent to *her*? Had there existed in the man a wellspring of love waiting to be tapped by the right woman . . . another man perhaps . . . or his very own child?

Had the battlefield somehow made a better man of the man she had known only for a few hours? Had he *survived* the battle? Was he alive and well in Butte, Montana, living a far better life than he himself ever dreamed possible? Should she make it her business to find out for Hubie's sake?

She dismissed the thought. Johnny Wayne had planted the seed, but a man could sow thousands of seeds and scatter them to the winds. It was those who cultivated the soil and nurtured the delicate plantings who had to take responsibility for the eventual harvest. Johnny Wayne was as much a stranger to Hubie as he was to her. No, she had to put her trust in the people who knew and loved her and Hubie, and served them well – Jeffrey (whom she had to forgive one tiny lapse) and Rupert, who had given her his pledge.

Rupert proved his worth as an ally when he accompanied her to the meeting at Wheaton. Amazingly enough, he put the whole matter into perspective quickly, with charm and humour, managing to smooth everyone's ruffled feathers, even the doughty Mrs Horton who had been convinced that Hubie had influenced her Peter into misbehaving.

First he got the two boys to admit that indeed, they *had* jumped deliberately but only for the sheer joy of jumping. Then he pleaded their case eloquently before the stodgy Wheaton bunch. Who was so old that he had forgotten the pleasure of being young and jumping for joy into a puddle, and who was so hardened that he could punish a boy simply for being so joyously young? Before the meeting was over, both boys swore that they would certainly think twice before they leaped the next time and all the adults were pleased though no one quite believed them. Then everyone was shaking hands and laughing, saying things like, 'Boys will be boys', and 'Would we want them to be any other way?'

Then Rupert brought the tears to everyone's eyes when he suddenly bent down to hug Hubie to him. 'He's my brother by adoption, you know, and he's quite a boy, the very best, and I couldn't love him more even if he were my very own.'

On the way home Nora suddenly took Rupert's hand and pressed it to her cheek. 'You were wonderful!'

'Much as your praise is music to my ears, I really didn't do very much.'

'To me it was a lot. It was everything. And I was just thinking that, after all, blood *will* tell.'

'Now, what does *that* mean?'

'It means that this afternoon I could really tell that you

211

were Hubert's brother,' she teased. 'For the first time I could see that you and he shared two very significant characteristics.'

Rupert chuckled. 'In that case you better tell me quickly what these two significant characteristics are so that I'll know whether to be pleased or alarmed.'

'Oh, no cause for alarm. They were two of Hubert's best qualities, those that I hope Hubie will *always* be blessed with too – his charm and his loving ways.'

Seeing Rupert's face darken, she quickly asked, 'Does that upset you?'

'Of course not. Who wouldn't be thrilled to be called loving and charming by the lovely Nora? But why did it take you so long to discover that I'm as charming and as loving as my brother?' he asked, chiding her and smiling. Then he stopped smiling. 'And I was marvelling at what an extraordinary man Hubert really was.'

'Extraordinary? Yes, he was, in many ways. But extraordinary is like beauty, seen through the eye of the beholder. How do you see Hubert as being extraordinary?'

'Out of the many qualities that make up a man and out of all the *uncharming* things Hubert actually was – if we're to be honest – to be remembered best for being a loving and lovely man? I must say that takes an extraordinary man.'

She turned away to look out of the car window at the increasingly darkening day, depressed that so much bitterness still rankled in Rupert's heart for his dead brother. And then she saw two lovers kissing on the street and another thought, even more disturbing, popped into her head. Was it only bitterness that rankled or was it *still* jealousy? But she was no longer his brother's love. She was his father's wife . . .

She turned to look into Rupert's face to try to read his heart, but his eyes were burning into hers and she had to look away again. Then the car pulled into the courtyard and Parks opened her door and she gently touched Rupert's arm. 'Come, let's go and find Jeffrey and tell him how wonderfully it all went and how it was *you* who won the day.'

19

Nora was ready to leave for the reception at the American Embassy – a farewell party for Hugh Cantington who was going home after serving as his country's ambassador to the Court of St James's for over ten years. But when she went in to say good night to Hubie, he begged her to stay at home with him. 'I have a stomach-ache and my head hurts, too,' he said piteously.

After speaking to the doctor, she went down to tell Jeffrey that he should go on to the reception without her. She found him impatiently striding back and forth in the library. 'We must leave at once or we're going to be late.'

'I think I'm going to stay at home with Hubie, Jeffrey. He's not feeling well and—'

'Did you call the doctor?' he asked severely.

'Yes. He said it was probably a flu that's going around and that we should keep him in bed, give him an aspirin and lots of fluids and report back with him in the morning.'

'Well, has Hubie had his aspirin?'

'Yes, but—'

'And you *can* leave instructions with the staff that he's to be given fluids frequently and checked on constantly?'

'I suppose,' she said reluctantly.

'Well, then, that's all that's necessary, isn't it?'

'But you know how Hubie's been lately. When he's feeling sick he wants me, only me.'

'I know all too well. Did you ever stop to think that the reason he doesn't feel well so often is only to get more of his mummy's attention? You're spoiling him, Nora, giving in to his eternal complaints just like Miranda did with Hubert. At one point it got so bad it took a reception at Buckingham Palace to get her to leave the house. Believe me, you're not doing Hubie any good giving in to him and I *won't* have it. Besides, Hugh will be deeply disappointed if you're not there tonight. You know how fond he is of you. And Rita will take it as a snub. You know how she is – just looking for an opportunity to feel slighted.'

'But with five hundred guests there tonight neither Hugh nor Rita will notice I'm not there. And if they *should* ask for me, you can tell them I was sorry to miss their party, but it couldn't be helped. Please understand. I think this time Hubie's *really* sick. He's even running a slight fever.'

'I'm sure he is,' he snorted. 'There isn't a schoolboy living who doesn't know more than a few ways to raise the temperature artificially and I assure you that rascal probably knows every one of them. Now, will you say good night to him and get your wrap? You know I detest being late.'

She really couldn't blame Jeffrey for being annoyed. If she didn't go with him this evening, it would make the fourth time this month. But Hubie had been in tears and he hadn't been himself for weeks now. 'Why don't you go on ahead and then later if—' She broke off when Rupert walked in, after knocking on the open door.

'I hope I'm not interrupting a nice, private quarrel or anything cosy like that,' he said jovially. 'I'm planning a quiet evening at home and I thought I'd find myself a good whodunit. An Agatha Christie, maybe. She's not half-bad for a woman,' he teased, glancing slyly at Nora. 'But I see it's top-ho for you two tonight and I must say, you're both looking wonderful. You look especially spectacular tonight in that bare-back gown, Nora, even

214

more so than you did at the Coronation Ball. So, where are you chaps off to?'

'It's the affair at the American Embassy for Hugh Cantington if I can get Nora to tear herself away from Hubie.' Jeffrey's voice was thick with irritation.

'Oh? What's the problem with Hubie?'

'He's not feeling well. I know he's been complaining a lot lately and it usually turns out to be nothing, but I think he's really ill tonight. I thought I'd stay at home with him, but your father is very annoyed with me.'

'And if I were he, I would be too. You look far too smashing to stay at home and he wants to show you off. I think he wants all the men there, including old Hughie, to ogle you and eat their hearts out. Isn't that right, Father?'

Jeffrey permitted himself a smug smile. 'I do think Hugh is a bit soppy for Nora, but a lot of good it will do him.'

'Oh, stop it, both of you. What utter rot.'

'Well, you really will be a rotten sport if you spoil Father's good time when there's no need. I *am* staying in anyway and you know how good I am at playing nurse. First, we'll watch *I Love Lucy* on the telly, then I'll challenge Hubie to a hot game of Scrabble. He's not half-bad. He *is* a bit lazy about using his mind, but I know how to keep him interested. I allow slang words even though it's against the rules. I even allow slightly naughty words and then for every one he uses, I teach him another, slightly *more* vulgar.'

'Oh, wonderful!' Nora giggled. 'Just what any eight year old really needs in the way of vocabulary training.'

'Sounds like a splendid offer to me,' Jeffrey said, 'and Nora accepts. Now, may we please get going?'

'Are you sure you *really* don't mind, Rupert? I don't want to take advantage of you and I'm afraid that I do—'

'Off with you, wench!'

'Oh Rupert, you really are a dear!'

★　　★　　★

Dancing with Hugh Cantington, she felt slightly self-conscious remembering Jeffrey's 'I do think Hugh's a bit soppy for Nora'. Hugh *was* holding her a bit close, but he probably wasn't even conscious of it.

'I'm going to miss all my English friends,' he smiled at her wistfully. 'But no one more than you and Jeffrey.'

'And Jeffrey and I will miss you.' It was true. Hugh was a dear man and a thorough gentleman.

'You must plan on visiting us in the States.'

'That would be fun. I've never been to America.'

'When do you think that you might visit?'

'Well, I'm not sure.' She was having difficulty concentrating. Her thoughts kept drifting back to Hubie.

'You'll enjoy Washington.'

She couldn't get the picture of Hubie sobbing out of her mind as she answered, 'Oh, I'm sure.'

'Washington is particularly lovely in the spring.'

He'd been almost hysterical. 'So I've heard.'

'But the weather's dreadful in summer. In the summers we go to Cape Cod. We have a place there on the beach.'

'Oh, lovely.' *I shouldn't have left him, no matter what.* 'You must be eager to get home.'

'Yes and no.' She felt the pressure of his hand on her bare back increase. 'But I expect to be kept busy. Ike asked me to take a cabinet position. I told him no, but that I'd be happy to serve his administration in an advisory capacity.'

'Oh, how interesting!' This had to be the most inane conversation ever but she really wasn't up to small talk.

'So, you *will* visit?' He tightened his hold on her hand now. 'Perhaps you'd prefer to visit us in Cape Cod instead of Washington? Our compound, oddly enough, is right next to Joe Kennedy's, my esteemed predecessor.'

'Oh, that's nice. Are you friends or simply neighbours?'

Hugh laughed. 'Hardly friends. We did have a bit of a row over certain of his anti-Brit sentiments.'

216

'But that's such a long time ago. Before the war. Surely you've made up by now?'

'More or less. At least we've acted neighbourly on those occasions we've bumped into each other which, naturally, has been infrequently since I've been serving here.'

'Naturally . . .'

Wondering what they'd talk about next, she smiled into Hugh's face but all she saw was Hubie's face, flushed and frightened, the tears rolling down his cheeks in torrents.

When she'd gone upstairs to tell him that Rupert was going to stay with him until she returned, he had clung to her convulsively. *What am I doing here having this silly conversation with Hugh Cantington when Hubie needs me?*

She pulled away abruptly. 'You'll have to excuse me, Hugh. Hubie was ill when I left. I *must* go! Will you tell Jeffrey that I've left? That I'll send the car back for him?'

Jeffrey came running out just as she was stepping into the Rolls. He was very angry. 'What is this sudden madness, Nora? Hugh was terribly upset!'

'I'm sure he'll get over it. And *you* don't have to leave. *Please* go back to the party, Jeffrey.'

'I insist you come back inside with me.'

'I can't. I have this feeling that Hubie needs me!'

'But Rupert is taking care of him.'

'I should never have left—'

'Very well,' he said huffily. 'I'll return home with you so that we may both attend to this terrible emergency.'

Nora raced up the stairs with Jeffrey close behind her. She supposed he wanted to be in position to turn to her the moment they saw a peacefully sleeping Hubie to crow: 'There, are you satisfied? Pleased that you forced us to leave the party?'

But he never had the opportunity to deliver those words for when she opened the door very, very quietly so as not to wake Hubie in case he was sleeping, what they saw by the scant light in a room full of shadows was a silent Hubie lying completely naked in his bed, face down, his legs spread apart. Then it took another moment to register that Hubie was gagged and that astride him was Rupert, his nude body glistening with sweat, as he thrust and shoved, thrust and shoved . . .

Then as she screamed out, she heard Jeffrey gasp, 'Oh my God, it *was* true!'

And she knew then, as she ran to the bed, that this wasn't only Hubie's nightmare they were living, but Hubert's as well . . .

20

Nora stayed on at Hartiscor House for several months until Jeffrey was well again, grateful for both their sakes that his stroke had only been a minor one. Then, his first week out of bed – promoted to a wheelchair – she told him that she was leaving.

She had just wheeled him out into the garden so that he could take the noonday sun and now he reached out to grab hold of a bordering row of yew hedges as if for support.

'*Leaving*? Are you taking a holiday? Why won't you wait until I'm well enough to go with you? It should only be another fortnight. Three or four weeks at the most. We'll go to the Riviera. Cannes or perhaps Monaco, stay at the Hotel de Paris. You always liked Monaco. And there's an invitation from Ari Onassis. He wants us to join him next month for a cruise. Winston will be on board and – or would you like to go to the States? We have an invitation from Hugh to—'

'I'm leaving for good, Jeffrey. I'm leaving *you*.'

'But why?' He clutched his chest.

She exhaled deeply. 'Please don't do that thing with your heart, Jeffrey. It won't work – the doctor said there's nothing wrong with your heart. And do you have to ask *why*?'

'But Rupert's gone!'

'Not quite. Living in a suite at the Savoy and taking care of Hartiscor business as usual is hardly *gone*. But that's beside the point in any case.'

'But it isn't! Rupert *is* the reason you're leaving and I have a plan that will take care of him! Listen to me!'

'I won't. Not this time. And the fact is that while Rupert has been the catalyst, he's not *the* reason I'm leaving, at least not the principal one. Hubie is. He was the reason I joined the Hartiscor family in the first place and he's the reason I'm cutting my ties with it now. To be frank, I can't get away from here fast enough. This is a haunted house – full of terrible ghosts. So *many* dead souls!'

A bit of the Jeffrey of old flashed in his eyes. 'Poppycock! You're being theatrical, as usual. I know all too well what a nasty thing happened here that night, but we *can* put it behind us! We *will*! I tell you I have a plan!'

'And I tell you that I'm not interested in your plan. It was difficult enough just to stay on here with Hubie until you were well enough for me to leave with a clear conscience.'

His eyes reproached her. 'A clear conscience? To walk out on me after all I've done for you?'

She should have expected he would say something like this, act like this, and she wondered how it was that she had never seen before how full of little tricks he really was.

'It's better, Jeffrey, if we don't talk about what you've done for me. Remember the day you asked me to marry you? I said that you had been *so* good to me and I meant it. Then you said that I had always given as good as I received. But while the words pleased me, I didn't believe you. I felt that I owed you so much more and I agreed to marry you for *that* reason, and for Hubie's sake. Because you were going to adopt him. But they were the *wrong* reasons and most probably I got what I deserved. But Hubie didn't deserve what *he* received. And as I see it, my staying here with you until you recovered was giving you a gift of time and, emotionally speaking, it's been a very expensive gift. It hasn't been easy being here after what happened. Hubie still wakes up in the middle of the night crying and so do I. Crying for Hubie *and* for Hubert.'

'You blame *me* for what Rupert did? Is that fair?'

Fair! Such an inadequate word!

'Did Hubert come to you, a terrified little boy, to tell you that his brother was buggering him?'

'Yes, but—'

'And were *you* fair? Did you believe him? Did you even *think* to try and find out what the truth was? Or did you call him a despicable liar and let it go at that?'

Jeffrey didn't answer, his fingers nervously toying with the fringe of the plaid throw covering his legs.

'Then I *must* blame you, mustn't I?'

A little cry escaped Jeffrey's dry, white lips. 'But who would have believed Hubert? Would *you* have?'

That was a tough question. One she had asked herself over and over again. But how could she in all honesty answer for that period in Hubert's life? By the time she'd met him it was all past history and Hubert's future was already a foregone conclusion – death by hanging.

'If Hubert had come to me when he was a child I think that I would at least have *tried* to find out the truth, as I would have *if* Hubie had come to me. But he didn't. He was afraid to tell me and why was he afraid? Because Rupert had convinced him that no one would believe him, that he'd be punished and reviled for telling lies. And Rupert was *so* persuasive only because it had all happened before in exactly the same way. Who would believe Hubie, the little liar, over him, the respected

Rupert Hartiscor of sterling character who one day will be the thirteenth Earl of Hartiscor?'

'But he won't be!' Jeffrey cried. 'Let me tell you what I plan to do! I'm not going to let Rupert go unpunished!'

Nora shook her head. 'The point I'm trying to make is not whether Rupert's going to be punished. The point is that what happened with *both* Hubert and Hubie could only have come about because you and Miranda had already created a hell on earth here, a place where something so evil *could* occur. You two made this house a breeding ground for terrible events – for tragedy. You made it all part of the Hartiscor legacy and Hartiscor history. And you're the one who taught me that history always repeats itself. Well, I'm getting Hubie out of here before any more bad things happen to him . . . before he, too, is laid to rest in the Hartiscor mausoleum of dead souls.'

Jeffrey smiled at her slyly. 'Would you call Hubie sitting in the House of Lords being confined to a mausoleum? And do you consider it such a *bad* thing to inherit the Hartiscor fortune? What woman in her right mind would turn down such a legacy for her son?'

She adjusted the plaid blanket higher to cover Jeffrey's shoulders since the sun had already begun to lose its warmth and there was a decided chill in the air.

'*This* woman could when that legacy includes a killing hostility that's bred in the bone. Abominable acts that generate more evil, more hatred, a cycle that never ends. And I have another kind of legacy in mind for my son, as absurd as it may sound to you – decency and good character, the ability to appreciate the important things in life, like love, laughter and hope. What hurts me most is that Hubert knew this – knew what the important things in life were and was reaching out desperately to find them, but he never had a chance. He was already too crippled by the past . . .

'Words!' Jeffrey said with contempt. '*Empty* words.

Do you think when Hubie is grown up he'll thank you for denying him his peerage and his fortune?'

'Not that I'm tempted, Jeffrey, but I *am* curious. It sounds as if you're offering Hubie that which is already Rupert's. Do you imagine Rupert is so contrite over what he's done that he'll step aside for Hubie to inherit in his place?'

Now Jeffrey leaned forward eagerly, thinking that he had her hooked, after all. 'That's what I've been trying to tell you, Nora. That I'm prepared to go to court to have Rupert's rights abjudicated.' He smiled at her triumphantly.

'You mean taken away from him?'

'Yes. On the same grounds, using the same words he wanted to smear Hubert with – moral turpitude, degenerate behaviour.'

She was astonished that Jeffrey actually believed it would be that simple. 'Don't you know that Rupert will fight you every inch of the way? Or do you think . . . hope . . . even *pray to God*, that he'll just crawl away to hang himself from a rafter at Hartiscor Castle?'

Jeffrey recoiled. 'That's unworthy of you, Nora. Are my sins so great that I deserve this from you?'

'Great enough,' she said bitterly, hugging herself, suddenly feeling cold. She looked up into the sky. 'Do you want to go inside? The sun's already gone.'

'What do you mean – *great enough*? Yes, I made a mistake in not believing Hubert and yes, I should have looked into it. But that was an error in judgement, not a crime?'

'What about Miranda falling down the stairs? Was that a crime? And what about Anne? Wasn't that a crime?'

At first Jeffrey stared at her uncomprehendingly. Then, when it came to him to what she was referring, he looked at her with as much hostility as Rupert had when she had gone to call on him at his suite at the Savoy . . .

Rupert was lounging on a gold velvet sofa when she

entered, poised, very much in control of himself, and at first as correct as he was icy. He stood up as he asked her to sit down, inclined his head in a small bow, then took a cigarette from a gold case and lit it with a gold lighter, exhaled a stream of smoke from his nostrils before offering her a cigarette which she refused, and then lunch in the Grill. 'It's that time of day and the food is superb.'

She had promised herself that she wouldn't lose control, wouldn't fly at him with pale polished nails extended to rake that arrogant face, would restrain herself from calling him all the terrible names that were on the tip of her tongue, burning to be shouted. All she said in clipped tones was, 'Yes, I know. Hubert and I often lunched here.'

'I should have known. If nothing else, Hubert always lunched at the best places in town.'

'I didn't come here to discuss Hubert.'

'Of course you didn't. Still, why *not* have lunch while you're about it?' He bared his teeth in a grimace of a smile.

'I didn't come to have lunch with you, either.'

He considered a moment, cocking his head. 'I suppose not. And now that we have *that* established, why don't you tell me why you *did* come so that I, at least, can go down to the Grill to have *my* lunch. Personally, I'm famished.'

'I came to tell you that I intend to file charges against you so that you'll be prosecuted for what you did. That I'm going to demand that you be arrested and be put away for—'

'No, that's not why you came here, Nora. If it were your intention to have me arrested, why *tell* me about it? Why not simply do it? Do you know what I think?' His voice rose and his eyes were slits. 'I think you came here for another reason entirely. I think you came here because you're a bitch on heat! My brother's slut! My father's whore!'

Oh my God, he's mad! And I was mad to come here!

223

She started to rise from the sofa, snatching up her gloves and purse, intending to make a rush for the door before he could say another filthy word. But, before she could straighten up, he was pushing her back down on the sofa.

'Where are you going so fast, whore bitch? You've just got here and you haven't had what you came for. We both know what you want. What you never got from either Hubert or Father!'

He unzipped his trousers.

'Get out of my way, Rupert! You're not stopping me from leaving! *I'm* not some frightened little boy!' She started to get up again, but again he pushed her back down.

He took his penis out of his trousers, but she tried not to look at it, keeping her eyes pinned to his face instead, trying to figure out her next move.

'Oh, yes, we both know you're not some frightened little boy, Nora. What you *are* is a hot, panting cunt who first married a pansy and then an old man. Poor Nora, she never did get a proper fucking, did she? Well, that's what you came for and that's exactly what you're going to get!'

And then he was on top of her, one hand reaching under her jacket to tear at the buttons of her blouse, ripping it open to expose her breasts barely covered by a lacy bra, while his other hand groped under her skirt. When she opened her mouth to scream, the hand mauling her breast formed a fist which he jammed between her lips and she bit into it, tasting blood. But instead of yowling with pain, Rupert laughed, his face glistening with a fine layer of sweat. 'So that's the way you want it? I should have known you'd like it rough!'

He slapped her, first one side of her face then the other. Realizing that she wasn't going to be able to stop him from doing whatever he wanted – he was simply too strong for her – she grew panicky and for a few moments lay there without moving, eyes closed, trying frantically to think what to do as he pulled off her stockings and then her panties, taking her silence and motionless state for compliance – mute desire – and she could feel his hot breath on her face.

And then she remembered the advice of the bouncer at the Cock 'n' Bull, a burly ex-sailor named Barney. 'When a matey gets too big for 'is britches, if you get me meaning, and too hard for a little bird like you to handle, you give 'im the old one-two-three. First you grab 'im by the ears, smashing 'is nob with your own and as 'e's seeing stars, you're letting go of the ears to thumb 'im in the eyes, at the same time bringing up your knee to wallop 'im in the old bollocks as viciously as you can manage. It's guaranteed to knock the wind out of any bloke's sails but, mind you, you got to take 'im by surprise and be quick about it!'

While she personally had never had occasion to try out Barney's technique, she *had* borne witness to Barney delivering the old one-two-three to more than one sorry bloke. But could she pull it off? If she tried and failed, Rupert might grow so incensed, so driven over the line, he might even kill her!

She heard him grunt, 'You know what I'm going to do? I'm going to give you what Hubert got, what sweet little Hubie got, since that's what you *really* want and I'm too much the gentleman not to oblige. So flip over!'

She knew then she *had* to do it now – try, at least – because if she didn't, and Rupert did to her what he proposed to do, *she* might slip over the edge herself and end up committing murder.

She opened her eyes to see him leaning back on his haunches to give her room to flip, his eyes glazed over.

Take him by surprise and then be quick . . .

'Oh yes, that's what I want! Oh yes!' Now she made her eyes shine with lust, and licked at her lips lasciviously. 'But first there's something I want to do. Something I *must* do! Stand up, Rupert, so that I can kneel at your feet . . .'

She wriggled off the sofa to stand over him as if in eager anticipation as his breath came in rapid, ragged gasps and he struggled to get to his feet. But before he could straighten up, she was quick to take him by surprise and delivered a vicious knee-jerk to his groin, successfully taking the wind out of his sails just as Barney had predicted.

If nothing else, Rupert was disabled enough so that she could take a few minutes to make some hasty repairs, enough at least to get her through the lobby. She did this in front of him rather than in the privacy of the lavatory so that she could keep an eye on him just in case he recovered enough to try to attack again. At least now she was positioned close enough to the door so that she could make a quick getaway.

But she doubted that it would happen. At least not today. Now, Rupert was darkly engrossed in making inroads on a bottle of Napoleon brandy. In fact, he no longer seemed to be aware that she was still there.

But he'd been correct in his evaluation of why she'd come there. She hadn't come simply to tell him that she intended to swear out charges against him. As he said, why bother to tell him about it rather than just do it? What she had come for was to ask him a question – get an answer that would enable her to close the Hartiscor chapter of her life for ever.

Now, with stockings in place, shoes on, the torn, blood-specked blouse discarded, her jacket buttoned to the neck to cover her breasts, and safely positioned at the door, she asked the question: '*Why*, Rupert, why did you do it?'

He looked at her with contempt. 'I gave you more credit than that, Nora. A simpleton could figure it out. There are acts of love and there are acts of hate – what the pros call acts of hostility.' He held his snifter of brandy up to the light, as if he were trying to see through it. 'And you know what they say – the line between love and hate is so thin, so fine, one is hard put to separate the two.

226

Now, I loved my Mummy, but she chose Hubert over me to play those little games with when I yearned for her to play them with me. So I performed an act of hostility against Hubert, but it was really an act of hostility against Mummy.'

He looked at her obliquely. 'That should be perfectly clear even to one as naïve as you.'

'But why Hubie? Surely he was innocent and he loved you! Trusted you. He didn't deserve your act of hostility!'

His look was one of pure hate. 'But you did! I loved you, but you loved only Hubert and Hubie. Then, with Hubert dead, I thought you would love *me*. But you didn't – you chose Father over me.'

'So what you did to Hubie was really an act of hostility against *me*?' she asked haltingly, the horror of it seeping slowly through her.

'*Now* you've got it! So you see, Nora, you aren't so simple or naïve after all. And you must understand that if you try to have me prosecuted, I will have to fight back.'

'But how can you? There were two of us who *saw* you – your father and I. Your own father. Two witnesses and Hubie. We'll support each other's testimony.'

'I know you. You'll never allow Hubie to testify, to go through all that. And Father will never testify against me.'

'He will!'

Rupert shook his head, smiled coolly. 'He won't. He can't. Father will never testify against me because if he does, I'll expose *him* and then he'll have no choice, but to go and hang himself.'

She was afraid to ask but forced herself to, her hand reaching out for the door knob. '*How* will you expose him?'

'Haven't you guessed yet? The night Mummy fell down the stairs, Father *pushed* her. No one else saw his hand on the small of her back as he pretended to put his arm around her in affection, but I was standing behind them and I saw!'

'I don't believe you! And no one else will either.'

He shrugged. 'Believe it or not. It's all the same to me. But I'm prepared to swear to it and it will be my pleasure to testify *why* he did it and then they'll *all* believe. It will be *their* pleasure to believe,' he laughed.

She turned the knob. She didn't want to hear any more, but Rupert went on, hissing: 'Don't you want to know *why* he pushed her? But you already know, don't you? Father pushed Mummy down the stairs to *silence* her. You see, *she* was going to blow the whistle on him – that he'd been fucking my sister Anne and had been doing it for years! Why do you think Anne ran away and even after she ran away, couldn't live with it and ended up hanging herself from a tree? But poor, little Anne, as I understand it, she botched the job, and lingered for hours . . .'

This was the moment of truth and she could not shrink from it now. 'If we go to court, Jeffrey – I to press charges against Rupert for what he did to Hubie, or you to have his right to inherit reversed – Rupert is prepared to make countercharges. He's going to swear that you *pushed* Miranda down the stairs the night she fell to her death.'

She watched him closely for some sign, but Jeffrey only sneered, 'Let him swear! He has no proof!' Then she still wasn't sure about Miranda – if it were true. She would never know for sure.

'And he's prepared to swear that the reason you pushed Miranda was because she was going to reveal that you and Anne were—' she forced herself to say the word '– lovers.'

She prayed that Jeffrey would sneer again, would say: 'Rot! Let him swear!'

But this time he didn't. This time he bowed his head and began to sob . . .

She held out her hand to make certain. Yes, there was a fine mist of moisture on her upturned palm. It was beginning to drizzle and she wheeled her husband into the house. He was still convalescing and she didn't want him to catch cold.

21

'I'll never give you a divorce!'

'I think that in the end you will,' Nora said, her voice quietly firm. They'd been arguing all afternoon, Jeffrey refusing to leave her room as she went through her wardrobes and drawers, choosing and discarding. 'I just wish you wouldn't make it harder, forcing me to do things I don't want to do.'

'Do you think you'll *force* me into giving you a divorce by blackmailing me with those charges of Rupert's? If you do, you're barking up—'

She shook her head wearily. 'How can you think that I want to dig up all your family skeletons? No, I'm quite willing to leave all the secrets and even the punishments to you and Rupert. All I want to do is to get all this behind me. All I want is a divorce, as fast and as simple as it can be.'

'Well, I have no intention of co-operating in this *simple* divorce and without my co-operation you'll never get one, you know. Adultery is the only grounds for divorce.'

'Yes, I know.'

'Then what do you propose to do? Set me up, as they say in the American thrillers? Will you send a scantily-clad tart to attack me bodily while a photographer leaps out of the closet to snap our picture?'

She smiled slightly at the ridiculous scene he conjured up. 'No, Jeffrey, I have no wish to tarnish your reputation. I'm prepared to be the adulteress and have you divorce *me*. And then you can tell everyone how the wife you took into your bed and heart proved so ungrateful as to be unfaithful, and I'm sure everyone will be properly sympathetic.'

'What about Hubie? Are you prepared to brand *his* mother an adulteress?' he taunted, thinking that this was one argument that would carry weight with her.

'I'm prepared to do anything I must to free us both.'

'It won't work, Nora. No matter what you do, I'll *never* divorce you. Never!'

'Oh, but you *will*, Jeffrey! I only wish you didn't have to make it more difficult by forcing me to hurt you. That was never my intention.'

She checked into the pretty little inn in Stratford-upon-Avon in Warwickshire with her friend, Tony Nash, but they were early. The detective whom her lawyer had hired to document her act of adultery wasn't due until two hours later.

'You must have more experience with this sort of thing than I do, Tony. What do we do until Mr Humboldt arrives?'

Tony, testing the bed by bouncing on it gingerly, laughed, which was the thing he did best as an actor who played romantic leads since he had perfect white teeth. 'Experience with this sort of thing? I've never been a co-respondent in a divorce before, if that's what you mean. This is a new, though entirely delightful, role for me.'

'But you *have* checked into a hotel with a lady who wasn't your wife?' she asked archly, checking the bathroom. Small but adequate with a large tub on clawed feet though she doubted she'd be there long enough to take a bath.

'Of course I have, especially since I've never had a

wife. But I've never before checked into a lovely country inn with so lovely a lady on my arm.'

Nora laughed. 'Really, Tony, you sound just like one of those silly charmers you're forever playing in your films.'

Tony pretended to be offended. 'What kind of role would you have me play? No one's exactly proposing Macbeth.'

'What a shame!' she said in mock sympathy. 'But tell me, Tony, how is it you've never married?'

Tony stretched out in the bed with his hands folded under his head. 'For the same reason I've never done Macbeth. No one's ever proposed. But that doesn't mean I'm not prepared to entertain an interesting proposal. And I can tell you what we should do while we're waiting for Mr Humboldt to smash down the door.' He fluffed up the bed pillow next to his and patted the empty space beside him. 'We can rehearse.'

'No, I don't think so,' she laughed. 'For one, you've always told me what a quick study you are so *you* don't need any rehearsing. And I'll just do what comes naturally.'

She wondered for a moment if she had made a mistake in allowing Tony to play her lover instead of the stranger her solicitor had suggested. But Tony had insisted that he'd love to help her out . . . that it would be marvellous fun. 'And who can fill the bill better than I?' he'd urged. 'I'm tall, dark and handsome, a most devilish rake – everyone says I would have made a damn fine Rhett Butler – and I've been in bed with the best of them. I ask you, whom do you know who has better credentials?'

And he hadn't changed his mind even when she warned him that it might not all be simple routine – that it might get nasty and that the pictures might well end up on the front pages of the more scandalous rags. All he'd said was, 'Oh, smashing! I hope so. I'd love to have people sit up and take notice that old Tony is as hot between the sheets as he is on the screen. It would probably do wonders for my career.'

She had preferred Tony to a stranger because it seemed less awkward this way and it could only help her purposes to have someone with a measure of celebrity, someone easily recognizable. But she had never imagined that there might be a problem with Tony forgetting that they were only *pretending*. They'd been friends for years and never once had he made an overture that might have been construed as overly familiar. Then again, he had never had reason to believe that she would be receptive to such a move. But now, under these circumstances, there was no reason for him not to believe it.

She went over to the bed to tug at his arm. 'Come, old chum, on your feet. Let's take a walk around town while we're waiting. We can visit the Royal Shakespeare Theatre and the house William was born in, and who knows? Maybe you'll grow so infused with the spirit of the Bard some great director will take one look, snap his fingers and say, "Tony Nash, I always thought you'd make a great Rhett Butler but I was wrong! What you are is perfect for my production of *Macbeth*!"'

'Oh, very well, let's take a walk if we must.' He grinned at her engagingly, stood up, bent down to kiss the crown of her upswept golden-blond hair. 'But are you quite certain that's the best suggestion you can come up with?'

Now that he mentioned it, she wasn't all *that* certain. Tony was very attractive and she was experiencing an odd sensation – as if an exotic butterfly had somehow flown into her vagina and was fluttering its wings . . .

Elston Humboldt was hardly the type of man Nora would have envisioned in this line of work. He was slight, sported a very small, neat moustache, wore rimless spectacles and a black suit – the sort of man she would have taken for a mortician, or even a vicar. But then, he did take a conservative approach.

'It's only necessary to bare the upper part of the body, Mr Nash. If you will, please remove your coat, tie, shirt, undervest and pop under the covers. And you, Lady Hartiscor, if you'll remove your blouse and join Mr Nash under the covers, we can commence.'

'Masterful direction,' Tony muttered, as she followed instructions, shushing him. 'Let's give the man a chance.'

But it seemed Mr Humboldt required only staid and static poses. The two of them sitting up with their backs upright against the bed's headboard while they looked straight ahead directly into the camera. Another with Tony's arm draped half-heartedly about her shoulders. Then the two of them lying supine, their arms languidly at their sides doing nothing more than staring listlessly into the camera.

When Tony complained that it all seemed rather bland and tepid considering they were documenting allegedly illicit behaviour, Mr Humboldt explained prissily: 'The two important things are to make sure the bed is recognizable as a bed and that we get a clear view of the faces so that positive identification can be verified.'

A shot of Tony kissing her ear was as passionate as the proceedings got.

'Can't I at least *bite* it?' he begged, but Mr Humboldt remained unmoved. 'Not at all necessary.'

'Oh hell, foiled again!' Tony grumbled, withdrawing his mouth from her lobe. 'I must say, Nora, this afternoon's a big disappointment. Doesn't it get any hotter than this?'

'It will,' she whispered. 'I promise.'

'When? Oh God, when?'

'Soon,' she giggled as the detective frowned.

Finally, he was finished. 'That should do it. I'll be in touch with your solicitor when the photographs are ready.'

But now she told him that she'd require *another* set of photos – this time in total undress and in more *explicit* positions, and Tony enthused, 'I say, that's more like it!'

233

But the detective blinked and said stiffly, 'I beg your pardon, Lady Hartiscor, but the pictures I have already taken will satisfy the courts as evidence of misconduct. Strictly routine in matters of this sort. It's not necessary to be more, as you say – *explicit*. No need for what may be construed as pornography,' he clucked, turning to pack up his equipment. 'No indeed, that wouldn't do at all.'

'Mr Humboldt, please understand. I'm not asking you to take *dirty* pictures. All I require is more – well, shots of what only *look* like compromising positions, but pictures no judge will ever look at.'

Mr Humboldt didn't respond, but they could see even the hairs of his moustache bristling.

'Listen here, old man, the lady says she needs more compromising positions and it's making me very cross that you seem to have a problem with that. Believe me, you *don't* want to get me angry,' Tony growled in imitation of a tough guy Hollywood-style, elbowing Nora in the ribs and enjoying himself thoroughly.

'Hush, Tony,' she whispered. 'This isn't a joke. You'll really spook him. Can't you see how nervous he is about getting involved in something other than just taking routine divorce stuff? He's afraid we're up to something else – something nefarious, hard-core stuff . . .'

'Some kind of blackmail?' Tony suggested, eyes sparkling.

Blackmail's not far from it, she thought, whispering: 'I really *need* these pictures, Tony. We have to manage to talk him into taking them or this whole thing's been a waste of time.'

'Don't worry, if you *need* those pictures, you're going to get them! I have the perfect convincer.'

A *convincer!* For a crazy moment Nora thought Tony was referring to a gun but he jumped out of bed to go to the Queen Anne desk to retrieve his wallet. Then, winking at her, he counted out several banknotes and handed them to Mr Humboldt and when the detective silently accepted and pocketed them, Tony winked at her

234

again and proceeded to divest himself of his remaining clothing. And then, still under the covers, she removed her chemise and panties.

They remained in bed until Mr Humboldt left. Then, suddenly embarrassed, she wrapped herself in the crumpled sheet and got out of bed, leaving Tony fully exposed. Then, self-conscious, she tried to avert her eyes from that which was very much in evidence – Tony in a state of arousal, a condition, she discovered, she shared. There was that sensation in her vagina again – the beating of butterfly wings, and she could feel her inner thighs growing moist.

'That *was* fun,' he said, but he wasn't so much as smiling.

Hoping to break the tension that was as thick as fog, she teased, 'If it was so much fun, why aren't you laughing?'

'Because I'm sad.'

'Oh, poor baby. Why is it sad?'

'Because I'm thinking how much *more* fun it would have been if we'd been doing it for real instead of faking it . . .'

First, she thought, he's absolutely right. It would have been lots of fun. And then she thought, it's *supposed* to be fun and never had she done it strictly for the fun of it. Then she allowed the sheet to drop to the floor.

At least once, just for the fun of it.

Nora spread the first set of photos – the relatively inoffensive poses of Tony and her – out on the library table before calling Jeffrey in to look at them. 'You can use this set of pictures to sue me for divorce.'

'But I told you there'd be *no* divorce,' he said coldly, before glancing at the pictures. Then, as his eyes quickly flicked from photograph to photograph, his normally ruddy complexion paled to grey. 'Where did these pictures come from?' he asked in a hoarse whisper.

235

'An inquiry agent took them.'

He picked up one to examine it closely then threw it down to pick up another, and repeated the process until he had examined all eight exposures at length. 'Who is this man?' he demanded, his voice low and harsh.

'A friend of mine.'

He laughed nastily. 'Yes, considering you're in bed together, one would think you'd classify him as a friend. But who is he? What's his name?' His voice was rising.

'Oh Jeffrey, it doesn't matter who he is.'

'How dare you? You've been carrying on like a common whore, you show me this filth, and you tell me it doesn't matter who he is!' His hand whipped out to slap her.

Her head snapped back and she staggered as much from the shock as from the impact of the blow. Though her impulse was to hit back, she struggled to contain herself, seeing his face go from pale back to bright red again, but now in fiery splotches. *Oh God, don't let him have another stroke!*

'For your own good, Jeffrey, I suggest you pull yourself together. You may be out of your wheelchair, but you're still not entirely recovered.'

It struck her then that, very possibly, she'd gone about things the wrong way. Still, he had given her no other choice and she didn't know what else she could have done. She only hoped he'd let her spare him the *other* set of photos. If he thought *these* were filth, what would he think of the others? How would he react? She was afraid to find out.

'Look, Jeffrey! These pictures were only taken for one purpose – as evidence so that you could divorce me. That's why I say it doesn't matter who the man is. He was only helping me out. He was simply a . . . a convenience.'

'Yes, I can see exactly how convenient he *was*. Or is it, how convenient he *is*? How long has he been your lover?'

His eyes bored into her as if expecting her to disinte-grate beneath his gaze, then drop to her knees to beg his forgiveness. She should have known that it would turn into this fiasco. That it wouldn't be clean and quick. Not with him trying to hold on to her with a growing desperation.

'He was always my friend, not my lover.'

He looked at her shrewdly. 'You say he *was* your friend. Past tense. Does that mean that now he *is* your lover?'

She was growing nervously impatient. She desperate-ly needed to have this business done with. 'It's not your business if he *is* or *isn't* my lover. Suffice to say that while you and I were living together as man and wife, I had no lover. Never even entertained the thought. But now that our marriage is over I have no obligation to be faithful to you.'

'Faithful! What does the word mean to a woman like you? But you still haven't answered my question? *Is* he your lover or not?' he thundered at her.

'And what if I said yes? Would you then agree to use these pictures to sue me for divorce?'

'No! As for your pictures, they're an obscenity and this is what I do with obscenities!' He scooped up a few of the photos, spat upon them repeatedly, then tore them and flung the pieces on the table like a furious child.

She looked at the scraps regretfully. 'I'm sorry you did that but there are copies should you change your mind.'

'Never!'

She moaned. She hadn't wanted to be cruel but he was leaving her no choice. Maybe she never had a choice. 'I think you will when I show you my other set of snaps.'

She went to the Georgian secretary to get the envelope and held it out to him. 'Before you look at them, I think you should know that if you don't go into court with those *other* photos, I intend to go to the tabloids with *these*. And believe me, I *will* do it though it will

237

cause me as much shame as it will you. But I think that in order to be entirely fair, you *do* have a right to know who the man in the pictures is, after all, since his celebrity will make the photographs even more valuable to those rags. I'm surprised you didn't recognize him even if you hardly ever go to the cinema, but I'm sure you've heard of him. He's the film star, Tony Nash.'

His eyes glazed over with contempt. 'An *actor*! I might have known!' He snatched the envelope from her, tore it open and let the pictures fall to the table. Then he picked them up one by one to let each flutter to the floor after he examined it as he began to weep – terrible, anguished cries. Then she knew that she had her divorce, hard won as it was.

She stooped to pick up the evidence of her 'adultery' – she lying spread-eagled with Tony on top of her, his mouth to her breast; another of his head buried in that space between her thighs; another, she kneeling on the floor as Tony sat on the edge of the bed, her mouth somewhere in the vicinity of his groin; all a medley of avaricious loins, of breasts, and buttocks and tongues, of frank abandon, lust and fulfilment.

The afternoon deepened into a melancholy twilight but neither of them made a move to turn on the lights. Somehow, now that it was all settled, they were, in a kind of way, at peace with one another and nothing seemed quite real.

'What kind of settlement do you expect?'

'I don't expect anything. Those pictures *aren't* blackmail, Jeffrey, no matter what you think.'

'You do understand that Hubie will get nothing? That—'

She cut him off. 'I understand. That was my intention.'

'Still, I'd like to give you and Hubie something.'

'I can't accept anything.'

'But what will you live on?'

'I haven't sorted it all out. I thought I'd sell my

238

jewellery. That should probably last us a couple of years. By then I shall have managed something.'

'And Merrillee Manor? It *is* yours, in your name. Will you sell it?'

'I would hate to.'

'Will you go to live there, then?'

'I thought I might, for a while. To think about what I'm going to do. I have Hubie's future to think of. But eventually, I'd like to go out into the world and bend it to *my* will, for a change. And . . .' she hesitated, not wanting to hurt him further, 'well, I'd like to have a little fun, too.'

I haven't had much of that.

'But what about Rupert?'

She looked at him, puzzled. 'What about him?'

'Are you resigned to seeing him go unpunished?'

'I don't think he *will* go unpunished.'

'What do you expect will happen?'

'I have this feeling you and he will work it out – fight it out, and one of you will be the victor and—'

She almost said, 'And the other will probably go hang himself,' but that would have been mean and unnecessary. 'And may the best man win,' she said instead, thinking that the best of the Hartiscor men, with the exception of Hubie who wasn't really a Hartiscor, had already lost.

She rose from her chair to go about the room turning on the lights. 'I'll ring for your tea.'

He looked at her then beseechingly. 'Will you join me?'

She hesitated. Having tea with Jeffrey seemed like such a small favour to grant and it was difficult not to feel pity for him. And he had, in his fashion, loved her and been good to her and Hubie. But once she started making room in her heart for pity, she'd be lost, lost again in the past.

And she *had* promised Tony she would come by at five-ish.

'I'm sorry, Jeffrey, but I have an appointment.'

At least once in a while, just for the fun of it . . .

PART FIVE

AND ONCE FOR THE FUN OF IT

England and Hollywood
1957–8

22

When Tony came down to Merrillee Manor for the weekend Nora assumed it was only for the pleasure of her company, but Tony soon confessed that he had come with an ulterior motive in mind – to ask her to tag along with him to Hollywood.

'Hollywood? You're going there to do a film then? Oh, Tony, that's wonderful!'

'*Hopefully*, to do a film. But Grantwood Studio – one of the biggest in the States – has asked me to test for a very famous role in a sequel to a very famous film that's in the works and you get three guesses as to which film it is.'

She thought a few moments. '*Gone With The Wind*?'

'You witch! How did you know? Someone told you! Tommy Purcell? He's the only person I've told. I'll murder him.'

'No, it wasn't Tommy. I haven't spoken to him in ages. I was just gazing into my crystal ball and I saw you playing Rhett. You made a dashing Rhett, but something was odd—'

'What?' he jumped on it quickly. 'You thought I looked too young for the part, is that it?'

'No,' she said thoughtfully. 'Maybe more like too *old*.'

'I beg your pardon,' he said, offended. 'May I remind you that Clark Gable was probably older than I am now when he played Rhett almost twenty years ago?'

She laughed. 'I wasn't serious, Tony, you nit. I don't even *own* a crystal ball.'

Apparently she could tease Tony the man and Tony the lover – his sense of humour was one of his most endearing qualities – but she should have known better than to tease Tony the actor. When it came to these things – age and looks – it seemed an actor's ego could brook no nonsense.

'Well, all right,' he said, only partially mollified. 'But *I'm* quite serious about your coming along with me to Hollywood. We'll really have a time of it!'

'It sounds very exciting, Tony, but I don't think so. I'm not ready.'

'Why do you have to be ready? I'm not asking you to marry me. All I'm asking you to do is come along for a bit of fun and games. You certainly could use a little of that and this is your chance, all expenses paid.'

'Oh Tony, it's sweet of you and I would love to, but I *can't*. I need time to—'

'Time for what? You've already had too much time hiding down here like a nun. Except, of course, for those times I took pity on you and came down to visit.' His eyes sparkled now that *he* was teasing *her*.

'But I haven't been hiding, I've been refreshing my spirit, renewing my energies and making plans for the future. I can't afford any rash moves. While I'm a single woman, I'm not free of my responsibilities as a mother and a breadwinner. And I just can't pick up and go running off with you, especially now that I'm on the brink of—'

'On the brink of what, for God's sake?' Tony demanded. 'A nervous collapse? Suicide? Middle age?'

It was the last that she pretended to take objection to. 'Middle age?' she shrieked. 'If you recall, I'm only thirty-two. And who'd know that better than you, you rat, since you're the one I celebrated my thirty-second birthday with at the film festival in Cannes? Did you forget? You know, on second thoughts, considering that you *are* seven years older than me, and already beginning to grow forgetful, maybe you *are* too old to play Rhett. It's possible senility is already setting in and how will you even remember your lines?'

'I may be senile, m'dear, but that doesn't change *your* condition. Only thirty-two you may be, which is hardly the bloom of youth, but your state of mind is at least twenty years older, not to mention that you're not exactly basking in the rosy glow of virginal innocence either. Some might even say Nora Hall Hartiscor is somewhat damaged goods,' he retaliated for the crack about his possible senility.

She in turn retorted by throwing a sofa pillow at him, but he ducked out of its way. 'As such, my girl, you'd do well to take my offer seriously and consider yourself fortunate that a dashingly handsome, incredibly sexy, tremendously successful, eligible *young* bachelor like myself is giving you this opportunity to have a high old time. Besides, you're no longer a countess and that does reduce your eligibility a bit.'

'I think I'll manage to cope,' she laughed.

He studied her solemnly for some seconds over the rim of his whisky and soda. Then, as if startled by a sudden and upsetting thought, he put down his glass. 'Tell me, Nora, if it's not middle age, suicide or a mental collapse, what is it you're on the brink of – another marriage?'

She threw a second sofa pillow at him.

'If you must know, I was going to say that I was on the brink of making the manor a paying proposition. That I've just leased two parcels of land to two tenant farmers.'

'Well, fine. That's all to the good. But does it mean you can't take a few weeks off for a smashing time? It might not even be for that long. It's possible that the whole thing will fizzle out. These Hollywood chaps *are* notorious for starting projects and then abandoning them. And then there's the possibility that I'll test for the role and not get it.'

'Oh my goodness, never!' she said with a straight face. 'Once you test for the part, it's yours. These American filmmakers are devilishly clever. They know a Rhett when they see one, no matter how old and senile he might appear.'

This time, Tony, his sense of humour fully intact, advanced on her with a sofa pillow of his own, but suddenly neither of them was laughing as they paused to make love in front of the fire.

'Come with me!' he urged. 'We're so good together.'

'I'd love to go, but Hubie's doing so well in school, *finally*. He's been at Mayberry's for eight months now and we haven't had a single problem. I'd hate to take him out.'

'But you don't have to take him *out* of school. All I'm proposing is a *brief* holiday while he's *in* school all safe and sound so you can go with a clear conscience. If I get the role we can proceed from there, but in the meantime, the world is ours. Did I tell you that they're paying for a bungalow at the Beverly Hills Hotel?'

'And that's good, I take it?'

'Oh baby, that's more than good! When they pay for you to stay in a bungalow at the Beverly Hills, it means you've arrived in America! It's their ultimate in star treatment.'

Why not? she argued with herself. Hubie *was* in school with no problems and Merrillee Manor *was* in fairly good shape. It really was the perfect time for a bit of fun.

Once just for the devil of it!

After taking two hours to dress, his hair perfectly arranged in a wave curling rakishly over his forehead, Tony announced he was off for his test at Grantwood Studio.

'But you haven't had a proper breakfast, love,' she protested. 'How are you going to test on an empty stomach?'

'They just rang while you were in the shower. The test has been rescheduled for this afternoon.'

'Then why are you leaving now? We can have breakfast

246

in the Polo Lounge. I understand that's where Hollywood people have what they call a "power breakfast". Doesn't that sound exciting . . . unless, of course,' she smiled provocatively, 'you think breakfast in bed sounds even more exciting?'

'Mmmm, that does sound enticing but I'm breakfasting at the Studio with T.S. Grant himself.' He sounded pleased.

'Oh, I see,' she mocked him. 'That certainly seems more powerful than breakfasting in the Polo Lounge and certainly more exciting than breakfasting in bed with this old girl.' But seeing his wounded expression she said quickly, 'I was only fooling. Really, Tony, I think that breakfast with T.S. Grant sounds very positive. A good omen.'

She knew how upset Tony had been that while they'd arrived three days before and had been nicely lunched, wined and dined and even taken to a rather wild party in the Hollywood Hills and a more formal one in Beverly Hills, he had yet to meet the head of Grantwood Studio.

'I really better dash. They've sent a car for me,' he said with satisfaction. 'Now, *that's* what I call proper star treatment. Do you know no one has ever sent a car for me before? I didn't even realize what I've been missing. I really like how they do business in this town. Now, if you need anything while I'm gone, just pick up the phone and ask for it.'

'Yes, Tony,' she laughed. 'While this *is* my first time in the States, I *have been* in first-class hotels before and I know all about how one picks up a phone to ask for things.'

'Yes, of course you do. I just want to be sure that you know how to announce yourself when you do pick up the phone.'

'Really, Tony, what's got into you? We've only been here three days. Has all this California sunshine gone to your brain so quickly? I'm a big girl now and I *think*

I've known how to announce myself properly for years now.'

'Yes, of course, but I want to be sure that you call yourself Countess Hartiscor.'

'Oh, Tony! How could you? I'm an ex-countess and I'm not about to go around calling myself the ex-Countess Hartiscor. If it weren't for Hubie, I'd stop calling myself Hartiscor at all so can we please drop the countess business once and for all?'

'Sorry, old girl, but you're *already* registered here as the Countess. You see, titles knock the stuffing out of Americans. It impresses them no end and Hollywood's a town that thrives on being impressed. You have to understand.'

'What I *don't* understand, Tony, is why it's necessary for me to impress the staff of the hotel? Do the desk clerk or the waiter really care if I'm of the aristocracy?'

'Maybe *they* don't, but the reporters they rang up the minute we checked in do. Now it's in all the dailies and on the Hollywood grapevine that that hot English star, dashing Tony Nash, is doing the local scene with the ravishing Countess Hartiscor at his side. And, as a result, do you know what is on everyone's lips even as we're talking here?'

'I'm sure you're going to tell me in any case, so you might as well get it over with and be on your way.'

Tony put one hand on his hip and dangled the other from a very loose wrist: 'They say the countess is mad about him, dar-ling, and she being as divine as *she* is, she must know – that *he's* absolutely divine!'

She giggled. 'I'm sure they're absolutely right.'

She lunched in the Polo Lounge on her own, amusing herself by watching all the milling and table-hopping going on, and people constantly being paged to the phone. But while it was fun, the incredible din of it all was exhausting, and she went back to the bungalow to change into her swimsuit, thinking she'd relax by the pool, a seemingly tranquil oasis of bright blue water, tropical flowers and tall palms. But no sooner had she finished oiling herself down with lotion, than she heard the Countess Hartiscor being paged over the speaker.

'Really, Tony, you are naughty,' she said into the phone, trying to keep the annoyance out of her voice. 'I thought I told you that – oh, never mind. How did the test go?'

'It didn't go. It's been rescheduled for tomorrow.'

'Oh Tony, that is a shame. But how did your breakfast meeting with T.S. Grant go?'

'Not too bad.'

'What does not *too* bad mean?'

He laughed ruefully. 'It means that he sat with me for as long as it took him to drink a cup of coffee before he had to leave – an emergency on one of his sets. But he seems a nice chap. He laughs a lot. And he said that he really felt great about having a star of my stature testing for the role, and then he left a couple of his people to finish having breakfast with me, and *that* was very informative.'

'Oh, good! What did you learn?'

'Well, I finally found out what the TS stands for – Thomas Samuel, or if you prefer, tough shit.'

'But what does *that* mean?' she laughed.

'I think it describes a certain down-to-earth quality about the man. You know, he's one of these real American types who's very honest, blunt and forthcoming . . . says exactly what he means and doesn't pull his punches, and if you don't like it, well – tough shit!'

'And that's good?'

'I think so. At least one knows where one stands.'

'That *is* good. And where do you think you stand with him other than that he feels good about your testing for Rhett?'

'*That* seems to me my problem – I'm not certain. But he wants to meet *you*, so we're having drinks with

249

him at five and maybe you'll help me sort out where I stand. They're sending a car for you so just climb into your sexiest get-up and—'

'Sexiest?' she laughed. 'Why? *I'm* not trying out for a part. Besides, the sun will still be high in the sky at five. Don't you think I'd look a bit odd in clinging satin and a plunging neckline before sundown?'

'Don't be silly. This is Hollywood, the sun never sets and anything goes. Besides, we'll probably be going on to dinner with him and then after that maybe we'll do some of the clubs. Oh, and don't be surprised when I introduce you as—'

'No, don't tell me – the Countess Hartiscor! Tony, I'm going to brain you!'

'I beg your pardon! I was going to say that I intended to introduce you as the loveliest woman in the world.'

'Oh Tony, that's sweet.'

How could she ever be mad at this man? It was so much easier to be mad *about* him . . .

When she stepped out of the limousine dressed for evening, but circumspectly so in a cocktail suit, Tony was waiting for her on the sidewalk in front of the Tropical Flower Lounge, all alone and seemingly immersed in melancholy.

'What is it, Tony?'

'It's TS. He isn't here.'

'Is he delayed or what?'

'He isn't coming. He had to go down to Palm Springs.'

It was foolish, she knew, but then *she* was disappointed. She'd been looking forward to meeting the famous T.S. Grant. Actually, she was more than disappointed – she was annoyed. She knew how silly it was, even odd, considering she didn't know the man, but somehow she felt as if he had stood *her* up.

'Well, these things happen, Tony, but never mind. We'll have drinks and then we'll have dinner, just the two of us.'

'Oh no,' Tony brightened. 'There's a big gang inside. Some of the other people TS asked to meet him for drinks. After that we're going on to the Coconut Grove at the Ambassador Hotel. It'll be lots of fun and that's what we're really here for, isn't it? To have a whale of a good time?'

And it was fun . . . lots of fun. Still, when they returned to their bungalow at four in the morning, she turned on Tony accusingly. 'How could you introduce me to those people as your fiancée? A total lie.'

He kissed her on the back of her neck. 'It just kind of popped out. I suppose it was wishful thinking on my part.' He grinned at her but there was a beseeching quality in his eyes and she realized that he was quite serious.

'Oh, Tony! We agreed that my coming with you was just a fling. A holiday. You made it very clear that you weren't thinking of marriage. You can't change the rules in the middle of the game. It's just not fair.'

'You're the one who's not playing fair. All my life I've been told that it was the female's prerogative to change her mind. Well, who says a man can't change his mind, too?'

His lips grazed her eyelids, her mouth, her throat. 'I love you, Nora. Isn't it fair that I tell you *that*?'

He was confusing her. She couldn't think . . .

'It's late, Tony, and you have your screen test tomorrow. You must get some sleep or you'll have bags under your eyes and who ever heard of a Rhett Butler with baggy eyes? We'll talk about this tomorrow. Tomorrow *is* another day.'

'Yes, Scarlett, tomorrow is another day, but tonight is tonight and this is the night I swoop you up in my arms to carry you up the stairs to make love to you against your will. But after – ah, *after*, you realize how much you really love me.' And he advanced on her.

She backed away. 'Tony, it's late and you're being

251

ridiculous! Besides, there are no stairs here.' She ran to stand behind a chair.

'A good actor can always improvise!' he laughed menacingly and kept coming, shoving the chair out of the way, swooping her up in his arms, carrying her into the bedroom and kicking the door shut after them . . .

As the sun began its ascent in the east, Tony asked, 'Now, what do you have to say, my love?'

She giggled. 'I *always* said you'd make the most marvellous Rhett and I'm not about to change my mind.'

Two hours later, the studio called to announce that they had to cancel the screen test for that afternoon. This time Tony said, 'Perfect,' and an hour later they flew to Las Vegas to be married in a wedding chapel on the Strip that offered a plain ceremony without music and flowers that took five minutes and a de luxe version that included both and took fifteen. They opted for the latter and as the groom kissed the bride, he murmured, 'These Yanks! They certainly know how to expedite a situation before a chap has a chance to change his mind.'

'Or a woman . . .' she murmured, and congratulated herself that this time around she had married a darling, amusing and very dear man for the best of reasons – for the sheer pleasure of it – and that *had* to be a brilliant marriage!

23

'What do you think is going on?' Nora asked after three weeks had passed and Tony still hadn't had his screen test.

'Who knows?' Tony shrugged. 'But what do we care? We're having fun and they're paying the bills.'

'But how long will they *continue* to pay the bills?'

'You worry too much. My mother taught me never to look a gift horse in the mouth. What about your mother? What did she teach you?'

'Not to trust anybody too much.'

'Ah! That's why you're such a worry-wart instead of relaxing and going with the flow.'

'Going with the flow? That's a new one on me. Where did you get that?'

'From TS just a moment ago. I managed finally to get him on the phone and asked him what was happening with the picture and he told me that if I wanted to survive Hollywood without suffering a mental crack-up, I was going to have to relax and go with the flow. Actually, I think they're having trouble with the screenplay.'

'I didn't even know there was a screenplay.'

'Of course there's a screenplay, at least in development, I *think*. There's usually a screenplay before they start casting though there are films that are shot as the script's being written on a day-to-day sort of thing.'

'So, what *is* the problem with the screenplay?'

'I don't know but I'm going to try and find out today. I'm lunching at the Brown Derby with Bob Rankin. He's the head of publicity. Care to tag along?'

'No, I don't think so.'

'Oh, come on,' he urged. 'It will be entertaining to see how much studio gossip we can bleed out of the bloke.'

'No, Tony, I'm really not in the mood.'

He studied her for a moment. 'Something's bothering you. Is it that letter you received yesterday from the headmaster at Hubie's school?'

'Yes. How did you know?'

'Elementary, my dear Watson. The only thing that really upsets you is anything to do with Hubie. Now, *your* problems are *my* problems, so why don't you tell me what's wrong while I dress for my lunch date?'

253

She followed him into the dressing room while he selected what he would wear. 'The point is that I'm not sure *what's* wrong specifically. You know how vague these academics can be. He just referred to certain difficulties—'

'That's all?' He held up a tie for her approval and she automatically nodded her approval. 'In that case, what you should have done was get on the horn this morning and called the bloody school and found out precisely what difficulties they're referring to.'

'But that's what I did do! At five this morning.'

'And—?' He went into the bathroom and took his shaving things out of the cabinet.

'It seems that Mr Haskell – he's the headmaster – won't be back till tomorrow.'

Tony lathered up. 'Why didn't you ask to speak to someone else?'

'I did. The assistant headmaster. But then *he* said he wasn't at liberty to talk about a matter of this nature on the phone and that I would have to wait for Mr Haskell.'

'And you couldn't manage to worm anything out of him?'

'Oh, Tony, *that's* one of the problems. I *did*.'

Tony laid down his razor. 'And—'

'He said the problem was of a *sexual* nature.'

'But that's ridiculous!' Tony laughed, picking up his razor again. 'How old is Hubie? My God, the boy's not thirteen yet. What kind of a problem can he have that's of a sexual nature when he's at school where there are *only* boys?'

When she burst into tears, he said, 'Oh. I see.'

He put the razor down again and took her in his arms. 'But, Nora, you can't – you mustn't! It really can't be a case of history repeating itself, so why assume the worst?'

'But there *was* that experience with Rupert. And Hubert had the same experience. Oh God, will the curse of the Hartiscors never end?'

254

'My! That sounds like the title of a Twenties' film. *The Curse of the Hartiscors*.' He kissed the top of her head, smoothed her hair with his lips. 'Look, why assume anything until you get to speak to Haskell and know more. What probably happened was that they found the kid masturbating – what twelve-year-old boy doesn't bloody play with himself? And they can't hang him for that. They can't even expel him for it or they'd have to expel half the school."

She wiped at her tears with a sodden handkerchief and tried to smile at him though it was the *other* half of the school that she was concerned with. If they weren't masturbating then what, of a sexual nature, *were* they doing?

While she was counting the minutes until she'd be able to talk with the headmaster – she'd figured out that taking the time difference into account, she could call at 2 a.m. LA time – she was trying her damnedest to concentrate on what Tony was saying just as he was trying his damnedest to distract her with the studio gossip he had gleaned from Bob Rankin.

'TS has a wife in a private sanatorium in Palm Springs. Some kind of mental disorder.'

'Oh, that's sad.'

'Besides which, there's a baby, a little girl.'

'But what's wrong with his wife? Will she get well? And how is he managing with the baby?'

'Well, as far as I could find out, it's a chancy situation with the wife. She's supposed to be seriously disturbed. As for the baby, she's with her maternal grandparents in Pasadena. It seems they're what's called "old money California", and TS says that since he's not in a position to take care of her and that all he could do would be to leave her in hired hands, he'd rather see her with them.'

'Oh, the poor man! It must be so hard on him not to have his baby with him.'

She sneaked another fast glance at her watch and Tony

255

said hastily, 'Oh, about the screenplay. It seems that there *is* one in the works, but there's some kind of problem there. They have a Pulitzer Prize winner working on it, but he's a novelist, not a screenwriter. Maybe *that's* the problem.'

'What's his name?'

'F. Theodore Rosen.'

Nora tried to concentrate. 'Though I hardly claim to keep up with who's writing what and who's winning what literary prize, the name *does* sound familiar.'

'That's probably not because of *what* he's written but because of *who* he's married to – Mimi L'Heureux.'

'You mean the French actress?'

'I mean the world's sex goddess. I met her once in the South of France and to meet the gorgeous Mimi is not to forget her.' He wiggled his eyebrows.

She forced a smile. '*That* sexy?'

'Not half. But she's got quite a fiery temper to go with the curves and those luscious lips.'

'So, what's the problem with the screenplay?'

'I'm not sure, but whatever it is, it's not working. Or maybe it's that the writer isn't working. I couldn't pin Rankin down, but I'd hazard a guess that the boy-genius – he won the Pulitzer right after he graduated from Princeton – has his hands full with the tempestuous Mimi. The storyline is that immediately after he won the Pulitzer, he met Mimi in Paris where he went to write his second novel. He fell madly in love with her and before the week was out, they were married.'

Despite the anxiety that lay like a stone in her belly, she was drawn into the story. 'That sounds very romantic, but what about *her*? Did *she* fall madly in love with *him* as well?'

'Who knows for sure except Mimi herself?' Tony grinned. 'Probably Teddy Rosen himself doesn't know for sure. You have to keep in mind that while the two of them are about the same age, there was a world of difference between them when they met. She was a

Parisian and you *know* no one's more sophisticated than a Parisian. And he was an American small-town boy. And despite his obvious brilliance, he was still a relatively unsophisticated college boy and she'd been this amazing film star ever since she was seventeen who had had dozens of love affairs with all sorts of men from princes to Greek fishermen. She's almost as famous for her hot love affairs as she is for her sizzling films.'

'She married him so she *must* have been madly in love.'

'You married *me* – does that mean you're madly in love with me?' he teased.

'You're fishing,' she attempted a laugh.

'What's wrong with a little fishing? But you're not answering—' he murmured speculatively.

'Oh Tony, of course I'm madly in love with you or I would have been on a plane back to England the moment I got that beastly letter from Hubie's school. Now, get on with the story.' Again she glanced at her watch to check the time. 'What happened after they were married?'

'As far as I could gather, just what you'd expect. The high life *à la* Scott and Zelda Fitzgerald. Only, of course, Zelda was an American girl who was mentally unstable and everyone knows that Mimi's not only a holy terror but a practical sort as well, who keeps an eye on her career and bank account even as she keeps her ass busy in bed.'

'Tony!' she laughingly protested and he was pleased that he was making her forget her troubles if only for a bit.

'Anyway, there was a house in Saint Tropez with the champagne constantly flowing and a continuous round of parties that didn't end till the wee hours and lots of holidays whenever Mimi wasn't working, which meant, I suppose, that the boy-genius didn't get too much time to do his own thing. Presto! His second book was a big floppo.'

'Oh, the poor man!'

Tony grinned. 'There are a lot of chaps who might say it was worth it to park their slippers under Mimi L'Heureux's bed *and* come to Hollywood to work on a sequel to *Gone With The Wind* which the great Tony Nash might possibly star in if he ever gets his screen test. At least, let's *hope* he's working, not just cleaning out the drinks cabinet, rubbing Mimi's feet, and playing nursemaid because Mimi's not the maternal type.'

'They have a baby, then?'

'Yes, a little girl. They're out in Malibu in the Colony, and as I understand it, the partying goes on. I wish we could get an invite, but it appears Mimi has a sign on her front door that says: ONLY FRENCHMEN MAY ENTER HERE.'

'You're fooling?'

'Well, only partially. But it seems Mimi has taken a distinct dislike to anything American.'

'Oh dear, I hope that doesn't include her husband.'

'That would be kind of ironic considering that they only offered *him* the screenplay in order to *get her* here.'

'Oh, that can't be true.'

'Why can't it be true?'

'Because of who *he* is. *His* stature as a Pulitzer Prize winner. Doesn't that mean anything?'

Tony's smile was wistful. 'Not in this town. They have a saying here: "You're only as good as your last picture." Since that wouldn't directly apply to Mr Rosen, I think what does apply is, "But what have you done lately?" And lately he hasn't done so well.'

'And Mimi? Did she make a film here?'

'Yes. A quickie. I surmise that knowing how mercurial Mimi could be, TS was afraid she'd turn around and go back to France at the drop of a hat so the minute she got off the plane, they shot the film in four weeks in South Dakota.'

'Where *is* South Dakota?'

'I haven't the foggiest but the film was a western, so I

suppose it's somewhere out there in the great American West one always hears about.'

'You mean they made a Cowboy and Indian film with the French sex kitten?' she giggled, and Tony was gratified that he had her laughing.

'Yes, and it seems she hated everything about it! Being on location in South Dakota – it was *hardly* Paris. And she hated the script, the director, the whole blooming cast, even her hairdresser. That was about a year ago.'

'You mean that Teddy Rosen's been working on the screenplay for *that* long and there's nothing?'

'I think they said there were a few pages.'

'The poor man. But Mimi's picture – what's it called?'

'I have no idea but I've got a hot one. *Sex and the American Indian* . . .'

When she didn't laugh he asked, 'Don't you think that's even a tiny bit amusing?'

'Sorry, I was thinking of something else. I just realized that I *did* read F. Theodore Rosen's book, after all,' she said. 'I had forgotten who the author was, but I remember the book. It was a *beautiful* book. Only a beautiful man could have written it. The title was *Celebration of Longing*.'

'And what does *that* mean?'

'Do you know how people say "you really had to be there"? Well, it's that kind of book. You really *had* to be there.'

'And the second book? Do you recall its title?'

She shook her head regretfully. 'I haven't a clue.'

So many emotions played across Nora's face as she talked to the headmaster, Tony couldn't tell whether she was exhilarated or crushed at what she was hearing and the moment she put down the phone he begged: 'Is it good news or bad?'

'You won't believe this! Hubie was caught having sex with the mathematics professor's eighteen-year-old daughter!'

'But that's marvellous! Aren't you pleased?'

'Of course I'm pleased! I mean, I'm awfully *relieved*. It *is* good news, isn't it?'

'Good news? I think it's *extraordinary* news. Our little Hubie fucking an eighteen-year-old woman! Amazing really. Nora, you should be proud of the boy!'

But then she reproved him. 'Really, what's there to be proud of? That my son is precociously promiscuous?'

He followed her into the bedroom where she began throwing things into a suitcase. 'What are you doing?'

'I'm doing exactly what it looks like I'm doing. I'm packing. I have to leave for home immediately.'

'Why? Everything's fine. Hubie was fucking a *girl*.'

'No, everything's *not* fine. You men think all is well as long as any male – even a boy of *twelve* – is screwing a female. They've expelled him and they're keeping him confined to his room as if he were a threat to national security until I come to pick him up. Can you imagine? I have to go back and transfer him to another school immediately.'

'But the planes don't leave in the middle of the night. You're losing your perspective. You're acting hysterical.'

'Am I? It's just that – Oh, Tony, I can't tell you how relieved I *really* am! I know I'm acting crazily, but I thought that—' She sat down on the bed and he sat down next to her.

'I know, Nora, I know what you thought. I understand.'

'Do you? Do you know that I blame myself for marrying Jeffrey?'

'For marrying Jeffrey? Don't you mean you blame yourself for taking up with Hubert?'

'No, I would never blame myself for taking up with Hubert. I've never regretted that. I *loved* Hubert! Oh, how I loved him! I loved Hubert so much that—'

'So much that what? That you'll never love anybody as much as you loved him?'

Tony looked as if she had stuck a knife in his heart and she was filled with remorse. He was so sweet and they laughed so much and they made such wonderful love together. 'Oh no, Tony, I wasn't going to say that. I was going to say that I loved Hubert so much that sometimes I forget that Hubert wasn't really Hubie's father. That sometimes they just merge into one. Hubie and Hubert. Sometimes I imagine that Hubie *is* Hubert. Does that sound ridiculous?'

'No, of course not,' he soothed her. 'But now I think we should go to bed and in the morning—'

'In the morning I *must* go home and see to Hubie.'

'I know. And I'll go with you.'

'Oh no, you can't. I appreciate your offering, but I can't let you leave without having your screen test. I'd never forgive myself if you missed out on the role you were born to play. I'll go home, arrange for Hubie to go to another school, then I'll come back and by that time, the cameras probably will be rolling. I bet they won't even bother with a screen test any more.'

'Do you really think so?'

'Yes.'

'And you'll rush right back?'

'The very second I can, I promise, cross my heart.'

'Well, jolly well do so then. You know, none of this is any good without you.'

'I know, and just *you* remember that.'

'And now that that's settled, shall we go to bed?' he leered. 'You might be gone a week and look at all the fun we'll be missing. We have to make up for the lost time starting right now!'

But then he showed no hurry as he undressed her tantalizingly slowly, kissing each square inch he bared. And she, giving herself up totally to the exquisite pleasure of his lovemaking, reflected that some men were born to enjoy life, to laugh and to love, and to make love . . .

And who would be so foolish as to love them less than

261

*the ones you loved who loved you back, but still managed
to break your heart?*

24

'It really wasn't my fault, Mummy.'

Hubie looked so forlorn, it was hard for Nora not to
just take him in her arms and forget the lecture. But she
couldn't – it was her job to help him grow into a good,
strong man.

'You're almost a man now, Hubie, and there are certain
urges a young man feels – we all feel them, women too
– but we have to learn to hold them in check until the
proper time when the circumstances are right.'

Oh God, I'm making a mess of this, she thought, and
wished that Tony was there to talk to him. At times like
these a boy needed a man more than a mother.

'Do you understand what I mean, Hubie, about waiting for the proper time and circumstances?'

Hubie was perplexed. 'You mean like Rupert should
have?'

Oh, dear God, what do I say to that?

'I've explained all that to you, Hubie. That Rupert's
a very sick man. Actually, what he did was a criminal
act.'

'Then why isn't he in hospital? Or in prison?'

Reasonable questions, to be sure. Why not, indeed?

'I know it's hard for you to understand, but sometimes
things are not the way they should be. We just have to
trust that time will sort things out. But now we have to
talk about you. What you have to learn about this business of growing up – that along with the pleasures come
responsibilities.'

'But I told you, it wasn't my fault. She *made* me do it.'

'Part of growing up, Hubie, is also learning to take responsibility for your actions instead of blaming others. That's what *little* boys or men do who refuse to grow up.'

But Hubie was adamant. 'She *made* me. I swear it, Mummy. She tricked me into going to the caretaker's cottage and when I got there she was naked and she started – you know – touching me . . .' He faltered, embarrassed.

She sighed. While Hubie, so tall and well-built, might appear to some as nearly full-grown despite his actual years, there was no guile in the still innocent face. It was very possible he was telling the truth, that the woman – a girl of eighteen *was* a woman – had seduced him totally, that she was entirely to blame. But what had the young woman been thinking of? Had she been so sex-starved that she had to pick on a boy who – no matter how manly he appeared – simply didn't know how to deal with her except to do what came naturally?

She kissed the angelic face. 'All right, darling, we shan't talk about it any more. I've enrolled you at a new school and we'll be driving up next week. And you will be good, won't you, and you'll try very hard to stay out of trouble? And if it should happen that you *do* get into trouble – I understand that sometimes it happens regardless of how hard we try not to – well, just face up to it like a man and not try to lie your way out of it or put the blame on others.'

Then it occurred to her that she had another rule to add to the list – to avoid all sex-starved young women until he was at least eighteen. But she could hardly put it that way. Hubie was such an innocent he might misunderstand her and run in the opposite direction.

After depositing Hubie at Brewster, she called Tony to tell him that she'd be another week. She wanted to be sure Hubie was adjusting to his new school before she left.

'Are you sure this is what you want to do? Don't you think you're overdoing the protective mother? And what about *this* old boy? Aren't you afraid you're neglecting me?'

'No, not at all. That's what so nice about marrying a *man* and not a boy. You know that he's mature enough to understand that sometimes a child *has* to come first.'

'Oof!' he said. 'That pointed arrow really hurt.'

'Good, and you be good and don't get into any trouble, at least not until I get there and can properly attend to you.'

'All kidding aside, I miss you, Nora.'

'All kidding aside, I miss you, Tony. See you in a week.'

It was by chance that she picked up a copy of the international edition of *Variety*. She was meeting Sally Whitehead for lunch at the Savoy and while she was waiting in the lobby – Sally, as usual, was late – a man seated near her left, leaving his paper behind, and she glanced through it to spot the death notice of TS's wife, Elise Parker Grant, twenty-three, who had suddenly died in a sanatorium in Palm Springs. The only details were that the deceased left behind her husband, T.S. Grant of Grantwood Studio, a daughter, Samantha, and her parents, the Edward Parkers of Pasadena, and that the service would be held at Forest Lawn Memorial on Friday, the twenty-seventh, at 2 p.m.

How terrible for them all! The parents, TS and his baby daughter, as well as the poor woman who had barely tasted life.

Then she thought of Tony. She recalled his telling her that he couldn't *bear* funerals – they actually made him ill and that he never attended them if he could help it. But under the circumstances, he couldn't help attending this one.

And I should be there by his side, she thought. She had intended to fly back Sunday, after seeing Hubie on

Saturday, but it really wasn't necessary. She'd seen him just yesterday and he seemed to be adjusting to the new school beautifully and Tony really needed her. He'd been so wonderfully considerate of her, surely she owed him the same consideration. That was what a good marriage was all about.

She rushed to find a phone to call the airlines. If she could get a plane out this afternoon, given the time difference and even with a wait in New York for a connecting flight, she should land in California in time for the funeral with a couple of hours to spare as far as she could figure it.

She was racing out the hotel door just as Sally Whitehead came sailing through. 'Nora! Where are you going?' she called out. 'We're supposed to be having lunch!'

She waved to Sally. 'Sorry, darling, but you were *so* late and I grew *so* bored waiting that I decided to fly back to Hollywood immediately. Ta, ta!'

When she arrived at LAX at eight in the morning, she decided that there was no point in calling Tony to come and pick her up. She would just grab a taxi and surprise him by jumping into bed with him before he even opened his eyes.

But then, when she walked into the bungalow, it was *she* herself who was surprised as the camera clicked in her brain to add yet another picture to join two others that would never fade from her memory: Hubert making love to his dusky assistant in his art gallery and Rupert sodomizing Hubie.

But one thing she had to admit even as she stood there transfixed and shattered at the same time – the dashing dark-haired Tony Nash and the breathtaking, blond Mimi L'Heureux made for a much more attractive and colourful photo than the other two. In an exhibition of photographs it might even have had as its title – *Sex as Poetry in Motion* . . .

*　　*　　*

265

Nora was disappointed in Tony. She would have thought he'd be more original than to spout all the old clichés: *it didn't mean a thing . . . It was just one of these things that happen . . . It has absolutely nothing to do with you and me or the way I feel about you . . . It was just a one-time thing and will never happen again . . .*

And then he began the 'it wasn't really my fault' routine in which he tried to make *her* feel guilty: 'A chap does get lonely, you know, and I was so upset by this funeral business. I don't understand why it took you over two weeks to see to Hubie's ridiculous little scrape. Good God – you'd think the problem was that the empire was crumbling! What the hell *were* you doing there all this time? If you had been here where you were supposed to be, this never would have happened . . .'

Any minute, she thought, he'd use the old saw that in her extreme youth a persuasive lad might try on a gullible girl – that he was so horny his balls were turning blue and would probably drop off and only she could save him from this fate worse than death. Only Tony would have to tell it a bit differently – that he was so randy his balls were turning purple and since his wife was neglecting him, he had to turn the poor, hard things over to a handy alternative for servicing.

And then came the third stage in which he attempted to lay all the blame on the sex kitten herself while at the same time belittling her character as well as her attractions, probably thinking that *this* would please and appease her.

'She's no more than a slut. She came creeping around at the crack of dawn, practically breaking down my door with some kind of a crappy story – she was supposedly breakfasting with a producer in the Polo Lounge, but the *merde* was overdue and she was hungry and did I want to join her? Three guesses as to what the tart was hungry for.

'Well, before I knew it, she'd pulled off her dress – the French cow wasn't even wearing so much as a pair of panties and what was a man to do? But, believe me, she was a big disappointment in bed – she just lay there like a sack of beans and where she got this reputation for being the sexiest woman in the world is beyond me. Even her body's been overrated. She's too wide in the bum and her boobs are already beginning to sag—'

The last three or four sentences of his statement – which were obvious misrepresentations of the truth – told her that his whole story about Mimi pounding on his door that morning was a lie. The goddess of cinematic sex, whom she had seen cavorting in bed with her own two eyes when she had flung open the bedroom door, had hardly been lying there like any sack of beans. Rather, she had been delivering a performance easily living up to her reputation.

As for the famous body, Nora herself could attest that it too lived up to its reputation. She had had an unhampered view of it when the sex kitten, upon sighting her lover's wife, had without a word – as slick as perfumed bath oil and as cool as iced champagne – slithered out of bed to undulate across the room as gracefully as any jungle cat to pick up her discarded white slip of a dress and pull it on in one motion before thrusting bare feet into high-heeled pumps, move sinuously to the dresser to pick up Tony's silver-backed brush and pull it through the wild mass of pillow-rumpled hair. And all in all, she had to admit the actress's whole performance had been every bit as extraordinary as her flawless figure.

After finishing with Tony's brush Mimi had tossed it to him as he lay vanquished and sheepish in bed, then glided over to the bedroom door where she herself – the wife who had yet to utter a word in this scenario – moved hastily out of the way to allow the star to make her exit unimpeded.

But, before she left, Mimi tossed off as spectacular an exit line as Nora had ever heard in any play or film. First she flashed an incredibly white smile and then in that throaty voiced tossed off: 'Not to worry, *ma chère* . . . *C'est magnifique, mais ce n'est pas la guerre* . . .'

With that, she was gone leaving a chagrined Tony muttering, 'What was that bloody remark?'

'She said, I believe, "It is magnificent, but it is not war". I think it was a French officer who said that watching the Charge of the Light Brigade at Balaclava. But what I think Mimi was doing, *mon cher*, was rating *your* performance.'

After Tony had settled down sufficiently to offer a graceful apology, to take full responsibility for his misconduct and promise as sincerely as he could that it would never happen again, he assumed that the matter was over and done with. Then she had to tell him that it was their marriage that was over, but Tony found it hard to believe.

'Over one little incident? You have to look at the broad picture. Weren't we having a wonderful time? Jolly sex and lots of laughs? We did have loads of fun, didn't we?' he appealed to her beseechingly, much as Hubie was wont to do.

'That's the problem, Tony – the fun's gone out of the thing, or maybe it's that the fun of it was a success, but the marriage itself is a failure.' Then she suggested that since they'd been married in the States, they might as well divorce in the States. 'Why don't you establish residency in Nevada where the divorce will only take six weeks? You loved Las Vegas – the shows, the gambling, all those neon lights – and then you'll be having fun at the same time you're divorcing me instead of just sitting around here waiting to see what's happening with the picture. Then if anything *does* happen, you'll be just a hop and a skip away.'

While she could see that the Las Vegas idea basically appealed to him, he was still reluctant to let go. 'But you make it sound so easy . . . it's just not right.'

'Oh Tony, it was the marriage that wasn't right and deep down you know it, too. But I blame myself for that – for not seeing that it wasn't right *before* we got married.

I should have known better. I should have known that one can't marry just for the fun of it.'

He mused over that somberly for a while before he brightened. 'I have a grand idea! Why don't you come with me to Las Vegas while we're getting our divorce? It's really no fun doing this alone.'

She burst out laughing. 'Oh Tony, we might not be suited to be husband and wife, but I just *know* we're going to continue being wonderful friends. In fact, while we may not have had the most successful of marriages, I do think we're going to have an absolutely brilliant divorce!'

She'd been back at Merrillee for over two months when Tony came down to visit carrying a bottle of champagne from California's northern vineyards under each arm. 'Don't tell me you brought that champagne all the way from the States? And what are we celebrating – our divorce?'

'Yes, that, and I thought it only fitting that we toast the end of my California débâcle with California wine instead of French. Besides, you can understand why I'm a little wary of anything French these days,' he grinned and she grinned back, glad to see that his sense of humour was still intact.

'So tell me all about it – the end of the débâcle,' she said after he popped the first bottle of wine and they settled down before the fire.

'You go first. What's happening with you and Hubie?'

'Oh, I'm pretty dull. I'm just trying to make ends meet while I try to get one of the barns in shape. I thought I might keep a few Jerseys. As for Hubie, *his* life is anything but dull. He and a few of his – shall we say less-than-sterling? – schoolmates are currently in a bit of a jam *again*. It seems they sneaked into town and made total fools of themselves at the local pub.'

'Ah, Nora, when are you going to learn that no matter what *you* do, boys *will* be boys?'

269

'I'll try to keep that in mind if you'll tell me what happened with my boy in Hollywood.'

'You're not going to believe this—'

'Oh, I might. Try me.'

'Would you believe Grantwood Studio never *had* the rights to make a sequel to *Gone With The Wind*?'

'You're right, I don't believe you! How could a major studio do a thing like that – hire a screenwriter, bring you over to test and all the rest of it without securing the rights first?'

'The story is that T.S. Grant gave the order to get the rights and then no one had the guts to tell him that they hadn't been able to—'

'That's incredible.'

'Not as incredible as it gets. Remember when we used to lie in bed at night speculating – among other things to be sure – as to whom they were going to get to play Scarlett?'

'Yes, I remember.' She would never forget those nights in bed at the Beverly Hills Hotel, speculation or no.

'Well, three guesses as to whom they had in mind for Scarlett the whole time—'

'Oh, no, don't tell me!' she shrieked. 'Not Mimi L'Heureux?'

'But how did you know?' He seemed crestfallen that she had spoiled his fun by guessing correctly.

'It was nothing, really,' she said smugly. 'All I did was think of the most incongruous casting imaginable – the sex goddess with the thick French accent as the quintessential Southern belle, and it was an obvious choice. But tell me, before they found out they didn't have the rights, did Mimi *agree* to play Scarlett?'

'Well, it seems that since our star was barely out of her nappies when they made the original and had never seen it even with French subtitles, much less even heard of the Civil War, they took her into a screening room so that she could take a gander at Vivien Leigh playing Scarlett, and I went along, too.

'Well, Mimi sat through nearly the whole first half of the film in complete silence and everyone figured she was enthralled and were already congratulating each other that they had found their Scarlett. But then came that scene in the railroad depot when all the Southern boys, thousands of them, are lying on the ground wounded and dying as far as the eye can see. A really impressive shot if you recall?'

'Oh, absolutely, and—?'

'And Mimi stands up, sticks that *retroussé* nose disdainfully in the air and just before sweeping out of the screening room she says, '*Gentlemen, c'est magnifique, mais ce n'est pas la guerre . . .*'

Nora stared at him, her blue eyes wide in shock, until she realized that she had been *had*! Tony had set her up, drawn her in, knowing exactly *who* she would guess the studio had picked to play Scarlett! Then she burst out laughing, beating at him with her fists. She might marry a hundred times more, but she would never again marry anyone who was quite as much fun as her own sweet, lovely, dashing Tony Nash.

25

Tony came down to Merrillee about once a month to stay for the weekend or occasionally Nora went up to London to meet him for lunch and a matinée of one kind or another after a morning's shopping if he weren't working, or to spend the evening with him if he were. But Tony always took the trouble to make their time together special, filling his flat with flowers to welcome her; getting tickets for a show she'd been dying to see; taking her to the hottest new club or discovering an Indian restaurant in the West End he knew she'd like. Moreover, he listened to her when she recited a litany of problems with running Merrillee as a money-making proposition or with Hubie and his little scrapes. He told her over and over again that she worried too much, that she was too beautiful to risk getting worry lines, and she told him over and over again that she didn't know why she'd ever married him, considering he was so much better as a best friend than he'd ever been as a husband. Then he'd counter with: 'I was an excellent husband except for one slip, which you shouldn't have held against me. You should never have held anything *against* me except for one thing – yourself!'

It had become a ritual, one she treasured as much as she treasured Tony's affection. Still, when he turned up at Merrillee after she'd seen him only three days before, she demanded: 'What are you doing here again so soon?'

'Such a charming welcome, and after I brought you a present – a jar of that bilious green chutney from Fortnum's you're so fond of.' He reached into the pocket of his Burberry to bring forth the jar, but then held it a few inches out of her reach.

'Really, you're *such* a child,' she said, grabbing for it, and after a few moments of grappling, he let her have it. 'All right, what else did you bring me?'

'Aren't you the greedy one? Can't you give a chap a chance to catch his breath? You haven't even offered me a drink.'

'It's eleven o'clock in the morning. You don't get a drink until at least noon.'

'Not only are you greedy but cruel as well.'

'Tony, I'm warning you. If you don't tell me what else you have for me, you're not going to get lunch either.'

'How do you *know* I have something else for you? You really are a bloody witch.'

'Just hand it over, matey, and cut the gab.'

He stretched out on the sofa expansively. 'It *is* cosy

272

here and I demand a whisky and soda – I've sworn off vodka until after lunch – before another word or action transpires.'

Sighing, she gave him his drink then stuck out her hand which he looked at disdainfully. 'It's not a *thing* I have for you. It's an invitation. A verbal one.'

'Uh-oh . . .' She sat down opposite him in the club chair. 'I have a feeling I should be sitting down to hear this one.'

'I've been offered an interesting role in a film that's shooting in Italy and I'm asking you to come along.'

'Why does this all sound so familiar? Is it *déjà vu*?'

'Not quite. And if you'd wipe that smirk off your face, I'd appreciate it. If you'll recall, the last time I asked you to come along with me I was careful not to mislead you by pointing out that I was *not* asking you to marry me.'

'No, you waited until you had me cornered, then you *demanded* I marry you.'

'You could have said no.'

'Oh, sure. There I was, friendless in a strange land and you said that if I refused you, you were going to drive me out into the desert and leave me there!'

'That's a lie if ever I heard one. Besides, there's no chance of that happening again because this time I'm asking you to marry me *before* you set one foot out of England!'

But, by this time, she was not surprised by his proposal and they discussed the pros and cons of remarriage over a lunch of shepherd's pie, or rather, Tony offered the pros and she the cons, and at first it was all in fun. He said, 'Think of the grand sex,' and she said, 'But we have that now,' and he said, 'But under the present circumstances, not often enough,' and she said, 'But that's what keeps it interesting.'

Then, gradually the discussion veered towards the serious. She said, 'But we're such good friends now. I'd hate to give that up,' and he said, 'But we don't have to.

We were good friends when we were married, weren't we?' and she said, 'Not really. When we were married, you betrayed me. And while one might betray a wife, one would never betray a friend.'

'Well, that's a cynical view and petty of you to bring up the past. Besides, I have affairs with other women now which you know all about and you don't regard them as betrayal.'

'Exactly. If we're friends and only occasional lovers, they're not betrayal. Once we're married, they are.'

'But I've repeatedly said that I was sorry about the L'Heureux incident. "To err is human, to forgive divine."'

'And as I'm most definitely divine, I *have* forgiven you. But to forgive is not to forget.'

'Well, suppose I promised you that I would never again be guilty of infidelity? Would you trust me then?'

'As a friend, yes. As a wife, it's a risk.'

'But that isn't fair!' he whined, reminding her of Hubie. 'Didn't we agree *not* to talk about the bloody incident again? You promised, Nora, and here you are bringing it up again.'

'That just goes to show that *you* can't trust *me*, either.' She sighed elaborately. 'One can't trust anyone these days.'

'I can't believe you! You've always accused me of thinking that life is only fun and games and of never taking anything seriously and here I am trying to talk to you seriously about something very serious and you're making fun.'

'Which goes to prove another point – as friends we make a wonderful team. We can support each other, yet present an opposite point of view when necessary. Today, for example. You're being much too serious *and* unrealistic so I'm showing you the error of your ways. On the other hand, when *I'm* being serious, *totally* realistic, worrying about *important* things like Hubie and money, you always make me laugh which is

274

good. That's friendship! Do you see what I mean?'

'Frankly, no. Who can make sense out of that? And it sounds as if you're more interested in giving yourself good marks for character and me poor ones than in making sense. But from what sense I managed to make out of all that natter, I think you spelled out a fine basis for a good marriage.'

'Don't be silly. I spelled out a fine basis for *friendship*. For marriage, it spells out as *incompatibility*.'

'I can see there's no talking to you today, Nora,' Tony said, pained no matter how much she had tried to avoid exactly that with her bantering. 'But since I'm not leaving for Italy until two weeks hence, perhaps you'll still change your mind.'

Then she said softly, 'Don't count on it, Tony.'

'But why not?' he asked, digging into his trifle. 'I don't understand why you refuse to give us another chance.'

'Because no matter how much I'd love to, I can't *afford* to give us another chance or even the benefit of the doubt.'

'If you're talking about money you don't have to worry. I am not a poor man,' he said huffily.

'I'm *not* talking about money. Well, not primarily anyway, though I won't say it isn't a consideration. But Hubie *needs* a father and if I marry again I can't have any doubts. I have to be sure it's right.'

'And I don't fill the bill as a father, is that it?' Though his tone was jaunty she knew he was hurt.

'It's not that you're not a wonderful person with wonderful qualities, Tony, but I think Hubie needs – well, a more serious man, a man of substance and stability.'

'For you, it always boils down to Hubie, doesn't it?'

She nodded. 'I'm afraid so, Tony.'

He tried to smile. 'What's our boy been up to lately?'

'Trouble, but this time it was serious. He and three friends broke into a house and vandalized it. And while he's not going to be prosecuted – the other parents and I made good the damages and I managed to talk the owners out of pressing charges – I *do* have to think about his future.'

'But what did Hubie say? Why did he do it?'

'The usual. What he always says. These boys were his friends and it was their idea and he had to go along with them. But probably he did it because it was *fun*, but there's no malice in him. He just can't resist temptation and he always ends up with these kind of friends.'

'And you propose to make it all come out right by marrying a man of substance and sterling character? One who has never yielded to temptation, who knows duty comes before a good time, who'll be a role model. Is that it? Ah yes, even I can see that Tony Nash is not that sort of chap.'

The ironic part of all this, she thought, was that Tony, in his pain at being rejected thought *he* was being ironic, but the fact was if she had tried to describe the man she had in mind to marry to provide a proper father for Hubie, it wouldn't have varied much from the man he'd just described.

Oh, maybe she could enhance it a bit. She *could* wish for this same man to be a very rich and handsome specimen who would come riding up to Merrillee Manor on a white steed to claim her and swoop her and Hubie up to carry them off to some wonderful never-never land where all women loved madly and were so loved in return, and all sweet, beautiful boys grew up to be splendid men who did their mothers proud. But that was too much to hope for. That was too much to even dream about.

'You know, the least you could have done was tell me all this when I first walked in with a proposal on the tip of my tongue so I wouldn't have made a bloody fool of myself.'

'But you didn't. You just proved that you're my love-ly, loving Tony – my best pal.' Her eyes begged him to understand everything, even that she would always love him in a very special way. 'You are my best pal, aren't you?'

'I suppose so, but only because I *am* a bloody fool – foolish enough to have a silly twit like you for my best chum.'

Then she knew that whatever else happened – handsome, rich stranger with all the sterling virtues notwithstanding – she would *always* have dashing Tony Nash as her friend if not her lover. No woman had a right to expect it all.

'Now, tell me all about this film you're doing in Italy. What makes it so interesting? Are you going to be working with one of those fabulous Italian directors?'

'Well, no. Actually, I've never heard of the director.'

'Oh? But you are shooting in Rome? No wonder you're so excited. *La dolce vita* and all that. Are you planning on becoming the British Marcello Mastroianni?' She slunk across the room affecting smouldering eyes. 'Oh, yes, I can see you skulking about Rome every bit as sexy as Marcello.'

'I hate to burst your balloon, but no, I am not going to be skulking about in Rome.'

'Oh Tony, don't tell me Venice or I *will* be tempted to run away with you, after all.'

'Really, Nora, do you think that's all there is to Italy? The high life in Rome or the romance of Venice? There are other places, you know,' he said with a note of irritation.

'Oh, Tony! I know! You're going to be shooting in Sicily. You're going to play one of those Cosa Nostra thugs. Now, I do think that *is* interesting, a real challenge considering that you're such a sophisticated type.'

'No, I am *not* going to Sicily to play an Italian mafioso,' he said querulously. 'If you must know, and if you will stop this ridiculous guessing, I will tell you—'

'Wait, it just came to me. My crystal ball, you

know. You're going to Italy to be in one of those spaghetti westerns!' She burst out laughing. 'Tell me it isn't so!' When he didn't, she asked, 'But can you really ride a horse?'

In September, Tony was back from Italy and came calling, deeply tanned, wearing a black sombrero, sporting a beard, his moustache long and curling, and carrying a long salami under one arm and a redolent Gorgonzola under the other. But then, after all the kissing and all the jokes about his chronic case of bowed legs, he reluctantly handed her a newspaper. 'I didn't plan on coming down until the weekend, but when I saw the paper this morning I thought you could use a little company when you read this. Or have you already heard?'

'Heard what?' But as soon as she glanced at the paper, she didn't have to ask any more questions and it took her only a few seconds to absorb the import of the prominently featured story: *After Lord Jeffrey Hartiscor had accidentally but mortally wounded his son and heir, Rupert, at a duck shoot at Hartiscor Castle, the grief-stricken father had taken his own life by hanging.*

'Shall I get you a drink, Nora?' Tony asked anxiously. 'I know that this must come as a terrible shock.'

'No, I was rather expecting something like this. The only surprise is that it took Jeffrey this long to take that shot.' Still, she sunk into a chair, shaken. 'I guess it's really over at last.'

'I'll escort you and Hubie to the funeral if you like.'

'No. Hubie and I will not be attending this funeral.'

'But you must, Nora! At least Hubie must. Jeffrey adopted him and now Hubie's legally the Earl of Hartiscor!'

'No, he's not.'

'Nora, what are you talking about? You must be in shock! With Jeffrey and Rupert both dead—'

'No. When Jeffrey divorced me I signed affidavits

278

agreeing to have the adoption nullified, relinquishing Hubie's claim to the Hartiscor title and estate.'

'But how could you, no matter how desperate you were for a divorce? Look, I'll talk to my solicitors. You'll file to have those affidavits declared invalid. You'll say you signed them under duress – that Jeffrey forced you to.'

'But that's not true, Tony. I signed them willingly and I don't want anything set aside.'

'But the Hartiscor fortune! Are you mad? How can you do that to Hubie? Rob him of his legacy?'

'What legacy – the Curse of the Hartiscors? There are more important things than titles and fortunes. In fact, I was thinking that Hubie would be better off if he dropped the name Hartiscor altogether . . .'

The day after Rupert and Jeffrey were buried in a joint service, Nora had a gentleman caller who had come to England for the funeral. And though it had been several years since she had last seen him, she recognized him at once – just the hero she needed, who arrived in the nick of time to carry Hubie and her off to safety and a better life. And while he rode up to her door in a white Bentley rather than on a white steed, and though he was hardly handsome and would never make her heart beat madly, he bore a most prestigious name and boasted all the sterling virtues that any mother could wish for in a father for her son – the man who, as her late former husband and stepson claimed, had always nursed a secret yen for her, the recently widowed Hugh Cantington, former ambassador to the Court of St James's, distinguished elder statesman and adviser to presidents, possessor of one of America's great fortunes, and, not incidentally, the father of four grown, successful sons.

PART SIX

THE ONE THAT REALLY COUNTS

Washington, DC
1958–68

26

Her wedding day dawned bright and clear, the Florida sunshine delivering on schedule – the temperature, a perfect seventy-five degrees – and Nora thought that a good omen. Somewhere she'd read that blessed was the bride the sun shone on, or something like that. She was too tired to try to remember exactly. For three weeks now she'd been trying to get Palm Haven in shape for the elaborate reception Hugh was hell-bent on having, and while it hadn't been a major overhaul – that would come later – it hadn't been easy. It seemed that she had worked harder here in the past three weeks than she had at Merrillee in a year.

Actually, it had been a shock to see how badly neglected the Cantington waterfront estate was when she arrived in Palm Beach after having spent a fortnight in Washington getting acquainted with his sons before all the wedding fuss began.

'Will they be interviewing me for the position of your wife?' she had joked with Hugh the night before he left England to precede her arrival in the States. 'Suppose they decide that I won't do? Will you throw me over?'

'What a thought!' he had laughed. 'Besides, they're going to love you as much as I do. How could they not?'

But no sooner had she and Hubie stepped off the plane in Washington than she discovered there would be problems when Peter and Paul, Hugh's twin younger sons, met them at the airport. While they were polite and efficient, taking care of all the tiresome business with the customs and luggage, they weren't what she'd call warm. As for Hubie, eager as a puppy to meet Hugh's sons – he'd been so excited when he heard that he was going to have *four* big brothers – Peter and Paul barely looked at him when they shook hands. Still, she was determined she'd wear them down with her own warmth.

'Where's your father?' she asked when they were settled in the limousine. 'It was naughty of him not to come and meet us. I'm going to have to give him a piece of my mind.'

The young men exchanged looks before Peter said, 'Dad's waiting at the house with Billy and Bobby and their wives. We thought it would be best this way – less excitement for him.'

'Less excitement? But I don't understand. Isn't Hugh feeling well? He was absolutely glowing when I saw him last.'

More than glowing, she thought. After she'd agreed to marry him, they'd consummated their troth by making love over and over again, and he'd been almost lyrical.

Peter smiled tightly. 'Our father's not a young man, Mrs Nash, and we're concerned that he doesn't overdo it.'

'Please, call me Nora.' She thought of telling them to call her, 'Mummy', just to see their reaction – they could use a bit of shaking up – but she decided to behave herself until she got to know them better. She supposed it was as difficult for young men in their twenties to accept any woman other than their mother as their father's wife as it would be for a small child.

'Patty, Bobby's wife, says that getting married at Father's age is bound to be a strain, especially when he's marrying a much younger woman.'

Hubie laughed. 'Mummy's not so young. She's thirty-three,' which earned him a frigid stare from Paul. But she wasn't concerned since Hubie – who always assumed everyone would like him – didn't realize he was being chilled.

284

But then, Peter – a bit nicer than Paul, she thought – explained to Hubie, 'Our father's *sixty-three*,' and Hubie thought that over and conceded, 'That really *is* old.' Then he confided, 'I'm only thirteen but Mummy says that your father's not really *too* old to be my father and we'll get along fine. But I think it's great that we're going to be brothers. Then if your father can't play soccer, *we* still can.'

Now Peter and Paul exchanged raised eyebrows and Paul told her, 'Patty said it was up to *us* to see that Father doesn't overdo things.'

'Patty must be very clever and I'm sure she's right. I'll certainly have to see to it that he doesn't.'

Then Hubie chortled and Peter and Paul looked at him as if they were thinking, *what is this idiot kid laughing at now?*

'What's funny, Hubie?' Peter asked and Hubie said, 'That you chaps are in your twenties and I'm only thirteen, but I'm taller than both of you already,' and she could see that the brothers didn't find that amusing at all.

But it would all work out, she thought. It was just a matter of everyone getting used to one another and that was *her* job – to see to it that they were one happy family. And she thought she knew the answer to that – the perfect link in the chain that would draw them all closer – a baby brother or sister that would be half-Hubie's and half the Cantington boys'. What could be a stronger link? And for that reason alone, she was thrilled that Hugh was such a virile lover.

Then the shocks came thick and fast.

For one, the enormous house on R Street was incredibly *shabby*. The front lawn was brown and patchy, the marble floor in the entry scarred and cracked, and in the drawing room where she and Hubie were left to cool their heels while the twins ostensibly went to fetch Hugh, the table tops were unpolished, the upholstered chairs threadbare and the down pillows badly in need of a restuffing. There was only one conclusion that she could come to – that even though Hugh Cantington was a very rich man with most likely a huge staff – what he really needed more than a wife was a good gardener, a capable housekeeper, some able helpers and a talented interior designer, all of whom he was clearly doing without.

Hubie wanted to know when they were going to eat – he was famished – and she told him to be patient. Finally, Peter reappeared to take her and Hubie upstairs to where his father and the others were waiting. Of course! she thought, this explained it all – why Hugh hadn't come to the airport to meet her and why he hadn't at least been waiting for her downstairs. They had some kind of a surprise party waiting upstairs with welcoming banners and a table full of party food. She whispered to Hubie, 'I have a strong feeling you're going to get something to eat any minute now.'

'Good! I could eat a horse!'

'Don't be silly, darling, they don't eat horses in America. All they eat all day long are bon-bons, ice cream and chocolate cake,' she giggled happily.

But, when Peter opened the door and stood to one side so that Nora and Hubie could precede him into the sitting room, what greeted Nora was no party but a family gathered together as if to take a serious family portrait with Hugh, the aged patriarch, sitting with his sons and daughters-in-law grouped all about him. But that wasn't all. In his arms Hugh held a crying baby while a boy of two or three was busy trying to climb up a leg and one of the daughters-in-law was attempting to sit a girl of perhaps five, fat and kicking, on his knee. Though he hadn't said a word to her, Hugh was a grandfather!

Delighted, she rushed to him and he tried to rise to greet her, holding the shrieking baby with one arm and attempting more or less to push the fat, blond girl back at its mother with the other, but the child pulling at his leg defeated him and he fell back into the chair.

Laughing, she took the crying baby from his arms, giving it a hug before handing it over to a grinning Hubie – he loved babies, 'even beastly ones', he'd once confided – while she leaned over to give Hugh a kiss. As she did, he whispered, 'Now, if you can get rid of that monster trying to amputate my leg, I'll be able to reciprocate properly.'

Once this was accomplished – she plucking up the boy by force to give him a kiss before setting him on his feet – and the baby stopped crying because babies always responded to Hubie, the introductions were made all around. And if the sons and the daughters-in-laws were cool, Hubie made up for it with his boyish enthusiasm. He thought the large and noisy scene was jolly good fun, and she thought that once she won over Hugh's sons and Patty and Daisy, what a wonderful time they were all going to have.

She could just picture the big family dinners they'd have at least once a week and of course, at Thanksgiving and Christmas. And on the Fourth of July they'd have huge picnics with fireworks and on Easter Sunday, they'd have their very own egg hunt with the very youngest Cantington – hers and Hugh's – given a head start because it was the baby. And the master of the hunt would be none other than Hubie Cantington himself, the eldest of the younger set of Cantingtons, at long last part of a big and happy clan.

She and Hubie had really fallen on their feet this time, she thought and anything she had to do to make the dream a reality she'd do and thank God for the privilege of doing it.

Then, *sotto voce*, Hugh asked *her* to ask his children to go home so that they could be alone.

'But Hugh, it's not *my* place to do that. I can send Hubie to look around the house or something so we can be alone, but I can't ask *your* children to leave. I have my work cut out here just getting them to like me. Naturally enough, I suppose, they think I'm nothing more than a fortune hunter and I – well, I don't want to get off on the wrong foot. I think that it would be better if *you* asked them to leave.'

'No, my dear, *you* must. It's the only way you're going to establish any authority around here. If you don't, all is lost.' He smiled at her, his 'all is lost' a spoof, but she could see that he was in dead earnest.

'But dinner—? Weren't they planning on us all having dinner together here?'

'I'm sure they were,' he chortled. 'And they were probably planning on feeding me pablum along with that wretched baby. Now, Nora, you must be firm or they'll walk all over you just like they've always managed to do to me.'

She couldn't argue the point with everyone pointedly waiting for the private conversation to end, and there was nothing else to do then but for her to tell them that their father *was* tired as she herself was, and it would be best if they came back tomorrow when everyone was feeling fresh.

'Of course, he's tired,' Bobby's wife, Patty, said severely. 'I should think! And before I leave I'm going to see to it that he has something to eat – he's on a special diet, you know – and then I'll see him settled in bed and—'

Be firm, Hugh had said. She set her teeth in so firm a smile it made her jaw ache. 'Oh my dear, I know *exactly* what Hugh should be eating and if there's one thing I'm *really* good at, it's seeing that a man is properly settled in his bed. So all of yōu can run along with easy hearts and see to your kiddies while I see to mine. And tomorrow we'll have a proper get-together. I know – I'll have the cook prepare a real English feast, roast beef and Yorkshire pudding and—'

'But that's exactly what Dad *shouldn't* be eating,' Patty said, horrified, and Daisy said, 'And you'd better not be upsetting the cook. She's been here for over thirty years and she doesn't like any interference. Isn't that right, Billy?'

Billy said indeed, that was right, and added, 'And you better keep Hubie out of her kitchen. She might get miffed and walk out and then where will poor Dad be?'

'With a new cook in *his* kitchen, I dare say,' she laughed and started gently edging them all towards the door.

'We'll see you tomorrow then, Dad,' Bobby said, but as if with misgivings. 'And we'll have some papers for *you* to sign, Nora. We thought it best if we got everything tidied away right from the start. Isn't that right, Dad?'

'Of course, son,' Hugh said with a little chuckle. 'The boys all have their law degrees,' he told her proudly. Then he waved to his children. 'See you all tomorrow.'

Then, once they were gone, Hugh suggested that since Hubie was dying of hunger and it would be sometime to dinner, if that was what anyone chose to call the pap that would be served, he should go down to the kitchen and see what he could scrape up for himself while he and she got reacquainted.

'But you just heard what Billy said about keeping Hubie out of the kitchen. That Cook might become annoyed enough to leave and where would that leave us?'

'Yes, I heard Billy, and I also heard your answer. You said it would leave us with a new cook. That was wonderful!'

'And that's what you *really* want?'

'My God, yes! And once you taste the tyrant's cooking, I'm sure you'll concur.'

Accordingly, she sent Hubie down to the kitchen, then asked Hugh, 'What's going on here? If you don't like the cook or her cooking, why haven't you simply given her the sack?'

'But I couldn't do that. She's a great favourite with Patty and Daisy as she was with Rita, and I have my reputation to think of,' he said, smiling at her beguilingly. 'Washington is a small town as far as gossip goes, and just think of the bad notices I'd receive in all of Georgetown's kitchens if I gave Cook the boot. Before you knew it the back-door gossip would be front-door gossip and then I'd no longer be the charmingly diplomatic Hugh Cantington but a nasty old man. Besides, you heard the children. The woman's been here for thirty years. I can't fire her any more than I can fire the rest of the menagerie that work here.'

'But you're quite willing that she or the rest of them *quit* if things around here become not to their liking?'

'Willing? I'm *counting* on it. All I know is that I'm damn tired of having the worst-run house in Washington and serving up the worst meals in town. Do you know that even before Rita became ill, an invitation to dine at our house was enough to send people into paroxysms of laughter? You can't imagine how I felt when I was in England and we'd go to yours and Jeffrey's home for even an informal dinner—'

'How?'

'Jealous to the core. Not only did Jeffrey have you – the desirable, young and beautiful Nora in his bed – but also the hostess with the most illustrious salon in London.'

Then she realized that while Hugh had begun the conversation facetiously, he was no longer smiling, but angrily sincere. 'But I don't understand, Hugh. You're an important, rich man and you've had a most distinguished career. Why *didn't* you have things the way you wanted them?'

'It was Rita. She hated my being a public figure. If it weren't one thing she was complaining about, it was another. Either she wasn't feeling well or someone was snubbing her and it made no difference if we were here or abroad. Why do you think we left England when

290

we did? All she wanted was to be at home with the children. And when we *were* home with the children, they always came first before everything, certainly before me or my career. And she refused to consider anything else. If I told her the house was in deplorable condition and we had to do something about it because it was an embarrassment, do you know what she said? Only the *nouveau riche* worried about these things. As far as *old* money was concerned, shabby was a badge of honour.'

'Oh . . .' she said, not really understanding.

'But do you know what the truth is? She acted out of spite. She tried to smother me with those children just like those children are trying to smother me now – trying to make an old grandpappy of me with their horrid brats crawling all over me, telling me I mustn't overdo things, feeding me their milk toast, trying to relegate me to a rocking-chair on the back porch. They want to take over not only the family fortune, but my very life. They're jealous of my position, just like their mother was. Do you realize if it weren't for Rita I could have been president?'

President? She was startled by the word. She had had no idea this was something Hugh had wanted for himself. She studied him now, mesmerized by the harsh look of frustrated ambition that shot from his angry eyes like fiery sparks. This was not the winsome, dignified, unfailingly pleasant Hugh Cantington she knew, a man content to rest on his laurels . . . the man she *thought* she was marrying . . . the man she thought was marrying *her* only for her own winsome charms.

'But it's not too late, you think? For the presidency?' he asked hopefully.

Ah, he still wants it . . .

She spoke slowly, choosing her words. 'No, I would say sixty-three seems an excellent age if a man still has his vigour, his health and his mental capacities . . .'

These were the very qualities she'd been considering when she thought that they would have a baby. Now she saw that it was much too late for *that* – what Hugh envisioned for their future was something else altogether and there was no room for a baby in *that* scenario. But, as it wasn't too late for a man of Hugh's calibre and reputation to shoot for the presidency, it wasn't too late for Hubie, either. He couldn't help but turn out marvellously if his adoptive father was elected as the leader of his adopted country. And she was willing to do her part. Whatever role Hugh wanted her to play, she could learn the lines. And if he needed a woman to clean house, so to speak, then she could be that woman, too. If nothing else, she was prepared to give at least as good as she got.

'I don't know very much about politics, certainly not American politics. But I'm willing to learn and I'll do my best to help you get whatever it is you want.'

Hugh leaned back in his chair with a sigh of relief as if at least half his battle had already been won and his face settled back into its usual sanguine expression. 'Now, let's get down to cases. You know those papers Bobby was referring to – the ones he said he wanted you to sign tomorrow? Most of them don't amount to a hell of a lot – insurance forms and permits, that sort of thing. The important document is our marriage contract which spells out what you *will* and what you *won't* get under various circumstances and contingencies.'

'I'm prepared to—' she began, but he held up his hand.

'But that doesn't mean that the contract has to be accepted and signed as it stands. Oh, they're hoping you're foolish enough to do that, but the thing to remember is that everything is negotiable.'

'But I'm not worried about the negotiations,' she smiled. 'I assumed that a marriage contract was what the boys had in mind when they mentioned papers to be signed and I can understand that they'd want to protect their inheritance, as well they should. But since it is *our* marriage contract, it means that we both have to sign it and I'm willing to take *you* on faith – that you wouldn't sign any contract that wasn't fair to me. I'm sure you'll negotiate on my behalf since I don't even know an American lawyer to represent me and *you're* the great diplomat . . . *the* negotiator.' She thought she was speaking in jest, that *naturally* Hugh would look out for hers and Hubie's interests.

But then he said, 'I'm going to do something better for you than simply negotiate for you, Nora. I'm going to teach you how to *negotiate for yourself*. And the secret is: you give a little here to get a lot more there. And what you have to watch out for are those contingencies.'

All this was getting to be a bit much and Hugh was really going too far. He made it all sound like a game of chess or a board game with the contestants playing war games.

'Look, Hugh, I don't want to think about contingencies. I'm not marrying you to divorce you, but to have a good life with you, and I hope that I'm going to be such a wonderful wife that you won't ever dream of divorcing me. And I refuse to think about your dying – I *won't!*'

'That makes you a fool and I'll be damned if I'll marry a fool. I want to marry a winner! And if you refuse to think about your own future, what about Hubie's? How do you think *my* sons will feel about my adopting *your* son, who *you're* going to insist is cut in for his fair share of the loot when their old man takes his swan dive? You're going to have to fight them tooth and nail and you're going to have to be tough.'

'Oh, Hugh, you mean you haven't told them yet that you're adopting Hubie?'

'No, of course not.'

'But why not?' *It was the least he could have done* . . .

'Because it's *you* who must do the negotiating and so it must be *you* who lays the cards on the table. But cheer up, my dear, during the next few days you're going to learn enough about negotiating and politicking to last you a lifetime.'

'I see,' she said, then asked, 'and this campaign

we're going to be waging for the presidency? When does it officially begin and what year are we talking about?'

'The election year is 1960, but the campaign has already started. It began the moment you stepped off that plane.'

She glanced at her wrist-watch. 'In that case, we're wasting time. What's the best restaurant in town where Washington's most élite will be dining tonight?'

Hugh was startled. 'By élite do you mean socially or politically powerful?'

'The latter, to be sure.'

'Hmm . . .' he considered. 'It's been a while since I've even been out to dinner. My jailers, you know. But I would say the Vendome would be as good a choice as any.'

'I'll call for a reservation. Then I'll go downstairs to collect Hubie so we can change into our best clothes.'

'You mean we're going out to dinner?'

'Exactly.'

'But you must be tired. You just got off the plane—'

'But we have to eat and you yourself said the food served here is beastly and you haven't been out to dinner in ages and one thing Jeffrey taught me was that direct action beats legislation every time. If we go out to dine you'll be sure to meet old friends and you'll be able to introduce your future wife and your handsome new son . . . remind everyone that Hugh Cantington's still around and a force to be contended with. Doesn't that all sound sensible?'

Hugh beamed. 'Absolutely. I'm in your hands and I *am* a shrewd old goat. I *knew* you were going to make things fun.'

She went downstairs to find Hubie, hoping he hadn't stuffed himself to the point where he wouldn't be able to eat dinner, but she needn't have worried. Hubie had never made it to the kitchen at all. It seemed he'd first been waylaid and then detained in a parlourmaid's bedroom in the basement.

'What *were* you thinking of?' she demanded, but it was a foolish question. Obviously he hadn't been thinking at all.

'She said I had a beautiful body and she just wanted to feel my muscles,' he grinned beatifically.

Now, still standing at the window, she looked down at the back lawns with the white-and-pink striped tents, watched the catering people setting up their buffets; the florists adding the last-minute touches to the flower arrangements of white roses and pale pink tulips, azaleas and giant hydrangeas; the musicians arriving early to tune up their instruments. And it occurred to her that she was going to feel like a stranger at her own wedding.

A thousand guests had been invited – a mixture of Washington senators and Palm Beach socialites, foreign dignitaries and governors from all over the country, Supreme Court justices and theatre people from New York, Democrats and Republicans (while the Eisenhowers had sent their regrets, they had sent a lovely telegram that arrived practically at dawn), sports figures and stars of the media. Soon they'd all be wishing her well (some of them kissing her on both cheeks), milling about, sipping champagne while Meyer Davis's orchestra played for the dancing, and tasting of the four-foot-tall wedding cake, but she actually knew very few of them, and none of them well – people like the Kennedys who were their neighbours here in Palm Beach and up in Cape Cod, too.

Hugh had told her that the whole Kennedy tribe had to be invited, not only because they were neighbours and socially and politically 'eligible', but also because they were the competition. 'And you always have to be friendly with the competition so you can keep your finger on their pulse and try to guess what they were thinking and planning.'

She had laughed. 'The *whole* clan is *our* competition?'

'Yes, the word is out that old Joe has decided that

295

Jack is going to make his run for the presidency in '60, too, and the whole family will get into the act of campaigning just as they did when Jack ran for the House and Senate.'

'But he's so young. Surely he can't be real competition for an old seasoned performer like you with your track record. I just can't believe it.'

But then she began to wonder about that. Her adopted country did appear to be not only the land of the free, but a land best suited for the young. For the old it seemed like an uphill struggle just to keep up, demanding enormous energy and then she wondered if Hugh was really up to it.

She would just have to have energy enough for two. That was her job just as it was her job now to get dressed for her wedding, putting on her pale pink taffeta faille wedding gown, her crown of orange blossoms interwoven with pearls and her wedding present from her groom – a necklace composed of diamonds and pearls set to resemble so many flowers all in a row. Then, lastly, she'd have to put on her biggest and best smile although today – for some vague, nagging reason – her heart was heavy and her feet felt like lead.

But then just as she was about to turn away from the window, she spotted Hubie, already dressed in his white usher's cutaway, racing across the lawn to – what?

She had no idea and wondered if *he* himself did. He was just so eager to *go* . . . a racehorse tearing out of the gate to run at full speed towards life just for the sheer joy of embracing it. For a moment she thought of flinging the window open to call to him, to stop him in his flight, to ask him where he was heading, to caution him not to go down to the beach, not to soil his white suit, not to fall and break his slender racehorse's leg. But he was so beautiful in the white suit with his lovely yellow hair catching the sun that her heart quickened and she couldn't bear to stop his poetry in motion.

Then her own feet barely touched the floor as she

began to dress and she hummed to herself, '*Oh, how we danced on the night we were wed . . .*'

Hubie Cantington was not only going to have the best of everything, he was going to be happy, too.

27

In January, Nora sent Hubie away to boarding school in Massachusetts feeling very much like a mother who had sent her son off to war. She knew she was being silly, but he was so young and so new to being both a Cantington and an American he really needed hands-on supervision. She'd thought that in the beginning, at least, she would keep him with her, but Hugh insisted that since Hubie was now a Cantington, he had to be educated as a Cantington, which meant an excellent prep school and eventually, Harvard.

'The Cantington men have always gone to Harvard with the exception of Peter and Paul who went to Yale because Rita insisted on it – her father was a Yalie. In fact, there was a Cantington in the first Harvard commencement class in 1642.'

'That's nice, but I doubt that Hubie's Harvard material.'

'I must say that's a negative attitude. Not at all what I would expect from my positive and optimistic Nora.'

'I *wish*,' she sighed. 'But I've learned that it doesn't help to deny what's as clear as the nose on your face.'

She touched the tip of his nose with the tip of her finger and he immediately grasped it to bring it to his lips to kiss, and she sighed again. Hugh was so sure of what he wanted – no shillying about – and had the conviction of those who *know* they're right, that he made it difficult to argue with him. Then when he was so sweet and loving in addition, he made it impossible for her to go against him.

'But you have to realize that Hubie *does* have a history.'

'My, my, already at *his* age?' His eyes sparkled mischievously. 'Isn't he the lucky boy?'

'Hugh, I'm serious! I'm talking about Hubie's scholastic record. It's never been what it should be and there's been a behaviour problem ever since he started school.'

'Then that's all the more reason to send him only to the best schools so that he'll do better in all departments.'

He makes it sound so simple.

'And he *must* go away to school because it will be easier for him to develop self-discipline away from his over-solicitous mother and his doting dad, because I warn you – I intend to be most doting.'

Did he know that that 'I intend to be most doting' *softened her heart to such a degree that she could only be agreeable to whatever he wanted?*

'Besides, if I'm to announce my candidacy by the end of this year we must get started at once so that I'll be a *viable* candidate by then. And once I announce there'll be the campaign to get the nomination and once that's in the bag, the real campaigning will begin. So that makes two years during which you'll be much too busy for this hands-on supervision that Hubie is better off without. And I'm sure you'll feel it's all been worth it when Hubie ends up living in the White House. Hah! I'd just like to see them try to keep the president's son out of Harvard.'

Then as it worked out it was just as well that she didn't keep Hubie at home because almost immediately she wasn't at home either but off and running. Before the month was out – just after she'd finished restaffing the Washington house and just before she started its renovations – they were off to Paris for a week, the honeymoon trip Hugh had promised her, after which he announced they'd be spending some time in the Soviet Union.

298

She was amazed. 'Russia? But we have so much work to do here and it will be *so* cold in Russia this time of year.'

'Exactly. I thought that you and I might drop in and warm up the atmosphere somewhat. Ever since the war ended I've been very vocal speaking out against the Soviets, but I'm beginning to reverse my thinking about that – that perhaps the better way is to make friends with them. And if a man wishes to be president, he must have something special to offer and since my field of expertise is foreign relations – well, I believe it's time to forge a dialogue with the Soviets and Khrushchev . . . it's time to heal the breach.'

Heal the breach . . .

The words had a lovely ring to them, she thought, and she spent the days before they left boning up on Russia and especially its Mr Khrushchev, which amused Hugh no end. 'I'm taking you to Moscow to *charm* Khrushchev, not debate him.'

'You said we were going there to warm things up. Well, how can I do that if I walk in *cold*? I may not be the wise man my husband is, but I do know that the best way to charm a man is to talk to him *about him* even if it is through an interpreter. Now, don't you think I'm right?'

'What I think is that the supposedly wise man married a woman infinitely wiser than he and certainly more charming.'

She was so charming that when Khrushchev toured the States in November, he not only demanded to see Disneyland, but the Cantingtons as well. And while he wasn't permitted to go to Disneyland for security reasons, the house on R Street was sufficiently secured (and by now sufficiently beautiful with its pale chintzes, gleaming Georgian silver and awesome art collection) for the Cantingtons to host a reception for the chairman that was viewed by Washingtonians as the coup of the political

299

season. Even the Eisenhowers deigned to attend which made it a *double* coup despite the necessity to beef up the security twofold as well.

In the end, the guest list grew so extensive that they purchased the house next door which opportunely was for sale, to accommodate out-of-town guests and even some of the Khrushchev entourage at the behest of the Soviet Ambassador. She then had a little bridge constructed that linked the two houses which was facetiously dubbed in the Press as the Cantington link to the Kremlin, which delighted Hugh. (The name stuck and later on sometimes it would have a good connotation and sometimes not – it all depended how the political wind was blowing at the time.)

But as extensive as the guest list was, it did not include Hugh's sons and the wives. She had wanted to invite them, but Hugh refused to allow it because of the existing hostility that had started with the haggling over the marriage contract and the announcement that he was adopting Hubie, and was then intensified by the children's disapproval of his trip to Russia and his new political ambitions. And it hadn't helped that when they wanted to bring their children over to visit their grandfather, or even see him on a business matter, Hugh insisted they arranged an appointment through his wife, which of course didn't endear her to them.

'They're just too nasty to have around,' Hugh said decisively. But then when Hubie was sent home from school on suspension pending the results of an investigation into a rash of petty thefts at St John's, he had no problem with Hubie being at the party though she herself had reservations about his being allowed to participate in the festivities.

'I don't want him to get the idea that he's being rewarded in any way—'

'Rewarded? The poor boy been's maligned and under no circumstances will I allow him to return to St John's. And before we send him off to another school, I think we

300

should do everything to make his stay at home a pleasant one. I'm very surprised that you don't agree with me.'

'But as yet we don't have all the facts,' she protested weakly in the face of Hugh's vigorous championing of Hubie.

'I refuse to believe that our Hubie is guilty of theft.'

'But he *is* friends with the boys who seem to be the culprits.'

'So are we, his parents, to pass judgement on him and confirm that he's guilty merely by association?'

'No, of course not.' How was she to explain to the man who had promised to 'dote' on him that Hubie lacked the fortitude to resist temptation and the wrong sort of friends? And then how could she not take pride when, at the grand reception, Hugh remarked how taken everyone was with the charming Hubie Cantington, even the dour Mrs Khrushchev?

But then just when Hugh looked like a hero for helping to cement good relations between the two world powers enabling him to win some of the early primaries, the relationship between the Soviets and the United States began to deteriorate again – there was the business with Cuba and then with the U2 being shot down by the Russians, and before long Hugh was no longer a hero – he was simply another presidential hopeful. A *tired* presidential hopeful who had bet on the wrong horse, and even before the Democratic National Convention was convened, he told her he was withdrawing from the race.

She was devastated. She couldn't bear the tone of resignation in his voice . . . in his whole bearing. 'But you can't just give up.'

'But I don't intend to just give up. I'm going to ask my supporters to swing their backing to Kennedy and I intend to support Jack's nomination at the convention. And then I . . . we . . . will work for his election. He's young and strong and full of vigour and that's what our country needs right now. Jack Kennedy is the voice of the future.'

'But we've been on the campaign trail all this time working *against* him.'

'But that's politics. The important thing is the welfare of the nation and the party. You know what they say, Nora. "Now is the time for all good men to come to the aid of their party." Do you know what that means?'

She shook her head too crushed by the turn of events to think about slogans.

'It means it's time to heal the breach so that what is really important can survive.'

Heal the breach . . .

That was the second time Hugh had used that phrase. And of course he was right. That was what was truly important, more important than anything else. And the least she could do for this man who had given her his love and her son his name and both of them a sense of identity was to heal the breach and give him back his natural sons so that *all* of them could survive in the best possible way – as a family.

She started her campaign that summer by inviting Hugh's children up to Cape Cod to spend some time with them at the compound in Hyannisport, even though Hugh was highly resistant to the idea. But it was something she was determined to do for him no matter how much he objected. In the end he'd be the happier for it. And it was something she needed to do for Hubie, too, make him part of the whole.

First came Bobby and Patty with their children and Billy and Daisy and their daughter and infant son. There was a lot of cheerful noise and pleasant confusion with all the little ones running around, and when Hugh complained, she told him it was good for him, otherwise he'd get old and stodgy.

And there were picnics on the beach with Hubie, ever the little boy at heart, building castles in the sand

302

with the small fry. And there was even a birthday party for Billy's and Daisy's daughter – she herself and Hubie canvassing the neighbourhood to round up children the right ages to fill out the guest list.

Then came Paul who was in a quandary. Though he was with the State Department as was his twin, Peter, it seemed he was more interested in the administration of the family's financial interests. The problem was that he thought that Hugh would be disappointed if he weren't a career statesman and Peter would feel abandoned because they'd always been inseparable, not to mention that Billy and Bobby might feel he was trying to invade their territory.

Armed with certain facts – Hugh didn't give a damn what career Paul followed, that Billy had complained to his wife that he really wanted to be in politics and felt burdened down by his obligation to help Bobby oversee the family's fortune, and that Peter was so involved with a girl he couldn't have cared less about Paul leaving him behind in the State Department – she set to work solving the dilemma.

Actually all she had to do was nag Hugh into telling Bobby he'd support his political career with money and influence, and suggest to Paul that he fill Billy's void helping Bobby out in the family office. She herself invited Peter to bring his girl up to the Cape so that the family (and especially Paul) could get to know her better. Then Peter was so grateful he asked her help in making the very pretty but shy Christy feel at home since he wanted to ask her to marry him. He was afraid she'd be overpowered by Patty and Daisy.

She assured Peter that she'd do what she could, setting to work again urging Hugh (who insisted that it wasn't so much that the physically well-endowed Christy herself was shy as it was her head – shy of intellect) into taking long walks on the beach with the young woman which would not only make her feel that he liked her, giving her confidence, but provide *him* with exercise and

Christy with the benefit of his conversation so that she wouldn't be all *that* shy of intellect.

Then she finished out the summer season by giving Peter and Christy an engagement party (with almost all the Kennedys from the neighbouring compound present) that was the talk of the Cape Cod season which brought the family together in what she hoped was an act of solidarity guaranteed to make Christy feel 'at home'. As for keeping Daisy and Patty from overpowering her, there were some things people had to learn for themselves or their character would never develop along with their intellect.

Then they all returned to Cape Cod in November to celebrate a truly wonderful Thanksgiving, Hugh's boys bending sufficiently – the supreme test of their willingness to be friends – to include Hubie in their rough-and-tumble touch football. But for her, the high-light of the four days they spent together came after Hugh gave the official Thanksgiving blessing and before he started to carve the huge turkey when she suggested that they go around the table with each family member telling what he was most thankful for.

When it was Hubie's turn, he looked around the table with a glowing face. 'I'm thankful that me and my mum are sharing turkey dinner with all of you. But, most of all, I'm thankful we all share the same name and the same Dad, who's the greatest!' Then she had to bite her lip not to cry and the table went quiet except for the baby who started screaming and banging the tray of his high chair with a spoon.

But then she did cry, after all, when Hugh walked from the head of the table to where Hubie sat near her at the foot and placed his hand on Hubie's shoulder to say just one word, 'Son . . .'

And when she heard Patty stage-whisper to Bobby, 'I bet she put him up to it just to impress your father,' she pretended not to hear, knowing that you could never convince anyone to believe anything when they

304

had already convinced themselves of what they wanted to believe.

Then came the Christmas holiday in Palm Beach with his children which Hugh claimed should suffice until at least the first of April. But she paid him no mind, convinced that everyone was enjoying the togetherness despite the few, inevitable discordant notes.

First, Daisy complained about her children's accommodation – it seemed they weren't used to sharing a room. Then Patty wondered aloud if a fifteen-year-old boy who was failing physics (Hubie having confided this himself) really deserved a state-of-the-art telescope from Hugh which had to cost in the thousands as a Christmas gift and demanded to know why Hugh had not seen fit to select comparable presents for his *real* flesh and blood when they *never* failed to excel. (No one gave her an answer.)

Then there was a bad moment when Hubie took a couple of the younger kids sailing and didn't come back until well after dark and Bobby called him 'an irresponsible jerk'. She could scarcely blame Bobby. She was furious with Hubie herself – it was such a thoughtless act and had caused all of them so much anxiety. Still, Hugh defended Hubie. 'He's a competent sailor who always has the situation well under control.'

And even when she and Hugh – and luckily no one else – discovered Hubie and Christy on the back patio in what could only be described as a *clinch* ten minutes after midnight on New Year's Eve, Hugh said this was excusable since it *was* New Year's Eve and probably Christy and Hubie – though *he* had been forbidden more than one glass of bubbly – had had too much champagne and it was best not to make a fuss.

'Hubie's only a teenager with a healthy dose of male hormones and she—? Well, I hate to say that I told you so, Nora darling, but I *did* tell you that that girl, even with her healthy pair of boobs, is a total nincompoop.'

305

Still, all things considered, she felt that they had made some headway in healing the breach . . .

28

Nora would always remember the day of John Kennedy's inauguration – Friday, 20 January – as vividly as most people would remember the day he was shot. She and Hugh were scheduled to attend the inaugural, their places on the stand with JFK assured by the prominent role they had played in his election. But the day before the inauguration, following a week of particularly bitter cold, a fresh snow had fallen covering Washington with a frozen white blanket, accompanied by an icy wind blowing in from the Potomac and the tidal basin. And then on Friday morning, though the snow had stopped falling and a cold sun shone, the temperature still hovered below freezing and the frigid winds continued to blow. Then she decided it would be better if they watched the proceedings from the warmth and comfort of home. Hugh hadn't been feeling *really* well for a couple of weeks already and he'd been coughing for the last few days.

At first, he objected strenuously when she announced the change in plans. 'Do you propose to start treating me like an invalid as my children tried to do? I warn you, if you do, I'm going to have to turn *you* in for a new model.'

'And I warn you – just you try it and see what you get. More trouble than you ever bargained for, believe me. But seriously, Hugh, tonight's going to be a really long evening what with the dinner we're giving before we even start out for the Inaugural Ball. It makes much more sense for you to take it easy during the day so you'll be rested and ready to charm your dinner guests and able

306

to keep up with me later on at the ball where I propose to dance you off your feet. So you see, I want to keep you at home for purely selfish reasons. Besides, I myself dread sitting out there in the beastly cold and this way I'll have more time to supervise the arrangements for the dinner.'

'Well, when you put it that way, I have no choice but to cave in to your bullying as gracefully as possible.'

Having said that, he flicked on the television in the study and sat down rather heavily in the big leather easy chair by the fire to watch the pre-inauguration coverage. Surprised that he hadn't put up more of a fight, she wondered if he were secretly relieved that she'd made the decision to watch the event on television. He *did* seem really tired and he did have that persistent cough.

By noon the temperature had risen somewhat, still it was below freezing, and she knew she'd made the right decision – it was so warm and cosy in the study.

At 12.20, JFK made his appearance on the stand, hatless and coatless, and Hugh smiled sadly. 'See, Nora? Twenty degrees above zero and Jack's not even wearing a coat. Who could take that punishment except a *young* man with an iron constitution?'

'What rot! Whoever said the ability to freeze was a qualification for the presidency?'

Still, when he coughed again, she thought of covering his legs with the plaid throw but then didn't, thinking that it would be bad psychological timing.

They watched Richard Cardinal Cushing give the invocation after which Robert Frost rose to read a poem, but the glare of the sun on the snow was so blinding that he had to recite a poem from memory, and then, finally, at 12.51 Justice Warren administered the oath of office and the new president began his speech: 'Let the word go forth from this time and place, to friend and foe alike, that the torch—'

It was then that Hugh cried out softly and slumped over in his leather chair.

★ ★ ★

She didn't know if it really took so long for the ambulance to get there or if it just seemed that way, knowing with a sinking heart that it just had to be a terrible day for ambulances what with that icy blanket covering the city and the impossible Inaugural Day traffic.

Then, when the ambulance finally did arrive, they tried to persuade her from riding along with Hugh, but she refused to be dissuaded. She knew better than they her rightful place and knew she was right about that when Hugh, regaining consciousness, gripped her hand as if holding on for dear life even as they were monitoring him and administering oxygen. '*You're* my oxygen,' he whispered. 'Don't leave me, Nora.'

And she didn't, not for a moment, until he was past that critical point when life triumphed over death, and he smiled up at her from his hospital bed. 'We beat the rap, didn't we?'

'We did indeed,' she laughed, trying not to cry, and not telling him then that the doctors had said he'd have to lead a 'cautious' life, that most of his activities would have to be curtailed, and even at that, the prognosis was uncertain.

She only knew that she was committed to him as she had never been before, to seeing to it that he enjoyed as fulfilling a life in 'curtailment' as he had in robust health. And then, as she always did when faced with life choices, she thought of Hubie. Who commanded top priority – her son or her husband? She already knew who came first in her heart, but whose *welfare* would come first if she were forced to choose? She concluded then they'd have to *share* top priority. They were, after all, father and son, and what wise woman would ever choose between a good husband and a sweet son?

She took Hugh home whereupon Billy and Bobby, Peter and Paul, as well as Patty and Daisy but at least not Christy, resumed their campaign to relegate Hugh to a rocking-chair on the back porch again, blaming his heart attack on his arduous political activities, implying at the same time and none too subtly that it had been she, the ambitious wife, who had imposed it on him.

But neither impressed with their arguments nor intimidated by their insinuations, she decided it was time for a new course. Much as she'd striven with a gentle hand to reconcile Hugh with them in order to improve the quality of his life as a complete man, she was now prepared to protect him from them. Trying to heal the breach was one thing, cowardly appeasement was another and she was willing to get as tough as she had to – it was a matter of assuring Hugh's survival as any kind of man at all.

'He may be a bit more fragile than he was before, but he's still not a teacup, he's a man. And only those of you who remember that are welcome in our home.'

29

If the Cantingtons' parties had been frequent and wonderful prior to Hugh's heart attack, they became even more frequent and wonderful after it, since Nora was determined that if Hugh couldn't get about Washington as he had before, she would bring Washington to him.

As the profile on the Cantingtons in *Washington Today* put it;

Nora Cantington surrounds her husband with Washington's finest – its most brilliant intellects and its most beautiful people – so that Hugh Cantington can stay at home and still feast his eyes as well as his mind, much as the fortunate guests feast their eyes on one of the town's most beautiful hostesses even as they feast at her bountiful table . . .

When Patty protested that Nora was wearing poor Hugh out by 'giving all these eternal dinner parties', she responded by correcting her: 'There's really no such thing as a *dinner party*, my dear. There are parties and there are dinners, as in we *give* parties, but we *eat* dinner.'

Then when Bobby suggested that her entertaining Washington celebrities did Hugh no medical good, she corrected him as well: 'But you have the wrong object of the verb – we're not entertaining *Washington celebrities*; we're entertaining *Hugh*.'

And then she announced that just as she had brought Washington to Hugh's doorstep, she wanted to bring the world to him as well. But since that wasn't possible other than by inviting the same old crop of foreign dignitaries to their home, she intended to take Hugh to the world. She would begin by accompanying him to China.

'*China?*' they cried, astounded.

'Yes, China,' she said blithely, as if talking about nothing more exotic or strenuous than a stroll in the garden. 'Hugh's never seen China and he's terribly keen on it. And you know how he feels about keeping an open mind to new ideas, how he always says, "Rigidity's the first sign of old age".'

After a few moments to allow that nugget to sink in, she continued ingenuously, 'So, while it's impossible for him to go in an official capacity – it's difficult enough to go at all with things the way they are – it's all been arranged for him to serve as a kind of unofficial ambassador-at-large.'

'What are you trying to do – kill him?'

'Oh, not at all. In fact I've arranged for Dr Steinfeld to be part of our little entourage.'

'*Entourage?*'

'Of course. I wouldn't dream of going without our own interpreter. It would get so confusing if we had to use one of theirs – we couldn't be certain of getting an accurate message across.'

'But what about the food? Suppose Dad can't stomach it?'

'Why wouldn't he? He's always adored Chinese food and the problem's with his heart, not with his stomach.'

'Doctor or no doctor, it sounds as if Dad will drop from exhaustion.'

'Not at all. I'm taking along the best possible motorized wheelchair, not knowing what will be available there, just in case he should tire walking about.'

'And what about the *travelling* from one city to another? Travelling conditions can be very primitive in China.'

She laughed. 'The things you children worry about. We're going to be flying over in a jet so I've decided we might as well buy our own since chartering one is so expensive. And then I'll be able to keep it there, pilot at the ready. So if we go any distance, we'll use that. As for getting around in general, I'm arranging for a couple of limousines to be at our disposal and I'm taking along Thomas to drive to ensure that Hugh will be completely comfortable.'

'Is *any* of this going to be absorbed by the Government or is it all going to be at Dad's personal expense?' Paul demanded.

'All of it will be at your father's expense since he *is* travelling in an unofficial capacity, but why do you ask?'

'Because it sounds like a very expensive proposition.'

'But I thought we were talking about your father's health and comfort, *not* about money. Or *are* we?'

'No, of course not,' Peter mumbled uncomfortably.

'Well, that *is* fortunate, specially since it *is* still your father's money we're spending. Now,' she said brightly, 'does anyone have anything else to add to the discussion?'

'I certainly do,' Patty spoke up snappily. 'I think that if you're determined to pursue this insane course, you leave Bobby and me no choice but to join your *entourage*. Then if there are any problems there will be

311

a family member present to help you cope. When you get down to it, that's all you can really count on, you know – family.'

'That's funny. Hugh and I have been thinking along those same lines – about taking a member of the family to count on. But we wouldn't dream of upsetting *your* lives. *You* have the children to think about and Bobby his work. So we've decided to take Hubie.'

'Hubie! But he's only an eighteen-year-old boy, and let's face it, hardly the most mature. And while most boys his age are going off to college, he hasn't even managed to graduate from prep school yet and how could he? He's gone through schools like they were revolving doors. Of what possible use can *he* be to Dad? What can you be thinking of?'

'Well, actually I was thinking that since he's such entertaining company for Hugh and always manages to make him laugh when he's tired or depressed, I can count on him to help keep Hugh's spirits up, no matter what. And Dr Steinfeld says that the spirit is as important as the body and I couldn't agree with him more. As for Hubie's immaturity, Hugh's thinking is that our counting on him might be just the answer to that problem. And his schooling? Well, everyone knows travel is both educational and broadening. Don't you agree?'

She was delighted with many things during their trip, but the main thing was how well Hugh was feeling and how re-energized. Hubie was proving to be a thoughtful and considerate travelling companion, surely a sign of his blossoming maturity. But best of all was his devotion to Hugh and how Hugh returned that devotion to a point that amazed her. She wondered over and over again how a man could seemingly love a son who wasn't his own flesh and blood more than those who were, but it appeared to be an undeniable fact.

At first she'd thought that this mutual devotion just *seemed* more pronounced since they were in an exotic land, dependent on each other in a way they weren't at home, coping with all the little things that went awry and then laughing about the funnier instances later. Then she thought that perhaps the reason Hugh seemed fonder of Hubie than of his own boys, and more tolerant of his failings, was that Hubie's own feelings for Hugh were so uncomplicated – no past resentments, no sparring for power the way it often was between sons and fathers, the sons seeming to say: 'Move over, old chap, it's our turn.' No demands, only mutual admiration and respect.

Finally, she concluded that the reason Hugh loved Hubie so much was because he loved *her* so much that it just spilled over. Love generating love, a never-ending circle, and she knew that the love she felt for Hugh wasn't diminished in any way because it was conceived in gratitude and respect, rather than in romantic fantasies or sexual passion.

After dinner and after being cheerfully and roundly beaten at chess by Hugh, Hubie went back to his own room in the Peking Royale, and Hugh observed, 'You know, Nora, I have no regrets about Hubie not making Harvard. I'm hoping now he'll attend college in Washington so that he can live at home with us.'

'I'm not sure he's going to make it to any college,' she sighed. 'And what will he study if he does? Let's face it, he's never going to be a lawyer like your sons.'

'What of it? They have their law degrees but not one of them actually practises law.'

'But they do practise honourable professions for which they're well prepared. Even if Hubie gets to college, what will he prepare for? To be a professional charmer, or maybe one of those – what do they call them? – sex surrogates?'

Hugh laughed though she hadn't intended to be amusing.

'Don't worry, Nora. If nothing else, he can go to work in the family business. Public relations, that sort of thing. Or, if we can nurture him through college, we'll see to it that a place is found for him in the State Department. They can certainly use a little charm over there. But, don't worry, we'll come up with *something* that will best make use of Hubie's talents. Once we get home we'll go to work on it.'

Once we get home we'll go to work on it.

The words reassured her and she was overwhelmed with affection for her good husband. Then, after they made love and she successfully brought him to climax, she lay in bed thinking about going home. Yes, it was time to go home. She'd begin planning their departure in the morning.

But in the morning they woke to the news that President Kennedy had been assassinated, and on hearing the tragic report, Hugh suffered a devastating stroke.

With Hugh almost totally paralysed and completely confined to his wheelchair, but still the partisan Democrat he'd always been, Nora established the Cantington Foundation for Democratic Political Action, essentially a fund-raising group and a think-tank for all Democrats seeking election or re-election, on both national and local levels.

With the foundation's offices right on the premises and politicians from all over flying in for checks and consultations, and with many of the fund-raising parties taking place right there, the house on R Street was constantly filled with the excitement of people coming and going, resounding with ideas and stimulating conversation, with an air of purpose and energy. And in the centre of it was Hugh and that was where she intended to keep him though there were the family's usual objections.

'What are you trying to *do* to the man, Nora?'

'The question is not what *I'm* doing, but what *Hugh's* doing and the fact that he *is* doing and not just vegetating.'

'But he's not up to all this activity. Good God,

314

he's almost completely paralysed.'

'Yes, his body is, but his *mind* isn't. And that's what we're going to keep active.'

'But you're killing him in the process.'

She laughed at that. She could have told them that what she was trying to do was help him live his life fully instead of like a man already dead, but it would have done no good. They preferred to believe that she wanted him dead so that she could get her hands on the money.

This was confirmed when Billy and Daisy came calling one evening just as Hugh was retiring for the night. When they refused to be turned away by the butler, she came downstairs to tell them herself that it was impossible – that Hugh was otherwise engaged in his bedtime activities and rituals. Undaunted, Daisy angrily demanded to know what bedtime activity could the paralysed Hugh be engaged in that precluded their looking in on him for a few minutes.

'That all depends on your attitude towards sex. Some people like it *with* an audience, and some without. Hugh prefers without as I do. Now, if you'll excuse me—' she smiled pleasantly, pulling her filmy négligé more tightly about her, 'I'll rejoin my husband so that we may get on with it. You know how it is, I don't like to keep him waiting.'

She left them standing there nonplussed as she turned to go back upstairs, but not before she heard Daisy gasp and Billy curse and Daisy say, 'Did she mean what I think she means?' and Billy swore again. Then she heard Daisy whine, 'But I don't understand. How does a paralysed man *do it*? Will you tell me that?'

Nora was tempted to turn around and tell her step by step, but then thought better of it. Daisy was a big girl – she could figure it out for herself.

Then she heard Billy say, 'We were right about her. One way or another she intends to fuck the old guy to death!'

315

30

Soon after returning to Washington from Palm Beach where they had welcomed in the New Year with a toast to '1968 – the best year ever', Nora finally gave up any hope of Hubie ever graduating from college. She discovered that while he left the house every day ostensibly on his way to classes at American, he rarely got there, waylaid by all manner of things – trysts with women of all ages, the gymnasium where he worked out, friends who talked him into driving up to New York for a special party or sports event, or the flying field where he kept his plane – Hugh's present to mark his twenty-second birthday the year before.

Oh, it wasn't *terrible* in the light of what else was going on in the world, she told herself, still it *was* discouraging to realize that after all her hopes, dreams and resolve, the only thing her sweet son really excelled at was being an irresponsible playboy.

January was also the month when Hugh became permanently bedridden, no longer strong enough to sit in his wheelchair.

For months, though he'd been getting weaker by the day, she'd insisted that he be dressed and shaved every morning for a daily foray into the world, even though it was a very small world now consisting of a four block square, she herself at the helm of his wheelchair.

And because she couldn't bear him to be shut out of things, she had also insisted that he continue to preside at the head of his table when there were guests for lunch or dinner, though his mind wasn't quite as fast and

316

his eyesight and hearing were beginning to fail and his speech to falter. Then she'd carry on as if all his senses were completely intact, making sure he was included in every conversation: 'Did you hear the point Governor *Whoever* just made about the space programme, darling?' she would ask, repeating what the Governor said, and then quickly she'd turn back to Whoever, 'Hugh says he couldn't agree with you more.'

But now even that would no longer be possible. A depressing beginning to the new year, for sure, and then February wasn't much better. February was the month Nixon announced his candidacy for the presidency as well as the month Hubie enlisted in the Marines.

Hugh tried to console her. 'You must be proud of him – he did the right thing as he saw it.'

But it was one thing to be proud and another to be terrified that he would soon be going off to Vietnam. And it was hard not to speculate – had Hubie enlisted out of patriotism or out of an urge for adventure? She remembered the little boy who had always wanted to wear a uniform.

March was a little better. Bob Kennedy announced his candidacy and that was good news. If anybody could give Tricky Dicky a run for the money, it was Bobby. Then Hugh even rallied a bit and sat up in an armchair for a few minutes every day for five days running.

But April was the month Dr King was assassinated, which was a terrible loss and equally terrible were the riots triggered off by his murder.

April was also the month Hubie showed up at their doorstep beautifully resplendent in his Marine dress blues, grinning and looking as wonderful as she had ever seen him. And for one brilliant moment the clock turned back twenty-five years and – but for Hubie's shorn yellow hair – it was as if it was the first time she was looking at Hubert Hartiscor resplendent in *his* uniform, and her heart turned over.

Then it almost burst with pride and she thought she

317

might cry until she learned that Hubie was AWOL, and then she was furious. He was no longer the careless boy playing pranks, but a man of nearly twenty-three, a man other men under fire would be depending on, relying on to do the right thing.

Hubie was, as ever, remorseful. 'I was afraid I'd be shipped out without having a chance to say goodbye. And it wasn't you, Mum, I was so much worried about, but my Dad. I know I'd get to see you again, but how could I be sure I'd ever see *him* again? I just had to make sure I did . . .'

And then, of course, she did cry. And when he went in to Hugh to sit by his bedside, hold his frail hand and kiss his withered cheek, they all cried – she, Hubie and Hugh. Then when she made arrangements for Hubie's immediate return to his base, she cried some more and was reminded of the poem that began: *April is the cruellest month . . .*

But then she had to change her mind about that when Hubie shipped out in May and another Kennedy warrior fell slain in June.

In July, the United States, the USSR and fifty-nine other nations signed the Nuclear Non-proliferation Treaty and that was a hopeful sign that perhaps everything in the topsy-turvy world would right itself after all.

July was also the month Hugh said he had to set things right and asked her to send for his old and trusted friend, the attorney, Ward Prouty.

'But why do you need a lawyer?' she asked, anxious that Hugh sensed his end was near and wanted to start setting his affairs in order. 'You have four lawyers of your own that come to see you every day,' she tried to make a joke of it, however feeble.

'They don't come to see me. They come to see *you.*'

She laughed. 'Me? Have they suddenly fallen in love with me then, after all this time?'

'Hardly. They come to see what you're up to, to see

318

if you're wearing down a dying man to get him to turn all his money over to you . . .'

'Oh no, Hugh,' she protested, not knowing if she were protesting that she would ever think of such a thing or the fact that he was dying or that his boys came for any other reason but out of their love for him. Then she asked, though she already knew the answer, 'Why *do* you want to see Ward?'

'To turn over all my money to you, just like they're afraid I'm going to do. I want to have that prenuptial set aside and leave everything to you. Then you can let the boys have whatever you think best, whatever you think fair.'

'No, Hugh. When we were married I negotiated a contract at your insistence and *under* your tutelage – all your sons, including Hubie, and I having equal shares, and that's the legacy that's fair. The boys have been your sons for most of your life, and I—'

'Have made my life a celebration,' he finished for her.

She took his hand, the skin worn shiny and silky, and pressed it to her lips. 'If that is true, then let it be a celebration of love, not a celebration dulled by a legacy of bitterness and greed.'

It was so hard not to think of the past and even harder to think of the future.

August was the month she and Hugh watched the Democrats nominate Hubert Humphrey, but then she had to turn off the TV because the riots in the streets of Chicago were too upsetting for Hugh to view. August was also the month she went about the house with her portable radio in hand for constant news of the fighting in Vietnam. Inadvertently, she also heard a lot of music: the Beatles singing 'Hey Jude', the Doors, 'Hallo, I Love You'. But her favourite was 'Sunshine of Your Love'.

September was a month for vigils, waiting for the postman to bring a letter from Hubie, fear that a terrible telegram might arrive instead, all this interspersed only by the round-the-clock marathons of reading to Hugh at

319

his bedside. She had got the notion into her head that it was an act of faith for both Hugh and Hubie, and that only if she kept reading, death wouldn't come to claim either of them *unless* she ran out of reading material, which, of course, was an impossibility, so the odds were with her.

While she *knew* it was a crazy notion and no letter from Hubie arrived, neither did a telegram from the War Department, nor did the Angel of Death come to call on Hugh.

In September she regretted not having risked moving Hugh to Cape Cod for the summer so that, even with his eyesight failing, he could have had the pleasure of once again seeing the sun rise over the Atlantic. So in September she did just that and took him there. It still wasn't too late for him to see the rising sun one last time and it was better than simply sitting a death watch.

Being on the Cape reminded Hugh of the Thanksgiving when Hubie had blurted out that he was thankful that Hugh was his dad, and the memory made him weep. 'But that's a wonderful memory, Hugh. Please don't cry.'

'But I failed him . . . and you, too, Nora.'

'Oh Hugh, how can you say that? It's not true. You were a wonderful father to Hubie.'

'But you were counting on me to provide him with a future – to find a place for him when he comes home, and now I won't be here to do it.'

She didn't protest his saying he wouldn't be there – she couldn't dishonour this honourable man with false protestations. 'You gave him love and a sense of belonging and you can't do more than that for anyone. While I didn't always know it, I realize now that people can only have the future they make for themselves.'

All you can do is point them in the right direction.

She planned on taking Hugh straight to Palm Beach at the end of October once the foliage turned – the Cape's loveliest time – in order to bypass the grey days of a Washington November, but Hugh said that he wanted to go to Washington. 'It's *our* home town, the one we lived in together. We really turned the town on its ear for a while, didn't we, my love?'

So that's what they did in the month of October. They went home.

In November when she had despaired of ever hearing from Hubie again, she heard *of* him, if not from him. The second she heard the news she rushed to Hugh's room, more hospital room now than bedroom. Though the nurse told her that she had just given Mr Cantington his sedative, she burst out, 'Oh Hugh, Hubie's *alive*! He's wounded, but he's alive!'

'But what—? How—?'

'You won't believe this but he jumped into a puddle and he came out of it not covered with mud and slime but—' her voice was full of awe '—drenched in glory! *Our* Hubie!'

'But what puddle?' Hugh asked groggily.

Then Nora tried to explain that it really wasn't a puddle at all, but a rice paddy. 'There was a squad of North Vietnamese regulars holed up there and it seems that after wriggling over on to his stomach to be in the right position, Lance-Corporal Cantington lobbed in a grenade, then jumped right in to mop up with his M16, whatever that is. I think I have it straight, but I was so excited I – Well, they say he's not too badly hurt, something with his leg . . . Oh, Hugh, he'll be home before too long!'

Please wait for him!

'Before too long,' Hugh whispered. 'But why did you call a rice paddy a puddle?' he asked as he drifted off to sleep.

Because once there was a little boy who jumped into a puddle just for the sheer joy of it and they made such a fuss, they called him a scamp. Who would have ever thought that the little scamp would jump into a puddle again when he was all grown up . . . to emerge a hero?

Maybe somewhere along the line she had done something right, after all. She and Hugh . . .

321

Or had Hubie jumped once again just for the hell of it?

December was the month she buried Hugh.

Two weeks after the actual funeral in Cape Cod where Hugh was buried in the family plot next to his first wife, Rita (she owed that much to Bobby, Billy, Peter and Paul), Nora organized a memorial service at the National Cathedral in Washington. Every last seat of the cathedral's two thousand seats was filled, she having personally arranged the seating in the roped-off section so that no national or international figure was slighted. The entire diplomatic corps was accommodated along with President and Mrs Johnson, the defeated Hubert Humphrey and President-elect, Richard Nixon and his pretty wife, Pat. Hugh would have wanted that. He believed in healing the breach.

Attired in a chic black suit with only a small diamond pin affixed to its lapel, she walked up the steps of the cathedral on the arms of her only family – Hubie with his campaign ribbons and a slight limp, and dear Tony who had flown in to lend his support. And she was smiling proudly. She had shed her tears in private and now she was through with it, she thought, but then when Hubie went up to the podium and held up the medal he'd been awarded for valour and said: 'They gave it to *me* but *I* didn't really earn it – my father did. It was Hugh Cantington's hand that was on my shoulder giving me a push and it was his voice whispering in my ear: "Do it, son . . . do the right thing," and so I did . . .', she wept.

Oh, he had jumped but this once not just for the sheer fun of it . . .

After Hubie went back to his base she went to Palm Beach for a bit, not quite ready to resume life at the house on R Street, and Tony went with her so that she wouldn't be alone.

'It's so sweet of you, Tony, to stay with me.'

'There's no place I'd rather be than with the charming Nora Hall Hartiscor Nash Cantington. Besides, this *is* the height of the Palm Beach Season and you know how old fun-loving Tony loves being any place at the height of its season.'

'Oh Tony, you're such a good friend. The *best!*'

'But *not* the best of husbands, seemingly. What a pity. When I offered to come down here with you under the *ruse* of keeping you company, I really had an ulterior motive in mind.'

'Yes?' She played along with his teasing.

'I thought that just maybe I might catch you again between husbands.'

Is he teasing? Maybe. Then again, maybe not. With Tony, it was hard to know.

'I beg you to remember, sir, that I am a widow in mourning and not to be trifled with—'

He lowered his eyes then, realizing she was sending him a signal – a stop sign. When he raised them again he pretended to be outraged. 'I beg *you* to remember, madame, that I wouldn't dream of—' Then suddenly he was serious. '*Was* Hugh the best husband? I hope so. You deserve the best.'

'Oh, Tony, I don't think I can define *best* any more than I can define *love*. Both come in so many forms. But I will say that Hugh was the best of men and I loved him dearly.'

I married him for name and fortune and for love of Hubie and I ended up getting so much more.

'So what does the future hold for my friend Nora now? Will you be going back to England? To Merrillee Manor?'

'Sometimes I long to – for the serenity of it. But no, I can't do that. I'm an American now and more importantly, *Hubie's* an American and his Cantington legacy is here and that's where I have to make a place for him as Hugh would have. I'm going back to Washington to continue my work with the foundation – being a Democrat was very important to Hugh and so much a part of him – and I hope Hubie will be part of that. I think that would be making the best use of his Cantington heritage.'

'But *you* personally, Nora? Do you see another husband in that crystal ball of yours?'

'I don't think so,' she laughed. 'For one thing, I've had more husbands than any one woman deserves, and for another, I've married for all kinds of reasons and now – well, I think I've run clear out of reasons.'

PART SEVEN

THE BRILLIANT MARRIAGE

Los Angeles
1969–70

31

Afterwards, Nora would remember all the particulars of the evening down to the last detail. The date: 20 December; the occasion: a dance and silent art auction for the benefit of the National Council For Underprivileged Children; the place: – the Smithsonian; and the guest list was composed of the usual Washington luminaries: the Republicans who were in and the Democrats who were out, with a large contingent of Hollywood stars flown in from the coast to add additional sparkle to the glitter of the evening.

The colour theme was black and white, with the men requested to wear white tie and the women black only, and there were gardenias for each lady, their heady scent filling the room. The flower arrangements consisted of tall, white lilies paired with black-dyed bristly foxtail grass, and the Dom Perignon was accompanied by black caviar, while the after-dinner brandies were served with the white chocolate mousse.

She, the co-chair, wore black lace off-the-shoulder, her necklace a choker of alternating white and black pearls, her ring a giant black pearl, and her hair swept back into a French knot to reveal white pearls at her ears. She tucked her gardenia into her cleavage.

She was dancing with Vice-President Agnew, who really liked to dance (whereas the president didn't), and Lionel Hampton's orchestra was playing 'Leaving on a Jet Plane' when *he* cut in . . .

At first, she didn't recognize him. Actually, there was no reason she should have since she had never actually met him. Still, she went into his arms quite

327

willingly – an animal magnetism emanated from him, though he was hardly what anyone would call handsome. A rugged homeliness was more like it. He had a huge frame, a craggy landscape of a face, and oversized features. But when he said in a warm, deep voice, 'Nora *Nash* Cantington, I presume,' she knew exactly who he was and said, 'Well, it's about time you showed up. How many years ago was it that you stood me up at the Palm Lounge in Hollywood? Twelve?'

He laughed heartily. 'I was a fool. That's why I'm here tonight, to rectify the error. I hate making a fool of myself, but I must admit that I'm a fool for the smell of gardenias.' He bent his head to the gardenia tucked between her breasts to breathe in its scent. Then he raised his head to smile into her eyes. 'Intoxicating . . .' he murmured.

And foolish as she knew it was – but not anything she could control – she felt something she hadn't felt since she'd been divorced from sexy, dashing Tony Nash. Those flutterings of butterfly wings deep within the centre of her sexual desire had shown up again, along with T.S. Grant.

He showed her the painting he'd bid for – an English landscape with a manor house square in the centre. It could have been Merrillee Manor and the beat of her heart quickened. 'Why did you choose this particular painting? The artist doesn't have a famous name.'

He laughed. 'I don't care about names. I don't even know anything about art,' he said almost as if it was something he was proud of. 'I just know what I like and I like this picture. I love the English countryside and the house reminds me of my own – Grantwood Manor. It's a grand English manor house but run down since I don't have either the time or a wife to see to it properly.'

'You haven't remarried, then?'

He looked at her obliquely. 'You *knew* my wife died?'

'Oh yes, I was in Hollywood the day of her funeral.'

'But you didn't attend? I don't remember who was there.'

'No, I wasn't there. I intended to go but fate intervened, I'm afraid, in the form of a woman. Actually, that was the day my marriage to Tony ended, you see.'

His arm slid about her and she could feel the goose bumps.

Don't be a fool, Nora. A forty-four-year-old woman is much too old for goose bumps.

'Tony Nash was an idiot,' he whispered in her ear. 'Whatever possessed him to let that happen?'

She laughed. 'A she-devil . . . a very sexy she-devil.'

'I bet I know her name.'

'What will you wager?'

'That painting, if I get it.'

'How much did you bid?'

'Fifty thousand.'

'That's a lot of money for a picture painted by an unknown artist. You'll get it.'

'And you? What will you put up as a wager?'

'I don't know.' She already felt certain she was going to lose the bet. 'What do you suggest?'

In answer, his eyes met hers in a frank challenge. Then he picked up her hand, kissed it, ran his lips up her arm and across her shoulder to rest on the back of her neck, and those butterflies quickened their flutterings so violently she looked around, sure that everyone could hear then.

Then he said, 'Mimi L'Heureux,' and she could not but admit that she had lost the bet. But then both of them had known that she would.

At midnight at the Hilton where TS was staying, drenched in the sweat of passion, she screamed out in an ecstasy she had never known before, Tony Nash notwithstanding.

At twelve thirty, *he* fleetingly thought of Tony. 'I was right about Tony. He *was* an idiot. You're the

329

goddess and Mimi – she was nothing. I've known a thousand like her.'

At one thirty, she remembered that he had a daughter and asked about her. He muttered that she was at school in Connecticut, but then he was kissing the insides of her thighs and she forgot about everything, including his daughter.

At two, he paused for a cigarette and she told him about Hubie, how sweet and charming he was but how unfocused, how she worried about his future. He stamped out the cigarette, told her that Hubie sounded perfect for the movie business and that she needn't worry – she could always send Hubie to him and he'd make a place for him. Then, though she was gratified to hear the reassuring words, as TS trailed a path of kisses across her belly, she forgot about Hubie completely.

At three, they climaxed together and he groaned into the hollow of her throat that he loved her and she whispered back, 'I love you, too.' Then realizing that it was *really* true, she laughed in delight and then he laughed and it was a roar.

It was nearly dawn when he said, 'In one of my films the couple eloped to some place in Maryland to get married, but I can't think of the name of the place but I bet you can.'

And, for the second time that evening, TS won his bet. She did indeed know the name of the place.

Once for love and once for the name, once for the fun of it and great sex, and once for the money and loads of affection and respect. But finally – once for the best of everything rolled into one and the marriage that would last for ever. This time around, there could only be sweet dreams.

32

The next day after the wedding, back at her house in Georgetown, Nora was surprised to discover TS packing up his one small bag, ready to go back to Los Angeles.

'Wait a minute,' she laughed, 'aren't we moving a little quickly? I can't simply pack up and leave on a day's notice.'

'Of course, *you* can't, sweetie, and I wasn't proposing that you do. *I* have to go back to LA since I only planned on staying that one night for the party and I do have appointments. But you stay, do what you have to. Tie up your loose ends, make your goodbyes and then when you're ready, you'll join me.'

What's going on here? Yesterday he had declared he couldn't live without her and here he was traipsing off with a breezy: 'When you're ready, you'll join me.'

He saw that she was upset and murmured, 'Nora, Nora,' lifting up her chin and kissing her lips. 'It's God-awful that we're going to be separated so soon. Believe me, it's killing me. But what's there to do? I have to get back to the studio and you have to do your thing. If nothing else, you have to get this house ready to put on the market.'

She was *shocked*. 'Put my house on the market?'

'Of course. What did you think? You knew marrying me meant moving to California. Unless you're proposing one of those, bi-coastal marriages, and I wasn't figuring on one of those, were you?' he chuckled, patting her rump.

'Of course not. But I wasn't figuring on selling my house either.'

He shrugged. 'How many houses do you need in the

East? You've the house in Palm Beach and the place on the Cape—'

'But I don't. I let Hugh's children have them.'

She saw a look of what – *annoyance?* – cross his face.

'You *let* them have those houses? What does that mean? You could have kept them but you chose not to?'

Was it her imagination or was his tone *scornful?*

'But those homes had been in their mother's family. I thought that was only fair – that it was their heritage.'

'Let me teach you one thing. Playing fair is a sucker's game but I guess it's too late for that advice. Regardless, I don't see any point in keeping a place in Washington.' Then he smiled as if remembering to do so. 'I intend to keep you far too busy for you to get to Washington much and when you do, that's what hotels are for.'

'But you don't understand. I thought of this house as Hubie's legacy, *his* heritage. I wanted to keep it for him.'

'But you told me you were worried about Hubie's future. What good will his heritage do him if he doesn't *have* a future? I told you *I'd* take care of his future, that I'd make a place for him at the studio.

'Don't you have faith in me, Nora?' Now, he was hurt and gazed into her eyes as if begging her to trust him.

'Of course I have faith in you. I'd hardly marry a man I couldn't trust.' And she realized that she *would* have to sell her house since TS was putting it on that basis – an act of faith. After all, a house was only bricks and mortar and it was the marriage and the man that were important.

'Just make sure you don't throw in the paintings and antiques when you put it up for sale,' he said as if it were a joke. 'They must be worth a fortune all by themselves. Besides, they'll fit right in at Grantwood Manor. Now, *there's* a house for you. It's on nine acres, a real showplace, and it's just dying for the Nora Grant touch as I am . . . right this minute.' He held out his arms to her.

332

'Are you sure you have the time?' she asked ruefully, but going into his arms at the same time.

'For you, always. Besides, my plane doesn't leave for another three hours,' he grinned.

'Do you realize tonight's Christmas Eve! You *can't* go back tonight. And what about your daughter?'

He made a little gesture of impatience. 'What about her?'

'She's at school spending Christmas with strangers. The least you should do . . . the least *we* should do,' she corrected herself, 'is go up to Connecticut to see her, take her some gifts and let her meet me.'

'Out of the question. I have this appointment in LA. Anyway, Sam's *not* at school. She's in New York for the holidays staying with some schoolfriend.'

'But you can break your appointment – it *is* Christmas Eve. Then tomorrow we can go to New York to see her.'

'You got all the answers,' he laughed. 'But I bet you don't have this one – the name and address of the friend she's staying with.'

'Of course I don't,' she admitted. 'But you *do*, don't you? At least the family's name? A phone number?'

'I *did*. At least I *had* the phone number on a piece of paper. I was going to call the kid to wish her a Merry Christmas, but I'm afraid I lost it, so that's that.'

She was upset. He sounded so cavalier, as if it really didn't matter much. But how could a father allow a thirteen year old to visit a family whose name he didn't even know. 'But how could you—' she began, then saw that look of irritation on his face.

Well, why wouldn't he be irritated? She *was* being critical, and one thing she had learned from all her marriages was that *no* man enjoyed being criticized. Why would he? Especially by his bride of only two days.

'It's just that I'm sorry I didn't get to meet her.'

'Don't worry – you'll get to meet her soon enough. Sooner than you'll want, probably. That kid's been nothing but trouble since the day she was born.'

'Well, is it any wonder? Her mother died when she was a baby, her grandparents a few years later, and then she was packed off to school across the country.'

'I did the best I could . . . I had the studio to run,' he said defensively and she rushed to assure him that of course he had. The poor darling, he was probably feeling all kinds of guilt towards Sam and she was just making him feel worse.

She drove him to the airport, reluctant to let go of him until the very last minute. 'Tell me, what is this appointment that's so important that you can't break it even for a new bride?' she chided him playfully, never dreaming that he'd say, 'A Christmas Eve party in the Hollywood Hills.'

Then she was so *outraged* that for a fleeting moment she considered stopping the car and pushing him out bodily. 'You mean you're leaving me for a party? A stupid party?'

'A party yes, but stupid? No. A very important party. I don't go to parties just for a good time. Parties are where I do business, *studio* business. Now, you ought to be able to understand that. From what I hear, you're one of the champion party-givers of all time and I'd bet that most of them aren't just for a good time, that usually you have some kind of an axe to grind. Now, ain't that so?' he grinned at her disarmingly.

And finally, after much prodding and cajoling she had to admit that he was right. But, as she accompanied him to the gate, she had another thought: 'If you don't go to parties to have a good time but to do business, how come you flew across the country to attend the party at the Smithsonian? What kind of business did you think you were going to do there?'

'Monkey business,' he winked, his face breaking into that craggy grin she found irresistible. Before she could think of a reply, he pulled her to him, kissed her hard and was gone, leaving her to wonder why it hadn't occurred to either one of them that she could have flown with him

334

to LA, spent a couple of days there – gone with him to the party – then flown back to Washington to do what she had to do.

She could have gone to any number of parties herself that night instead of spending Christmas Eve alone, but too many people already knew that she'd married T.S. Grant of Grantwood Studio – Washington was a town that thrived on gossip – and would wonder what was going on with them since he had left her all alone so soon after the wedding.

Instead, she sat at home trying to figure out exactly what kind of monkey business had brought TS to the fund-raiser at the Smithsonian. Then, going through some bits and ends that in his haste he'd left behind, she found the publicity piece about the coming event torn from the *Post*, a picture of her, its chairwoman, included, and then she knew. TS had flown to Washington not to buy a painting by an unknown artist or to make a contribution to a charity – one could always mail a cheque if that was what one had in mind. He had come to the party only to meet her, and if that *was* monkey business, it was the nicest and most flattering kind.

The next morning she waited expectantly for the special delivery of a Christmas present, or at least a call from the coast. Finally she decided to call him. They weren't a couple of kids playing the dating game, so why stand on ceremony? Then she realized that she didn't *have* his phone number. How could she have been so careless to marry a man whose number she didn't even have?

Information couldn't help since it was an unlisted number, which put her in a really foul mood. Ordinarily she had her source whereby she could obtain an unlisted number, but since it *was* Christmas, she couldn't access that source.

Alternately angry, despondent and frustrated, she went to bed early, but having given the entire staff the day off, when the doorbell rang, she tore out of bed to run downstairs to answer the door. And she wasn't disappointed –

it was a late delivery of a roomful of roses and she wondered how she could have ever doubted him. A roomful of roses was worth a dozen calls, she told herself. *Wasn't it?*

The day after Christmas, a Friday, he *did* call. Or rather, his secretary, one Allison Parnis, did. 'Mr Grant was about to phone you, but he was called away so he asked me to call and tell you that he was thinking of you. And by the way, Nora, congratulations!'

She thought of telling Ms Parnis that you congratulated the groom on his good fortune, but you wished the bride good luck, and that you didn't call the boss's wife by her first name unless she specifically told you to, but what was the point in taking her frustration out on a secretary? Besides, the woman was only doing things the California way. So all she said before hanging up was, 'Have a good day, Allison,' since that, too, was the California way and, hopefully in a couple of weeks she herself would be an Angeleno.

On Sunday, 28 December, he called again, this time in person. 'I've been phoning day and night. Where the hell have you been?'

Should she tell him that mostly she'd been at home sorting out – deciding what to send on to California, what to save for Hubie or give away to charities or Hugh's children, not wanting to be petty? And should she pull him up short by telling him that even if she hadn't been home when the phone rang, there was staff on hand to take messages?

She didn't. A wise woman so recently married kept her mouth shut and let her husband do most of the talking, especially when he spoke such lovely words of love.

On Monday, 29 December, Mary Beth Jones, who'd headed up the committee on the art auction for the party, called to tell her that she was a naughty girl. 'The whole town's talking about how you ran off with that charmer, T.S. Grant, without so much as a word to anyone. Is it really true?'

'True as true love.'

'Oh, lovely,' Mary Beth breathed. 'By the way, your new husband won the painting that he bid on. Shall we send it over to your house or on to California?'

'You might as well send it over here since I'm having all my paintings crated for shipping. That will save the committee a bit of bother. And while you're at it, you might as well send your so-delicately worded request for payment here, too, and I'll pass it on.'

'No problem. You married a positive man. He was so sure he was going to win the painting, he left a cheque with his bid. So *forceful*! He said he always gets what he goes after. I do so love a man who's forceful. No wonder he talked you into eloping with him the very next day. So romantic.'

Nora hung up bemused. While her elopement *was* decidedly romantic and it was titillating to think that not only had TS flown across the country just to meet her and had possibly even made up his mind to 'go after her', it was somehow strange to think that without ever actually meeting her, she had already been his 'quarry'.

But then she smiled, remembering how it had actually been. Mary Beth had said 'no wonder he talked you into eloping', but the truth was she had needed no persuasion – if he hadn't suggested it and if he weren't so physically large, *she'd* been prepared to drag *him* to Maryland by force.

On Tuesday, the 30th, she thought about flying out to California to take TS by surprise so they could spend New Year's Eve together. But then remembering what happened when she took Tony by surprise, she decided it really wasn't such a good idea. Not that she believed she'd find TS in a compromising position, but a surprise could lead to confusion.

But, just as she was about to call TS at the studio to tell him of her intention, there was – *talk of the devil*! – a call from Tony in London.

'I thought I had better wish you good luck with your

latest marriage. I figured it was the least I could do since I feel responsible . . . that somehow I was instrumental in bringing you two together.'

She laughed at his nonsense. 'I hereby absolve you of all responsibility. But how did you hear about it so soon in London? I didn't give out any announcements to the Press.'

'Well, you know how it is – bad news travels fast,' he said dolefully.

'No, really, Tony, who told you?'

'I got it right from the horse's mouth – none other than the big man himself. I just ran into him at a cocktail party at a mutual friend's in the West End.'

Talk about your surprises . . .

Well, as TS said, he did a lot of business at parties.

She spent New Year's Eve at home on the off-chance that TS would call. He didn't. But he *did* on New Year's Day from Palm Springs to make up for not calling the night before – he'd been flying back from London, he explained. And then he made up for any dereliction by telling her how much he missed her and what he was going to do to her, step-by-step, when he got his hands on her again.

She knew there was one more thing she had to do before she left for the coast, something she had to do for herself as well as for TS and his daughter. She had to go and see Sam, difficult as this might be without TS to ease the way.

Realizing what a shock it would be if she suddenly appeared out of nowhere to announce, 'Like it or not, kid, here I am, your father's new wife, your new step-mother,' she called ahead to tell the school that she was a family friend coming to visit Sam and take her out for the day. Once she had Sam alone, she'd break the news to her gently, making sure that the girl understood that she wanted to be her friend and that she posed no threat.

★   ★   ★

338

From the second she saw the tall, slender girl enter the restaurant – she'd thought it best if they first met on neutral ground – she could tell that her task wasn't going to be easy. Maybe it was the way Sam held her head, high with her nose tilted in the air, or maybe it was the surly look that sullied the fine, aristocratic features.

She stood up to greet Sam with a warm smile as the hostess escorted her to the table. Then, though she hadn't planned on it, she moved to kiss her, but Sam recoiled before taking her seat, spitting out, 'I don't like to be touched.'

No, not easy. Nora sat down again, her smile still intact. 'I know you have no idea who I am, but—'

'You're wrong,' Sam said coolly, 'I know exactly who you are. A liar, for one thing.'

'I beg your pardon?' Nora was shocked.

Now Sam was the one who smiled – very much in control as she spread her napkin across her lap. 'You heard me correctly. You told the dean that you were a friend of the family, but I already know that you're the woman who snagged my poor unsuspecting father. Yes, I heard all about the marriage while I was in New York spending the holidays with Jody Thornton. Someone from Washington called Mrs Thornton knowing I was Jody's friend and this someone also filled her in on your background – that you've been married a zillion times and *always* to very rich men, and once you lived with a man who turned out not to be your husband and there was some terrible scandal. So you see, I *do* know all about you.' Then she picked up the menu to study it intently.

No, not easy. Harder than she'd ever dreamed. *This poor child is in so much pain . . .*

She pasted her smile back on again. 'Mrs Thornton's informant wasn't *quite* correct. I've been married three times and only two of my husbands were very rich. My second husband was an English actor who wasn't really what you'd call *rich-rich*.' Best to ignore the scandal part, she thought. 'But there's a lot more to know about me than that, just as there's more to know about *you*, I'm sure, than what people might suspect at first sight.'

Sam looked up from the menu warily, as if intrigued despite herself. 'What might people think about me?'

'That you're beautiful, probably intelligent, sure of yourself and physically mature for thirteen. But also that you're rude, arrogant and closed-minded.'

Sam flipped her long red hair as if to show how little she thought of what her stepmother had just said. Still, she was interested enough to ask, 'And what might they find out if they got to know me better?'

'Maybe that you're as beautiful inside as you are outside and that underneath you don't really feel as sure of yourself as you pretend, and that's the reason you are sometimes rude and arrogant . . . and that you're capable of being a wonderful, really mature young woman, if only you'd let yourself be.'

'And what else is there to know about you? That you really want to be a mother to me?' Sam asked with a sneer.

That was exactly what she had been hoping to be, what she had had in mind when she set out this morning. But she saw now that this pathetic *little* girl trying so hard to be grown up, sophisticated and tough, was already too damaged to accept her as a mother, no matter how much love was showered on her.

Instead, she would have to try for a lighter touch. 'No, not a mother. But you might discover that I'll make a good friend – even a best friend – and every girl, young or old, can use one of those. Try me. What do you have to lose?'

For a second she thought she detected a crack in the hard façade, a *yearning* in the beautiful green eyes, even an eagerness to believe, and a wellspring of hope sprang up in her own heart, strangely like an ache. And quickly she added what she thought might be the clincher, 'And once you get to know me better maybe you'll even come to believe that I married your father out of love, a desire to make him happy.'

But then she saw the face close up again, the eyes turn as hard and brittle as thin green glass. She had, after all, said the wrong thing. She realized too late that Sam didn't want to believe that she had married her father for love, didn't want her stepmother to be the one to make him happy. She had had so little of him all her life – had seen him so infrequently – was so starved for his love that she *ached* to have him all to herself and for him to love only her.

Now, Sam asked cunningly: 'What's really on your mind? To try and make friends to impress Daddy with how wonderful *you* are, while you see to it I don't get too near him?'

Nora smiled so that Sam wouldn't see how much her words hurt. But they didn't hurt so much that she was prepared to give up. Hugh's sons had already been too old and hostile when she'd met them to let her into their hearts. But Sam was still young enough, so vulnerable underneath that veneer of toughness, that maybe it wasn't too late to go for love.

'Why don't we order now?' she suggested, picking up the menu, 'and when you come home for your spring break, we can *really* talk about all this.'

'But I never go home for spring vacation,' Sam said, with a gleam of suspicious hope in her eyes. 'Daddy never knows when he has to take off on business.'

'Well, this time you will come home because even if your father isn't home the whole time, *I* will be.'

'Sure. I'll believe it when it happens,' Sam sneered.

Nora smiled as she continued to study the menu. *I'll make a believer out of you yet, Samantha Grant.*

Oh yes, she would try – for TS, for Sam and for herself, because somehow – in spite of all the anger, hostility and arrogance – she suspected that she had just fallen in love again for the second time in a matter of a

341

couple of weeks. And how many times in a lifetime did one actually fall in love?

33

From the moment she saw it, Nora fell in love with every green inch of Grantwood. It was as if she'd been transported back in time to the countryside of her youth and the house itself reminded her of Merrillee Manor even though it was surrounded with tropical plantings, and ivy trailed from its tiled roofs. But, like the Cantington house when she'd first seen it, it too, was badly run down, even more so since Grantwood was that much larger and the Georgetown house, in the heart of the city, had had no grounds to speak of.

'There she is, yours to fix up to your specifications. I hereby grant you *carte blanche* to restore this grand old English lady to her former glory,' TS said grandly.

'How does *carte blanche* translate into dollars?' She didn't want him to go into shock when the bills came rolling in. 'Restoration and importing antiques from Britain doesn't run cheap, especially if you want fast results.'

'The sky's the limit. Just work that famous Nora Grant magic.'

After having said that, he removed himself totally from the project which, she was quick to learn, was his way. He was so absorbed in his movie business that everything else had to take a back seat. But she didn't mind. She understood his obsession with his studio since she'd spent much of her adult life similarly obsessed . . . with her son.

Besides, she was thinking of the wonderful example of devotion to duty he'd set for Hubie once he came home and went to work at Grantwood Studio, and she set to work with her customary energy and determination. If a showplace where he could give the most marvellous parties was what TS wanted, there was no reason he shouldn't have it – he'd earned it.

When the bills started pouring in, not wanting to bother TS with money talk – they had little enough time to play at being newly-weds with the arduous schedule he kept – she paid them herself as she did the household expenses. Since money was no problem to either one of them, it really didn't matter who paid what now that they were a team. But when the cumulative amount began to assume the sky-high level TS had alluded to, and she was running out of ready cash since most of her funds were tied up, she asked TS what to do with the bills. 'Shall I put them in an envelope and send them on to your business manager?'

TS grinned wryly. 'I don't have one of those any more – I fired him months ago. Who needs someone to take his cut off the top only to tell me how much money I can spend? Now, I ask you, does that make good business sense?'

'No, I guess not,' she laughed. 'So what *shall* I do with the bills? Send them to the studio?'

'They'd most likely send them right back to you and then what would you do?' He laughed. He enjoyed posing silly questions to her just to see what answer she'd come up with.

'I haven't the vaguest.'

'In that case maybe you'd better pay them and I'll pay you back when my accountant straightens out my accounts.'

'Oh? Is there a problem?'

'There wouldn't be if I fired him too and got myself someone a little sharper. Maybe once you finish with the house stuff you could take care of that for me. After all,' he grinned, 'who'd know more about that than a billionairess?'

343

She was taken up short, not sure whether he was kidding. She smiled uncertainly. 'Where'd you get the idea that I was a billionaire?'

'Come on, you sly fox,' he chided. 'You can't keep secrets from the old man. Everybody knows Hugh Cantington was worth over a billion and was completely devoted to you.'

'That doesn't mean I was left a billion dollars. Hugh's estate was divided seven ways *after* taxes, with his four sons and Hubie and me getting equal shares.'

'You mean you let them pull a number on you?' he demanded brusquely and she stiffened at his tone.

Then he put his arms around her. 'It just riles me that those big money boys took advantage of you.'

'But they didn't. I got exactly what I bargained for and it was a *lot* of money. Between me and Hubie, we inherited a quarter of a billion! I wasn't greedy for more. It was important to me *not* to be greedy. Can you understand that?'

'Sure I can, sweetheart. But you and Hubie and four sons – I'm not much for figures, I admit,' he grinned at her, 'but I can add up to six. Who got that seventh share?'

'Various charities.'

His eyes opened in astonishment. 'That's about one hundred and thirty million bucks left to charity? Couldn't you talk that sick, old man out of leaving them that big a bite?'

'I could have. I didn't try,' she said, feeling sick.

'Why the fuck not?'

'Because that's what Hugh stood for. That's the kind of a man he was. He believed in giving back. I would never rob him in death of what he stood for in life.'

He stared at her uncomprehendingly and she realized then that it wasn't that TS wasn't a good person, or even ungenerous. She'd seen him hand out hundred-dollar tips to valet parkers, give money to a friend down on his luck without being asked, and the staff adored him not only

344

because they were so well paid, but also because he spoke to them as if they were his friends. It was just that he didn't understand . . . didn't really think about anything outside making movies. And it didn't mean that all the wonderful things about him were any less wonderful. Besides, TS was a great filmmaker – a genius, and what did geniuses know about money? And she was ashamed of the suspicion that had crept unbidden into her mind that he had married her for her supposed billion dollars.

He scratched his head, smiling ruefully. 'I guess you have to forgive me for being so ignorant about how the *really* rich do things. When it comes to money, I'm just a wash-out, I guess. If I were better at it, I wouldn't always be in a mess with the *overs*.'

'The what?'

'The overs – over-budget, overextended and over-due at the bank,' he chuckled. 'But not to worry – in Hollywood they don't call it being broke, they call it a cash-flow problem. Anyway, that's what my accountant tells me.'

She laughed. This was much better – this was the famous T.S. Grant light touch, the humour for which he was known.

'A cash-flow problem isn't unique to Hollywood, you know, and not unknown even in the poshest circles. You have all your money tied up in films and they have it tied up in paper. But you were foolish to let me spend all that money fixing up and buying all those outrageously expensive antiques. It could have waited.'

He turned serious again. 'But it's a matter of *image*. You might understand about money, Nora, but image is one thing *I* know something about. It's my business. In Hollywood, if you don't keep up the image, everyone doesn't just *think* you're broke, they're positive of it, and then you can't borrow a dime from the banks. And if *they* won't lend you money to make a movie, who will? Besides, I love Grantwood Manor and I love you. I want it to reflect properly that it's the castle of a very special

345

lady, not a countess but a queen! As for those bills, I was just kidding when I said you should pay them – just send them over to the accountant – let him wrestle with them. That's what he's getting paid for.'

She thought then of telling TS that the bills which totalled several million dollars by now, didn't *really* pose a problem. In a couple of days she could free up some cash, and a good marriage was, after all, a partnership. But then she decided to hold back, thinking that he might be embarrassed to have the woman he called a queen and for whom he wanted Grantwood Manor to be a castle, foot the bills, and he might even be upset with her – think she was trying to take over his male prerogatives.

Still, instead of mailing the bills to the accountant – actually a huge firm – she took them over personally, making an appointment first to talk to Andy Donovan who glanced at the bills and shook his head woefully. 'No way,' he told her and she said, 'No problem,' and wrote out a cheque.

Encouraged at how quickly the cheque was forthcoming, Andy Donovan felt free to be frank. 'The problem with TS is that not only is he grandiose, both in his personal spending and moviemaking, he can't separate the two and refuses to plug up the holes. But the sad truth is that if he doesn't have a really big winner at the box office soon or pull off something really spectacular, he's going to lose both Grantwood Manor and Grantwood Studio.'

She smiled faintly. 'What do you mean by pulling off something spectacular?'

'Well once, when the studio was virtually going under, he came up with fifty million dollars like a magician pulling a rabbit out of his hat. Maybe it doesn't sound like so much today what with the cost of making movies zooming, but back in '56, it was a hell of a lot of money.'

'Yes, I would think,' she said and she was indeed

346

thinking hard – 1956 was the year his daughter, Sam, had been born. 'And it's still a hell of a lot of money. But since it didn't really come out of a hat, where did it come from?'

Andy shrugged. 'TS would never say. But would you believe that after paying back the banks, he was back in their debt again after only one year and a run of bad luck at the box office? And again he pulled off the spectacular, only this time he didn't pull any fifty million out of the hat for the banks. The magic was that he got a bank to pull *its* money out of a vault for him,' he chortled.

'Only one year later? That would make it '57?'

1957 was the year she was in Hollywood with Tony.

'If '57 comes after '56, then that was the year.'

'But how did he do it?' she asked and the accountant said admiringly, 'With a really cute manoeuvre. First he went to the bank and pitched them with a sequel to *Gone With The Wind*, the movie that up until then was the biggest grosser of all time. So they got all excited and instead of asking him if he had secured the rights, which normally they should have done, they asked who he was casting. Well, when TS said he had Mimi L'Heureux, the French sexpot, to play Scarlett, they went bananas. Someone *did* ask how Scarlett would play with a French accent but TS just winked and said they'd dub – with Mimi's body and name who cared whose voice it was and they agreed. Then when he told them that along with Mimi came her Pulitzer Prize winning husband as the screenwriter, they didn't recognize *his* name, but they did recognize the name *Pulitzer*, and that was sufficient.'

'And for Rhett Butler—?' she asked innocently.

Andy laughed. 'That was the one that clinched the deal. TS told them he had an English actor, Tony Nash, on the line who not only was the spitting image of Gable, but who could be got *cheap*. These were bankers, after all, and their bottom line is spelled budget.'

'And what spells cheap?'

347

Andy laughed again. 'That was *really* the cute part. Tony Nash, the poor fish, never got a contract and since the picture never got made, all Nash cost the studio was a couple of plane tickets and a few weeks of expenses for him and his girl-friend, an ex-countess. Some creative bookkeeping you might say – we put *her* down in the ledger under publicity.'

'I'll just bet you did.'

'Anyway, once TS got the bank's commitment he went to France and signed up Mimi and her husband. L'Heureux was a smart cookie – she would never have signed unless she saw that commitment in black and white. Then when the bank saw *her* name on the dotted line, they forked over the cash.'

'But since the picture never got made didn't TS have to give the bank back their money?'

'Well, of course he did . . . *eventually*. But he would have had to do that in any case, win or lose. The point is they lent it to him when he was desperate, which they wouldn't have done without a very *spectacular* package.'

'Not only spectacular but very creative, you might say.'

'That's what TS's always telling me *I* should be. "You have to be more creative, Andy" he always says.' He shook his head affectionately. 'What a guy!'

'Yes,' she agreed. 'What a guy!' *A guy I thought didn't know anything about money. That goes to show what I know.*

'But I'm sorry if I upset you painting a dire picture of TS's financial situation. I shouldn't have done that. He's sure to pull something spectacular again.'

'I'm sure,' she said, rising to leave, shaking hands.

'It was good to meet you, Mrs Grant.'

'You must call me Nora, Andy,' she smiled sweetly. 'Unless you want to call me Mrs Creative Bookkeeping.'

He looked at her, puzzled.

'You know, that girl-friend, the ex-countess, the one you put down under publicity – she married the poor fish, Tony Nash.'

348

'I had an interesting visit with Andy Donovan today,' Nora said provocatively as Nora and TS lay in bed, she flipping through a magazine, he totally absorbed in a copy of *Variety*.

He didn't stop reading. 'Interesting? Then you're lucky 'cause I find Andy pretty boring myself.'

'That's mean. And he says such nice things about you.'

TS turned a page. 'What kind of nice things?'

'Oh, how you can pull rabbits out of hats to save the day. Like when you needed money and out of the hat came the sequel to *Gone With The Wind*. And then, really a fabulous magician, you looked up your sleeve and there was Mimi L'Heureux, F. Theodore Rosen and none other than Tony Nash.'

He put down the paper to roar with laughter. 'Andy Donovan's not only boring, he's got a big mouth. All right, let's hear it. What's bothering you? Are you worried that I pulled off a scam that the late Mr Cantington would view as less than honourable?'

She picked her words carefully so as not to offend him. 'Well, it *was* kind of double-dealing, wasn't it?'

'Come over here,' he said, putting his arm about her to draw her closer till she was lying in the crook of his arm. 'What I did wasn't anything people in Hollywood or those politician friends of yours in Washington don't do everyday: making something work by stepping fast and talking even faster. And who got hurt? The bank got its money back, Mimi made a bundle, her husband got paid for a screenplay he never wrote, and Grantwood Studio is still here. That says it all as far as I'm concerned.'

And then she knew a little more about the man she'd married – he might be all the wonderful things she thought he was, but he was something else as well. Not only a magician, but a pragmatist for whom the ends justified the means.

'But what about Tony?' she gently chided him. 'What did he get beside a run-around?'

TS grinned down at her. 'He got better than he deserved. He ended up with the big prize only to lose her because he couldn't resist the French slut. That shows he was a sucker and a wise man never gives a sucker an even break.'

Then his hands were all over her and his lips, and she never asked the question she meant to – had he *ever* truly intended to make the sequel? She guessed not, but it didn't really matter. It was thirteen years ago and a lot of movies and even marriages had been made in the intervening years . . .

But after TS was asleep she thought of a few more far more interesting questions she could have asked him. One was if Mimi was the slut Tony, the sucker, couldn't resist, had *he*, the wise man, been better able to resist her?

Or she could have asked him if he had met Mimi *before* he signed her up as Tony had – at one of those film festivals where people apparently spent more time flitting from bed to bed than they did viewing films – and if so, when? She tried to remember when Tony had said he'd met her. *Late '55?* It would be a funny coincidence if all three of them had been there at the same film festival at the same time . . . a kind of preview of things to come.

And she might have asked what exactly was the spectacular trick he had performed to save his precious studio in 1956, the year Sam was born. *Married Sam's mother?*

But the question more pertinent even than fascinating was what spectacular feat would the magician pull off this time to save his studio from the banks?

Then, looking at the man she had married in such haste, sleeping the sound sleep of the strong and the untroubled, she wondered what was his secret? Did his strength come from his pragmatism, from his belief in himself and in the righteousness of his cause – his beloved studio. Then she whispered a final question from a poem she had learned long ago when she was innocent and untroubled: '*How much do I love thee? Let me count the ways . . .*'

No, that *let me count the ways* wasn't quite right, she thought. It would have to be: *I must count your ways.*

34

Nora had given top priority to redoing Sam's room so that it would be ready by the time she came home for the spring vacation. She had lavished attention on every minute detail, using Sam's favourite green as the primary colour in the decorating scheme, to ensure that the finished product would be a teenager's dream. When it was finished down to the last accessory only a couple of days before Sam was due to arrive, she led TS into the room to take a look.

He smiled patiently. 'Very pretty.'

'Is that all you can say?'

'What do you want me to say?' he laughed. 'Tell me and I'll oblige. You know I'm an obliging kind of a fellow.'

'I think you're a maddening kind of a fellow. Say it's magnificent and that Sam will adore it.'

'I'll say it's magnificent, but I will not say she'll adore it, because she won't. She's never going to adore anything *you're* connected with. In the past, every time I saw her, all she did was question me about the women in my life. She's always been insanely jealous, terrified that I'd marry again and now that I have, she's going to hate your guts no matter what you do.'

'Of course she's jealous. You're *the* only person in her life and it's natural that she'd resent any woman who took her mother's place in her mother's house and in her

351

father's heart. It's up to us to dispel her fears – you with your love and me with sheer persistence. I don't like to give up, you know, and I'm not going to until I wear her down.'

'Don't count on it – that kid's tough.'

Of course, Sam was tough, she thought. People on their own learned to be tough and Sam had been on her own – away at school and hardly ever coming home, and it didn't help that her father was seemingly and oddly unsympathetic.

'Well, maybe between us we'll soften her up and I hope that while she's here, you'll make it your business to be at home a lot more than you usually are, so we can do a lot of things together like a real family.'

His eyes crinkled up and he put his arm around her. 'Sure. How about if the three of us go down to Disneyland?'

She smiled but just barely. TS thought he was kidding, but she'd been dying to see Disneyland, but had had no one to go with and going by one's self was no fun at all.

Nora had hoped that TS would go with her to the airport to meet the plane, but then he called only ten minutes before she had to leave for LAX to say that he was tied up. 'But I'll be sure to make it home in time for dinner.'

So she went to the airport with Olaf, the chauffeur, who'd been with TS for some years. She was glad that Olaf was there because Sam, instead of crying in disappointment that her father wasn't there, threw her arms around the chauffeur. Then Nora had to turn away so that they wouldn't see her tears. *The poor baby.* Sam was so glad to see Olaf because at least, *he'd* been a constant in her life. He'd been there on each of the infrequent times she'd got off a plane in LA and she knew that he was fond of her.

While Olaf went to get the luggage, she asked Sam if

she'd had a good flight, and Sam answered, 'Not really. They showed a movie I'd already seen twice, the food was disgusting and the stewardess was fresh.'

My, is that all? That's not so bad. Just think, the plane could have gone down in flames.

Then as soon as they were in the car Sam complained that she was freezing. Accordingly Nora turned down the air-conditioning to accommodate her, but then Sam lowered her window, declaring that she was suffocating from the heat. Then she sniffed and sniffed, her features screwed up in total revulsion until Nora felt compelled to ask, 'What *is* it?' and Sam answered with another question: 'What *is* that nauseating scent you're wearing? You'd think that with all my father's money you could get yourself a perfume slightly less revolting. Or maybe it's just that once it touches your skin, it turns putrid.' At last, she smiled at her own malice. 'That's a chemical reaction I've read about.'

Nora dug the fingernails of one hand into the other while managing to smile. 'Isn't that interesting?'

They were already on the freeway before Sam demanded, 'Why didn't Daddy come to the airport? What did *you* do to keep him from coming?'

But Nora was only surprised that it had taken her stepdaughter this long to get around to the accusation.

No, it wasn't going to be easy.

She could tell Sam loved her room from the look of delight in her green eyes and the sigh of contentment that escaped her lips before she remembered to wrinkle up her nose and toss her hair in disdain. 'The colour scheme's kind of obvious, isn't it? But then I suppose a woman of your background would hardly understand about subtlety.'

'My background?'

'Yes. I already knew about all your marriages and that you were involved in a big scandal from Jody Thornton's mother. But all the girls at my school have very *informed*

353

mothers, and now I know a lot more of the *details* of those marriages.'

Nora laughed. 'Only a very *uninformed* thirteen year old would have the arrogance to think she could possibly know *anything* about what goes on in a person's marriage no matter how much gossip she's foolish enough to listen to.'

'But I am *not* uninformed. And it's not just gossip. I did some checking on dates and one thing I *know* is that one and one make two. So I do know what was going on when you were married to that actor and living in Hollywood that first time.' Now her tone was more bitter than malicious.

What was this poor tortured child getting at?

'What do you think was going on?'

'What was going on was that you were cheating on him and the year was 1957 – the same year my mother killed herself and do you know *how*? She fucking killed herself by cutting her own throat until she bled to death and do you know *why*?' Sam's voice began to rise until it was a scream. 'Because my father was fooling around with another woman while she was sick – a woman who was beautiful enough and clever enough to take advantage of his grief over my mother's illness!'

Then she threw herself down on the pretty, pristine floral bedspread to sully it with a torrent of tears and Nora ran to comfort her, to try and put her arms around her, but Sam shrank back from the attempted embrace. 'Don't touch me! *You're* the woman who seduced my father – who's responsible for my mother killing herself! I know it!'

'It's just not true, love. I never even met your father then and you don't even *know* that your father was having an affair with anyone. You *can't* believe malicious gossip from those girls at school who got *their* information fourth or fifth hand from people who didn't even know your mother.'

Sam turned around to look at her with eyes bruised

with misery. 'But they're not the ones who told me about *that*. The ones who told me were people who knew my mother very well – who went to see her constantly when she was sick in that sanatorium. Her parents . . . my grandparents!'

'Your grandparents? How could that be? They died when you were only five. How could they tell you such a thing?'

'They told me all about it just the same.' A sick smile twisted Sam's lips. 'And don't *you* tell me that I was too young at the time to get the facts right or to remember. It's something I remember every day of my life!'

A wave of horror swept through Nora. It wasn't that she doubted Sam. No, it was that she believed her and wondered how it could be that the grandparents of a five year old could be so brutal. Then she thought she understood. Even the nicest people, if they'd ever been that, could be driven to brutality by a bitterness that was so acute it was consuming. A daughter's death by her own hand but generated by a husband's faithlessness – that could cause that kind of bitterness.

A woman so beautiful and so clever . . . She knew one woman who was around at the time who could fit that description . . .

'And did they tell you who this woman was?'

'No, why would they? They didn't care who *she* was. They blamed *him*. But I know better who's to blame. Daddy's so trusting! Oh, it must have been so easy for *you* to fool him.'

'I doubt that he was fooled by anyone. The truth's probably that your grandparents weren't lying but were, in their grief, mistaken. Your father loved your mother too much to be tempted or fooled by any woman. He's often told me how much he loved her, that he was mad about her.'

She didn't mind telling a little white lie if it helped this child in torment.

'Of course, I can't say for sure since as I said I didn't

355

know TS then. And if you don't believe *that*, why don't you ask him yourself tonight? Maybe he'll even tell you how the one time I was *supposed* to meet him with Tony for drinks back then, he actually stood me up.'

But if she was hoping for even the tiniest response to her pathetic little attempt at humour, she was disappointed. Rather, Sam turned away to bury her face in a pillow and she decided it would be best to just leave her be until TS came home for dinner. Then he could reassure her that not only hadn't he known her, Nora, at the time, but that there'd been no other woman at all, not even a sex-pot movie star.

When it became clear that TS wasn't going to make it for dinner, she went upstairs to suggest to Sam that they start without him in the hope that he would get home in time to join them for dessert. But by now Sam was asleep and she didn't have the heart to wake her to what would most likely turn out to be yet another disappointment – when TS didn't make it for dessert either – in what had already been an emotionally exhausting day.

Instead, she gazed at Sam, her features softened in repose and so much more childlike asleep than awake. There was nothing tough about her now, with those tear-stained cheeks and her lips curling up at the corners as if she were dreaming and the dream was sweet. She took the duvet folded at the bottom of the bed and covered her with it carefully so as not to wake her. Still, Sam stirred, the eyelids fluttered for a moment and the lips curved into a real smile as she breathed, 'Mommy . . .'

Oh yes, she thought, Sam's dream was very sweet.

Was a needy child any less needy for being a stepchild, or a stepdaughter any less deserving of love for not being one's own flesh and blood? And if she had learned anything at all by now it was that hand in hand with love went obligation, and that you didn't give up on a child no matter what . . . even if there were certain problems . . . certain deficiencies of character.

356

No, I won't give up on you and that's a promise . . .

Quickly she bent to brush Sam's forehead with a kiss then went downstairs to wait for TS to come home.

35

TS tried to mollify her when he came home at one in the morning with kisses, hugs and jokes but she refused to be placated. 'What you did today and tonight, not showing up at all, might seem like nothing to you but it was a very cruel thing to do to Sam. Don't you realize how she adores you?'

He shrugged. 'She's a hysteric just like her mother, Elise.'

'Well, that's a pretty callous attitude, I must say.' And she wondered how much one owed a callous man? Was there an obligation to overlook certain deficiencies in character, an obligation to work with him to try to overcome them?

'Look, Nora, it's late and I'm pooped. Let's say, I tried to make it but I couldn't, and leave it at that.'

Ordinarily, if he had said he was tired, she would have fussed over him, taken him upstairs to bed to coo over him, but now she was too angry. 'Why *couldn't* you make it?'

'Business. Studio business,' he said as if that was all the explanation necessary.

'Is that the only thing that matters? That damn studio?'

He smiled not quite as warmly as was his usual style, but it *was* late and he *was* tired. 'Not *the* only thing. *You* matter to me. *You* matter very much.'

But it was not the answer she wanted to hear right now. 'What about Sam?'

'What about her?' He was running out of patience. 'You constantly worry about Hubie. *Is he safe? Is he keeping out of trouble? When will he be coming home?* Isn't that enough for you? Why don't you leave Sam to me to worry about?'

'But you *don't*. That's the problem. Do you know what your daughter thinks? That you and I were having an affair when I was married to Tony and while her mother was in that sanatorium, and that's the reason she killed herself.'

His eyes slitted and he muttered, 'That crazy kid . . .'

'It's not her fault she believes it. That's what her grandparents told her – that you were having the affair with *some* married woman. Sam's only guessing that it was me.'

When he made no response other than an expletive, she knew that the story of the affair was true and she was incredibly saddened. She'd been hoping that it wasn't but that wasn't the issue that had to be dealt with now.

'For *my* sake you're going to have to straighten her out, TS. Convince her that you and I were not even acquainted at the time, and while you're about it, try to convince Sam for *her* sake that her mother didn't cut her own throat because her husband was fooling around with *any* woman. She needs desperately to believe in you.'

By now TS seemed to be his usual unflappable self again and his voice was low when he spoke, which made what he said that much more bloodcurdling: 'I'll straighten her out all right, and you know how I'm going to do that? I'm going to tell her the truth, the God's honest truth, that her mother killed herself for only *one* reason – because she was *always* mentally unstable . . . before and after she married me, in and out of institutions her entire life . . . off the wall. I'm also going to tell sweet Sam that she'd better watch her own step because madness often runs in the blood.'

She was appalled. 'What kind of a man are you? How can you even think of saying something so awful, so devastating to your own daughter?'

'Maybe because she's *not* my daughter.'

Now he smiled at her shocked expression, more be-mused than anything, and she knew that whatever he was or wasn't, TS *was* an incredible man. Otherwise, how could he just drop a bombshell like that and *smile*?

'Whose daughter is she, for God's sake?'

He shrugged. 'Your guess is as good as mine. I think it was one of those society boys from old Pasadena. All I know is that she isn't mine. The timing's off. But what does it matter now? He wouldn't marry her and I can't really blame him, considering how many loose screws were rattling around in Elise's pretty head.'

'But *you* did?' *A foolish question to say the least.*

'I did indeed.'

'Knowing she was pregnant?'

'Knowing she was pregnant.'

'Did her parents know she was pregnant?'

This time he laughed. 'Did they not? Do you think those hypocritical snobs were prepared to let their little girl marry someone in the movie business, *dar-ling*, unless they needed someone to play daddy real fast? Come on, Nora, why are we playing questions and answers when you already know the answer and I'm a man who doesn't mind laying his cards on the table? TS Grant and the Parkers cut a deal.'

They cut a deal! *Of course!* The spectacular magician's stunt that had saved Grantwood Studio in 1956. Actually that stunt had been quite simple to pull off. All it had taken was one marriage and one birth.

But then a year later in 1957, the spectacular stunt that saved Grantwood Studio a second time got a little more complex – one that involved one French movie star and an affair, one movie never meant to be filmed, one suicide and a motherless year-old baby. And what would TS the pragmatist have to say about that – only that sometimes things in the movie business got a little out of hand like a production going over budget?

359

But while, as TS said, they weren't playing questions and answers, she still needed a few questions answered since the man she married was a gambling man who played the angles and he had just said that he knew Sam wasn't his daughter because the timing was off.

'You married Elise in '56, but you *did* know her before?'

His eyes twinkled. 'I met her at a charity ball early in '55. Just cultivating the field, so to speak, in case I would want to reap a harvest someday.'

'And you brought Mimi L'Heureux over here in '57. But you had cultivated *her* before, too?'

He smiled, nodded. 'In late '55. Once again just sowing some seed for an eventual harvest.'

Now, *she* nodded. This incredible man she had married never ceased to amaze. He was a virtual jack-of-all-trades. As in 'rich man, poor man, beggarman, thief', TS was lover-man, movie-man, gambling man, magician, and now, apparently – farmer *extraordinaire*.

'And what about now? Are you *still* the farmer working the fields?'

It was a question conceived in sarcasm, still it was a serious question, and *crucial*. She was pretty sure she already knew the answer – how could she not? – but she was hoping against hope that TS was the magician supreme who could pull off another spectacular feat – make a believer out of her again.

'What I *am* is a businessman who likes to put his cards on the table,' he said looking directly into her eyes and placing his hands on her shoulders and she wondered what the tricky devil was up to now – trying to disarm her with candour? Still, she held her breath.

'I might be ploughing the fields but it's not for pleasure. It's only for business. Studio business.'

And she let out her breath with a silent but mournful moan. She had her answer – TS was a better businessman than he was a magician.

'And tell me – how much did you eventually harvest from the Parkers?'

He shrugged. 'Fifty million. You *could* call it Elise's dowry. Just an advance, really, on what they were going to leave Elise in their will anyway. But once she was married to me the hypocrites cut her out of *their* deal fast enough.'

'And did they leave Sam anything?'

'Of course not,' he said reasonably. 'They were afraid it would end up in my pocket. They were suspicious people, you see, not really very nice no matter how la-de-da.'

'Then Sam really was left with absolutely nothing – no money, no father to love her and a dead mother.'

He scratched his head. 'The hour is late and I'm a little dull. Is there a point you're trying to make here?'

'Yes, there is – the point is Sam's legacy. You got fifty million dollars and she—? She got short-changed.'

'Come off it, Nora, don't kid an old kidder. What you're trying to say is that I'm responsible for Elise's suicide and it just ain't so. She had suicide written all over her from the day she was born. Didn't you ever meet anyone like that?'

It was a rhetorical question – she had indeed and he knew that she had.

'And didn't you ever make a deal, sweetie pie? You know, like marrying someone to get something you want and give them back something they want in return? People marry for so many foolish notions it's enough to make your head spin – some people marry for money, some for sex and some just because they need a name for their kids. It's all fine as long as everyone knows what they're getting and what they're willing to pay. Can you disagree with that?'

She couldn't and he knew that she couldn't, and what he was getting at was that she and he weren't that far apart after all. Both of them had in their time married for love – he for love of his studio, and she for love of

Hubie. But not this time. This time she had married for love of a man who, while he was very clever at so many different trades, wasn't clever enough to recognize when he was loved only for himself, and maybe that was the saddest thing of all . . .

But the hour was late – much too late for all manner of things, and certainly for mourning a marriage that had died before its time, a marriage that had been a first for her – the only time anybody had married *her* for her money. It was time for them to start laying all their cards on the bargaining table with new stakes, a time to renegotiate the terms of their marriage contract, now obsolete.

'All right, TS, I already know what *you* want, now I'm going to tell you what I want. Are you ready to cut a deal?'

And then when they were through she realized that, at the very least, she had married a man who would never cease to astonish her and a man who, if nothing else, was a sporting kind of fellow. First he laughed, and then he shook his head in admiration. 'When I married you I knew you were a beauty, an ex-countess, a fabulous decorator and a famous hostess, as well as a woman with a head for politics. What I *didn't* know was that you were one hell of a negotiator, too. I'll have the papers drawn up tomorrow.'

'No, not tomorrow. Tomorrow you'll be much too busy taking your daughter around the studio and spending the entire day with her. It will be good for the two of you to have the time alone together and she is really mad about the film business. She told me so when I went to visit her at school. Do you know what she said? It really was quite precious. She said, "When I grow up I want to make great movies just like my father. I guess things like that just run in the blood." '

A couple of days before Sam (almost but not *quite* as unfriendly as she had been that first day) was ready to go back to school, Nora told her, 'I don't expect that you'll ever love me. I'm not asking you even to be my friend, though that *would* be nice. But if you would care to sign a truce, which means that you will be at all times civil, reasonably respectful, generally pleasant to be around and co-operative, I think it can be arranged for you to spend the summer at home instead of away at camp. What do you say?'

At first, Sam's eyes lit up with sheer joy before she grew suspicious. 'What else do I have to do?'

'Nothing more than what I've mentioned.'

'Do I have to promise to obey?'

She laughed. 'They don't even include that one in the marriage vows any more.' Then she grew serious. 'But you're right, of course, that *is* a point to be taken under consideration. We *will* have to have some ground rules as to what constitutes appropriate behaviour. But that's negotiable. I'll be reasonable if you will, which means that you can't be running to your father every minute to appeal some ruling of mine. You'll have to understand that he's a busy man and that he's in charge of the studio and I'm in charge of running our home. But I promise to be fair if you will.'

Sam's eyes narrowed. 'And what about *after* the summer? You're planning to pack me off to school again in the fall, is that it? You're willing to have me around this summer so you can show my father you're *trying* to be nice, but—'

'Hold on – let's see how the summer goes. If all goes well, we can renegotiate. Deal?'

Sam was guarded but she nodded, 'Deal.'

'Jolly good,' Nora said cheerfully. 'Now we must do something to seal the bargain.'

Sam cocked an eyebrow. 'You said "civil and reasonably respectful". You said nothing about kissing. I told you I don't like to be—'

'I *know*, touched. And I didn't mean that we should seal our bargain with a kiss. I had something entirely

363

different in mind. I don't know about you, but I've never been to Disneyland and I thought that if you didn't mind, we could—'

'Seal our bargain by going to Disneyland?' Sam's eyes opened wide before she rolled them and groaned expressively. Then she said, 'Well, I did agree to be co-operative, so I guess so . . .' Then, almost as if she couldn't help herself, 'I hope you're not a fraidy cat because they have an attraction that's really scary that I'm dying to try and—'

'Oh, I am kind of a fraidy cat, but I think that if we do it together, I won't be too terrified . . .'

And then Sam smiled – smugly, perhaps – but it *was* a smile and Nora thought, *what do you know about that*?

That was what was so nice about negotiating. Sometimes there was a surprise at the end . . . a kind of bonus you weren't expecting . . . maybe sometimes, even love.

36

Hubie came home with his discharge soon after Sam went back to school. It was a time, Nora would think later, that Grantwood Manor looked its most beautiful – the foliage and lawns greener in the first, lush burst of the season; the flowers perkier, their colours brighter than they'd be once the summer heat set in; the pool sparkling in a somehow more brilliant sun.

She had worried that there might be a difficult period of adjustment, that Hubie and TS would not hit it off, or that Hubie would not like Los Angeles. But both worries proved groundless. TS went out of his way to be nice to the always friendly Hubie, who, in turn, thought TS was a great guy, especially so after TS presented him with a welcome home gift – a red Ferrari, the twin to his own bearing the licence plate Studio 2. (TS's own licence plate read Studio 1.)

At first she wasn't sure whether she was pleased by TS's extravagant gesture. A Ferrari was a car for a play-boy and she herself had had a more 'serious' car in mind for Hubie since in LA a man was judged more by the car he drove than the company he kept. But she supposed it'd be all right – TS drove the same car and he was no playboy, being very serious about his work.

But for Hubie, the Ferrari was the embodiment of the Southern California lifestyle and he was off and running, exploring the pleasures of his new milieu – the beaches to the west (TS had a house fronting the ocean to which he immediately gave Hubie a key), and the Hollywood clubs to the east. He was also zipping down to Palm Springs where the studio kept a condo for entertaining, or flying up to Aspen where the condo was even lusher, and usually in the company of a woman, each prettier and sexier than the last, the most common Southern California commodity of all.

But after a few weeks she was impatient to see Hubie off and running into his future, and with this in mind, she addressed TS. 'You've been wonderful with Hubie—'

'Not at all. Just keeping up my end of the bargain. A deal's a deal and I promised to be a real father to your boy.'

'Let's not get our terms confused, TS. For one, Hubie's not a boy – he's twenty-five and he's *had* his share of fathers. What he needs at this stage of his life is a friend, a mentor and an employer . . . which is what you agreed to be. *Sam's* the one in need of a real father and *that's* one of our terms of agreement, too. Remember?'

His smile was wily. 'Of course. But it's easy to under-stand how I get confused every now and then with these

365

terms of agreement. You want me to be Hubie's employer, but it's I who is employed . . . by you.'

Her smile was just as wily. 'As long as you remember that we shouldn't have a problem.' And then she reminded him that she hadn't brought her son to California to be a playboy.

'What's your rush? He's just home from the war. Let him have a little fun before he decides where he wants to fit in at the studio.'

'Who says he can't have fun while he's working? Isn't that what life's all about, combining both? In any case, I want him to start at the studio right away in a post he has an aptitude for, and one that will teach him the business.'

'You're the boss,' TS grinned amiably, 'and I think I have the answer to the question of where to start him off.'

True to his word, TS put Hubie to work, but Nora soon found out that TS's solution, pragmatist that he was, as to what you did with an incredibly handsome young man whose main assets were his charm and a talent for pleasing women, was to apply these talents to the three major Ps of the Industry – publicity, promotion and public relations. But it took only a couple of weeks for her to learn the job description of Hubie's assignment – influencing, entertaining and the gentle persuasion of those females who needed to be persuaded for whatever reason. A sideline was those actresses who needed direction to wherever – première, party or bedroom.

Furious, she reminded TS that the future she envisioned for her son was not that of a male whore.

TS only laughed. 'I thought you were a woman of the world who understood how things worked. Don't you know that *everyone's* a whore? Especially in Hollywood. It's the fastest track of all and if you don't know that, you're never going to last the race.'

'Oh, I'll last the race. I might even outrun *you*.

Even Hubie might and without being a whore. Start him in production and let him learn the business from the bottom up.'

He quirked an eyebrow. 'You're calling the shots, but I've been in this business a long time and I know my people. Production will bore the pants off Hubie and he has problem enough keeping them on already. You'd be better off trying to make an actor out of him. He has the looks and the personality – he might even have the talent.'

'No. Actors don't become heads of studios. Only people who learn the business properly do.'

TS gave his customary shrug as if to say it was no skin off his ass. 'I'm genuinely fond of Hubie and I, too, want only the best for him, but as you say, it's *your* race.'

The first day of summer – the same day that Sam was flying home – was a scorcher with the temperature soaring into the high nineties, giving promise of a long, hot season. And though TS had given her his promise that this time he would make it to the airport, at the last moment he begged off claiming the usual crisis in Burbank. Instead, he sent Hubie, explaining to Nora on the phone that it was a deliberate tactic. 'Sam'll be so excited at meeting her new, big brother – as you yourself said, the poor kid's starved for family life – that she won't even notice that I'm not there.'

Nora was only partially appeased. What TS said was probably true, but she didn't know how wise it was for Hubie to go alone, with no one to make the preliminary introductions and smooth the way. She wasn't so much worried about how Hubie would take to Sam – he was unfailingly friendly and had been happily anticipating having a younger sister about. Sam's reaction to Hubie was the unknown factor.

How was Sam going to adjust to having yet one more person around to vie for her father's attention?

Especially since Hubie went off each day with her father to that place where she herself longed to be. Perhaps if her *own* situation with Sam were better resolved than the shaky truce they'd arrived at, she wouldn't be so anxious.

Still, Nora was determined to maintain a positive attitude and as she waited for them to arrive, she busied herself with the final touches for the family party she was planning for the four of them – a combination homecoming and birthday party since Sam had just turned fourteen.

For once keeping his promise to be home early, TS showed up before Sam and Hubie did to find her a nervous wreck. 'The plane came in at two, now it's six and they're still not here!'

TS was unperturbed. 'Did you check with the airline?'

'Of course I did. The plane landed on schedule.'

'It *could* take an hour to pick up the luggage if it were a crowded flight, especially if it wasn't non-stop.'

'So that would make it three o'clock.'

'Well, there could be a lot of traffic coming back from the beaches today, it was so damn hot.'

'That would take us to four. Four thirty at the most.'

'You checked for accidents?' He poured himself a drink.

'Of course.'

'And I assume what you heard was reassuring? And I dare say they didn't just disappear into thin air and it's not likely they were kidnapped. After all, Hubie's a twenty-five-year-old decorated Marine who made it through Vietnam and Sam *is* five feet ten and could kick the shit out of anyone dumb enough to mess with her. So what are you worrying about?'

Easy for him to say. Hubie isn't his son and Sam isn't his daughter in any sense of the word. He doesn't even know what it means to love a child. Life is simple when one really doesn't give a damn . . .

'*Anything* could have happened. Maybe Sam was

so upset by Hubie showing up instead of you that she decided to run away or something and Hubie had to take off after her. All I know is if they don't show up soon, I'm calling the police.'

'If you do you're going to feel awfully foolish when they come waltzing in with a perfectly reasonable explanation.'

In the end, she didn't call the police, though she did feel kind of foolish as well as relieved when they finally arrived at ten, not exactly waltzing, but arm-in-arm with big smiles on their freshly sun-bronzed faces. She felt not foolish but angry when she heard Hubie's reasonable (to him) explanation: 'It was so goddamn hot when Sam got off the plane and LAX is so near the beach, it seemed a shame not to take the poor kid for a swim so she could cool off.'

Nora was about to ask if, in all his years, he'd ever come across a handy invention called a phone when Sam, eyes shining with excitement, blurted, 'Then when we were drying ourselves off these kids were getting up a game of volleyball on the beach and they were short of a couple of players so we decided to be good sports and help them out, right, bro?'

'Help them out?' Hubie howled. 'What we did was whip their bloody asses! Little sister here didn't mention that she was a varsity champ at that school of hers.'

'That's right, I was,' Sam shrieked, throwing her arms around the bemused TS. 'And we sure did whip those asses!'

'Well, then the losers had to buy and it wouldn't have been gracious not to let them,' Hubie grinned at Nora. 'You know how you always taught me to be gracious, Mum.'

'But *I* didn't have any beer, Nora,' Sam said quickly and primly. 'I just had a coke. Right, Hubie?'

'Mmm . . .' he considered. 'I guess. Well, you didn't beg for *too* many sips from my glass.'

'Oh you,' she giggled, punching his arm while he

pretended to shield himself from her blows. 'That's a big fat lie. Don't you believe him, Nora.'

Nora was amazed, her anger considerably dissipated. It was as if the girl she'd seen that spring had evolved into a different person. She glanced at TS to gauge *his* reaction, but he just seemed to be enjoying the by-play. She turned back to Hubie. 'Even so, that would have taken you up to what – six o'clock? And now it's past ten.'

Sam giggled again. 'Well, you know what they say? Time sure does fly when you're having fun, right, bro?'

Hubie guffawed, and Nora sighed. *Sam's acting like any fourteen-year-old teenager but so is* he. *I guess no matter what else he is, does or becomes – the warrior in Vietnam or Hollywood producer, he'll always remain a child at heart.*

'All right, Hubie, what *did* you do between six and ten?'

'Well, we *were* already at the beach and when sis here said she was famished—'

'I hadn't eaten *all* day,' Sam interrupted to explain. 'The stuff they pushed on the plane was totally gross.'

'Well, then I remembered that Harv Feldman who has a place in Carbon Beach had mentioned that he was having a barbecue, if I cared to drop by. I fully intended to call from his place but his dumb phone was out of order.'

'It was *so* super eating out on the deck and the place was crawling with movie stars!' Sam enthused.

'Stars?' Hubie hooted. 'Extras and bit players is more like it but the kid here is easily impressed, specially since one of the jerks tried hitting on her,' and Sam punched his arm again. 'She's just pissed off because I told him to lay off my little sister unless he really craved a bloody nose.'

Sam pretended to pout. 'He ruined my romance.'

TS finally spoke up. 'Sounds like the kids had a real good time, Nora, but since *they* ate and *we* didn't and now *I'm* famished, do you think *we* might have *our* dinner?'

'I don't see why not,' Nora answered happily and they trouped into the dining room, a family of four.

When Sam saw the room and table decorated for her combination homecoming and birthday party, she screamed, threw her arms around her father, then around Hubie, and finally, even Nora, before declaring, 'This is the very best day of my life! And tomorrow is going to be the second best.'

'What's happening tomorrow?' Nora asked.

'Tomorrow my big brother is taking me to Disneyland and then after that, we're going to a rock concert.'

Nora thought of saying something about Hubie having to go to work, but how long could she ride herd on a man in his twenties and how could she ruin the best day of a young girl's life by ruining the plans for the second best day of her life?

As summer wore on, TS observed, 'I have to hand it to you, Nora, you're doing a great job. You have Hubie ensconced at the studio and with his able assistance you've even conquered the formidable Sam. And now that we're one big happy family and everybody loves everybody else, I hope we're all going to settle down and it will be business as usual.'

There it was in a nutshell, she thought. For TS, their being a happy family was a secondary, at most, a pleasant detail. Business as usual – *studio* business – was the only thing that truly counted and he didn't really care if Sam and Hubie were friends so long as Sam was out of his hair, just as it made no real difference to him if Hubie worked or not as long as it didn't prove inconvenient to the running of the studio.

It didn't even matter too much to him that legally he no longer owned the studio so long as he ran it. Grantwood Studio itself was *the* only thing that mattered – that it existed, that it endured; the rest was mere detail.

How then could she discuss with him the vague unease she felt about the intense intimacy struck up

371

between Hubie and Sam, one that, considering their age difference and experience, seemed somehow unnatural? And what would happen when, inevitably, Hubie tired of horsing around with a younger sister, however adoring, and turned his attention to more adult (and sexually rewarding) pursuits? Sam could be left adrift, devastated and any progress they'd made as a family, and she and Sam as mother and daughter, could self-destruct.

Then she decided that maybe TS was right, after all, about the importance of things settling down and getting on with business as usual. And now she looked forward to the fall when everything hopefully would be brought into sharper focus. Sam would start school, would make friends with kids her own age and develop her own teenage interests, leaving Hubie to pursue his own more mature interests and his career.

Summer was winding to a close the day when things were brought into the sharpest of focuses for her, a Sunday no different from any other lazy summer Sunday except that TS was at home reading scripts in his study as she played sounding-board, he insisting she had a good ear for an exciting project.

But suddenly she forcibly removed a script from his hands. 'I know what your difficulty is.'

He grinned up at her. 'I didn't know I had one. Now, be a good girl, Nora, and give me back my screenplay.'

'No. I'm the boss and the boss says enough work for today. I've figured out that your problem is that you've never stopped to smell the flowers, and who knows? If you had, you might be a better man for it.'

He laughed heartily. 'I've always said you've got a great sense of humour. Tell you what I'll do since I'm a sporting kind of a fellow – I'll take a fast walk around the gardens with you and sniff the hell out of those flowers.'

'But I wasn't talking literally.'

'I know you weren't, but it's all I have time for.'

'Wrong. You're going to the beach. We haven't been all summer and that house is sitting there going to waste. A few hours sitting and watching the surf roll in and reflecting on the mysteries of life might do wonders for you. Then we'll stop and have dinner at some little place on the way home. At the very least, it will be peaceful and relaxing.'

He made a face. 'Didn't the kids go to the beach today? It's hardly my idea of relaxation having Sam bury me in the sand or nag at me to ride the waves with her and listen to her shriek all afternoon. And then if we go out to dinner with her and Hubie, they'll drag us to one of those beach joints where the music is loud enough to burst my eardrums. And I thought you were a woman with a heart.'

She laughed. 'But they didn't go to the beach today. First they played a little tennis, then they took off for the zoo at Griffith Park. It seems that poor little Sam has never been and Hubie insisted that the situation had to be rectified but immediately. So now that you don't have them as an excuse not to go, you might as well give in gracefully.'

It wasn't the image that came into focus first. First there were the sounds coming from behind the door even before Nora finished turning the key in the lock – the heavy breathing, the sighs and the moans, a male's husky groans furiously mounting, a girl's high-pitched scream of joy.

Nora recoiled, dropping the key, then came TS's 'Shit!' as he pushed the door open to reveal the shot: three brightly-coloured scraps of bathing attire discarded on a white-tiled floor. Pan to couple also lying on white-tiled floor, boy mounted on girl. Boy: tanned, beautiful muscular body glistening with sweat, blond head buried in her throat. Girl: long red hair spread in disarray, head thrust back in wild abandon, eyes shut

373

tight, long, shapely legs spread to accommodate boy's still shuddering body . . .

Then, before Hubie turned around or Sam's eyes flew open, Nora heard TS say, 'Shit,' again before he said, 'I hope you're not going to go all to pieces, Nora. This isn't exactly the end of the world, you know. It can be handled.'

She laughed bitterly. Any minute now he would shrug and say, 'Well, what did you expect? Boys will be boys and I told you right from the beginning that that girl was trouble . . .'

It was all a matter of how one viewed the situation, she mused sorrowfully, each of the four players involved seeing this final development in a different light.

Hubie saw it sheepishly as a slip in behaviour, a misstep that could be rectified with abject apologies and an honourable shouldering of responsibility: 'It was all my fault.'

Sam saw it as an act of romantic passion needing no defence save an equally impassioned, 'We love each other!'

Nora herself viewed it after the fact as inevitable, blaming herself. She'd been so relieved that Sam and Hubie had hit it off that she had closed her eyes to the obvious – that Hubie was *not* a responsible man, didn't know what constituted *inappropriate* behaviour, much less a betrayal of trust, and that Sam, despite her physically ripe body and assumed sophistication, was still only a child too vulnerable in her need for any kind of love.

As for TS, in his desire for 'business as usual', he saw the incident only as an inconvenience.

Then each of them viewed the solution to the improbable situation according to his own light: Hubie presumed that his promise that it would never happen again was solution enough; Sam thought that her screaming protestation that she and Hubie loved each other madly was sufficient; TS, ever the practical CEO, knew only that if someone became inconvenient, you rid yourself of the someone and if there were *two* someones, you got rid of the one most expendable. And this time, Nora agreed with him – one of them had to be exiled.

She knew beforehand whom TS would choose, arriving at his choice by pragmatic deduction. He himself needed *her*, Nora and he assumed that she needed Hubie, making them a package deal. But who really needed Sam? She was extraneous baggage. *Ship her back east to school as soon as possible.*

But she knew better who had to go. Never having loved another person, TS didn't really understand any kind of love, was unable to fathom the depth of love a woman might have for a child not of her womb. He couldn't comprehend that sometimes a mother didn't really have a choice, as in the case of a mother who had two children whose lives hung in the balance and it was already established that only one could live . . . that she would have to choose not on the basis of love but which child had the best chance of survival.

It is time to let go . . .

She had tried so hard, but now she had to give up her son to the gods of destiny to find his way for himself. And she could only pray that he would make it back to claim his legacy – her enduring love and his half-share in the magic kingdom.

Yes, it was too late for Hubie, but it wasn't yet too late for Sam. Sam was a second chance much as a second marriage was and this time round she wouldn't make the same mistakes. This time round it would be 'tough love' so that Sam could discover the truth for *herself* . . . that she was a strong woman worthy of all the different faces of love and that the legacy she thought was hers by right of birth had yet to be earned. Still, there were certain truths she could never let Sam learn – not only that TS wasn't her blood father, but that no matter what she did, he was incapable of loving her.

Still, despite all her brave resolutions, it wasn't easy to let go, and it wasn't much of a consolation for her to tell

375

herself that Hubie, with his innate inability to withstand temptation in any form, was best off out of Hollywood – the fastest, deadliest track of all where he was bound to stumble again and again. But then she had a marvellous idea! Maybe Hubie would do better, after all, in the land of his birth where she had an old and very dear friend – who was only incidentally her ex-husband – to call upon for help.

When she called Tony to tell him she needed a really big favour he told her it was hers even before she explained what it was. Then after she had, he didn't hesitate for a moment.

'Of course, Nora. I always *meant* to be a good husband to you and a father to Hubie if only you hadn't been in such a bloody rush to divorce me. Well, I'm at your service now, a little bit older, a little bit wiser, better-late-than-never Tony Nash. I will not only take Hubie under my wing and be a real father to him, I'll even show him a good time.'

She had to laugh. 'Hubie doesn't need any help in *that* department and at this stage, he doesn't really need a father. What he needs is a friend, a place to *be* and a fresh start. I'm hoping you'll get him started in films so that he can learn the business.' *And someday – when he and Sam are both grown up, he can come back to claim his heritage . . .*

Nora wasn't surprised that Sam turned on her, the old dormant hostilities reawakened with a fresh fury and new accusations: *you were jealous . . . you wanted him to love only you . . . you wanted to break my heart . . . you sent him away to punish him for loving me . . .* She even went so far as to accuse Nora of wanting Hubie's sexual favours for herself.

But Nora neither defended herself nor lashed back as she yearned to hug Sam to her breast, to rock in her arms, to assure her that it hurt only for a little while before it got better. But she didn't do any of these things either. All the old bets were off – from now on it would be tough love and that meant telling Sam that she didn't give a tinker's damn whether Sam liked her or hated her, but if she wanted to stick around the place where her father was and go to school locally, she'd better straighten up and fly right, which meant keeping a civil tongue in her mouth and toeing the mark.

And then, not much later, it really didn't come as *that* much of a surprise when Tony called in tears to report that he had failed her again – that much as he had tried to get Hubie started in films and as hard as he had tried to keep him interested, Hubie had become bored and taken off.

'To find some fun, was what he said. And he said to tell you that he loved you and that he would be in touch.'

'But, Tony, where did he go?'

'I'm sorry, Nora, but – He joined the Foreign Legion.'

'The *what*?' If someone would have asked her she'd have guessed that the Foreign Legion was something that no longer existed – something they'd once made movies about but didn't any more . . . a romantic notion that had become obsolete. But then she said: 'Don't feel bad, Tony, it isn't your fault. I guess Hubie just has a few more puddles to go. . . .'

'I don't understand. *Puddles?*'

'Puddles. When Hubie was a little boy he loved nothing more than to jump into puddles just for the fun of it.'

PART EIGHT

THE FIRST SWEET TASTE OF THE SEASON

Los Angeles
1970–74

37

Honey sat by herself at a table in the corner of the lunchroom, taking disspirited stabs at her salad. Since it was the first day of the semester at Beasley and she was a freshman – her first day – she didn't know a single girl there. But looking around she saw everyone else talking to everyone else a mile a minute. Surely there had to be other girls who didn't know anyone. But where were they?

But then a girl bounced up – a very short girl with a shiny dark fringe hanging low over sparkly, dark eyes who, even before she set her lunch tray down, demanded: 'Are you Playmate or Bunny?'

'I'm not sure,' Honey said tentatively, not having any idea what the girl was talking about but not wanting to admit it, afraid that the girl might just bounce off to try someone else who was more clued up. 'Which are you?'

'I'd *like* to be a Playmate, but I guess I'm a Bunny.'

'Well, then I'll be a Bunny too,' Honey responded quickly, thinking this was the friendly thing to say.

But now the girl looked at her thoughtfully, considering: 'No, I think *you* have to be a Playmate because *you're* beautiful and a true Playmate is beautiful as well as voluptuous and therefore, makes it to the pages. But I have to be a Bunny because while I'm cute I'm definitely not beautiful. Also, I'm short and *too* voluptuous for my height. Mostly a Bunny's just cute and all she gets to do is bob her bushy tail up and down and jiggle it all around like this—' She leaped up to execute a couple of fast dance steps – boogie mixed with wiggle – and finished off with an old-fashioned bump and grind. 'See?'

Honey laughed revealing a blindingly white, near-ly rectangular smile and the girl enthused, 'Even your smile is gorgeous. Yep, I'm cute but you're centrefold material.'

Centrefold material! Playmates and Bunnies! Of course! While she had never seen it, she knew that the Play-boy Mansion, situated in Los Angeles' prestigious Little Holmby Hills, was only a couple of hundred yards down the street from Beasley, and she had heard the joke that a Beasley girl didn't have to go far to get a higher educa-tion. She merely walked down the street to the mansion and jumped the fence.

'You *do* mean the *magazine*? *Playboy*?'

'Now you've got it! That's the frame of reference.'

'But I don't want to be a centrefold in *Playboy*.'

'Not even if you were Playmate of the Year? That would make you the only girl in the entire school who didn't.'

'You know most of these girls, then? This isn't your first year here and you're *not* a freshman?' She was dis-appointed. If this girl whom she already liked wasn't a freshman they'd probably end up not being friends.

'Freshman? I might be fresh but there are at least a dozen boys who will testify to the fact that I'm no man. That's a joke in case you're wondering. A piss-poor one, I guess, since you're not laughing. But soon I'll tell another and then you'll laugh, OK? Actually, I *am* a freshman, but I know most of these girls – we've all been on the same loop.'

'Is being on the loop like being on the pill?'

The bouncy girl giggled. 'Hey, *that's* funny, but being on the same loop simply means we've all gone to the same schools ever since we were little buggers. You know – the Hampton Playschool, the Good Preschool, Miss Watley's Day School, the Brentwood School of the Dance . . . You name it – wherever our mothers thought was the right place for the right girl to be – we've all been there. And now we're up to Beasley and I recognized most of the girls even before I followed them through the door this morning. I probably can recognize almost every girl here *from* behind *by* her behind and the way she shakes it.'

This time the two of them laughed together.

'Where *did* you go to school?'

'Beverly Hills. That's where we live. My father and I.'

'I live in Bev Hills too. So if you've always gone to school there, how come you're not going to Bev Hills High?'

'Well, my father went to Princeton and now that it's gone co-ed he has his heart set on me going there, too, and he thought that maybe if I went to private school instead of Beverly Hills High I'd be more . . . well, acceptable.'

'*Acceptable!* That's a word my mother always uses. "That's *acceptable*. That's *non-acceptable*",' she said in obvious imitation. 'Almost everything is *non*-acceptable, you understand, but I'm sure your father and my mother don't use the word in the same way. What does he do for a living?'

'He's a writer, F. Theodore Rosen. The F is for Franklin, but I call him Teddy. He's a novelist and a screenwriter.'

'That's neat. Do you know what my father does for a living *and* for fun? He sends people to jail!'

Honey laughed.

'No, I'm serious. He's a judge. It's just that he really *enjoys* his work,' and Honey laughed again.

'Anyway, I'm really glad your father sent you to Beasley for whatever reason. I'm just glad you're here because I know we're going to be friends.' She put down her cheeseburger to stick out her hand. 'My name is Babette Lee Tracy but everyone except my mother calls me Babe.'

Honey shook her hand. 'I'm pleased to meet you, Babe.'

'Just make sure you don't call me Babe in front of my

mother or she'll have a primal screaming fit. She thinks Babe sounds common. She's a Lee of the Virginia Lees who would fart Chanel Number Five if she farted at all, but she doesn't – she's too tight in the asshole department for that.'

'Oh . . .' Honey didn't know if she was supposed to chuckle at that or what. It was such a weird thing to say about one's mother. 'I'm Honoria L'Heureux Rosen, but I'm called Honey. And you can call me that in front of anybody, I guess.'

Even my mother, but that would be quite a trick since we don't exactly hang out together.

'Oh, Honey's a great name for you! It fits you to a T. But Honoria? I never heard that name before. It's French, I gather, like the L'Heureux?'

'Yes. L'Heureux is my mother's family name.'

'Oh, God! I *thought* you looked familiar! I mean, you look just like her – the French sex-pot! I should have known. All that gorgeous blond hair and those eyes. They're really the colour of topazes. And those lashes out to there that I would gladly die for. Mimi L'Heureux *is* your mother?'

Honey blushed. 'Yes . . .'

'Hey, you don't have to turn pink because your mother's a beautiful, sexy woman. My mother'd be a beautiful, sexy woman, too, except for one thing – she's never had sex in her life. I'm the original stork-delivered baby. I was dropped complete with a bundle of disposable nappies as part of my accessory kit! Honest! And even if Catherine did have sex just *once*, she did it with her eyes shut tight and you know why? Because she didn't want to see my father enjoying himself.'

Honey giggled. 'What a thing to say about your mother.'

'Oh, don't you worry about Catherine the Terrible. She can take care of herself. I'd match her against anybody's mother if it came to slugging it out. Only she'd do it with her pinky extended as if she were taking tea with the president which, you understand, *is* her prime ambition.

'Anyway, I've seen a couple of your mother's old movies on late-night TV. When Catherine wasn't looking. With English titles, natch, since my French is as good as my Japanese. And I think your mom's super. Way sexier than Monroe ever was. But I haven't seen any *new* movies lately. Doesn't she make movies any more?' Then, stricken, 'Oh, did I put my tiny foot in my big mouth? She's not dead, is she?'

'Oh no, she's alive and well and living in Paris.'

'Whew! I'm glad. I thought that maybe – Well, you *did* say you lived with your father and all . . .'

'I know. It's just that my parents are divorced and I live with my father and *not* with my mother.'

'Lucky you,' a voice drawled and they looked up to see an extremely tall girl with bright red hair licking a spoonful of yoghurt, but managing to do it elegantly. 'I'm Samantha Grant and I'm a freshman, but don't ask me if I'm a Playmate or a Bunny because if another person asks me that I'll scream. *Boring!* And while I'm an Angeleno bred in the bone I've always gone to schools in the East so I don't know anyone here and from what I've seen, I don't think I really want to.'

She sat down, crossing her long legs. 'Tell you what I'm gonna do, I'm going to join you two for lunch today and if you're very, very good and very careful – for the rest of the week, as well. And after that, well – we'll see.'

Honey, thinking she'd never seen a girl more or less her own age exuding so much sophistication and self-confidence, glanced at Babe to see how she was taking the cool Samantha. But, proving that she was up to the challenge Babe said, 'I'm Babe Tracy and my beautiful friend here is Honey. But are we really supposed to call you Sa-*man*-tha? Now my mother would Sa-*man*-tha you to death, but if we're going to be eating lunch together, I think you'd better come up with something more informal or you'll have to call me Babette. Right, Honoria?'

385

'You may call me Sam,' Sam said, bright green eyes glistening. (Green as bottle glass, Honey thought.) 'That's what my intimates call me. I'm named for my father. He's T. Samuel Grant, *the* T.S. Grant of Grantwood Studios.'

'I think Sam's a lovely name,' Honey said and Babe enthusiastically agreed. 'Absolutely. Sam's Jake with me.'

'Good, now that that's out of the way, how would you two like to join my club? It's called GAMs.'

Babe giggled. 'I'm game for GAMs. I've got the sexiest legs in the business.'

'I'm sorry to say that GAMs doesn't stand for legs, sexy or otherwise. It stands for Girls Against Mothers.'

Babe gave a shriek of joy. 'That's groovy! I'll join but you have to promise *not* to tell my mother.'

'Who else belongs?' Honey asked.

'No one. It'll be just us three. Half the fun of belonging to a club is keeping other people out.'

'Now that you mention it, I believe you're right,' Babe agreed. 'We'd be honoured to join GAMs. Right, Honey?'

Honey wasn't sure she wanted to join a club aimed specifically against mothers. While she scarcely knew her mother and though she had no real reason to feel loyal to her, it would still seem like an act of betrayal to belong to a club whose main *raison d'être* was to be against her.

But Babe and Sam were looking at her expectantly, waiting for her affirmative response and she wanted them to be her friends. She just knew that if she said no to being a GAM, the two of *them* would be close friends and she'd be left on the outside, looking in, just like her father always was. 'But I don't know if I'm really *against* my mother. I've hardly ever seen her.'

Sam shrugged. 'So, what does that have to do with anything? I've never *ever* seen mine as least as far as I can remember.'

'You haven't?' Honey was surprised. She had assumed

386

that she herself was one of a tiny minority – children of divorce whose mothers *chose* not to have their children live with them.

'No. My mother – she was a debutante from Pasadena – died before my second birthday,' Sam offered flatly and her eyes were suddenly opaque.

'Oh, I'm sorry. But then, how can you be against her?'

'Oh, it's not my mother I'm against – it's my *stepmother* who's my enemy of choice,' Sam exulted. 'You know something? I think our meeting here at Beasley was preordained. Kismet! The second I saw you two sitting here by yourselves I had this funny feeling deep inside that I had found two true comrades in arms. Now, all that GAMs stands for can be represented by just us three: you, Babe, who lives with your real mother; you, Honey, who has a real mother you *don't* live with; and I who live with my steppie Nora, the Wicked Witch of the West.'

'That's cute. Come on, Honey,' Babe urged. 'You heard Sam. It's Kismet! You've got to join. OK?'

'OK!' Honey blurted and Babe got to her feet to do a quick time step, ending up by throwing out both arms in an extravagant, all-encompassing gesture.

'Wonderful!' Sam said. 'Now, put out your hand, Babe, palm up, and you put your hand over hers, Honey, palm down.' After they complied, she put her hand over both of theirs. 'Now, let's say it all together: "Friends for ever more . . ."'

They said the words in one voice just as the bell signifying the end of lunch-hour rang out.

'Look, we've lots to do,' Sam said, getting up. 'We have to write a constitution – all the rules and by-laws and a Bill of Rights so you'll both come home with me when Olaf comes to pick me up after school and you'll stay for dinner.'

'But don't you have to ask your moth — I mean, your stepmother first?' Babe asked. 'If I invited kids over without asking first, Catherine would shit a duck.'

387

'God, no! It's my home at least as much as hers, if not more. Besides, if Nora has *one* good quality it's that she loves company. It's part of the role she plays. The hostess with the mostest. She loves everyone to death . . . except me, of course.' Then she added, 'And probably not Hubie any more, either.'

'Hubie? Is that a man's name?' Babe asked, helping Honey to clear their places at the table.

'Yes, a *real* man's name. And what are you two doing cleaning up? What is this, McDonald's?'

'We're supposed to clear the table. It's the rule.' Babe picked up Sam's yoghurt container to dump along with the other debris. 'So, who is this Hubie? And why doesn't your stepmother love him any more?'

'Because he loved *me*. But there's no time to get into that now. Now, don't forget, wait for me outside.'

Babe chewed at her lip nervously as they walked out of the lunchroom. 'Look, I'll have to call my mother before I can definitely say whether I can make it or not. I'll have to dream up a good story like we have to work on a school project together or something. But I'll let you know at three. What about you, Honey? Don't you have to get permission?'

'No, it will be fine with Teddy. I'll just call him later to tell him not to hold dinner for me.'

'He must be really easy to get along with, just like my father,' Sam said proudly. 'Just wait till you meet him! You'll love him. I just wish you two could have met Hubie. But now you probably never will. *She* took care of that.'

Babe was fascinated. 'Your stepmother?'

'Yes, Nora the witch. Just watch out for her when you meet her. I mean, she's sneaky. She can charm the panties right off your butt and make you think she's mad for you, but before you know it she's taken away everything you love, including your soul. That's why I call her a witch.'

Honey and Sam exchanged glances. Sam sure did have

a case against her stepmother. Then just before they split up in the hall to follow their individual schedules, Honey asked, 'Tell me, Sam, did you *really* have that feeling the minute you saw us that we were fated to be friends?'

Sam laughed so hard there were tears in her eyes. 'You want to know the *real* truth? I looked over and saw you two: one cute, small, dark-haired chick and one medium-sized beautiful blonde and I thought, add one exceedingly gorgeous, tall redhead, and what have you got? One dynamite trio who'll make waves wherever they go, not to mention that the guys will be standing in line to drool. It's as simple as that.'

Then her eyes widened and she grew serious. 'But you know? I think I really hit on something *big* here. I really do think that, together, the three of us will make such a great team no one will be able to stop us. Together, we'll conquer the world! You know what they said about the Duchess of Windsor? Wherever she goes, so goes the world. But she was only a duchess and we three are *princesses*! Three princesses of Hollywood where all dreams can come true *if you believe*. And Grantwood Manor's a Hollywood castle, a magic kingdom, and I'm going to share it with you two and wherever we go the world and all the Prince Charmings will fall into line behind us. I, Princess Samantha, have spoken!'

Honey laughed, *hardly* believing, but then later that afternoon, after she went home with Sam to Grantwood Manor, she both believed and disbelieved. Grantwood Manor did seem like a magic kingdom, but she was convinced that Sam was all wrong about her stepmother. If she herself and Sam and Babe were the three princesses, then surely Nora Grant had to be the queen, and not a witch at all.

If only Nora could have been my mother!

The girls got off the school bus at the corner of Rodeo Drive and Charleville. 'That's our house down the block,' Honey pointed. 'The pink Mediterranean with all the Australian ferns and bougainvillaea in front.'

'Oh, it's so pretty,' Sam cried enthusiastically.

'I think Teddy chose it because it reminded him of the house in Saint-Tropez he and my mother once lived in when they were first married.'

'But when you told me you lived in BH, I had no idea you meant the *south* side of Beverly Hills,' Babe said, as Honey fished around in her big leather bag for her house key.

'I didn't know I was supposed to be so *specific*,' she mumbled, flushing.

'Of course you didn't have to be specific. It's just that when you said you lived on Rodeo I just naturally assumed you meant *North* Rodeo. I wasn't making a crack just because the north side is considered better than the south. Oh God, I didn't mean *better*. I meant—'

'More expensive?' Honey smiled faintly, as she continued to grope around in the bag for her key but without success.

'I didn't mean that either. I just meant that certain people think the south flats are less desirable but—'

'You're getting in deeper and deeper. You'd better give it up before you make it worse,' Sam chortled. 'Besides, we understand perfectly. We know you can't help being a snob,' she teased. 'After all, you are your mother's daughter and as they say, blood will tell.'

'You haven't even met my mother yet though she *is*

a snob, but that doesn't mean *I'm* one. Besides, while we *are* north of Santa Monica we're only in the eight hundred block of Rexford at the corner of Sunset, which is very good but not *as* good as being north of Sunset. And we don't have a zillion acres in old Bel-Air like the aristocratic Grants.'

'I'd hardly call Nora an aristocrat. But *I*, who truly am one, am not the one making snobby cracks. You are. Just listen to yourself. *Less desirable . . . north of Santa Monica . . . eight hundred block . . . north of Sunset.* You sound like one of those snooty real-estate ladies who trip around on four-inch heels and wouldn't be caught dead driving anything less than a Cadillac if, poor babies, they can't afford a Jag.'

'But there's no one snootier than you. At least I don't go around telling everyone that my mother was a debutante from Pasadena. Anyway, Catherine says Pasadena is *passé* – that it's outlived it's social significance.'

'That's really a hot one! Social significance! And who says your mother's the last word on what passes for social significance in California? She's not even a native Californian like I *and* my Pasadena debutante mother *and* her mother before her, which makes *me* fourth generation California. And what about all that cornball mush about being one of the Lees from old Virginny? If I recall my American history correctly, or at least my favourite movie – *Gone With The Wind* – General Lee and the dear Old South *lost* that war. Now, that's what I call really *passé*!'

'Will you two stop?' Honey begged. 'You sound like two alley cats and we're supposed to be best friends, remember?' She gave up on finding her key in her handbag and tipped back a stone urn of pink geraniums to feel around for the house key hidden there for emergencies. 'And I know you didn't mean anything by what you said, Babe, and my feelings aren't hurt. And you, Sam, stop teasing her. You're being mean.'

Still, as she retrieved the extra key with a triumphant

'*Voilà!*' and threw the door open with a flourish, she drawled, 'Welcome to the Rosens' humble abode but keep in mind, folks, that it's not all *that* humble. While it *is* in the less desirable southern flats, it does have two and three-quarters baths including an imported marble bidet in the master bedroom, and it's only one and a half-blocks *south* of Wilshire which, while not great, is not *excruciatingly déclassé* either.'

She gave the chagrined Babe a swift peck as they walked into a foyer furnished with only a long narrow Spanish table on which sat a blue pottery bowl filled to overflowing with a simple arrangement of garden flowers. There was a sense of cool and quiet in the dark room except for a spill of mail on the burnished planked floor.

Honey stooped to gather it up, explaining, 'The mailman slips it through the slot in the door around noon but by that time Teddy's at work upstairs and forgotten that there is a downstairs or even a mailman. That's how real writers are when they're absorbed in their work – they don't know anything else exists,' she said affectionately, but her attention was focused on shuffling through the mail.

'What are you looking for so hard?' Sam asked curiously. 'Have you been holding out on us? Do you have a secret lover from whom you're expecting a letter? A boyfriend in Vietnam?'

'If you must know, I'm looking to see if there are any cheques here but it doesn't look like it.'

'Cheques?' Babe was puzzled. 'Who would be sending *you* a cheque? Your mother?'

'No, not my mother, though I once got a hundred-franc note from her tucked between two sheets of stationery imprinted with her name but not another word, but the pages *were* scented with Arpège. And occasionally she sends me a picture postcard from Biarritz or a Greek island or some place like that and sometimes there's a card on my birthday and usually a present. There's *always* a present for Christmas. I guess it's hard

392

to forget Christmas . . .' her voice trailed off and Babe and Sam waited silently for her to go on.

'The present is usually something really lavish like an immense bottle of ultra-expensive perfume that's sure to turn bad before I could possibly use it up. That was the year I was eight, I think. And once she sent me a pink satin négligé trimmed in marabou that I could have worn to a Halloween party maybe. Then when I was twelve, there was a pink plush elephant as tall as I was. I guess she just forgets from year to year how old I am.' She shrugged, trying to smile. 'I wouldn't be surprised if this year she sends me a walking-cane or maybe even a wheelchair.'

'Either that or a topless bikini,' Babe suggested, trying for a laugh since Honey sounded so pathetic.

'Let's hope it's the bikini,' Sam said cheerfully. 'It'll come in handy when we vault the wall at the Playboy Mansion. If we're wearing a topless anything under our school uniform we can just shed the uniform once we're over and be ready for anything. I bet we could even sit around the pool without anyone guessing we didn't really belong.'

'Nope, no cheques.' Honey placed the mail on the table, visibly disappointed. 'You have to understand that writers who don't get a weekly paycheque are forever rushing for the mail hoping to find an unexpected cheque. Royalties on an old book or maybe an advance on a new edition or something.' But having said this, she didn't explain why her father, the writer in question, always left the mail just lying there for her to find when she came home from school.

'You two go on into the living room while I go see if Teddy's still working. If he is I won't disturb him and you'll meet him later on.'

She led them into a big curtainless room bathed in light emanating from a skylight and a wall of glass overlooking a patio and a small jewel box of a garden. Though there was an austerity to the room with its white walls and all white slipcovers, there was also a warmth – in the glazed terracotta tiles aged to a faded rose that covered the floor, the brightly rendered impressionist paintings hanging from the high ceiling, and the multicoloured dust jackets of the books lying on tables in orderly stacks and lining the shelves of bookcases that formed a border around the room.

'What a super room!' Babe raved.

'It really is,' Sam agreed, 'though it's kind of a jolt coming from that dark room into this one.'

'I know,' Honey said. 'That's the effect my father wanted. He says that's the way they do it in the Mediterranean. When you first come in from the outside where the sun's hot and the light's blazing, you need a dark, cool room to calm and refresh the spirit, and then you walk into another room awash with light to warm the soul. That's the way Teddy talks,' she said with pride. 'But you'll see for yourself. I'll be right back.'

She knocked on the closed door lightly and when she didn't receive any response, she opened it and tiptoed in to find Teddy asleep on the day bed, his longish hair tousled, a few errant strands curling down over his still-boyish brow, a half-empty bottle of Scotch standing close by on the floor.

Her eyes darted to the old Smith-Corona on the desk with some sheets of balled-up paper lying beside it. There *was* a sheet of paper rolled in but she could see even from where she stood that there was only one word typed on it. She could also see the photo partially sticking out from under the discarded sheets of paper and she didn't have to come any closer to see which picture it was. She knew it by heart.

In the background there was the sea and in the foreground, a young man in white swimming trunks with a sweet and gentle smile holding up a blond and laughing baby while a blond woman in dark sunglasses – her masses of hair whipped by the sea breeze, her body voluptuous even in a plain striped T-shirt and white sailor pants – sat on the sand looking up at them, her gaze inscrutable, her lips set in a pout. On the back of the photo was written in violet ink: MALIBU – 1957.

Even though she'd pondered this photo at least a hundred times she wondered each time that she looked at it what Mimi was thinking – that, even then, she was wishing she was free of the two people she was looking at?

She tiptoed over to the couch, covered her father with the mohair throw, picked up the bottle of Scotch and set it on the desk carefully averting her eyes from the discarded sheets of typewriter paper and the photo that lay beneath. Then she went downstairs to tell Babe and Sam that Teddy was deeply involved in the screenplay he was writing which he had promised to deliver the day after next – his deadline – and that if he got enough work done by dinner time, he'd join them since he was dying to meet her new friends.

The girls came into the kitchen to sit at the yellow-and-white tiled counter on yellow, wooden stools while Honey set out cans of Coke, an orange bowl of corn chips and quickly mixed up a batch of guacamole. 'We've an avocado tree out in back so we eat guacamole a lot.'

'It's yummy, but I didn't know you could cook,' Sam said, her mouth full.

'This is hardly what you'd call cooking, but I do cook a little. Teddy does most of it. He just got used to doing it, I guess, taking care of me all by himself since I was a little girl. You know, after he and my mother split up.'

'Didn't he have a housekeeper?'

'At first, I think.'

'And you don't even have a maid now?' Babe was amazed. She looked around the kitchen – at the gleaming tiled floor, the shiny copper pans hanging from a butcher's hook over the polished black stove, the little pots of herbs lined up on glass shelves in front of the sparkling, stained-glass window. 'But everything's so clean! Spotless! And those other rooms too! Everything's so perfect and neat and shining!'

Honey laughed. 'Well, don't sound so shocked! What did you expect? A six-month layer of dust, piles of dirty dishes with cockroaches crawling all over? I bet everything at your house is neat and shining and you take that for granted.'

'Well, that's true but my mother's middle name isn't *Immaculoso* for nothing. This woman needs resuscitation if she finds a piece of lint on the carpet and she doesn't allow roses in the house because a petal might fall on the floor. And we have a cook and a full-time maid to keep up, not to mention the services of a professional cleaning crew that comes in to sterilize everything including the occupants every month or so.'

Encouraged by their laughter – Sam was inelegantly sputtering guacamole and corn chips – Babe warmed up. 'And while *Senora Perfectionata* doesn't actually work I have to say she is kept pretty busy interviewing the domestics, not to mention gardeners and pool men and other assorted minions. She does have a very real problem with employee turnover since it not only takes a strong back to keep up with her unceasing demand for perfection, it also takes a certain humility. It's not everyone who's willing to kiss her feet first thing in the morning and kiss her ring at noon, and it's awfully hard in this day of equality to find anyone willing to call her "Mistress of the Universe" and the Judge, "Massa Tracy".'

Honey was laughing so hard now she found it hard to speak. 'Well, we do have Mrs McCarthy who comes in every other week for five hours. She's been with us for the past three years since Teddy is not what you'd call difficult. And I help out a little. But Teddy does most of the work himself every morning. He says it's good discipline and a writer must have discipline and that orderliness of surroundings is essential to promote an orderliness of the mind, which is essential to the writer, too. But to tell the truth I think he's just naturally a neat person and I get the impression that my mother was *not* and he just got in the habit of picking up after her . . .'

She also had the impression that Teddy used his excessive housecleaning as an excuse to postpone facing his scary Smith-Corona monster, but she wasn't about to tell Sam and Babe that. That'd be a betrayal just as it would be if she disclosed her suspicion that when Teddy was scrubbing and scouring, he wasn't so much trying to eradicate dirt as the memories of past glories and broken dreams that haunted him.

When Babe and Sam asked to see her room she said they couldn't go upstairs because they might disturb Teddy. Instead she showed them the rest of the downstairs.

The dining room, with a bleached pine floor, was drenched, like the living room, with light and was simply furnished with a white pine table, a matching hutch and country French chairs with checked blue-and-white seat pads.

Then Honey took them into the library, intensely dark with its drawn window hangings of heavy satin. She flicked on a lamp to reveal a room furnished with an eclectic mix of bergeres striped in green-and-white satin, a plump sofa covered in grey velvet, a collection of enamelled boxes on a Napoleonic campaign table along with a bronze bust, with plants in porcelain cache-pots scattered here and there, a television incongruously perched on a painted tea table embellished with gilt, and two huge armoires, their doors standing open to disclose shelves filled with books.

'I guess you could call this our Parisian salon, although,' Honey laughed, 'I really haven't the slightest idea what a Parisian salon looks like. All I know is that after my mother left California to go back to France my father bought this house and this is the stuff he brought with him from their old house in the Malibu Colony. I guess Mimi liked it there because it reminded her of the French Riviera. There was a circle of French movie people, artists and writers living there and my mother had a kind of salon – you know, all the French people

397

hung out at their house, drank wine and talked about how much they missed Paris and everything. I don't like to ask Teddy too many questions about it because he gets too sad then . . .'

Babe and Sam sat transfixed with big eyes until Babe asked, 'But why *did* she go back to France?'

'I really don't know, but if she was leaving, where else would she go? It was her home where she had all her friends and Teddy said she adored her friends. Besides, Teddy says she never really liked California . . . *hated* Hollywood. She made one film here and hated the picture, too. She said American directors didn't understand European actresses and they only wanted to exploit her sexuality instead of interpreting it artistically.'

'It's too bad she didn't make a movie at our studio,' Sam said. 'I bet my father would have made an artistic movie that would have pleased her.'

Honey shrugged. For all she and Sam knew her mother could have made her picture for Grantwood Studio. 'Not taking anything away from your father, Sam, I doubt that *anything* would have pleased her here.'

Sam's eyes narrowed. 'So is *that* why she left? Because of her career? Because she didn't want to make movies here?'

'I don't know for sure, but if that was the case, she wouldn't have had to leave *us* – Teddy and me – behind,' Honey blurted angrily. 'Don't you understand? He would have picked me up and followed her to the ends of the earth!'

'Really?' Babe's dark eyes gleamed. 'But that's so romantic! Don't you think so, Sam?'

'You're incredible, Babe. How romantic can it be when obviously he *didn't* follow her. Why didn't he, Honey?'

'That's pretty obvious, too. Because she didn't want him to! Because she didn't believe in husbands and daughters!' Her voice had slowly been rising but now it dropped to a whisper as the tears started to roll down her cheeks.

'She only believed in lovers. *Still* does, as far as I know. I saw a picture in a magazine a couple of months ago at the dentist's office. It was of Mimi at a Beaux Arts Ball in Paris, surrounded by all these swains, the magazine called them. But they were all so sleazy-looking and my father is so—' she groped for a word, 'so *fine . . .*' She went over to the writing table in an alcove and picked up a photograph in a silver filigree frame. 'This is a picture of my father when he graduated from Princeton.'

'Wow!' Babe exclaimed. 'I had no idea he was so handsome. He looks like a movie star himself.'

'I think he looks like a poet,' Sam pronounced. 'And he does look like a fine person. Does he still look like this?'

'Of course. You'll see for yourself later.' She picked up another photograph. 'And this is he when he won the Pulitzer in Literature – the youngest person to win it ever!'

'*The* Pulitzer Prize?' Sam asked, incredulous.

'Of course, *the* Pulitzer Prize. How many do you think there are? He won it for his novel, *In Celebration Of Longing*. He won it the year after he graduated from Princeton and the book won a load of other literary prizes, too.'

She flipped open a big leather portfolio. 'It's all here. All his reviews and interviews . . . everything. They called him the Golden Voice of his generation. Everyone predicted he'd win the Nobel before he was thirty-five.'

'And did he?' Babe asked. 'I don't exactly keep track.'

Honey closed the portfolio. 'No, he didn't.'

'How come?' Babe looked as if she might cry.

'Really, Babe, that is a *very* dumb question,' Sam said, but she looked as if she might cry too.

Honey came downstairs to report that Teddy was still struggling at his typewriter. 'He apologizes but he said we should go ahead with dinner without him. So

399

I'm just going to warm up the *coq au vin* that he prepared this morning.'

'Not for me, Honey,' Babe said dolefully. 'I called my mother while you were upstairs. She says I can't stay for dinner because I was granted permission only to come over after school and that now I am trying to take advantage. That if staying for dinner was what I had in mind all along, I should have said so, but now it's too late.'

'Couldn't you get her to change her mind?'

'Oh no! My place is already set at the table,' Babe said as if *that* was an irreversible situation.

'How about you, Sam? You can stay, can't you?'

'Sure. Is your mother coming for you, Babe?'

'Oh, darn, we didn't discuss it. I guess she assumed one of Honey's parents would drive me home—'

'*One of my parents?* You didn't tell her that I lived just with my father?'

'Frankly, Honey, I didn't. I didn't say *anything*. I just let her assume whatever she assumed. I never told her who your mother is, either. I mean, if I told her your mother was the French actress who made all those sexy pictures, it would be all over. She'd never let me be your friend. All I actually told her was that your father was a writer and that he went to Princeton and that was sufficient for her to overlook his major shortcoming—'

'What shortcoming?' Honey's voice shook. *That he drank?*

'That his name is Rosen,' Babe said, ducking her head in embarrassment. 'It's not that she *hates* Jews, exactly. She says that they have their place in the scheme of things, only their place isn't in her living room. I'm sorry.'

'*You* don't have to be sorry. I understand. Neither of us exactly picked our mothers,' Honey said softly.

Actually, she was relieved. If she had to choose between the two, she preferred that her father was scorned as a Jew rather than as a man who drank. Teddy took pride in his Jewish heritage and he had taught her to take pride in it, and it mattered not at all how other people felt about that. But she couldn't bear for Teddy to be known as a man who had to find his solace in a bottle – that would take away from all the other wonderful things he was.

'But what am I going to do now about a ride? If I have to call her back and tell her I don't have a ride, she's going to ask me all kinds of questions and make me give her all kinds of explanations and – Do you think that your father could possibly tear himself away for a few minutes to drive me home? It wouldn't take more then twenty minutes or so.'

Honey was stricken. How could she explain that Teddy couldn't possibly drive anyone?

Sam looked from Babe's agonized face to Honey's, equally agonized. 'Oh damn!' she said. 'I just remembered. Daddy's bringing home someone for dinner tonight – an actor who's in that new soap they're shooting in Palm Springs. Daddy's thinking of casting him in a picture and he wants to know what I think of him – you know, his sex appeal quotient. So I have to go, after all. So, I'll just call and have Nora send Olaf to pick me up and then he can drop you off too, Babe.'

'You know, Sam, if you weren't so snotty, I'd kiss you,' Babe said, relieved.

'And if you weren't so snobby, Babe, I'd kiss you back.'

Honey was so happy the problem was solved she kissed them both.

39

Babe shoved her Beasley Chicken Supreme aside.

'It *does* look gross,' Sam agreed, nibbling at a spoonful

of peach yoghurt. 'You really should know better. They dump chicken à la king straight out of the can, plunk a canned peach-half on top and present it as gourmet cooking à la Beasley. You should have stuck to your usual cheeseburger. There's not much they can do to ruin a slice of cheese sitting on a skinny beef patty garnished with two limp slices of pickle, all slapped together on a soggy, untoasted bun.'

'I didn't want to become a slave to habit. But it doesn't matter. In fact, I may never eat again.'

'OK, what's bothering you?' Sam demanded and Honey urged, 'Yes, Babe, you'd better tell us.'

'OK, I have to tell you some time today so I might as well get it over with. We all *have* to go to my house. I've put it off for as long as possible, but Catherine insists on meeting *my little friends* and she's arranging her schedule today so she'll be free. So for once, Sam, don't give me a hard time and just say you'll come.'

'I wouldn't dream of giving you a hard time, Babe darling,' Sam said happily. 'Specially since I've been *dying* to meet Catherine the Great from the very first day we met. I'll just call home and tell them that Olaf doesn't have to pick us up.'

'Why do we have to go on the school bus? When we go to your house we never take the bus. Olaf always picks us up.'

'That's because I *never* take the school bus. The driver on the Bel-Air run wouldn't even recognize me. What diff does it make if we go on the bus or if Olaf drives us?'

'The difference is that it will impress Catherine if we arrive in a chauffeured Rolls and we need all the help we can get with the impressions. When I told her who your father was she was not what you'd call thrilled. She's *not* crazy about show-biz people and she already knows Nora – they bumped into each other at some function, and she *knows* Nora's active in the Democratic party and if there's anyone she frowns on more than a *Jewish person* or a *movie person*, it's a *Democrat*!'

'OK, if you think it makes me more acceptable to be the stepdaughter of a Democrat if I ride in a chauffeured Rolls rather than the stepdaughter of a Democrat who takes the school bus, we'll go in the Rolls. Believe me, I don't want to make any problems for you and if you want, I'll personally disavow the whole Democratic Party since at the moment I have no political affiliation. Will that help?'

'Oh, stop being such a smartass. This isn't funny. If she gets a bug up her butt about you two, that's it. Finis!'

'Yes, Sam, stop, it isn't funny,' Honey said.

But Sam was having too much fun to stop. 'I can see where *you* wouldn't think it's funny, Honey, you having a Jewish father. You're *already* on probation. Right, Babe? Do you think it would help if Honey disavowed the Jewish religion altogether? If she said that she was thinking of becoming a Buddhist? Or do you think that it would be even better if she disavowed her *father* altogether?'

'If you'll remember what I said before, Sam Smartass, it was that Catherine was willing to overlook Mr Rosen's Jewishness because he was a writer and a Princeton graduate. But ever since I told her that he won the Pulitzer, she's *impressed*, so Honey now has more going for her than *you* do.'

'I see,' Sam sighed heavily. 'Do you think it would help if I told her how many Oscars Daddy's flicks have won?'

'Uh-uh. The movie business, you know. *Déclassé.*'

'And it won't help that my mother was a real, live – well, once she *was* alive – debutante from Pasadena?'

'Uh-uh. We've already discussed that, remember?'

'I remember – *passé*. Well, in that case I'll just have to fall back on being my natural self and hope that she'll be impressed by my charm, intelligence and good breeding.'

'Oh, no! The *last* thing you want to do is act your natural self. Are you trying to sabotage the effort?' Then seriously, Babe added, 'You know what I think you should emphasize?'

'Tell me quick before I kill myself.'

'Talk about Grantwood Manor. About how grand it is, how large a property, how Nora imported most of the antiques from Britain and how you have that golf course and the reproduction of the pro shop at St Andrew's. Keep in mind the things that will do Catherine in every time – if there's something about the person that even *smells* of being landed gentry or of riding with the hounds, of being to the manor born.'

Sam chortled. 'Far be it from me to toot my steppie's horn, but if your mother ever got to *really* know Nora, she'd get a strong whiff of all those things. She's not the *real* stuff, but Nora can talk as good a game as any about being landed gentry – she was married to it, she lives in a grand manor house and in her time, she's even ridden with the hounds.'

Digesting this information Babe finally said, 'I think it would be best if all this was somehow revealed by you, but not in an obvious manner. Oh Sam, you *will* behave yourself, won't you?' Babe begged and Honey was relieved to hear Sam say: 'You can count on it, Babe. I promise to be as good as gold.'

Then Babe cried: 'Oh, I almost forgot! Remember, you're not to call me Babe in front of Catherine. It's Babette!'

'We'll do our best to remember,' Honey vowed, but now *she* was worried. What was she going to say if Catherine asked about her mother or what great literary work her father was currently writing? She could kind of fudge, but she didn't think she could out and out lie.

As they waited in front of the school for Olaf to show up, Babe briefed them again: 'Remember, no calling me Babe. And Honey, try *not* to say that your mother and father are divorced. In fact, don't mention your mother at all. I'm hoping that by the time Catherine learns who she is, she'll like you enough to overlook it. And actually there should be no reason for it to come up that your father is working on a screenplay and not a novel. Just

404

don't volunteer any info, just answer direct questions without disclosing anything damaging. And Sam, try not to talk about your father.'

'Will you relax? If the Inquisition gets too tortuous we do have an out – we can always kill ourselves, right?'

Babe nodded. 'Right. You're right.' But then a bright yellow Jaguar pulled up in front of the school and Nora got out and waved and Babe cried, 'I don't believe this! Honestly, I have no luck.'

'I'm sorry, Babe, I guess Olaf was busy,' Sam said as they walked to the car and Honey put her arm around her shoulder. 'Oh, come on, Babe, probably your mother won't even know who drops us off unless she's watching through the window.' And then Babe said, 'But Catherine is *always* watching through the window even when she isn't . . .'

Babe heaved a sigh of relief when Nora dropped them off at the kerb in front of the huge white colonial mansion and whizzed off. She'd been terrified that Nora might pull into the circular driveway and stop at the front door and then Catherine might have come to open the door herself and then Nora would have got out of the car to say hallo and even before they were inside, Catherine would have had her back up.

'You know, I think your mother got her states mixed up,' Sam crowed as they walked up the driveway.

'What are you drivelling about now?' Babe asked nervously.

'This house is Tara personified and Tara was in Georgia and I thought you Lees were supposed to be from Virgin-i-ay.'

'Really, you're *so* ignorant, Sam. If you *must* know, the style of this house is late-Georgian, an architectural statement that's found throughout the *entire* south-east.' And then she forgot herself and executed a quick time step, throwing out her arms and singing, '*And that's what I like about the South* . . .' Then she remembered that she

405

might be under observation and her eyes darted quickly and guiltily to the windows to see if any of the draperies were askew.

A maid answered the summons of the door chimes, Babe confessing that she didn't own a house key since she was not deemed responsible enough for this privilege. 'Your mother's waiting in the morning room, Miss Babette.'

As Babe led Honey and Sam down a long hall to the connecting wing, she whispered, 'My mother uses an employment agency that specializes in kidnapping assorted European types off the plane the minute they land at LAX. She says she prefers this type of foreigner because the Europeans speak better English than the locals, which you spell L-a-t-i-n-o which is spelled the same way you spell *prejudicio*.

'Incidentally, don't get uptight that we're on the way to the morning room. It's spelled like the first part of the day, not like the state you're in when someone dies. All it really is is the same room other people call a sun room or the den. You know, the room where you entertain guests you don't want to bother messing up the living room for.'

'I guess that tells us how we rate with quality folk like your mom,' Sam said. 'It also reinforces what I've always known about Nora – that she really *is* riff-raff. She'd mess up our living room for just about anybody, whether it's the president – well, probably not Nixon – or the L-a-t-i-n-o gardener if he has something he needs to talk over.'

'Do you realize that you just said something *nice* about Nora?' Honey laughed.

Sam was stunned. 'I guess I did. Well, I'll just have to watch my step in the future so that I don't do *that* again! Still, whatever Nora does, doesn't really count because she's a phoney, always putting on an act for effect.'

'Sh!' Babe shushed her abruptly. 'We're here,' and she ushered them into a conventionally attractive room. Even Sam, who would have liked to have been able to say later that it was tacky, couldn't honestly say so. Then, a surprisingly young and attractive and incredibly slender (as Babe had told them, her mother *was* a disciplined size four which meant a willingness to embrace starvation) Catherine Tracy graciously rose to greet them, and she was *smiling* though Babe had given them the impression that that was something she never did.

'How nice, finally, to meet Babette's new friends.'

Her dark, bright eyes – bright like a bird's, Honey thought – moved from Sam to Honey and back again, giving the impression that they were a high-powered, double-lensed, fast-speed camera recording pictures meant to last a lifetime.

'It's a pleasure to meet *you*,' Honey said.

'Oh yes,' Sam said quickly, 'a real pleasure.' Having promised Babe that she'd behave herself, she was determined to be as sweet as Honey

'Well, Babette? We're waiting—' Catherine smiled.

Sam and Honey looked quickly at Babe who seemed to have lost a couple of inches from her original five feet nothing. They, too, were waiting, though they had no idea what for, hoping that whatever it was, Babe would come through real fast so that they could all at least sit down.

But Babe was at a loss. 'Waiting for what?'

'Perhaps if you think about it, it will come to you.' Catherine was still smiling but there was steel in her voice and her eyes bore into Babe as she hung her head and stared at the flowered carpet as the seconds passed like hours.

'Oh, Christ!' Sam muttered under her breath and Catherine turned the burning spotlight of her eyes directly on Sam. 'Did you say something?'

'Oh no, something was just caught in my throat.' She made a big show of trying to clear it.

Catherine's eyes turned back to Babe and laughing sourly, she said: 'I suppose I must tell you then, Babette, if you have so forgotten your manners. We were waiting

407

for a proper introduction, isn't that so, girls?'

Honey gazed from the red-faced Babe to Catherine who was now waiting for an answer from her and Sam. Not knowing what else to do, she just smiled and, as surreptitiously as possible, prodded Sam with a sharp elbow to the ribs who said, 'Sure. Anything you say is fine with me.'

'But you introduced *yourselves*,' Babe mumbled. 'You said you were glad to meet them and they said they were glad to meet you. Isn't that an introduction?'

Catherine shook her head in dismay. 'My, my, what will your friends think? That Judge Tracy's daughter doesn't know that a proper introduction means an exchange of *names*?'

'Names?' Babe was so humiliated she wanted to cry. 'But they *know* your name. They know you're my mother and that my name is Tracy, and so is yours. And you know *their* names because I told you about them—'

The smile was gone. 'I think that perhaps it's time for you to make a decision, Babette. Do you wish to *argue* or do you wish to make the proper introductions? We're waiting for your decision . . .' She began to tap her foot.

Honey silently prayed that Babe would comply and get it over with and Sam silently prayed that Babe would tell Catherine to go fuck herself. After a few more moments, Honey's prayer was answered as Babe mumbled: 'Sam, Honey, I'd like you to meet my mother, Mrs Tracy.'

Honey immediately stuck out her hand fervently hoping that this would be the end of it, then Sam, taking her cue from Honey, followed suit. But Catherine did not extend hers.

'That's not *quite* right, Babette. You gave me no indication which young lady is Sam and which is Honey, and one always introduces a person by using their family name as well as their Christian name. And in *my* case, the same rule applies. It should have been, "I'd like

408

you to meet my mother, *Catherine* Tracy," relying on their judgement to address me as *Mrs* Tracy.'

'I don't *believe* this—' Sam burst out.

Catherine's gaze focused on Sam. 'Can't believe what, my dear?' Her tone was icy enough to freeze the blood and Sam looked at Honey whose eyes pleaded with hers to be *good* and then at Babe whose eyes just begged . . . *period.*

'I can't believe that Babe – I mean Babette – doesn't know how to make an introduction properly. But I really don't think it's her fault, Mrs Tracy. I believe that the responsibility lies with the schools we've attended.' It was a quick and probably adequate recovery, but now Sam was warming to her task, even beginning to enjoy herself.

'I know that *my* parents – my father, T.S. Grant, and of more recent date, my stepmother, Nora Grant – my poor mother who made her début at the Pasadena Grand Assembly having passed away when I was only a tiny baby – have always sent me to the best of schools. Before Beasley, I went to a fine school in the East, you know, and they relied on these schools to teach me at least the *basics* of proper etiquette, but unhappily—' she threw her hands up '– they've failed us all.'

Towering over the tiny Catherine, Sam reflected how – if she chose – she could probably floor the bitch with one left hook. But she smiled ingratiatingly. 'It's really too bad that we don't have women like yourself working in the private school system. I'm sure if we did, girls like us would surely know more about proper social techniques and—'

'Quite.' Catherine cut her off frigidly, putting an end to the monologue and dispelling any notion Sam might have had that she was successfully snowing her. 'Now that we have *that* settled, shall we sit and have some refreshments? I know how ravenous teenagers are when they come home from school. Babette, will you please advise Hilda that she may serve?'

'On the intercom?' Babe asked, frightened now to commit another *faux pas* that might incur another to-do. She had anticipated that the afternoon might go badly, but even in her wildest imaginations she hadn't visualized this nightmare.

'Of course, on the intercom! What did you think I had in mind? For you to go into the hall and *bellow* like a foghorn?'

'No, I—' She buzzed the kitchen and when the cook answered, she said, 'May I speak to Hilda, please?'

'For heaven's sake, Babette! *May I speak to Hilda please?*' Catherine repeated in cruel imitation. 'Will you just tell her to tell Hilda to bring in the tray?'

'Yes, ma'am,' Babe said quickly, unbearably rattled. Then she corrected herself: 'I mean, yes, Mother.'

But it was already too late. Sighing heavily, Catherine turned to Honey and Sam to include them in the lesson. 'I have told Babette repeatedly – only servants and tradespeople use the term *ma'am* as a form of address.'

Out of nervousness Honey almost said, 'Yes, ma'am,' to that but she was cut off in the nick of time by Sam who gave a little cry of discovery, 'Oh my! It just came to me who you look exactly like, Mrs Tracy! Nancy! Nancy Reagan!'

'You mean the governor's wife?'

Who do you think I mean – the fat lady in the circus? 'You could be her twin but, of course, you're much younger.'

'Well, as a matter of fact, I am,' Catherine beamed. 'By several years – at least ten. But I'm delighted that you think I resemble her. She's a charming woman and actually, a great friend. We often have lunch when she flies down from Sacramento for her weekly appointment with her hairdresser here in Beverly Hills. Poor thing! She says it's impossible to get a decent manicure in our state capital, which is a sorry state of affairs. Oh yes, we've been friends for years. Actually, the Judge and I had a lot to do with Ronnie being elected governor. We

410

worked hard to help get him there. How astute of you to notice the resemblance.'

'And that dress you're wearing. It's so much Mrs Reagan's style. I bet it was you who advised her what to wear when she was hitting the campaign trail!'

'Well, yes, I must admit I did,' Catherine allowed. 'But Nancy always had marvellous taste. Such a well-bred person even if she did appear in those less than tasteful films.'

'But as I was saying just last week to my father who's known for his integrity as a filmmaker that whatever Nancy appeared in she lent it a touch of class.' She shot a look of triumph at Honey. She had Catherine in the palm of her hand.

'Yes. But speaking of class, dear, don't you think that Sa-*man*-tha is nicer than Sam? Whatever is your stepmother thinking of to allow you to be called by a boy's name?'

Here we go again, Sam thought. Was there to be no end to the toadying necessary to satisfy this bitch?

'Well, Nora's British, you know. And she *was* married to landed gentry who rode with the hounds and always lived in very grand houses, as grand as Grantwood Manor, which, while Nora may have some weird political beliefs, she has decorated very tastefully with fine English antiques. But you know how it is, those old landed gentry think differently from us, the descendants of fine old *American* families.'

She took a breath and seeing how well she was doing with the bitch, she felt honour-bound to continue in the same vein. 'Personally speaking, I myself am fourth-generation native Californian and when I say native, I *don't* mean *Indian*. And Babette has told us how you're descended from General Lee! Wow, I can't tell you how much that impresses me. And I can't tell you how I cried at the sight of all those gallant Confederate boys lying on the ground by the thousands in that railroad depot scene in *Gone With The Wind*. Really, I cried at that even more

411

than I did when Rhett told Scarlett that frankly, he didn't give a – well, you know – damn. I guess you might even call me a southern sympathizer.'

When Catherine's laugh tinkled out pleasantly, Sam leaned back in the green wing chair, satisfied that she had won not only the day but the war. Then as Babe shot her a look of gratitude and Hilda set down a tray of assorted cookies and balloon glasses of iced, frothed orange juice, Sam looked to Honey as if to say, 'Well, I've done more than my share of brown-nosing. Now it's your turn.'

'Did you ever?' Sam gasped once she and Honey were on their way home in the Rolls in a state of hysterical laughter.

'But I could have *died* when you said that we'd stay for dinner,' Honey said.

'Well, I figured, how could we desert Babe at that late stage? Besides, did you think I was going to leave without seeing the Judge? Frankly, I thought I'd *shit* when you addressed him as, 'Your Honour, the Judge, sir.'

Honey writhed in embarrassment. 'By that time I was so crazy I didn't know *what* I was saying. Besides, I figured that way, I could cover all bases, not mess up too badly. I almost threw in, "Your Highness", for good measure.'

Suddenly Sam groaned. 'Do you realize we're going to have to do this over and over again because Catherine is going to want to keep tabs on us? It turned out OK today and once was fun, but repeats are going to get to be a real drag.'

'I guess it'll get better,' Honey said hopefully. 'Babe says that next time we'll be able to hang out in her room.'

She hoped so. Today she'd been lucky. While she *had* revealed that her parents were divorced, she hadn't revealed who, exactly, her mother was, or that her father seldom worked on his novel and made a precarious living

412

writing screenplays that seldom got made even when he completed one.

'Well, now that we've met Catherine and His Honour, the Pompous Bore, all that remains is to meet *your* father, Honey.'

'I know. He was so sorry that he wasn't able at least to say hallo when you were over, but he promised that next time he's not only going to spend a lot of time with us, but he'll prepare his specialty – *Bifteck hachè à la Lyonnaise.*'

'It sounds wonderfully French.'

Honey laughed. 'It's only ground beef with onions and herbs. Teddy says it's the herbs that make the difference.'

'Do you think we'll ever get to meet your mother?'

Honey sat very still. 'It's not likely.'

'I know! When we graduate the three of us will take a trip to Europe – a continental adventure where we'll each have sex with at least one man from each country! But first stop, Paris and Mimi L'Heureux!' She gripped Honey's hand. 'At the least she deserves to see what she's been missing and she's going to be one miserable lady when she does!'

'But how do you know she'll be miserable?'

'Oh Honey, how can she help it? You're the sweetest and isn't that exactly what I told Catherine the Asshole when she enquired why you're called Honey when your name is Honoria? Because you're as sweet as bee's honey and don't you ever forget it, no matter who else does . . .'

40

Sam had been talking about the Christmas Eve party the Grants were having ever since they'd first met in

September, and that Saturday afternoon was no exception.

'Even I must admit Nora knows how to throw a really groovy party. She says it all starts with the guest list – the right mix. First you invite a few brilliant people, but only a handful because if you have too many geniuses it makes the other guests feel like dorks and they get uptight and tight people make for a dull evening. Besides, geniuses are usually egotists who monopolize the conversation which isn't good either. But once you have your Einsteins, you invite *tons* of famous people because the other people who aren't famous only know they're at a great party if they can tell other people they rubbed kneesies with Mick Jagger.'

'Who wants to rub kneesies with Mick?' Babe giggled. 'I can think of better things to rub and it rhymes with Mick. But are you absolutely *positive* Nora's invited him?'

'I was just using him as an example but she probably has. She says the idea in inviting a load of celebs is that out of all the ones you *do* invite only a few accept. Most of them won't admit they have a free evening or that they'll even be *in town*. They'd rather stay home playing with themselves than let on they're not busy jetsetting around. And even out of those who say they'll be there, only half actually show because it's a power trip to leave you hanging or just plain ditch your pow-wow at the last minute for a groovier blast.'

It appeared that not only every worthy on the Hollywood scene was coming including the 'A' list, but even those who were having their own parties were planning on dropping in during the night, including the prize plum, Liz Taylor, who adored Nora for reasons Sam couldn't fathom except that they were both British and/or married a zillion times.

And what was more, Nora had engaged hired help for the night in addition to the caterer's staff so that all the regular staff could enjoy the party as a guest. 'But don't get too carried away thinking what a lovely person Nora really is to do that, because she's *not* doing it out of kindness. It's only that that's how things are done in merry old England. Everyone who lives and works on the estate comes to the manor house for a big party on Christmas Eve with presents for everyone. I guess she enjoys acting the Lady Bountiful who's nice even to the little people. And there *will* be presents for everyone at our party, but what does Nora care about money? She doesn't mind spending it as long as it's my father's money she's throwing around and not her own.'

'But it's his party, too, so that's fair,' Honey said.

'Well, of course it's *his* party. He's a wonderful host and even if Nora does have a knack for parties who would she be in this town without him? A nobody! And where would she throw her parties if she didn't have *our* house to throw them in? But wait till you hear what's on the menu—'

There would be Eastern oysters on the half-shell plus Oysters Rockefeller plus huge oysters from the northwest. 'They're big and fat and dipped in batter, then deep fried. Lushy. The caterer came over and we had samples.'

There'd also be baked salmon since everyone was dieting these days and wanted fish. But since Hollywood people loved *smoked* salmon so much – 'You know, lox, the kind you get at Nate and Al's . . .', there'd be pounds and pounds of that, too.

And there'd be caviar. All kinds and colours: black and grey, pink, red and gold. 'The caterers are going to set up a station where they're going to make the blinis right on the spot.' And there was going to be crab. 'King crab and crab salad, but who wants to eat crab salad when you can eat those tails? But that's only the beginning. There's going to be roast turkey and roast beefs plus roast goose since, I suppose, that's Englishy for Christmas and Nora makes sure to remind everyone constantly how British she is. I guess that's why she invited that colony of

415

British actors – David Niven, Roger Moore and Sean Connery—'

'Yikes!' Babe practically swooned. 'I *adore* Sean Connery! I think he's the sexiest! But you know, Sam, I don't get it. Sure, it's going to be a wonderful party and personally I can't wait, but you're always having parties at Grantwood, so why are you so excited about this one?'

'Because it's Christmas Eve, you little old asshole. Every other year for as long as I can remember I've been away at school or at other girls' homes. This is the first time I've been home for Christmas in years and years.'

Then she burst into tears and Honey was shocked. Sam just wasn't the crying kind. 'Oh Sam, what is it?'

'It's just that sometimes I miss my mother *so*!'

Honey was silent – she knew exactly what Sam meant. But Babe said, 'How can you miss a mother you never knew?'

'I always miss *not* knowing her, but especially at Christmas. All those Christmas Eves I wasn't even home. If my mother had been alive, I would have been.'

Babe and Honey said nothing then, but they didn't understand why her father hadn't made sure she came home for the holidays. Then Sam burst out in a fresh torrent of weeping. 'Hubie,' she gasped between sobs.

'What about him?' Babe asked, puzzled. While Sam mentioned him once in a while, she never really talked about him at length except to say he was so sweet.

'What about him? I'll tell you what about him! I begged Nora to let him come home for Christmas, but she's so mean, she won't even talk about it . . . won't even consider it.'

'She must have her reasons,' Honey offered. 'Besides, it's not like he's a child. He's a grown man.'

'So what?' Sam sniffled. 'He's still *her* child.'

* * *

416

The party was only hours away, but Honey was still trying to talk Teddy into going to the party with her, instead of just dropping her off and going back home to be alone.

'No, sweetheart, you go and have a wonderful time and don't worry about me. I'll be just fine.'

'But *why* won't you go? You're invited.'

'Yes, and it was very nice of the Grants to include me in their invitation, but they're your friends, baby, not mine.'

'But they all want you to come. Sam says she adores you and that after her father, you're the sweetest man she knows.'

That made Teddy laugh. 'And while I don't know if *adore* is quite the word I'd use, I certainly like Sam very much. After you, she's the sweetest girl I know. She and Babe.'

'And Nora said she's dying to meet you, that she read *Celebration of Longing* and loved it so much that even after she finished reading it, she couldn't get it out of her mind.'

He smiled his gently ironic smile. 'And did she say that she read *Night's End*, too, and couldn't get *it* out of her mind?'

'No,' Honey admitted reluctantly. 'If she did read it, she never mentioned it . . .' She dropped her eyes unable to bear the pain she saw in her father's. She knew that even now, years after, her father still mourned the publication of his second novel which had been greeted with devastating criticism. Possibly he mourned its demise as much as he mourned the loss of his Mimi. It was so unfair that he had so much pain to bear, he who was so sensitive to everyone else's.

'Teddy, what's the real reason you won't go tonight?'

'Honey, it's settled. I sent my regrets.'

But Honey persisted. 'Is it that you'll be uncomfortable because you won't know anyone there? If it is, you don't have to worry – there's going to be over five hundred guests there and at least half of them will be movie people. And Nora's invited some literary people from the East. Even William Buckley! Though he's a conservative, Nora says she loves his mind. And there'll be guests from Europe, too. I bet some of them will be people you know from Paris or the Riviera. You're *bound* to know *some* people there!'

He smiled sadly. 'Maybe that's the problem – too many people I've known too well. People who'd rather run away than talk to me. They're afraid that what ails me is contagious and maybe they're right. Maybe failure *is* catching.'

'Oh please, don't say that, Daddy!'

He looked sad now, regretting his words, knowing how they hurt her. She could tell from his expression that he wished he could take the words back but it was he who'd told her that words – once spoken – were irretrievable.

It was when she was in the seventh grade and they had had one of their rare disagreements. She'd been wearing a miniskirt to which he objected as *too* mini and she told him that all the girls in her class were wearing them that short. 'It's the style,' she'd said. Then he told her about the time when he and Mimi had had words about a dress *she* wore – one of her sex kitten dresses, Honey guessed – that he thought too extreme and it became clear that he was telling her the story to make a point how style reflected how a person felt about herself.

But suddenly in the middle of the telling he forgot the story and said morosely, 'It's a funny thing about words. When you put them down on a page, they can be eradicated – crossed out, erased, wiped out with that little bottle of white stuff, but when you speak the words *out loud* to someone else – someone you care about very much, you can't take them back no matter what. No matter how sorry you are, no matter how hard you ask to be forgiven, no matter how strongly the other person says they've already forgotten them, they're indelibly there, imprinted on the brain for ever . . . or at least until death wipes them clean.'

Then she'd wondered to whose words he was referring, his or Mimi's, or even if his theory was sound. But then was then and now was now and now she believed the theory to be true. She only wished it wasn't, since she didn't think she would ever forget what he had just said – his words were already imprinted on her brain to conjure up pictures of his humiliation – people running from him in horror and now she certainly couldn't continue to urge him to go to the party where he might be shunned as a leper . . .

Now, it would be hard enough for *her* to go to Grantwood Manor tonight and not look at each and every guest and wonder if he or she were one of the people who would dodge Teddy as if he were the bearer of a killing disease – her sweet father, who was their better by far, every last one of them.

When she came downstairs in a black, off-the-shoulder jersey with a short skirt, Honey thought Teddy might joke that she was almost out of skirt or tactfully suggest that perhaps a bit too much shoulder was exposed. But all he said was that sometimes it was a shock to him to realize that she was already a woman, and a breathtakingly beautiful woman at that.

'But who can believe you? You say that to me every day of my life even when I'm just going to school in my uniform!'

'Well, did you ever stop to think that it's true every day of your life? But I do have a question. Why are you wearing black to a party? I know I'm out of things, but it seems you're a bit young to be wearing black.'

'First I'm a beautiful woman and now I'm too young to be wearing black? If you must know I was going to wear red, but Sam said red is Babe's colour as green is hers and black is mine. That sometimes I *could* wear white but for real glamour and sophistication, I must always

419

wear black. Especially for those occasions when I want to look my most dangerous.'

'And tonight you want to look your most dangerous? I don't think I like the sound of that.'

Though she knew he was joking now she also knew he dreaded the time she'd start dating. Because it would mean that she was growing up, the sooner to leave him, or did it have something, as usual, to do with Mimi? Was he afraid that she'd be like her mother, a hot number, a woman men took one look at and, as Sam said, immediately took their dick in hand?

But if that were the case, Teddy had nothing to worry about. The last thing she wanted was to be a hot number, a sex kitten, a woman who provoked sexy images and leery jokes. The truth was that though a lot of the girls she knew were already dating and some of them had been since they were twelve, she wasn't at all eager for it. For that matter, neither was Sam, even though she talked about sex a lot and with her usual 'know it all' manner that drove Babe crazy, talked about it as if she were an expert on the subject.

Actually only Babe was eager for the dating which was ironic considering that Catherine was, as Babe proclaimed, not only the original ice cube to come out of a freezer, but the original virgin they'd named the state after . . .

'I don't think you have to worry about anything dangerous happening tonight, Daddy dear. *Most* likely there will be only older men at the party. Too old for me to even talk to. I wouldn't even know what to say to them.'

'Well, good. There's only one thing you *should* say to them – no! If you remember that, you'll do just fine.'

She knew he was just teasing, but she laughed tearfully, feeling suddenly emotional and strange – as if she were swelling up with the love she felt for him. 'I'll remember, Teddy. I'll never do anything that will make you unhappy.'

420

'No, don't promise me that, Honey. Promise me only that you'll never do anything that will make *you* unhappy . . .'

'But they're one and the same.'

He smoothed the silky hair that fell from a middle parting nearly to her waist in glorious perfection. 'You think so now – that they're one and the same, but you won't always.'

'What am I to do then?' she asked mournfully.

'You must follow your heart.'

'But what if I follow *my* heart and break yours?'

He thought about it. *Is he thinking about Mimi?* 'You'll still have to follow your heart wherever it leads you.'

But he'd done that and look where it had led him . . .

Then to break the spell of the air of melancholy that filled the room, Teddy said with a laugh, 'Would you mind if I asked you just one question? After all, if I'm to write screenplays that work, I need to know how things work in the real world these days. Tonight's party at fabulous Grantwood Manor with its more than five hundred guests is a formal occasion as well as a dangerous one, right?'

She laughed. 'Yes . . .'

'Then would you mind telling me why you're wearing a really short dress instead of a formal, long gown?'

'Oh,' she said, relieved that it wasn't a harder question, 'that's because of Babe. Her parents are letting her go to the party only for a little while, just to drop off her Christmas presents for Sam and the Grants mostly, so she won't be wearing a real formal, so Sam and I decided we wouldn't either so that Babe wouldn't feel out of place.'

'I think that was very considerate of you two. Now if you're ready to go, let's do it,' he said, suddenly impatient.

'I'll call Babe to be ready. We're picking her up.'

'OK, hop to it while I get the car out of the garage.' And he was out of the kitchen door. Then Honey realized that he'd been edgy for a while, eager to leave so –

what? So he could come back home and begin his own private celebration?

She knew he hadn't had a drink all day just so he'd be in condition to drive her, just as – excepting for the first time Babe and Sam had visited – he made sure to be presentable on those days her friends came over, presentable enough to talk to them and drive them home if necessary.

Still, before she went to the phone to call Babe, she tucked a note from the housekeeping money into her purse so that when she was ready to leave the party she could call a cab and not bother anyone for a ride home, especially since Nora had invited the entire staff as guests, which meant Olaf couldn't be expected to drive her home.

Honey rang the Tracys' bell – Catherine insisted that anyone picking up Babette had to come to the door instead of merely honking the car horn – while Teddy waited in the car with the engine running. But when Babe opened the door she didn't have her coat on. She whispered urgently, '*They* want to meet your father. Can you ask him to come in?'

Honey looked anxiously at her father sitting in the car. To ask him to meet the Tracys now with his nerves already jangly was really a bit much to ask. 'But we'll be late.'

'It'll just take a minute. Honey, please! She's *insisting*! She'll be offended if he doesn't—'

'Oh, let her be. I'm sick of – Oh God, Babe, he's not even dressed. He's not wearing a jacket – just jeans and a sweatshirt and then she'll say something about that, too.'

'Please, Honey!' Babe was practically jumping up and down in her anxiety.

But then Teddy was standing in the doorway. 'Is there a problem, ladies?'

'Well, yes, there is, Mr Rosen. My mother and

father are *dying* to meet you, but Honey says there's no time. But my mother will be *so* disappointed and – please, Mr Rosen!'

Teddy put his arm around Honey. 'It will be all right, sweetheart. It won't make a bit of difference if you get to the party a few minutes late. At these big parties people come and go at all hours and no one knows the difference.'

His chin was set resolutely – heroically, Honey thought – and his soft brown eyes reassured her.

A half-hour later both Tracys saw them to the door. Catherine said, 'I'm so glad that we had this occasion to chat,' and the Judge harrumphed, 'Yes, indeed,' and Teddy said, 'It's been my pleasure,' managing to sound as if he meant it. Then Catherine said, 'I'll remind you again, Babette, that you are not to drink any wine or eggnog with spirits in it, and that the cab I'm sending for you will be at the door at nine-thirty sharp, so you just make sure you're there ready and waiting,' and Babette said, 'Yes, Mother.'

Then when they were in the car heading towards Sunset, Babe said, 'You were *so* super, Mr Rosen, thank you!'

Teddy laughed. 'That's a dubious compliment. Did you think I *wouldn't* be and what did I do that was *so* super?'

'Well, my mother does have that way of interrogating people, sort of like in this movie I saw on TV with the Gestapo asking these frightened Jews a lot of questions.'

Honey could see Teddy's hands tighten on the wheel as they turned left on to Sunset. Still, he said, 'That was OK, Babe. Parents *should* be concerned about the people whose homes their children visit. It only shows how precious they think you are and I can understand that.'

'You always put things so beautifully, Mr Rosen. I just wish—' she sighed heavily.

423

But it wasn't the questions about Teddy's Jewishness that had set Honey's heart to racing, but those about his career. What right did the nosy Catherine and the judge think they had to do *that*? They really were insufferable. Teddy would have been right if he had just told them both to go to hell!

But he hadn't. He hadn't even accepted the judge's offer of a drink. All he'd done was answer all their questions in his soft and sincere way, a complete gentleman, which should have shamed them both but didn't, since the judge wasn't a gentleman and Catherine was no gentlewoman.

'You know, I could just kill myself that I can only stay at this party for an hour and a half. Sam says Mick Jagger is coming, and Paul Newman! Do you believe that, Mr Rosen? That they are *really* coming to the party?'

Though Honey laughed, Teddy didn't. 'I'm sorry, Babe, but I can't answer that one. It's been my experience that you can never tell about these things . . . about who will and who won't . . . really come to the party . . .'

Sam, in bright green taffeta, came running over to them the minute they stepped into the hall which had the biggest Christmas tree Babe or Honey had ever seen, its branches reaching to the vaulted ceiling, and hung with gold balls, silver stars and red and green velvet bows.

'Where have you two been?' Sam accused. 'The party began almost an hour ago and I hate to tell you this, Babe, but Mick Jagger has already come and gone . . .'

'Oh, no!' Then, 'Are you telling the truth, Sam, or are you just being mean?'

'Of course I'm telling the truth! Do you think I would tell a lie or be mean on Christmas Eve? Really!'

'I think I'm going to kill myself right now!'

'Well, don't do it here. People are coming and going and we don't want them to get the wrong idea. If you want to kill yourself, you'd better go upstairs.'

'It's all my mother's fault. She made Honey's father come in and talk and – Oh, why am I so cursed?'

'Honey, your father!' Sam suddenly wailed. 'Is he still out there? I thought maybe Nora would go out and persuade him to come in for a while. I wanted him to meet my father.'

Honey shook her head. 'He's gone. Besides, he wasn't dressed for a party. In fact, those security guards down at the gate didn't even want to let him drive us up to the door. They said they'd valet us up, but Teddy insisted on his rights. He told them I wasn't allowed to ride with anyone but him.'

'Look,' Babe said, squirming out of her coat and handing it to the waiting maid. 'I've only got an hour and a half so let's get rolling. I can't waste my time standing around. I can talk to you two any old time. Where do I stick these presents?' she demanded. 'And where's the food and where's the dancing, and above all, where are all the hot celebs?'

'You put the presents under the Christmas tree in the living room,' Sam said as if she were talking to a small child. 'And you'll find the buffet in the dining room where you'd *expect* to, with several bars set up throughout the house just in case that's of interest.' She rolled her eyes. 'And the dancing is in the conservatory where the two bands are alternating. As for stars, you'll just have to take your chances going from room to room. They're all over the house. Even in the bathrooms, and if you're lucky, maybe you'll even find a couple of them upstairs making out,' she giggled. 'Oh, and in case it turns you on I just saw Henry Kissinger in the library talking to the political types.'

'Kissinger? Catherine will never believe this! Maybe I should call her and let her know and then maybe she'll let me stay an extra hour?' She thought it over. 'No, I guess not, so I might as well not waste what little time I do have.'

'Also, Babe, there's mistletoe hanging over every

425

doorway. As a matter of fact, I kissed Mick under the mistletoe right there!' Sam gloated, pointing. 'I nailed him just as he was practically out the door.'

Babe went pale. 'But why didn't you tell us right away the minute we walked in?'

'I didn't want to break your heart.'

'Did you take him by surprise?'

'Kinda.'

'So what did he do?'

'He kissed me back.'

Then Babe was off and running with Sam and Honey frantically running after her trying to keep up, pushing through the assorted groups, dodging waiters balancing silver trays of champagne and waitresses offering canapés.

'Babe, you maniac, what do you think you're doing?' Sam shouted at her back.

'Trying to make up for lost time!'

When she grabbed a glass of champagne off a waiter's tray as it crossed her path on her way to the dining room, Honey blanched. 'Oh God, what will Catherine say about Babe drinking champagne? She forbade her to even taste eggnog.'

'She can't say *anything* if she doesn't know, silly, and who's going to tell her?'

'She's sure to have one of those machines that test your breath at the front door when Babe walks in. We have to make sure she doesn't take another glass!'

Then, Honey was stopped by a couple conversing in a mixture of French and English who demanded to know if she was related to the French actress, Mimi L'Heureux, since she looked exactly like her. When Honey admitted to being Mimi's daughter they practically detained her by force and called over some of their friends to take a look at Mimi's *baby*.

'*Some* baby!' seemed to be the consensus of opinion.

By the time Honey got away from them, she'd lost sight of Sam and Babe and went to look for them at the buffet tables. Probably, Babe was trying to stuff herself on as many goodies as possible in record time so that she could get on to the next activity with an even higher priority – stargazing.

But then she was stopped again. This time it was Sam's father who put an arm around her to draw her into the group with whom he was having an animated discussion, introducing her as Teddy Rosen's beautiful daughter, and one man, looking pointedly at her breasts, said she was indeed a beauty. A woman, thin to the point of emaciation, snickered and another man, with a glint in his eye, drawled, 'I know old Teddy. What's he up to these days, Honeychile?'

When Honey replied that he was working on both a screenplay *and* a new novel, the man snickered, and the woman smirked, and Honey could feel her face glow with heat. She wanted to toss off a clever retort of some kind that would wipe the smirks off all their collective faces, but she couldn't think of anything and she looked to TS to say *something*. *If* only he would.

Even though he doesn't actually know Teddy, couldn't he say, 'He's a brilliant writer', or words to that effect?

But he just kept chewing on an unlit cigar, silent.

But then Nora came rushing up to give Honey a big hug. She took a quick questioning look at Honey's flushed face then another at the faces surrounding them, and immediately twinkled, 'Has everyone met our Honey? She's *such* a love. You all must have heard of her father, F. Theodore Rosen, the novelist? He writes such beautiful books. And why wouldn't he? He's an absolutely beautiful man.'

Honey could have shouted with gratitude. *How did she do it?* Sam was right about her – she *was* a witch . . . but one of the good kind.

'Run along now, Honey, and have some *real* fun instead of hanging around these fuddy-duddies,' Nora suggested. 'I saw Babe and Sam boogieing up a storm in the conservatory.'

Honey flashed her a look of appreciation, mumbled a

427

'Nice to meet you', to the others, unable to suppress her instinct to say the right thing even though she didn't want to.

Honey spent most of the next hour nervously keeping track of the time for Babe since Babe seemed to have lost all interest in doing so herself. After one turn around the floor slow-dancing with a tall, dark and suave older man who held her too tightly – one of those men to whom her father would have insisted she say, 'No!' – Honey excused herself to search out Sam whom she found in the library delivering a heated monologue about the sorry state of the art of film making in the Soviet Union to a short, blond middle-aged man who seemed more interested in trailing his fingers across Sam's nearly bare back than in Soviet films.

'I can't find Babe!' Honey wailed and the cab her mother's sending for her will be here in five minutes!'

'Oh, shoot! I saw her go to the powder room off the living room about ten minutes ago. Do you think she's still in there throwing up or something? She did have an awful lot of lobster Thermidor though I told her not to make a pig of herself. And she had *two* more glasses of champagne.'

'Why did you let her?'

'Let her? What did you expect me to do, wrestle her to the ground? We better go check the powder room.' Slapping away at the man's hand, Sam jumped to her feet and snapped, 'Dirty old man,' and he muttered, 'Cock-teasing bitch!' but they were already off and running.

Sam pounded on the locked door while Honey called, 'Babe, are you in there? Your taxi is going to be here any second!'

They heard Babe inside, giggling.

'Babe, what's going on in there?' Honey asked and Sam commanded, 'Unlock this door this minute!'

'Who do you think you are giving orders around

428

here – my mother?' Babe yelled back and then there was more giggling.

'Babe, you better come out this minute or your mother's going to kill you!' Honey implored and Sam threatened, 'If you don't open this door, I'm calling somebody to break it down!'

'Oh, all right!' Then there was a few seconds of fumbling around with the lock and then they were astonished to hear a distinctly male voice cursing under its breath.

'I could understand if it was Warren Beatty in there with you, but one of the guys from behind the bar? That has to be the tackiest thing I ever heard of and you deserve any punishment the Judge doles out,' Sam lectured as she and Honey buttoned Babe into her coat since the cab driver waiting for her had been threatening to leave for ten minutes. 'Would you mind telling me exactly *what* you were doing in there?'

'That's for me to know and you to find out,' Babe smirked just before she threw up, and Honey moaned and Sam said, 'I better go and get Nora to clean up this mess one way or another.'

Nora explained to Catherine that there seemed to be something wrong with the lobster Thermidor – several people had been taken ill – and they'd put Babette to bed in Sam's room and called the doctor who said she'd be fine by morning. 'So I thought that if it's agreeable with you, we could just let her sleep and bring her home first thing tomorrow.'

Catherine could hardly say no.

Then Nora suggested that Honey sleep over as well, so Honey went to the phone to call Teddy, but when after seven or eight rings he still hadn't picked up, she hung up thinking that she *had* to go home to see that he was all right.

'No answer. I guess he went out. He told me he

might and told me to take a cab in case I didn't get him in.'

'So you'll call him later and tell him you're sleeping over. He won't mind, right?' Sam said, matter-of-factly.

'No, I think I'd better go home now. I wouldn't want him to come home late and not find *me* home before I could reach him to tell him that I wouldn't be. He'd worry. So I'll just call a cab like he told me to.'

'No,' Nora said. 'I don't want you taking a cab to an empty house at this hour. It's not a good idea.'

'But I don't want to bother Olaf. He's a guest tonight.'

'We're not going to bother Olaf. I'll drive you home.'

'But you can't leave your party.'

'I won't be gone long and this party will get along fine without me for a little while. Besides, I can use the fresh air. And I'll let you in on a little secret. The real fun of a party is *before* the party – the anticipation . . .'

'Always?' Honey asked, disappointed.

'Of course not *always*. Sometimes you get lucky and the party is even better.'

'Thanks so much for the ride.' Honey opened the car door ready to bolt, her house key already gripped in her hand, but Nora said, 'Wait, I'll go in with you in case your father's not home yet so that you don't walk in alone.'

'Oh, there's no need,' Honey said hurriedly. 'See, some of the lights are on. He must be home now.'

'But doesn't he leave a few lights on when he goes out?' Nora got out of the car. 'I'll just check. It will only take a second and *I'll* feel much better.'

Honey opened the door and called out, 'Daddy?'

Oh, if he would only answer, Honey prayed. Then Nora would be satisfied that everything was OK and leave without coming in. But there was no reassuring answer.

She sighed. There was no sense going from room to room with Nora to check for an intruder. There were only two rooms Teddy would be in – downstairs in the library or upstairs in his bedroom-study – and she might as well get it over with by checking out the library since Nora wasn't about to let her go upstairs by herself.

'Maybe he's home and just fell asleep in the library, reading or something . . .' She could only hope that if Teddy had passed out, it was in some non-compromising position. But then just as she was reaching for the knob, the door opened and Teddy blinked to see them standing there. 'I thought I heard you come in, sweetheart,' he said a *little* thickly, appearing only a *little* confused. Honey was somewhat relieved. It could have been worse.

'And this must be the wonderful Nora of whom an angel sings.'

'Daddy!' Honey protested, embarrassed.

'But you have, sweetheart. You have not damned her with faint praise.'

Nora laughed, offering her hand. 'Yes, I'm Nora Grant and I'm pleased to meet you, Mr Rosen.'

Teddy smiled his sweetest smile, the smile that could break your heart, Honey thought, when he looked unbearably young and boyish. 'You must call me Teddy. And you, Honey Bunch, shouldn't have bothered Mrs Grant to drive you home. You should have called—'

'Oh, it was no bother,' Nora said quickly. 'Actually, I was glad to get away from all the noise for a bit and I'm glad we had this opportunity to meet. But now I best be getting back. I hope we get to know you better, Teddy. Will you come to dinner with Honey some time soon?'

'I'd be delighted,' he said and she said, 'Good. I'll ring you then. Good night.'

Teddy made a sweeping bow. 'Good night, fair lady, and a Merry Christmas to one and all . . .'

41

When Honey and Babe stepped off the schoolbus, Sam was eagerly waiting for them in the parking lot. 'Guess what *I* have? A half-lid of the *really good* stuff,' she whispered.

'What good stuff?' Honey asked before turning away to talk with a girl from her French class, but Babe chirped, 'A half-lid! Wow! How good is this good stuff?'

'Keep it down! The whole school doesn't have to know—'

'Right. How good is good?' she asked *sotto voce*.

'Acapulco Gold!'

'Where'd you get it?'

'From Roberto.'

'Who's Roberto?'

'One of that tree cutting crew that was working at Grantwood last week. He said it's *real* Acapulco Gold and every bit as good as *Panama Red*.'

'Panama Red! I guarantee you this tree snipper never *saw* Panama Red, much less smoked it,' Babe scoffed loudly.

'Sh! How do you know he never smoked it?'

'Because there is no such thing as Panama Réd. They sing that song about it and you hear kids rap about it as if it were some mythical experience, like dying and going to heaven, but when you pin them down, it's never *they* who smoked it but somebody else. It's a fantasy potheads only dream about. But Acapulco Gold's fine. Where have you got it stashed?'

'In my purse.'

'Oh, my God! You're carrying two fingers of grass

432

in your purse? Are you crazy?' Babe screeched.

'OK, Babe. If you can't keep your voice down, forget the whole thing, OK? We won't say another word about it.'

'But suppose it fell *out* of your purse? They'd throw *you* out of school and Catherine would never let me talk to you again. You should have left it in your room. Nora doesn't go through your drawers like Catherine does mine and then we could have smoked it after school. But since you *didn't* and you *do* have it with you, when do we go for it?'

'OK, Sam, let's see the colour of your grass,' Babe demanded as they hunked down on the cement floor at the back of the furnace in the utility room which Sam had deemed safe – the janitorial staff took their lunch at noon, too. 'Since we're short on time you'd better roll just one joint.'

'Yes, one will be plenty.' Honey was as nervous about smoking dope for the first time as she was about being caught.

'Of course we're going to roll only one joint! What did you think?' Sam asked indignantly. 'That we were going to blow the whole bag in one sitting?' She took a packet of rolling paper and a plastic sack from her handbag along with a small box of wooden matches. 'This shit didn't come cheap. You have no idea what I had to do to get it.'

'Oh?' Babe smirked. 'You mean no cash changed hands?'

'No, but as my father always says, there's no such thing as a free lunch.'

'Oh Sam, you didn't—' Honey began but Sam cut her off. 'You don't want to know the details, Honey Bunch, or you won't enjoy one puff of the old magic dragon. Suffice to say that Roberto has this nasty-looking wart on the tip of his—'

Honey covered her ears. 'I thought you weren't going to give any details.'

'I was *going* to say: on the tip of his *nose*. OK, who's rolling?'

'I've *never* rolled a joint,' Honey said in a rush.

'Didn't they teach you anything at all at that school in Beverly Hills? At Miss Devon's School they had a special course in the refinements of modern living and the first refinement was how to do drugs with panache,' Sam giggled. 'But here,' she shoved the bag and papers at Babe, 'since you're such an eager beaver, you do the honours.'

'No, it's OK,' Babe pushed the bag and papers back. 'The honour should be yours since it *is* your shit and you earned it by doing things that would turn a weaker sister's stomach queasy. Besides, due to your superior education, you know how to do it with panache and *we* can do with no less.'

'Well, to tell the truth, I never *did* get the hang of it,' Sam confessed. 'I always bought my dope by the stick. Loose joints, as they say in the East.'

'Sure.' Babe winked at Honey. 'We understand how it is.'

'Look, why don't we postpone this whole thing until we have more time?' Honey proposed. 'We can do it *after* school.'

'Where?' Sam demanded, stalling for time, not sure she was ready for this big moment after all.

'Look, we're wasting time,' Babe said. 'Or is it that you're really chicken, Sa-*man*-tha?'

'Me?' Sam was outraged. 'I'm the one who sacrificed everything I hold dear to get the damn stuff!'

'If we postpone it we still have time to go and have some yoghurt or something,' Honey urged eagerly.

'No,' Babe said resolutely. 'For everything there's a time and *this* is the time and we're going to do it *now* even if Sam won't admit that she never rolled a joint in her entire life and probably never smoked one, either.'

Sam made half-hearted protests while Babe carefully shook out a little of the pot on to a page ripped from

434

her notebook and groaned, then recklessly dumped the entire contents of the bag. 'Would you look at *that*?'

Sam stared at the marijuana. 'What about it?'

'*What about it*? Did you or did you not say that this grass went by the name of Acapulco Gold?'

'OK, Babe, spit it out. What are you getting at?'

'What I'm getting at is that for a girl who took a refinement course in drugs, you sure got taken, girl.'

'I gather you're making a point but it escapes me.'

'Take a look at this shit. Obviously you've never seen any before. *Shit* is exactly what it is! At least *half* seed and stems! Whatever you did to get it, you grossly overpaid.'

'No, I didn't! Mostly I just let the crud touch me but no place important and when he took his own cruddy joint out of his cruddy jeans I insisted he put it back immediately.'

'Well, don't feel *too* bad,' Babe consoled her. 'You didn't make *such* a bad deal. Out of this mess we should be able to make a few cruddy joints of our own.'

Then she quickly rolled one, lit up, took a deep drag inhaling sharply before passing it to Sam who did exactly what Babe did before passing it to Honey, who gingerly took a puff and, trying to imitate Sam and Babe, sucked in her breath for so long that she grew dizzy and thought she'd pass out.

'Easy does it,' Babe said, taking the joint back, and they repeated the process until they were down to a tiny, sticky roach which Babe wrapped in a tissue. 'We'll save it for another time when we have a toothpick handy,' and began to roll a fresh joint. 'Nice and fat this time,' she murmured happily though Sam, more *numb* than high, protested, 'No use getting carried away, Babe. Why don't we save some thrills for another day?' And Honey, feeling dizzier every second and sick to her stomach, seconded the motion.

'Don't be silly. You two are just green but you'll see! The more you smoke the better it gets.'

435

'We only smoked three joints between us which comes
down to only one apiece so if we share one more that's
only one and a third each.' Then Babe merrily began to
roll a fourth when the bell rang signalling that lunch-hour
was over.

'Oh damn, isn't that inopportune?' Sam greeted the
bell with relief as Honey staggered to her feet.

But more inopportune was the appearance of Dean
Perkins who was escorting several members of Beasley's
Board of Directors to see for themselves how seriously
antiquated the furnace was and how desperately the
school needed a new one.

Even before they were dismissed from the Dean's presence with a warning that they were on probation and
that the next infraction of the rules would bring instant
expulsion, letters were on their way to their parents via
messenger service.

'God, if this had happened at any other school I would
have had at least a day before Catherine got the fucking
letter,' Babe moaned. 'But does Beasley use the US
mail like a normal school? No, they have to use the
Hollywood Star Messenger Service as if they were some
hot-shot movie actor or some big mogul. Maybe I
should just kill myself now.'

'You can come home with me,' Honey offered. 'Teddy
probably won't even answer the door when they deliver
the letter, then the messenger will slip the letter through
the slot and I'll probably see it before Teddy does. I'll be
able to prepare him for the shock before I give it to him
to read.'

'You'll get it before he does and you'll still let
him read it?' Babe demanded. 'Are you crazy?'

'I *have* to let him see it. Otherwise, it would be like
cheating. But it'll be all right even if he reads it before
we get there. He won't yell at us, I promise. The most
he'll do is tell us a story that has a moral to it.'

'Better still, come home with me,' Sam urged. 'Nora's in New York doing an interview with Gloria Steinem for this new magazine *Ms.* For some dumb reason they think Nora's some kind of positive feminist figure which is ridiculous. She's done nothing but live off men her whole life. And my father won't even bother to open the stupid letter. He didn't get to own a major studio by wasting his valuable time.'

'No, I better go home and face the music. I only hope the music that's playing isn't "She's a Lady". Catherine gets really worked up about me *not* being a lady and she's not going to look on this little escapade as very ladylike behaviour. But just in case dear old Dad decides to send me to a home for delinquent girls, you'll be sure to visit, won't you?'

Honey and Sam promised that they would though they doubted things would go that far. Then they offered to go home with her to be there when Catherine confronted her, but Babe shook her head. 'It would only make things worse . . .'

The next morning Sam was waiting in the parking lot again to catch Honey and Babe as they got off the bus, but only Honey was on it. 'Where's Babe?' she demanded, frightened.

'I don't know. She didn't get on at her stop. And last night I kept calling but the maid – they've got a new one again – kept answering and said she wasn't home. I kept calling you, too, but your line was always busy.'

'I know. I kept calling Babe, too, that's why. And I got the same rap with the maid until finally I got the *Judge*. He said that Babe was *incommunicado* and would I be so good as to desist from calling again.'

'Incommunicado? But what does that mean?'

'It means you can't communicate with a person.'

'I *know* the word. I mean, what do you think it means as far as Babe is concerned?'

'I don't know. You don't think they *already* sent her to that home for delinquents, do you?'

'I don't think so. Even *they* wouldn't be *that* mean . . . *would* they? Besides, it wouldn't happen that fast, *would it*?'

'I don't know,' Sam said dolefully. 'It's possible, I guess. Who knows what that woman's capable of. Even Nora, who bumps into her now and then, thinks she's a woman of mystery with lots of secrets. You know that bull she feeds Babe about her being one of the aristocratic Lees of Virginia? Well, it just ain't so. Catherine the Great doesn't come from Virginia at all. She actually comes from Memphis, Tennessee.'

'Nora told you that?' Honey was astonished.

'Of course not! Would Nora tell me anything really important? But I overheard her telling it to one of her friends from some committee or other. I forgot to tell you.'

'How could you forget a thing like that?'

'It slipped my mind, all right? But do you believe it?'

'Nora wouldn't say it unless it were true.'

'Ordinarily I'd argue the point but I guess this time you're right. Anyway, Nora also told this woman that the info was to be considered confidential – if Catherine chose to be a Lee from Virginia, that was her biz.'

'But why would Catherine *tell* a lie like that?'

'If you wanted to cover your tracks, you wouldn't go around advertising where you're really from, would you?'

'I guess not. But why did she pick Virginia?'

'Well, if you're making up a place you're from and you *are* southern and you want to present yourself in the fanciest light, why *not* as a Lee from Virginia? And give poor Babe just one more thing she has to live up to.'

'I guess you're right. But I don't think we should say anything to Babe about this, Sam. She'd be upset and what's the point? I know I'd be upset to find out that my father had lied to me about something. Wouldn't you?'

'I guess. OK, we won't say anything.' They walked dejectedly around to the front entrance. 'But wouldn't you just die to know Catherine's real story? I wonder how much *more* Nora knows about her. Actually, I wouldn't put it past her to keep a complete dossier on Catherine.'

'A dossier – a *file*? On Babe's mother?' Honey laughed. 'Why would she do that? Nora's not in the spy business and Catherine Tracy certainly isn't. You've said a lot of crazy things about Nora, but that's the craziest yet.'

'You just don't know *anything* about politics. Both Nora and Catherine are politically involved and that's how it works. Try to follow. Nora's a rabid Democrat, one of their biggest fund raisers on the West Coast and that makes her a Democratic kingmaker. And the Tracys are fervent right-wing Republicans. They're not only Nixonites but Birchites which makes Nora and the Tracys kingmakers on opposite sides of the fence. And kingmakers always play dirty to get their way, hence the use of dossiers which come in handy when a bit of blackmail is in order. Besides, judges always know where the bodies are buried so Judge Tracy probably has more than his share of dossiers. *Now* do you understand why Nora probably has a dossier on the Tracys?'

'Maybe, or I would if I knew what a kingmaker was.'

'It's pretty self-explanatory. One who makes kings. Activists who don't run for political office themselves but back those with similar points of view,' Sam said judiciously. 'They want to be the power behind the throne either because they're plain power happy or for personal gain maybe, or because they're just born manipulators. You know, like Nora.'

'But why doesn't she run for public office herself?'

'Because she already has a major occupation – gathering husbands and feathering her nest.'

Ordinarily, Honey would have argued that point

with Sam, but today she didn't have the heart for it.

At lunchtime they weren't hungry and went to sit dispiritedly on the front steps of the school again. 'What *are* we going to do, Sam?'

'Go to the athletic field and have a cig?'

'You're out of your mind! That's all we need now – to be caught smoking again!'

'But only cigarettes. They can't expel you for smoking cigs *outside*. We've got *some* civil rights. It's not even like being caught smoking in the bathroom, which is no big deal anyway. But if you're nervous about it, we can go and smoke in the parking lot. We can hide behind the cars.'

'No, I don't feel like it. But if you want, I'll go with you and—' She jumped to her feet. 'Look, Sam – at the kerb! It's Catherine's Mercedes and Babe's getting out!' She started down the steps but Sam pulled her back.

'Wait until Catherine pulls away.' But then Catherine got out of the car too and Sam muttered, 'Arrogant bitch. She's leaving her car in the street instead of parking in the lot like everyone else is supposed to.'

'I guess she's going to see Dean Perkins. Poor Babe!'

They waited as Catherine and Babe walked up the path from the street and began to mount the steps. 'Do you think we should say hallo to Catherine as if everything was normal before we speak to Babe?' Honey whispered.

'I guess—'

But before they could utter a word, Catherine – her dark hair in a pouf of curls with an upward thrust and wearing a muted grey suit and matching inch-heeled pumps – sailed right past them, with a silent Babe shuffling behind her, her eyes glued to the ground. Then Honey looked helplessly at Sam who mumbled, 'I guess we'll just have to catch her later.'

Babe looked nervously round the locker room as if there were spies everywhere. When a locker door slammed shut with a bang, she jumped as if she'd been shot. 'I'm not supposed to talk to you at all,' she whispered. 'There's to be no contact. Catherine says that you two are a bad influence. She told Dean Perkins that both of you have been raised in a permissive environment which she and the judge disavow. And while she herself will enforce the rule *after* school she expects her, Dean Perkins, to enforce it during school hours with no exceptions. And that means lunch hour too, even if Dean Perkins has to assign a teacher to do nothing else but watch us.' Then she spun around to make sure that there was no teacher already assigned to observe them.

Honey moaned and her eyes filled with tears but Sam was enraged. 'What is this – the Russian Secret Police? And you're going to submit to this?'

'Oh Sam, get real,' Babe said in resignation. 'It's either that or getting transferred to another school or some kind of place for bad girls.'

'But you're *not a bad* girl,' Honey cried.

Babe smiled grimly. 'Tell that to the Judge.'

Honey and Sam sat on the floor in Sam's room seeking consolation in barely unfrozen Sara Lee fudge brownies. 'So what *did* your father say when you showed him the letter?'

'He said exactly what I expected,' Honey sighed. 'Or rather, he told me a story with a moral to it like I thought.'

'What was the story?' Sam asked through a mouthful of brownie so cold it hurt her teeth.

'He told me how his mother caught him smoking when he was fourteen. He was in a playground with a bunch of boys and she yelled at him right there in front of them, which humiliated him. Then she dragged him to a store where she bought him a box of Marlboro, asking him if that was his brand in front of the storekeeper, which embarrassed him too. Then she took him home and made him smoke over half the pack, one cigarette after the other, until he was sick. Then she tossed him the rest, telling him to let her know when "the big smoker" – that was what she called him – needed more so that she could buy them for him just like she bought him milk or orange juice. She thought that by being sarcastic and shaming him and letting him get sick, he'd never smoke again, or at least until he was grown. But he kept on smoking and never stopped, even though it makes him cough and he says it doesn't even taste good any more.'

'That's the whole story? Did he tell you what point he was making?'

'It's pretty clear. That once you have an addiction it's stronger than almost anything. It doesn't matter what other people do or say, shame you or hurt you, or even what you tell yourself. And if you don't want to have an addiction, it's better not to get the taste. I guess he wasn't just talking about smoking cigarettes or even dope, but all drugs and whatever else is bad for you.'

Like alcohol and women like Mimi . . . they're his addictions worse than any tobacco habit could ever be . . .

'That's pretty neat, that instead of yelling at you he just told you a story that made his point.'

'What happened with you? Did your father say anything?'

'No. He never read the letter. It was with the rest of the mail and he never looked at it. But I have an idea! Ask your father to tell Catherine one of his stories!'

Honey laughed. 'I can just imagine Catherine listening to one of my father's stories and at the end saying, "Oh Mr Rosen, how delightful! Please, won't you tell me another."'

'Don't get funny, Honey Bunny. I meant a story with a moral like to forgive is golden or something. Or maybe he could tell her a story about a girl he used to know – a girl whose mother wouldn't let her play with her friends and as a result she drowned herself?'

Honey shook her head. 'I know we're desperate,

442

Sam, but it won't work. When she met my father on Christmas Eve she was polite but hardly friendly. Besides, she's got a much stronger personality than Teddy. She'd overpower him. It would probably end up with her lecturing *him* on how he's messing up with me. But what about your father? *He* has a strong personality. She'd never overpower him. Do you think he'd be willing to talk to her?'

'Well, he might if I explained everything to him, but I doubt it would work. She's bound to piss him off and then he might tell her to piss off and then we'd be worse off than we already are. No, there's probably only one person in the world that's a match for Catherine the Bitch and that's Nora the Witch and even that wouldn't work because Catherine already hates her. Even Babe said so.'

'So what are we going to do?'

'I don't know,' Sam said gloomily. 'And to make matters worse, Nora is coming home from New York late this afternoon and my father isn't coming home to dinner and that means it will be just the two of us for dinner, unless you stay. Will you? In the meantime, should I go down and get another cake out of the freezer? I think I saw a Sara Lee Cherry Cheese hiding out beneath a box of cauliflower . . .'

'Before we sit down to dinner there's something I want to get out of the way,' Nora sat them down in the library. 'I read the letter from Dean Perkins but I'm not going to lecture you two. Besides, I'm sure your father has already discussed it with you, Honey. As for you, Sam, if I tell you that smoking pot is not a good idea and not to do it again, you're not going to listen to me anyway, so I won't bother.'

'Thank God for small favours,' Sam said sullenly, but Nora ignored her and went on. 'But I will say that smoking it at school was an incredibly stupid thing to do and if you're smart, you certainly won't do that

443

again. And now that I've had my say and not that I think any one of you really deserves a present considering – well, as I've already dragged them from New York, I might as well hand them out. Since the women at *Ms* told me that no matter how liberated a girl might be, she still loves gorgeous undies that come in a Bloomie's shopping bag, that's what I've brought back – matching teddys in different colours for the three of you. By the way, where *is* Babe? No, don't tell me. Catherine Tracy has grounded her and I can't say as I blame her.'

With that, Honey burst into tears.

'Now, come on, it can't be all that bad.'

'But it is! Babe can't *ever* speak to us again, much less be our friend.'

Babe bit into her cheeseburger with great gusto. 'I don't know what Nora said or how she did it but after she left our house last night they called me down and told me that after much thought and soul-searching they decided that their previous decision was a bit harsh and so they were going to give me, as well as you two, a second chance to demonstrate that our friendship is not detrimental to my character, health and general well-being.'

'It's a miracle!' Honey declared in wonder. 'And you don't know what Nora said to make them change their mind?'

'No. I thought maybe you two might.'

Honey shook her head but Sam looked like the cat that had swallowed the canary and Babe asked: 'Do *you* know, Sam?'

'No, she didn't tell me anything and I don't know *what* she said. But I think I know *how* she did it. Blackmail.'

Babe started to choke on her hamburger. 'Blackmail? My mother and father, of all people?'

Sam looked smug. 'Laugh if you like but remember what we talked about yesterday, Honey?'

'What did you talk about yesterday?'

444

'Dossiers,' Honey said. 'Sam said that probably Nora has a dossier on your mother.'

Babe whooped. 'That's the funniest thing I ever heard! But if it's true, I'd *kill* to see it.'

42

It was two weeks before the fall mixer – an annual event at which the Downey School's boys joined Beasley's girls for dancing and punch, and the girls were hanging out in Sam's room, listening to music and discussing which movie they wanted to see when Babe suddenly announced, 'My parents have been asked to chaperone at the dance.'

'And they accepted?' Sam asked, leaping up to turn off Janis Joplin, needing silence to digest this news properly.

'Of course! There's nothing they'd rather do than supervise people's behaviour even if it's only a bunch of kids. Then when it's slow-dancing time they'll probably walk around with rulers measuring the distance between bellies.'

'That does it for me!' Sam grimaced. 'If Catherine's going, I'm not. But it's OK – I wasn't crazy to go anyway. I mean, who really wants to mix it up with that bunch of doofuses anyway? Between the zitzes and the sweaty palms, not to mention that they're either dwarfs or goony gawks, who needs them? And to have Catherine breathing down my neck really puts the finishing touch on the deal. What about you, Honey? Are you going to submit to this torture?'

'I don't care either way. I'll do whatever you two do.'

'What do you mean: whatever you *two* do?' Babe demanded. 'Do I have a *choice*? Would my mother let me *not go* when they *are*? And if I have to go, so do *both of you*. And if you don't, then you two *really* suck and I'll—'

'What?' Sam scoffed. 'Kill yourself? You're forever threatening but you never follow through, not even once.'

'No, that wouldn't be punishment enough to pay you back. But if you don't support me I'm prepared to resign from the GAMS and I'll give you two minutes to answer my ultimatum.' She made a display of checking the time then went to Sam's desk and started rummaging through the drawer.

'What do you think you're doing?'

'Looking for a pen and a sheet of paper to write out my formal resignation.'

Sam said, 'Uh-huh,' and Honey laughed nervously.

'OK,' Babe clapped her hands. 'Time's up. That's it. I'm writing.' Then she said in disgust, 'For Pete's sake, isn't there even a stupid pen in all this mess?'

'I guess you can't resign after all,' Honey giggled.

'Oh yeah, she can,' Sam offered coolly. 'She can type it. Hey, Tracy, I give you permission to use my typewriter.'

'You'd better be careful, Grant. I might *throw* that typewriter at you!' But her lips began to twitch.

'Oh yeah? You and who else? I'm bigger than you.' She advanced on Babe who ran to the bed for a pillow to shield herself with as Sam pounced, forcing her down with the weight of her body. But then Sam allowed Babe to pummel her into submission with the pillow until she begged her to stop. 'OK, I give up! I'll go to the stupid mixer!'

Babe smiled smugly. 'I knew you'd go and that goes for you, too, Honey. I didn't doubt it for a minute.'

'How come?'

Babe got to her feet to snap her fingers and jiggle in accompaniment as she sang:

446

'Friendship! Friendship!
Just a perfect blendship
Should other friendships be forgot
Ours will still be hot . . .'

It was the night before the mixer and in her excitement Babe screamed into the phone, 'There's good news tonight!'

'It *better* be good because you just broke my eardrum,' Sam complained. 'What is it?'

'My mother has the flu. She can't go tomorrow night.'

'That *is* good news. I can think of only one thing better.'

'I hope you weren't going to say that the only thing better would be if she never recovered. She *is* my mother.'

'Really, Babe, I wouldn't say *that*. I might *hope* it, but I wouldn't *say* it. Ha, ha . . . only kidding. I wouldn't even hope that about Nora. What I *was* going to say was that the only thing better than your mother not going to the dance was if your father couldn't go either.'

'Oh, I agree. And he *isn't*! He said it was clear where his duty lay and that was home with Mother.'

'Super! You really don't appreciate your father, Babe. What dedication! And to Catherine of all people! Amazing!'

'Well, I better go now and ask her if she wants a cup of tea or something since my father fired the new maid for insubordination and the cook is acting up again. She says she was hired as a cook-housekeeper and she's tired of doing all the fucking work around here. Of course, if the Tsarina was on her feet she'd give that serf a taste of the whip to straighten her out, but in the meantime Father says we must all do our part to keep Mother comfortable.'

'Did you ever stop to think, Babe, that this might be your one big chance to even the score? Now that Catherine is at her weakest, you *could* take advantage.

447

You could hose her down with ice water or take away her blankets and as she's shivering, tell her you're only doing it for her own good to lower her temperature. And then you could withhold all nourishment. You know, feed a cold and starve a fever?'

'I think it's starve a cold and feed a fever.'

'But you're allowed to make mistakes – you're only fifteen.'

'Well, I *have* sort of thought of torturing her a little since she's too weak to strike back, but then I thought about what would happen to me once she got better. Oops, I think I hear her calling in that pathetic little sick voice demanding that hot tea. Hold on one minute while I check.' She held the phone a few inches from her mouth: '"Yas'm, Miz Tracy, ah's a comin' and ma head is bended low and you ain't just woofing Dixie." You heard it, Sam, and away I go.'

An hour later, Sam called Babe back.

'I thought you'd want to know. The school called to ask if Nora and Daddy would chaperone tomorrow night. It seems that that flu bug that bit your mom didn't die immediately after exposure to her, as expected. It lived another day to infect a few more parents who were going to serve.'

'So are they going to do it? Your father and Nora? That would be really cool. At least they're lots of fun.'

'Nora is but Daddy can't. He's going out of town.'

Teddy hung up the phone to tell Honey, 'That was Nora.'

'Oh? Did she invite you to dinner again? I hope this time you accepted. I don't think it's nice to keep giving her excuses. The Grants don't bite, you know.'

Teddy laughed. 'I didn't think they did. At least, I didn't think *Nora* did,' and Honey wondered if this meant he thought that possibly TS did. Then she wondered if TS was the reason he never accepted Nora's invitations to dinner – that Teddy was avoiding him.

'And no, she *didn't* invite me to dinner, but yes, I

did accept an invitation from her to serve at her side as a fellow chaperone at the big shindig tonight.'

Honey was surprised. 'And you said yes? How come?'

'Because she presented her offer in terms I couldn't refuse. She asked me to come as a special favour to her – to keep her company as she faces a "fate worse than death" – a roomful of rocking teenagers and the Beasley faculty. Only I promised not to quote her on that so you can't repeat it.'

'Oh, I won't. And I think it was really nice of you, Teddy, to go just to help her out.' She also thought it was nice of Nora to ask him, suspecting it was a ploy on Nora's part to try and draw him out of the house . . . out of himself.

Sitting on one of the gold leatherette chairs lining the walls of the gym, Sam refused all offers to dance. Honey, sitting next to her, also said, 'No, thank you,' to all comers, thinking she should keep Sam company since Babe, the most popular girl there, hadn't missed a dance all night.

'It's not too hard to figure out Babe's popularity with Downey's finest, Honey. She's the only girl here who's shorter than they are.'

'She's also the best dancer. And you didn't *have* to wear those high heels. You did it to make *sure* you'd be taller than every boy here so you'd have an excuse not to dance.'

'So what's *your* excuse?'

'I'm sitting here to keep you company.'

'No, Honey, that's only what you're telling yourself. I think the truth is that we *both* don't fit in. Me, because I'm too mature, and you because you're afraid.'

'Afraid of what – *these* boys?'

'No, not *these* boys. You're afraid of being popular. Any other girl with your looks and body would be setting all these little boys on fire just for the fun of it, but you hang back. You always hang back when a boy

449

so much as looks at you. Look how you acted last week in the Hamburger Hamlet when those boys from UCLA tried to pick us up. Babe was practically ready to crawl under the table with any one of them but you acted like you had turned to stone.'

'And what about you?' Honey was defensive. 'You weren't exactly friendly. You were definitely snotty.'

'But I *reacted*. I was being *provocative* and I got off some really fabulous cracks and I threw my hair around a lot.'

'OK, my friend Sam the amateur psychologist, why do you think I'm afraid to be popular?' While Honey was annoyed, she was also piqued, curious as to what Sam would say.

'I'd say you're afraid to turn out like your mother.'

Honey was upset but she said, 'I'll have to think about that. And you – do *you* want to be like *your* mother?'

'We were talking about *you*, not me.' But now Sam was visibly agitated and Honey was sorry she'd asked the question. She knew Sam didn't like to talk about her mother except to say that she was a debutante from Pasadena every once in a while, the remark that was guaranteed to drive Babe crazy. But then Sam said, 'No, I don't want to be like my mother. Why would I? She died practically before she ever lived,' and Honey asked softly, 'What did she die of? You never said.'

'What do you think she died of? From being seriously ill. She certainly didn't die from old age. But my father's the one who really suffered. It took him a long time to get over it. He didn't marry for a long time until he let the ex-countess get her claws into him and just look at her now.' She pointed to Nora dancing with Teddy, she animatedly talking as he smiled down at her.

'Looks like she's charming him utterly, doesn't it?' Sam smirked. 'Even though she's probably at least eight years older than he is. She's totally shameless. The minute my father goes out of town—'

'Sam! All she did was ask my father to come tonight since he's a parent too.'

She'd been feeling so happy that her father had come tonight and that he was looking so beautiful in his dark suit and white shirt with his longish yellow hair curling down over his collar. And she'd been feeling so happy that in anticipation of the evening he hadn't taken even one drink – not so you could tell anyway – which proved that he really didn't *have to*. And no matter what Sam said about Nora's reason for asking Teddy to come, she wasn't going to let it spoil her pleasure that he was here.

'Of course,' Sam said, 'it doesn't hurt anyone that he's so good-looking and brainy too, does it? But not to worry, Honey. If nothing else, he's not rich enough for her to take him really seriously or make him number five.'

Honey stared at her in disbelief. 'You really are out of your skull. And now if you don't want to dance and you refuse even to talk to anyone, let's at least get some punch.'

Sam made a face. 'Why? It's only unspiked pink piss straight out of the can and if we turn it down all week long at school, why should we drink it tonight?'

Honey thought about it for a while. 'Maybe because it's the only drink in town and we're thirsty?'

When they were ready to leave they couldn't find Babe. It was as if she had disappeared into the gymnasium's very close air and both Teddy and Nora were upset, feeling that somehow they'd been derelict in their duty.

'Don't worry,' Sam said, rolling her eyes. 'We'll find her, won't we, Honey? We know just where to look.'

After they pounded on the door of the girls' room in the basement for nearly five minutes, Babe finally emerged with a boy shorter than she by at least two inches and Sam drawled, 'Really, Babe! You're going to have to curb yourself of this fixation for males and bathrooms before it becomes an addiction – one you'll

451

never be able to break. *Then* what are you going to do for the rest of your life?'

43

As soon as the date for the Beasley Spring Follies was announced – an event in which every sophomore was expected to take part as a performer or in some facet of production, Sam volunteered to be its executive producer. Then, though no one had planned on having an executive producer, the faculty adviser assigned to the project seized on Sam's offer since it would mean that much less work for her. Then, Sam appointed Babe and Honey her associate producers whereupon Babe immediately asked if the term *associate* was movie-talk for assistant to the big cheese, and Sam told Babe that if she didn't like the word *associate* she was quite willing that Babe pick her own title. 'But it's a multiple choice – choose one: subordinate, junior, gofer or stooge.'

Then Sam talked Honey, who was reluctant to perform, into doing a dramatic presentation – something from Shakespeare maybe, since Honey *was* interested in the theatre and was seriously considering pursuing a career as a serious actress. 'How are you ever going to perform on the legitimate stage if you don't get over this shyness of yours?'

'And what's the big-cheese producer going to do by way of entertaining us?' Babe asked good-naturedly enough.

'Really, Babe, as *executive* producer I can't possibly be expected do anything else. After all, does my father act in his own movies? But I do have the most terrific idea how we can best utilize *your* remarkable talents for singing and dancing. I'm thinking of a big musical number as a finale – the kind of number they used to do in the Forties' movies à la Garland and Rooney. You know the kind of act I mean, like when all the kids in the neighbourhood get together and someone shouts, "Come on gang, let's put on a show!" and then suddenly there's swing music playing and everyone starts jumping and singing and dancing? It could be a real big production number with the whole cast jitterbugging! What do you think?'

'I think it's not *le idea hot*, or if you prefer, I think the idea sucks,' Babe stated unenthusiastically.

'Well, I think *your* reaction sucks, or rather, your gratitude quotient does. I only thought up the idea to showcase *your* talent – for you to be the lead performer.'

Babe was contrite. 'Listen, I appreciate that. I really do. But this is only a crummy school show and you're talking *Judy Garland* and *Mickey Rooney* and *finale* and *showcase*. The trouble with you, Sam, is that you think of everything in terms of movies. Don't you have anything else on your mind?'

'Like what, for instance?'

'Like boys, for instance. Here my mother has given me permission to start dating providing the boys are from the right schools and families and you two won't co-operate at all by refusing to triple-date with me.'

'No, I *don't* have boys on my mind, Miss Teeny-bopper of 1972,' Sam huffed wearily. '*I'm* not boy-crazy. Besides, you *know* I prefer older men,' she smiled condescendingly.

'Preferring doesn't mean getting and as far as I can see you haven't had anything to do with the opposite sex except for some long-distance flirting – like the guy's in one room and you're in the next so he really can't get at you, and that goes for all of them, young and old.'

'But that doesn't mean I didn't have something to do with an older man before I ever met you, does it? Or that the experience so scarred me that I haven't the heart to—'

'Look, you're always hinting at this mysterious older man and this earthshaking love affair, but I've had it with listening to all your bull. Unless you're prepared to back it all up with some hard evidence, I suggest you take it and—'

'Let's get back to the Follies,' Honey quickly interjected before things really heated up. 'Babe's right about one thing, Sam. The number you're talking about is way beyond us. It would take hours and hours of rehearsal, co-ordinating costumes, choreographing and who'd do the choreographing anyway? I think we should just have solo numbers and if you like we can have a simple finale with everyone in the show on stage singing a tune that everyone can carry without a problem and without a million rehearsals.'

'Very well,' Sam said coldly, 'I will accede to the majority opinion.' Then consulting her clipboard and muttering under her breath about no one having any artistic integrity, she demanded: 'Well, Babe, since you have no interest in being a real star, what *do* you want to do by way of an act? Will you do one of your silly tap dances and *call* it modern jazz or do you want to do a gymnastic routine?'

'Neither.'

'Oh, are you going to sulk like a baby just because I – Don't tell me you want to sing! *Everyone* wants to sing.'

'No, I don't want to sing. What I'd like to do is a comedy routine. You know, stand up and tell jokes . . .'

It was the girls' obligatory once-a-week afternoon at the Tracys which Catherine insisted on so that she could 'touch base' with the girls and know 'where their heads were at'. The first phrase was one Catherine liked to use when discussing the task of child-rearing; the latter was one she had recently picked up on from an article on the turbulent teens in the turbulent Seventies in order to show that she was *hip* to the young people's *scene*, two more words she sprinkled into her conversation to show the girls that she spoke their language so they could let her know what they were thinking.

But Babe knew better. 'She's been pulling that confidence routine on me for years. First she sucks me into telling her how I feel about things then she says something like, "idiotic" or even "disgusting", or makes a nasty crack about my less-than-average IQ and how was I ever going to manage to do halfway decent on my SATs. Or she gets me to tell her what I'd really like for Christmas and then makes sure it's exactly what I *don't* get because anything I'm so dumb to want is *inappropriate*.'

In order to forestall Catherine getting even an inkling into what was on their minds whenever they were ensconced in Babe's room, they made sure to cover every surface with textbooks and Cliff notes and looseleafs so that no matter how often Catherine popped in on them with only one fast knock they were ready to cease all normal conversation to be found immersed in their schoolwork.

But today they didn't bother with the usual subterfuge since they were actually working on a *legitimate* school project – the Beasley Spring Follies. First, they had a run-through of Honey's Portia from *The Merchant of Venice*, which left her friends speechless.

'God, you're a natural!' Babe raved and Sam cried, 'For once I have to agree with Babe. You really *are* Portia!'

Honey, pleased but blushing furiously, sat down on the floor next to Sam. 'Are you sure you don't have *any* suggestions? Do you think I should use my hands more?'

'Next time I'll concentrate on that facet of your performance,' Sam offered judiciously, 'but now I think we'd better check out Babe's routine, see if she's come up with some material that's more original than what we heard before.'

'Excuse me, Madame Producer,' Babe said, getting to her feet, 'but *I'm* the original, the one and only – Babe Lee Tracy!' She threw out her arms and took a few steps to simulate running out on stage as Honey giggled.

'Honey, if you laugh before she even begins how are we going to maintain the proper objectivity?' Sam objected. 'Let's be serious, OK? Babe, you're on!'

Babe rubbed her hands together. 'Good evening, ladies and germs—'

'Babe, that is *lame*! Now start over and why, if I may ask, are you rubbing your hands together?'

'I've been watching the comics on *The Johnny Carson Show*. They *all* rub their hands together.'

'But what does it *mean*? Every gesture is supposed to *mean* something.'

'Who says? This is comedy I'm doing, not method acting.'

'Good. In that case, why don't you try being funny?'

'OK, here I go! Good evening, ladies and gentlemen *and* members of the Beasley faculty—'

This time Sam giggled. 'I like *that*!'

'A funny thing happened to me on the way here tonight. A guy came up to me and said, "I haven't had a bite in three days" so I bit him! Then he said, "Will you give me ten dollars for a cup of coffee?" so I said, "But a cup of coffee is only fifty-cents," and he said, "I know, but I need nine-fifty for the valet parking."'

With both Sam and Honey laughing, Babe really began to warm up. 'It's getting so crazy out there, I can't believe it. I have an aunt who got a phone call from her husband which isn't crazy except that he died a few months ago.

'So she said, "Edgar, I can't believe it's you," and he says, "It's true, Harriet. I've come back!" And she says, "You mean you've been reincarnated?" and he says, "Yes, and I'm in such a nice place with a lot of cows. One of them is really beautiful!" Then she says, "But *where* is this nice place?" and he says, "I don't know but this cow – *she's* gorgeous!" Then my aunt says, "Edgar, why do you keep on talking about a dumb cow?" and he says, "I don't think you understand, Harriet. I've come back as a *bull*!"'

The three of them were convulsed with laughter until they heard: 'What, may I ask, is going on here?'

The girls snapped to attention to see Catherine standing in the doorway, eyes boring, lips compressed. 'We're wor – working on the Follies,' Babe stammered. 'I told you that's what we were going to do—'

'If you are working on the Follies, may I ask why you were telling that disgustingly vulgar story?'

Babe looked to Sam and Babe for help and Honey scuffed at the carpeting with her loafer. 'Oh, that was just a – We weren't really going to *use* it. Were we, Sam?'

'No. We wouldn't dream of using it,' Sam said. 'Someone told Babe that dumb joke and she just wanted us to hear it – she had no intention of using it in her comedy routine. I mean, she wouldn't tell a vulgar joke like that, would you, Babe?'

'My daughter's name is *not* Babe. It is Babette. But now I want to hear more about this comedy routine. *What* routine?'

'The routine I'm doing for the Follies,' Babe blurted.

'I'm just going to pretend you never said that, Babette. Young ladies of good breeding do *not* do comedy routines for school productions and that's my final word on the subject.'

Sam recognized a final word when she heard one and she threw an apologetic look at Babe before saying, 'Those are my sentiments exactly, Mrs Tracy, especially since Babe . . . Babette . . . is such a great dancer and terrific at gymnastics. No one else in school is the whiz she is at gymnastics—'

'Yes, she could do gymnastics or dance,' Honey said quickly. 'Or she could sing . . . something uh . . . classical.'

'No!' Babe said between clenched teeth. 'I don't sing *classical*. I've never sung classical in my life. And if I'm going to dance, I'll do the kind of dancing *I* like—'

'That will do, Babette. And don't you *dare* raise your voice. If you're to perform at all in what appears to be turning into a circus, you will play the piano since your father has provided you with lessons for some eight years from which he's never derived one moment's pleasure.'

'I'm *not* going to play the piano! I hate playing the piano and you can't make me!'

Honey gasped and Sam opened her mouth to say something, then shut it again.

'Oh, I think you will, because you will either play the piano or you will not take part in the Follies *at all*, which also means no behind-the-scenes participation. But don't make a hasty decision. Talk it over with your friends by all means. You can let me know what you decide by this evening.'

She left the room and once she was gone, Babe put her ear to the door to hear if she was truly walking away down the hall. Then she turned back to Sam and Honey. 'Now I'm going to say this once and one time only so you better just listen to me. I am *not* going to play the piano and if you're truly my friends you won't say *one* word urging me to. And you *won't* quit the show as a gesture of support either. Gestures suck!'

It was their first rehearsal in the school auditorium without Babe and Honey and Sam were deeply depressed.

'Did you get a chance to speak to Nora about her talking to Catherine?' Honey asked wistfully.

'Yeah, but she won't do it. She said she couldn't *meddle* in a matter like this, tell Catherine that she shouldn't insist on Babe playing the piano. She said it was *absurd*.'

'But she did it last time. She made Catherine change her mind about letting Babe be friends with us again.'

'Don't you think I reminded her of that? I didn't use

458

the word blackmail, but I *did* remind her that she had *persuaded* Catherine to listen last time but all I got was a lecture. She said being involved in politics had taught her a lesson. That sometimes you pushed and sometimes you held back. That not everything was worth pushing for because if you pushed too often, you had nothing left to push with for the bigger battles. And she said that since Babe was making an issue of choosing *not* to be in the show as a matter of principle – taking a stand – no one had a right to mix in.'

'I guess that makes sense,' Honey said thoughtfully.

'Maybe it *would* if Babe could keep on doing it – standing up for herself, but she can't. Catherine and the judge are just too strong for her and Babe's too scared of them. You know that as well as I do. Still, I *did* learn something from my little chat with Nora even if I didn't get anywhere with her. Remember when I said that Nora must have a dossier on Catherine or at least had the goods on her, and you didn't believe me. Well, now I know it for a fact. After our talk was over and I was already walking away, she said something that convinced me I was right. She said, "Anyway, you don't use a cannon to squash a mosquito." Now, just think about what *that* must mean.'

It was an hour before showtime but Honey was already anxiously peeking from behind the stage curtain at the empty auditorium while Sam stood behind her.

'Nobody's here yet,' Honey reported.

'It's too early. Besides, who cares? This whole thing is a disaster as far as I'm concerned. Once Babe wasn't in on it, it stopped being fun.'

'I know, but you've done a wonderful job, Sam. Everyone says so. Even Dean Perkins.'

'Dean Perkins?' Sam sneered. 'She hasn't even seen it.'

'She has. Part of it, anyway. Yesterday at rehearsal.'

'Well, who cares what *she* thinks? I only care what my father thinks and he isn't even going to be here!'

459

'You didn't tell me that.'

'I didn't know it myself until this morning. He had to fly to Yugoslavia, of all places. One of his dumb prima donnas is acting up and slowing up production.'

'Well, I suppose that had to come first. You always say that, Sam – that making movies is important business and always comes first. But what about Nora? Will she be back in time to come tonight?'

'Who cares if *she* comes? Besides, she won't. She's too busy stomping for McGovern's nomination to be bothered with a school production. With Nora, politics come first.'

'No matter who comes you did a great job and you should be proud of yourself. I know *I'm* proud of you.'

'You ain't doing so bad yourself, kid. You're going to knock them right out of their socks. And you look mighty fetching in that white chiffon dress. Where'd you get it?'

'It's my . . . my mother's. There's a trunk of stuff she left behind. It was always padlocked so I never saw what was inside. But when I told Teddy that I was going to do Portia, he . . . well, he went and took this dress out of the trunk. He said I would be as beautiful as my mother—'

'I've got news for you, Honey Bunch. You've already left your mother in the dust. Sure, she's sexy but you're sexy, too, and in addition, you have something even better.'

'Yes?' Honey was sure Sam was going to say something like inner beauty, a special radiance or even just a great personality. 'What do I have that's better?'

'*Me* as a best friend!'

A half-hour before curtain-time the auditorium was filling up and there still was no sign of Teddy and Honey was almost in tears. She had asked him to come early so that he'd be sure to get a good seat up front, but now she wondered if he was going to show up at all.

Sam, frantically rushing about and issuing orders, caught her peering into the audience again. 'Look, Honey, don't I have enough to worry about without you popping up at that damn curtain every two minutes? He'll be here. Would *your* father miss your first public appearance?'

He might if all the memories became too much for him.

'Now will you get back to business? You *are* supposed to be my assistant and Pam Folstein has misplaced the bow from her dumb violin. Do you think you could help her find it?'

Honey walked out on stage heartsick. She just *knew* she was going to be awful. But it didn't matter. Of the three people she was really eager to see her perform tonight, one was absent by default – immersed in the misery of his past; a second was at home with her mother, quite miserable in the present; and the other was backstage, giving everyone holy hell. There was no one out there watching her to tell her later, 'Oh Honey, you were really *good*! You made me proud.'

Before she began, her eyes swept the audience – from left to right and from front to rear the way both her father and Sam had told her it was done. Mostly the faces were a blur and she didn't know if this was because of the lights or the tears in her eyes. But there was a frantic waving down in the front row so that she couldn't miss it even if she tried. It was her friend Sam *out in the audience*, just making sure that there was someone out there who loved her, who just knew she was going to knock them out of their socks . . .

After the grand finale the cast took bow after bow since the audience, composed of supportive and enthusiastic friends and family, insisted on it with their thunderous applause. And then the girls on stage started chanting,

'Producer! Producer,' following Honey's lead until Sam, snappy in the forbidden strapless green mini she had changed to (for which she would be subsequently censured), came running out to take her bow, followed by her backstage staff which consisted of nearly a quarter of the entire student body.

'I guess I'd better call Olaf to come and pick us up,' Sam told Honey backstage as the small space was overrun by proud parents and general well-wishers. 'We *could* ask someone for a ride home but I'd rather not, if you know what I mean.'

Honey nodded. She knew exactly what Sam meant. It was as embarrassing as it was depressing that neither one of them had a single person in the auditorium ready to claim them.

'What the hell, Honey, it doesn't matter. What matters is that we did good, you and me both. And we didn't do it for the old Gipper either,' Sam laughed. 'We did it for the GAMS and we did the GAMS proud even if Babe wasn't here. Right?'

'Right,' Honey agreed after she recalled that the line – *do it for the Gipper* – was from an old black-and-white movie with Ronald Reagan that they had recently watched on television. Babe was right about Sam – she *did* think only in terms of movies. But tonight, it was just as well. There were so many things it was better *not* to think about – that Teddy hadn't made it there tonight or that in a weak moment she had actually written her mother a note telling her all about the Follies and that she was going to do the monologue from *The Merchant of Venice*.

She didn't even know what she expected in return. A note of encouragement? A word or two dashed off about how she, Mimi, was proud of her daughter, or simply rooting for her? Or even just a postcard from someplace glamorous and foreign that said, 'Wish you were here', and signed, 'Love, Mother'.

'Where have you two been hiding? We've been looking all over for our two stars!' Sam and Honey couldn't believe their eyes. It was Nora, all smiles and exuberance, and behind her was Teddy, his smile almost as big as Nora's. *Where had they come from?*

'Oh, Daddy,' Honey flew into his arms. 'Where *were* you?'

'Right here, sweetheart, bursting with pride.'

'But I looked for you and looked for you and I couldn't find you—'

'We were seated way in the back. Nora called me from the airport. She said she wouldn't be arriving until the very last minute and that she hated going places alone and would I wait for her so that we could go together. And so I did. How could I not after she took about a half-dozen different planes and travelled all day just to get back here in time for what she called a very special night?'

Honey whirled around to tell Nora how glad she was that she had made it, to see Sam and Nora sort of waltzing around one another, taking each other's measure the way she'd seen prizefighters on television doing, just before they came out slugging.

'What are *you* doing here?' Sam demanded. 'I thought you had a rendezvous with destiny or something at that rally for McGovern in Minneapolis, or was it Duluth? I hope you didn't let old George down just for little old me . . .'

'No, certainly not. You know I don't believe in letting anyone down, not even my worst enemy.'

'So, what happened with the rally? Did you miss it?'

'Oh, that. No, I didn't miss a thing. The rally was called off – we were rained out.'

'Oh? Of course. I bet you were disappointed.'

'At the rally being called off?'

'No, disappointed that you came to see the show that I produced and that I didn't fall flat on my face.'

'Quite the contrary. I wasn't disappointed at all. Rather, I'm pleased that I can report to your father about what an extraordinary job you did. You see, I wouldn't want *him* to be disappointed – he thinks his daughter can do just about anything better than anyone else.'

'Really?'

'Yes, of course, really,' Nora said crisply before turning to Honey. 'And you love, you were *so* beautiful!'

And Honey was gratified, knowing that Nora was talking about her performance and not just how she looked in her mother's dress.

44

After dinner at the Grants' Babe had to go home – mother's orders – and she asked Honey if she wanted a lift home. 'If you do you have to be ready to leave in ten minutes, me mither is picking me up at eight-thirty.'

But Sam urged Honey to sleep over. '*M*★*A*★*S*★*H* is on tonight and we can watch it together. I just love that show!' But when Honey called home to tell her father that she was sleeping over, there was no answer.

Honey tried calling several more times thinking maybe she'd dialled the wrong number or that Teddy was in the shower . . . had taken out the trash . . . had run out of cigarettes and driven over to the liquor store on Beverly Drive which stayed open late. He might even have driven over to the market for a carton of milk or a loaf of bread. But finally she stopped dialling. He just wasn't going to pick up. He'd been so dejected lately, ever since he'd been signed to rewrite someone else's original screenplay and then after he'd worked on for weeks – he hadn't

464

even touched his novel – he'd been replaced by another screenwriter.

He had tried to console *her*. 'It doesn't really mean that much, sweetheart, it happens all the time because *they* don't know what they really want. By the time you hand in a script they've already changed *their* minds and then they tell you it's not what they were really looking for. You can't take it to heart because if you do, it will kill you.' He laughed, but the laugh had a hollow ring to it.

'But it's so hard *not* to take it to heart, Daddy,' she'd said. 'I don't see how you can't.'

'When I first came to Hollywood someone gave me what he considered good advice. Right from the horse's mouth, as he put it. He said, "You have to go with the flow or you might just as well pack it in – put a gun to your head or drive your car into a wall with a heavy foot on the accelerator." And he was a very clever man.'

'Who was he?'

He smiled enigmatically. 'T.S. Grant.'

'You *do* know him then?' Honey asked.

Actually, she had sensed *that* since the Grants' Christmas Eve party the Christmas before last when Mr Grant had introduced her to his friends as Teddy Rosen's daughter instead of using his full, formal name, the way you would if you didn't actually know the person but had only heard of him. And now she instinctively knew that she was also right about something else – the reason he never accepted any of Nora's invitations *was* because he was avoiding TS.

'Not *know*. *Knew* is a better word. It was a long time ago and I haven't spoken to him in years.'

'Did you have a fight with him? An argument?'

'Let's just call it a parting of the ways.'

It had been a fight . . . some kind of argument.

'Did he know Mimi too?'

'Yes. TS produced the one movie she made here.'
And then that haunted look she knew so well had crossed

his face and she knew that the reason Teddy had had that parting of the ways with TS had *something* to do with Mimi. And she wanted to ask him more questions, but then Teddy said, 'And I wrote the script. It was a Western and it was awful. Hollywood called it the bomb of all time but Mimi had another word for it – one I don't care to repeat to my innocent daughter.' He had laughed, making a joke of it, and changed the subject.

Still, he hadn't honoured his own advice to her not to take the rejection to heart and he hadn't followed TS's advice either – to just go with the flow. Rather, he'd sunk into a depression, seemingly deeper and deeper with each passing day, and started drinking more heavily again just when she thought he had begun to drink less . . .

'I have to go home,' she told Sam urgently. 'I think our phone must be out of order and I can't stay if I can't tell Teddy that I'm staying.'

Sam would have liked to argue with her, but Honey's logic was irrefutable. 'OK, but since you've already missed your big chance to ride with Catherine, I'll get Olaf to do the honours since he's still around, waiting to pick up my father later on. And I'll go along to keep you company and then I can go in and say hallo to your father. I haven't seen him in a while and I love talking to him. He's so soothing.'

The last thing Honey wanted was for Sam to come in with her. 'But my father might not be home. I mean if the phone *is* working and he's not answering, then he went out. And even if he *is* home, he's probably busy. Besides, I think I'll survive the ride without you, fascinating as your company is.'

'OK, so I'll go to keep Olaf company on the ride back. *He* loves my company.'

'But you'll miss *M*A*S*H*.'

'So who cares? I'll see it on the re-runs. I just feel like going for the ride. Do you mind? *God!*'

But then Honey was saved. When Sam stuck her head

into the library to tell Nora that she was going along with Olaf to take Honey home and that she thought she'd stay for a while and visit Teddy's father if he was home, Nora said she'd better think again. 'It's too late for you to first start visiting.' She suggested that instead Sam go upstairs to check out her homework.

Honey was worried that Sam would argue with Nora, even refuse to obey her – a not infrequent occurrence – but this time Sam just made a face, deposited a kiss on Honey's cheek and went trudging up the stairs muttering, 'I might as well be in prison, or even living with Catherine and the judge,' which ordinarily would have made Honey laugh, but not tonight. Tonight, she was too anxious.

Honey fumbled around as usual in her big bag filled with just about everything any teenager could possibly need but what she really *needed* – her key – she couldn't find. She waved at Olaf, waiting in the Rolls as per his orders, to signify that she had everything under control and he didn't have to get out of the car. Then she tipped the urn of geraniums to get the spare key, but it wasn't there! Teddy must have used it and never put it back. In a panic she alternated between pressing the buzzer and pounding on the door furiously. But still nothing happened!

Then Olaf got out of the car to see what the problem was, which was exactly what Honey was praying wouldn't happen. 'The spare key isn't here and my father must have gone to bed and can't hear the bell,' she explained to him, trying to appear calm, wanting desperately for him to leave. 'But it's OK. I can climb in a window on the back patio. I do it all the time. I'll be fine. You can go.'

'I don't think I can. Mrs Grant wouldn't want me to. Now let's go and find that window.'

When they found Teddy lying unconscious in a small

puddle of blood in the library, Honey didn't utter a sound but sank to the floor to pillow his head in her lap, to kiss his bleeding forehead and sob soundlessly. Then she saw Olaf at the telephone and whispered hoarsely, 'Are you calling 911?'

'No, I'm calling Mrs Grant. She knows how to get things done and fast. The ambulance will be here before I hang up.'

Honey nodded, then suddenly remembering, looked around the room frantically for evidence that might incriminate. She saw the empty liquor bottle lying on its side on the coffee table but realized she couldn't do anything about it. Teddy's head was in her lap, slowly staining her grey pleated skirt a bright red and she couldn't do anything but wiggle out of her navy blue jacket to take off her white shirt to try to staunch the determined flow of blood and wipe it away from his eyes.

She had to fight not to pass out. She never realized how nauseating the smell of fresh blood was, especially so mixed with the stink of alcohol. It seemed to be exuding through his pores, even as his head was exuding his life's blood.

The ambulance took Teddy to the Emergency Room at Cedars where they treated a cut so deep it required twenty stitches. (The police who arrived about the same time as the ambulance ascertained that he had fallen, and in falling had struck his head on the sharp edge of a table. As bad luck would have it, it was the French campaign table fashioned out of steel.)

'He lost a lot of blood,' the doctors told Nora, assuming that she was in charge, while Honey listened more scared than she'd ever been. 'Lucky you found him when you did. The blow wouldn't have killed him but he could have bled to death without ever gaining consciousness. It's happened before.'

Two hours later, conscious and bandaged, and after

it was determined that he had suffered only a minor concussion, Teddy insisted he wanted to go home, but the doctors insisted even harder that he stay overnight so that they could check him out properly.

'I don't think you have much of a choice, Teddy,' Nora smiled cheerfully, 'but to listen to these doctors.'

She put her arm around Honey who was still wearing her stained skirt and her blood-streaked blazer. 'Come on, love, you're coming home with me. If nothing else, we have to get you into some clean clothes.'

'But I want to stay here with Teddy. Can't you ask them if I can stay overnight with him? He *needs* me.'

'Not tonight, Honey. Your father's getting all the care he needs and I'll bring you back first thing in the morning.'

Teddy smiled at Honey. 'You go home with Nora, I'm fine. And thank you, Nora, thanks for everything but most of all for looking after my girl.'

Then Nora said something Honey thought odd. 'That's the easy part.'

When they were in the car, Nora took her eyes off the road for a moment to look at Honey who sat crouched over, her head buried in her hands. 'You know, Honey, you can love your father very much, but you can't really help him.'

'But when he comes home from the hospital all he'll have to do is rest, won't he? And I can miss a couple of days of school to take care of him. It won't matter.'

'That's not what I'm talking about, Honey. I'm talking about your father's drinking,' Nora said as kindly as she could. 'You may *think* you can help him or *wish* that you can but you can't.'

At first Honey tried to deny that her father drank. Oh, if only she had managed to hide that bottle before Nora arrived, she agonized. 'Oh, you saw that bottle,' she said lightly as if to dismiss it with a shrug. 'Sure he has a drink once in a while, like maybe

469

once a week. But don't most people? Don't you and Mr Grant?'

'I learned a long time ago, Honey, that it doesn't help to deny the truth either. The truth is funny that way . . . and stubborn – it refuses to go away. And no matter what you do or say, you really can't protect your father from the world.'

Honey began to cry then and Nora took one hand off the wheel to press her hand.

'It's not his fault . . .' Honey sobbed. 'He's a wonderful man. It's all *her* fault. She left him.'

'You mean your mother? Nothing's ever *all* one person's fault. And it's possible that you don't know all the facts. Perhaps she had to leave him.'

'But she left him and me!'

'Sometimes, that's all people *can* do. Leave . . . cut themselves free . . . to save themselves.'

'You wouldn't. You'd never do that.'

Nora's mouth curved into a sad smile. 'Sometimes *one can't* stay, no matter what. And as far as helping anyone that person has to *want* to be helped. Mostly, the only one who can really help anyone is the person himself.'

'But can't we try to help someone to help himself?' Honey asked in a small voice. 'Do you think—?' she faltered, not knowing exactly how to put it. 'Do you think that maybe *you* could try to help me help my father to help himself?'

Nora burst out laughing. 'You don't give up, do you?'

But then she stopped laughing and said soberly, 'The problem with never giving up is that *sometimes* you win, but many times all you end up with is what the French call *chagrin d'amour* which loosely translates to a broken heart. But I'll think about it.'

Having no choice but to be satisfied with that, Honey sat back in her seat and thought about the phrase *chagrin d'amour*. It was deceiving. It sounded so romantic and at the same time it was deadly. Then a thought occurred to her. 'Sam said you were living here at the same time that my mother and father were in Malibu when you were married to an English actor.'

'I wasn't really *living* here. I was just visiting you might say – two or three months.' She sensed the question that was coming and she was right.

'Did you ever meet my mother?' Honey whispered.

'Well, yes, once. Briefly. For a few minutes only.'

'And what did you think of her?'

'That she was the most smashing woman I'd ever seen.'

Then they were zipping up Grantwood Manor's driveway and there was no more time for any more questions or answers . . .

Sam was waiting at the door in her long Lanz nightgown. She threw her arms around Honey and turned to Nora accusingly. 'When Olaf came back and said Mr Rosen went to the hospital I was sure you'd call to let me know how he was!'

Nora apologized. 'You're right. I should have realized that you'd be waiting to hear. But he's going to be fine. So now you can run along to bed with a clear mind.'

'But isn't Honey coming up with me?'

'In a while. But first we have to get her cleaned up and then I'm taking her into the kitchen to have a cup of tea. My mother always said that a drop of whisky was fine, but for a bit of real comfort there was nothing like a nice cup of tea.'

'Well, can't I have a nice cup of tea too?' Sam asked piteously. 'I'm very upset about Mr Rosen too.'

'Of course you are,' Nora said quickly. 'And yes, you can certainly have a nice cup of tea.'

As Nora, Sam and Honey, now wearing the twin nightgown to Sam's, sat at the long scrubbed pine table in the kitchen working on a second pot of tea along with a platter of assorted biscuits, TS appeared in the doorway wearing an old, homely plaid bathrobe. 'I thought I heard a big commotion down here. It's a strange time of day to be having a tea party,' he grinned at the trio.

471

'Oh Daddy,' Sam cried, 'it's Honey's dad. He fell and hurt his head and they had to take him to the hospital.'

'Olaf told me all about it and that you went to take care of things, Nora. I knew then that everything was going to be fine. It is, isn't it?' and Nora nodded.

'Good. Keep smiling, Honey. Now I'll say good night.'

'Don't you want to sit down with us, Daddy, and have a nice cup of tea, too? It's very comforting.'

'I'd love to but I've got a heap of work still waiting for me. Be sure and say hallo to Teddy for me, Honey. Tell him I send him my regards.'

But Honey knew she wouldn't tell Teddy anything like that. Though she didn't know what happened between TS and Teddy and Mimi she trusted what she felt in her heart and she certainly trusted her father. Whatever happened was *bad* and TS was the perpetrator . . .

45

Though Honey's birthday wasn't until July and Babe's not until September, the girls decided to celebrate their sixteenth birthdays officially together in June on Sam's birthday. It looked like it was going to be very special since TS said he'd throw the girls a party at the restaurant of Sam's choice. Sam chose Ma Maison's since it was also the restaurant of choice for many of Sam's most favourite film stars like Steve McQueen and Rock Hudson whose Fifties' movies with Doris Day were among her top twenty best of all time. In addition, Ma Maison's host, Patrick Terrail, always kissed her hand on those occasions when Nora took her to lunch on the restaurant's famous patio under its infamously hot, plastic, flowered canopy, and that made her feel special – as if she were really part of the movie scene.

'It's going to be fabulous! Daddy's going to invite a big bunch of movie people,' Sam enthused.

'But won't that cut down on the number of guests *we* can invite?' Babe asked, worried.

'What are you afraid of? That we won't have room for the tons of boys you want to ask?' Sam smirked.

'Well, it *is* supposed to be my and Honey's party, too. And what's a Sweet Sixteen without boys?'

'You know, Babe, there *is* another life out there without boys. And some girls actually have *all-girl* Sweet Sixteens.'

'Yeah, but there's also a life out there that doesn't centre around movies, movies, movies. What would you have done if you grew up in Sioux City or some place like that?'

'But I wouldn't have been T.S. Grant's daughter then, and moviemaking wouldn't run in my blood so I wouldn't have the same interests.'

'Do we have to fight about this, too?' Honey sighed. 'Since Nora said we could each invite twenty guests and I don't have any boys I particularly care to invite and the three of us have the same list of girls, I hereby donate nineteen of my invitations to you, Babe.'

'I wish you'd think twice about this, Honey,' Sam chortled. 'You know what she'll do with them? She'll post them on the bulletin boards of every frat house at UCLA and USC and in every boys' locker room in town.'

'Oh, I couldn't do that,' Babe giggled. 'If my mother found out, she'd skin me alive and not even let me go out with the boys from Downey's. But tell me, Honey, why are you offering me only nineteen invitations? Who are you saving that last one for? Some mysterious stranger?'

'Yes, very mysterious. My father. Do you mind?'

'Do you *have* to invite him?'

'Yes, I *have* to!' Honey was exasperated.

'Well, you don't have to take it personally. It's not that I don't want your father there – I adore him! It's just that if my mother finds out you've invited *your* father, she'll want to know why I didn't invite her and my father, and they're the last people I want there.'

'I can well imagine,' Sam drawled. 'But if you don't want them there you'd better tell Nora because she says Honey's father and your parents are getting *official* invitations. She says that since this is a party for the three of us and she and my father are going to be present, then your parents and Honey's father have to be there, too. But if you can change her mind, good luck! Oh, and before I forget – Nora also says that since we're sharing this birthday party and she thinks it's not nice to expect guests to bring *three* presents, she's stipulating on the invitations that presents are strictly *verboten*. Sorry, girls, but you know that old saying, "I can't do a thing with my hair"? Well, I can't do a thing with my steppie.'

'I knew it was a terrible mistake to invite my mother and father. Now, Catherine says that if it's *my* Sweet Sixteen as well as yours and Honey's, and she and my father are going to be there, then she'd like to invite some of *her* friends.'

Sam was furious. 'But she can't do that! I refuse to have my party ruined!'

'She did say that she'd be more than willing to pay whatever extra it costs,' Babe offered miserably.

'Oh!' Sam held her stomach. 'I think I'm going to throw up! If that isn't the tackiest thing I ever heard of – to bring money into it!'

'Well, don't blame me. I don't even want to go to this party myself any more. I think I'll just kill myself in the least painful way I know. How many 'ludes do you think it would take to overdose?'

'I don't know but if you find out, let me know. Maybe I'll join you. How about you, Honey? Care to join us?'

Honey forced a smile. She no longer was thrilled about this party herself. She was sure that at the last minute Teddy would find some excuse for not going, that he'd *never* go to a party where TS was playing the host.

'Well, let's wait to hear what Nora has to say about your mother's latest demand, Babe,' Sam chuckled. 'She thinks she's so smart, let's see how she gets out of this one.'

But Honey could see that even Nora didn't know how to deal with Catherine other than to let her have her way, after she offered to pay for the extra guests. Forced to deal with the money part *first* by saying, 'Don't be absurd,' gave Catherine permission by default to ask anybody she pleased.

Then it came to Honey how the whole party was going to turn out. Catherine and the judge would come with their friends and Babe would be so inhibited by their presence, *she'd* have a miserable time. And she herself would be miserable because her father hadn't come because he knew TS would be there but then TS himself wouldn't show up because some business thing came up, and then Sam would be miserable. And then to top everything off, some of the kids would bring presents despite Nora's request that they didn't and then those who didn't would be embarrassed and miserable too. *And a great time was to be had by all!*

Then Honey wondered if Nora was thinking all these same thoughts because suddenly she said, 'You know, I've been thinking that instead of having this party – for the next couple of months you girls are going to go to Sweet Sixteens till they're coming out of your ears – we should call it off and do something more original to honour the occasion.'

Sparks glinted from Sam's eyes. 'Like what?'

'Like I would take you girls on a trip the first week school is out.'

'Wow!' Babe said but Sam demanded, 'Where to?

475

Disneyland?' thinking this the height of sarcasm.

'No, what I had in mind was flying to Washington, DC, to see all the sights.'

'First-class?' Sam asked immediately.

'Of course, first-class, dear. Would I expect a first-class girl like you to travel any other way?' she asked drily.

'And we'd stay in a hotel? Which one?'

'I haven't planned an itinerary yet but trust me – your accommodations will be all that you deserve or at least, all that you desire.'

'All right,' Sam agreed. 'If Babe and Honey want to go, I'll sacrifice the party.'

'But I don't know if I'll be *able* to go,' Honey said. 'I'd love to but I don't know if I can leave my father for a whole week. He might even forget to eat.'

'Try it, Honey,' Nora said. 'It might be a surprise. He might get along without you better than he does *with* you.' But then she smiled as if to take the sting out of her words.

'Well, I know for sure my parents will never let me go,' Babe said dolefully. 'They'll be afraid you'll take me to a demonstration or even a McGovern rally.'

'Oh my, that *would* be awful!' Nora laughed. 'But don't worry. I'll speak to your parents. I'm sure I'll be able to persuade them to let you go.'

'You're sure? But what will you tell them?'

'I'll promise them that you'll attend neither a rally nor a demonstration and that I'll get invitations to all the right places. Even to the White House, maybe even for dinner.'

'How can you? The Nixons are in the White House!'

Nora laughed again. 'Oh, that's right, they are, aren't they? But don't worry. I lived in Washington for several years and I still have wonderful friends there on both sides of the aisle. Even, would you believe, old Dicky?'

'*I'd* believe it,' Sam said, unrelenting even though now she was excited about the trip. 'I'd believe that there isn't a man you ever met that *isn't* your friend one way or another, if you get my meaning. Except for Hubie, of course. I bet he doesn't feel so friendly towards you now, does he?'

But when Sam saw how decisively she had scored with that one as Nora's face darkened, she felt a little twinge – she didn't know if she were glad or not. For one thing, it certainly put a damper on everyone's upbeat mood.

46

Just as Honey and Babe had celebrated their birthdays early so that they could share Sam's birthday with her, Sam and Honey waited until September when Babe turned sixteen so that the three of them could go down to Motor Vehicles in Santa Monica and get their drivers' licences at the same time. And once they had their appointments to take their tests, Sam called a meeting of the GAMS to discuss the momentous event.

Now that the big day was almost at hand there was a question of who would drive them there and in which car. While it was Olaf who had taken them out practice driving, it was out of the question, Sam claimed, that he take them for the test in the Rolls. 'Can you imagine what would happen if a chauffeur drove us there to take our road test in a *Rolls*? They'd automatically fail us out of sheer class resentment.

'And my father's going to be in New York so he can't take us in the Ferrari which might be worse than the Rolls anyway. All those guys who take you out for the test drive would probably *kill* for a Ferrari. And we can't count on Nora to be in town. What with with this being an election year and she being one of McGovern's biggest supporters, she has *her* priorities and *I'm* not one of them. Besides, I don't know if the class resentment would be any less if we took the test in Nora's Jag rather than in a Rolls or Ferrari. A Jag's probably worse than a Mercedes. They see lots of *them*.'

Babe turned pale. 'If you're thinking what I *think* you're thinking – of my mother taking us in her Mercedes – don't even think it! She won't do it! She doesn't think sixteen year olds should *have* licences – that it's giving them a licence to murder.'

'She's right,' Sam said cheerfully. 'The first thing I intend to do when I get my licence is drive over to your house, call Catherine outside and plough into her. Then when she's lying in the driveway bleeding I'm going to put the car in reverse and run her over again. Back and forth a few times should certainly do the trick. But actually, I was thinking more along the lines of your *father* taking us in his car.'

'My *father*?' Babe screeched. 'Are you out of your glue-sniffing mind? With him watching me drive away in his Lincoln I'd probably drive straight into a wall and then the inspector would fail me for sure. Why would you even *want* my father?'

'For his registration, fool, what did you think? Before you take the test they check the registration of the car you're driving and when they see the name *Judge* Terence Tracy on the old reg, who would *dare* fail us?'

'But why do you have this obsession with us failing?' Babe complained. 'Why *should* we fail? Nobody could possibly *not* pass us, unless, of course, you start driving like a cowboy on wheels, which you have a tendency to do.

'Besides, Vanessa Casey said all the inspectors are guys so all you have to do is wear a really short, tight skirt and if he puts his hand on your thigh you just moan as if he's getting you *so* hot it's hard to keep your mind on your driving. Or you accidentally put your hand on

478

his weenie until *he* moans at which time you know you're doing fine because what with his hard-on, it's difficult for him to concentrate on your driving. Then there are other alternatives. Cambria Shoemaker claims she knows a girl who was such a lousy driver that the only thing she could do to get her licence was get down and give the creep a blow job.'

'And you *believe* that story?' Sam scoffed.

'Of course I believe it. Why wouldn't I?'

'You're a momo. How could that girl drive a car and give head at the same time? She'd have to be a contortionist.'

'You think you're so smart, but I'm just a little smarter because I figured out exactly how she did it.'

'I'm dying to hear *this* one.'

'He told her where to drive – which road and all – which is what they do, right? Then as soon as they passed an alley or a dead end or some deserted place, he told her to cut a left and pull over because he wanted to check her out on her left-hand turns and how well she pulled over. Then he told her to turn off the ignition and put on the emergency because he had to check her out on *those* little items, and just *one* more. And then before she could say, 'Oh my goodness, you don't mean—?' she was down on the floor of the car and he was really checking her out and there you have it – *passo!*'

'That's disgusting! Sometimes I think that after everything your poor mother's gone through with you, she's failed, after all. I mean, sometimes I'm forced to think that you've just got no class.'

'Oh, ho, ho, listen to you! Don't you think it's rather *déclassé* of you to try and use my father's judgeship to intimidate a poor cop into passing you when your driving really *sucks*? Besides which, my father simply wouldn't do it. Actually, he and Catherine are working to have the driving age *raised* from sixteen to *eighteen*, forget seventeen completely. I'm just lucky she's letting me get my licence at all.'

479

'Yes,' Sam agreed. 'That *is* a surprise. How come?'

'Well, she's not *altogether* mean. I guess she thinks it would be cruel and unusual punishment if you two got your licences and I didn't. And remember, she *did* let me go to Washington with you two and Nora even though it was against her and my father's better judgement, so she isn't *all* bad.'

'Well, good. Let's pin a medal on her for that.'

Finally, Honey, who'd been lying on Sam's bed through Babe's and Sam's discussion so silent they'd almost forgotten she was there, spoke up, her voice clipped and distant. 'I'm sure my father will be willing to take us.'

'But why didn't you say so in the first place and spare us all this discussion?' Sam demanded.

Honey shrugged and didn't answer. Maybe it was because once Sam said both Nora and her father would be too busy to take them, she'd been reluctant to offer her father's services, to admit that he was available because *he* wasn't too busy, that he had nothing else to do that couldn't wait until the next day or the day after except maybe to stay sober enough to take them.

Or maybe it was that magazine article she'd read last night about people who abused alcohol which made the point that unless a person was willing to stand up and say, 'I'm an alcoholic,' he couldn't *ever* recover. And how could *she ask him* to say it when she herself couldn't say it except for that one time with Nora and Nora said that you could only help someone who wanted to be helped.

'Anyhow, Sam,' she continued in a frigid voice, 'since all we have is our old Ford, you won't have to worry about being failed due to class resentment. And as for the matter of what you're willing to wear and what you're willing to do to ensure passing, Babe, that's up to you. Personally, I'm going to wear jeans and keep my hands on the wheel and my eyes on the road at all times since I'm satisfied that all it takes to get a licence is to drive a car *adequately*, and I

480

hope *you* won't do anything to embarrass me or my father.'

'Oh come on, Honey, don't be such a doofus. Can't a girl have a little fun?' Babe stuck out her bottom lip.

'Really, Honey, you *are* in a snit. What did we do or say to bring this on?' Sam was really upset and sat down on the bed to try and put her arm around her. 'What's the problem?'

Honey shook her arm off brusquely and then Sam was hurt. 'All right, if that's the way you want it—'

'OK, if you really want to know what my problem is I'll tell you!' Honey sat up straight. 'My father is an alcoholic! There. I've said it, and I hope you're satisfied . . .' There was a stunned silence before Honey began to cry.

'Oh, Honey, Honey.' Sam threw her arms around her. 'Don't you cry. It will be all right.'

'No, it won't,' Honey said. 'It never will be!'

'Of course it will,' Babe said, hugging her too.

'There's hope for him,' Sam insisted. 'He's so sweet and *alive*. And I never told you how my mother died, did I?'

Honey's sobs abated somewhat. 'No . . .'

'She was in a sanatorium for the seriously disturbed—' She smiled a weird kind of smile, made circles with a finger and pointed to her head. 'And then one night she got hold of a razor and—' She drew a line across her neck and made a funny croaking noise in her throat. 'And it was all over. She bled to death and she was only twenty-three.'

'But who told you that?' Honey asked, horrified, not sobbing any more. 'Your father?'

'No, of course not my father! He would never tell me a thing like that. My grandparents did. My mother's mother and father. I lived with them until I was about five because my father was so devastated by my mother's death he couldn't take care of me himself. Then they died in a car accident.'

'You mean they told you that when you were only five?' Babe asked, her eyes as big as saucers.

'Yes. *They* were the ones who were really sick even though I didn't know it at the time. How could I? I was a little girl. I think they were just trying to punish me.'

'But how could they be so mean to a little girl?' Honey wondered, the tears slipping down her cheeks again. 'And why would they want to punish you with such a terrible story?'

Sam shrugged. 'I guess they didn't like me because they were mad at my mother for what *she* did. And they couldn't punish her, so they punished me instead.'

Then *she* burst into tears and Honey put her arms around her, but instead of getting into the act of trying to comfort Sam, Babe got to her feet. 'OK, since this is show and tell, or at least *tell*, I've got an announcement to make too.'

Honey was wary. 'Babe, if this is going to be something really terrible, tell me now so I can prepare myself.'

Sam, wiping at her eyes with her hands, looked nervous, too, but she said, 'Don't let her fool you. She can't bear not to be in the spotlight so she's going to make something up just so she isn't left out. Go ahead, Babe, let's hear what you have to say but try not make it too big a whopper, OK?'

'No whopper,' Babe said. '*I think I'm adopted.*'

This time, nobody cried. Rather, there was a stunned silence until Sam, not doubting Babe's sincerity after all, asked shakily, 'What makes you think so?'

'Because the other night after my date with Evan Layton, which Catherine thought was an excellent date because his mother's prominent in the Blue Ribbons, when I came home just a *few* minutes late and just a *tiny* bit rumpled, the Judge took one look at me and said to Catherine who was already crying, "This is what comes of taking in another man's trash . . ."'

482

Sam was aghast. 'But how could you keep that to yourself? Why didn't you tell us before?'

'If you were called another man's trash would you go around bragging about it?' Babe laughed.

No, you didn't brag, Honey thought. *You just cried yourself to sleep until you told your friends about it and laughed so that it didn't hurt so much.*

But Sam said, 'You have to look on the bright side of things. If you're some *other* man's trash, then at least you're not *his*. But didn't you ask Catherine what he meant?'

'I tried to but all she'd say was I was never to mention the subject again but that I should get down on my knees every day in thanks for having a man like him for a father,' to which Sam asked, 'Do you think that's what *she* does?'

'What?'

'Gets down on her knees every day to give . . . um . . . *thanks?*'

Teddy, sober as a judge, made cheerful chit-chat to relax the girls as they drove to Motor Vehicles in the old blue Ford. Still, they were nervous and they discussed who should go first without coming to a conclusion, but it worked out that Honey, wearing jeans and a blue denim workshirt went first, accompanied by a middle-aged officer and came back soon, smiling widely. Everything had gone smoothly.

Then Sam in a long denim skirt that topped her cowboy boots got into the Ford with a very young and good-looking inspector and she returned in fifteen minutes, giving Teddy, Honey and Babe the high sign.

Then it was Babe's turn. In a tight and very short denim skirt and wearing high heels Sam and Honey had never seen before (where *had* she dug them up?) Babe wiggled her hips over to the Ford to await the officer who was going to take her out for her spin. And in a couple of minutes the officer appeared, a snappy looking young *lady* (Babe's eyes popped) who took one look at Babe's towering high heels and sneered, '*One* . . . *just one* false move, kid, and you're dead in the water . . .'

47

Sam called Honey just as she was getting up at six – it was her day to prepare breakfast and set the table with the flowered Limoges china that came from the old house in Malibu. She and Teddy took turns making breakfast. It was both ritual and routine, which Teddy maintained was good for people. And part of their morning ritual on schooldays was that after breakfast he kissed her goodbye at the door and waved as she ran to catch her bus. Then he'd pick up the *LA Times* to go back into the house ostensibly to read the paper over another cup of coffee. But lately, she'd come home to find the paper still neatly folded, unread, which meant one thing to her – he was growing increasingly uninterested in what was going on in the world. Or, sometimes she'd see that only the page with the book reviews was read and crumpled and then she knew that he had had a bad day.

But this morning with Sam calling so early, everything was *not* routine. Usually, Sam didn't get out of bed until the last possible moment. 'What are you doing up so early, Sam?' she mumbled into the phone. 'And why are you calling? I'm going to be seeing you in approximately two hours.'

'I'm calling to tell you not to get on the bus today. Just wait for me and for once don't ask a million questions.'

At ten to eight there was a great blasting of horn coming from the street and Honey ran to the door. It sounded like some kind of emergency. Teddy, in his bathrobe and slippers, followed on her heels. But when Honey threw open the front door it was quiet outside and there wasn't anyone on the street, only Sam madly waving from a bright green Alfa Romeo!

'Oh, Sam finally got her new car!'

'Meet the new Beasley Express!' Sam yelled, getting out of the car and running up the path. 'Isn't she gorgeous? Did you ever see anything so beautiful, Mr Rosen?'

Teddy laughed but Honey, ever sensitive to his every word and expression, observed that it wasn't his best laugh. What was wrong? Was he worried about her driving with Sam? True, Sam was a bit reckless with a tendency to speed but she'd been riding around for months with Sam at the wheel of her parents' cars, just as she'd driven Sam and Babe in the Ford. Was it different now because Sam had her own set of wheels?

Then with a pang she realized what the problem was – Teddy was *jealous* of Sam's car, of the fact that Sam had a shiny new Alfa Romeo while his Honey didn't! And she wished she knew how to tell him that it was OK – that having him for her father was worth a million new cars and that Sam having the Romeo was almost as good as she herself having it. But that would be acknowledging that it was painful for him and that was not part of their ritual. So she settled for squeezing his hand and a big kiss as Sam pulled on a pair of racing driver's gloves and said, 'Ready? Then, let's boogie!'

'In a sec.' Honey dashed back into the house to grab her bag and books and dashed out to find Sam and Teddy at the kerb for a close-up inspection of the car. 'It's truly a marvel,' Teddy said, kissing Sam on the forehead. 'And as my mother would have said, "Drive it in good health".'

'Oh, that's cute!' Sam giggled. 'Most adults would say, "Now, drive carefully". I like your advice better. Ready, Honey? Then let's burn rubber!' Then as they

485

roared to a start and the tyres screeched in protest as they tore away from the kerb, Honey waved fiercely to Teddy as he stooped to pick up his paper, a disconsolate droop to his shoulders.

'We're going to pick up Babe.'

'Why didn't you call me yesterday when you got the car?'

'I didn't get it until almost midnight and Nora said I wasn't to dare call anyone at that hour.'

'You got it at *midnight*?'

'That was when Daddy got home and it was *his* present though the card said it was from him and Nora. But you know that he'd put her name on the card no matter what. But he was so funny. He said, "It's all yours. Now don't do anything in it I wouldn't do." But do you know what Nora said, the old witch? That even though it's only April, the car's my *seventeenth* birthday present so I should try my best not to crack it up before my birthday in June. Did you ever hear anything so mean? But I was so thrilled I didn't care. You should have seen it! Daddy had it all tied up in pink plastic wrap, yellow ribbon and all these purple balloons!'

'Sounds good enough to eat but that doesn't sound like your father. He's not the purple balloon type, you know?'

Sam laughed. 'I guess you're right. It does sound more like something Nora would dream up, like she was decorating for a party. But why not? What else does she have to do?'

'Still, it *was* a nice thing to do,' Honey said wistfully, thinking of the last gift that had arrived from Paris. For a Christmas present to one's daughter one hadn't seen in years, it was weird – a tall, white chef's hat and an apron that said, '*Bon Appetit!*' Sometimes she thought that maybe it wasn't that her mother didn't give a damn about her but that it was that she was on *something*, stoned out of her mind for the duration of her daughter's lifetime.

When Babe, waiting in the driveway, saw the car

heading for her as if with intent to kill and coming to a stop only inches from her she let out a shriek but it wasn't fear – it was joy. 'Do I see what I think I see or am I dreaming?'

'Climb in quick, short person. We're already late and I'm going to have to do eighty to make it to school on time.'

'Where am I going to sit?'

'Don't be dumb. You sit sort of scrunched on top of the seats. Haven't you ever ridden in a sports car before?'

'I'm dumb? There are three of us, there will *always* be three of us and you get a car that seats only two?'

'Well, what did you want me to get? A station wagon? The cool cars all seat only two. Half the fun of riding in this car is scrunching up. Even when you're scrunching you're still higher than the people in front and you can sort of hang out the window and yell out insults to other drivers. Come on, climb in. You know how it's done.'

'Oh, all right. Get out, Honey, and let me go scrunch. Unless you want me to climb over you? Better still, how would you like to scrunch since it's half the fun and I'll just sit in front like a plain person who's not having any fun.'

'I don't think so,' Honey said, laughing. 'Since you're the shorty, it's better for you to scrunch because that way you'll be higher than us and we'll all kind of come out even.'

Babe slammed her books and bag into Honey's lap and without waiting for her to get out, proceeded to climb over her to get to her perch as Sam helped with a shove and the three of them screamed with laughter until the front door opened and there was Catherine in a pale blue satin robe demanding to know what was going on.

'Oh shit!' Babe hissed into Sam's ear. 'You woke her up!

'I woke her up? You were—' She broke off to

487

wave at Catherine. 'Hi, Mrs Tracy. How are you this great morning? Isn't it a beautiful day? The sun's really shining and—'

'The sun's usually shining,' Catherine said sourly. 'What I want to know is what do you think you're doing making this racket at this hour of the morning? And why aren't you at school by now?'

'I just got my new car last night and I thought I'd pick up Honey and Babette this morning since – well, I know we're a tiny bit late but—' She gave Honey an elbow in the ribs.

'But we'll make up the time,' Honey blurted. 'We'll be at school in ten . . . fifteen minutes at the most, right, Sam?'

Sam gave her a withering glance. 'No, twenty minutes is more like it. I wouldn't dream of going over twenty-five miles an hour and I believe in defensive driving.'

Catherine gave Sam a withering look and fixed Babe with an eagle-like eye as Babe tried to appear to be sitting normally. 'I have always trusted you, Babette, to get on the school bus every morning without supervision and now I must wonder if you're to be trusted. Do I have to stand out here and see that you get on the bus as you're supposed to?'

'I'm sorry,' Babe whined. 'I thought that this once it would be all right since Sam just got her car and I didn't want to wake you just to ask you if it would be all right. And now I've already missed the bus—'

'Do I have your word that this won't happen again without your asking permission?

'Oh, definitely, Mother. Without a doubt.'

'Actually, I'd refuse to pick her up if I didn't know for a fact that she had your permission,' Sam said quickly.

Catherine gave Sam another withering look. 'Very well. This one time since it's not my intention to keep you girls from having *fun*.' She said it like it was a dirty word. 'But as you're already late and I won't have you

488

speeding, if you'll get down from that ridiculous perch and come back in the house, Babette, I'll write a note for the three of you asking that your tardiness be excused. Then perhaps Honey will exchange seats with you since she's taller and has more square inches to absorb any possible shocks to the body just in case—'

'We get rear-ended?' Honey chuckled, but nodding though it meant she'd have to double over in half. Then she grimaced as Babe clambered over her to get out of the car to follow her mother into the house. But just before Catherine disappeared through the doorway she turned as if suddenly remembering her manners and smiled tightly. 'Good luck with your new car, Samantha, and be sure to drive carefully.'

Sam groaned. 'I was hoping she wouldn't say that.'

In a couple of minutes Babe emerged, smiling smugly to take her place in the vacated passenger seat. 'OK, move it!' she directed. 'But take it easy. She's watching.'

'I can't believe she actually let you go,' Sam said, easing the car into the street as if it were made of eggshells, then slowly inching to the corner before she took her left into Sunset and exploded into a burst of speed.

'I knew she would the moment I saw her in the doorway.'

'But how could you?'

'Because I remembered why she was up so early. It's Friday and she's got a standing ten o'clock at Elizabeth Arden's and since I had already missed the bus and if I didn't take the ride with you, *she'd* have to drive me which would make her late for her appointment. By the by, when you come to the turn for school don't make it. Just keep on Sunset and keep moving until you hit the old PCH, then hang a right!'

'The Pacific Coast Highway? We're already late by nearly an hour. Are you crazy or what?' Sam demanded.

'Crazy like a fox. This is the first day you have your car and you have to do something special to break her

489

in, right? Well, what's so special about driving to school? But if we meander up the coast to the Malibu Pier and – well, the surf's up and it's a superiffic day! There's going to be a lot of action at Surfrider's Beach.'

'But what about school?' Honey protested. 'Tomorrow's Saturday. We can go to the beach tomorrow.'

'But then it's not special any more. *Anybody* can go to the beach on a Saturday,' Babe said reasonably.

'But what about the letters they'll send home if we don't show up? Your mother's note only excuses us from being a little late, doesn't it? What does it say, exactly?'

'There is *no* note,' Babe said happily. 'Knowing that my mother was anxious about *her* time – she needs at least an hour to put on her face *before* she goes to Arden's to have them remove the face before they work to improve the face – I suggested that she just *call*, which she did, telling the office clerk that we were going to be late, but she didn't specify *how* late. Get it? We can show up at two o'clock and still be in the clear and have about five hours to catch some rays and check out the action. The surfers always have such cute little butts in those rubber tights. Now do you see why I'm crazy like a fox?'

'Crazy!' Sam agreed, whizzing past the school turn.

'But if we get caught you're the one who's most vulnerable, Babe,' Honey pointed out. 'Your mother won't let you out of the house for a month! Maybe a year!'

Babe sighed breezily. 'Sometimes you just have to go for it.' She clicked on the radio to hear the strains of 'Aquarius' and bopped up and down. 'This really *is* the age of Aquarius.'

'But how are we going to go on the beach in our uniforms?'

'We don't, Honey, my love. We take them off.'

'To put on what or do we go on the beach bare-assed naked? Then we'd be *sure* to get all the surfers' attention.'

490

'I don't believe in being *that* obvious. We put on our bikinis which we buy at that little shop right near the pier.'

'With what or are we just grabbing them and running?'

'Would I be so crass as to suggest we commit larceny? We use the credit card Nora gave Sam.'

'Hold on. Anything I buy that Nora hasn't authorized comes out of future allowances. She's chintzy that way.'

'Well, don't *you* be so chintzy. Oh all right, we'll pay you back out of *our* future allowances. Right, Honey?'

'That's fine, but that's not what's bothering me.'

'We know what's bothering *you*, Honey – your conscience. Or should I ask what *else* is bothering you?' Babe asked.

'Won't the water be a little cold today?'

'Who said we're going in the water? All we're going to do is lie in the nice warm eighty degree sun working on our tans while the boys check out our terrific bods. Now, will you relax? I swear, sometimes you sound just like my mother . . .'

As Sam made her right turn on to the PCH, Babe pointed at the ocean sparkling in the sun. 'Now, I ask you, aren't you glad we're here instead of in American Lit?'

She turned up the volume on the radio to let 'California Dreamin' ' blare through the air to mix with 'Me and Julio Down by the Schoolyard' blaring from the MG in the right-hand lane cruising in tandem. Its driver, a surfer type with bleached white hair, wearing black Raybans and a T-shirt with the sleeves cut off at the shoulders, yelled, 'Where you headed, doll?'

'Surfrider's,' Babe yelled back. 'You?' She turned down the radio's volume and flashed her most provocative smile.

'Zuma,' he said, 'but maybe we can negotiate.'

But just as she opened her mouth to answer Sam stepped on the gas to zoom ahead, leaving the MG in the distance, and Babe, outraged, demanded: 'Are you insane? He was *cute!*'

'Come on, Babe, he had Valley Boy written all over him.'

'What are you, some kind of a West Side snob?'

'I was just acting in *your* own best interest. I didn't want to see you waste your valuable time because he'd never past muster with Catherine and the judge.'

'What did you think I was looking for? A lifelong commitment?'

When Sam and Honey, who had dozed off in the sun, came awake, they looked around for Babe. 'Where do you think she is? It's time we headed back,' Honey said nervously.

'You go down and check the water and I'll check out the rest rooms. A bunch of kids always hang out there.'

When neither of them met with any success, Sam said, 'Let's go back to the car. Maybe she's there.' But as they approached the car, Sam screeched, 'Do you see what I see?'

'If you mean Babe and that guy from the MG getting out of *your* car, then I see what you see.'

No one said anything at all until they were heading back, Babe, subdued, in the scrunch seat. Finally Sam said, 'May I ask what you were doing in my car with that creep?'

'What do you *think* I was doing?' Babe was defensive.

'Oh, stop trying to imply that—'

'But I'm not *implying*. I'm—'

'You mean—?'

Babe looked as if she might cry. 'I mean – all the way.'

'Oh my God! You mean you actually *defiled* my new car?' Sam's eyes darted frantically around the car while Babe looked frightened. 'What are you looking for?'

'Semen, if you must know! But there isn't any! Did you *swallow* it all?'

Honey gasped, whispered to Sam, 'Don't,' while Babe said, 'I might never forgive you for that!'

'You defile my car and *you* won't forgive *me*?'

'Damn you, Sam, why are you acting like this? And you Honey, Miss Goody-two-shoes, you haven't said a word. I thought the least my best friends would do was ask me how it was. And you're both acting like my mother!' The tears rolled down her cheeks.

'Well, who did you expect me to act like? Nora?' Sam demanded, suddenly remembering *her* first and only time and how Nora had reacted. But hers had been a beautiful experience and Babe – her first time seemed to have been a bummer and she herself was only making it worse. 'OK, I apologize for acting like your mother, but only if you tell us every last juicy detail.'

'That's better,' Babe said, only sniffling now.

Now Honey knew she had to say *something*, anything that would show Babe she wasn't being judgemental. And she wasn't, it was only that she would have wished for something more meaningful for Babe this first time out – as she wished it for herself. 'OK. I'd like to take this opportunity to congratulate you, Babe, and wish you many happy returns of the day . . . I *think*.'

'OK,' Babe tried to smile. 'That's better. As for details, Sam, I want you to know one thing about your new car – it's *awfully* hard to do *it* in a car that has no back seat and bucket seats in front. It's just lucky I'm so good at gymnastics or it might never have happened at all!'

'Well, I'm *so* glad that you managed and I have only one question. Tell us, did the earth move for you?'

'Oh, so *that's* what that was! I thought we were having an earthquake, but that turned out to be only a tremor.'

493

48

Beasley kept its own calendar with September the month when freshmen were given precedence. But once October came the emphasis swung to the seniors who had to be prepared for their entrance into the future and there the emphasis remained for the rest of the school year.

First, there was the SATs with a great effort expended to see that the girls were properly prepared for the exams, but once the SATs were out of the way, everything else took a back seat to the college applications. It was understood that it was incumbent upon a girl to attend the finest school she could get into – she owed it to Beasley and to the Beasley girls who came after her. Accordingly, each student was encouraged to apply to at least four of the most prestigious schools in the country with an emphasis on the seven Sister schools in the East regardless of her SATs scores and academic standing, Beasley subscribing to the theory that character was as important as scholastic achievement, as were social standing, prominent ancestors, and the ability/willingness by parents to make a donation to the school in question. Then to allow for the vagaries of the registrars of admissions at these schools, it was suggested that at least three additional colleges, slightly less desirable, be applied to as 'safety schools'. Accordingly, letters were sent out to set up appointments with the parents so that they could be in on these strategy-planning sessions along with the students and guidance counsellors.

When Honey found the letter to Teddy in the pile of unopened mail, she tore it in half before depositing it in the trash. There was no need for Teddy to meet

with her guidance counsellor since she already knew
which school *he* wanted her to attend – his own alma
mater, Princeton. And there would be no problem with
the counsellor. She would heartily approve of Princeton
as top choice. Beasley had had many of its girls go on to
the Sister schools, but not one had gone on to what some
viewed as the most élite of the élitist schools which had
only recently elected to take in women.

The only hitch with Princeton as the school of choice
was Honey herself – much like the girl in the nursery
rhyme who couldn't leave her mother, Honey couldn't
leave her father.

Who would watch over him?

Since all the mail that was of any interest to him went
to the studio in Burbank, TS never bothered to open any
of the letters delivered to the manor and it was Nora who
opened the letter from the school, but she brought the
letter to the breakfast table – the one time of the day
the three of them were sure to be together – so that TS
could be consulted as to what day and hour would best suit
him. She knew that Sam would not only *want* her father
in on the discussion but would be crushed if he wasn't.

But it was a surprise to Nora when Sam didn't object
when TS said it was impossible for him to commit to an
appointment – *Gone Yesterday* was weeks behind schedule
and millions over budget and he had no idea when he'd
be free. But she did object when he told Nora, 'You and
Sam can take this meeting without me. Just get her set up
at Vassar or Radcliffe. Smith wouldn't be a bad choice,
either.'

'But I don't want to go to Vassar or Radcliffe, Daddy.'

TS picked up a piece of toast to lay it down. 'Nora,
the toast is cold. You know how I hate cold toast,' he
said, sticking his bottom lip out like an aggrieved little
boy.

Nora smiled and rang for the maid.

'Didn't you hear what I said, Daddy? I said I have

495

no intention of going to Smith, Vassar or Radcliffe.'

'That's fine. You and Nora decide where you want to go, then Nora can tell them at school what we all want.'

The maid appeared, but then TS said to forget the toast, he was running late. He scraped back his chair to rise, picking up his cup to grab a last gulp of coffee. 'Coffee's cold, too. What's going on around here, Nora?' he grinned. 'What's happening to my perfectly run household?'

'Oh? I didn't think you noticed.' She went to the sideboard to fetch him a fresh cup.

'Daddy, we haven't finished discussing my plans!' Sam cried petulantly.

'I told you. You and Nora work it out. And whatever you decide tell that school that if they can't get you in, Nora will. She has all kinds of fancy connections and lots of negotiating skills. That's what comes from marrying an earl, a high-falutin' diplomat and being a big shot in the Democratic party. Ain't that right, Nora?'

'But nobody's listening to *me*,' Sam shrieked. 'I'm not going to college at all!'

'Then what will you do with yourself? You have to do *something* to keep busy. Oh, I know what it is you want to do,' his face creased into a grin and Sam relaxed. *Of course he knew!* 'You want to disco the nights away, right? Then sleep in the next morning and maybe around eleven get dressed to bomb around town in your car or maybe get in some shopping on Rodeo. Then you'll zip over to the Polo Lounge for lunch, after which you'll just have time enough to get your nails done—' He shrugged. 'Well, why not? That's fine for killing time until you grab yourself a husband. It sure beats the hell out of being one of those hippies with dirty feet who go around protesting every damn thing.'

If it had been anyone else who had said what her father had just said, Sam would have torn his head off but she couldn't be angry with her father. Besides, he was

496

probably just teasing her. Or maybe it was Nora he was teasing with that grabbing a husband bit.

'Daddy, maybe getting a husband was all Nora had on her mind when she was a girl way back when—' she cast a sly look in Nora's direction but Nora merely sipped her tea and smiled – 'but it couldn't be further away from what's on *my* mind, or Honey's, or even Babe's. Women want to do something on their own these days and—' She laughed. 'Look how Billy Jean King whipped Bobby Riggs' little old ass.'

TS looked pained, shook his head at Nora who could barely suppress a smile.

'Spare me that women's lib stuff. There's only one woman I ever knew who *really* didn't want a husband. As for the rest of you, that's all you have on your mind no matter if you're Billy Jean King swatting tennis balls, a Bev Hills princess who gets her hair done at Jose Eber's or one of those flower children with dirty hair! But what do I know about these things?' He drained his coffee cup. 'Why don't you tell Nora all about it? She understands *everything* and she won't steer you wrong.' And he was gone.

Nora and Sam studied one another silently until Nora said, 'If you don't want to go to college, what is it you *do* want, Sam?'

'Just like Daddy said, you know everything, so why don't you tell me?'

'That's not what your father said,' Nora pointed out. 'Anyway, I'm afraid he has this unrealistic conception of me and what I can and can't do.'

'Still, you *do* know what it is I want, don't you?' Sam insisted, at first cool then impassioned. 'I want to work at the studio! Making movies runs in my blood. It's my life!'

'When you graduate, Sam, you'll only be eighteen and when a girl's eighteen, no matters *what* runs in her blood she really has no idea of what she wants her life to be.'

Sam looked at her with narrowed green eyes and

said with what she perceived as great shrewdness: 'I bet I know what ran in *your* blood when you were eighteen and that you knew exactly what you wanted. Shall I tell you?'

Nora thought of the young and, in her way, innocent girl who had gone to London in 1943 with her blood running hot only for a good time, dreaming of all the men who would love her and make her laugh . . . the girl who had never given a thought to the future. It had never even occurred to her to think about what she wanted her life to be.

'No, Sam, *don't* tell me. Since you'd only be guessing it doesn't make any difference what you think. And, this way, I can fantasize that you were going to say only the nicest things. But what I will tell you is that I *wasn't* prepared for the future, which is always a mistake for anyone.'

'You mean like Hubie, for instance?'

Nora closed her eyes for a few seconds so that Sam wouldn't know that she had scored with that one.

'The only future you need to concern yourself about, Sam, is your own. And you'd be wise to prepare for it. It's not enough these days to go into the movie business and think you're going to make it big because you're the boss's daughter. Just suppose this scenario: for some reason your father is out of Grantwood Studio soon after you begin there not knowing a thing about the business. Then *you're* out of there, too, and you still don't know a bloody thing. But if you learn the craft of making movies first, then you have a basis from which to proceed. Gain experience, and after that, who could stop you from being anything you want or can be?'

'You think I should go to college to learn the basics?'

'That's the gist of it.'

'Would you consider making a deal with me?'

'I might . . . if your terms are reasonable.'

'Since my father listens to you and he doesn't seem to take anything I say seriously, would you talk him into giving me a job at the studio next summer after I graduate, and then in the fall when I'm in film school at UCLA or USC, I can work at the studio part-time. Now that's reasonable, isn't it?'

'Perhaps, but it all depends on where you're willing to start – at the bottom so you can learn the business?'

'If those are *your* terms.'

'Those would certainly be my terms. But we're talking a deal here and, so far, we know what *you* want to get out of this but you still haven't told me what *I'm* going to get.'

'Well, I know what you want in general. You want to do a great job on me in order to show Daddy how great you are. Isn't that how it works? In return for everything you're getting out of this marriage – his love, devotion and prestige, all the advantages of being Mrs T.S. Grant – you run a great household, make great parties and give great—' She smiled slyly and said, 'Oops! I mean – raise his daughter to be a credit to her father or something like that.'

Nora smiled coolly. 'Something like that . . . So, what are you offering in return?

'I'm offering to be a really good girl, not to give you a bit of trouble and no back lip, either.'

'Well, *that* would be a pleasant change. How could I possibly turn down a deal like that?'

'So we *have* a deal?'

'Done.'

'Done,' Sam repeated, giddy with pleasure. 'If I wanted to risk melting that icicle of a heart of yours I could almost forget myself enough to give you a big hug. But I won't. I mean, then what would you do for a heart?'

'Fortunately, we'll never have to find out.'

'Are you sure your father couldn't come to this meeting, Honey? Perhaps we should postpone it until I have a chance to talk to him,' the guidance counsellor asked.

'Oh no, Mrs Durand. He's immersed in his new novel

499

and you know how writers are. Their muse is all! He doesn't even stop to eat or sleep.' She thought that surely Mrs Durand would be impressed with that line. Most people were. 'Besides, there's nothing to discuss. I'm going to UCLA – they have a very fine school of drama and there's no reason for me not to go there since drama is what I want to study and I can still live at home.'

'But we were counting on you going to Princeton. And that *is* what your father told us when he enrolled you – he wanted you at Princeton. You're letting us all down.'

Honey pushed the long hair away from her face nervously, feeling the need to apologize. 'Our plans have changed and – besides, we don't know if I could have got in to Princeton.' She stood up thinking that if she did so, Mrs Durand would dismiss her. 'Probably, I wouldn't have—'

'Of course you would have. You scored almost perfectly in the SATs and you're a Beasley girl who is number one in her class, one we *hoped* would be our valedictorian. And your father's a Pulitzer prizewinner who himself went to Princeton. They never would have turned you down except maybe for – Well, there is one thing they might have turned you down for,' she said, slamming books about in her frustration.

'Because I'm half-Jewish?' Honey suggested softly.

'Of course not,' Mrs Durand said. 'They took your father, didn't they? And that was over twenty years ago. If they turned you down it would have been only for your looks.'

'My looks?' Honey asked, bewildered.

'Yes. It's hard to take a girl as pretty as you seriously, you know. But I suppose it won't hurt you if you want to be an actress.'

'But I want to be a *serious* actress.'

Mrs Durand smiled cynically. 'In that case, you may have a problem and I can only wish you good luck.'

'I do have one more question. You said something

500

about me possibly being valedictorian. Since I'm not applying to Princeton does that mean I'm out of the running?'

'I didn't say that,' the counsellor said defensively. 'But what does it matter anyway? What does it mean on an actress's resumé to say she was valedictorian?'

'It's an honour, isn't it? And if I earned it fair and square, then I want it! I want it for my father. It will make him glad.'

When she came home Teddy was waiting for her. 'Mrs Durand called.'

Honey sighed. 'I thought she would.'

'Don't you think you should have talked this over with me before you came to your decision?'

'Maybe. But I had made up my mind and there was no use talking about it. Are you terribly disappointed?'

He shook his head.

'Are you mad?'

He shook his head.

'Then what are you?'

'Glad. I would have missed you so.' He opened up his arms and she ran into them.

'But they may not let me be the valedictorian now, Daddy, and there was a good chance I might have been.'

'Do you mind, sweetheart?'

'Yes. I wanted you to be proud of me.'

'Then it really doesn't matter since I couldn't be prouder of you than I already am. But that doesn't matter so much either.'

'Oh, Daddy, you're not making any sense. Of course it matters if you're proud of me. What could matter more?'

'Your being proud of yourself . . .'

Babe was torn between wanting to go away to school and staying in Los Angeles with Sam and Honey. Going to school on the East Coast and living away from her

501

mother and father would be liberation at last. Of course, if she could have gone off to school *with* Honey and Sam, that would have been heavenly liberation. But it wouldn't be *her* decision in any case. Only Catherine's and the Judge's. She wouldn't even be asked what she wanted or where she wanted to go. Still, it was one of the few times that even they didn't make an instant decision. Rather, Babe overheard them toss it back and forth for a while and it sounded like a two character play:

She: (Wistfully) It would be rather nice if we could say that our daughter was going to Radcliffe. Janet Rush is always bragging that *her* daughter goes to Radcliffe – it means that a girl is intellectually superior and will get a fine academic education. It was my father's dream that I'd go to Radcliffe . . . (Voice trailing off)

He: (Severely) We agreed a long time ago that we would not talk about your father just as we agreed that we didn't want Babette to go to Radcliffe, isn't that so? All she would meet at Radcliffe would be boys from Harvard, which is a hotbed of radical professors, drugs and Jews. Besides, Babette is *not* intellectually superior and has no need of a fine academic education since she's never going to be a scholar. Most likely she will never practise a profession no matter what she majors in.

She: (Subdued) Well, there are other schools. Alicia Madison went to Smith and she married a lawyer who graduated from Harvard who isn't even Jewish. Kevin O'Keefe. He's practising in Boston.

He: (Scoffing) Boston Irish! Catholics! And we know what we want, don't we?

She: (Sigh) Yes . . .

He: (Sternly) And considering everything, I don't

502

	have to remind you that Babette needs constant supervision.
She:	(Tremulous) Yes, of course.
He:	And we don't want her traipsing off to the East to find herself a husband and stay there after all our work. We want her right here, don't we? Isn't that what we agreed on?
She:	(Resigned) Yes, Terence, of course.

End of discussion, end of liberation . . .

To Babe it sounded as if there had been no need of a discussion – it sounded as if everything had been decided a long time ago. And she didn't need a superior intellect to gather that many years before, some kind of a deal had been struck between her mother and father and that a big part of the deal had to do with her – she whom the Judge had referred to that one time as another man's trash.

But one thing *was* a big surprise. She had always thought that Catherine ruled their roost leaving only the courtroom for the judge to strut his stuff. Now, she wasn't so sure. The conversation she had just overheard almost sounded as if her mother was the defendant who had already copped a plea.

'We've decided that you're going to the University of Southern California, Babette.'

'But both Honey and Sam are going to UCLA. I'd really rather go there, too. Can't I, please? Since both are really good schools, what difference does it make?'

'The difference is that UCLA's part of the state university and USC is private and we feel that it's to your advantage to go to a private university. As far as Honey and Sam going to UCLA, well, it's time to broaden your horizons. We can't have the same friends for the rest of our lives.'

'But I thought you *liked* them. You've always said that no matter what else, Honey *was* a lady and very bright. And you said that in spite of everything, Sam had a certain style. You *did* say that, Mother, you *did*!'

'Yes, but what of it? We have to move on in life. We must grow! And I never said you still can't be friends with them just because you're going to different universities.'

'They'll develop different interests—'

'Let's hope so, since Samantha is going to be in film school and Honey is taking drama, and *you're* going to major in political science.'

'That's another thing. *Why* am I going to major in political science? I don't even like it.'

Catherine indulged in that laugh Babe hated. 'More reason you should study it. We must extend our interests. That's the reason we educate ourselves. Now just suppose you meet and marry a man who's interested in a political career. You'll be all prepared to make him a wonderful wife—'

'But what about what *I'm* really interested in?'

Catherine smiled at her in that annoying, condescending manner. 'You mean there *is* something besides boys?'

'It's possible,' Babe snapped. But what could she do? Tell her mother that she was interested in being a stand-up comic? She'd shit a duck. She would go straight to the phone and call the judge.

'What would you say if I told you I was interested in becoming a brain surgeon?'

'Considering everything, I'd say you were making a *joke.*'

'Talking about jokes, would you like to hear one? Do you know what everyone says USC is short for?'

'Tell me,' Catherine said with that patronizing smile. 'I'm sure your father would appreciate knowing.'

'University of Spoiled Children . . .'

This time, Catherine didn't smile. 'Well then, dear, you'll fit right in, won't you?'

49

Ever since Teddy had told her over three years before that people avoided him because he was addicted to failure, Honey hadn't been able to get it out of her mind. And for months now she couldn't stop thinking that if Teddy could stop drinking, he'd be able to write the novel that would re-establish his literary genius. And ever since, the puzzle of which came first – the chicken or the egg – had plagued her. Did her father drink because he couldn't write the novel to equal the genius of his first, or was he unable to write the novel because he drank? Or did he drink because Mimi – the woman he still loved – had left him? Had he lost her because of the drinking or the failure? Which addiction had come first? The bottle? Mimi? Failure? And could he recover from one without being cured of the others?

Nora had told her that the only person who could really help someone was the person himself. But maybe some people just needed more help than others and maybe the only way to help Teddy was to cure him of all his addictions at the same time. Then she got it into her head that the only way to find out for sure was somehow to effect a meeting between Teddy and Mimi. Maybe if they could just see each other something might happen. Maybe with the passage of time Mimi might even reciprocate the love Teddy still felt for her and it could turn into a reconciliation. Stranger things had happened and Mimi was neither so young nor the star she had once been. Perhaps that would make a difference.

But how could she bring them face to face? They hadn't seen each other for years, hadn't as far as she knew, even been in touch. But then when it was announced that she was to be valedictorian, after all, she thought that maybe that was some kind of a sign – that this was her big chance.

She'd write a letter her mother wouldn't be able to resist. She would *beg* Mimi to come to her commencement to hear her deliver the valediction. She would throw herself on Mimi's mercy. She'd *vow* that if Mimi did this one thing for her she'd never ask another favour of her for the rest of her life and she would *swear* that if Mimi would only come she'd love her for the rest of her life no matter what. What mother, even an alley cat, could resist an offer like that?

Having left Teddy downstairs in the library watching a movie on television (with a bottle of vodka close at hand) – one he himself had written which had never made it into the theatres before being sold off for TV viewing – she sat herself down at her desk to compose the letter to Mimi. But then the last thing she expected was to have Teddy walk in on her as she was nearly through with the first draft. Quickly she covered the letter with an open copy of *Cosmopolitan*. 'Movie over already?'

'No, but I decided I'd seen enough since I already know how it all comes out,' he smiled, his speech a tiny bit slurred. 'I thought I'd see what you were up to.'

'Nothing much. Just looking at this magazine Sam gave me. There's an article she wanted me to read.'

'Come on, Honey,' he grinned. 'I saw you cover up something you didn't want me to see. I know – you were working on your speech, right? But you don't have to worry about *me* seeing it before it's finished. Let me take a look.' Then before she could stop him he uncovered the letter and started to read and she was terrified at the look on his face. Never before had he looked at her this way – with such cold rage! Her sweet, gentle father . . . *It has to be the liquor!*

'How *could* you write to that *ugly* woman *begging*

506

her to come to your graduation? After how she's treated you!'

How can he call her ugly? Everyone knows she's beautiful!

'Where's your pride? Never once has she asked to see you. All she's ever done is send you those ridiculous presents all these years, and those stupid cards. I never said anything to you – I didn't want to fill you with my poison and I kept hoping that maybe she'd do better. But she never has. And now, this—'

'Daddy, please!' She tried to put her arms around him, but he pushed her away and she was stricken.

It has to be that he's even drunker than he appears.

'You're not a little girl any more. You're grown up and you're smart. I thought by now you'd have the intelligence to figure out for yourself what she is but obviously you haven't. Otherwise, you wouldn't shame yourself by writing to her like this, begging her to what – *love you*? And I was so proud of you, the way you turned out. I thought you were the one thing I'd done right! And now I see I've failed again. By writing this letter you not only shame yourself, you shame me!'

'No, don't say that!' she screamed. 'I did it for you! I only wanted her to come to my graduation on the chance that you two could reconcile – because you love her so much!'

He stared at her, the soft brown eyes wild. 'Love her? I *hate* her! I've hated her practically from the moment I married her!'

After she cried and he cried and they apologized to each other over and over, they went down to the kitchen and Teddy made them hot chocolate and she took out the cookies.

'But Daddy, why didn't you ever tell me before that you hated her? You'd never talk about her, you were always so sad when I brought up her name.'

'I thought only a bad father would tell his daughter that he hated her mother. He would have to tell her *why* and

507

I couldn't do that to you. And I was *sad* for *you* . . . that you'd been so badly cheated by having her for a mother.'

'But when you married her, didn't you love her?'

'I was bedazzled by her, spellbound . . . It was as if I were a fly caught in her web, completely in her thrall. I still remember the moment I first saw her and to this day I can't imagine any young man who didn't know what she really was, *not* falling in love with Mimi L'Heureux.'

'But how could you love her so much and end up hating her so? How can that be?'

'Disillusionment. There is no one who hates so much as one who's disillusioned.'

'But how were you disillusioned?'

'By betrayal. There is no one quite so disillusioned as one who's been betrayed.'

'Betrayed? How?'

'Well, think of a very young man, starry-eyed in love with an irresistible woman. A woman most men would die for, one who made you think that out of a world of men she loved and desired only you. What kind of betrayal do you think would practically destroy such a besotted fool?'

There was only one answer. 'Sexual betrayal,' Honey said.

'Yes.'

'But *not* right away?' she begged.

'Yes, right away. At first, I couldn't believe it . . . wouldn't accept it. I thought I had married a goddess but all I had married was a whore.'

The word sent a shiver through her. 'But why did she marry you only to betray you like that?'

'Because I believed in her . . . in the golden myth of her. Because she thought that with my help she would transcend what *she* knew she was – nothing more than a face and a body with a golden tarnish – to become a great actress with a timeless image. She married me so she'd have her very own writer to help her make the big leap. But it didn't work out that way. In the end we both

508

turned out to be what we were intended to be all along –
I the failed writer and she the eternal slut!'

'Oh Daddy! But once you found out what she was
and you no longer loved her, why didn't you leave her?'

'I couldn't.'

'But why not? If you hated her—'

'Because by the time I was ready to admit that my
marriage was a failure she told me that she was pregnant.'

'You mean *me*?'

'Yes. And she said that if I left her she'd have an
abortion. It was a kind of blackmail because she knew
how much I wanted a child.'

'And she didn't?'

'No. Women like Mimi don't really *want* children.
Pregnancy can put one out of commission for months
and it's always a worry about what it will do to the
figure. And then once a child is born, one has to do
something with it – it's a burden if not a responsibility.
And worst of all, a child is always a reminder of one's
age both to the public and to one's self. And if one is a
sex goddess – well, age *is* a consideration as much as the
figure.'

Everything Teddy said made sense but for one thing.
'But if she never loved you and things weren't good
between you and nothing that you were doing for her
professionally was working out and she didn't really *want*
a child, why was she willing to have a child just to keep
you?'

'Ego and greed. The ego couldn't bear that there was
a man who didn't love her . . . want her . . . and the
greed wouldn't allow her to give up anything she already
possessed.'

'So you had me. And after I was born you left France
and came here to Los Angeles . . .'

'Yes . . . for the money. I told you, Mimi was greedy.'

'But that didn't work out either?'

'It didn't. Not for either of us. And then she wanted to
go back to France where she was still the sex goddess.'

509

'And by then she was through with both of us – you and me? She didn't want us any more.'

'Wrong. She wanted us. By then we were part of the total baggage she toted around – all those Vuitton suitcases and trunks and jewellery boxes and make-up cases – and she never wanted to give anything up that was hers. Who knows? Maybe she thought she could make use of us some day – her faithful husband, the beautiful little girl that looked just like her. If nothing else, it *was* a great publicity shot.'

'But she wanted us and yet we *didn't* go with her.'

'I refused for both of us. By then I knew you were better off without a mother who didn't love you. It's a terrible thing to love and not be loved in return.'

'Yes, and you loved me enough for two,' she said and even though it wasn't a question, he whispered, 'Yes.'

Still, there *was* one question that remained since Mimi L'Heureux was a woman who slept around so widely. *Was she, Honey L'Heureux Rosen, really Teddy's daughter?*

Honey studied herself in the long mirror before she went to bed – the golden hair, the topaz-coloured eyes, the nose, the cheekbones, the dazzling white smile. Then she stepped back from the mirror the better to examine her body, the full breasts, the narrow waist, the round swell of hips. Oh, she was Mimi L'Heureux's daughter for sure but there had never been a doubt about that. If only there was something as positive to prove that she was Teddy's.

Then again while this might be nice, it *was* of no real importance. Not to Teddy and not to her. As far as either one of them cared she was the daughter he loved completely and he was the father she loved without equal. And he was *such* a lovely man who had been no less than that for as long as she could remember. Oh no, proof was immaterial.

Still the dirty word *betrayal* crept into her bed as she switched off the bedside light. Who were the men Mimi

510

had betrayed Teddy with? Was one of them anyone she knew?

50

'OK, this is the big day,' Sam said over lunch in the school cafeteria.

'I'll bite,' Babe said taking an extra large nip out of her cheeseburger. 'Why is it so big?'

'Well, we're all familiar with that famous saying: "All a Beasley girl has to do to get a higher education is walk down the street and jump the fence of the Playboy Mansion." But so far as I've heard, no one's ever really done it. And we'll be graduating soon, but before we do, *we're* going to make Beasley history and actually *do* it.'

'And today's the day?' Babe asked.

'You got it. Do you want it?'

'I want it,' Babe said.

'Do we have to?' Honey asked. 'I don't see the point.'

'There is no point and that's the point,' Sam sighed. 'We do it just to do it.'

'Let's plot the action,' Babe was gung-ho. 'Do we go over the wall at the main entrance or over the back wall?'

'We can't go over the back wall,' Sam said flatly. 'That's where the sentry house with the uniformed guards are, we'd be spotted in a second.'

'So then we *have* to go over the wall on Charing Cross. The gate's electric so that's out but the wall's low, even with the iron spikes mounted on top and that chicken wire stuff at the back's not too high. The whole business can't be more than four feet tall. I can hop it easy and so can you two if you're careful not to get one of those spikes up your ass,' Babe chortled.

'But it can't be *that* easy,' Honey said. 'If it were, they'd have a mob climbing it every day. It must be wired to give electric shocks.'

Babe howled. 'They can't do that! If they were allowed to do that, it would be like giving them a licence to electrocute and the lawn would be littered with fried bodies.'

'True,' Sam agreed. 'At the same time, the wall *has* to be wired to an alarm system. The minute you start to climb an alarm must be set off. Otherwise, it just doesn't make sense. I mean, why would they have such a low wall if it's not wired for security? It would be an open invitation for all kinds of weirdos who want to see all those girls walking around with their boobs exposed and those rooms with the mirrored ceilings and video cameras.'

'Those rooms are in a separate building apart from the main mansion,' Babe said with authority. Then when Honey and Sam stared at her, she rolled her eyes. 'No, I'm *not* speaking from personal experience, I'm quoting from an article I read.'

'What we have to do is get around that security system,' Sam said, thinking hard. 'The important thing is not *how* we get inside but just that we *get* inside one way or another, just so we know we've done it and we can describe it all to the rest of the girls, and *it* and *we* become part of Beasley lore. And I think I know how we can do that without any bodily risk. We just saunter up to that *rear* entrance where the guardhouse is and Honey, bold as brass and shaking her ass, says, "Hi, I'm Mimi L'Heureux's daughter and Mommy said I should drop by and say hallo to old Heff for her." And then the guard takes one look at the figure and the mop of hair and says to his buddy, "Hey man, this is the real stuff!" and they call up to Heffie boy who says, "*The sex kitten's daughter?* By all means, send her and her friends ahead!"

512

And then we're *in* and I wouldn't be at all surprised if, besides meeting Hughie in his silk pyjamas, we get a guided tour – grotto, pool, sex rooms and all!'

'Great scenario, Sam,' Honey said, 'only there's one hitch. I refuse to announce myself as Mimi L'Heureux's daughter. As far as I'm concerned, there is no such person. She doesn't exist.'

'OK, this is the plan,' Babe gave Honey and Sam last-minute instructions as they stood in front of the mansion on Charing Cross where all was quiet serenity with not a security guard in sight. 'When I say go, it's over the wall. It should take three or four seconds at the most, before we land on the other side and the security alarm starts blasting like mad – count on it. But don't stop for a second – just keep running to the rear of the house. It will probably take them at least a minute or two to get here from the guardhouse and by that time we should be out of sight, so they'll have to hunt us down. Then by the time they catch up with us, we'll at least have got an eyeful.'

'If they don't cart us off to jail,' Honey said, 'and then we'll have to call the judge.'

'Don't say that even in jest. You *know* all they'll do is show us out of the gate. Isn't that right, Sam?'

'I suppose . . . if they don't shoot first.'

'OK, wiseass, but if they do, just remember that this was your idea, not mine. OK, I'm going to count. At three, we go.'

At three they went but only Babe managed to make it over the wall before she was immediately surrounded by guards with walkie-talkies transmitting the message: 'We've got a live one.'

'Yikes, there must be twenty of you guys!' Babe giggled. 'But no problem. Just don't shoot and don't call the Judge and I'm sure we can work out something here,' Babe smiled at the men ingratiatingly and winked at Honey and Sam watching goggle-eyed from the other side of the wall.

'Oh, oh,' Sam whispered to Honey. 'I don't like that wink.'

'What shall we do?'

'You stay here and talk to them. Stall for time while I try and get Nora on the phone just in case they don't just show her the gate.'

'But what will I talk about?'

'Anything! Tell them you're Mimi L'Heureux's daughter.'

But before Honey could even retort to that, the guards were showing Babe through the gates with a 'Come back in a couple of years, kid, and we'll give you an escorted tour'.

51

When Honey didn't feel well during graduation rehearsal and it was discovered that she was running a fever, Sam immediately volunteered to drive her home but the office refused her offer. They'd follow their usual procedure – the school nurse would drive her in the Beasley station wagon.

'My father's going to be surprised to see me at this hour of the day,' Honey told the nurse on the way home, but when they pulled up to the kerb and she spotted the Jaguar behind their Ford in the driveway, *she* was the one who was surprised. And then she was glad they hadn't allowed Sam to drive her after all, since it was *Nora's* Jaguar and when it came to Nora, Sam had a very active imagination. And then she realized that her own wasn't doing badly, either.

What is Nora doing here at eleven in the morning?

She was hardly in the habit of dropping in at their

house and had never even made a formal visit. And Honey found herself wishing that she wasn't thinking what she was thinking.

'I'll walk you to the door, Honey. And I should speak with your father,' Nurse Laughlin said.

'Oh, I'm not *that* sick – I probably just have that twenty-four-hour thing that's going around. And I see that my father has a visitor, a business appointment, probably. I'm sure he'd rather not be disturbed.'

'But I'm supposed to—'

Honey laughed. 'I'm almost eighteen, Mrs Laughlin, and I'm not really very sick. Not only can I get to the door on my own, I think I know enough to get into bed, turn on the television, and drink lots of fluids. I'll probably be back in school tomorrow. So really, you don't have to bother.'

'OK, Honey, I guess it'll be all right. But I'll sit here until you're inside just the same.'

Honey walked up the path slowly, her heart hammering wildly. If the nurse weren't watching, she wouldn't even walk into the house. She'd just hide in the backyard until she saw Nora leave, just to be sure that she wasn't walking in on something . . . something that she really didn't want to see.

Then she told herself that she was being silly.

Nora's probably here just to ask Teddy to be on a committee or something, or maybe they're planning some kind of a surprise for me and Sam – a graduation party.

Still, if she tiptoed into the house and they *weren't* downstairs having coffee in the kitchen or a conversation in the living room, she wouldn't go upstairs at all. She'd just keep on tiptoeing until she was out of the back door.

Careful to do it as soundlessly as possible, she turned her key in the lock, waved to Mrs Laughlin, tiptoed in and – her heart sank. Everything was in order, everything was as neat as a pin, and except for a bird chirping from the side patio, it was as silent as a graveyard . . . which *meant* that they were upstairs!

515

Oh, Daddy, how could you? Of all people, with Sam's father's wife! And Nora! Sam had been right about her after all . . .

Well, she'd do what she'd planned – keep on going through the house and out of the back door. But she wouldn't hide in the backyard. She wasn't all that sick. She could go for a walk . . . a long walk . . . and come back in a couple of hours. By that time, Nora's car was bound to have gone and she could pretend she'd just come home and didn't know a thing.

But nothing will ever be the same again.

She wouldn't be able to look her father in the eye for a long time to come and she wasn't sure she could ever act normally around Nora again.

But then she saw that the door to the library was *closed. They were in there!* And then, though she'd always believed eavesdropping to be despicable, she tiptoed to the door to listen and when she heard the low hum of conversation, she was relieved that they were talking and not moaning and groaning.

But she couldn't make out what they were saying and maybe that was just as well. Maybe it was the conversation of sated lovers caught up in the afterglow . . .

She went out of the back door but instead of walking around the block, she crossed the street to wait and watch and before too long she saw them come out of the front door together – Teddy was walking Nora to her car. Well, Teddy would do *that*, she thought. Didn't a gentleman always walk the lady to her car afterwards? And even if he *were* having an affair with Sam's father's wife, wasn't her father always the gentleman?

Besides, Teddy wasn't as much to blame as Nora. *He* wasn't the one who was married. And maybe it was because he was so vulnerable, Nora was just one more person or thing he couldn't resist becoming addicted to . . .

After Nora's car pulled away, she walked back to the house and let herself in, calling out, 'Teddy, it's me!'

He came rushing out of the kitchen, alarmed. 'Honey! What are you doing home so early? Is something wrong?'

'Not really. I wasn't feeling so good so the nurse drove me home. She said I had a little fever. But it's nothing. I'll just go to bed for a while.' She started for the stairs, eager to go to her room so she wouldn't have to talk to him.

'All right, you get into bed and I'll bring you up some soup. Or would you like scrambled eggs and toast?'

'No, thank you. I don't want anything. I'm not hungry.'

She was halfway up the stairs when he said, 'It's too bad you didn't get here a few minutes ago. You just missed Nora.'

He was actually *telling* her that Nora had been there, so maybe it wasn't what – She turned around, trying to sound casual, 'Nora? What was she doing here?'

'Bringing me some good news. News so good she had to come and tell me herself.' His voice was full of excitement and she came rushing downstairs again. 'Tell me, quick!'

'Some friends of hers are doing a special for CBS and Nora suggested me as the writer and I had a meeting with them, but I didn't want to say anything until it was definite. I didn't want you to be disappointed. But today she came over to tell me I got it! I'm going to write the special!'

'A *television* show? *Not* a screenplay.' Honey was disappointed.

'Yes, a television show, but what a television show! It's going to be a Thanksgiving story – a two-hour drama about a sick man who's made a mess of his life, coming home for Thanksgiving after being away for twenty years. I don't think you understand what an opportunity this is for a writer, Honey. When I get an assignment to do a screenplay it's just hack stuff. They won't take a chance on me for a quality movie. But this is something I can sink my teeth into – this is very possibly Emmy-winning material.'

She threw her arms around him. 'Oh, Daddy, that *is* good news!' How could she have suspected that he would fool around with another man's wife?

And *Nora . . . How could I have doubted her? She was helping Teddy help himself . . .*

'I'm very grateful to Nora,' he said, almost as if reading her mind. 'I think she did a lot of fancy talking and fast footwork to pressurize them into giving me this chance.'

'I'm sure they're giving you this chance because they *know* you're the best writer in Hollywood. Probably all Nora had to do was tell them that you're a genius.'

Teddy laughed. 'I think you're a bit prejudiced. As a matter of fact, I think Nora is too. Anyway, I'm going to have to work very hard not to let her down.'

'Yes,' Honey agreed, 'you can't let her down. But to tell the truth all along I've been disappointed that – I was always hoping that—' She caught herself. She'd almost said that she was hoping that Nora would help him help himself but she couldn't say *that*. She amended it to: 'I always wondered why she didn't get her husband to give you a really wonderful assign—' her voice trailed off.

Now why did I say something so stupid as that? She really had botched that one up.

Teddy looked at her sharply and said stiffly, 'I guess because she knows what you and I know – that I would never work for TS no matter how much I needed the work.'

She could have asked him how Nora would have known this but today was not a day for questions – today was a day for celebration.

'You know, Daddy, I feel so much better now I don't even have to go to bed. And I'm starving. Why don't we go in the kitchen and celebrate by sharing some scrambled eggs? If you'll scramble, I'll toast. Deal?'

'Deal.'

He put his arm around her as they walked into the kitchen and then she saw the two *empty* liquor bottles on the counter next to the sink and she could still smell the alcoholic fumes coming up from the drain. And when Teddy turned to the refrigerator to get out the eggs, she quickly snatched the bottles and threw them in the dustbin on her way to the bread box. Some things you didn't talk about – you just kept your fingers crossed and whistled a lot.

52

'Where's Daddy?' Sam asked, as she sat down to breakfast.

'And a good morning to you, too,' Nora offered drily. 'As for your father, he had an early breakfast meeting.'

'Well, it's only seven-thirty now. How much earlier than that can you get?'

'Would you believe six o'clock?'

Sam looked at her suspiciously. 'Not really. Where would he eat at that hour?'

'Plenty of places. Twenty-four hour coffee shops, for one.'

And hospital testing rooms that serve up barium and nasty things like that – hold the toast please.

Sam shook her head. 'He shouldn't be racing around in the middle of the night. He'll get sick. You really should try to make him keep more regular hours, Nora.'

Nora, not in the mood to parry words, said, 'Quite. Was there something you wanted to discuss with him?'

'Actually, there's something I want to discuss with *you*. I was thinking that it would be nice if we had a graduation party. Right after graduation, I thought.'

'There's a reception at Beasley after the exercises.'

'I didn't mean *right* after. I meant that evening.'

'I don't think so, Sam.'

'Why not? I didn't have a birthday party this year.'

'I'm afraid I have to say no. Perhaps we can arrange to go out to dinner somewhere that night with Babe and Honey, some place you like – Chasen's, maybe?'

'What's special about that? We go there all the time.'

'Well, let me think about it.' She had a splitting headache. 'Perhaps I can come up with some place you'll feel is properly special – flying to San Francisco or something.'

'You're saying that you refuse to make me a party?'

'It's just not a good time, Sam.'

'Not a good time? For whom? You? You're always giving parties for everything and everybody. Just last month you gave that party for that senator from Colorado. And when I ask you for one little party, you say no?'

'But that was last month. *This* month is not a good time. You're not a baby. It can't be so hard for you to understand that I might not have the time to make a big party now.'

Sam's eyes narrowed. 'Well, I guess it's a matter of priorities. You haven't found it difficult to find the time to spend visiting Teddy Rosen lately.'

Nora tried to keep her temper and ignore Sam's innuendo. 'True. I believe that helping out a friend in need of assistance does take priority over making a party for a *mature* young woman who's had her share of parties and will be going to loads of graduation parties this month anyway.'

'Since I *am* a mature young woman I'll accept that that's a priority, but could you explain to me of what possible assistance *you* could be to Teddy Rosen? Do you clean windows, or have you added typing to your list of accomplishments or is it only that you give good—' she broke off grinning slyly.

For a moment Nora considered giving her a crack across the face but she forced herself to smile. 'What

I do is give good *ear* since Teddy Rosen asked me to listen to him read his teleplay so that he could get some feedback.'

'Oh? Is that what they call it these days? *Feedback?* Maybe you ought to tell Daddy about it. Maybe he could use some of that feedback stuff at the studio, you know?'

Again Nora was sorely tempted to slap the insolent face but again she resisted. It wouldn't do any good. Sam was going to need a lot more than that to get her through the next few months.

53

'Do you believe how they're wasting our time?' Babe groaned. It was graduation practice but mostly they'd been sitting around for what seemed like hours while the members of the faculty in charge of the proceedings got things organized. 'We could be at the beach or shopping for our formals for the prom. Have you decided yet if you're going to wear one of your mother's movie star dresses, Honey?'

'I've decided and I'm not.'

'Then how do you feel about *me* wearing one of them?' Sam asked. 'There must be a gown in there that would fit me. *All* of them are spectacular. It's a shame for them to go to waste no matter how you feel about your mother.'

'They're not going to waste – last week we donated the trunk complete with contents to the Salvation Army.'

Sam was outraged. 'You didn't? How could you?'

'We just decided we didn't want them hanging around the house any more.'

Just like we don't keep bottles of vodka hanging around either.

'But you know what they say, dresses don't kill people, people kill people,' Babe said, cracking up at her own joke. But Honey didn't laugh and Sam just shook her head in disgust.

'Well, *I* think it's funny and all I meant was that keeping those dresses couldn't really hurt you or your father,' Babe explained.

'It's not that they hurt us. It's more that they had become . . . well, superfluous. Teddy always thought he owed it to me to keep them just in case when I grew up I'd want them, sort of like a legacy. Then when he showed them to me I wore one of the plainer ones – you remember that white dress I wore to our first mixer – and I saved the rest. I hoped, even dreamed, that maybe by the time I grew up, I'd have reason to *want* to wear my mother's dresses, the way boys sometimes want to step into their father's shoes. But now that I'm *pretty* much grown up–' she laughed, '– a young woman graduating into adulthood as they keep reminding us, I've outgrown that dream. I know now that I'll *never* want to wear her dresses. And so giving them away to the Salvation Army is sort of another kind of graduation, if you follow me.'

'I guess I can see what you mean,' Sam acknowledged.

'But why did you pick the Salvation Army?' Babe asked. 'You should have picked a more up-scale charity. I don't mean to sound snobby – *au contraire* – but the people who shop at the Salvation Army store aren't exactly in need of a movie star's gold lamé evening gown, if you get my point.'

Honey smiled, eyes sparkling. 'Not that I want to sound too, too *contraire*, *ma petite*, but I think that some of those people may be very much in need of a movie's star glamorous evening gown . . . more so even than someone who can afford to shop in an *upscale* resale store. Just suppose some girl from an underprivileged home is shopping for a dress for her prom and like a dream come true she finds a movie star's glamorous gown she can buy for a few dollars. After all, you know what they say,' she said giving Babe a sharp poke in the ribs, 'one woman's nightmare can be another woman's dream . . .'

54

It was getting to the stage when Babe relished the game of pulling the wool over her mother's eyes, more so every day.

'Why is Sam picking you up instead of your date?'

'It's easier this way since the party's at some fraternity house and our dates are on the hosting committee.'

'But I never met this boy, Babette.'

'Neither have I – he's a blind date.'

'You know I don't like you going on blind dates or dating young men I haven't met.'

And I like the ones you haven't met best of all. 'Well, look at it this way, Mother. If I like him, you'll meet him and if I don't, you didn't waste your time.'

'What's his name?

'I told you, I don't know. I'm just doing Sam a favour by going on this blind date since she's dating his buddy.'

'Well, you must know the name of the fraternity?'

Why are you asking, sly boots? Are you planning to call me just to check if I'm really there?

'Uh-uh. All I know is that the frat house is on Hilgard. You know, UCLA's Greek Row.'

'And is Honey going to this party, too?'

Why, are you planning to question her, too?

'No, it's a pity but she can't go. She says she has to stay home to practise her valedictorian speech.'

'What a pity you couldn't say that.'

OK, Catherine, you scored but she who laughs last laughs

523

*best and if you knew who I was really dating tonight, you'd
just about croak . . .*

'You have to cover for me in case my mother calls,
Honey. The story is that I'm double-dating with Sam
and we're going to a frat party.'

Honey sighed. She hated the stories Babe invented so
she could go out with boys Catherine didn't approve of
and she hated having to lie for her. And worse still, she
herself worried about the boys Babe went out with on
the sly. And now she had a new mysterious boyfriend
she wouldn't even tell her and Sam about – he really had
to be *bad* medicine!

'But if you told her you're double-dating with Sam
and I'm not even involved, why would Catherine even
call here?'

'You know how tricky she is. She might get it into
her pointed head to check if what I told her is the same
thing you *know*. She thinks you don't lie even if you are
part Jewish and part French Catholic.'

'Isn't she more likely to call Sam's house?'

'I'm covered there, too, since Sam's picking me up
so she won't bother calling the Grant house. Then Sam's
dropping me off to meet my date and don't bother asking
who he is because I'm not telling.'

'Where's Sam going after she drops you?'

'She didn't say. Maybe she's going over to the Beverly
Wilshire Hotel to ask Warren Beatty . . . ha, ha . . .
to take her to the prom since she hasn't asked anybody
yet and it's count-down time and she insists she's not
going unless it's with a movie star. But that's a story
for another day. Right now, all I'm asking you to do
is to corroborate *my* story, keeping in mind that you're
not testifying in court so you don't have to get in a sweat
about lying, OK? Probably Catherine won't call anyway
because either I'm getting better at my stories or she's
getting older and slipping. Gotta go, love ya!'

Honey thought a moment, then dialled Sam's number

and was relieved when she got Sam in. 'I was afraid I wouldn't catch you before you left to pick up Babe.'

'I was just about to leave so talk fast.'

'Well, she said you were going to drop her off to meet her date and I was wondering if when you drop her off you could sort of hang around or something – you know, try to see who he is. She's acting so mysteriously that – I don't know, but I'm worried. Why won't she tell us who he is? She always has before. This one must really be bad news.'

'I'll try. But if it gets too complicated, like hanging around for a long time, I *can't*. Not tonight. I just don't have the time.'

'Why? What do *you* have to do?'

'I got to go. Talk to you later, OK?'

The phone went click, leaving Honey more upset than ever. What was going on? First Babe, now Sam was being mysterious. What did Sam *have* to do tonight that was so urgent? Go and see Warren Beatty at the Wilshire? She had assumed Babe was kidding but who knew? Sam was capable of practically anything. And she did so love to throw everyone into a state of shock and what would be more shocking than if she really walked into the Coconut Grove on prom night on Warren's arm? Every last Beasley girl would *die* on the spot! Still, would Sam give even Warren Beatty priority over finding out if Babe was in over her head? She seriously doubted *that*.

An hour later Teddy walked into her room as she still sat at her desk mulling gloomily. 'Something wrong, sweetheart? You look like the troubles of the world are settling on your weary shoulders. Is it that bad?'

She smiled at him. 'Not really.'

For a brief second she considered telling him what was troubling her, but thought better of it immediately. It would sound so ridiculously trivial and Teddy had enough to deal with, what with writing his teleplay which was really important, and at the same time

525

staying sober. That was enough for *any* man without having the added concern of with whom Babe was possibly exchanging bodily fluids or whether Warren Beatty would or would not attend a prom with Sam.

Then she noticed that Teddy was wearing his dark grey suit – the one he wore for really serious occasions – for the second time that week, the suit he'd already worn at least four or five times that month. 'You're going out?'

'Yes.'

'Heavy date?' she tossed off trying to sound casual.

'Heavy, but I don't know if it's what *you'd* call a date,' he said haltingly as if he were about to say more, then thought better of it.

Oh, great, now he's *acting mysterious.*

'Well, what would *you* call it?'

'More like a meeting.' Again he acted like he might say more but then there was a horn honking from the street and he said, 'I have to go. See you later.' He kissed the top of her head and left. She went to the top of the stairs to see him racing out of the front door, slamming it shut behind him. She ran down the stairs, meaning only to yell after him, 'Have a good time,' but it was too late – the Jaguar was already pulling away from the kerb. *Nora!* And then she saw a bright green Alfa Romeo shooting past as if in hot pursuit. *Sam!*

She trudged upstairs again wondering what was going on. Teddy was going somewhere with Nora and Sam was tailing them. Apparently Sam thought that playing detective with Nora was more important than playing detective with Babe since she had had to race back from dropping Babe off to pick up Nora's scent. But why? Did she *know* that Nora was picking up Teddy? What did she suspect? *Clandestine meetings?*

Meeting was the word Teddy had used with her, but he *had* been acting mysteriously. And why *was* he having *evening* meetings with Nora? It was one thing to meet her

526

during the day since she was helping him with his teleplay, everyone knew about *those*. But evening meetings
were another thing altogether – especially since no one
else knew about them.

That did make it all sound less than innocent. And
Teddy hadn't simply come out and said, *I'm meeting Nora*,
or *I'm going to a meeting with Nora*, which would have been
his usual straightforward style. And even though it was
hardly unusual for Nora and TS to go out in the evenings
separately – he busy with studio affairs and she with her
political affairs – *something* had aroused Sam's sleuthing
instincts.

Suddenly, it came to her and a bolt of relief shot
through her. Teddy had used the word 'meeting' and
Nora was forever going off to political *meetings*. And she
was helping him now in whatever way she could – was
responsible for getting him the Thanksgiving teleplay
assignment in the first place. It made sense that Teddy
was trying to help *her* with her activities in any way that
he could. That would be the honourable thing to do and
Teddy *was* an honourable man. And the reason he didn't
mention it to her was because she always teased him about
being a totally apolitical animal.

Now she felt ashamed that she had doubted him even
for a few minutes, and Nora as well. But then she had to
laugh thinking about Sam following the two of them
to what she presumed was a *clandestine* rendezvous. Was
she ever going to have egg on her face! Then the thought
of clandestine meetings brought Babe back to mind and
again she was plunged into gloom.

Anxious not to lose sight of the Jag, Sam made an illegal
left into Pico on red without even bothering to check the
stream of traffic coming at her. And then it hit her! Talk
about your *déjà vu*! This was the same trip she'd taken
only a while ago when she'd dropped Babe off at that
slimy joint in Hollywood halfway down the street from
that little fleabag motel with the neon light flashing its

name – Stardust Heaven – and its main attraction – adult movies – before she hightailed it back to Bel-Air not to miss Nora taking off.

But she reminded herself, as her pulse seemed to race in pace with her engine, that Pico ran for miles and it would be *too* much of a coincidence if Nora and Teddy were heading for the same bedbug haven as Babe and her obviously slimy date.

Still, wouldn't it be a howl if Nora and Teddy and Babe and her sleaze-squeeze met in the parking lot when the two couples were leaving. They'd have so much to talk about. If nothing else they could exchange critiques about the adult movie they'd all just seen. Maybe the four of them would even go for drinks. No, make that coffee! Babe was underage and Teddy, that fucking hypocrite, was supposedly off the stuff!

But then as she saw the neon light flashing Stardust Heaven on and off she sent up a silent prayer that the Jag *wouldn't* make a left into the motel's parking lot and it *didn't!* But then just as she was saying, 'Thank you, God, for small favours,' the Jag made a right into the parking lot of a small, shabby church right across the street!

You have to hand it to Nora – she's smart as a fox and twice as sneaky. Why park a distinctive looking car in Trash Heaven's lot where anyone might spot it when all you had to do to find heaven was cross the street? Who, after all, would even notice a car parked by a little shabby church you could just as likely overlook as not.

Honey jumped when the phone rang though she'd been half-expecting it to ring – a kind of terrible premonition ever since she'd seen Sam whizzing by in pursuit of Teddy and Nora. She didn't know what she expected to hear when she picked up the receiver – a report of a car accident or Sam telling her she'd discovered Teddy and Nora doing unmentionable things to each other after all. But she breathed a tentative, 'Yes?' to hear Babe breathe back raggedly, 'Honey, do you have the car? I need you to come pick me up. Please, Honey, come fast before I do something terrible . . .'

Sam waited several minutes for Nora and Teddy to come out from the church's parking lot and cross the street to the motel and when they didn't, she was puzzled. What had happened to them? Where had they disappeared to? Was there another exit at the back? Leaving her own car parked in the street, she got out to investigate. No, there was no other way out of the lot and yes, there was the Jag, parked next to a pickup.

It was crazy! Had Nora and Teddy Rosen driven all the way to Hollywood only to desecrate a church with their unholy screwing? Then a Buick pulled in and she saw an elderly couple get out and enter the church through a side entrance. *What the hell is going on here? She had to see! Quickly she followed the couple in to find herself at the back of an auditorium where some kind of meeting was going on. And then up towards the front of the room she spotted Nora sitting and Teddy standing. Then she heard Teddy's beautiful, resonant voice: 'My name is Teddy Rosen and I'm an alcoholic . . .'*

She ran out, desperate to get out of there before they saw her. She'd die of shame if Teddy Rosen found out that she'd been spying on him – what she'd suspected him of . . . or that she had heard him declare himself. He was such a fine, sensitive man and he was sure to consider this the most horrible betrayal of his privacy . . . of his very soul. He would never forgive her and if he told Honey what she'd done, Honey would never forgive her either.

She jumped into her car, stepping on the accelerator even before she turned the ignition key and the engine coughed but didn't catch. *Oh God!* Was she going to be stuck here to be discovered when the meeting was over?

For a second she thought about abandoning the car and fleeing on foot when the motor caught. *Thank you, God!* Then in order to make a swift U-turn in the middle of the street, she took a left into the flow of traffic without

*so much as a fast look to the right or the left, not noticing
that she barely missed being slammed into by a blue Ford
making its own way left into the drive of the motel across
the street.*

Honey's eyes searched the motel lot anxiously even as
she made her turn, fearful of the condition she'd find Babe
in – she had sounded so desperate, had even threatened
to do something terrible. *Like what?* But even after she'd
completed the turn she still didn't see Babe though
she'd said she'd be waiting near the entrance.

Honey circled the lot on foot. Maybe Babe was hiding
between the cars, not wanting to be seen.

*Oh God, where is she? What's happened to her? Did she go
back into one of those dreadful rooms? Had someone dragged her
back?*

Then Honey prayed that she wouldn't have to go
knocking on the doors of all those sordid rooms to
find Babe. But even worse would be to look *beyond*
those doors and *still* not find her. Then she'd have to call
somebody to help her search and whom could she call?
Not the police! *Oh God – not the police!* And certainly not
Catherine and the judge! That would be betraying Babe
so badly she might never recover.

And she couldn't turn to her father or Nora. She
didn't even know where to reach them. But maybe Sam
would be home by now. Having discovered that Teddy
and Nora were engaged in some innocent activity after
all, she might have raced home to nurse her embarrassment. Yes, if she didn't find Babe on her own, she'd call
Sam and maybe between them, they'd figure out what to
do short of calling the cops.

Driving home, Sam found herself wishing that she could
find the courage to confess to Honey what she'd done,
taking her chances that Honey would forgive her. It
would make her feel so much better not to have any
secrets between them. But would it make Honey feel

better or would it just give her something more to worry about? And what about Teddy? If he wanted Honey to know that he was going to AA he would tell her himself. *Whatever, it's not my secret to reveal* . . .

As for Nora, *tonight* she'd been innocent but that didn't mean she *wasn't* guilty of being unfaithful on numerous other occasions with someone other than Teddy Rosen. For days now her father had had the look of a haunted man – something very serious had to be worrying him. And it couldn't be the studio that was worrying him since they had a terrific smash on their hands – *Dead On Target* had been number one at the box office for weeks already. It had to be something else and what else could gnaw at a man as trusting and good-natured as TS than to be betrayed by the woman he adored?

There was only one more thing for her to do before she started knocking on those doors, Honey thought, sick to her stomach. She would check in the little office to see if the desk clerk or the manager, or whatever they called the person who gave out room keys in places like this, had seen Babe hanging around in the lot.

But just before she entered the office, she saw a car partially hidden behind a clump of shrubs alongside the small structure and she walked round to take a look. And then her heart began to pound wildly. But it couldn't be! Not *his* Ferrari! But then she saw the vanity licence plate and she knew that there was no way she was ever going to be able to call Sam – the vanity plate read STUDIO 1. There was nothing like advertising but really not quite the thing to do if one wanted to make Stardust Heaven one's home away from home.

Oh, Babe!

'Honey . . .'

She spun around to see Babe, seemingly tinier than ever, tear-stained cheeks, eyes ringed with smeared mascara, her bright yellow party dress an incongruous note in the dimly lit lot. At first, Honey shuddered with relief. At least Babe was safe. Then she was overcome with rage, shaking Babe like a rag doll. 'Where were you? You said you'd be in front!'

'I started walking. I was thinking of . . . of just disappearing.'

'I thought you were dead!'

'I thought of that, too. Just killing myself.'

Honey looked at the Ferrari and back at Babe. 'Maybe you should have thought,' she said angrily.

Then they both burst into tears before Honey hustled Babe towards her car. 'Let's get away from this place before he comes out. It's bad enough looking at you. I don't think I could *bear* looking at *him!*'

Actually, it had been quite a while since she was able to bear looking at TS anyway, thinking of all the possibilities . . . of all the reasons that Teddy might have for not being able to bear looking at him, too. If what she thought might be true, then it had to be very hard for Teddy . . . hard for the betrayed to look into the face of one who was instrumental in the betrayal without wanting to kill him. And it would be especially hard for Teddy – he was such a gentle man.

They drove for several blocks, silent except for Babe's soft weeping, until Honey said, 'You'd better stop crying before you get that mascara on your dress. It's going to be hard enough to get your face cleaned up in a hurry so I can take you home to your mother.'

'Honey, are you ever going to forgive me?' Babe asked in a small, piteous voice.

'It's not I who has to forgive you,' Honey said in despair. 'It's Nora! And Sam! Oh, Babe how *could* you?'

'You don't understand. When he first asked me to meet him I thought he was kidding. And then when I realized he *wasn't* – that the great T.S. Grant who could have his pick of beautiful women, of practically every sexy wanna-be in Hollywood, wanted to fuck *me*, well . . . I was flattered. I mean, if he picked *you*, I could understand it. Or even Sam, if she weren't his daughter.

But me? It was like suddenly I was special and no one ever thought I was special before – certainly not my mother or the Judge.'

'Oh Babe, but you *are* special – you always have been.'

Babe shook her head. 'No. Well, anyway that was the first time and it was over so fast – he said he had an appointment – it was like I didn't get enough. I wanted to hear him tell me he loved me. And then after the second time I realized that he never was going to say it because he *didn't* love me. He was just another Hollywood letch with the hots for anything *young*, like it would rub off on him and the only reason he picked me was because he *knew* I was an easy lay. As if it were written all over me.

'But then I met him a third time because if nothing else, I was putting it over on everybody, especially my parents. I thought that was really cool and I didn't even *think* about Nora or Sam. But tonight when I started to take off my dress and he told me to hurry – he had another appointment in an hour – I realized that it *wasn't* cool and that the only person I was really putting anything over on was – me. And I did think of Nora then, and of Sam. How heartbroken she'd be, and I felt really scuzzy. So I never took off the dress and I told him I was leaving. And do you know what he called me? A cunt! But that was OK, I guess, because that's what I am.'

'No, Babe, you just made a mistake! And what he saw written all over you was that you were vulnerable. And that's probably who he always searches out – the vulnerable. He's a . . . a spoiler. But his car's still there. Do you know why?'

'No, I can't figure it out. After he called me a cunt he just buried his face in the pillow and started to *cry*.'

'Cry? But that doesn't sound like him.'

'He *cried*. But somehow I *knew* that it had nothing to do with me, that it really didn't matter to him if I stayed or went, that he was crying only for himself.'

They were silent then, thinking about why T.S. Grant

would cry – the man who always smiled, no matter what.

Then Babe asked anxiously, 'Do you think I *have* to tell Nora and Sam?'

'No. What you *have* to do is *never* tell them. I'm not sure about Nora, but I am about Sam. She adores TS – this would break her heart. It has to be our secret for ever.'

'What about TS?'

'He's not about to tell anybody.'

'But how will I ever look at him again? I can't.'

'Well, maybe we'll both get lucky and we won't have to.'

Honey had barely crawled into bed after taking Babe home when she heard Teddy coming up the stairs. *God!* What with Babe she'd almost forgotten about Sam following him and Nora.

When he tapped lightly on her door, she said, 'It's OK, you can come in. I'm not asleep.' She clicked on her lamp.

'Good,' he said, coming in and sitting down on her bed. 'There was something I wanted to tell you. I hesitated to before . . . well, I didn't want you to be disappointed in case I slipped. But I don't want there to be any secrets between us so I want you to know that I've been going to AA.'

Oh God! 'And that's where you were tonight?'

'Yes,' he said with eloquent satisfaction. 'And Nora went with me for back-up.'

Honey wondered if Sam, following them, had ever found this out. She hoped so though herself she could never bring it up. It wasn't her secret, if that's what it was, to reveal.

'Oh Daddy, I'm so glad you told me and I'm so glad you're going. And I *know* you won't slip . . .'

'That's what Nora said. It was she who urged me to go, you know, and – well, I don't know if I would ever have gone if she didn't offer to go with me to be my own private cheering section. I'd hate to let her down.'

'You won't. You're not a man to let anyone down and I think Nora Grant is wise enough to know that . . .'

And a whole lot more.

55

'You have to go to commencement tomorrow, TS, if it's the last thing you ever do!'

He shook his head in admiration, managing a wry smile. 'You're really something, Nora. You never give up. Going to that graduation tomorrow before I check into the hospital on Monday might very well *be* the last thing I'll ever do, but all that's on your mind is getting me to that damn commencement.'

'I'm sorry, I shouldn't have phrased it that way. It was stupid of me but it's only an expression. You *are* only checking into the hospital for an exploratory.'

'Checking in only to be told I'm checking out?' he laughed. 'Sure sounds like a hell of a waste of time.'

'I refuse to listen to all this gloom and doom. Even if the news isn't, well – *good*, it doesn't mean you're not going to have a full recovery.'

'Still playing the cheerful optimist, eh? Well, that's generous of you, considering everything. But that's *one* of the reasons I married you, you know. Your generosity, cheerful optimism and positive attitude. I know you think it was only the money but your many other fine qualities counted for a lot, too. For one, I've always admired your guts.'

'And I yours, which is why I won't tolerate all this self-indulgent whining.' Her tone was chipper but it pained her to see in the too-bright glare of the descending sun streaming in through the conservatory's windows how pale he was – his year-round LA tan all but gone – and how worn, the creases of the craggy face having deepened to that point when they no longer presented the image of one who had only laughed well and looked too often into a noonday sun. She went to the windows now to draw the draperies closed, musing on the perversity of nature – how in these minutes before it disappeared into the horizon, when all too soon it would be twilight, the sun seemed to shine its most brilliant.

'But what I've *most* admired about you, Nora, is your straightforwardness. How you never hang back or hold back. It's disappointing that you're holding back on me now.'

Smiling, she sat down next to him on the chintz covered couch. 'I don't know what you're talking about, TS, and one thing I always gave *you* credit for was speaking clearly.'

He chuckled. 'Don't you know better than to try to crap an old crapper? We both know the score, so why don't we lay the cards out on the table in the best Nora and T.S. Grant tradition and get on with it?'

Get on with it? Business as usual? But it's too late for business as usual and TS knows that. Now he's only asking that I acknowledge that and not demean him by being less than honest with him in these twilight hours. But did she really owe that to him considering how painful it was? So much easier to gloss it over with optimistic phrases and glib assurances right up till the end rather than help him accept and prepare for the relentless inevitable.

Count up the score, Nora.

Yes, he *had* deceived her badly when he married her and yes, it *had* been a devastating blow to discover that he didn't love her. But she'd recovered and they'd made their peace and ever since they had both been as honest with each other as they knew how to be. At the very least, they had both kept scrupulously to the terms of their agreement. No, he didn't love her because he was incapable of that kind of love. Still she knew that he not only admired and respected her, he *liked* her thoroughly . . . probably more than he ever had liked anyone, and while it wasn't love, it wasn't nothing, either.

True, they'd often been *adversaries*, but they had never been *enemies*. Rather they'd been partners, in a manner of speaking, and even cohorts. One might even say, though they hadn't been lovers save for that falsely sweet beginning, by now they were intimate friends. And even after they had sat down to deal and her terms had emerged far tougher than he had imagined, he had remained – as he liked to describe himself – a sporting kind of a fellow. And he had never held it against her that she had held him up. Even now he was being a good sport though the odds were against him and he'd been handed the dirtiest deal of all.

No, it hadn't been what most would call a brilliant marriage – on the other hand, it hadn't been a disaster either. And even if she had come up short on one end, in many ways she had got far more than she'd bargained for and sometimes that was all one could reasonably expect. And yes, she owed it to him to lay the cards on the table but very carefully so as to spare them both as much pain as possible.

But what she hadn't bargained for now was he showing her new cards to reveal more than she wanted to know.

'It was an act of unfaithfulness,' he began.

'But confessions aren't necessary,' she broke in. 'Our agreement never specified fidelity. Discretion only, was implicit.'

'But I committed an *indiscretion* and a pretty lousy one at that. And while I might not have violated the letter of the contract, I violated its spirit.'

'Please, don't do this, TS. Whatever it was – well, it just doesn't matter any more.'

'But it does and since we're spelling it all out it's the only honest thing to do. If nothing else, won't you indulge a dying man by letting him confess his sins?' he chided.

'If you must—'

But then she was sorry she'd given him permission. When he said 'I screwed little Babe,' in a flat monotone and then she could only whisper, '*Our* Babe? Oh, damn you, why *her*?'

'My only excuse is that I was depressed about my condition and was reaching out . . .'

'But that doesn't explain choosing *Babe*,' she cried in despair. 'She's so young and so vulnerable. You took advantage of her desperate need for a father's love. You could have had your pick of hundreds of women!'

'But I thought only sweet and tender flesh could save me. I thought, how can I die if this sweet young woman loves me? I thought there was a magic to it – some kind of strength, some kind of redemption. Can you understand?'

This is what he calls being honest? Laying this grotesque aberration on me? How dare he talk of redemption? How dare he ask for my understanding now?

What she understood was that while she'd been bending over backwards to rationalize everything he did and didn't do and didn't feel . . . had spent tortuous hours trying to *understand* and forgive, he – when looking into the face of death – remained as selfish and calculating as ever with his usual disregard for every other member of the human race.

'So Babe was your choice of victim to prey upon. But why not Honey?' she demanded, voice rising in fury. 'She's as young as Babe and so much more beautiful . . . easily as desirable as her mother whom you didn't hesitate to screw when it suited your purposes . . .'

'I *never* considered Honey.'

'Why? Because she wasn't an easy mark like Babe? That you knew she'd reject you? That she has your number and shies away from you? I've seen her do it.'

'It's true she avoids me just like her father avoids me.

Maybe it's because she's figured out – as Teddy Rosen has – that it's quite possible I could be her father . . .'

Of course. She could not deny that she hadn't thought of that herself a long time ago.

'And that's why you didn't try with her? How admirable! How noble! You didn't try to fuck the girl who was possibly your daughter! And Sam? What about Sam? You knew *she* wasn't your daughter and she would never have resisted you! Oh no, never,' her voice was low now, ragged with her bitterness. 'She's always been so hungry for your love, she would have done anything you asked of her, and with a passion. Tell me, why not Sam?'

She didn't know what she hoped to hear in answer. Maybe that he'd say, 'Because even though *I* knew she wasn't my daughter, *she didn't*, and that made it impossible – that the idea of sex with her own father would, in the end, prove too damaging for her to live with.'

But he didn't say that or anything that she could in some way find redeeming. Rather he said, 'It never even occurred to me. Frankly, I never found Sam sexually appealing.'

With that such an uncontrollable rage swept through her that her hand whipped out involuntarily to slap him, but he didn't even blink, he only smiled that little ironic smile and then she ached to spit into the smile.

'But you didn't let me finish. I was going to say that the reason I never found Sam appealing or wanted to be around her is that the sight of her makes me feel guilty as hell.'

Did this guilt – guilt, but *not* love – constitute one small measure of redemption? She was too heartsick to know and wanted him to stop talking, but he refused to be denied and insisted on telling her all about the short-lived affair which had proved to be unsatisfactory finally to both him and Babe, and had ended with her walking out on him, leaving him to weep into the Stardust's mouldy pillow.

'So why did you weep? Because Babe came to her

539

senses and was rejecting you or because you were being denied your sex? Cheated of this magic that you hoped would save you, but at the same time knew that *nothing* could?'

'Wrong on all counts. I wept because of the realization that I had *had* the magic that would have saved me right in the palm of my hand—' he cupped her face in the heel of his palm '— and I didn't know it and bargained it away.'

She went to the windows to open the draperies this time, to let in the last light of day now that the sun had fully set and buried her face in the curtains to weep because it was so late . . . too late for everything . . . even for that magic potion called love.

'All right, Nora, I'll go to the commencement to please you but it will have to be a trade-off.'

'What do you want in exchange?'

'I don't know how long this damn business will take, but however long, I'm prepared to play out my losing hand with as much grace as I can muster. But the one thing I refuse to put up with is having Sam sitting by my bedside fussing over me, moaning and whining and carrying on, begging her daddy not to leave her. You have to spare me that, Nora. Send her away some place . . . as far away as possible.'

And she agreed for Sam's sake, if not for his. Sam had to be spared the pain of watching the man she believed to be her father die. And now that she knew that TS had acquired this penchant for confession presumably in the name of all-cleansing truth, she also had to protect Sam from a possible deathbed confession that would reveal that she wasn't his daughter after all. It was a truth that could destroy her.

He took her hand. 'But you'll be there? Till the end, for as long as it takes? I know I don't have the right to ask, it was never part of the deal but what the hell — a dying man deserves a little something extra and you always were a good sport as well as a damn good winner.'

Was she a winner? At best that was open to interpretation. But she was determined to be a good loser. 'I'll be there.'

And then it was inevitable – as inevitable as the violet twilight deepening into a velvety darkness – that he would take her in his arms. There was even a fitness to it and a timeliness, she thought, that she would go into them as passionately as that first night they had met . . .

PART NINE

COMMENCEMENT

Los Angeles,
1974–5

56

She made her call at 2 a.m. LA time to awaken Tony, still in his bed. 'In case you're too groggy to recognize the voice, old chum, this is your friend Nora Grant.'

'I'm not too groggy to know when you start calling me old chum, it's a favour you're after and not a marriage proposal.'

She laughed. 'I'm calling strictly to present you with a business proposition.'

'But I'm an actor, remember, not a businessman.'

'But I'm offering you a marvellous opportunity to be both. In fact, I'm offering you a chance to be something else, too, that you always said you were dying to be – a producer.'

'Either I'm still asleep and dreaming or you're trying to pull a fast one.'

'Wrong on the first, right on the second.'

'It's too early in the day to sort that out,' he groaned. 'What am I right about?'

'That I'm trying to pull a fast one. Fast as in tomorrow, first thing.'

'As you well know, Nora, there's only *one* thing I'm good at this early in the morning so if it's speedy action you're after, maybe you'd better spell it all out for me fast.'

After she did, he moaned, 'I *knew* I'd be sorry it wasn't a marriage proposal. All I can say is I hope I won't let you down. The first time around I didn't hold on to you and the second time around I didn't manage to hold on to Hubie.'

'But that's what's so wonderful about life, Tony

545

darling. Each time around it's a new deal. Only this time hold on for dear life, please, don't let this one get away . . .'

Teddy woke Honey for breakfast at seven-thirty even though graduation was scheduled for two.

'But Daddy, I didn't have to get up until nine or ten,' she complained.

'I just couldn't wait any more, I have a surprise.'

'Belgian waffles with strawberries or blueberry muffins?'

'Sorry, we will entertain no guesses. Just put on your robe and slippers and come downstairs.' Then he practically pulled her down the stairs, made her close her eyes and threw open the front door. By now Honey had an idea what the surprise was – her graduation present – but when she opened her eyes and saw the white Thunderbird in the driveway, she screamed, 'A T-bird!' and burst into tears.

'I hope those aren't tears of disappointment,' he smiled. 'You weren't by chance expecting a Maserati—?' But they both knew she was crying tears of joy and it wasn't because the T-bird was far beyond her expectations, but that it meant *they* had accepted the teleplay and paid out the final cheque.

'Oh, Daddy, did they *really*, *really* like it?'

'Did you say *like* it, kid? They *loved* it!'

'Oh!' She gave him another hug. 'Does Nora know?'

'Well, *she* helped me pick out the car and she said *white*. She said beautiful blondes should always drive white. And you know Nora's unfailingly right about these things.'

'Unfailingly. But the question is what *are* we going to have for breakfast? Belgian waffles or blueberry muffins?'

'I think *you* should tell her when she comes down to breakfast which should be any moment now. She said she was setting her alarm for nine so she'd have plenty of time to get ready, allowing an hour for make-up and an hour for hair.'

'Why do I have to be the one to tell her?' TS, on his third cup of coffee, demanded. 'You're not playing fair, Nora. All you said I had to do was go to graduation. Why can't *you* tell her about London and the movie?'

Nora took a sip of tea to wash down a second aspirin. 'Because it's her graduation present and it will mean a lot more to her if *you* tell her about it. If I do she'll only get suspicious that I'm trying to get rid of her for the summer.'

'But she'll carry on so! All those tears and kisses and general hysteria. You know how I hate hysterics. That's what I like about you, Nora – you take things in your stride.'

'She *is* only eighteen – she's entitled to make a fuss. Especially about such an exciting offer! To fly off to London to live and work on a film! I remember when I was eighteen and going down to London-town to have myself a time! Oh, I didn't take it in my stride. I was *so* excited . . .'

Her eyes shone with the memory and TS looked at her longingly. 'I wish I had known you then,' he said finally.

'Oh, you wouldn't have liked me,' she laughed. 'I was hardly your film star type. I was so – well, *unformed* – kind of like a lump of unmoulded clay and I was in a constant state of excitement as Sam will be. Especially when she hears that she'll be working on a film with Tony. You know how she loves her movie stars just like her father does.'

But TS was in no mood to be teased. 'That's the reason *you* should be the one to give her the big news. After all, Tony was *your* idea and *your* husband.'

He cracked the top of his soft-boiled egg and grimaced, 'Nora! This egg is *not* soft-boiled. Raw is what it is and you know how I hate eggs that aren't cooked the way

547

I like them. And you *know* how I count on you to see that they are.'

Babe called Honey at ten. 'Only got a minute. We're going for breakfast at the Hotel Bel-Air in honour of the big day. I just called to see what kind of car you got.'

'You're amazing! *How* did you know I got a car?'

'Easy. Half the girls at Beasley already have a car like Sam, and the other half are all getting them today since it's the practical gift that serves a twofold purpose – graduation present *and* necessity. And the Beasley mother considers today her graduation too – the end of chauffeuring her pain-in-the-butt daughter around. So, what kind of a car *did* you get?'

'A white T-bird! I love it! You *did* get a car?'

'Yeah,' Babe said without enthusiasm. 'A Mustang.'

'But a Mustang's super. Don't you like it?'

'A *brown* car is super? *You* get a white car, *Sam* has a green one and I get asshole brown. Well, it figures. As I once told you, I get that shitty end of the stick every time.'

'Oh, come on, Babe. It's graduation time all over America today and how many girls do you think are getting brand-new Mustangs? Really, you should be ashamed.'

'Yeah? Do you know what my fakey father said to me when he handed me the keys to the *refined* – that's how Catherine describes the colour – shit-brown car? He shook hands and told me he hoped that I appreciated it, while Mrs Ice Cube stood there and nodded. But I guess I shouldn't complain. At least he never sexually abused me – at least not that I can remember. And *she* never beat me except for those few times she lost it and cracked my face with a hair brush. But now I gotta go – our very refined breakfast awaits. Tell me, did you ever hear of shit-brown scrambled eggs? I wouldn't be surprised if *that's* what we're going to have as the graduation special. I hear it's the last word in refined dining.'

'Honey, where have you been, girl? I've been calling you for the last half-hour every minute on the minute.'

'Well, if you really want to know I was taking Teddy for a spin in my beautiful white Thunderbird!'

'A T-bird? That's *neat*. Happy graduation, Honey Funny!'

'The same to you, Sammy. But why were you calling me every minute on the minute? Did you get a *new* set of wheels?'

'No, not a car. Something much more exciting. Wait till you hear this! I'm going to England! Daddy told me this morning. Grantwood Studio is making a movie there and *I'm* going to London to work on it! And guess who's going to be the executive producer and the star? This will *really* blow you away. Nora's ex, Tony Nash! Can you believe it? I bet it must be *killing* her because the whole time Daddy was giving me the details she kept interrupting to remind me that while she *hoped* I'd enjoy the experience, *my dear*, the purpose of my going was to learn, learn, learn and she hoped I would take proper advantage of the opportunity and not forget why I was there, blah, blah, blah. Honey, why don't you *say* something?'

'I will as soon as I recover from the shock. How long will you be away?'

'As long as it takes to make the flick, I guess. Maybe a whole year. I don't think they have a shooting script or anything yet, but Daddy says it will be the best training if I'm right there from the *very* beginning of the project.'

'That means you won't be starting UCLA with me in the fall,' Honey said forlornly.

'No, but I'm going to have my very own flat so you and Babe can come visit as soon as you get your first school break and we'll really have a blast! I'm leaving tomorrow!'

'*Tomorrow?* How can you leave so fast? And why? It's not like it's an emergency, is it?'

'Well, you know what Daddy always says: "It's *always* an emergency in the movie business." And I guess he should know. Anyhow, Nora made the reservation and that's the flight she booked me on, tomorrow at the crack of dawn. I don't know why she made it *that* early, but I suppose she figured if I was leaving, the sooner the better as far as *she* was concerned. Honey, you still haven't told me that you're happy for me.'

'Of course I am, but it's all so sudden. Oh, Sam, I'm going to miss you so . . .'

'Me too you, but I'll be back, Honey Bunny, and you'll be coming over to visit. Now I have to call Babe and tell her. See you soon, Honey Moon, at the grad, with your dad.'

She hung up before Honey could tell her that Babe was out for breakfast.

Even before they were out the driveway, the Judge – sitting next to Babe who was at the wheel of the Mustang – launched an ongoing litany of complaints and criticism of her driving until she was ready to jump out at the next red light. Or maybe even, while the car was still in motion.

Finally Babe asked him if he'd feel more comfortable if *he* took the wheel and he took the question in the sarcastic spirit intended. 'Since you haven't a trace of appreciation in you and don't even know how to keep your fresh mouth shut I'm more inclined to take back *the car* than the wheel.'

She was dying to snap back, 'Why the fuck don't you since you're dying to anyway and then I won't have to hear about how ungrateful I am and how I'm no lady, which is getting pretty boring, but still not *as* boring as *you* are to start with . . .'

But she *didn't* say it because then he might well do just that – take back the stupid car and she'd really be stuck for the long hot summer without any wheels of her own. Then, in the fall, she'd have to rely on *them* even for transportation to school and the whole point of going to college as far as she was concerned, was to get away from the two of them and gain a little breathing space. But then, even though she hadn't said it, Catherine demanded that she either apologize for being fresh to her father as well as unappreciative, or they would simply forget about breakfast *and* the graduation exercises as well.

Babe was tempted then *not* to apologize even if it meant missing graduation, but the idea of spending the rest of the day and the evening, too, locked up in the house with the two of them was too dismal even to contemplate and she mumbled the required words. Still, when she brought the car to a halt in front of the hotel's canopied entrance, she hit the brake so hard that if it hadn't been for his safety belt, the Judge would have certainly gone through the windshield.

But, alighting from the car, she winked at the parking attendant, smiled prettily at the Judge and apologized as nicely as any father could have wanted. Then once they were seated in the elegant, crowded dining room with Catherine looking around to see if there was anyone worth noticing and the Judge intent on studying the menu, she got their full attention when she said to the Judge with wide-eyed innocence, 'While you have been a really wonderful father to me, I *know* you adopted me and even though Mother told me I was never to mention the subject, I thought that now that I'm graduating you might want to tell me who my real father is.'

They answered simultaneously. Catherine, pale with either shock or anger blurted, '*Was*, not is, and that finishes this discussion,' while the Judge sneered, 'You wouldn't want to know and believe me – if you did you'd understand why you have so much difficulty being a lady.'

★   ★   ★

'So, what happened then?' Sam demanded, her blood boiling.

'She ordered eggs Benedict, he ordered apple pancakes, and since I wasn't very hungry I only had a glass of hemlock.'

'Babe!' Sam barked into the phone in exasperation. 'I wasn't asking for a rundown of the menu – I mean, what did you say after he said you wouldn't want to know who your father was or about you having difficulty being a lady—?'

'I didn't say anything,' Babe said miserably.

'Why not? You have every right to know the facts – who your father was and why your mother refuses to talk about it!'

'You just don't understand, Sam. I *have* no rights. All I have is Catherine and the Judge. And if I don't let them call the shots and behave myself, I won't even have them. And who cares who my father was if he's dead – where was he when I needed him? Besides, from what the Judge implied, he must have been a murderer or a rapist or something equally wonderful. Anyhow, it's the Judge who counts because he's the one who married good old mom and adopted me, forgiving her her terrible mistake and me, my bad blood. So I guess Catherine's right and I'm wrong – I *should* be grateful that he gave me his name and all, considering everything, and it's no wonder she wants to keep it all a big, dark secret.'

She began to cry. 'Anyway, I don't even care about *him* or what he says even if he is the big man. It's *her* – she's my *mother* and she's *supposed* to love me. But she doesn't. She's *ashamed* of me, and that's what really hurts.'

'Did you ever stop to think that maybe she's really ashamed of *herself*?'

Then Babe had to laugh, even through her tears. 'That's a hot one! Catherine the Great ashamed of herself? Shame on *you*, Sam Grant, for forgetting that she's not only a Lee from Virginia but a perfect size four and a perfect lady who's married to *the Man*!

552

'But tell me more about *your* news. Oh God, what I wouldn't give to be you – being on your own in London, not having anyone breathing down your neck or giving you orders!'

'And what about working with Tony Nash? I saw his picture in a magazine. He's still devastatingly groovy looking even though he must be pretty old considering he was married to Nora. Though I don't plan on holding that against him,' she giggled. 'Wouldn't it really be a howl if I had an affair with Nora's ex? Besides getting *her* where it really hurts, an affair with him wouldn't exactly hurt *me* considering how I've always had a thing for older men.'

'Yeah,' Babe offered dully. 'I know.' The last thing she needed or wanted now was to discuss having an affair with an older man, *especially* with Sam. 'I better go now and get ready. Though I already took a shower this morning Catherine suggested I take another. I guess she thinks I really stink!'

Nora found Sam in the library, buried in thought. 'We have to leave soon. Hadn't you better shower and dress?'

Sam looked up. 'Do you think I *need* a shower?'

'*Need?* Don't you usually shower before you dress?'

'Usually. But Babe just said her mother told her to take a shower though she'd just taken one a couple of hours before. Babe thinks it's because Catherine thinks she stinks.'

'That's silly. If Catherine suggested she take a second shower, so what? Why is Babe making a fuss over nothing?'

'But it isn't *nothing* to Babe. It's her state of mind. She really believes that she stinks as a person. And it's Catherine the Bitch and the asshole, the Judge, who've talked her into it. And I think *you* should talk to *them* about it.'

Nora stiffened. 'Even if what you say about them

is true what makes you think I'm the one to talk to them?'

'Remember that time we got caught smoking pot and Catherine said Babe couldn't be friends with us any more? You talked her into changing her mind. I'm convinced she caved in because *you* know where some of her bodies are buried.'

'That's nonsense.'

'Is it? Babe guessed that the Judge adopted her and now he's admitted it, but they still won't tell her *who* her real father is. All they said was that he was someone pretty bad, which makes Babe think she's bad, too. And I overheard you tell someone that Catherine wasn't from Virginia at all, but from Memphis, Tennessee and that her maiden name wasn't really Lee. *Why* did she lie? And if you tell me you don't know I won't believe you. I'm convinced that you do!'

'In that case, I won't bother affirming or denying. But I'll ask *you* a question. Even if I knew these answers what makes you think *I* have the right to interfere in another's woman's life – tell her what she should or shouldn't tell her own child? And what makes you think I have the right to divulge other people's secrets? And, finally, if you have it in mind to tell Babe even so much that her mother wasn't really a Lee from Virginia, you'd better damn well be sure that this is what she's *ready* to hear, *wants* to hear and will be the better off for the knowing.'

'But everyone's better off knowing the truth!' Sam cried.

'Not always, Sam, not always,' Nora said, though she herself had often been tempted to tell Babe the facts as she knew them. 'As for Babe finding out that she *doesn't* stink – that has to come from her own self-discovery or it doesn't mean a thing. Now, if you don't get ready to go, we'll really be late and your father's already dressed and waiting – impatiently, I might add. And since we're pressed for time, why don't you skip the shower? You

554

already smell as sweet as a rose, even a rose by any other name . . .'

'Now how am I supposed to take that?' Sam said in exasperation. 'That you're serious or making fun of me?'

'You're eighteen and graduating today, Sam. And you have a fairly good mind and you are supposedly mature, so why don't you figure it out for yourself?'

It's a beautiful day for an outdoor graduation, Nora thought, much like the day an eager bride might choose for her wedding day. *Happy is the graduate the sun shines on today.*

The TV weather person had predicted a perfect day, with the temperature at a sanguine seventy-four degrees in Los Angeles (seventy-one at the beaches, several degrees higher in the desert and several degrees lower in the mountains), with near-zero humidity and a minimum of smog. Even the setting was perfect – Beasley's Shakespeare Rose Garden, in which every Beasley girl took a proprietary pride since all its varied specimens had been raised in Beasley's own hothouse of roses (symbolic of the bevy of young women entrusted into its nurturing care) before they were transplanted to the outdoor beds, each named after a fair maiden from one of the Bard's works (this, a scholarly reference to its hallowed soil).

They were a little late which meant that Sam, in her blue robe and tasselled hat, hair streaming behind her, had to run to join her classmates lining up for the procession to take their places on the stand, while Nora and TS took the first two small white chairs they spotted. Looking around, she saw the Tracys to the left of them in the next row forward and Teddy sitting in the front and to the right, head turned, eyes searching the rows and she thought: *he's looking for me to make sure I'm here.* Then he spotted her and waved and she waved back as TS watched with a little smile and enigmatic eyes. He was about to say something but just then the band struck up and the girls – lined up by size, Babe first, Sam last and Honey somewhere in the middle – began their spirited march up the aisle.

'Sort of like a wedding but without any bridegrooms,' TS whispered to Nora drily.

'Oh, the grooms will come along soon enough. After all, this is commencement and that means it's all just beginning.'

Each girl took part in the programme. When Sam joined with three other girls in song Nora heard only her sweet voice above the others; saw only her tall, graceful figure and her fine uplifted head; and felt her heart beat with love, pride and prayer. She glanced quickly at TS to see if there were *something* showing in his eyes, but he was studying his hands. Who knew what he was thinking or if he was even listening?

But it doesn't really matter except that Sam thinks he heard her. All the good qualities are there just bursting to emerge and it has nothing to do with whose daughter she is – she's Sam, and with lots of love, she'll do just fine. She'll even find out who she is and who she's capable of being. And as always, her thoughts leaped to Hubie from whom she only occasionally received a card, and her heart raced again with love and silent prayer. She'd done what she could, she'd provided him with the right name and protected him with secrecy. Now she could only hope he'd find the maturity to know for himself who he truly was.

Now Babe took her place at the white Steinway (Beasley priding itself on having only the finest in the way of equipment) to offer up a piece by Chopin and again Nora glanced at TS to see what emotion played on his face – shame, regret, even some small trace of affection? But he was studying his shoes now as if admiring their high polish.

Then with Babe's adequate, if not brilliant, rendering floating on the balmy air, Nora looked over towards the Tracys to catch their faces in profile. The Judge's face was devoid of expression, his head moving from side to side like a metronome, but Catherine's head was tilted back high as if she were holding it proud and her eyes were shut closed all the better to hear. And while she wasn't smiling, her lips pressed tight, her determined chin nodded as if in approval.

And then the realization hit Nora that while Catherine *wasn't* a nice person, the truth was that in her own way she probably did love Babe! And the bottom line was that Catherine had done no more than she herself had – woven a swaddling cloth out of secrets and lies to secure a name and a future for her child and to give that child a good life according to her lights. How dared she, Natalie Nora Hall Hartiscor Nash Cantington Grant, presume to sit in sanctimonious judgement on pretty Katya Marcus?

What was her crime, after all? That she'd fled her Russian-Jewish immigrant father's dry-goods store in Memphis to marry comic Jackie White who had changed *his* name from Jacob Weiss? And who could blame her that she fled that life, too, when instead of being exciting and fun, it turned out to be a series of dismal one-night stands in dreary clubs, the newlyweds holed up in even drearier hotels? And perhaps it was Babe's birth that moved her to leave Jackie behind to find safe haven with the Judge, who offered both her and her daughter his name, prestige and Protestant heritage, asking in return that Katya Marcus Weiss be brutally obliterated and that she take on his colouring and be what he wanted her to be.

Have I done in the final analysis any less? Does she love Babe any less than I love Hubie or Sam? Who's to say what form love may take . . . what path it can make you walk? Have I lied that much less – white lies though they may be – or do I keep fewer secrets? How can I condemn her? How can I even dream of divulging her secrets when I'm not prepared to divulge my own? And like Hubie, Babe has to find out for herself who she really is or it won't count for much.

557

After the presentation of the diplomas it was time for Honey's valediction. First Honey with her usual grace and charming self-assurance – *oh, she already knew who she was, F. Theodore Rosen's proud daughter (and let no one dare tell her differently)* – favoured the assembled with that fabulous, glowing smile, and then she began to speak . . .

Then without looking at him, Nora could *feel* TS squirming. Was he bored or only uncomfortable sitting so long on the small chair not really built to accommodate a man of his frame? Was he in physical pain or only mental? 'It won't be long now,' she whispered. 'After Honey, it's all over.'

'But it's not over until the fat lady sings.'

'Finally, here at last!' Honey spread her arms in an all-encompassing gesture. 'Our commencement! And now it all begins for us – life! And we greet it with open arms for we, Beasley's class of '74, so beautifully endowed with the love and learning bestowed upon us by all of you – our friends and teachers, our mentors and parents—' she blew a kiss to Teddy '– are now ready to go out into the world prepared to embrace it in love and in truth and in celebration . . .'

Her voice was clear and rang out with a sincerity no one could deny and an enthusiasm that was contagious, and when she finished, there was thundering applause as once again the band struck up and the new graduates, diplomas in hand, rose to their feet to march back down the aisle triumphant.

'Great delivery. Our Honey is going to make a hell of an actress,' TS commented in an aside to Nora as Teddy, on his feet and applauding wildly, turned to wave again at Nora, revelling in *his* triumph. And Nora waved back just as enthusiastically with tears of shared pleasure in her eyes.

'You *really* like him,' TS observed, and though it was a statement rather than a question, Nora answered, 'Of course, I do. Why not? He's such a lovely man.'

Now TS shook his head to say, bemused, 'And I always figured him for a loser, which just goes to prove that I wasn't as good at casting as I thought I was.' He laughed. 'No wonder I find myself in this lousy predicament.'

No, Teddy wasn't a loser. And if one were casting a movie, one might even cast him in the role of hero.

The graduates quickly broke formation to hug one another and rush to their parents and friends to kiss and hug and be kissed and hugged in return. Sam embraced her two best friends before rushing to her father to throw her arms around him so violently, he thought she would solve his problem by strangling him. 'Oh, Daddy, isn't this the most wonderful day? I'm so happy I could die!'

'In that case, before you do,' TS said, disengaging himself from her embrace, 'maybe you'd better give Nora a hug, too, since she's the one who decided you should go to Beasley.'

'Of course,' Sam agreed now that he had made a point of it. And it was true enough that Nora *had* made a wonderful choice – without Beasley there would have been no Honey or Babe in her life. But she made a quick job of it before she dashed off to join Babe and Honey in hugging Teddy to pieces.

It was out of the question that she and TS would remain for the reception, Nora decided. For one, TS was champing at the bit and for another it would be awkward with both Babe and Honey, each for her own reason, trying to avoid him. Any minute now Sam would try to drag the girls over to be congratulated and they would surely resist, and then Sam would be puzzled and hurt.

'Why don't you sit here for a minute, TS, while I pay some respects and tell Sam we're leaving, then we can go.' She made the rounds – the graduates that she

559

knew, the Beasley people, the Tracys and some of the other parents, and girded herself to tell Sam she and TS were leaving.

'You stay here with your friends.'

'But why can't Daddy stay just an hour or so?'

'He wants to write a few memos to Tony so that you can take them with you tomorrow morning.'

'But what about our graduation dinner? I thought we'd be going out with Honey and Babe and their parents. It's the last time I'll be seeing them for a long time.'

'But you have to pack yet and I thought you'd want to spend this last evening alone with your father.'

'I didn't think of that. Of course I do.'

'Good. Now before I leave, I must congratulate Babe and Honey.' It would be the last time she'd be seeing them for a while too. She doubted very much that they would be coming to visit Grantwood Manor again until Sam came home . . . after TS was gone.

Teddy caught up with her just as she was about to claim TS and leave. 'You didn't say goodbye to me.'

'Did I ever tell you I sang songs in a cabaret during the war? Well, I did and the club was filled with soldiers and sailors and one of the songs I sang was "I'll be seeing you, always . . ."'

'I know that song but you're a little mixed up,' he said with a teasing smile. 'There's no "always" in there. It goes: "I'll be seeing you in all the old familiar places that my heart embraces all day through . . ."'

'You're right,' she blushed. 'I was thinking of another song that had *always* in it. I guess I got the titles muddled. It *was* thirty years ago and you know how it is . . .'

'Yes, I think I know how it is.'

57

When the doctors suggested and Nora insisted that
TS undergo radiation and chemotherapy, he demanded,
'What for? The reviews are in and it's a dog and when
the movie's a dog, there are two ways to go. You can
prolong the torture by waiting for the box office receipts
to kill the dog off or you can get it over with by pulling
it out of the theatres immediately. I always believed in
the fast kill.'

'But life isn't a movie.'

'No, it's a magazine,' he retorted acidly. 'When I was
a kid, that was considered a joke. Someone would say,
"What's life?" And the answer was: "Life's a magazine."'

'But I'm not laughing.'

'Neither am I. What's there to do with an old magazine
that's read and finished but get rid of it?'

'No TS! Do the radiation and chemotherapy for me.'

He looked at her for a long time before saying, 'I
would if I thought I'd be doing it for you, but I wouldn't
be. You want me to do it for *Sam* so that after I'm gone
you can tell her, "He tried against all odds . . . he fought
valiantly so that he could be here for you." Deny that if
you can.'

She didn't. She couldn't. She said nothing.

'Well, since it's my show I'm going to do this my
way. I'm going to go to the studio every day until I
can't go any more. Then I'm going to sit by that damn
pool that I never had time to use until I can't sit up any
more. Then I'm going to lie down in my own bed in my
own house and wait for them to carry me to the cemetery.
And that's what you can do for me – *let me*. Promise me

there'll be no treatments, no hospitals and that you'll let me go out in my own style.'

She nodded. He had hardly made a brilliant husband and had certainly been a lacklustre father, but at least she'd be able to tell Sam that her dad had been a stylish kind of guy.

58

Nora knew that TS wasn't planning to go the studio again when he came home and asked if they still kept the pool heated now that it was autumn and Sam and her friends weren't there to use it.

'I forgot to have the heat turned off at the end of the summer,' she lied, not wanting him to think that she'd been preparing for the day when he'd stop going to the studio. 'Are you planning on taking a swim before dinner?'

He laughed. 'You know that joke about the guy who gets his finger chopped off and they sew it back on and the doctor says, "There you are – good as new. Now you can sit down at the old piano and bang out Mozart." And the guy says, "Gee, doc, medical science sure is great these days. I never even knew how to play the piano before." The point of which is I never swam before, so why the hell should I start now?'

No, the point was *not* that he had never swum before, but that he was telling her not to get her hopes up by expecting him to die a better man than he had lived.

'And I never said I planned on *swimming*. All I said was that I was going to *sit*, in peace I hope.'

'Well, if you're not interested in swimming what about a nice, relaxing jacuzzi? All you have to do is *sit* and let the jets do the work. The night air's cool but the water's hot

. . .' she said provocatively.

'Sounds good but only if you'll join me.'

'That's what I'm here for.'

The next morning TS was already sitting poolside when she awoke. 'What are you doing here even before breakfast?'

'What does it look like I'm doing? I'm reading scripts since your cute ex and clever stepdaughter still haven't come up with a worthy project and I hate to see all that money you gave them go down the drain. Maybe you ought to call up your winner-friend, Teddy, and see if *he* has any bright ideas . . .'

'I just might at that,' she said, going back into the house to get a breakfast tray, wondering if TS, so close to the end, was just teasing her, being sarcastic, exhibiting jealousy, or simply trying to mend his fences before he was off into the wild blue yonder . . .

When Teddy answered the door to find Nora he was surprised and then elated. He hadn't seen or even spoken with her on the phone since the girls' graduation. But he drew her into the house and closed the door behind her before he said, 'Long time, no see. Dare I ask to what I owe this pleasure?'

'You may dare, but I'm not sure you'll think it quite so pleasureful when I tell you—'

The flow of exhilaration coursing through him ebbed to be replaced by concern. 'Is anything wrong? Is it Sam?'

'Partially, but not entirely.' Then after she finished explaining she asked, 'So, will you help me out? As you see I'm in a race against the clock. For both their sakes I'd like to see a film in the can before – well, the end.'

Teddy paced back and forth. 'But why *me*? With all the hungry and gifted screenwriters loose in Hollywood and the eager and equally gifted writers floating around in London, *why me*? Even with the Thanksgiving special showing this month I'm not out of the woods yet. I still have a long way to go. How do you know I can come up with something good enough in so short a time?' Then he looked at her suspiciously. 'Are you sure you're levelling with me? That this isn't another one of your philanthropic projects to help the needy – read Teddy Rosen – and just incidentally, of course, make nice-nice all around? Because I personally have no *need* to make nice with T.S. Grant, no matter what.'

'I know that, Teddy. But I think *he* does.'

'So, I *was* right.'

At first he'd been disappointed to learn why she had shown up on his doorstep, but now he was angry as well. 'You want me to write this damn screenplay just so he and I can kiss and make up before he meets his maker, not because you *need* me or even *think* I can come up with a great screenplay in a race against time. I *thought* it was a little strange that in all these months Tony Nash couldn't find a decent screenplay to go into production with.'

'You are only partially right about the making-up part. I *do* need you and I *know* you can do it and it's not so strange, really, that Tony couldn't get it together to find the right screenplay by now. That was a miscalculation on my part. You see, I needed a friend to do me a favour – a loving and old friend I could trust with something very precious to me. But while Tony *is* that friend and is in his fifties it seems I sent a boy to do a *man's* job and now I'm trying to rectify that error. Can you understand?'

He sat down beside her to look into her clear as-a-cloudless-blue-sky eyes and traced each eyebrow with the tip of a finger, which was as close to a caress as he dared allow himself. Then he smiled into those eyes and said, 'I understand that you make it difficult for a *man* to refuse.'

She had to fight down the impulse to touch his yellow hair, but she smiled back into his eyes. 'I must confess – I was *sure* you wouldn't refuse me though I knew I was asking a lot. Probably more than I have any right to considering your and TS's history.'

'How could you be so sure I wouldn't refuse?'

She laughed. 'Because I'm Nora Hartiscor Nash Cantington Grant and that means I know my men.'

It means that by now I can tell the men from the boys, the losers from the winners – can even pick out the few heroes from a field of winners . . .

'It's almost lunchtime. Let me make you lunch. We can eat by the window overlooking the garden.'

She gazed around the living room ablaze with sunlight. 'I think not. It's too bright in here. One sees too clearly and too much. Sometimes it's better not to see *everything*.'

'We don't have to eat in here,' Teddy said, studying her face. 'There's the library – it's very dark in there.' But before she could answer he shook his head, 'No, that won't do either. In the dark you can't tell one thing from another – can't even see what you might be stumbling into. Besides, it's too early in the day to go into such a dark room . . .'

'Yes . . .'

'Maybe the best thing would be if I took you *out* to lunch. That way, there's no conflict . . .'

'No, the best thing would be if I went home to have lunch with my husband. He gets lonely and restless when I'm not there. He depends on me.'

'Yes, I'm sure.'

But she wasn't sure just *what* he was sure of – that she should go home and have lunch with TS or that it was true that TS depended on her. There was really a world of difference there.

She asked about Honey before she left. 'How's she doing at UCLA? Is she enjoying her classes?'

'She's in seventh heaven. Her drama class is doing *Romeo and Juliet* and guess who's Juliet?'

'The starring role? How wonderful! Honey is a natural.'

'Honey's a honey,' he agreed. 'And how's Sam doing, movie-producing efforts aside?'

'Oh, she's having a marvellous time, seeing the sights, driving here, jetting there. Between you and me I don't think she gives a damn whether they ever get started on that film at all. One thing I must say about Tony. He might not make a great producer, but he sure knows how to show a girl a good time.'

Teddy smiled rather wistfully. 'That's a talent too.' And she could not disagree.

When she came home she found TS in a rather petulant mood but she understood – it was hard to sit by a pool while life went on around you.

'Where were you?' he demanded. 'I'm starved.'

'You should have asked Mrs Barry for your lunch.'

'It's not the same as having you here to eat it with me. Where were you?' he asked again and when she said, 'At Teddy Rosen's,' he said, 'It figures.'

'Now what does *that* mean? It was *you* who put the idea in my head to ask him to come up with a screenplay,' she reminded him, not wanting him to be upset even if he had no right to be. 'That's why I went to see him – to ask him if he'd like to try and help out – fill in the gap, you might say.'

'Hah! And I bet he just leaped at the chance!'

'Not really. I had to talk him into it. He definitely held back.'

In more ways than one . . .

59

Sam called to wish her father a happy Thanksgiving but TS – who had insisted on eating his turkey dinner in the library and washing it down with bourbon while he watched Astaire and Crosby cavorting in the old classic, *Holiday Inn*, wouldn't pick up the phone. 'I can't now.

I'm up to the part where Bing's singing, "I have plenty to be thankful for" and I'm dying to hear every word.'

'Your father can't come to the phone right now,' Nora told Sam, 'but he says, "Happy Thanksgiving to you".' But there was so much noise on Sam's end, Sam couldn't hear very well. 'It sounds festive there. Did some Americans take pity on you and invite you to Thanksgiving dinner?'

'Not exactly,' Sam giggled. 'I'm on this darling Greek island and all that noise you hear are Tony's friends celebrating something or other. I haven't the slightest idea what but it's so much fun. We're dancing and drinking wine and breaking dishes. This is the most fun Thanksgiving ever!'

'I can just imagine.'

Yes, she had sent a boy to do a man's job and now she was beginning to wonder what else the old boy was up to.

After *Holiday Inn*, they watched Teddy's Thanksgiving Day special and when it was over, there were tears in her eyes and yet another shot of freshly poured bourbon in TS's hand. 'I have to hand it to you, Nora,' he said thickly. 'That was really beautiful. You sure know how to pick those winners. Is he going to be Number Five?'

Nora struggled with her temper, reminding herself that TS was a dying man and quite drunk for which she really couldn't blame him. *What does he have to gain by staying sober?*

'Oh, I don't know, I think it might be time to call it quits,' she drawled.

'But you can't quit yet,' TS smirked and she was foolish enough to respond, 'Oh? Why can't I?'

'Because after I go you have to try and even out the score. If you count Hubert Hartiscor, whom you were practically married to, you've been widowed three times but only twice divorced. You're entitled to one more divorce.' He raised his glass in salute. 'Better the gay divorcée than the merry widow!' Then he shook his head.

'No, I got that wrong. I should drink to the *real* winner – Mr Number Six. After all, better divorced than dead.'

60

When it became necessary to increase TS's pain medication and he remarked that the days were really growing too cool to be sitting by the pool except at high noon, Nora decided to hold their traditional Christmas Eve party after all. 'We haven't had a party in a long time and it's high time we did,' she told TS, but he disagreed. 'It's too late into the month,' he said, although it was only the first week in December. 'There's not enough time to do it up right and we can't have people saying that the latest Grant party was a fizz at the box office.'

Having said that he went upstairs to bed and the next morning refused to leave it. But instead of outfitting the bedroom with all kind of hospital equipment – a total waste of space, he said – TS demanded that the projection equipment be brought up to the bedroom along with his extensive library of films – stacks and stacks of reels. With all of that, plus the giant projection TV, plus the usual bedroom furniture and the king-sized bed, Nora could see that there wouldn't be room for medical monitors and machines and all those wires that would only get in the way. And she complied with all his requests – a dying man was entitled to fill his space as he saw fit which included only those people he chose to entertain.

But when Teddy called the second week of the month to tell her that he had a first draft of a romantic comedy he'd tentatively titled *In The Name Of Love* and asked if she wanted to take a quick look-see, she asked him to bring it over immediately. While she had no hope now

568

of TS seeing the film in the can, it would be something if production could at least get underway in his lifetime, and Sam would be able to take some small comfort in that.

'I was thinking of sending it over via messenger.'

'No. I want you to take it up to TS *personally*.'

'Must I?'

'Yes, you must. Please, Teddy – that was part of our deal. You're not going to welch on me now, are you?'

'I can think of many things I might do to you but welching is not one of them.'

She played it straight. 'Good. I'll be expecting you.'

But when Teddy arrived, screenplay in hand, TS said he had no time to see either Teddy or any scripts. 'I like the old ones better and I'm right in the middle of a great little oldie. *The Man Who Wouldn't Die*. I have to see how it comes out. Then after that, I'm going to watch *The Thing That Wouldn't Die*. But my last selection for the afternoon sounds the most intriguing though it's not what you could really call a golden oldie, but it's got a real catchy title: *Wives and Lovers*. I hope you can watch them with me, Nora. It's not the same without you.'

Then she went down to tell Teddy that since TS was only into black humour that afternoon and *In the Name of Love* was a romantic comedy, he wouldn't be able to evaluate it properly. 'I think what I'll do is send it off to London as is so they can get started and we won't waste any more time. And since time *is* of the essence, you'll forgive me if I don't ask you to stay for coffee or anything. We have an awful lot of films to get through before . . . well, before we're done. Hundreds and hundreds of titles . . .'

'I understand, but speaking of titles, remember when we were talking about song titles at graduation?'

She nodded, remembering and flushing.

'At first you said the song went "I'll be seeing you, always", and I corrected you. I said there was no always in there, that it went: "I'll be seeing you in all the old

569

familiar places that my heart embraces all day through"
and you agreed that I was right – that you had got that
song mixed up with another that had the word *always* in
its title.'

'And—?' she said warily.

'And I was thinking about it the other day and it
came to me. The song you must have been thinking of
– "Always" is the complete title. Would you like to hear
the lyrics just to refresh your memory?'

She flushed again, lowered her eyes then raised them
to gaze steadfastly into his. 'I don't have the time now.
TS is waiting for me and he has first call on my time.'

But her memory needed no refreshing. She remembered the song quite well and the lyrics went something
like 'I'll be loving you always . . . with a love that's true
always . . .'

Then for days she couldn't get those lyrics out of her
mind until another song took over as the holidays grew
nearer and she thought of Sam and Hubie so far away:
'I'll be home for Christmas . . .'

This Christmas would be the saddest and loneliest
she had ever experienced. And it didn't help when TS
insisted on viewing all the old Christmas classics, one
after the other – there were so many of them! – beginning
several days before the 25th and going at it for punishing
hours at a time. It was as if he were trying to go through
those towering stacks of film reels with an urgency and a
vengeance.

But there were two pleasant surprises on the 23rd. One
was a Christmas card from Hubie from some illegible
place in Africa postmarked a month before. There was
also a brief but lovely visit from Honey and Babe who
came bearing gifts. Honey had two presents – one from
her and one from Teddy. 'Daddy said he wouldn't get a
chance to bring his over so he asked me to.'

No, he wouldn't want to come himself, Nora thought,
tucking the gifts under the tree. 'I know how it is,' she
said. 'The holiday season is so hectic. And now that

you're here, I can save a trip, too. I was planning on dropping these off tomorrow.' She handed Babe one gold-foil wrapped box and Honey two. 'Will you please give this one to your father for me with my very best wishes?'

'I certainly will,' Honey promised. 'And if you'll give me a hug, I'll pass that along, too.'

Babe got into the act demanding that she wanted a hug, too, which she'd keep just for herself. Then the three of them laughed and Nora was relieved. She'd been afraid that the girls wouldn't feel comfortable at Grantwood Manor with TS permanently 'at home', but she supposed what made the difference was that now TS was permanently 'upstairs'.

'And now I want to hear what's going on with you two. Your father told me that you're going to play Juliet, Honey. That's so exciting! How's it going?'

'Wonderful! Of course it's only a class production, not really such a big deal. Still, it would mean a lot to me if you'd come to see it, Nora.'

'I'd love to. When is it?'

'Not till the spring. I don't know the specific date yet, but I'll send you a notice.'

'Well, I'll certainly try to make it. And you, Babe? What are you up to?'

'As you know I'm majoring in political science and my classes don't exactly thrill me, but I am having fun. At least I'm meeting lots of boys and going to lots of parties.' They all laughed at that. 'But – Well, I wanted you to know, Nora, that I'm getting along a lot better with my parents. My mother and I had a long talk and she told me that she realized that she was being unfair. You know, not to tell me anything about my *real* father.'

Nora leaned forward to kiss her. 'Oh, Babe, that *is* good news. I'm so glad.'

'Yeah. She said she never wanted to talk about it before because it was so painful even to think about it because they'd been so much in love and he died in a boating accident not long after I was born. But she said I had nothing to worry about when it came to his background – you know, his bloodlines – because he came from a fine, old Southern family. And the only reason the Judge sometimes made disparaging remarks about him was only because he was jealous. You know, because *he* was her first husband and I was really *his* daughter and they'd been so much in love and all. So I can understand why the Judge would be jealous. I even kind of feel sorry for him, you know.'

'Yes, I know,' Nora said, glancing at Honey. Her face was inscrutable but her hands folded in her lap were clenched so tightly, they were white. *Honey knows what's what without really knowing the facts, but she, like me, knows that sometimes people have to be protected from too much truth.*

'Mother even told me his name. William Butler Cranford of the Charleston Cranfords. Isn't that a beautiful name?'

'Beautiful,' Nora agreed.

And if Catherine Lee of Virginia and William Butler Cranford of Charleston had moved to Atlanta, they could almost have lived out an updated version of Gone With The Wind. *But the important thing was that Babe was happy and that for the time being anyway, she and her mother were friends. Making up, after all, was a healing process.*

And that's a thought!

Then she asked the girls if they'd like to go up and wish TS a Merry Christmas before they left, keeping her tone light and easy. 'It will mean so much to him to see a young face around here since Sam isn't at home and – well, it *is* the season when all good men and women should come together in the spirit of peace and good will.'

The girls hesitated only a few seconds before they agreed and Nora asked them to wait while she checked to see whether TS was napping. But TS, as usual, was watching a movie. 'Babe and Honey are downstairs. They'd like to pay you a short visit – just to wish you a Merry Christmas.'

TS didn't even bother to move his eyes from the screen. 'I'm sure they're just dying to—' he laughed. 'Up to your old tricks again, are you, Nora? But we agreed, didn't we, that I was going to go out in my own style? Tell the girls that I wish them the best of the season, but I can't be disturbed. I'm watching *Christmas In Connecticut* and Babs Stanwyck is having the boss over for Christmas dinner. I gotta see if everything turns out OK.'

After Honey and Babe left she retrieved Teddy's present from under the tree. No one would know if she opened it before Christmas. She tore off the gay wrapping and opened the little box to find a gold charm – a replica of a musical note. She smiled to herself. They were certainly two people with a single thought. Her present to him was the same musical note fashioned into a tie pin.

I'll be loving you always . . . with a love that's true always . . .

Sam called on Christmas Eve. 'You won't believe where I am, Nora!' she gushed. 'I can't believe it myself! At the Ritz in Paris! Can you imagine? Christmas in Paris!'

'What are you *doing* there, Sam?'

'Scouting locations. Tony thought the Ritz Hotel would make a great background for one of the scenes in *In The Name Of Love so* we hopped over to check it out.'

At first she thought of demanding to speak to Tony. But then she told herself not to lose her cool. And after all, if Babs Stanwyck could spend Christmas in Connecticut why couldn't Sam and Tony spend Christmas in Paris? That made perfect sense. As a matter of fact, maybe they ought to retitle *In The Name Of Love*. Make it *Christmas In Paris* instead . . .

61

When TS could no longer keep down the meat-and-potatoes kind of food he liked and she couldn't interest him in custards or gelatin surprises, they struck a deal. For every portion of rice pudding he ate she'd reward him with an ounce or two of bourbon. But then when even the custard didn't go down easily she let him cheat. The supply of bourbon, at least, was something she could count on. Conceivably Sam's and Tony's movie *might* begin shooting in TS's lifetime and it *was* barely possible that he could get through all his reels of movies before the end, but there was no way they'd run out of bourbon. All she had to do was call the nearest liquor store.

But she was fast running out of a commodity she'd been counting on to see her and TS through – her cheery optimism. She had promised TS she'd keep smiling no matter what, but it was getting harder and harder to deliver. And it didn't help that when the rain the state had been praying for began to fall, it fell for weeks. While it was welcome it was also depressing to those used to sunnier days. But then that last week in January, both out of the blue and out of the rain came a miracle, when Elena, newly-hired, told her that there was a man downstairs waiting to see her. 'What's his name?' she asked but Elena, short on English, lifted her shoulders and threw out her arms. *Who is to know?*

'Did he tell you what he wanted?'

Elena repeated the gestures. *Who is to say?*

His back was to her, but she'd know that back anywhere. Then he turned, smiling, and it was as if the sun had come out. Oh, nobody had a more beautiful smile than her Hubie! And he was as handsome as ever despite the differences the years had wrought. He was brawnier, his blond hair was bleached almost white by the sun, he sported a moustache and a beard that were the colour his hair used to be, and there were fine lines etched into the tanned face where before there'd been none. But there was something else indefinable and she struggled to think what it was as they hugged.

'I missed you so, Mum, and it was different, somehow, than how I missed you when I was in Nam.'

'Oh, Hubie, that doesn't make sense. How many different ways are there to miss a mother?' she laughed through tears.

'I don't know but when I was in Vietnam I used to get scared sometimes and wished that you were there to make things all right. But this time, in the Legion, I'd wish you were there just so I could hear you laugh or talk and make things fun. It was like I missed you as a person more than I missed you as a mother. Does that sound screwy?'

'No, it sounds wonderful.' What it sounded like was that he hadn't missed her as a boy might but the way a grown man would. Was this the indefinable difference then – that the boy had finally grown into a man?

Then she realized that he was still in his dripping wet raincoat and they were standing in the middle of a puddle. Hubie and his puddles! 'Let's get you out of these wet things. And it's almost dinnertime. Are you hungry?'

'Starved,' he grinned at her. 'I could eat a horse.'

There were some things a boy never grew out of and there were some things that never changed. Then there were all kinds of things you wouldn't want to change even if you could . . .

Though TS had forbidden anyone besides Nora and over vociferous protests, Dr Ross, entrance to his bedroom – no visitors, no nurse and no member of the

575

household staff other than Olaf to load the projector (or the housekeeper to bring in a tray or change the bed linens when Nora was forced to be elsewhere), he gave Hubie frequent access, explaining: 'Hubie's got that big smile which I don't see too much around here any more. I gotta tell you, Nora, though I hate to complain, you're kind of losing it lately. And Hubie doesn't tense up even when I'm spitting up blood. That's my kind of man. You know how I believe in people going with the flow.

'And to tell the truth, I'm getting kind of bored with the old movies and Hubie was always good company, like his mother used to be before she started losing her sense of humour. And now that he's been around the world a little, Hubie's got some great stories to tell and a lot of what you might call he-man jokes. And I need some good laughs. You know what I always said – always leave 'em laughing.'

But then, though he tried to smile, he couldn't quite make it and couldn't hold back a moan. And this time she called in Hubie to give TS his injection since she had just about lost the energy it took to administer the needle or at least, the stomach for it, and Hubie had both the good stomach and the energy of the young, as well as a gentle hand.

It seemed as if Hubie had shown up in the nick of time just as she herself was flagging and she thought back to when he had arrived in time to help ease the agony of Hugh's passing both for Hugh *and* for her. It was *good* to have a son she could lean on and she wondered if Hubie was at last ready to assume the responsibility of his legacy now that it was nearly time to do so.

Perhaps she wouldn't have been so furious with Hubie when he told her he'd be taking off soon if she hadn't been so disappointed in him leaving when she was counting on him to help TS 'leave 'em laughing'. This time, his behaviour was more than inappropriate or irresponsible – it was the height of insensitivity, so unfeeling as to be bordering on the cruel. If this was Hubie the man, she would gladly take back the immature but warm and loving boy he had once been.

'Where will you be off to this time – to join up with the circus?' she asked bitterly. 'Or are you going to join some hippie commune? Aren't you getting a bit old for this sort of thing? And is this need to run away from responsibility so strong that you can't put it off for three, four weeks? At least until it's spring?'

'I don't think you understand, Mum. I'm *not* running away. It's that I have a commitment, one that commands a higher priority.'

'Commitment . . . higher priority?' she sneered. 'Such high-sounding words. Tell me, what *is* this noble commitment?'

'I've joined the Peace Corps.'

'You *what*? You must be joking!'

But Hubie wasn't laughing; he wasn't even smiling. 'You're serious!' she said then, and laughed though it wasn't the least bit funny and she could see that a commitment to the Peace Corps might presume a higher priority.

'But, Hubie,' she said perplexed, all anger gone now, 'what will you *do* in the Peace Corps? You never went to college, you have no profession or training other than that of being a soldier and making war.' But, even as she spoke the words, it struck her how incongruous they sounded – loving, gentle Hubie making war. Still, the big question remained: of what possible use could he be to the Peace Corps?

'For one thing, Mum, when I was serving I learned a few other things other than just combat. There was always a guy who needed a letter written or help filling out some forms, or someone just to read to him so that he could hear a human voice. At least my fancy, prep-school education came in handy there. And there was always some poor chap who needed a hand held or a few sympathetic words and it was you who taught me about that. Sometimes all it would take to cheer up a bloke would be a joke and I tried to remember all the jokes Tony told me when I got into trouble so I'd laugh instead of feeling sorry for myself.

'But even more important were the things I had to learn under fire, when there was no trained personnel around. You learned fast how to use equipment you hadn't been trained in, or even how to give last rites if pressed, or give emergency medical treatment. Once I had to cut off a friend's smashed leg to free him up so that we could carry him to safety. I know all this sounds as crass as hell but the point is that what I had to offer without training was better than *nothing*. And that's how it is in some of these Third World places – *something* is better than nothing which is what they have now. And who taught me that if not you and Hugh? So you see I'm better-trained than you think.'

'So I see,' she said ashamed now, and so choked up it was an effort to get the words out.

'And what's more, the man you see before you *is* a man with a real craft.'

A craft? What kind of craft could Hubie possibly have?

'A couple of years ago I was stationed in this tiny village in Africa and we had nothing to do except hang around, drink whatever we could get our hands on and play cards. Then one day I saw some natives struggling to put together some kind of primitive structure with almost no materials, no machinery and no know-how, so I pitched in to try and help.

'To be honest I wasn't doing it for any other reason than that I was bored out of my skull. But we got it built even if it was pretty shabby. Then it struck me – if I had had the least bit of training I could have done it better and faster and the fact was, *I liked* doing it – loved working with my hands to build something. So I took a correspondence course in simple carpentry and then another in basic construction. And you know what, I found out I had a real knack! So I do have a trade and I

578

can *do* and *teach* wherever they don't have something or someone better.'

Then he laughed joyously the way he had when he was so young and so foolhardy as to jump recklessly into schoolyard puddles. 'Next, I'm going to take a correspondence course in plumbing. I figure wherever I go it will come in handy. At worst, it can't hurt.'

Oh no, my darling Hubie, it can't hurt! And it can't hurt to jump into a few more puddles – each bigger and more beautiful than the one before – before you're too old and too grown up for that kind of thing.

But even as she hugged him she thought of the people that he said he'd learned from – herself; Hugh, the loving public servant who had adopted him; Tony, the actor, with his good humour and love of life. But there were the others – the substitute fathers who surely had left their mark no matter what. Dear Hubert whose sweetness and loving nature had probably influenced Hubie whether he had memory of him or not, and Jeffrey who no matter what, had had many fine qualities. And TS? They had hardly known each other and she was sorry. How wonderful it would have been if he could have learned something from him, too.

But this craft . . . this skill . . . this love Hubie said he had for working with his hands, this knack that obviously had been there all along, unplumbed and undiscovered, had to come from somewhere, from someone. And who else could it be but the Duke of Butte, Montana . . . Johnny Wayne?

For a brief second it occurred to her that all she had to do was make one call and in a matter of a day or two she could know everything there was to know about the Duke. But no, she didn't have to. In the final analysis, Hubie was his own man and that was enough for her to know.

'When do you leave?'

'In a few days. I thought I'd be able to stay till the spring but I can't.'

'That's all right. I have a feeling that spring will come early this year.'

'But, Mum, you really have to let him go to the hospital. You can't keep this up. There's nothing left of him – he's just skin and bones and you're not far from that yourself.'

'I *can't* send him to the hospital. I promised him that he would die in his own bed and that's the way it has to be. You didn't fail your friend when he needed you to remove his leg so he could live, did you? Well, I can't desert my friend when he needs me to help him die the way he wants.'

'What can I say then except that I'm proud of you? It takes courage and sheer guts to do what you're doing. And TS, too. I've seen a lot of men die bravely in the field, but TS has shown me how a man can die bravely in his own bed, laughing even when the laughing hurts as much as the thing that's killing him. That's *something . . .*'

Despite her own pain, something inside her rejoiced. TS, never a father to Hubie in the remotest sense of the word, *had* left his mark on her son after all in a positive way. And that would be something to tell Sam, too – how valiantly her father had faced death.

'Oh, Hubie, I'm so glad . . .'

'Glad about what?'

'That you learned that from TS. If someone teaches you a valuable lesson about dying it's the same as if he'd taught you something about living. It's like a legacy. And speaking of legacies, I think it's time we talked about the money you inherited from Hugh.'

'What is there to talk about? Dad, being the wise man he was, left it to you to keep in trust for me for a very good reason – because he knew it was better entrusted to you than me. He knew you'd keep it safe for me until I was ready.'

'I think you are ready. At least ready enough to know what I've done with it.'

'Right now it's enough for me to know that I'm

earning my own keep, it's more important. As for what you've done with it – whatever it is I know that it was the right thing. There is just one thing that worries me – about what happened between me and Sam.'

'Oh, Hubie, there's no sense talking about what happened. It was terribly wrong but you were really only a boy then and now that you're a man, well, it simply doesn't matter any more.'

'It isn't that. I was wondering how she's going to take her father's death when she doesn't even know he's dying. It's going to be a terrible shock. Don't you think you should prepare her?'

'I thought I was doing that and at the same time trying to spare her.'

'You know, Mum, you really can't spare anyone anything.' And she wondered if Hubie, in his new-found maturity, was right . . .

Nora couldn't tell whether Dr Ross was angrier with himself or with her. 'I can't do it any more, Nora . . . I won't give you any more morphine! I was crazy to let you talk me into the morphine injections without a registered nurse here to administer them instead of you. Don't you realize the untenable position you've put me in, not to mention yourself? If they took away my licence I wouldn't blame them. It was irresponsible, unethical and dangerous! The day he couldn't keep the Dialuid down was the day I should have insisted you send him to the hospital or withdrawn from the case.'

'But you couldn't have withdrawn. You're my friend.'

'Friend!' he said in despair. 'What friend puts a loaded gun into a friend's hand when that person isn't even thinking rationally? Who would believe, if it came down to it, that you didn't give him an overdose intentionally to end his suffering, or screw up the injection by mistake?'

Sam's the only one who might question my motivation . . .

'On top of that, and without telling me, you've been

581

giving him whisky along with the morphine! Don't you know that's like playing Russian roulette?'

'I never gave him whisky at the same time and never a *lot*. Besides if you had put him in the hospital, you would have probably given him glucose – sugar. At this stage, the whisky isn't much more than that, it's probably what's keeping him alive since he can't keep anything else down. But why are we arguing about this? It's all immaterial. He can't keep the whisky down any more either. Spring is coming early this year.'

'Let me at least bring in a nurse.'

'No, I promised and I don't break promises. And if you won't give me the morphine then I'll get it some place else.'

'Where?'

'For a doctor, you *are* naïve. The same place where anybody who's hell-bent on feeding his habit gets his.'

But soon after she knew that spring had come, she gave TS his last needle and he opened his eyes wide and gave her what passed for a smile. 'You'd better get married again, Nora. You're too good at it to give up the habit.'

And that was it. All that was left was to arrange for a cremation, set a date for a memorial service and call Sam . . .

62

Nora had anticipated that Sam, crazy with grief, might very well turn on her with a litany of accusations. It wouldn't have even surprised her to learn that Sam had a mental picture of her grinning as she withheld the agonized TS's painkiller, threatening to flush it down the toilet unless he signed over everything he owned. She was even ready for that final and inevitable accusation – that she, the avaricious wife, was so greedy for an ill-gotten inheritance that she had hastened her husband's death by murderous means. But what she wasn't prepared for was to have Sam get off the plane with Tony's arm protectively about her to announce: 'Allow me to introduce my husband, Tony Nash.'

'Oh no!' she cried out involuntarily only to have Sam snap back, 'Oh yes,' her eyes gleaming with vindictive relish while Tony looked sheepish and moved forward to kiss his ex-wife and new stepmother-in-law. But Nora aborted this act by recoiling from him. *You sneaky, betraying son-of-a-bitch!* She wanted to kill him!

As he usually did when faced with an uncomfortable situation, Tony reacted with a joke: 'May I call you Mummy?'

'Only if I call you Sonny Boy,' she cracked back, forcing herself to smile, unwilling to let Sam see her anguish. What Sam obviously wanted was to see her stepmother out of her mind with jealousy, and if she showed any signs of being wounded, Sam would only assume that she had achieved her goal.

Then when she saw the copious amount of luggage the newlyweds had brought with them, she was more reflective than surprised. It would seem that Sam had no immediate plans to return to England with Tony, but was planning to dig in for a long stay, and she expected that Sam would choose to do so at Grantwood Manor. It would seem the natural choice since Sam viewed the manor as her ancestral home and what better place to flaunt the pleasures of her new marriage, intent as she was on sticking her knife ever deeper into what she perceived as Nora's jealous heart?

Once they were in the car Nora asked as if it were no more than small talk, 'When were you married?' and Tony answered, 'The day after you phoned with the terrible news.'

But his bride corrected him. 'That's not exactly right, Tony darling,' she kissed him lingeringly before fixing Nora with eyes glazed over with bitterness. 'We were married the *same* day you had my father cremated. Or was it the day you called to let me know he was dead *and* the day you had him burned into a pile of unrecognizable ashes one and the same? If one was of a suspicious nature or addicted to mystery stories where the guilty party is quick to destroy the evidence, one might wonder at this unseemly haste to get rid of the body.'

Nora sighed. *Yes, there would be the inevitable litany of accusations . . .*

'We must have some champagne so we can properly toast your marriage,' she said when they arrived at Grantwood Manor, 'but first I'd like to speak to you, Tony, *alone.*'

Sam voiced immediate objection. 'Anything you have to say to my husband you can say in front of me,' she said, linking her arm possessively through Tony's.

'But Tony and I have *business* to discuss, Sam, so why don't you take a stroll around the garden until we're through? Spring came early this year and everything's in bloom.'

'What business do you have with Tony that you can't discuss in front of me?'

We might as well get this over with once and for all. '*Studio* business – between the boss and the man who works for her. How many employees do you think drag the little wife along when they're talking business, even when she's as cute as you and the boss's stepdaughter besides?'

It took a few shocked seconds for Nora's words to sink in, then Sam shrieked, 'So it's true! First you got rid of me, then you kept my father from getting proper treatment, then you tricked him into leaving you his studio, *my* studio, and you didn't care if you had to kill him to do it!'

Yes, we might as well get it over with . . . with the old

formula of one part truth, one part little white lies, one part secrets kept and one part love. Mix well and hope for the best.

'Don't be a little fool. You're letting your imagination run away with you. But I suppose that's natural considering that you're only eighteen and immature despite your marriage to a man – what is it? – *three* times your age?'

She paused to glance at a shamefaced Tony and shook her head. 'My goodness, I never stopped to consider, but you *are* getting rather long in the tooth, aren't you, Tony?'

She turned back to Sam. 'Now, let's get a few facts straight before you make a complete ass of yourself. First of all, *I* didn't *have* to get rid of you – your father did that when *he* decided to send you away because he wanted to spare you the pain of watching him endure his own. And *I* didn't *have* to keep him from getting treatment because that was *his* decision – he's the one who wanted to go out in style, *his* style, which was, incidentally, a very courageous act. And *I* certainly didn't *have* to kill him. Why would I? The cancer did that. As for tricking him into leaving me the studio, why would I have to do that when I *already owned it*?'

Sam gasped and Tony tried to wrap his arms around her protectively but she pushed him away. 'What do you mean – you *already* owned it?'

'I owned it from the beginning of our marriage. You've heard of prenuptial agreements? Well, ours was what you might call a postnuptial agreement since your father signed it in the spring of 1970, not long after we were married.'

'He signed the studio over to you just like *that*? I don't believe you!'

'But you don't have to believe *me*. I'll show you the signed agreement, all very legal. And if you don't believe the rest of it all you have to do is check the records down the line – the lawyers', the doctors', the death certificate. As for who sent you away I'll show you a studio cheque signed by CEO *T.S. Grant* made out to

Producer Tony Nash to finance a Grantwood production to the tune of several million dollars, which, not incidentally, I, as the owner of record and present CEO, am demanding the return of immediately.

'That is what I wanted to talk to you alone about, Tony. I didn't want to embarrass you in front of your wife. But the fact is that I regard what you did as close to fraudulent, as well as an act of betrayal. You were entrusted with that money to produce a film . . . *not* to marry the boss's daughter.'

While Sam shrieked in rage that Nora was just jealous, a crushed Tony mumbled, 'That's not fair, Nora.'

'*Why* isn't it fair? Do you have a single foot of film? Have you even begun to cast? Do you have *anything* to show me – a scrap of paper, a scribbled memo? Anything at all beside your marriage certificate?'

Tony was silent.

'I didn't think so,' she said sadly and turned to Sam. 'As for your accusation that I'm jealous, why would I be? I *chose* to be divorced from Tony; I *didn't* choose to be the widow of the remarkable man who was your father.'

At these words Sam began to howl and Tony, disgruntled, dismayed and depressed over how things had turned out, sought to comfort her, but without success. He'd anticipated some bad blood emerging this afternoon but he had never suspected it would be *his*. For one thing he never would have believed that Nora was capable of being so snide about his age. And he *had* counted on her understanding about the marriage as he had on her knack for smoothing things over. He certainly hadn't counted on her making Sam feel worse than she already did. And he hadn't expected her to make such a stink about that fucking film or pull the rug out from under him so quickly. He would have got around to doing something about the picture sooner or later.

Actually Nora felt sorry for Tony, watching him fuss over Sam without effect. And most likely most of this was her *own* fault rather than Tony's. She'd sent a boy to do a man's job and the boy simply hadn't been up to it and thus in a way she was to blame for Tony's present fix – married to a woman who didn't love him. And he, poor lad, had that sensitive ego which was in for a severe jolt when he realized that Sam had married him only to spite her stepmother.

She felt completely drained but she knew that the afternoon's drama was not quite over. There were other matters still to be resolved and questions Sam had yet to ask which were as inevitable as the rest of it, so they might as well get on with it. She herself already knew what all the answers had to be – in a nutshell, tough love.

'Well, what's done is done and since you're my *near* son-in-law, Tony, and since you and Sam are so much in love, we won't allow *In The Name Of Love* to stand between us and a harmonious family relationship. Just return the advance money and we'll forget all about your participation in the film. The studio will make the film here with a Hollywood producer since it's too wonderful a script *not* to be made and you and Sam will be free to return to London to get on with your married life.

'Ah, how well I remember the thrill of starting a new marriage. There's nothing quite like it. Now, when do you plan to return to England? The same day as the memorial service or the day after? Seeing as it's so soon you may want to make your plane reservations early . . . like today.'

Sam stopped crying to sit straight up. 'Wait a minute—'

'In the meantime,' Nora went on, 'I'll call the Beverly Hills Hotel to reserve a bungalow for you two lovebirds.'

'Hold your horses!' Sam snapped. 'Why should we go to the Beverly Hills Hotel when there's a zillion bedrooms right here? As a matter of fact, what's wrong with my old room? It has the king-sized bed and closet space enough for six.'

'Oh?' Nora said in surprise. 'I hardly thought you

587

and Tony would want to spend your honeymoon in *my* house—'

'What do you mean *your* house? For your information, I was *born* in this house!'

'Yes, you were, and I don't mean to be unkind but being born in a house doesn't give you squatter's rights. There are legal considerations like who presently owns it. Besides,' she giggled, 'a bungalow at the Beverly Hills Hotel is perfect for newlyweds. Remember, Tony? Didn't we have a time of it?'

Tony grinned foolishly but Sam was too distraught to take notice. 'So you ended up with both *my* house and *my* studio! I can't believe Daddy didn't leave me *anything*! I'm his blood . . . his child. For God's sake, he was my father!'

Nora ached now to take Sam into her arms but she couldn't, not if she was to do what had to be done. 'Of course he was and he *was* thinking of you to the very end and there *is* a kind of trust fund—'

'A trust fund!' Sam uttered and Nora could see a wave of relief light up the green eyes. 'Then he *did* leave me something! He didn't forget me. But what do you mean by a *kind* of trust fund?'

'Well, he didn't specify how much it was to be or when you're to get it. He left everything to me and told me – practically his very last words – that he trusted me to disburse it as I thought suitable whenever I thought you were mature enough to handle it. And – well, I have no choice but to follow his wishes, do I?'

'But that means I'm at your fucking mercy! That's totally unacceptable!'

Nora shook her head regretfully. 'I'm sorry you feel that way, Sam, but I don't think you have any choice but to accept it. But your father *did* leave you something outright. His library of films. It takes up practically a whole room – stacks and stacks of reels. TS said you *had* to have them because you and he felt the same way about films – that the love of movies ran in both your blood.

'And now I'll call the hotel to make the reservation. You'll be my guests, of course. It will be my wedding present. Then I'll tell Edmund to bring out the champagne and Olaf to stand by to drive you over. Oh dear, what a shame we bothered to have all that luggage carried into the house only to have it all dragged out again. Oh well,' she smiled her brightest smile. 'That's life . . .'

After the first shock of the marriage wore off, Nora found herself hoping that it would somehow work out for the two of them. It *was* possible, after all, that she'd been wrong about the union – God knows she'd been wrong about marriages before (quite a few of them, actually) – and that Sam and Tony could help each other grow up. Did it really matter that Tony was so much older than Sam if they were at the same level of maturity? And while Sam *had* married for the wrong reason, maybe she'd come to discover something she didn't yet know – that she really loved Tony.

Perhaps it all hinged on the reason Tony had married Sam. It *was* his second time round and after that first time there were so many damn reasons for marrying one could hardly keep score. Well, she'd hope for the best even though reason told her not to be surprised if the marriage didn't last the year.

But then she *was* surprised when a woebegone Tony came calling the morning after the memorial service.

'Tony! You *are* an early bird today! I was just having my breakfast. You must join me or have you already eaten?'

'I haven't but I'm not hungry.'

'Sit down anyway and have a cup of coffee or do you prefer tea?'

'Tea, please. I was brought up on tea for breakfast and it's too late for this old dog to learn new tricks.'

She gave him a look. Was he trying to tell her something? 'Tea it is, then,' she said. 'You're the boss.'

'But that's it. Maybe I *should* be the boss, but I'm not.'

'Not the boss? Maybe you'd better start from the beginning, Tony, so I know what you're talking about.'

'I told Sam that now that the memorial service was over we should think about going back to England but she absolutely refuses to consider it. And it doesn't seem to matter to her that I told her that I can't sit around the Beverly Hills Hotel for ever even if you are paying the bills.'

That was a joke and she acknowledged it with a smile. They both knew that if her paying the hotel bill posed a problem for Tony, he could easily pay the bill himself.

'Well, if you want to stay on in LA and you don't like living at a hotel, you *could* rent a house—'

'No, we can't. England is my home. That's where I live and work.'

'Look, Tony, while I think that essentially I was fair in my assessment of our movie deal perhaps I was too hasty and even a little mean. Would it help solve yours and Sam's problem if you got involved in the production here?'

'No.'

She sighed and nodded. She hadn't thought so.

'The idea of working in films in Hollywood was fun when you and I were married, Nora, but while it's hard to face up to it, the fact is I was twenty years younger then and, well . . . this old dog is too *old* to learn to be an expatriate.'

'I see.' But what she saw was that Tony was starting to grow up, however too late, and now he would leave Sam behind in more ways than one.

'I know you'll probably think I'm running out on my responsibility to Sam, but if she refuses to go back with me, what can I do?' He banged his teacup down in its saucer. 'The whole damn thing was a mistake. She doesn't love me. She's not ready to love any man. Since we've been here she's spent more time with Babe and Honey than she has with me. I don't even know why she was so hell-bent on us getting married, except maybe that

590

she'd just lost her father and was looking to replace him – saw me as a father figure.'

Not wanting to hurt his feelings, she suppressed a smile. Even Sam wasn't immature enough to see Tony Nash as a father figure. But did it really matter *why* Sam had wanted Tony – whether to make her stepmother jealous or to find an older man to replace the father she'd just lost? It all added up to the wrong reasons for getting married. And now that Sam realized she hadn't succeeded in making her stepmother jealous, she was ready to abandon the marriage . . .

'Tell me, Tony, why *did* you marry Sam?'

'Because at the time it seemed the right thing to do. She was so disconsolate at losing her father I didn't know what she was capable of doing and I remembered how her mother had died – how she'd taken her own life and I was afraid. When you put Sam in my care you specifically told me, 'Tony, don't let *this* one get away.' And I knew that no matter what else, I owed that to you – not to let Sam get away. Don't you know, Nora, that I married Sam for you?'

'Oh Tony!' she wailed. He *had* married Sam out of love, but for love of the wrong woman.

She drove Tony to the airport herself, that being the least she could do for him and when she returned home she found Sam being helped out of a limousine by a uniformed chauffeur who then proceeded to unload her many pieces of luggage. Seeing Nora, all she said was, 'Good. Now that you're here, you can pay the driver.'

'Lucky me,' Nora chuckled, taking out her purse. She wasn't about to argue with Sam in front of the driver any more than she would allow the man to go unpaid. But once they were in the house, she demanded, 'What's the story, morning glory? You didn't care for the accommodation at the hotel?'

'Well, how could I stay there? Once Tony left I knew the honeymoon was over and you wouldn't go on paying

591

the bills. And I don't have any money. I'm just a penniless orphan.'

'I find it hard to believe that Tony would leave you high and dry, without the limousine fare,' Nora said drily.

'Tony was very sweet. He tried to force all kinds of money on me.'

'Which you wouldn't condescend to accept, I take it?'

'Of course not. *I* didn't marry him for his money even if some other people did.'

'That's commendable. You wouldn't want to be a cheat.'

'I suppose there's a point to that remark?'

'Well, if you *had* married Tony for money he hardly got *his* money's worth, did he? But it's over. Let's talk about your plans instead. I take it you came to pick up your car? Well, why wouldn't you? It's yours. Shall we have Olaf load it with all that luggage . . . if it fits, that is. Well, we can always send it on to you when you're located.'

Sam's eyes opened wide as her mouth fell open. 'You mean you're actually throwing me out of my own home?'

'We've already established that this house is *my* home and since you're over eighteen I'm under no obligation to provide you with shelter even if you were my own flesh and blood.'

'But you know I have no place to go,' she cried. 'I never thought you'd be mean enough to throw me out on to the street. I thought that at least you'd be fair.'

'But are *you* being fair in your expectations? You expect me to give you a home, but what are you offering in return? Friendship, good company, good cheer? No, you're offering hostility. Well, I'm not a masochist and that's no bargain as far as I'm concerned. But I'm willing to give you a chance. You'll always have a home here at Grantwood Manor if you're prepared to do your share. And I don't think I have to spell out what that means as I did when you were thirteen.

592

You should be able to figure that out for yourself by now.'

Sam stuck out her hand, having the grace to smile politely, if falsely. 'It's a deal. But there *is* one more thing. I *will* need some spending money. Do you want to give me an advance on that trust fund money? A few thousand, say?' she asked innocently.

Nora laughed. 'Don't push it, kid. But, of course, you *will* need money. And the way to get money is to do what most people do – work for it. So, you can start at the studio next Monday if you like—'

'As what? A glorified gofer?'

'Yes, at the bottom if that's what you mean. But if that doesn't please you, get your own job. I'm sure there's plenty of work for a girl with all her faculties and as clever and attractive as you. There is one other alternative. A schoolgirl is entitled to an allowance and I'm willing to go for that if you want to start college.'

Sam sighed in grand affectation. 'You certainly know how to drive a hard bargain, Nora. That's one thing I can definitely learn from you. I'll have to think about that. Job or school. But, in the meantime, I'll need an advance – on either my salary, my allowance, *or* my trust fund money.'

Nora shook her head admiringly. 'When it comes to driving a hard bargain, you're no slouch yourself.'

Pleased, Sam smiled, picked up one of her pieces of luggage and headed for the stairs. 'Oh, it *is* good to be home again.'

Nora watched her go up the stairs, reflecting that while it was indeed good to have Sam home again, there'd probably be a lot of moving in and moving out for Sam before they were through. Maybe even a few more husbands. As a matter of fact, she wouldn't be at all surprised if one of these days Sam didn't up and marry a diplomat or even a duke . . .

One of the good by-products of having Sam back at Grantwood Manor was having Honey and Babe charging in and out again, swimming in the pool, playing tennis, filling the house with their effervescent beauty and the sound of their youthful voices. Of course, it wasn't *quite* the same now that TS was gone and the girls had more purpose to their lives and less free time for play – Honey and Babe busy with their classes and Sam involved in her production assistant's job at the studio until the fall term at UCLA got under way.

As for herself, it seemed just the opposite – she had *more* free time and *less* purpose to her life. She was hardly running the studio herself and having dropped all outside activities so that she could give TS 100 per cent, there was now definitely a huge void in her life, which for the first time she could remember, she was reluctant to fill. But she knew the reason – she was waiting for the other shoe to drop. What she was waiting for was Teddy Rosen's call.

They hadn't really spoken since the day he had brought over the script. Of course, he'd given her her golden charm for Christmas and she had given him his tie pin, but it had been silently acknowledged that they wouldn't *really* be in touch . . . not while TS still breathed the essence of life through his wife.

Then he had sent flowers after TS breathed his last, along with a note of condolence signed Teddy and Honey. But at least a hundred people had sent flowers and three hundred more messages of sympathy. And of course he had come to the memorial service with Honey, but so had six hundred others, including the Tracys along with Babe and her new boyfriend, Greg. And, of course, he had shaken her hand and murmured all the right words. He was too much the gentleman not to do that and he was too much the correct gentleman to look too lingeringly into her eyes . . .

Then she realized that he *wasn't* going to call her. Not Teddy Rosen, the infinitely sensitive gentleman. He would wait for *her* to call him so that he'd be sure he wasn't trespassing on another man's marriage even though that man had passed on. He would wait for her to signify in some way that she was ready.

But though all of her yearned to make that call, she couldn't. Not yet, and it had nothing to do with TS – she was satisfied that she had completely fulfilled her commitment to *him*. It had to do with the fact that a call to Teddy Rosen could never be simply a call – it would be a commitment as well. And she didn't know if she was ready for *that*.

But as he had come with Honey to pay his respects to her and Sam at TS's memorial service, she would go with Sam to see Honey play Juliet in the same spirit. Out of respect and friendship for the father as well as the daughter. But just as he had done she would only shake his hand as she offered him her congratulations . . . and she would not look too long into his eyes . . .

63

Babe could tell that Catherine was trying her best not to let her irritation show, but at the same time she was determined to have her way. 'I want you to go to the phone this minute, Babette, and invite Greg to go with you to the play tomorrow.'

'What's the big deal? I've been out with him twice this week already and it's not as if I wasn't inviting him to some really big event. It's only Honey's school production. And after the play Mr Rosen is taking me, Sam and Honey out for a little private celebration. That's all. I assure you, Greg wouldn't even want to go. A drama class production of *Romeo and Juliet* is not his idea of a big time.'

He'd only sit there and make snide, superior little cracks the whole time and spoil the whole damn thing for me.

'That's not the point. You want to invite him so he'll know you're not excluding him from any part of your life.'

She can't make me do this! It's not like it was when I was fourteen and if I didn't listen to her, she could send me to my room and force me to miss the play altogether.

'You're going to be mighty sorry if you do anything to spoil *this* relationship, Miss. Greg's a young man with a brilliant future. Even your father says he's going places and if you had half a brain you'd make sure that you're there right by his side. For once in your life can't you try and please your father? Is that asking too much after all he's done for you?'

'Oh, all right! I'll ask Greg to go if it will make both of you so goddamn happy!' *And get you off my back!*

'Good. But try to control yourself sufficiently to refrain from using swear words. At least when you're in Greg's company. Anyone can see that he's a young man with old-fashioned values who wouldn't dream of marrying a woman who might embarrass him by presenting a bad public image.'

'*Marrying?* Give me a break, I'm only *dating* him – not getting ready to march down the aisle with him!'

Catherine was disdainful. '*You* could do a lot worse and probably *will* if you're fool enough to let this one get away.'

She had no one to blame but herself for being in this jam, Babe berated herself. If only she'd had the sense to run the other way the day she literally bumped into Greg in the law library instead of dragging him home to show *them* that she was capable of attracting an 'acceptable' man. But how could she have foreseen that it'd be love at first sight between the handsome, smooth-talking, third-year law student with the beautiful manners *any* mother would love, and her parents? And that the moment they laid eyes on Greg they wouldn't see him as just another date, but their long-awaited white hope who, with a little grooming, a bit of a financial push, a dash of influence and the right wife, could go the 'big' distance?

And how could she have known right off that he (so affable as well as ambitious) *was* very much interested in a career in politics, would fall like a ton of bricks for the rich and powerful Judge, his socially savvy wife and *all* their paraphernalia – the big Beverly Hills house, the membership in the LA Country Club, the correct dinner parties Catherine gave with all the right people sitting at her table?

Looking back, she realized that he had never really seemed all *that* enthralled with *her*, but at the time, she'd been too busy being pleased with herself to notice. For the first time she was actually basking in her parents' approval, even their admiration, and it was pretty heady stuff. It even made her feel that at last she was worthy of their love. But that was before she began to see the tiny cracks in Greg Ryan's façade, defects her parents failed to see or were determined not to. They found him so genial, so amiable, but she had seen him angry. (Once it was only over a movie he wanted to see and she didn't.) And an angry Greg wasn't a pretty sight. But when she said as much to the Judge all he said was that any man who didn't react with anger once in a while was a man without backbone, and after a little reflection, she regarded this as a reasonable statement.

But when Greg drank too much at a party she recalled what she had once heard Nora Grant say: 'Anybody can drink too much on occasion. The test of a man is not whether he can hold his liquor, but how he behaves once he's drunk.' And on that occasion Greg had turned plain *nasty*, had even accused her of upstaging him by trying to get a bigger laugh with her jokes than he had with his, which was absurd.

But try telling that to Catherine and the Judge!

When she did they missed her point and told her

that they, too, found a young woman telling jokes un-attractive and unfeminine, and wasn't she the silly girl to risk offending a fine young man by humiliating him in public? Then she stopped telling them *anything* about Greg, even stopped telling jokes. She didn't *have* to tell jokes. There were other things in life to do that were more worthwhile . . . *weren't there?*

And that's how a girl gets herself into this kind of a predicament – going out with a guy whom her parents adored, but whom she didn't even like . . .

Babe put down the receiver. 'He's going,' she told Catherine. 'Are you satisfied now?'

'Don't be silly,' her mother said. 'I'm not the one who has to be satisfied. *You* are, Babette, and you *should* be. You should be delighted that out of all the young women Greg Ryan could be going out with, he's chosen you.'

Sam hung up the phone and turned to Nora. 'That was Babe. She's going to the play with Greg Ryan so if you want to save a little gas, you can ride with me.'

'I appreciate the offer but tonight's hardly an intimate occasion when Babe and her boyfriend might want to be alone, so why can't the three of you go together?'

'Because *I* don't care to make it a threesome. I've been out with them a couple of times and I found him a total dork. What an egomaniac! A few minutes with him and I discovered homicidal instincts I never even knew I possessed.'

Nora, grateful to be having this kind of friendly, girl-to-girl conversation with Sam, laughed. 'He can't be all that bad if Babe likes him.'

'Care to try that one again?'

'*Loves* him?'

'Once again.'

'Is *mad* about him?'

'How about: those fucking Tracys are mad about him?'

598

'If that's the case Babe's the one to point out the error of their ways. In the meantime, I'll take you up on your offer of a ride. I do hate going places by myself.'

'Are you *sure* you're not already spoken for?' Sam asked, eyes oblique.

'Who'd offer me a ride to see a play at UCLA?'

'Teddy Rosen maybe? You and he were always pretty tight.'

Sam's tone was offhand, but Nora could see that she was probing and her reply was equally casual. 'Tight? That means close friends, doesn't it? Of course we're friends, but I haven't seen him since the commencement at Beasley, except for the time he came over with the script for *In the Name of Love* for your father to see and then again at the memorial service. How tight does that make it?'

'Not *too* but we're only talking about going to see a school play, not a commitment. And I *know* you'd never make a commitment to Teddy Rosen,' Sam laughed.

'How did we get from going to a play to making a commitment?' Nora asked with irritation. 'And just as a matter of curiosity, how do you *know* I'd never make a commitment to Teddy Rosen?'

'With your record, that's easy,' Sam drawled. 'He doesn't have enough money for you.'

Nora sighed. *That's Sam for you. First she dazzles you with footwork – a friendly offer of a ride – then when your guard is down, she clobbers you with a left-right combination to the heart.*

'You're going to be just wonderful so there's no reason for you to be nervous,' Teddy reassured Honey as they walked into the theatre which was empty since they were early.

'I wouldn't be but Professor Beaumond has invited a few of his friends – *real* professionals – to come see the play and that kind of makes me a *little* nervous. Even

599

Joshua Prince, the head of Royal Productions, is coming.'

'*Even!* Well, I *am* impressed,' Teddy teased. 'The crown prince of TV's night time soaps is actually coming to see my little princess play Juliet. What an honour!'

'Daddy, you're making fun and that's not like you. Looking down your nose at TV now that you're writing a really big movie. You didn't mind accepting that Emmy for the Thanksgiving show, did you?' she teased back.

'I beg your pardon, Ms Honey. Do you really want to compare *my* show with one of Prince's *t and a* series, or one of those shoot 'em up and car chase fantasies?'

'Those are called *action* series for your information and Professor Beaumond says Josh Prince's company is providing more prime-time hours for television than any company in TV history and has consistently boasted more top-rated shows. Now that's *something*, isn't it, even if it's only what you snob types consider "entertainment fluff", and not "art".'

Teddy laughed. '*Touché.* But I wasn't trying to downgrade Mr Prince's achievements. I just wanted to impress upon you that you don't have to be nervous over the likes of him since you're a *serious* actress and he probably couldn't tell a real actress from a bimbo if she hit him in the eye. But it sounds like your Professor Beaumond is really tooting Mr Prince's horn. I wonder why.'

'Well, he *is* his friend, so naturally he'd say nice things about him. Besides, while Professor Beaumond *is* a serious dramatic arts professor, I think he's eager to direct a few episodes of Josh Prince's strictly entertainment fluff. He says a dramatic arts professor does not live by Shakespeare alone – he needs some *real* bread, too,' she giggled.

Teddy nodded. 'I'm sure he's right.' Still, he wondered why it was necessary for Beaumond – who'd been around Hollywood for ages and who was a friend of Prince's – to drag the producer down to a class play just to see how well he could direct. Surely by now Prince knew his work well enough.

'I'd better go backstage now, Daddy. They're probably worrying where I am. Why don't you sit down in front and save a couple of seats for Babe and Sam? Oh, I forgot. Do you know who else is coming tonight? That Italian director, Vittorio Conti, who's here making a movie for Columbia. He's a friend of Professor Beaumond's, too.'

'Look Nora, there's Teddy in the front row with two empty seats next to him. He must be saving them for me and Babe so we might as well take them.' Sam started down the aisle before Nora could protest and she had no choice but to follow even though she found the situation awkward.

Teddy stood up, a touch flustered. 'Sam . . .' he gave her a hug. 'Nora, it's good to see you. I didn't know you were coming. I—'

'Oh, I wouldn't miss Honey's first dramatic appearance for anything,' she said quickly. 'But I see there are only two free seats here and Babe's coming, so—'

Sam rolled her eyes. 'Look, folks, I understand there's some confusion about who's coming and who's sitting where, but why don't we all just sit down and cool it? Besides, Babe's coming with the big man. That's her boyfriend, Greg Ryan, in case you didn't know—' she explained to Teddy. 'And they can find their own seats. Whoops, there they are just coming in! You two sit while I zip up to tell Babe what the seating arrangements are. By the way, Teddy, do you think you want to include Nora and Greg the Great in our celebration after the show? He'll probably be a drag, but I don't know if you have much choice. What say you, Nora? You always know the right thing to do. If Teddy was going to take Honey, Babe, me and now you out for a celebration, does he have to include Greg too?'

'I—' Nora began, thinking she'd like to throttle Sam, but Teddy saved her. 'By all means invite Greg on my behalf, Sam.' Then Sam was off and running up the aisle and Teddy appealed to Nora, 'You *will* come, won't you? I have a feeling I'm going to need some help with all this exuberant youth.'

'Yes, of course, I'd love to. Besides, I owe you one. I still remember how you came to my rescue when I was serving as chaperone at the Beasley mixer. Recall?' She was careful not to meet his eyes which led her to look at his tie to see that he was wearing the tie pin she had given him for Christmas.

'Oh,' she said and he said, 'I recall,' while looking at her hair to avoid looking into her bright blue eyes and he thought: *It really is the colour of gold.*

Then she flushed and fumbled for the little gold musical note that she wore suspended on a chain that reposed inside the V of her dress to finger it as if it were a good-luck charm. Still, they avoided each other's eyes.

Sam came back to take the seat on the aisle and report: 'The happy couple can't make our party after all – they have to go back to the Tracys. It seems the Judge has offered Greg a clerkship or something while he's waiting to pass the bar and tonight the four of them are going to hold their own private celebration. Poor Babe . . . What about you, Nora? Coming along?'

'Yes, indeed. Thank you for thinking of me, dear.'

'Super! And guess who I saw sitting in the back of the theatre? Josh Prince . . .'

'Where's he sitting?' Teddy asked and when Sam pointed Prince out to him, he asked, 'Where did you meet him?'

'Oh, I never met him but I recognized him from his picture. There was an article about him in the paper – publicity release, I guess. He's casting a new series called *Three Wise Gals*. It's about three investigative reporters with lots of jiggle and it seems he's looking for fresh faces,' she laughed. 'Aren't they always? And guess who he's searching for? One sexy, gorgeous blonde; one sexy

602

but classy redhead; and a sexy, perky brunette. Now what three wise young women with fresh faces does that bring to mind? It's too bad that I'm only interested in *making* movies and Babe's parents would rather see her dead than performing and Honey's only desire is to be a serious actress. But what a team we would have made!'

Neither Teddy nor Nora made any comment.

'And did you see who's sitting next to the Prince? The Italian director, Vic Conti. Now there's a man whose talent you have to really respect – it's awesome!'

'So is his ego and his talent for manipulation,' Nora commented drily.

'You know him?' Sam sat up straight.

'I met him years ago in Europe when – well, believe me, the man is bad news.'

'Really?' Sam's eyes lit up and she smiled slyly. 'Maybe you just didn't press the right buttons.'

Nora was sorry then that she'd opened her mouth, realizing she had just pressed the worst button possible as far as Sam was concerned – the button marked 'challenge' or was it simply the button marked 'Nora'?

Then the lights dimmed and the house went quiet as the curtain started to rise.

When the curtain came down on the final curtain call, Teddy, already on his feet applauding, turned to take another look at Joshua Prince to see how enthusiastically *he* was applauding. But both Joshua Prince's and Vic Conti's seats were empty and he guessed that Prince had gone backstage to make a move on Honey. 'I can't wait to tell Honey how proud I am so I'm going backstage now,' he told Sam and Nora. 'Do you two want to wait here for us or—?'

'I should say not,' Sam said. 'We can't wait to tell Honey how proud we are, too, right, Nora? Oh look, here come Greg and Babe. I guess they want to congratulate Honey, too, before they go home to Mommy and Daddy Tracy.'

Teddy saw that he had guessed correctly. It was a scene right out of a movie – Conti, the prestigious director, standing to one side viewing the proceedings with a jaded eye, while Beaumond, the professorial director, draped a proprietary arm about his protégée – a flushed, radiant Honey, beautifully virginal in her Juliet dress, her mass of hair a golden halo framing a rosy face, locking enthralled topaz eyes with the tenderly admiring brown eyes of a seemingly equally bedazzled Prince Joshua.

Reluctantly Honey tore her eyes away to greet her father and her friends and excitedly to introduce everyone to everyone else. Then Teddy could not help but admire how silkily Prince managed his part of the introductions.

'Ah, the legendary Nora Grant,' Prince said and while he didn't actually kiss Nora's hand it almost felt like he had and he followed up by offering her his sympathy on the recent death of her equally legendary husband. Next he proclaimed what an honour it was to meet the fortunate man who possessed such treasures – the remarkable Honey, a Pulitzer and an Emmy – which showed Teddy that Joshua Prince was a man who did his homework. Undoubtedly he also knew that Honey's mother was the legendary French sex kitten – a bit of information that wouldn't hurt a campaign to publicize a potential sex kitten of the American television screen. Then Prince politely acknowledged Greg Ryan's existence, but when he came to Babe and Sam, he laughed with pleasure. 'The beauty in this room is blinding!'

And then Teddy saw that he was right (and Sam a fine prophet) when Prince said, 'And what's amazing is that I have a series coming up – *Three Wise Gals* – that I could cast right here and now if I could talk three lovely young women into a great career move. Isn't that so, Vic?'

But Vic Conti didn't hear nor did an entranced Sam. They were already deep into an intense discussion of the artistic superiority of European films over the American.

But Babe heard and said wistfully, 'You could talk *me* into this great career move, but I doubt you could talk my mother into it.'

Then Greg abruptly prodded her, 'Speaking of your mother, Babette, we'd better get moving. Your parents are waiting.'

Once Babe and Greg left Teddy suggested that Honey change so they wouldn't be late for their reservation. But then Honey enthused, 'Oh Daddy, can you call and tell them that there will be a few more of us? I've asked Mr Prince, Mr Conti and Professor Beaumond to join us and they've said they'd love to.'

Joshua Prince told Honey she had to call him Joshua, even before Teddy spoke, about to say that it was too late to change the reservation. But Nora placed a staying hand on his arm. 'I'll take care of it, Teddy. I'm really good with headwaiters.'

There was a scramble for transportation to The Scene, the newest and hottest place in West Hollywood that Teddy had chosen thinking the girls would enjoy it. Since Vic Conti had come with Josh who asked Honey to ride with him in his Lamborghini which seated only two – an offer she accepted enthusiastically – Vic was left without a ride, a void Sam quickly offered to fill and since her car was also a two-seater, this left Nora without a ride.

'I'm afraid you're stuck with me,' Nora told Teddy who said, 'I can think of worse predicaments. Being stuck with Jacques Beaumond, for instance,' and they both laughed because he *was* stuck with Beaumond as she was since his was the only car that accommodated more than two.

The Scene was noisy and the music hot though the food was lousy and the drinks watered, which really didn't matter to anyone but Jacques since he was the only one who sat continuously downing Margaritas and stuffing his face.

Teddy and Nora, sitting at the table with him, ate little and drank only Perrier as they watched the others dancing. Sam and Vic, preoccupied with rubbing bodies on the dance floor and ceaseless conversation, were too busy to eat while Josh and Honey, having shared only a few sips from a single flute of champagne, kept a couple of inches between them as they danced, more into staring into each other's eyes than making direct physical contact, without saying much at all.

'Vic and I are leaving,' Sam said, picking up her purse.

'But why?' Nora asked, startled. 'Where are you—?'

'If you must know, we're going back to the house to screen *Citizen Kane* and Bertolucci's *1900* to compare their relative artistic merits. That's OK, isn't it, since Daddy did leave me his library of films?'

Teddy watched Nora watch Vic and Sam make their exit, anxiety written all over her face. He reached across the table to take her hand. 'You can't stop her even if you know she's going to get hurt. You yourself told me that that's part of the growing-up process.'

'I know but I can't help wishing she could grow up in a hurry without so much trouble and pain.'

'At least you don't have to worry about her getting into trouble tonight,' he offered wryly, trying to get her to smile. 'Even without *Citizen Kane*, the cut version of *1900* runs at least fours hours. Which version do you have?'

She laughed. 'The original – six hours.'

'There you go. Nothing to worry about. That will take them through the night.'

But then when Honey came running over in a flurry of excitement to tell him that she and Joshua were leaving – 'Josh wants to take me on a tour of Royal Productions!' – Teddy stood up to protest the lateness of the hour.

'Oh, it's OK, Daddy. I don't have any classes to-morrow,' she said and Joshua Prince was there to reassure him, 'She'll be fine, Mr Rosen. I promise to take good care of our Honey Rose and not bring her home too late. And thank you for a wonderful evening.'

He then thanked Nora for the pleasure of her company, completely ignoring Beaumond who was busy working on yet another Margarita, while Honey threw her arms around her father to thank him for everything, and then they were gone.

Dazed, Teddy sank down into his chair to ask Nora: 'Is this it? After all these years, is this it? One evening and I have to let go? Is it over that fast?'

She reached her hand across the table to take his. 'But it's not over . . . for either of you. For her, it's just the beginning and for you – it's the beginning of another time . . . a new time . . . a different time. Like with me and Sam.'

'But Honey isn't *like* Sam. Honey doesn't have Sam's defences. Sam's tough and worldly-wise and Honey's still an innocent . . . vulnerable.'

'It's very possible, you know, that it's the other way round – that Honey's really the tough one with more inner resources to fall back on and Sam's the vulnerable one. Who's to say, really? Only time will tell . . .'

'But how can I trust that man with my daughter? He's way too old for her.'

'He's not *that* much older. Thirteen . . . fourteen years at most. Honey probably wants . . . *needs* an older man because she looks up to you so much.'

'But you saw him . . . heard him. He's *too* smooth. His manners are *too* good to be sincere.'

She smiled faintly. 'Your manners are very good, too, but you're certainly sincere. I imagine that's one of the reasons Honey is attracted to him. She would never like a man with bad manners or a surly disposition.'

'But I'm sure he only wants to use her. You can't deny that.'

'I can't deny or predict anything. He *may* want to use her by casting her in that series of his but that's not to say he couldn't or wouldn't love her. Only Honey can

607

determine that. She will have to find that out for herself.'

'But you heard him – he called her Honey Rose. He just met her and already he's trying to change her name . . .'

'That's silly,' she smiled at him gently. 'Think about it. All he did was leave the "n" off the Rosen – he didn't call her Honey Princess.'

'Yet . . .'

'Yet . . . But I don't think we have any choice but to let go of our girls and let them grow up in their own time.'

He nodded. 'I suppose you're right. Aren't you *always* right? Isn't that what everyone *always* says about you?'

'I think you're teasing me and it's time for us to go.'

'No, not yet. Have some caviar.'

'But I'm not hungry.'

'You don't have to be hungry to eat caviar. Have some anyway. I'd like you to.'

She laughed. 'Why?'

'I want you to have something rich and wonderful.'

'Then give me a twenty-dollar bill.'

As Jacques Beaumond said plaintively and drunkenly, '*I'd* like something rich and wonderful,' Teddy handed Nora the twenty and she got to her feet, went over to the band leader to whisper in his ear. By the time she made her way back to the table the band had switched from boogie to the strains of a melody old and sentimental, and she held out her arms to Teddy and he rose from the table to clasp her in his.

I'll be loving you always
With a love that's true always.

As they danced – her arms around his neck, his arms encircling her waist – they looked directly into each other's eyes to see the same, raw compulsion there – a compulsion that could no longer be denied and her trembling body confirmed it. It was time, she thought, the right time. And then *he* confirmed it by demanding of her, 'Where?'

Oh, not her place, for sure. Not this time, anyway
. . . not this first time. Sam was there and so was
TS's ghost. And not his place either – his house had its
ghosts as well. It had to be some place neutral and not
the Beverly Hills Hotel with its ghost of Tony Nash. It
had to be some place *new* for them both . . . a beginning.

'Why don't you let me make the arrangements?' She
leaned her head back so his lips could find her throat.
'You know what they always say about me?'

'What do they always say?' he murmured, finding
her throat.

'That I'm really terrific at planning a great party.
Trust me – it's what I do best.'

He laughed heartily, trusting her completely. 'But
what do we do about *him*?' he indicated Beaumond
with his head.

'Sometimes a person has choices in life, after all.
We could just leave him here, crying into his Margarita
and sticking him with the bill, which is no more than
he deserves. Or, we could be nice and pour him into
a cab.'

'Well, this is our time and we want to be nice. But
the hour is late, so let's do it quickly,' he whispered
urgently.

64

Babe knew it was an unusual evening as soon as she
and Greg walked into the house after the play and it
wasn't because her family was having this little celebration in the first place. Over the years they'd had quite
a few of these private parties to mark a special occasion
– when her father had been named man of the year by
some organization or other . . . when her mother had

been elected president of her Women's Club . . . when she herself had won a spelling bee. And she never forgot the time when she had performed extraordinarily well at a piano recital and her parents had toasted her with their wine glasses held high, her own glass brimming with grape juice. She could still remember how special she felt and how happy and proud, and how she'd thought she'd give anything to recapture the moment over and over again.

Catherine had always considered these little celebrations an ode to family solidarity, their own brand of 'togetherness' and never once had there been a fourth person present, and never had they celebrated in the drawing room, reserved for those social occasions which truly merited its use. But tonight, though it was still considered a family affair, they were honouring a fourth person – Greg – and they were celebrating in the drawing room! And there was a lavish spread, the kind of delicacies usually served only to her parents' most august and eligible guests: gravlax and Beluga caviar, *Foie Gras Truffle de Strassbourg* – the pâté Catherine had on special order, tiny sauteed lobster tails and escargots Bourguigonne, and because Greg was so fond of it, sushi. There was also a pitcher of martinis the Judge had mixed himself in addition to the Cristal champagne reposing in the silver cooler. It was assuredly a special, special celebration, and for what, she wondered – a crummy job down at the courthouse when Greg had yet to pass the bar?

And then, suddenly, she found herself all by herself on one of the twin sofas upholstered in palest peach, facing the three of them on the matching sofa. Then, as if it were a dream running in slow motion, she saw the Judge solemnly pouring the Cristal into four flutes, Greg reaching into his breast pocket, and heard Catherine's quavering voice: 'When Greg heard that we were making this little party for him he was so dear – he said that he wanted to make it *really* an occasion by sharing *this* moment with us.'

610

Then, amazingly, she saw the three of them raise their champagne glasses high. *They were toasting her!* Her mother was smiling tremulously, crying tears of joy, and the Judge was looking proud while Greg leaped forward to thrust this *thing* at her – a diamond ring winking up at her from a little blue velvet box.

Then Catherine said, 'Quickly, darling, pick up your glass so that we can all take the first sip together!'

The room was dark except for the light emanating from the projector to illuminate Robert DeNiro grappling with Dominique Sanda, with the sexual electricity practically leaping out from the screen. But Sam and Vic Conti, each bare to the waist and grappling on the projection room's velvety red carpet, were totally oblivious to any other sexual electricity but their own.

Sweating profusely, his breath coming fast and laboured, he lay under her, his hands reaching up to fondle the breasts hanging suspended as she sat astride him. But she wouldn't permit the contact. Rather, she grazed his face with the tips of her dark pink nipples, teased his lips with them, moved them down to taunt his swollen bulge. Then as his hands attempted to pull down his zipper, she pushed them aside to do that herself, to draw out his engorged penis, to stroke it slowly with her hands while the master director grunted and groaned and begged for her lips. But she sat up straight and moved her own body down in order to pull his trousers free and then when he was completely nude, she parted his thighs to run her tongue lightly over the tautened skin.

Cursing her now, the director supreme attempted to take charge of the production – to maul her breasts; to bite her lips and shoulder; to tear away her skirt and panties until, finally, they were both completely nude, their bodies heaving and glistening in the darkness. Moving swiftly then, taking him by surprise, she rose to move to the door as he staggered to his feet to come after her, but she taunted him with a laugh before whispering, 'Not here . . .'

'Where?' It was an animal cry.

'Upstairs . . .'

Then she was out of the projection room, out into the hall and starting up the stairs with him hot after her. She had to run faster, she knew, because if the great director caught her on the stairs, he would take her then and there in a violent rage and she wouldn't be able to stop him. And she was determined that the only damn place Nora's 'bad news' was going to fuck her was in Nora's bed, where once Nora had fucked TS. And after that, well – who knew? Maybe she'd even marry the bastard. There was a lot she could learn from him about making movies.

Royal Productions's lot was an eerie place at night, full of shadow and half-light, but it was a beautiful, romantic place, too, Honey thought as Joshua proudly walked her around the sound stages showing her where they produced his different series – the cop show, *Hollywood Beat*; the fantasy, *Enchanted Isle*; the series, *Heartland*, about a family in Witchita, Kansas; something for everyone . . . It was a beautiful, romantic place because it was both a dream factory and the place where Joshua Prince's personal dream had come true.

Entranced, Honey watched his face in profile as he told her how he'd come to Hollywood ten years before with nothing but his vision and his belief in himself that he could make his vision a reality – producing entertainment not for the small, élite group who had access to legitimate theatre or even for the millions that went to movie theatres, but for the many, many millions who relied only upon their television sets to enrich their lives and make them happier. Hearing this, she was sure his dream was as noble as it was inspired.

Suddenly, it came to her whom Joshua reminded her of – her own father, but how he must have been before he had been derailed – youthfully exuberant and confident in his own abilities and in the rightness of his dream. And there was that same soft voice and gentle manner, even a slight physical resemblance – the same velvety brown eyes, the same fine, clean line of feature.

Joshua took her next to his administration offices and into his own private domain – an elegant room where he put a match to the gas jets of a large stone fireplace even though it was already late spring. Then, sitting on the sofa in front of the fire, he showed her all the planning materials for the projected new series which was only awaiting its star to go into production and become a reality.

'Star? You mean stars, don't you? Three of them?' she asked, herself starry-eyed.

'No, now that I've met you, I realize that the other two "wise gals" can only be supporting players. Only the Honey Rose can wear the princess's crown because she's the ultimate all-American dream girl come true.'

'The Honey Rose . . . the all-American dream girl,' she repeated after him. Oh, it *did* have a lovely ring and she knew for certain that she wanted to be part of Joshua Prince's vision . . . his princess come true.

And when he put his arms around her, bent his head to kiss first her eyelids, then her lips, then her throat . . . to bury his face in her breasts before he undressed her slowly and tenderly to kiss each and every part of her, she was ready at last to embrace love and lovemaking, with *all* of her – mind, body and soul. And when he entered her she knew that she was ready to be anything Joshua Prince wanted her to be.

A bemused Teddy pulled up in front of the canopied entrance to the Hotel Bel-Air. This was a new experience for him – he was forty-eight years old and had in his time checked into many hotels, but never before had he checked into a fine hotel at two o'clock in the morning. But obviously this was possible and in no way extraordinary since a parking attendant leaped to open his door and enquire after the luggage, while another ran to open the car door for Nora.

'Did we remember to bring the luggage, dear?' he asked Nora since she was the one who had made the arrangements.

'Of course we remembered to bring the luggage,' she said huffily, walking around to the trunk to direct the attendant which pieces were to be carried in. 'Mmm . . .' she murmured in deep thought as she surveyed the trunk's contents. 'That,' she pointed to a portable typewriter in a battered case, 'and that,' a bruised attaché case, 'and of course, *that*.' She indicated a new burnished leather briefcase. 'And this—' *This* was a tennis racket in sore need of restringing.

Then she smiled brightly and led the way down the canopied stretch into the lobby and up to the front desk where she stepped aside to allow Teddy to claim his reservation and register. '*My* name?' he murmured in an aside.

'Of course *your* name, my darling, though a Rosen by any other name would smell as sweet . . .'

Then when they followed the bellman to a bungalow in the rear of the hotel, he whispered, 'You give good arrangements,' and she whispered back, 'You ain't seen nothing yet.'

Still, when the bellman opened the door, he was amazed to see a living room with a fire blazing in the hearth and a midnight supper laid out on a pink-clothed table set with roses and candles, flowered china and sparkling crystal, with a magnum of champagne cooling in a silver bucket.

His mouth dry with a growing urgency, impatient for the bellman carrying the typewriter, tennis racket, briefcase and attaché into the bedroom to be gone, Teddy managed to mutter, 'You sure know how to throw a party.'

Leaning over the table to light the candles, she blew

him a kiss. 'As with all good parties, the best is yet to come.'

With those words hanging in the air, he sprang like a tiger to wrap his arms around her from behind, caressing each breast with a hand and pressing himself against her. But he jumped away when the bellman reappeared from the bedroom to collect his tip and ask if they would like a maid summoned to do the unpacking. At this, Teddy almost laughed though his body throbbed with its unbearable ache. Still he played the game, aware that every party had to follow its own schedule. 'What do you think, Nora? Do we want the maid?' But if she had said, 'Yes', he was prepared to throw her to the floor and take her right there by force.

She must have known this, for eyes laughing into his, she demurred. *No maid*. Still, she teased, 'The waiter, then to serve our supper?'

Then he knew it was clearly time to assert himself – she was the partygiver of all time, but he had his rights, too, since he was the man who had been so beautifully invited to come to this party. He walked over and blew out the candles first, then slowly bent to kiss her upturned lips. 'Everything in its time. And now, at last, I think *our* time has come and we can't delay any longer.'

He stood on one side of the room, she on the other. First, he watched her undress, then she stood perfectly still while he undressed. When he was nude she came to him and he picked her up and carried her into the bedroom and placed her on the satin spread to make love to her body with his lips, and it was so sweet she suddenly couldn't remember that there had ever been anyone else.

She felt the years slipping away and it was all new again as if it were the first time. And then she made love to him in the same way, sweetly and slowly so that *his* ghosts would dissolve into nothingness and it would be all new for him . . . as if it were his first time, too. Then, lying side by side, she feeling his body against

615

her feverishly demanding, he feeling her breath upon his flesh hot and ragged, they both knew it was time for the future to begin.

It was dawn when he asked her how, when and where they'd be married since she was the expert on this sort of thing.

Married? Of course he would want to marry. I should have known that he was the marrying kind . . .

She recalled what TS had said about her marital record – thrice-widowed if one counted Hubert and twice-divorced – and if she were to marry again, she still had one divorce coming to even the score. And while she knew it was foolish to give any credence to this sort of nonsense, she could not help but wonder: had this just been one more of TS's cynical remarks tossed off for effect or was it based on firmer ground – one of TS's frequently *shrewd* observations? *Was* she being silly regarding it as a possible curse . . . a kind of hex, a prediction foredooming the marriage to failure? She didn't believe in superstition. Still, why endanger something as precious as their love by marrying? Why tempt some evil, jealous, wrathful god by flaunting her good fortune? Better to savour its sweetness in secret and guard it well. One more secret couldn't hurt.

Besides, she had married different men for a variety of reasons with mixed results. Maybe she wasn't a woman made for marriage? Maybe it was high time she stopped marrying, but took herself a lover? It would be fun for sure . . . maybe it would even be good luck? Maybe it would turn out to be the most brilliant union of all?

One thing she did know – it was going to be glorious finding out.

PART TEN

AFTER THE PARTY

Los Angeles
June 1990

65

Nora let herself into the house as quietly as possible. Not that it mattered if the three women sleeping upstairs knew that she'd been out all night – how she spent her nights was none of their business. Still, she wasn't quite ready to reveal *where* she'd been though if the day went as she hoped it would she might even do that.

God knew, Teddy had been after her for years now to do just that – to dignify their affair with the shining light of truth since she wouldn't legitimize it with marriage. But Teddy was given to absolute truth much more than she and wasn't addicted to secrets. 'Don't you know that "the truth will set you free" are very famous last words? At least it can free this couple enough to let them live together openly even if the woman *is* diametrically opposed to marriage,' was one of his favourite arguments.

Well, today was the day she was ready at last to tell a few truths and the chips would just have to fall where they might. If those girls weren't ready by now, they'd never be, and she and Teddy deserved more of her undivided attention.

She glanced at her wristwatch – it was nearly six. There was still time to shower, do her face and pull herself together so that she'd be presentable enough to face what promised to be a long day . . . *and* Sam, Honey and Babe, when they came down to breakfast.

But as luck would have it, a slightly bedraggled Honey emerged in the hall just as she nearly made it to the sanctuary of her bedroom. 'Honey, what are you doing up so early?' She was grateful that Honey was too much of a lady to ask *her* what she was doing up so early with a coat thrown over her night-gown and négligé.

Honey smiled forlornly. 'I'm due in court at eleven so I thought that as long as I was just lying there awake, I might as well go home and change and generally prepare myself . . .'

Nora smiled sympathetically. 'I know how hard all this must be on you even if you do walk out of that courtroom with a quarter of a billion dollars. It isn't easy to destroy a man you once loved even though you might hate him now.'

'But I don't *hate* him! I could *never* hate Josh. I thought *you* understood. I just want a different life for myself from the one Josh wants for me and refuses to accept. But you used the word 'destroy'. How can you say that? Of course I don't want to destroy Josh! All I want is what's rightfully mine, what I'm entitled to, morally and legally.'

'Oh, my dear, I know you don't *want* to destroy Joshua . . . Still, that's what you're doing, isn't it? How do you think he's going to raise a quarter of a billion dollars? What does he have in the way of actual cash or property that he can so easily raise money on? He's going to have to liquidate . . . sell off a great deal of Royal Productions – its assets, its real property, its contracts, the different divisions. And once you start to tear apart the foundation, the whole thing will crumble. I know a little about these things and I know that the whole is worth a lot more than the sum of its parts.

'Oh, you're going to destroy Royal Productions, all right, and if you destroy the company, you will, in effect, be destroying the man. But of course that's not *your* concern. As you say, you're entitled to whatever is legally and morally yours. And you're your father's daughter, Honey. I know you'd never do what wasn't right, and if, as they say, you stick it to Josh, then I'm sure he richly deserves it.'

She kissed the agitated Honey. 'I won't keep you. I know how long it takes to get ready for court, especially when you're the Honey Rose and your public expects you to be every bit as dazzling and glamorous as your television image. But since it is only around six and you do have a little time to spare, why don't you stop off and have breakfast with your father? Maybe he'll be able to cheer you up. And be sure to let us know how things turn out in court.'

'Oh, I'll be back the moment it's over. Sam and Babe are counting on me to do that . . .' *Especially Sam.*

Though Teddy made Honey her favourite blueberry pancakes, she didn't eat more than a few bites. 'What's the problem, sweetheart? This is the day you've been waiting for. D-Day, you might say. That's what they used to call a big day in my youth. The reference then, of course, was to the Big War. I guess the contemporary reference would be the Divorce Wars.'

But though he was smiling at her, Honey took exception. 'Really, Teddy, is that supposed to be a joke? If it is, I don't find it very amusing.'

He poured a cup of coffee for her. 'No, it wasn't supposed to be a joke. Let's say it was more of a wry observation. But, seriously, this *is* the day you've been waiting for so you can get on with your life. So why *are* you so down in the dumps?'

She told him what Nora had said – that this settlement she'd been fighting for would destroy Royal Productions, and ultimately, Josh himself. 'So I'm confused.'

'I see. Then that D in D-Day doesn't stand for divorce but destruction. Is that it?'

'Daddy!' She stood up so abruptly she knocked over her coffee cup and they both watched the brown liquid dripping on to the tiled floor without doing anything to stop it until Honey grabbed for some paper towels to wipe up the mess. 'I'm sorry but I was startled to hear *you* of all people say that to me, Teddy. Were you *trying* to be cruel?'

'I think you know me better than that just as I know

you better than to think you'd ever *intend* to be destructive.'

'Then why did you say it? You think Nora is right?'

'Much as I respect Nora's wisdom and her knowledge of the human heart, I think that as far as you and Joshua are concerned, only you know the true answer.'

'But I *don't*! I don't have any answers. How can I when I don't even know who I am any more – Joshua's wind-up doll, Mimi's sexpot clone or Teddy Rosen's impossibly idealistic daughter? I thought life would be so simple. That all you had to do was love and then you lived happily ever after . . .'

'I think you know very well who you are better than anyone. Remember when you and I silently acknowledged between us that it was possible I wasn't your natural father since your mother was sleeping around with several men, including TS, at the time of your conception? You never blinked an eye because you knew that it really didn't matter. We both knew in our hearts that you were truly my daughter. And now the truth is that you're not Josh's Honey Rose any more than you're Mimi's sexy look-alike or even Teddy Rosen's disillusioned daughter – you're Honey Rosen Prince, your own person and a pretty special one at that. And all you have to do is look inside your heart and you'll find her there and then you'll know exactly what to do – what's right.'

Honey went home to Crown House, the castle that the Prince and the Princess of TV had built, to get ready for court, less miserable perhaps than when she'd entered her father's house but no less confused. What her father had given her was a vote of confidence, not any easy answers.

No sooner had Nora sat down to the breakfast table at a little after seven than Sam made her appearance wearing an emerald-green kimono with a Chinese dragon emblazoned on its back, and dark circles under her emerald-green eyes. 'Babe had a terrible night, but she's sleeping now.'

'Good. She needs all the rest she can get. It's going to be a tough day. But if you don't mind my saying so you look as if you could have used a little more sleep yourself.'

Sam looked at Nora warily. She had to weigh every word she said to Nora this morning since she was about to present her proposition that Nora sell the studio to her and Honey instead of to her mysterious buyer, but she couldn't just blurt it out. She had to feel her way.

'Why should I mind? It's not the worst thing you've ever said to me. I guess the worst thing you ever said to me was what you said last night – that you were selling the studio out from under me, which is why I never fell asleep at all.'

'Oh, I'm sorry to hear that. I saw Honey this morning before she left to get ready for court and she didn't look as if she had slept much either, poor thing.'

'Why do you say "poor thing"? I mean, naturally she's nervous about the settlement, worrying how much she's actually going to be awarded, but this is the big day she's been waiting for so she can get on with her life. That's what we *were* celebrating at the divorce shower yesterday, wasn't it?'

'That was our *intention*, but I don't know if Honey was really in the mood. I think she's taking this divorce harder than we realize. After all, she was married to Joshua Prince for almost fifteen years and she was so much in love with him – I never saw a girl so in love. It's not like *your* two marriages. You were married to Tony for about fifteen minutes and your marriage to Vic Conti lasted what—?'

'You know very well that the marriage lasted about six months, the separation for a few months more, but happily the divorce has lasted for years. It really took.' She couldn't suppress a bitter smile. 'But I can't say you didn't warn me about him – what a bastard he was and how he'd try to exploit me as TS's daughter. Sometimes I wonder about that. Like you *knew* all you had to do

623

was say something bad about him and that'd be enough to send me rushing into his arms.'

Cautioning herself not to lose control, Nora poured Sam a cup of coffee as she permitted herself a tight little smile. 'That's like saying I manipulated you into that marriage and even I always gave you more credit than that – that you were too clever to be manipulated into anything, especially into marrying the likes of Vic Conti. And, *of course*, I warned you against him. That was my duty since I swore to your father on his deathbed that I'd watch out for you.'

She sighed. 'I guess that was a no-win situation for me. I was damned if I warned you against him and damned if I didn't. Still, *children* blame others for their failures – not mature women in their thirties.'

Sam bit her lip. 'Yeah, you covered all that last night – about how immature I was, among a lot of other things.'

'Well, perhaps in the heat of the moment I said *too* much. Especially now with the studio – the real bone of contention around here – being disposed of, it doesn't really make that much difference how we feel about each other, does it? So I apologize for anything I might have said that was too cruel or perhaps even unjustified and we can put it all behind us.'

'Wait a minute—' Sam blurted. 'The studio! I have to talk to you about the studio. You said the papers weren't signed yet – that the sale hasn't gone through! And we have an offer to make!'

'*We . . . offer?*' Nora asked though she thought she knew what was coming.

'Yes, Honey's and mine!'

'Honey and yours—' Nora repeated. *Of course. We're right on schedule.* 'You're talking about making me an offer with Honey's settlement money, I presume?'

'Yes, and if it's not enough to satisfy you, I thought you could add my trust fund money to—'

'Don't start that trust fund business again, Sam. I told you – that's yours only when I decide you're ready and

624

I'm not satisfied that you are. So, until that time, what's your and Honey's offer? I'm waiting.'

'What are the other people offering?' Sam asked cagily.

'I'd be a bad negotiator if I revealed my bottom line.'

'Is that all that's important to you – the bottom line? Dollar signs all in a row?'

'I didn't say that – you did – and I'm still waiting.'

'But I won't know that until Honey hears what she's getting,' Sam anguished, forgetting that she was trying to remain cool . . . to be at least as cool as Nora. 'They might not give her the full quarter of a billion dollars and—'

Nora looked at her without emotion. 'I'm sure she'll get something close to it since she's been responsible for generating the larger part of Royal Productions' income for years and never actually received a share of what I suppose was simply shovelled back into Joshua's company. In any case, I'm sure there'll be enough for us, at least, to discuss it.'

Sam stared at her stepmother unable to believe that it had been this easy after she had anticipated that Nora would set up all kinds of stumbling blocks. 'And your other buyer?'

Nora shrugged. 'As your father always said, it isn't a deal until the name's on the dotted line and I suppose I owe it to you and Honey to entertain your offer first. But we really can't talk until we hear from Honey. Poor Honey – win, lose or draw, she's going to end up a loser.'

Sam's eyes narrowed. 'Why do you say that?'

'Because I know Honey has no interest in owning a studio. All Honey wants is to be a serious actress, to study and try the legitimate theatre. That has been her dream all along.'

'But she said she doesn't care about that any more. She said she *wants* to do this . . . own the studio jointly with me . . . wants me to run the studio while she does the acting, has her pick of the best roles.'

Nora smiled sadly. 'You *are* a lucky girl, Sam, to have a friend like Honey – willing to give up her dream for yours. And you know Honey – how sensitive she is, how deeply she feels things and how guilty she's going to feel about destroying the man she once loved no matter that she's divorcing him. As I explained to her, what she didn't stop to realize is that Josh is going to have to liquidate so much of Royal Productions to raise that settlement money that the company won't be much more than a skeleton when it's all over. That will be a terrible burden for Honey to bear.'

'But she herself says that she's morally *entitled* to that money, as well as legally. She earned it!'

'I know. But that will be cold comfort when she sees Josh so shattered. And I feel sorry for you, too.'

'Why should you feel sorry for me all of a sudden?' Sam asked sullenly.

'Because it's going to be a terrible burden on you, too – an awesome responsibility to make good so that both Honey's dream and Joshua's lifeblood aren't sacrificed in vain. For your sake and Honey's, Sam, I hope you're up to it.'

66

Honey knew that today, more so than at any other stage of her career, the lights would be flashing and the television cameras grinding. Even if the judge sent her out of the courthouse without a dime . . . even if there were an earthquake that registered a ten on the Richter Scale or if the sun fell out of the sky, she still owed it to her public to look her best so that the Honey Rose would go out in a blaze of glory.

She spun around in front of the mirrored wall of her dressing room to check out the total effect – face, hair, the Zandra Rhodes suit a modest but modish two inches above the knee. Then, after she finished the head-to-toe appraisal, she sat down at the dressing table for a close-up shot of shadowed lids to consider if she'd applied too much or too little of the faintly tinted gold colour. But she was unable to make even this simple decision. As she tried to concentrate on whether her lashes needed another sweep of mascara, the only thing she could think of was the four Rs – ratings, reruns, residuals, revenues. Fifteen years of them. Was that what Joshua was thinking of this morning?

She picked up the silver-framed picture standing on the dressing table – the wedding picture which had appeared on the cover of *People*. Josh wore a subdued but fashionably correct Armani grey and a self-satisfied smile. She, in her Saint Laurent wedding gown, wore the smile that was her trademark. The gown was traditional white satin trimmed with seed pearls and lace with a fourteen-foot-long train at the back, but an untraditional mini in front, four inches above the knees as Josh had insisted, unwilling to forgo a photo opportunity to display his star's superb legs. There had also been tears of joy in the topaz eyes that the camera hadn't caught.

Dissolve to last shot where brilliant marriage is being dissolved since brilliant marriage is not about love and passion and until death do us part – it is only about making a brilliant divorce, Hollywood style.

Dressed in jeans and a white pullover, Sam sat down at her dressing table to brush her hair and apply some make-up to the scrubbed-clean face, to cover the dark circles under the eyes with concealer. But when she peered closely into the mirror, she wished only that she could see some kind of answers there.

For both yours and Honey's sakes, I hope you're up to it, Nora had said. *Oh damn you, Nora, for making me doubt myself!*

But it wasn't the first time she was doubting herself.

Even last night after Honey had made her offer of the settlement money, she had asked herself if she were really up to running the studio, had even told Honey it was possible that she wasn't – that she was just full of hot air. Oh God, if only she had stuck to those crummy jobs she'd had in the Industry for more than a couple of months at a time, maybe she would know more . . . would be surer about her own abilities.

And was Honey sure that this was what she really wanted or would she regret this decision for the rest of her life? And how would she herself be able to deal with that . . . knowing that she had caused Honey so much pain? Oh, damn that stupid voice in her head that kept saying that Nora was right, that sweet Honey really wasn't cut out for divorces and settlements – it was too hard for her to go for the jugular.

She heard Babe calling from the bedroom and rose to go to her. Babe looked godawful. The dark circles under her eyes were darker even than her own. 'How do you feel, Babe?'

'Terrible, thank you. What time is it?'

'Almost ten.'

'Has anybody called? You know – to see if I'm here?'

'No, not yet, Babe.'

'Do you think I have to get up yet?'

'I don't know. Do you feel up to it?'

'I don't think so.'

'I'll go ask Nora if it's time for you to get up. But I'm going to take an aspirin first. Would you like one?

'Oh Sam, I just don't know.'

'Mr Rudman is downstairs, Mrs Prince. He said to tell you that you have to leave right now, that the traffic will—'

'Thank you, Gladys,' Honey said, fastening pearl ear-rings in place. 'Please tell Mr Rudman I'll be right down.'

She stared at the pear-shaped diamond on her third finger, left hand, then abruptly pulled it off as if it were searing her flesh and tossed it into the yawning jewellery case. She'd discarded her wedding band months ago, but had continued to wear this ring. But today was the day to let go once and for all. Besides, Babe, who kept up on this sort of thing, had told her a few months ago that Tiffany pear-shaped solitaires were out and Cartier emerald-cut solitaires were in, so how could a today's woman wear the former?

And that's who I am now, aren't I? A today's woman?

She contemplated selecting another ring from what Josh called 'the Collection', which meant a selection of jewellery suitable only for a princess, just as Crown House was the only palace fit for a princess of her standing to live in.

Briefly, she considered wearing three rings on three fingers, an acceptable fashion statement. But she was unable to decide which was frequently the case now. Josh had always made all decisions, however trivial, for her. Actually, breaking up with Josh was practically the *only* decision she had made for herself since the day they met. He had even ordered for her in restaurants without consulting her, without taking into consideration what she might be yearning for just that once.

Caviar? 'Too salty. You'll retain water and get puffy under the eyes.'

French fries? So obvious a no-no it wasn't even worthy of a comment.

Chocolate mousse? 'You know chocolate's bad for the complexion, Honey, and loaded with sugar. Besides, it's not even your birthday.'

A hamburger was too greasy and a *feuillete de poisson* in a white wine and butter sauce, which she adored, had too many calories. 'You're the luscious Honey Rose, not the fat lady in the circus, remember?'

As for babies, well! Certainly there could be no babies on the Honey Rose's personal menu this year or the next. Maybe a few years down the road . . .

Finally she decided to go with her naked fingers

embellished only with her French manicure à la Jessica's, currently Hollywood's manicure and manicurist of choice. And just in case anyone noticed, Honey smiled self-mockingly, her bare fingers *were* a kind of a statement. No rings, no attachments. Autonomy time and the appropriate manicure.

But then, suddenly, she picked up a diamond tennis bracelet and fastened it around her wrist. She'd bought it for herself all by herself only months before she and Josh parted – the only piece of jewellery she'd bought on her own since her wedding day. It was almost as if she'd taken the step not of her own volition. She'd been strolling down Rodeo, passing Van Cleef and Arpels, and suddenly it was as if some invisible force propelled her into the store, made her ask to see the entire collection of tennis bracelets – a style Joshua had ruled out as too pedestrian for her regal wrist. Then she'd made her selection within minutes, paying for it with a scarcely used Visa card instead of making it a house charge which would have been sent on to Josh's business manager, in itself a departure from the norm.

A Hindu saying she'd read once came to mind: 'He who buys a diamond purchases a fragment of eternity, but she who wears a diamond arrays herself in the rays of creation's dawn.' Pretty heady stuff, she thought, and wondered who had really dreamed it up – a wise Hindu or a Rodeo Drive jeweller?

Still, that probably *was* the moment she had decided to recreate Honey Rosen and the decision to buy the bracelet had nothing to do with tennis bracelets at all. But that wasn't so strange either since the wrangling over assets and settlements that pervaded the decline and fall of the brilliant marriage, the big money divorce, had never been about money any more than it had been about Joshua's destruction.

So what was she to do about Joshua's possible destruction? She had given Sam her word and she was never going to divorce her friend Sam . . .

'You're going to have to get dressed, Babe,' Nora said, sitting down on the edge of the bed.

'But I feel terrible.' She pulled the duvet higher about her shoulders. 'They haven't called, have they?'

'No,' Nora said and Babe sighed in relief before Nora added, 'but I called them.'

Babe gave a little cry. 'Oh no! But why? You said you wouldn't . . . you promised.'

'I said that I wouldn't call your parents last night . . . that we'd sleep on it.'

'But why did you have to do it at all?'

'Because if I didn't it would have only delayed the inevitable. And did you really want calls going back and forth between Washington and Los Angeles until either Greg or your mother thought to call here before they called the police? That's what a child does, Babe . . . runs away so that she has everyone's attention and everyone gets very upset and when they do catch up with her, they say, "poor baby", and forgive her, instead of punishing her for being naughty. But you're not a naughty child, you're a grown woman who hasn't sinned against anyone but herself and one who has a problem that has to be settled decisively so that she doesn't have to keep running away again and again.'

'But I'm afraid to face them,' Babe moaned. 'When are they coming?'

'In a couple of hours, that's why you must get dressed.'

'But can't I stay here in bed while I talk to them?'

'So that you can lie there cowering under the covers like a frightened child? That puts you under a psychological disadvantage. You should be dressed and meet them downstairs. Show them that you're strong and in fighting condition.'

Babe moaned again. 'Will you at least stay with me, Nora? Please,' she begged.

'No, I can't, Babe. This is something you must do for yourself by yourself. Otherwise, your parents will think that without me standing by you're going to fall apart and revert back to a little crybaby.'

'But they'll only say what they always say – that if I try to divorce Greg, they'll support him by saying I'm just a sick, confused girl who—'

'Not this time they won't. They're going to back off and they'll make Greg back off too. While I can't be at your side, I *am* going to give you some ammunition to fight back with and I promise you it will get them right between the eyes.'

Babe's own eyes opened wide. 'What's the ammunition?'

'A small synopsis of your mother's life and a bit of information about your real father. But believe me, it will be more than enough to blow them out of the water.'

Sometimes you tried to keep other people's secrets as you hoped they might keep yours. But sometimes those same people made it impossible and sometimes, as Teddy claimed, only the truth could set people free and set things right.

67

'How come we're not arriving at the courthouse in a limousine?' Honey – more to keep herself from thinking than anything else – teased Press Rudman who, using his silver Porsche as a weapon, ducked in and out of the clogged lanes of Los Angeles's morning traffic with the expertise of the native-born Angeleno, masterfully cutting off arrogant BMWs as easily as he did the more humble Hondas.

He laughed. 'Ordinarily I *do* make it a practice to

arrive at the courthouse in the stretchiest stretch I can find, complete with entourage, when the lady in question wants the flash since that's part of *my* image, too. But today I'm trying to spare you and I'm hoping to find an anonymous parking spot and sneak you into the courthouse on the q.t.'

He took his eyes off the road for a second to smile at her and she smiled back. She trusted Press. Known as the best women's lawyer in town as opposed to 'a man's attorney' whose specialty it was to defend a male clientele against greedy wives or live-in lovers, he had consistently acted the good friend rather than the divorce lawyer. Still, she couldn't bring herself to tell him what was troubling her now at this late hour – *Joshua's destruction.*

'You've been wonderful, Press, and no matter what happens I'm satisfied you've done everything you could.'

Press sighed. 'I tried. And I did try to spare you all this crap in court and I would have if Josh hadn't fought us every inch of the way. The truth is that, most often, my confreres in the divorce business *itch* to go to court – they want the publicity themselves not to mention the extra billing a court case involves. But this time nobody but Joshua Prince is responsible. If he had even tried to meet us halfway—'

But, of course, Josh hadn't. The bottom line was that Josh was furious with her for even *dreaming* of divorce and hadn't been willing to give her the time of day much less a tenth of what was due her. The truth was that he still didn't really understand *why* she wanted a divorce. The lack of co-operation in reaching an equitable settlement was the least of it. Josh, his general tone one of quiet hurt, had given out interviews, implying that the Honey Rose had bitten the hand that had fed her for fifteen years. 'It's an old Hollywood story,' he mournfully declaimed. 'I made her a star and she turned on me.'

'Not so,' she murmured now.

'What?' Press asked as he manoeuvred the Porsche

into a parking space on the street two blocks from the courthouse.

'Oh, nothing.'

'You call this brilliant bit of parking nothing?' Press grinned, elated at finding a space on the street so easily. 'This, madam, is what you call a good omen. But we'll have to run for it – we're due in court in five minutes.'

He had planned to enter the courthouse through a back door he was familiar with, thereby giving the slip to the crowd mobilized in front. But now he found the door locked against them and he kicked it, cursing his own stupidity for not having hired a couple of muscle men to keep the mob at bay, and hustled Honey around to the front of the building.

As they tried to fight their way through the onslaught of Press and fans that greeted them, the clamouring mob's attention was partially diverted by Josh's arrival in a white, gold-flashed limousine with his flamboyant lawyer, Cassius Bushkin in a ten-gallon Stetson, plus Bushkin's assistant and Royal Productions' publicist. Then, just for a moment, as Press shoved one photographer and another stuck his camera in Josh's face, Josh's and Honey's eyes met and Honey saw a look she had never before seen on his face – subdued, dignified, but total defeated *desolation*, and she wondered which loss was he mourning: *me or Royal Productions*?

'So now you know everything,' Nora said. 'Or at least as much as I know—'

Babe fell back on the bed pillows, her face as white as the lacy pillowslip. 'I can't believe it! My mother was Katya Marcus married to Jacob Weiss – But why did she do it? Lie to me all these years?'

Who knew if Catherine had done it for Babe or for herself, or for both of them? But it didn't matter.

'I imagine she believed she was doing it for you – to give you a proper background . . . a good life.'

'Don't defend her!' Babe's eyes were wild. 'She did

634

it to hide her Jewishness . . . because she was ashamed of marrying a comic called Jackie White. She did it for *him* – the Judge! She did it so she could be just like him! And you, Nora! I trusted you. Why didn't you ever tell me this before?'

Nora understood what Babe was going through – to have her true identity revealed within the span of a few brief minutes after a lifetime of thinking she was someone else, *had* to be a shattering experience. It would take her quite a while just to absorb the shock before she began to pick up the pieces, and the accusations and the anger were only the first and probably, necessary, phase in the reformation of her life.

'I'm not sure why I didn't tell you because there's no one easy answer. Maybe I didn't think it was my place to tell you. *I* wasn't your mother who had her own private dream for you. Or maybe I didn't think I had the right to play God. Or that I thought it would serve no good purpose to tell you – that maybe you didn't *have* to know or wouldn't *want* to know. Or perhaps I thought that sometime when you were ready, you yourself would look beyond what your parents told you to search out the answers for yourself.'

'Then why are you telling me now?'

'Let's say circumstances forced my hand and I felt I no longer had a choice but to give you the ammunition you needed to fight with. But *you* do have a choice, you know.'

'Me?' Babe asked bitterly. 'I never had a choice before, so what kind of a choice can I have now?'

'You *could* choose to fire your ammunition in the form of blackmail and your problem would be solved. I'm sure your mother and the Judge will back down rather than have the whole story made public, and once Greg no longer had their support, he'd back off just as quickly – give you whatever you wanted rather than risk being branded a wife-beater.

'Or–' she paused, 'you could do it all yourself *without*

635

any help from me and *without* blackmail, because you *know* who you are: a strong woman who's not afraid to stand up for what you believe in – yourself. And it doesn't matter if your name is Ryan, Tracy, White or Weiss. And you know, I have the feeling you might even fall in love with that woman . . . But it's a *choice* and only you can make it. Now get dressed and put on your face. This is your big moment of truth and I always say a woman must look her best for life's big moments.'

From the vantage of the conservatory Nora watched Sam and Babe sitting by the pool, each of them waiting – Sam for Honey's return, Babe for her parents' arrival. As always they made an incongruous pair – Sam so tall in jeans and trainers, and Babe so tiny, dressed in the same yellow Chanel suit and towering high-heels she'd arrived in for yesterday's party. They alternately spoke and fell silent, each staring into the blue of the pool as if to find answers there. Sam appeared somewhat calmer than Babe, staying put in her chaise while Babe jumped up to pace around every few minutes before throwing herself down again. Still, Sam kept running her fingers through her hair which she always did when she was anxious.

No, she wouldn't go out to them, Nora decided. She had done what she could, said as much as she was able, and now it was up to them. Perhaps the two friends, of the same generation and talking things over, might be able to help each other come to the right decisions.

The phone rang and she rushed to answer it. Maybe it was Honey calling from the courthouse, unable to wait until she got back to the house to report the final outcome. But it was Teddy and she was reassured just by the sound of his voice.

'Nora, did you hear anything from Honey?'

'No, did you?'

'No. Did the Tracys get there yet?'

'No. We're all just waiting.'

'I think I'll come over. We can help each other wait.'

636

'Oh, I don't know, Teddy . . . if it's the right thing
. . . for you to come over.'

'I'm coming over,' he said resolutely. 'What can be
wrong about a friend coming over to wait with a friend?
What are you so afraid of, Nora – that people will start
suspecting our terrible secret?'

And then, maddeningly, just as he hung up, he started
to hum a melody that she couldn't quite place though she
was sure it was another song she had once sung. Then a
phrase began to float back through time. How did it go?

People will say we're in love . . .

68

Leaving the courthouse was even more difficult than it
had been entering, the horde of media people hungrier
than ever for quotes from the principals since Joshua's
publicist announced that the final settlement had been
worked out in the privacy of the judge's quarters but
gave no figures.

Once again Press damned himself for not having hired
a couple of bruisers to get them through the crush. And
then as the mob – reporters, photographers and fans –
followed them all the way to his car, he cursed himself
for having parked the Porsche so far away. Some days,
no matter what you did you couldn't win, he thought as
he hit out blindly, sending a photographer, who stuck his
camera only inches from Honey's nose, sprawling. Then
he had physically to restrain Honey from going to the
asshole's aid. 'Let him sue!' he growled.

Finally, when he had the car doors locked and his client
properly buckled up, he collapsed against the leather
seat, gave a great sigh, took a deep breath and turned to

637

Honey, 'Well, I guess we didn't do *so* bad, did we?'

Concentrating on holding back her tears, unwilling for Press or the onlookers still peering through the car windows to see them, Honey said the first thing that came to mind – an echo of Press's words: 'No, I guess we didn't do *so* bad.'

'Is that *all* you have to say? Not so bad?' he asked as he guided the car into the stream of traffic. Stealing a sidelong glance he saw that she was lost in reverie and he wondered what she was thinking about – the settlement that had been hammered out at the last moment? Josh Prince? Or what the future held in store for them both?

A good divorce lawyer had to be at least half-psychiatrist and usually he knew what a client was all about, but in her own guileless way Honey was as much an enigma to him now as she'd been from the start. He'd never been sure whether she was still in love with the man she was divorcing, and he still wasn't sure. And he'd never been sure if she knew exactly what it was she wanted, any more than he knew now if what she had got was what she really wanted either.

Throughout their association he had often felt as if he were picking his way through yards of pink gauze to get her to see the necessity of certain moves – to make her realize that a few foul blows to the kidneys were obligatory for a successful divorce even as he wondered why it had been so difficult to make her understand what to him was a simple concept. It had taken him a while to realize that she had no killer instinct at all. Then he regretted that it had fallen to him to try to instil one in her – he, who had fallen in love – and who wouldn't love Honey just as she was? How could Prince have been such a fool?

He'd been glad for her sake that there'd been no kids and no need to get into all the messy custody business. While it *was* a lot easier to get big money and the title to the house for the woman who did have children, a custody tangle muddied up the important issues in a no-fault divorce – what constituted community property and was either of the parties squirrelling away any secret CDs. The couple who were also parents always ended up fighting over the kids, using them as a weapon when what they really wanted besides the money was to wound the other partner in the gut. Then the kids always ended up being used as pawns in divorce blackmail and the cases dragged on until one of the parents cried, 'Surrender'.

If there'd been kids he was sure Honey would have collapsed immediately and he would have had to alter his strategy to spare her any additional pain. As it was, there'd been more than one occasion when he had had to struggle to retain his juristic cool, to remember that it was bad form to let his personal feelings for his client impede his judgement.

Besides, Honey had endured enough gossip without further conjecture about whether the lady's lawyer was screwing his beautiful and extremely wealthy client.

He glanced at her again as he took the Sunset Boulevard exit off the freeway. She was still deep in thought, having said not a word since her only remark – that they hadn't done *so* bad – and he guessed that it was the divorce itself she was thinking about and *not* the settlement.

He took his right hand off the wheel to take hers. 'Believe me, Honey, it only hurts for a little while . . .'

But he was wrong. It was very much the settlement Honey was thinking about and what she was going to tell Sam.

Nora and Sam sat in the conservatory, tensely waiting while Babe was behind closed doors in the library with Catherine and the Judge. Watching her stepdaughter switch from running her fingers through her hair to biting at her cuticles – an even more extreme display of anxiety – Nora was tempted to forget tough love, to put her arms around Sam, smooth her long red hair and croon, 'There, there, my baby . . . everything will be all right, by and by . . .'

But, of course, she couldn't do this. For one it would

639

be a violation of the rules of the game, and for another, she still didn't know for sure that things would indeed be fine.

'Poor Babe,' Sam said, finally breaking the silence and Nora was pleasantly surprised. She had assumed that Sam was thinking so anxiously about her own situation and not so much about Babe's. Surely this was a good sign and one in Sam's favour – that she was thinking about Babe and not herself.

'Do you really think Babe's going to be able to stand up to them? That she won't fall apart even armed with that stuff you told her about Catherine and her real father?'

'I'm hoping she'll stand up to them *without* using that stuff.'

Sam stared at Nora in disbelief. Then she shook her head in despair. 'I guess that's the big difference between you and me *and* the problem we have with one another. *I'm* willing to settle for only a small miracle, not expecting even that, and *you* want it all! You always did. The big, splashy *miracle* with fireworks and balloons and you want it overnight! You not only want it or expect it – you *demand* it!' Sam's voice was slowly rising. 'And damn it and damn you, you just demand too damn much! Don't you understand that?' And then her voice broke and the tears began to flow down her cheeks.

Oh dear God, Nora thought, her heart pounding wildly. *Is it possible? Are we getting so close to an understanding? So close to that miracle?*

Still, she risked blowing it all to say, 'Don't be such an ass, Sam. Twenty years is hardly overnight . . .'

But that only made Sam cry even harder and she didn't stop, not even when Teddy walked in singing, *'Don't laugh at my jokes so much or else people will say we're in love . . .'* Then, seeing Sam in tears, ignoring Nora who was looking at him in exasperation, he sat down next to Sam to console her, 'Don't cry, sweetheart. I have the feeling that everything's going to turn out all right.'

'But how do you know?'

'Because I have faith.'

'In miracles?' Sam sniffled, looking at Nora.

'In miracle-workers . . .'

Then Sam looked from Nora to Teddy, a question on her lips, but before she could ask it, they heard the sound of the library door opening and shutting and then the front door slamming and she leaped to her feet. 'They're leaving! The Tracys are leaving! It's over!'

Nora got to her feet too, remembering what TS always said: 'It's not over until the fat lady sings.' And neither size-four Catherine nor little Babe exactly qualified.

But then a tiny woman in a yellow suit and high heels stood in the doorway, grinning with her arms spread wide and she was singing. The tune was 'My Way', but she paraphrased the last line so that it came out, 'I Did It *Your* Way . . .'

69

Press had to swerve abruptly to the right as he approached the entrance to Grantwood Manor to avoid a head-on collision with the Lincoln tearing down the driveway. 'Somebody's sure in a big hurry to get away from here.'

'Oh, God!' Honey moaned. 'It's the Tracys – my friend's parents. You know, Babe Ryan, the senator's wife. She was so terrified about having a showdown with them about divorcing her husband. And I was supposed to be here to lend her my moral support. But I'm too late. I've let her down.'

Press tried to console her. 'Well, you couldn't help it – you had your own problems to deal with and deal you did. But your friend's a big girl. Having a showdown with her parents is something she's old enough to do by

641

herself.'

Maybe. But Sam can't do it by herself. There's no way she can get the studio without my money and now—

Press pulled into the courtyard and Honey saw Teddy's car, knew that he had come to hear the results of her day in court. *Will he be proud of me? Will Nora? But what about Sam? She'll never understand! She'll never forgive me.*

'Are you absolutely sure you won't have lunch with me, Honey? It's all included in the fee, you know. Actually, it's *de rigueur* for the divorcée to go to lunch with her attorney after the settlement is done.'

'I'll have to take a rain check, Press. They're all waiting for me and I have to see how Babe made out. Besides, it's two o'clock. It's much too late . . . for lunch.'

Press got out to go around and open the door for her. 'We can always make it dinner, you know. It's never too late for dinner, right?' His large, teddy-bear figure enveloped her in a hug. 'Feel free to call any time you're in the mood for dinner, or even if you just want to talk.'

'Yes, I will,' she said, hugging him back. 'You've been wonderful . . . a real friend.'

'Them's kind words,' he said, his nice homely face assuming a look of mock humility. 'Just keep in mind that I look on you as a . . . well, a very favourite person rather than a client. OK? And if your friend Babe needs a divorce lawyer – the best in the business – just send her along because any friend of yours is a friend of mine.'

She watched the Porsche vanish around the curve of the driveway, then turned to face the manor's front door. First she had to find out how Babe had come through her personal ring of fire and then she had to tell Sam her news . . .

She assumed that Edmund or one of the other members of the staff would open the door for her, or perhaps it would be Sam herself, and she braced herself to face her. But her heart leaped with joy and relief when she saw Babe, grinning and wild with excitement, *bopping . . .*

642

'Oh Babe! I guess I don't have to ask how *you* made out. I should have known when I saw your mother and the Judge tearing down the driveway like someone had put a match to their tails.'

'Honeychile, you can say that again!'

'Oh Babe, I'm so happy I could cry. How did you do it?'

'I did it in the very best way – all by myself after being pointed in the right direction by my very good friends. But I'll tell you all the details later along with the rest of my news – stuff Nora told me about Catherine and my father . . . my *real* father. But right now everyone's waiting for you chewing their nails down to the nub and dying to hear all *your* details. In the meantime all I'll say is this: when Catherine and the Judge started reading me the riot act, I kept in mind the famous words of *their* favourite heroine, former first lady Nancy Reagan, which I thought was kind of fitting.' And then Honey started to giggle even before Babe could utter the words, 'Just say no!'

Nora and Teddy hugged her even before she said a word and she knew this was their way of saying that it didn't matter what had happened in court. They believed in her 100 per cent, and rich or poor, married or divorced, no matter what course of action she had taken – she was still their Honey. But even as she hugged back, her tearful eyes met Sam's – equally tearful – and she wondered whether she would still be Sam's Honey once Sam heard her news.

But before she spoke Sam said, 'I have something to tell you, Honey.'

'Please, Sam, let me speak first.'

'No, *I* go first. Don't try to push me around just because you're rich and famous. I *insist* on speaking first!' And she took a deep breath, glancing at Nora whose eyes were fastened on her, eagerly waiting for her to speak though she hadn't told anyone what she had decided to tell Honey.

'After I asked a certain widow, well known to all of

us, if she would entertain an offer from you and me to buy her studio and she graciously agreed to give us first consideration—'

'But Sam, will you please listen to me?' Honey pleaded.

'No, you're going to hear *me* out first! Remember, I'm bigger than you are and I always beat you at arm wrestling as well as at tennis. Now, as I was saying, after the merry widow agreed to give our offer to buy her studio first consideration, I *changed my mind*. I decided I didn't want to be your partner, after all.'

Sam cast another quick glance at Nora who – miracle of miracles – was grinning even as she was crying! *How about that?* She had actually pleased the *woman* there was *no* pleasing. *Would wonders never cease?*

Honey was too shocked by Sam's decision even to be relieved. 'But why *did* you change your mind? Why don't you want to be my partner?'

'If you *must* know the truth, Honey Bunny, I think you'd make a really crummy partner for a movie studio. You'd grab up all the best roles and . . . well, frankly speaking, I don't think you're quite up to doing movies right now and we'd end up with a bunch of bombs on our hands and before you know it we'd be out of business and a fine studio would be down the toilet. I'm afraid that at this stage of your career you're strictly TV material and what you really should do is what you planned on doing originally – go to New York, study acting, and when you're ready, shoot for the stage. The theatre is *damn* good training for those who want eventually to act in movies. Unless, of course, you don't plan to go to New York any more anyway and intend to stay in TV.'

Honey was flabbergasted. She didn't believe one word of what Sam was saying. Sam was clearly letting her off the hook so that she'd be free to do her own thing no matter how much money she'd been awarded today. A sacrifice on Sam's part equal to the one she had *planned* on making for Sam.

But what was that last thing she'd said? *Unless you*

don't plan to go to New York any more and intend to stay in TV? What was that all about?

She looked from Sam to Teddy to Nora to Babe. They were *all* looking at her expectantly, yet no one had asked her the big question: had she got the quarter of a billion and if not, how much *did* she get? And the reason they *didn't* ask is because they all thought that very possibly she had backed down at the last minute – that she'd been incapable of breaking Prince Josh into too many pieces for all the king's horses and all the king's men to put together again and had relinquished all that was rightfully hers. Or that possibly she had even agreed to stay on in Hollywood to do another series for Royal Productions. Or even that she had reconciled with Josh because she still couldn't resist his seductive persuasions because she was still in love with him . . .

'Well, why doesn't somebody ask me what the final settlement was?' Honey demanded now. 'Did you all turn shy all of a sudden? Oh, I think I know what *you're* thinking, Sam Grant. That even if I *did* get everything I asked for, I'm still too *chickenhearted* to do this to Josh and I'm just dying to turn around and give it all back to him. That's why you said what you did. You were giving me room just in case I wanted to do it so I wouldn't feel guilty about letting you down. You're even allowing for me to change my mind about studying for the theatre, thinking I might very well let Josh talk me into another series.'

'Not too chickenhearted, Honey, too *sweethearted*.'

Honey smiled. 'Well, thank you, Samantha.' She was suddenly feeling much better, having just thought of something she could do to 'fix' Sam for that *strictly TV material crack*.

She turned to her father. 'Daddy, don't *you* want to know how much I was awarded?'

Teddy looked at her gravely. 'It doesn't really matter. More money, less money, no money. The only thing that matters is whether you can cope with it, live with it, be happy with it. And I already know that you can.'

'I think this means that *you* think that I let Josh settle for a lot less than I originally demanded.' When he didn't answer, she turned to Nora. 'You gave me something to think about this morning. Don't *you* want to know the result of my thinking?'

'And as I told you, I have enough confidence in you to know that whatever you decided, it was the right thing. But I must admit I'm curious to find out if I was correct in my guess as to what you did do,' Nora laughingly acknowledged.

'Then you *do* have a guess. Well, tell me what it is and I'll tell you if you're right.'

Nora laughed again. 'I think I'll wait for you to tell first then I'll just say that yes, that was my guess, or no, it wasn't.'

'Oh, playing it safe, eh? Well, in that case I'll take a guess at your guess. Since you are basically a romantic at heart, no matter what you want us all to think of you, I think you think that I'm still in love with Josh and acted accordingly – like a woman in love.'

Nora only smiled enigmatically but Babe threw her arms around Honey. 'Oh Honey, it's OK. We all understand.'

'What do you understand and what's OK?'

'It's OK to admit to us that you still love Josh. After all, you loved him so much and I never even *liked* Greg. And I think I speak for all of us when I say we would understand if you wanted to marry him again.'

'Well, thank you, Babette Tracy, for your understanding.'

Again they all looked at her expectantly and all she had to do was *tell* – not make excuses, not offer explanations, not even clarify her actions because these were her friends, her family, her loved ones.

Still, she couldn't resist teasing, 'Well, since no one has the guts to come right out and ask how much money I ended up with or what happened I think I'll just let you all wait to hear it on the five o'clock news.'

But when they all began advancing on her with blood in their eyes, she backed down: 'Oh, all right, I'll tell you. We never got into the courtroom, never got beyond the judge's chambers. You're now looking at the half-owner of Royal Productions, officially, and I might say, even happily.'

They were all stunned, except perhaps Nora.

'Are you sure this is what you want, Honey?' Teddy asked.

'I'm sure. This way, I get everything I deserve – morally, legally, even financially, since it's more or less an even trade and I don't ruin the company or Josh.'

'Well, then I'm happy for you.'

'And is that it? Just a business relationship between you two?' Nora asked, a tiny, quizzical smile on her lips.

Honey laughed. 'Oh yes, I see that I was right about you. You *are* an incurable romantic. Isn't that right, Daddy?' Now she looked at him, smiling a tiny, quizzical smile of her own. 'And all I will say is: yes, for now that's all it is – a business relationship between two people who respect one another.'

'I caught that *now*,' Babe said. 'Perchance are you leaving a door open there for some future adjustments?'

'Really, Babe, for a woman who's going down the old divorce road, it seems to me you're being mighty cavalier about another woman's relationship with her ex. And no, I don't believe I'm leaving any doors open.'

'But are you closing them with a bang?' Babe asked.

Everyone laughed except Sam who said, 'Then I was right about *one* thing. You *are* going to stay here in Hollywood and you *will be* working in TV, after all. And why not? You are half owner of the biggest TV production company in the world.'

'Wrong, Sam, on *two* accounts. As soon as I talk to my lawyer, I'll only be a *quarter* owner of the biggest TV production company in the world. You see, since I *am* going to New York to study, I want to make

647

sure I'm leaving someone here I can trust to take care of my business interests, even if they are only *TV* interests and not as grand as, say, movie business interests,' she mocked. 'But be that as it may, I think between my able friend, Samantha Grant, and my able ex running Crown Productions, I should have nothing to worry about, wouldn't you say? And you won't mind too much being a quarter owner of a mere TV company, will you?'

In shock, Sam glanced quickly at Nora to see if she was as stunned by Honey's announcement as she, but Nora didn't appear surprised – she only seemed *interested* as if she were waiting to see what else would transpire that afternoon.

'I can't let you do this, Honey—'

'Oh, Sam, you *have* to let me. I know it's not your dream – your studio – but isn't it the next best thing?'

'But that's it, Honey. Nobody can hand anybody else their dream. It's just like with Babe. She had to tell Catherine and the Judge to fuck off herself. No one could do it for her. And that's how it is with dreams. You have to pursue them yourself and then if you catch them, it's really *something.*'

Then she lowered her voice confidentially even though Babe and Teddy and Nora were standing right there. 'And between you and me, kid – and don't tell my witch of a stepmother I said so – I'm not ready to take charge of a newstand, much less the greatest TV company in the world *or* Grantwood Studio. That wasn't a real dream, that was only an imitation – a pipe dream.' She turned to Nora, 'So what do you think?'

Nora laughed, 'About what? About you calling me a witch or about your very mature decision?'

Talk about your dreams! Am I dreaming or did I hear right? Did she actually use the word 'mature' in connection with something I did?

'Actually I was referring to neither of those things. But I *was* wondering if, when you speak to those buyers

648

of yours, you could put in a good word for me. Ask them if they can use a good but inexperienced all-round movie person who has a feel for movies. You could say that while I *am* arrogant — famous for it — I'm also beautiful, brainy and classy. You could even tell them that moviemaking runs in my blood.'

'I *could* do that. Or maybe, since you're big on people doing for themselves, you could ask one of the new owners yourself when he shows up next week.'

'Well, it would be better if you did it. After all, it's you who's famous for your charm. Isn't that right, Teddy?'

Teddy laughed. 'Right. Absolutely the most charming person I have ever known.'

'Never mind that now,' Nora said hastily, afraid that Teddy might even break into song. 'I really don't think you have to worry about this person not finding you sufficiently charming, Sam. You and he have already had the pleasure of meeting and his view of you is most positive, I assure you.'

'Nora, will you stop playing games with me? Who—?'

'It's Hubie. He's coming home next week and he's one of the two new owners of the studio. At least *he* will be once I put my name to the dotted line transferring that which I've been holding in trust for him.'

Sam sank down on the chintz sofa. 'I can't believe it! Hubie's finally coming home and he's going to own half of the studio? You've been holding it in trust for *him*?'

Honey and Babe instinctively ran to sit on either side of Sam as if sensing this was Sam's big moment of truth and she might need them for support. Then, Teddy gently pushed Nora down on the sofa facing the three women. She'd been waiting for this moment for years, on her feet and fighting, and now that it had finally come, he wanted her to relax and relish it. Then he sat down beside her and draped his arm possessively about her while Sam, Babe and Honey gaped.

649

'Nora, I think everyone's waited long enough. Why don't you explain?'

She looked at his hand gripping her shoulder. 'Explain?' *About that arm around her?*

'About the trust fund. Hubie's trust fund.'

'Yes, of course.' *Of course. The time has come for a lot of truth and only a few white lies . . .*

'It's not all that complicated, really. When I married Hugh Cantington, he adopted Hubie and because he was such a loving man, he held Hubie in as much affection as his four natural sons. Accordingly, he wanted Hubie to share in his estate equally. At the same time he realized that Hubie was not mature enough to cope with the responsibility of so large a legacy so he left Hubie's share in my name and in my care, trusting that when Hubie was ready, I'd make the transfer. Well, I feel that time is at hand.'

'But the studio——?' Sam cried, still bewildered.

'I'm getting to that. Soon after I married your father he told me that he was in big financial difficulty and needed a great deal of money to save Grantwood Studio from the banks. Actually, I think what concerned him most was saving the studio for you, his daughter whom he loved so much since he always regarded it as your natural legacy. He always said, "Movies are in that girl's blood as much as they are in mine."'

She paused as Sam moaned, 'Did he really say that?'

'Yes, he did,' Nora lied easily. 'So I did the only thing I could do – I gave him Hubie's money, but since his money was entrusted to me, I was honourbound to do it legally. We made a fair trade since Hubie's legacy was more or less equal to half the worth of the studio and there you have it.'

'But what about *your* legacy from Hugh Cantington? Surely he left you as much as he left Hubie and his other sons?' Sam asked cannily. 'Why didn't you give him or lend him *your* money instead of Hubie's?'

A natural question on Sam's part, Nora thought. Did

she reveal to Sam that she bought Grantwood Studio outright using *both* her own and Hubie's money or did she lie again?

Without a question, I lie!

'Because my money was tied up at the time in investments not easily liquidated.'

Sam nodded, accepting the explanation, then choked-up, she said, 'I'm glad that you did what you did, Nora . . . that at least my father was able to keep Grantwood until he died and I'm glad that Hubie will now own a part of it – he *is* my stepbrother and it's like keeping the studio in the family.'

Babe and Honey each took hold of one of Sam's hands to squeeze it in silent commiseration as Nora awaited Sam's next question: who was the prospective buyer of the remaining half interest in the studio? When it wasn't forthcoming – perhaps with her new humility, Sam didn't think she had the right to ask it – Nora stood up. 'Well, now that that's settled–' she looked at her watch '–and it's much too late for lunch, why don't we all have an early dinner?'

Teddy stood up, too. 'But don't we have a couple more matters to be settled, Nora dear?'

'All in good time, Teddy dear, all in good time,' she said leading the way to the dining room. But when she opened the dining-room door, what greeted them was a roomful of balloons, criss-crossed with streamers, and a table set not for dinner but for a celebration . . .

When Teddy and the girls looked at her in amazement, Nora shrugged: 'Well, you all know how much I like to give parties and today was such a long day with so much waiting involved that I needed something to keep myself busy. Besides, I thought it would be lovely to end the day with a commencement party since no matter how things went, we would all want to make a toast to a new beginning. Now, quick, everyone take your seats – there are place cards at each setting so you'll know where you belong.'

'Place cards for a party of five?' Sam wondered. 'Isn't that kind of overdoing it?' Then she saw the envelope at her place with her name on it and that Teddy, Honey and Babe each had one, too. She waved her envelope at Nora. 'What is this?'

'It's a party favour. What's a party without favours, after all?'

'What indeed?' Teddy chuckled. 'I know you won't mind, girls, if I open my favour first. I can't wait. Ever since I first met Nora I've been dying to get a favour from her.'

Giggling, the girls watched as he tore his envelope open to find a shiny, new gold key with an accompanying note. He took one glance and his eyes met Nora across the table. 'Do I read the note aloud or do I just sing?'

'You'd better read the note aloud if you know what's good for you,' Honey threatened him and Nora said, 'I think you had better listen to your daughter.'

'"This key to my heart is actually the key to my house since my house is your house."'

Honey said, 'Oh!' though by now she was hardly surprised and Babe sighed at the romance of it all while Sam asked: 'Does this mean he's moving in?' at which they all laughed.

'My turn,' Babe cried and tore her envelope open to find a key too and read aloud: '"Just in case you need a place to hang your hat till you find that home where your heart is, use my house. Nora Grant signing for F. Theodore Rosen."'

Babe started to cry until Teddy, as surprised as Babe was by this turn of events, said, 'There's no need for tears, Babe. It's not all that touching since it appears that I'm just *lending* you my house, not giving it to you.'

Babe gave a last sniffle and wiped at her cheeks with a hand. 'Oh, that's not why I'm crying. I'm crying because your key looks like real gold and mine is just plain brass.'

They all laughed again as Nora explained, 'Sorry about that. But since I didn't know until last night that you might need a temporary home, I didn't have a chance to have one made up in gold. All I had time for was to have them make up a plain one from the key I had hanging on my key chain.'

Still, though she was spelling out things pretty clearly all by herself, she flushed when Sam said, 'I guess if the little one here is getting the key to *his* house and he's getting the key to *her* house, it means he most definitely *is* moving in, no question about it.'

'And though no one's about to ask *my* permission, I heartily give it,' Honey said tearing open her envelope, 'and I can't wait till I get *my* key.'

But though Honey shook the envelope no metal key fell out, only a cardboard cut-out replica of a key, an aeroplane ticket and her note. She read: 'The real estate agent in New York will give you the actual key to the apartment of your choice – first, last and a month's security all paid up. As for the ticket – it's for a one-way trip from New York to LA so that you can fly back on the wings of love to those who love you best any time the spirit moves you.'

For a moment, Honey sat mute, then she rose, walked around the table to hug Nora and say, 'No mother could have said it better,' as they all applauded, Teddy the hardest.

'This is better than the Oscars and now I guess it's my turn,' Sam said, ripping her envelope open. 'And I think I already know what door *my* key is going to unlock – my own apartment so that I'll vacate the premises, which is only fair, I suppose. These two lovebirds should have this place all to themselves.'

But then an oversized key fell out – a fakey kind of key with a tag affixed and another envelope inside the larger envelope, and Sam asked, 'Which should I read first, Nora? What it says on the tag or what it says on the envelope?'

'The tag.'

And Sam read aloud, 'The key to the magic kingdom,' and laughed uncertainly. 'What is this? Some kind of joke?'

'Read what it says on the envelope,' Honey urged.

Haltingly Sam read, 'Certificate of Maturity.' Then she asked huskily, 'But what does that mean?'

'Just what it says.' Nora said. 'Why don't you open it?'

Slowly, Sam started to do that, but by now she thought she knew what she was going to find inside. Finally, that which her father had left in trust for her . . . her legacy. Then she took out the certificate to see that it was indeed a transfer of property and there at the bottom was Nora's signature. Silently, unable to speak or even look directly at her stepmother, she passed it around for Babe, Honey and Teddy to see for themselves that she was now the legal owner of 50 per cent of Grantwood Studio.

But she had to say *something* so, finally, smiling at Nora through the tears, she said, 'Well, all I can say is it's about time you handed it over . . .' to which Nora responded, 'Well, all I can say is, it's about time you grew up.'

She *could* have kissed me, Nora thought. She could even have said, 'Thanks, Mom.' But for now, it's enough. Everything in its time. She smiled brightly at Teddy. 'I think we're ready to make our toasts. Will you open the champagne or shall I call Edmund?'

'I'll do it. We want to keep this a family affair.'

'Wait a minute,' Sam said, jumping up from her chair. 'There's something else we have to discuss, Nora. I've grown up enough now to realize that I don't know enough to run the studio. And while I know Hubie's matured into a marvellously competent person and has done wonderful things in the Peace Corps, what does he know about running a studio or making movies? He knows even less than I do. I'm afraid that between the two of us we'll run the studio into the ground.'

'Now that statement shows how mature you really are, Sam. But there's no problem. Just because you and

Hubie own the studio doesn't mean you have to run it yourselves right off without experienced executives to rely on, to guide you, for you two to learn from. Those executives are in place now, many of them the same people your father relied on. So all you two have to do is "go with the flow", as TS always said.'

Satisfied with Nora's answer, Sam sat down just as Babe popped up. 'I just realized. With all the excitement about finding out about who I really am, then having to face the Judge and Catherine, I never asked you, Nora, about my father and you never said. *Is* he alive and if he is, *where* is he?'

'I'm sorry, Babe, but I haven't the foggiest. I never – But there's no reason *you* can't find out. You might even begin by asking your mother and the Judge what they know.'

'No, I don't want to talk to them . . . I won't.'

'But you'll have to some time, Babe. You must. You won't be able fully to face the future until you come to terms with the past, and that means trying to reconcile your differences with your mother and the Judge for all of your sakes. That's as important as finding out about your father.'

'And you also have to think about what you're going to do with yourself now that you're out of a job in Washington,' Sam said. 'How would you like to come to work at the studio? I'm sure we can find something that interests you, keeping in mind, of course, that we won't need any tap dancers. They're not making those kinds of films any more.'

'*Très* amusing, Sam, but from now on you can leave the jokes to me. You know how I always wanted to be a stand-up comic and now I know why – because my father was a comic and it runs in my blood! And now that I'm all grown up and don't have to ask anybody's permission, that's exactly what I'm going to be! Anyway, I'll give it a shot. And who knows? Maybe I'll find my Dad and he'll teach me the tricks of the trade.

And no one better dare laugh at *that*!'

And no one did except Honey who rushed to explain: 'I'm sorry, Babe. I was just thinking of the time you wrote that comedy material years ago and you began with, "ladies and *germs*", instead of ladies and gentlemen. It was—'

Babe waved a disdainful hand. 'Don't bother to apologize. I know your kind.'

Honey laughed uncertainly. 'My kind? Now what does that mean, you clown?'

'You know . . . *your* kind . . . the ones that are only *half*-Jewish.' When everyone at the table looked at her as if she had lost her mind, Babe laughed hilariously, 'I just realized something – that I'm *all* Jewish! Like you, Teddy. You're going to have to tell me all about it . . . how it feels and all. Maybe I'll even go to Hebrew school to study up.' She sighed happily. 'Wow! I'm really going to be busy . . .'

Laughing with the rest, Sam drawled, 'Honey's right – you really are a clown, but you're *our* clown and we love you.'

'On that note I think it's time we made our toasts or we're never going to have any dinner tonight,' Teddy said, reaching for the champagne standing in its silver cooler just as Edmund appeared to whisper in Honey's ear.

'I'll take it in the library, Edmund, thank you.' She rose, asking to be excused. 'Josh is on the phone.'

'Why don't you take the call in here?' Sam suggested innocently.

'No, thank you, Sam dear. But hold the wine. I'll just be a minute.'

'OK, what did the big man talk you into this time?' Sam demanded when Honey returned.

'He only wanted to have dinner with me tomorrow so that we could discuss putting Crown House on the market.'

656

'Oh sure . . . And what did *you* say to that?'

'I said I'd take care of it before I left for New York and it really wasn't necessary for us to meet right now. Are you satisfied?'

'The question is – was *he* satisfied?'

'He has no choice but to be. Then he asked if he could come visit me in New York sometime once I'm settled in and I said that would be very nice.'

'*I* wouldn't trust him. He'll try to get you pregnant just to get you back.'

Honey giggled. 'I don't think that's a very nice thing to talk about in front of my father. Besides, that still takes two consenting adults. End of discussion.'

'Let's hope so,' Teddy said. 'And if everyone is quite finished, I will now open the champagne. But before I do—'

But then Edmund came in to whisper in Honey's ear again and she excused herself again. 'Be right back.'

'Wow!' Babe rolled her eyes. 'For a lady who just got divorced she's sure scoring a lot of action.'

'OK, who was it *this* time?' Babe demanded. 'Warren Beatty?'

'Sorry to disappoint, but it was only my lawyer, Press Rudman.'

'What did *he* want?'

'For me to have dinner with him tomorrow night.'

'Just to discuss divorce business, of course,' Sam said.

'Well no, just to have dinner.'

'And what did you say?'

'Fine. But I suggested, that if he didn't mind, I'd bring my friend Babe along so that she could meet him and perhaps she would discuss divorce business.'

'Yeah?' Babe asked. 'Sounds intriguing. Is he cute?'

'Well, he's no Warren Beatty but *you* might find him sexy.'

'Well, that really *does* sound intriguing.'

At which the three friends dissolved into a gale of

juvenile giggling until Teddy demanded, 'Nora, will you *please* do something about the level of maturity at this table?'

Giggling herself – it reminded her of the old days twenty years before – Nora countered, 'Why don't you? Aren't you the master of the house now?'

'Absolutely not. In this house I've only been assigned the role of live-in lover, and as yet, I haven't decided whether to take on that role . . .'

Then all four women stopped giggling to stare at him.

'Would you mind clarifying that statement, F. Theodore Rosen?' Nora asked. 'Have you been leading me on?'

'You say that to me when all you've ever been since the day we met was manipulative?'

'Me manipulative? Girls, defend me!'

'Sorry, Nora,' Sam shrugged. 'You *are* manipulative. Even last night when you lied—'

'Don't be absurd. When have I ever lied to you?'

'What about last night when you said you had received an offer for the studio . . . that you had buyers all lined up?'

'Oh that!' Nora said in relief. She'd been afraid for a moment that Sam hadn't been kidding about the lying. 'I had to do *something* to get you moving on the road to maturity . . . That's what's called a little white lie.'

'No, I'm afraid not – that's more manipulation than a little white lie. And isn't that what I told you girls right along – that my old steppie was the master manipulator?'

'She did, Nora, and I'm afraid she's right,' Honey sighed dramatically. 'I think we've all been the victims of your fine manipulative hand. Especially today. In evidence, I point to the fact that even *before* any of us knew what was going to happen today – before *we* had completely made up our minds what *we* were going to do – *you* were all prepared with your party favours. That means you had to arrange everything at least very *early* this morning. And Sam's certificate of ownership

658

in the studio – you probably had to have that drawn up days ago. So what can the answer be but that you manipulated us into doing exactly what you wanted us to do? As for Daddy's key, that was real cold-blooded manipulation. Knowing what a perfect gentleman he is you knew he would never embarrass you by refusing to accept that beautiful gold key.'

'Well, as far as I'm concerned, she can manipulate me any time she wants. I'm perfectly satisfied,' Babe said.

'But that's precisely the point,' Teddy declared as if he were debating the issue in court. 'I am *not* satisfied with the quality of the manipulation. Actually, I'm dissatisfied on two specific counts.'

'Oh? Now it's fault-finding time, is it?' Nora demanded. 'Come, come, let's hear the source of your dissatisfaction so perhaps I can correct the situation. You know I'm not one to turn down a challenge.'

'I thought by this time you would have manipulated me into winning the Nobel, or if not that, at least into a brilliant marriage.'

'Well, let's put it this way – I'm still working on the former. As for the latter, if you're willing to be my *live-in significant other* for a while – after all, I've never had one of those – I'm willing to take the matter under advisement. What do you say?'

'I say,' Teddy said, popping the cork, 'we'd better drink to that. And while we're at it we might as well drink to Honey, Sam and Babe and to the last of the brilliant divorces.'

YEAR AFTER THE PARTY

Los Angeles

1991

Standing at her bedroom window, Nora gazes at the panorama that is Grantwood Manor – blue pool and green lawns, gardens bright with the varied colours of early summer flowers interspersed with massive tropical plantings, a vista uniquely Southern Californian though the manor itself is a great English country house.

To the far right is the rarely used, three-hole golf course – there never seems to be enough time – and to the far left, the tennis court where she can almost visualize Sam and Hubie in their tennis whites moving about the court – Hubie in slow motion, Sam much more competitive, darting to the net for the kill.

Just beyond the court is the oversized doll's house where a fourteen-year-old queen of France might have amused herself before she lost her head, but Grantwood's doll's house, covered with bougainvillaea and furnished with movie-set cast-offs, is uniquely Los Angeles. Now, Nora squeezes her eyes tight so that she can almost hear the girlish voices of the three Hollywood princesses – Sam, Babe and Honey – as they play at being adults, dreaming of that time when they'll be all grown up and life will be perfection, as perfect as it can only be in one of Grantwood Studio's star-studded productions.

But that was twenty years ago and, today, all of

Grantwood is getting ready for a wedding.

As she looks down at the wedding props – the little round pink-clothed tables circling the pool, the north lawn canopied over in pink-and-white chintz roses, the south lawn set with rows of little white-and-gold chairs facing the rose-covered gazebo where the actual ceremony will take place – Nora thinks of how she'd come to Grantwood Manor as a bride and how many brilliant parties she has hosted here. It seems only fitting that the last party she will be orchestrating at Grantwood should be the most brilliant of all – a many-splendoured wedding . . . a wedding made in heaven . . . a marriage impervious to those jealous gods of divorce.

She looks up at the cloudless blue sky, the sun is still well in the east – the wedding is scheduled for high noon. Time enough to put on the deep pink gown laid out on the bed, to add a last-minute touch of rosy blush to her still creamy English complexion. And she watches the florist's people putting their finishing touches to the floral arrangements, the band setting up their equipment while the catering manager drills his staff, gesturing madly at the buffet tables.

And suddenly she recalls another wedding day in Palm Beach – she standing at her bedroom window looking down at all the last-minute preparations, watching a thirteen-year-old Hubie in his white usher's cutaway racing across the lawn like an elegant thoroughbred, so eager to go . . . to run at full speed towards life for the sheer joy of embracing it. She remembers wanting to call out to him, to caution him not to go down to the water's edge, to warn him against falling. But she hadn't. He'd been so beautiful in the white suit with his lovely yellow hair catching the sun that her heart quickened and she couldn't bear to stop his poetry in motion. But that was a long time ago and today her beautiful son is all of forty-five and the gold of his hair is touched with silver.

And then her heart jumps as she sees not a boy, but a

man in a white cutaway stride across the lawn to approach the bandleader, *his* hair shining silver in the sun. Then she realizes it isn't Hubie at all, but Teddy, already dressed for the wedding though it's still two hours away.

She turns from the window at the rapping on her door. It's Sam in one of her many green négligés. Sam had even wanted to wear emerald-green today but she, maintaining her role of the stern stepmother, had forbidden it. 'We must keep to the colour scheme and we agreed that all the women in the wedding party will wear different shades of pink while all the men wear white,' and Sam, muttering under her breath about manipulative stepmothers who always insisted on having their way, had quickly given in.

'But Nora, you're not dressed yet,' Sam says now and Nora points out that neither is she.

'I know but I haven't been able to get off the telephone. I've been trying to locate Honey. When she said she couldn't possibly get here until this morning I just knew something like this would happen – that she'd be late – and I bet when she does get here, her gown will need pressing. And wouldn't you know it, Josh is already downstairs pacing back and forth, driving everyone crazy? I thought maybe you could think of something we could do to find Honey.'

'Yes. Since Josh is the only one around here with nothing to do, why don't you let him try to locate Honey while you get dressed?'

'Good idea. I knew the great little organizer would think of something. By the way, I spoke to Babe. She's coming with Press, but she wanted to know if it was OK to bring two extra people. I said "fine" but I bet those two people are the Tracys and who needs them here today?'

'Oh, Sam, it will be wonderful if they're here today! This is what I've been hoping for . . . that she would make up with them. You know what they say – a girl's best friend is her mother.'

'So they tell me. So what do you have up your sleeve

662

today, steppie mine? I hope it isn't *Honey's* mother. That might kind of spoil the day for Teddy.'

'I wouldn't dream of spoiling the day for Teddy,' Nora laughs and urges Sam to get dressed. Still Sam lingers as if there is something more she wants to say, and Nora asks, 'What is it, Sam? Is there something else you want to tell me?'

Sam's eyes fill up and she starts to say something but then she changes her mind and runs out of the room.

An image flashes through Nora's mind. A red-haired girl and a golden-haired boy-man making love on a white-tiled floor in a Malibu beachhouse. And she wonders if what Sam was about to say has anything thing to do with that by-now fading picture.

The house phone rings and Nora picks it up to hear *that* voice singing, '*Your eyes mustn't glow like mine . . . people will say we're in love . . .*' and she laughs, 'You are impossible, really!'

'Actually, I didn't call you up just to sing to you. I'm calling to let you know that yours and Sam's ex, Mr Tony Dashing Nash, has just arrived in the flashiest looking limousine you have ever seen.'

'How does he look?'

'Oh, a bit worn around the edges.'

'Oh, but don't we all?'

'Oh, but some of us more than others. But what will I do with him? He's demanding access to your bedroom. Shall I send him up to you or on to Sam's room?'

'Neither. We're both busy getting dressed. Don't you know there's a wedding today? But I understand Josh is already here making a bloody nuisance of himself, so why don't you let Josh and Tony talk to one another? They can start a club – the Mexes.'

'Mexes?'

'Try putting male and exes together and see what you get.'

'You *are* bright, Nora. No wonder I've been after you

so long to marry me 'cause I'm no fool either. When are you coming down? I miss you.'

Only an hour to go but suddenly everything starts falling into place as Nora's house phone rings again. She laughs when she hears that same voice again: '*Your sighs are so like mine people will say we're in love* . . . Just calling to tell you I *am* in love and that Babe's arrived with her petunia-pink dress already on and with a real cute couple in tow and she's on her way up leaving Press Rudman down here which is unfortunate because Josh is looking like he could kill, and Rudman looks like a real tough guy who might be handy with his dukes. But not to worry. I'm going to leave dashing Nash to act as a buffer.'

'But where are *you* going?'

'Well, Hubie just came downstairs and since the bar's open for business I thought I'd buy him a drink. But not to worry – I'm saving my one glass of champagne to toast the bride.'

Nora hangs up quickly because Babe is pounding on her door demanding entrance. And then, not waiting to be told to enter, she bursts into the room, with her arms opened wide, a grin on her face and a sparkle in her eye. 'Ta, ra! Here she is, folks! The ex Mrs Ryan with her Pop – the all-time greatest little comic in the world, Mr Jackie White and his lady, Blanche Weiss, who you better watch out for, Nora. She's about to give you some real, mean competition in the stepmother department, let me tell you.'

And then Nora is crying and Jackie White is crying and so is Babe. The only one who is not crying is Blanche Weiss, who is patting Babe on the shoulder, calling her darling, and cautioning her not to stain her pretty pink dress with her tears.

Soon after, Honey comes tearing up the hall. She waves wildly through Nora's open door, clutching her rosy-pink dress to her breast, before disappearing into Sam's room. Only ten minutes later she emerges picture-perfect and ready for a wedding, to race back down the hall towards the stairs.

Nora calls after her, 'Where are you going in such a hurry? You didn't even say hallo!'

'Oh Nora, I'm so sorry. I love you very, very much and you look so beautiful today, but I have to find my father. There's something I must tell him before I tell anyone else.'

'What is it, love? Is something wrong?' Nora wonders what it is that is so urgent. Is she in trouble? Is she *pregnant*? Or is it that she's given in to Joshua Prince's persuasions and is considering remarriage? Sam has told her that Honey told her that Josh has been flying back and forth between the coasts at least once a month ever since Honey moved to New York, although Honey keeps insisting that they are only friends . . . will always be friends.

'Oh, I might as well tell *you*, Nora, you witch. You always know everything before anyone else does anyway. No, nothing is wrong! Something is wonderful!' She breaks into her dazzle of a smile. 'I think I've landed a part in an off-Broadway production and guess what – I'm going to play all three acts without a drop of make-up. Isn't *that* wonderful?'

'Smashing, Honey! Your father will be so proud.'

Now they are almost ready to begin and the pianist is already playing songs of love as a prelude to the Wedding March as the guests take their seats and Nora is not at all surprised to hear the strains of 'People Will Say We're In Love' floating through her windows. It is time for all the members of the wedding party to assemble in the conservatory as planned and now only she and Sam are still upstairs.

There's a knock on her door and Nora assumes it's Sam checking to see if she's ready to go down. But when she says, 'Come in,' it is Hubie, and he rushes to her to take her in his arms to hug her tightly. 'I had to come up before the wedding to tell you how much I love you, Mum.'

665

She reaches up a hand to touch the sweet head, remembering the little boy who couldn't resist jumping into puddles for the sheer pleasure of it all and she says, 'Oh Hubie darling, I know, and I love *you* very much. And I was hoping you would come up because I have something for you.'

'Something for me? But you've already given me so much and I'm only beginning to realize *how* much in the terms of a lifetime.'

'This is something I'm replacing, in a way. The ancestral home I denied you a long time ago when you were still Hubie Hartiscor and you could have been a Lord and lived in a castle if I hadn't refused it for you. And now I'm giving it back to you–' she says, handing him a sheaf of papers. 'Your heritage.'

He still doesn't understand and glances at the papers. 'But these are the title-deeds to Grantwood Manor. I can't accept it. It's not my heritage. If it's anyone's heritage, it's Sam's.'

'Yes, I know. But if you look more carefully you'll see that it's made out to you and Sam both as joint tenants.'

'But Grantwood Manor is your home, Mum! I can't accept it and neither will Sam.'

'But it's not my home any longer. One has to move on in life, Hubie, as you and I have always done. When your father died and I married your grandfather, Lord Jeffrey, he gave me Merrillee Manor which he called my dowerage. But when I married Hugh I had to leave Merrillee Manor even though I loved it very much because I had a new dowerage – our home in Washington, which was very special to me. Still, I had to leave that, too, to come and live here with Sam's father. And now it's time for me to leave Grantwood Manor. Teddy wants us to have a home that's just ours, his and mine and with no history, and I can't deny him. We've bought a wonderful house high on a buff overlooking the Pacific, perfect for a prize-winning writer and I don't even know if it will have a grand name yet. We might just call it "home".'

They kiss again and Hubie offers her his arm. 'Will you do me the honour of going down with me so that we can finally get this marriage launched?'

'You go first and I'll come down with Sam in a sec.'

Now Nora knocks on Sam's door. 'It's time to go down, Sam. Are you ready?'

'Not yet. There's something I want to ask you first . . .' Her voice is muffled.

'Shall I come in then or would you rather talk through the door?'

'I guess you'll have to come in.'

Nora opens the door slowly to see Sam standing at the window with the noonday sun streaming in, turning her hair a burnished copper and lending a golden glow to her wedding gown of palest baby pink silk taffeta.

'Were you right?' Sam asks. '*Can* red-heads wear pink? What do you think?'

Nora thinks she mustn't cry. 'I think I've never seen a more beautiful bride – at least not a red-headed one,' she laughs, which is better than crying. 'Is that what you wanted to ask me?'

'No . . .'

'What is it then, Sam?' she asks gently. 'It's getting late—'

'Is it too late to change the wedding arrangements?'

Puzzled, Nora asks: 'Change how?'

'I know I told you I wanted to walk down the aisle alone since my father's – But I changed my mind. Nora,' she blurts, 'would *you* walk down the aisle with me?'

They look into each other eyes for long seconds before Nora hoarsely asks, 'You mean you want *me* to give you away?'

'Well, my father isn't here and . . . and you . . . well, you *are* my stepmother and some people think a stepmother is as good as a mom any old day,' Sam's voice trembles.

Nora's smile is tremulous as she picks up the crown

667

fashioned of baby pink roses to place it on the long red hair and smooths the veiling into place. 'Any old day . . .' she repeats. 'And no, it's not too late to change the arrangements. It's never too late for that . . .'

Then Sam whispers confidentially, 'I have a secret to tell you. I haven't told Honey or Babe or even Hubie yet. Can you keep a secret?'

'Oh yes, I'm the best little secret-keeper you've ever met. Try me.'

'Oh, Nora, I'm going to have a baby! Isn't it wonderful?'

Nora is too choked-up to speak. Finally she says, 'That's *too* wonderful a secret to keep.'

'But I don't want anyone to know I am pregnant before I march down the aisle. They might think Hubie and I are getting married just because of that, not because we're terribly in love. As for Hubie, I want him to get used to being married first before I tell him he's going to be a daddy. But he will be thrilled, won't he?'

'Oh yes, Hubie's a very loving man with loads of room in his heart for a child.'

'I guess he must take after his mom after all,' Sam says hooking her arm through Nora's as they walk down the hall to the stairway. 'And you *will* keep my secret? Is it a deal?'

Nora knows by now if she knows nothing else that there are all kinds of secrets, some far sweeter than others. But one of the sweetest has to be a mother/daughter kind of a secret. 'Of course I will,' she says. 'Your secret is now my secret and that's a deal you can take to the bank.'

Now the bride and the groom are kissing and the best man is grinning at the mother of the groom. Then the bride throws her arms around the mother-in-law who gave her away and kisses her almost as ardently as she kissed her groom and whispers in her ear, 'Thanks, Mum.'

Now the mother is kissing her son while the bride

668

kisses her maids of honour and the best man taps the bridegroom on the shoulder to say, 'Cutting in'. And now they're all marching up the aisle, arm in arm, bride and bridegroom followed by the golden-haired bridesmaid interlocking arms with the dark-haired bridesmaid, followed by the best man holding on tightly to the mother of the happy couple.

Now they are dancing and the orchestra plays: '*I'll be loving you always . . . with a love that's true always . . .*'

'What are you thinking, Nora?'

'I'm thinking they're playing our song.'

'What else are you thinking?'

'If you must know it just occurred to me that I've been married many times for all manner of reasons to all manner of men, but not once have I been married to the right man for the right reason at the right time, and while I've been both widowed and divorced, never once have I been married *for ever*! And that's really something I'll have to try before I call it quits altogether! What do you think?'

'Ah Nora, I think they're playing our song.'

THE END

THE MOVIE SET
by June Flaum Singer

They were young, beautiful, talented, and they all wanted to make it into the fastest set of all – the Movie Set, which fed on scandal, glamour, sex, and raw emotion.

Buffy fell in love with a hero, then found herself a victim of the ultimate degradation.

Suzannah, breathtakingly lovely, who mutilated her body and nearly destroyed herself by her own burning ambition.

Cleo who was dazzled by her clever intellectual lover, and spent the rest of her life trying to keep up with him.

Cassie who married to spite her mother, and was trapped in a nightmare of sadistic cruelty.

Suellen knew all the secrets, but still hoped for a happy ending.

They all made it into The Movie Set – and no one but them knew the cost.

0 552 12636 5

SEX IN THE AFTERNOON
by June Flaum Singer

She was the most beautiful and alluring woman he had ever seen. She was also the most elusive. But Jonathan West was a millionaire and knew how to get what he wanted. And he wanted her – the mysterious woman in the luxury suite on the *QE2*. He set his vast organization to find out who she was, where she came from, but even as he tried to subdue her, possess her, claim her as yet another of his conquests, he found himself drawn into a web of sexuality and mystery. All he could discover was her name – Andrianna DeArte.

As their devious and curious relationship grew, the secrets grew stranger. For Andrianna DeArte had many names and many lives. And no-one knew the real life, the life that had begun as the daughter of a Mexican girl and the ruthless man who had bought her, the life that had shattered into violence, lies, and passionate sexual betrayal until there was no man she trusted, no man she would not use.

Between her and Jonathan West exploded a raw sexual hunger, a passionate obsession that threatened to shatter both their lives.

0 552 13503 8

A SELECTED LIST OF FINE NOVELS
AVAILABLE FROM CORGI BOOKS

THE PRICES SHOWN BELOW WERE CORRECT AT THE TIME OF GOING TO PRESS. HOWEVER TRANSWORLD PUBLISHERS RESERVE THE RIGHT TO SHOW NEW RETAIL PRICES ON COVERS WHICH MAY DIFFER FROM THOSE PREVIOUSLY ADVERTISED IN THE TEXT OR ELSEWHERE.

☐	13648 4	Casting	*Jane Barry*	£3.99
☐	12869 4	Dreams Are Not Enough	*Jacqueline Briskin*	£4.99
☐	13395 7	The Naked Heart	*Jacqueline Briskin*	£4.50
☐	12850 3	Too Much Too Soon	*Jacqueline Briskin*	£4.99
☐	13396 5	The Other Side of Love	*Jacqueline Briskin*	£4.99
☐	13558 5	Ambition	*Julie Burchill*	£4.99
☐	13830 4	The Master Stroke	*Elizabeth Gage*	£4.99
☐	13266 7	A Glimpse of Stocking	*Elizabeth Gage*	£4.99
☐	13644 1	Pandora's Box	*Elizabeth Gage*	£4.99
☐	13255 1	Garden of Lies	*Eileen Goudge*	£4.99
☐	13976 9	Rachel's Daughter	*Janet Haslam*	£4.99
☐	12375 7	A Scattering of Daisies	*Susan Sallis*	£3.99
☐	12579 2	The Daffodils of Newent	*Susan Sallis*	£3.99
☐	12880 5	Bluebell Windows	*Susan Sallis*	£3.99
☐	13136 9	Rosemary for Remembrance	*Susan Sallis*	£3.99
☐	13346 9	Summer Visitors	*Susan Sallis*	£4.99
☐	13545 3	By Sun and Candlelight	*Susan Sallis*	£4.99
☐	13756 1	An Ordinary Woman	*Susan Sallis*	£4.99
☐	13934 3	Daughters of the Moon	*Susan Sallis*	£4.99
☐	12636 5	The Movie Set	*June Flaum Singer*	£4.99
☐	13333 7	The President's Women	*June Flaum Singer*	£3.99
☐	13503 8	Sex in the Afternoon	*June Flaum Singer*	£4.99
☐	13504 6	Brilliant Divorces	*June Flaum Singer*	£4.99
☐	13523 2	No Greater Love	*Danielle Steel*	£4.99
☐	13525 9	Heartbeat	*Danielle Steel*	£4.99
☐	13522 4	Daddy	*Danielle Steel*	£4.99
☐	13524 0	Message from Nam	*Danielle Steel*	£4.99
☐	07807 7	Valley of the Dolls	*Jacqueline Susann*	£3.99

All Corgi Books are available at your bookshop or newsagent, or can be ordered from the following address:
Corgi/Bantam Books,
Cash Sales Department,
P.O. Box 11, Falmouth, Cornwall TR10 9EN

UK and B.F.P.O. customers please send a cheque or postal order (no currency) and allow £1.00 for postage and packing for the first book plus 50p for the second book and 30p for each additional book ordered up to a maximum charge of £3.00 (7 books plus).

Overseas customers, including Eire, please allow £2.00 for postage and packing for the first book, £1.00 for the second book, and 30p for each subsequent title ordered.

NAME (Block Letters) ....

ADDRESS ....

....